Lilian Harry's grandfather hailed from Devon and Lilian always longed to return to her roots, so moving from Hampshire to a small Dartmoor town in her early twenties was a dream come true. She quickly absorbed herself in local life, learning the fascinating folklore and history of the moors, joining the church bellringers and a country dance club, and meeting people who are still her friends today. Although she later moved north, living first in Herefordshire and then in the Lake District, she returned in the 1990s and now lives on the edge of the moor with her three ginger cats and a black miniature schnauzer who has a fan club bigger than that of her mistress. She has a son, a daughter and two grandchildren, is still an active bellringer and member of the local drama group and loves to walk on the moors. Visit her website at www.lilianharry.co.uk.

LILIAN HARRY

The Bells *of* Burracombe

A Stranger *in* Burracombe

The Bells of Burracombe
First published in Great Britain by Orion in 2006

A Stranger in Burracombe
First published in Great Britain by Orion in 2007

This omnibus edition published in 2009
by Orion Books Ltd
Orion House, 5 Upper St Martin's Lane
London WC2H 9EA

An Hachette UK company

A CIP catalogue record for this book is available from the British
Library.

ISBN 9781407221229

Printed in Great Britain by Clays Ltd, St Ives plc

www.orionbooks.co.uk

The Bells *of*
Burracombe

Dedication

To the Bellringers of Devon – the 'Ringing County' –
especially my good friends in Peter Tavy and Tavistock

Author's Note

Readers just setting off to explore Dartmoor and South Devon may be disappointed to know that the villages of Burracombe and Little Burracombe do not actually exist. However, you may think of them as being somewhere in the triangle produced by Tavistock, Princetown and Plymouth. The other villages mentioned, and whose church bellringers take part in the Bellringing Competitions, do exist in this lovely part of Devon and are each worth a visit. You can even find the Watchmaker's Tomb in Lydford Churchyard, and although the inscription itself is now faint, it has been transcribed so that visitors can read the full text.

The villagers of Burracombe are like those of any other village in the 1950s, or indeed at any time – a mixture of human beings: some friendly, affectionate, humble and hardworking; some snobbish, self-important, misguided or slovenly; and yet all, I hope, entertaining.

This is the first story about Burracombe. I hope you will enjoy reading it, as I have enjoyed writing it, and that we will all enjoy those yet to come.

Lilian Harry

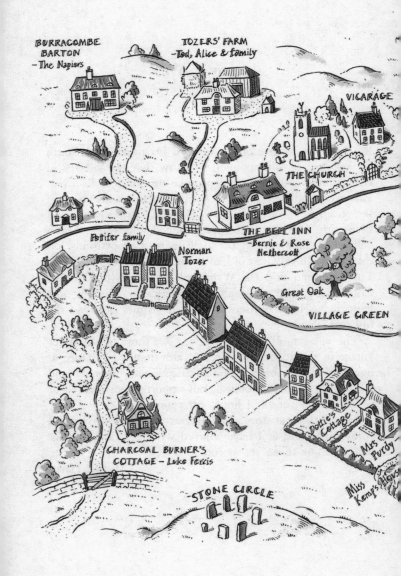

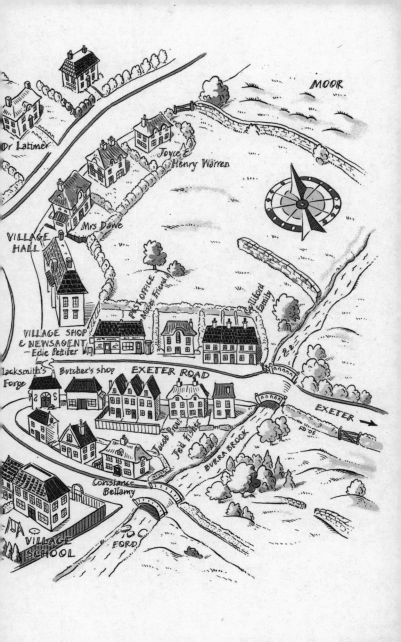

Chapter One

Burracombe, South Devon, 1950

'You must be the new teacher!'

Stella Simmons turned quickly. The little bus, that had trundled around several villages on its way from Tavistock where she'd got off the train, was already departing down the narrow lane. There was nobody on the village green apart from herself and the young man who stood a few yards away, watching her with dark blue eyes. Tall, very thin and loose-limbed, wearing what appeared to be an old gardening jacket and trousers splashed with paint, he looked rather as if he'd been thrown hastily together from spare parts. Yet there was an attractive friendliness in his face and the grin that showed white, if slightly crooked, teeth. He was carrying a large, flat book.

'Are you the vicar?' Stella asked doubtfully, and he burst into delighted laughter, his wavy black hair flying around his bare head.

'Do I look like a vicar?'

'Well, no, but he was supposed to meet me here. And I'm not the new teacher – not yet. I've come for an interview. How did you know about me, anyway?'

'In a small place like Burracombe,' the young man said, 'everyone knows everything. We all knew that someone was coming today, and I guessed it must be you as soon as I saw you get off the bus. You're the only stranger here, you see.'

Stella met his bright blue glance and then looked away. The October sky was a hazy blue, with the jewelled colours of the woods shimmering as if through a delicate silvered veil. Her journey had brought her through meadows that dipped and dived, across wide, flat fenland and fields of sunburned stubble, and then between the brown folds of the moors. Even as she stepped off the bus into this village, tucked into a soft valley clothed with oak and beech trees, she had felt as if she were coming home. Oh, she thought, I hope I get this job . . .

The village green still seemed deserted, with the church tower tall and grey above the cob cottages clustered around it, but as she gazed about she began to see signs of life. Along the lane was a forge with a big Shire horse being shod by a brawny, bald-headed man. A young woman a few years older than Stella, wearing breeches and a yellow jumper, was holding the horse's head. A cottage door opened and a woman in a crossover pinafore stepped outside and began to shovel up some dung that had obviously been deposited there only a few minutes before by the horse; she gathered it into a bucket and disappeared round the side of her cottage, but not before giving Stella a quick, sharp glance. And then hasty footsteps coming down the church path announced the arrival of the vicar, and the young man murmured in Stella's ear: 'Here he comes. He's just like the White Rabbit in *Alice in Wonderland* – always terrified of being late!'

The vicar opened the wooden lych gate and hurried across to them. He grasped Stella's hand and shook it vigorously, talking almost before he was within speaking distance. 'My dear young lady, I'm Basil Harvey. So sorry to keep you waiting. I'd intended meeting the bus but I was asked to give an opinion on marrows – not that my opinion's worth anything. All I could say was that they're very big!' He let go of her hand and stepped back a little.

'It's so kind of you to come all this way. I hope you had a good journey?'

'Very good, thank you,' Stella said, smiling at him. He did indeed look a little like the White Rabbit, with a halo of silver hair and a pink face that looked as if it had been scrubbed. 'I came on the train as far as Tavistock, just as you said.'

'Ah yes. A pleasant journey. And when you're settled you must try the branch line, from Whitchurch to Plymouth. Or in the other direction, to Launceston. One of the most beautiful railway lines in the country, to my mind. Railways are something of a hobby of mine,' he confided a little sheepishly. 'But I mustn't keep you standing here. The other governors are meeting at the vicarage at twelve-thirty, so I thought it might be nice for you to see the church before going on to the school. And there'll be lunch afterwards.' He glanced at the young man, who was watching them quietly, an amused twinkle somewhere deep in his bright eyes. 'I see you've met our other recent newcomer to the village.'

'We've had quite a conversation,' the young man said easily, 'but we haven't actually introduced ourselves.' He held out his hand. 'Luke Ferris, at your service.'

'Oh.' Stella took his hand, feeling unaccountably flustered. 'And I'm Stella Simmons. But of course, you know that already.'

He laughed. 'I had the advantage of you, didn't I! But to be honest, I've only been here a week or two myself. I'm renting a cottage on the estate. I'm an artist – or like to think I am,' he added a little ruefully. She realised that the book he was carrying must be a sketchpad. 'Trying my hand at the Devon landscape.' He gestured at the vicar. 'It was Uncle Basil here who suggested it. Thought I needed a change from smoky old London.'

'And so you did. I'm not really his uncle,' the vicar told

3

Stella, 'but his father and I have been friends for many years. Anyway, we mustn't stand here gossiping. Miss Simmons will be getting cold. Come along and look at our church, my dear.' He turned to Luke. 'Why don't you join us for lunch? I'm sure Grace can stretch the rabbit pie to another plate.'

At the mention of rabbit pie, Luke shot a swift glance at Stella, who shyly looked away. 'I won't, thanks.' I want to go over to Little Burracombe and catch the afternoon sun on Cuckoo Wood. The colours are magnificent now, but if we get a wind the leaves will be gone overnight and I'll miss the chance.' He said goodbye and loped away along the lane, his jacket unbuttoned and flapping round his lean body. The vicar looked after him and then turned to lead Stella up the path.

'Luke's been rather ill for the past two or three years – Grace and I do worry that he doesn't feed himself properly . . . However, that's not why you're here.' He bustled up the flagstone path and Stella followed him, peering at the leaning gravestones on either side. *Robert Tozer, Beloved Husband of Alice . . . Fell Asleep January 14ᵗʰ 1842; Albert Tozer, 1796–1875, Gone But Not Forgotten; Jemima Tozer, 1800–1879, Wife of the Above; William Tozer, 1833–1835; Susannah Tozer, 1834–1840; Eliza Tozer, 1836–1880.*

'There are a lot of Tozers here,' she said. 'Are they a local family?'

'Oh yes, and there are still plenty of them about.' Basil Harvey looked at the gravestones. 'Many of them died young, as you can see, especially during the 1830s. Cholera, you know.' He hurried on and opened the big wooden door. Stella followed him into the dim church and stood still for a moment, letting her eyes adjust.

'It's lovely,' she said, looking up at the wooden beams on the vaulted roof and the sturdy, tree-like pillars of the nave. The soft grey of the stone was lit and coloured by sunshine pouring in through a stained-glass window, while the deep crimson of the altar cloth glowed like a winter bonfire behind the carved railing of the chancel. The stone floor was cold but the dark wood of the pews seemed to give out its own warmth as if extending a welcome that had been sustained for centuries past.

'We're very proud of it,' the vicar admitted, standing beside her. 'As you see, we're preparing for our Harvest Festival service on Sunday – that's why I was asked to choose which marrow should go at the foot of the pulpit.' He moved up the aisle towards a young woman who was arranging fruit and flowers around the pulpit and chancel steps. Two enormous marrows lay like slumbering green hippos on the floor, with a pile of scrubbed orange carrots beside them and a great sheaf of golden chrysanthemums thrust into a bucket of water. There were boxes of other vegetables and fruits as well – potatoes, swedes, scarlet apples, gleaming bronze onions – all in glorious disarray at her feet, while Stella now noticed two or three other women busy arranging more produce on the wide windowsills.

The young woman looked up as they approached. She was about thirty and was wearing an old jumper and skirt, yet still managed to appear elegant with her slender figure and long, artistic hands. Her fair hair was loose, in a long page-boy style, and her grey eyes were cool but friendly as she surveyed the vicar and his companion.

'You must be the new teacher.' She wiped her hand on her skirt. 'How do you do? I'm Hilary Napier. Sorry, I'm in a bit of a mess – perhaps we'd better save the handshake for later.'

Stella smiled and shook her head. 'I'm not the new teacher – not yet, anyway. I haven't even had my interview yet. Mr Harvey's just showing me round.'

'Well, that won't take long – Burracombe's not much more than a handful of cottages and a dog. I hope you're not a city girl. You'll find it very dull and quiet here if you are.' She eyed Stella assessingly. 'You look very young to be applying for a teacher's post.'

'I'm twenty-one. I've done all my training, and worked as a pupil teacher where I used to live.' Stella felt a twinge of anxiety. She had done her best to make herself look older before setting out on the journey that morning – trying to brush her short, dark curls flat, putting on a brown hat and coat that had been passed down to her by one of the other girls, wearing lace-up shoes and thick stockings. But nothing could disguise her fresh, smooth complexion, nor the brightness of her hazel eyes. She had an uneasy feeling that she just looked like a little girl, dressing up in her mother's clothes.

'Well, we want someone young and lively for our children, don't we,' the vicar was saying cheerily. 'Miss Morgan was an excellent teacher, I'm sure, but I did sometimes feel that the little ones were getting a bit too much for her. There were times when she didn't even seem to *like* them very much, but I'm sure she did really. It was just that she was tired.'

'It wasn't that at all,' Hilary Napier said. She had a brisk way of speaking, in a clipped voice that Stella guessed indicated an upper-class background and private education. 'She *didn't* like them. And it wasn't just her age, either – she never did like small children. Totally unsuited to be a teacher, if you ask me.' She bent and picked up one of the marrows.

The vicar protested. 'Oh, I'm sure you're wrong about that, Hilary. She was an excellent woman. Every child who passed through her hands went on to the junior class able to read and write and do sums.'

'Too frightened not to.' Hilary balanced the marrow in both hands and flicked her eyebrows at Stella. 'It was a good day for Burracombe when she retired. And not a moment too soon, either – she must have been well over age. Eighty in the shade.'

Mr Harvey gave her a reproachful look. 'If I weren't accustomed to your sense of humour, Hilary, I might be cross with you. You shouldn't be talking like that, even if you don't mean it. You'll be making poor Miss Simmons wonder if she really does want to come to Burracombe.' He glanced suddenly at the watch on his wrist. 'Goodness gracious me! Where does the time go? We ought to be making our way to the school. And I haven't shown you the church properly at all. Never mind, there may be an opportunity later.' He whirled off down the aisle towards the door and Hilary Napier laughed.

'You'd better go,' she said. 'If Basil thinks you're late, you must be!' She gave Stella a friendly smile. 'I hope you get the job. Burracombe's quiet, but it's a nice enough place to live, provided you don't hanker for city streets and big shops.'

'I don't,' Stella said, smiling back. 'I lived in the country for a while when I was a child – evacuated, you know.' The usual shadow touched her heart, but she was so accustomed to it by now that she could ignore it – almost. 'I hope I'll see you again, Miss Napier.'

'Oh, I expect you will.' Hilary clasped the marrow to her chest as if it were a baby and carried it over to the altar. 'You'll be meeting my father, anyway – he's one of the school governors. Enjoy your visit to Burracombe. At least you've got a nice day for it. I warn you, it can be a bit bleak around here in winter.'

She turned to arrange the vegetables in a row along the chancel rail, and Stella followed the vicar out of the church.

The October air was as sharp as a russet apple as they trotted back down the church path. Stella looked about at the cluster of cottages and tried to imagine herself living here, in this tiny village on the edge of Dartmoor. A narrow

7

stream ran along the side of the road, and beyond the cottages the hills were clothed in woods, bronzed with autumn colour, with occasional splashes of deep purple. Above the woods she could see the moor itself, golden-brown with the dying bracken and scattered with the bright yellow of gorse flowers. *When gorse is out of season, kissing's out of reason* . . . Someone had told her that once, years ago. It never was completely out of season.

Luke had disappeared but there were a few more people about now. The Shire horse had finished being shod at the forge and was coming along the green. He was a huge beast with chestnut-brown sides, a creamy white blaze down his nose and feathery blond hairs covering his enormous feet. The young woman leading him paused as Stella and the vicar came down the church path, and the horse leaned his big head against her arm.

'Valerie!' Basil Harvey greeted her. 'Come and meet Miss Simmons. We're hoping she may come to be our new infant teacher.' He rubbed the horse's nose absently and felt in his pocket. 'I'm sure I've got a peppermint somewhere here . . .'

Stella smiled shyly. She was beginning to wonder how she would ever be able to remember the names of all these people. This young woman looked about the same age as Hilary Napier – a year or two under thirty, perhaps – and was about the same height, but her hair was dark and tied back from her face with a blue ribbon. She had a rather long face and her smile seemed tinged with sadness. She nodded at Stella.

'Nice to meet you.' She was the first person Stella had met who spoke with a Devon accent, although it wasn't very strong; perhaps she'd been out of the village for a while. She gave the vicar an apologetic glance as she added, 'Sorry, Mr Harvey, I can't stop, Dad needs Barley back on the farm. He cast a shoe in the night – got it caught up on the fence – and it's put us all behind.' The horse had his nose down in the grass and had begun munching, and she gave the head-collar a gentle tug. 'Come on, Barley, it isn't dinnertime yet. We've got work to do.'

She walked on and Stella saw the vicar look after her thoughtfully. Then he turned back to Stella with a cheerful smile on his rosy face.

'A nice person, Val Tozer. She lives at the farm just over there. Still with her parents – ought to be married with her own home and family, but she lost her fiancé in the war – a sad story. Right – the school's just along here and if we're lucky we'll get there while the children are still in class.' He gave Stella a conspiratorial glance. 'I'm afraid you won't meet the redoubtable Miss Morgan, though. Since Dr Latimer ordered her to retire, we've had the assistance of another of our old teachers, Miss Perriman – a very different kind of person. The children love her.'

He hastened on along the village street with Stella almost having to run to keep up with him. Her heart was beginning to beat fast and she felt again the tinge of apprehension that had accompanied her all the way on the train from Hampshire and then on the bus from the little market town of Tavistock.

I want this job so much, she thought. I don't know what I'll do if I don't get it . . .

Val Tozer strode along the lane, her hand stroking the soft skin under Barley's neck. The big, gentle horse nuzzled her as she walked but her mind wasn't with him. Nor did she notice the colours of the hedgerows, their summer green fading now to the browns of autumn with a few black-berries still glistening above the gateways, and the grey, spiky twigs of a sloe-tree in contrast with its purple fruits. Familiar as they were to her, they were far from her thoughts as she walked between the steep Devon banks towards her father's farm.

'Val!'

Even before she heard the voice, the sound of footsteps behind her had brought a prickle to her spine. Her back stiffened and she quickened her pace.

'Val, wait. Please. Look, you can't go on avoiding me all the time.' The voice was closer. 'Please talk to me, Val.'

Val took a deep breath, squared her shoulders and stopped. Barley came to a halt and turned his head enquiringly. Stubbornly, she stared straight ahead.

Luke Ferris came beside her and touched her arm. She shook it off and stepped away from him.

'Don't do that.'

'Val,' he said despairingly. 'Val, please. We can't pretend we don't know each other.'

'I don't see why not.' Her breath felt tight in her chest, like a hard lump, and her heart was thumping painfully. 'I don't see why we have to have anything to do with each other.'

'But I'm living here now. We're bound to meet—'

'No, we're not. Not if you keep out of my way.' She faced him at last. 'I'm perfectly prepared to keep out of yours. And why did you have to come and live here anyway? Couldn't you have gone somewhere else?'

'I didn't know you lived here,' he said quietly and, at the flash of angry disbelief in her eyes, added, 'I *didn't*. You never told me – or if you did, I'd forgotten. It was all a long time ago.' He hesitated, but she didn't speak, and he went on, 'Look, I really didn't come here to make trouble. I needed to be in the country and Uncle Basil – the vicar – knew of the cottage and asked Colonel Napier if I could rent it. It was as simple as that. It never occurred to me that you'd be here.'

She looked at him. His face was thinner than she

remembered, and rather drawn. Yet he was still sunburned, as if he spent a good deal of time in the open air. She wondered briefly what he'd been doing over the years since they'd last met.

'Well, you know now,' she said brusquely. 'And if you don't mind, I'd rather we didn't talk to each other. We've got nothing to say.' She lifted her hand to push Barley's damp nose off her shoulder. 'I've got to go now.'

Luke's eyes went to her fingers and a frown gathered between his brows. 'You're not wearing a ring.'

'No,' Val said shortly. 'I'm not.'

'But . . .' He seemed to be feeling for words and when he spoke again it was uncertainly. 'You – you didn't get married, then?'

'I couldn't,' she said. 'He was killed in the D-Day landings. We didn't have a chance to get married.' Her eyes met his again and she added bitterly, 'Not everyone had a soft job drawing pretty pictures.'

'They weren't pretty,' Luke said quietly. 'You know that, Val.' He paused. 'I'm sorry to hear about Eddie, though. And – there hasn't been anyone else?'

Val's eyes filled with tears. She turned away and jerked at Barley's head. He gave a whicker of protest and she rubbed his nose in apology, but was already striding on along the lane.

'No,' she said over her shoulder, 'there hasn't been anyone else. There never will be.' She stopped and turned again, facing him. 'Go away, Luke. You've done enough damage. Go away and leave me alone.'

Together, she and the big horse marched away down the lane. Her shoulders were stiff, her back straight, but Luke knew that if he could see her face he would find tears pouring down her cheeks. He started after her and then stopped again, knowing that it was no use.

He watched until she disappeared from sight round the

bend in the lane. Then he walked slowly back through the village, past the green with its huge ancient oak tree, past the grey stone church, past the Bell Inn with its thatched roof and benches outside, past the school where the children were spilling out into the playground. Almost without seeing them, he passed the vicar and Stella Simmons, standing at the door and talking to Miss Kemp, the headmistress, and then he turned up the narrow lane that led to his own cottage, on the edge of the Barton estate.

He had spoken the truth when he'd said he hadn't realised that Val Tozer lived in Burracombe. But he couldn't, in all honesty, say that he wouldn't have come to live here if he had known.

Chapter Two

Basil Harvey, standing in the playground of Burracombe School, saw Luke walk by and lifted his hand. But Luke didn't seem to notice him. He appeared to be deep in thought, his long face furrowed with creases that had come too soon for his age, and there was a droop to his thin shoulders as he passed the school railings. He turned up the lane without acknowledging Basil, and the vicar watched him thoughtfully and with a touch of anxiety.

Basil Harvey was more than a family friend; he was Luke's godfather and took his responsibilities seriously. He had been as worried as the rest of the family when Luke had developed TB, but the sanatoriums seemed to have worked a cure at last, and now all the young man needed was peace, quiet and fresh air to build up his strength. Basil had hoped that in Burracombe he would find all of these, together with the chance to build up his reputation as a landscape painter.

Miss Kemp and Stella had seen Luke as well.

'Isn't that the man you introduced me to on the green?' Stella asked. 'I thought he was going to paint some trees.'

'Yes, he was. He wanted to catch the colours. I hope he's all right.' Luke disappeared along the lane and Basil turned back to the others. 'Well, I dare say he just changed his mind. You ought to get him to come into the school and talk to the children sometime, Miss Kemp. He's rather a good artist.'

'Perhaps we will.' The headmistress glanced at her watch. 'We'd better go over to the vicarage. I expect Colonel Napier and Miss Bellamy will be there by now.'

Stella followed them across the playground. The children had either gone home for their midday meal or were crowding into the tiny canteen where she had met the school cook, Mrs Dawe, who was serving shepherd's pie for those who lived too far away to go home. She had seen both classrooms – the large one for the 'big' children of seven to eleven years, and the smaller one, which would be hers (if she got the job) for the infants. There were usually about nine or ten of them, Miss Kemp had explained, although it would probably go up next year when the Crocker twins arrived.

'Twins!' Stella exclaimed. 'Are they identical?'

'Well, they're certainly very alike.' The headmistress glanced at Basil Harvey. 'I'd say that George and Edward were identical, wouldn't you, Vicar?' She folded her lips wryly. 'I'm afraid there'll be fun and games when those two arrive in school!'

'Now, we mustn't put Miss Simmons off,' the vicar said hastily. 'Anyway, they're only four years old now and there's almost a whole year to go before they start. They'll probably change a lot in that time . . .' As if feeling that even this statement had a certain ominous sound to it, he opened the school gate with something of a flourish. 'What do you think of our little school, Miss Simmons?'

'I like it very much.' Stella had spent most of her life in larger schools, with up to forty children in each class. Even when she had lived in the country, as an evacuee, schooling had been difficult, with the village school shared between local and evacuee children, taking turn and turn about in the mornings and afternoons. The prospect of having only ten or a dozen children to teach, in quiet and ordered surroundings, seemed like a glimpse of heaven.

Burracombe School and its playground were situated at the edge of the village. The headmistress's cottage stood to one side and beyond it were fields, a wood and then the moor where Miss Kemp had explained that the children were sometimes taken on nature walks. 'There's a pretty stream and a pond where they can catch tadpoles for the nature table.' It was near enough to the green and the church for the school to feel very much a part of local goings-on, and the children were taken to church every Wednesday morning for their own service.

'I'm in and out a lot too,' Mr Harvey told Stella as they walked back towards the church. 'I hope you won't mind my popping in. I like the children to get to know me and feel that they can come to me with their problems even after they've left school and have gone out into the world.'

'Yes, we encourage several of our friends to drop in and talk to the children,' Miss Kemp agreed. 'Mr Tozer, the farmer, comes in when he brings our logs for the fire, and tells us all about what's happening on the farm—'

'You met his daughter, Val, with the horse,' the vicar interrupted. 'And Hilary Napier, whom you met in the church, came in once to talk about her time in the ATS during the war. She was a driver, you know, and met some famous people – Mr Churchill, Mr Eisenhower, Lord Montgomery . . .'

'Colonel Napier, the chairman of the governors, is her father,' Miss Kemp continued. 'The other governor is Miss Bellamy. She's from a very old Burracombe family and quite a character.'

They passed the church to go through the gate to the vicarage, a large house set back from the road in a big, untidy garden. Rhododendron and azalea bushes fringed the path and a few tall trees were shedding coloured leaves on the lawn. The vicarage itself had a verandah running all the way around three sides, and the front door stood invitingly open. Mr Harvey ushered them through and called out to his wife.

'Grace! We're here.' He sniffed appreciatively. 'Mm, that smells good.'

A tall fair-haired woman emerged from the kitchen, wiping floury hands on a cloth. She smiled at Miss Kemp and held out her hand to Stella. Her grasp was firm and her eyes intelligent. 'It's good to see you, Miss Simmons. I hope you had a pleasant journey.'

'It was lovely. I had such good views of the moors. I like wild countryside.'

Grace Harvey nodded and turned to her husband. 'Colonel Napier and Miss Bellamy are here. I put them in your study.'

The vicar led the way down the hall. Over his shoulder, he said, 'Grace wanted to put us into the drawing room but I knew Colonel Napier would prefer the study – it's more formal. He's our Squire, you know. We had to bring in another chair, but I think we'll be comfortable enough.'

He opened a door and the two women followed him into a large room lined with bookshelves. There was a French window opening on to the verandah at the side and looking out into the shrubbery, and a large desk littered with papers. A small fire was burning in the grate with a leather armchair on each side of it, one occupied by a large man in his mid-fifties wearing a tweed suit, and the other by a small, stocky woman with a face so creased by tiny wrinkles that she looked as if she had been crumpled up in a giant fist. She was dressed in a shapeless purple jumper and a sagging brown skirt.

'Ah good, you've made yourselves at home.' The vicar beamed at them as the man got up and held out his hand. He was the sort of man, Stella thought as she took it, who would dominate any situation – solidly built, with confident bearing and a head like a lion's, certain of himself and his

16

position and probably rather arrogant. She decided not to be intimidated by him and lifted her chin to meet his eyes.

'So you're hoping to be our new infant teacher,' he said. His voice was strong and deep, just as she'd expected it to be, and carried a slight undertone of warning. It was as if he were saying, *Don't expect it to be a foregone conclusion, whatever the vicar might have said*, and she felt a small thrill of challenge run through her.

'I hope so,' she replied steadily. 'I like what I've seen so far.'

There was a small change in his eyes, as if he had registered that she wasn't here to beg, and that it was as important that Burracombe should make a good impression on her as the other way about. They regarded each other for a moment and then the vicar said, 'And this is Miss Bellamy, whose family endowed the school almost a hundred years ago.'

Stella turned to greet the old woman, who was now standing up. She was little more than five feet tall, with iron-grey hair and eyes as black and lively as tadpoles. Her face was as red and wrinkled as a Cox's apple and she seemed to bristle with energy. She shook Stella's hand vigorously. 'You'll find us pretty quiet down here in the West Country.'

Stella smiled. 'I lived in a village for a while, as a child. I think I'll like being in the country.' She felt something nudge her foot and looked down at the rug to see the elongated body of a dachsund. 'Oh – a dog!' She bent quickly to pat him and he lifted his long nose and licked her hand. 'Is he yours, Miss Bellamy?'

'He is. He's called Rupert.' The little woman bent and rubbed his back and he rolled over and stuck four short legs in the air. 'And a shameless beggar he is too. No dignity at all. Make yourself decent, Rupert! The idea! And in the vicarage, too. Sorry, Vicar, but boys will be boys, as I'm sure you know.'

The Squire looked impatient and moved towards the desk.

'Let's get this interview started,' he said. 'I'll take your chair, Basil, if you don't mind.' The other three governors took the seats beside him and Stella sat in front of them, her brief moment of confidence deserting her as nervousness returned. 'Now then, Miss Simmons . . .'

At the farm, the Tozers were sitting down to their midday meal. Val, still feeling shaken after her meeting with Luke, was quieter than usual, but there was enough family chatter going on to conceal her silence, at least for a while.

'Well, it's been a warm start to the month,' Ted Tozer remarked, accepting a large plate of sausages and mashed potatoes from his mother Minnie. At eighty-two, she still cooked dinner for them every day, although once that was done her duties were over and she was content to sit by the kitchen fire in winter or potter in the garden in summer. Just now, she was beginning to think about Christmas and had already begun knitting new gloves and mittens for presents and for the church bazaar.

Ted was still talking about the weather and hoping it meant a mild winter. 'Don't speak too soon,' his wife advised him, helping herself to another sausage. 'Plenty of time yet, there be, for the weather to change. Just you remember 1947 – the snow didn't really start till halfway through January but once it started it didn't know how to stop. Us don't want that lot again.'

'No, you'm right, there, Alice.' The blizzard across the south-west of England at the end of January that year had cut off Burracombe for a fortnight. They'd lost any number of sheep up on the moor, and those that didn't freeze starved before the men could get fodder up to them. Work in the fields had been impossible too, with the ground like iron for weeks on end. The snow lying in the fields and on the moors and piled along the hedgerows became solid ice, impossible to shift, and had then melted all at once when the temperatures rose at last, and turned into floods. It was the worst winter yet, after years of severe winters all through the war, and they said that February itself had been the coldest since 1814.

'Still, we got a good summer to make up for it,' Joanna said cheerfully. She was sitting at the end of the table, with Robin in his high-chair opening and shutting his mouth like a goldfish as she spooned in potato and gravy. 'It was a lovely summer, 1947.'

'You only think that because you had the luck to marry me then,' Tom said, grinning at her. 'It could have rained the whole year and you'd still have thought it was lovely.'

'It's us who were the lucky ones,' Alice told him. 'The thought of our Joanna going back to London was as bad as – well, as our Val leaving home. Proper wound herself round our hearts, she had – just like this little one here,' she added, leaning forward to poke her grandson's tummy and make him squeal. 'It were a good day for the Tozers when you came home and had the sense to ask Jo to marry you.'

Joanna smiled, but her smile had a touch of sadness about it. She had lost both her parents in the Blitz in 1941, and when the war ended and she'd been demobbed from the Land Army, she had felt like a lost soul, cast adrift on an open sea. She'd been glad to stay on until Tom came home, and when he finally arrived, everything had changed. With one look, they both knew what their future must be, and Joanna had settled down as a farmer's wife as easily as if she'd been born to it.

'Mrs Warren was in the shop this morning, talking about this big Festival they're having in London next year,' she said, wiping Robin's chin. 'She's going to get up a coach-party to go and see it. D'you think you'll go, Mum?'

'Me, go to London?' Alice said. 'Oh, I don't know about that. I went once when I was a little girl, to see the old King's Coronation, but I didn't really like it. It was so busy! And I dare say it'll be even worse now.'

'I expect it will,' Tom said with a grin. 'They've got cars now, Mum. It was all horses then, wasn't it.'

'Well, there were cars about,' Alice said, 'but not very many. I don't think I could get used to all the traffic these days. I don't even like going to Plymouth or Exeter all that much. Tavistock's good enough for me, and the Goosey Fair's as good as any big festival in London.'

'Yes, but we won't have to worry about traffic,' Joanna said. 'The coach will take us right there and bring us home afterwards. You'll go, won't you, Val?' she asked her sister-in-law. 'You'll go on the coach trip to the Festival?'

'Haven't really thought about it.' Val's thoughts had been far away, further even than London. 'I might. It'll be something to do.'

Alice glanced at her sharply. 'Is something the matter, Val? You've hardly eaten a thing. You're just picking at those sausages.'

'Sorry, Mum. I'm not very hungry.' Val moved her plate away. 'I'll go out and start filling up the racks in the milking parlour, Dad. It'll save time later.' She pushed back her chair and left the table, and they heard her pulling on her boots in the outer kitchen.

Alice looked at her husband in consternation. 'Well, and what's that all about, d'you know, Ted? Our Val enjoys her food so much as a rule. And your mother's made a nice bread-and-butter pudding for afters, too – it's her favourite.'

Ted shrugged. 'You know what these young girls are like, never the same two days running. Look at our Jackie –

all smiles one minute, but you just got to say the wrong word and she's flouncing out and slamming doors till the house shakes. Val'll be all right when she's worked it out of her system, whatever it is.'

'Yes, but Val's not a young girl,' Alice said sharply. 'She's a woman of twenty-eight and she ought to be married with her own home by now. As she would have been, if Eddie hadn't been killed.'

'That was six years ago,' Ted said. 'She should have got over that by now. She met plenty of other young men while she was away nursing, you'd think there'd have been someone to take her fancy.'

'Valerie's like me,' Minnie said, sitting down at last with her own plate. 'A one-man woman. I never wanted to look at another man after your father died, God bless him.'

'Mother!' Ted exclaimed. 'You were sixty-nine when Father died. There weren't likely to be many other men for you to look at.'

Minnie wagged her fork at him reprovingly. 'That's all you know, Ted Tozer. There was Arthur Dawe for a start, him that farmed over to Shaugh. He asked me often enough. And I could have had George Crocker, any time I liked. He threw out enough hints about my cooking.'

Ted spluttered with laughter. 'Arthur Dawe! He's ninety if he's a day. And as for George Crocker – well, he was just looking for a housekeeper with her own bit of money. Mean old toad.'

Minnie sniffed. 'Never mind that, all I'm saying is I had my chances. Those weren't the only two. It's a good job I could run fast, that's all.'

'Good job they could run faster,' Ted muttered, and ducked sideways as she aimed a slap at him. 'Good job for us, I mean,' he added hastily. 'I don't know what we'd have done without you to cook our dinners for us, Mother.'

'You'd have had Alice to cook them instead, and she'm just as good a cook as me.' Minnie cut up one of her sausages. 'Anyway, all that's by the by. What us wants to know is what's eating our Val. You're right, Alice, there's something the matter there. Pale as a ghost she was, when she came in from taking Barley to the forge. Pale as a ghost.'

'I don't know, I'm sure.' Alice passed the cabbage over to Joanna. 'Take some more of this, maid, you've got hardly any . . . I tell you what, I've been worried about that girl for a long time now. Whatever you may say, she's not getting over that business with Eddie as she should. It's not natural for a girl of her age to grieve for ever. It's as if she's got stuck somewhere.' She looked round the table at them all and said, 'It's my belief something else happened to her – when she was out in Egypt during the war, most likely. She never talks about it much, but she must have seen some nasty sights, nursing out there.'

'I don't see what she could have seen that'd turn her off marrying,' Ted objected, swallowing the last of his sausage. 'Anyway, that was before Eddie was killed. What difference could anything that happened out there make?'

'I don't know, but she seemed different when she came back. Why, she was a real ray of sunshine when she was a girl and even after she joined the VADs she was always bright and cheerful. But when she came back from Egypt, she'd changed. That's all I'm saying.' Alice got up and began to collect the vegetable dishes and take them over to the sink.

The rest of the family finished their meal in silence. Minnie served out the bread-and-butter pudding and then Joanna said, 'I think Mum's right. I didn't know Val before the war, but I think she looks really sad sometimes, as if she's thinking about something she can't talk about. I don't know what we can do about it, though.'

'You can't do anything,' Tom declared, scraping the crispy bits off the pudding dish. 'Val's a grown woman and she's got to sort out her own problems. I don't know what you're all worrying about anyway – she seems all right to me. Just because she didn't want her dinner . . .'

The women looked at him and then at each other in exasperation, but Ted was nodding in agreement. 'Leave her alone. Everyone feels a bit down in the dumps now and then.' He scraped back his chair. 'Time you and me were outside, Tom. Can't leave the maid to do the work all on her own.'

'That's right,' Alice said. 'This is supposed to be her day off. She works all hours at the hospital, and then has to come home and do your work as well!'

The two men went outside. Minnie settled in her rocking-chair and Alice started the washing-up while Joanna cleaned her son's face and set him on the floor to play with some wooden bricks. She went over to the sink and began to dry the dishes.

'I shouldn't worry too much about Val,' she said quietly. 'Whatever it was that happened to her, she's as happy here as she'll ever be. She's got her family around her and a job she loves at Tavistock Hospital, and she's happy helping out on the farm in her spare time. There are plenty of people a lot worse off than Val.'

Alice paused and stood with her hands in the hot, soapy water, gazing out of the window at the yard where Val was disappearing into the cowshed.

'I know, maid,' she said, 'and most of the time she does seem happy enough. But you know what it is with your own,' she glanced down at the toddler playing at their feet. 'You want everything to be right for them. And it's not right for Val. I know it isn't.'

She sighed and went on with the washing-up, then

added so low that Joanna could barely hear her, 'But Tom's right. Unless us knows what it is, there's nothing any of us can do about it.'

Chapter Three

As far as Stella could tell, the interview had gone quite well. They had asked her a lot of questions and she'd answered them honestly: how she'd been orphaned during the war, then sent to a Children's Home in Hampshire. She looked at the four governors, hoping that she hadn't sounded self-pitying. She thought they probably knew most of her story anyway, from her letter of application and from the references they'd asked for from the Home.

'They were very good to me at the Home,' she said now. 'They let me stay on and work as a pupil teacher, and while I've been at college they've let me go back and live there during the holidays. Otherwise, I'd have had nowhere to go.'

'So you've had quite a lot of experience already, of working with children,' the vicar said with an understanding nod of his silver head.

'Yes,' Stella replied. 'I worked mostly with the infants – that's why I applied for this post.'

'And you'll be happy to come and live in Devon?' Colonel Napier asked, his voice gruff.

As local Squire, he must own a good deal of the land hereabouts, and Stella knew he would have a lot of influence. She could see too that he was a dominating man, used to being obeyed, but she didn't think he was a bully. He would appreciate someone who was ready to speak up for herself.

'Yes, I will,' she answered him. 'I love the countryside – I'd hate to live in a city.' She shivered a little, remembering the narrow streets she had lived in as a child.

'Hmph.' He glanced at the two women, Miss Kemp and Miss Bellamy. Miss Kemp began to ask about Stella's teaching experience and training, and the lines she would take with the children: how did she feel reading and writing should be taught, was she good at teaching crafts and handiwork? Then it was Miss Bellamy's turn and she leaned forward, her little black eyes bright.

'You say you've no other home now. Does that mean you'd like to stay in Burracombe during the holidays as well as termtime? You'd want to be part of the village – join in with the other things that go on here?'

'Yes, I would. I want somewhere to settle down – somewhere I can call home.' Stella thought of the village, its centre clustered about the green with the pub and the church close by, and the school only a little way down the lane. Although its centre was small, Burracombe was quite a large village, with its own shops and Post Office, its bakery, its butcher, and the little hardware store tacked on to the garage. And although she hadn't had time to read them, she'd seen several notices pinned to the board by the village hall. There'd be a Women's Institute, a Mother's Union, whist drives, dances – perhaps even an amateur dramatics group or a church choir. 'I'd really like to join in things,' she said, unaware of how wistful her voice sounded.

The interview had ended soon after that and they'd all gone to the dining room for lunch. Mrs Harvey had made a rabbit pie, with plenty of onions, fresh vegetables and a thick gravy. The mashed potato to go with it was light and fluffy. Afterwards, there was blackberry-and-apple crumble and, to Stella's amazement, clotted cream.

'I've never seen cream like this,' she said, spooning some

of the crusty yellow mound on to her plate. 'In fact, I've hardly ever seen cream at all!'

'Good Devonshire cream, that is,' Miss Bellamy asserted. 'You won't get it anywhere else. Well, they do make it in Cornwall, but then it's Cornish cream – not as good, is it, Gilbert?'

The Colonel, who had spooned a generous helping on to his own bowl of crumble, shrugged. 'Can't see any difference myself.'

Constance Bellamy snorted. 'Try telling that to Ted Tozer or Alice! Our cream's got to be richer, it stands to reason – look at the fields. You don't get that green down in Cornwall.'

'And it all comes from the rain,' the vicar told Stella with a smile. 'Plenty of rain means lush grass, means rich milk, means cream. Have some more, my dear.'

'Yes, you mustn't believe too much talk about sunny Devon,' Mrs Harvey said. 'We do get lots of sunshine, and of course it's generally milder here than in the rest of the country, but we get plenty of rain as well. You'll need a good mackintosh when you come here.'

'*If* Miss Simmons comes here,' her husband corrected her gently, and she looked startled.

'Oh dear! Have I spoken out of turn? I thought it seemed as if you'd decided.'

Colonel Napier and Miss Kemp glanced at each other, and then at the other two governors. Then the Squire cleared his throat and said, 'Well, since we've come to this point, perhaps we'd better say that I think we have.' He addressed Stella. 'We had a talk while you were out of the room, and we'd like you to know that if you're still interested in taking the post of infant teacher in our school, we'll be delighted to have you. We're in complete agreement over this.' He paused, while Stella's heart suddenly thumped. 'Welcome to Burracombe.'

Stella stared at him. She looked round the table at the others. Miss Kemp was looking pleased and encouraging, the vicar's pink round face was glowing and Constance Bellamy was nodding. She felt a sudden surge of joy and, at the same time, a prickling of tears in her eyes.

'Do you really mean it?' she asked, almost afraid to believe what she had just heard. 'Have I really got the job? I thought you'd need longer to think about it. I thought there must be other applicants.'

'There have been two other applicants,' Miss Kemp told her, 'but we've all agreed that you're the one we think most suitable. So if you can make your own decision and let us know . . .'

'Oh, I've already decided,' Stella said instantly. 'I'd love to come to Burracombe. I knew I wanted to, the minute I got off the bus.' She thought fleetingly of Luke Ferris's wicked grin and twinkling blue eyes, of the village with its beautiful surroundings and then of the school itself with its two classrooms and bright, active children. 'It's just what I wanted,' she added sincerely.

'Then that's settled. We'll go into details later, but we'll take it that you'll come to us immediately after Christmas. You'll start the New Year with us. We've already arranged lodgings with Miss Friend – known to the village as Dottie.' Miss Kemp beamed at her and then turned to Mrs Harvey. 'Grace, I'm sure Miss Simmons would like another helping of this delicious crumble to celebrate.'

Stella looked at her plate, sure she wouldn't be able to swallow a morsel. She felt dazed by the news, hardly able to take in the headmistress's words, and so full of joy that there seemed no room for food. Nevertheless, she spooned on more cream and found that she was able to eat it after all. The crumble was light and crisp, the blackberries and apple an ideal combination, and the clotted cream rich and buttery. She thought of her wartime childhood, with only a few sweets a week – and not that many more even now. Five years on and we've still got rationing, she thought. Not that you'd believe it, to look at the meal they'd just eaten.

'I hope I'm not taking your rations,' she said, looking again at the bowl from which they'd all helped themselves so liberally. 'I really didn't expect such a lovely meal.'

'Bless you, you're welcome,' the vicar's wife said, smiling. 'We do have to be careful, of course we do, but things are easier here than in the towns. We've all got space to keep a few hens, you see, and we're allowed to use our own eggs, so long as we don't have too many. And the milk's so rich it would be a crime not to make cream from it. I make my own – just pour the milk into a pan and simmer it very gently for two hours or so, and then let it cool. The cream comes to the top naturally, you see, and we can still use the skim. None of this came from a shop.'

'No, indeed,' Miss Kemp agreed. 'The apples are from the vicarage orchard, and I picked the blackberries myself on a nature walk with the children. They all took a basketful home. There are mushrooms in the fields too, but you have to be out early in the morning to pick them.'

'Why?' Stella asked. 'Don't they last long enough in the day?'

The vicar laughed. 'Well, if it's a hot day they might shrivel up a bit, but mostly it's just because people *do*, pick mushrooms early in the morning, so if you're not out there too, they'll all be gone! It's like a kind of silent race.'

'You'll soon learn country ways,' his wife said. 'You can't live long in a place like Burracombe without hearing all the old country lore.'

'Not that you have to believe it,' the Colonel remarked. 'Lot of mumbo jumbo . . .' He began to rise to his feet. 'Basil, I must be going. Plenty to do. Grace, the lunch was delicious. Miss Kemp – better get back to your class.' He gave Stella a nod. 'Welcome again, Miss Simmons. I hope you'll be happy in Burracombe. I'm sure we've made the right decision.'

'Yes, I must go too,' Miss Kemp declared. 'As the Colonel says, the children will be waiting. I left Mrs James reading to them all but I mustn't presume on her good nature any longer.' She turned to Stella. 'I'll be writing to you, Miss Simmons, and of course you'll be hearing officially about your appointment. I look forward very much to meeting you again in the New Year.'

She and the Squire departed together and Stella was left with her host and hostess and Constance Bellamy. She hesitated, not sure what to do next, and the vicar came to her rescue.

'What time is your train back to Hampshire? You must be sure not to miss the Tavistock bus – it goes at three-fifteen.' He smiled. 'You'll meet a lot of your new charges again – those who live too far away to walk use that bus to go home.'

'You'll be very late home tonight, I'm afraid,' his wife said, looking worried. 'Really, we should have asked you to stay the night. Shouldn't we, Basil?'

'Oh, there's no need,' Stella said quickly before they could offer her an invitation. 'I'll be back by ten. And I promised I'd be there in the morning, to get the little ones up.'

The vicar looked at the tall grandfather clock in the hall. 'Well, it's two o'clock now. What would you like to do? I could take you over to the church again – they'll have finished the harvest decorations by now. Or—'

'Well, if you don't mind,' Stella said, 'it's such a lovely afternoon, I'd quite like to walk round the village by myself. Just to get the feel of it, you know, and have something to think about before I come back again. I'll go into the church as well,' she promised hastily in case he was offended. 'I'd like to see the decorations.'

'Of course,' Mrs Harvey said, and added hospitably, 'You must come back here and have a cup of tea before catching the bus. We'll expect you in about half an hour.'

Stella put on her jacket and gloves and walked out into the afternoon sunshine, turning away from the village street with its small shops interspersed between the cottages, and walking along a lane that led into the countryside. I really am seeing Burracombe at its best, she thought, gazing at the green and gold tapestry of the hedgerows. A narrow stream glittered beside the road, and blackberries hung full and glossy over her head. The high, grassy Devon bank would be sprinkled with primroses in the spring, she thought, and perhaps violets too, and later there would be foxgloves and dog-roses and honeysuckle. But now the year was winding down, the trees and hedges getting ready to close down for the winter. The grass was fading to a pale, dusty fawn and the leaves on the hedges were turning brown, lit by the tiny red lanterns of hips and haws, and the more sinister purple of honeysuckle and deadly nightshade.

Stella loved the autumn. The rich golds and scarlets of the trees were like a huge damask quilt flung over the countryside, and the swelling moorland above the valley glowed auburn against the tender blue of the sky. A smell of fresh air and damp earth and woodsmoke tingled in her nostrils, and somewhere nearby she could hear a bird singing – a pretty, liquid song like the sparkling drops of the stream translated into music. Stella stopped for a moment and looked about, and then caught sight of the orange breast and bright black eyes of a robin, its brown body camouflaged by the tawny leaves.

By the time she came back after Christmas, the year would have turned and the leaves gone, leaving a tracery of grey, brown and black twigs. The birds would have eaten the red rosehips and the fruits of the hawthorn hedge, and even the bryony and deadly nightshade berries would have shrivelled and cast their seeds. The blackberries would be long gone and the flowers of spring still huddled beneath the cold earth.

Stella didn't mind winter. She liked the cold bite of a bright January morning and the full-bellied bruises of clouds that promised snow. She loved the occasional mild day when it seemed as if spring had arrived early, and enjoyed a walk in a clean, scouring wind as long as she was well wrapped up against it. She wasn't so keen on rain and hoped that the vicar had been exaggerating when he said what a wet county Devon was, but everywhere had rain and you just had to put up with it. And the little streams and rivers that abounded in this area would look all the better after a downpour.

She came to a small wooden gate which led into a wood and hesitated for a moment; then, as there was no *Private* sign forbidding her to enter, she opened the gate and walked along a narrow footpath between the trees. They were spaced quite wide apart, tall, thin oaks and beeches, and their brown leaves, mast and acorns crunched beneath her feet. Rocks and boulders lay scattered between them and everything was covered in thick green moss. It even grew up the trunks of the trees, well above her head. The tinted leaves rustled in the soft breeze and as she looked up, she could see that a few were already falling. Somewhere amongst the branches a bird screeched, and she heard the scuttering sound of small feet.

The path led her up a short, steep hill. The sun slanted down into her eyes and she climbed almost blindly, emerging at the top to find herself on the edge of the moor. A tumbled wall bordered the wood and she clambered through a gap and stood on brown, dead bracken, catching her breath.

'So we meet again.'

Stella gasped and turned quickly. The man who had first spoken to her when she got off the bus was sitting on a large rock, a sketchpad on his knee and a pencil in his hand. His mouth quirked in a grin and she laughed with relief.

'You startled me.'

'Sorry. I seem to be making a habit of it. I'll try not to do it again.' His dark brows gathered together in a small frown. 'What are you doing up here? I thought you were being interviewed.'

'I was. We've finished now and I'm just having a walk before I catch the bus.' She hesitated, then said rather shyly, 'I've got the job.'

'You have?' His grin widened. 'That's really good. I'm very pleased. When do you start?'

'After Christmas. I had promised to stay on at the Home, where I'm teaching now, until then.' She stumbled with her words, feeling suddenly unwilling to admit that she lived in an orphanage. 'I'll probably come and settle in some time in the New Year.'

'Come earlier, if you can, and I'll show you around a bit. Not that I know much myself, but I'll know more by then.' He laughed and Stella smiled. 'Do you know where you'll be living?'

'Miss Kemp says they've found somewhere for me to lodge. A friend, I think she said – or maybe a Miss Friend – but I'm not sure. Is that a surname?'

Luke laughed again. 'It certainly is! Half the village is called Friend, and the other half are either Pettifer or Tozer. And they're all related, one way or another. You have to be *very* careful what you say. The Burracombe village grapevine is extremely efficient.'

'I will be,' she promised, and then glanced at her watch. 'I'd better go. I said I'd go back to the vicarage for a cup of tea.'

33

'That's a pity,' he said, unfolding his long legs and standing up. 'I was going to suggest you come and have one with me in my cottage. Never mind, there'll be plenty of time once you're here. Anyway, I'll walk back with you.'

'I don't want to interrupt your work—' she began, but he waved a hand.

'The light's going anyway. I was just about to pack up.' He closed his sketchbook and led the way along the wall and through another gap where a broader footpath took them down through the wood, passing a tiny cottage on the way. 'This is my abode,' he said. 'It used to belong to a family of charcoal-burners, so I've been told – they lived here until the end of the war. Then the old man died and his son didn't come home from the war, and the old lady went to live with her daughter in Horrabridge. It had been empty for a couple of years when I moved in.'

'It looks very cosy,' Stella said, wondering what it must be like to live in such an isolated cottage in the middle of a wood.

'It is, when I've got the fire going, and there's certainly plenty of firewood around.' He gestured at the fallen branches and trees lying on the moss-covered earth and rocks. 'I can live quite cheaply.'

'It must be lonely, though.'

Luke gave her a swift glance. 'Not at all. There are plenty of birds and animals about – rabbits, foxes, badgers, they all come past my door, and if I sit quietly on that log there for a while, the birds forget I'm about. Listen to that.' Stella tilted her head slightly and heard a drumming sound somewhere in the trees. 'That's a woodpecker. You'll see him if you look hard enough – leaning out from the trunk and drilling at it with his beak. And look, there's a squirrel.' He put his hand on her shoulder and turned her. She caught a flash of red disappearing behind a tree-trunk and then spotted the animal itself, scurrying along a branch. It ran right to the end and then took off, almost flying across the wide gap to land in another tree and disappear amongst the leaves. Stella caught her breath with delight.

'Oh, that's lovely! They're really red, aren't they.'

'They are, but we've got greys moving in and I've heard that when they take over an area, the reds disappear. It's a shame because the red squirrels are the ones who really live here – the greys came over from America. Look, there he is again. He's collecting chestnuts from that tree and burying them for the winter.'

'They hibernate, don't they?' Stella asked, but Luke shook his head.

'No, they just spend a lot of time asleep in their dreys while the weather's bad. Then they come out and find as many nuts as they can and gorge themselves, ready for the next bad spell. You can see them when there's snow on the ground and the sun's out, scampering about looking for their hiding places. Half of them are lost, of course, and that's one of the reasons we get new trees – the squirrels have planted them!'

Stella laughed and then jumped as she heard the same screech as she had heard before. 'What's that?'

'A jay.' Luke pointed and she saw a brightly coloured bird almost as big as a rook flash between the trees. 'There are loads of them round here. They like woodland.'

'You seem to know a lot about birds and animals,' she said, watching the squirrel as he sat on a branch, a nut held between his tiny paws, chattering crossly at the noisy jay.

'I spent a long time in the country,' he said briefly. 'I had plenty of opportunity to learn. Right, how about that cup of tea now you're here?'

'Oh no, I mustn't. Mrs Harvey's expecting me. It would be rude not to go back.' She looked up at him and smiled. 'It's been really nice to meet you, Mr Ferris.'

'Luke, for heaven's sake. And your name? I can't call you Miss Simmons, as if I were a mixed infant.'

'Stella,' she said, and put out her hand as if they had only just been introduced.

He took it and held it in his, and once again she felt the warmth of his long fingers. 'Stella,' he repeated softly. 'A star. A nice name – it suits you.'

Stella felt her cheeks colour. She drew her hand away and gave a little laugh. 'I really must go. I've got a long journey – I mustn't miss my train.'

'No, of course. Look, if you take this path down to the road you can cross the field and come out just opposite the vicarage gate.' He walked with her, his long strides covering the ground swiftly so that Stella, who wasn't particularly short, had to move quickly to keep up. The wood opened on to a meadow grazed by a flock of white sheep with black faces, who glanced up as they came into view and then went back to their munching. In a few moments, Luke and Stella were at the road and she waved him goodbye and crossed to the vicarage.

Luke leaned on the gate and watched her go. The sun was lower in the sky now, dipping towards a band of purple cloud coming in from the west. It would almost certainly rain before morning. He had lost the light on Cuckoo Wood and before he got another chance like this, all the leaves might have been blown off the trees. But there would be something else to paint, some scene or trick of light he had never seen before, something new to try to capture on his canvas.

He glanced along the lane leading to the Tozers' farm, where he had met Val that morning. He sighed, straightened his shoulders and turned back towards the woods.

That was an artist's life. Leaving one lost chance behind and moving on to the next.

Chapter Four

Gilbert Napier got into his car to drive back to the Barton. It was a new car, bought when petrol came off ration, and he'd celebrated by treating himself to this smart-looking Armstrong Siddeley, selling the old Hillman Minx and handing on Isobel's boxy little Austin to Hilary. It looked pretty old-fashioned now, he had to admit, and she'd been murmuring about getting something more up-to-date – one of those little Morris Minors, perhaps, or an estate car. But there was Stephen to think of too; recently home from Cambridge, he ought to be provided with a decent motor-car.

Napier frowned a little. It was only natural for a young man of his age to want something sporty, but if anyone had an estate car it ought to be him, since he'd be working with his father learning to run the Burracombe estate, ready to take over when the day came. Not that that would be for a long time yet. At fifty-five, Gilbert Napier still had a good many years left in him – years in which Stephen could be trained to become as good a Squire as his brother Baden would have been.

The familiar pain washed over him. Nobody could be as good a Squire as Baden would have been. The boy was cut out for the job right from the start. You could see it in his bright eyes, his interest, his courage and determination. Napier could remember the way he'd stumped round the stables, only two or three years of age, clamouring to be lifted into the saddle. And the pretty little skewbald Napier had bought for the children to learn on wouldn't do – no, it had been Napier's own black mare, fiery Trespass, that the boy wanted to ride. He'd been persuaded in the end to accept a pony of the same colour, but the minute he could handle him he'd wanted to go on to something more lively, and so it had been throughout his childhood. Fearless, venturesome, intelligent and popular, he had been all Napier had ever wanted in an eldest son and heir. In his hands, the Burracombe estate would have been safe.

And it had been just those qualities that had killed him.

The sleek car never even reached fourth gear on the short journey from the vicarage and along the drive to the Barton. It was a car for the open road, like that TR3 that Stephen kept talking about. Well, maybe he should let the boy have his way after all. You were only young once, and the war had messed around with his life as well. He'd been only eleven when it had started, and it had curtailed any chances he might have had of going abroad, as Baden and Hilary had done, and he hadn't even been able to live in his own home during the holidays. The estate house where they'd had to stay while the Barton was being used for a school wasn't bad, but it had been pretty cramped when they were all at home. He wouldn't be surprised if the difficulties of living there had played quite a large part in Isobel's death.

Another pang struck at his heart and he gave an impatient shrug and brought the car to a halt outside the front steps. Crocker, the gardener and stableman, could put it away. Napier never allowed the man to take the car out on to the road, but he liked to give him the small pleasure of driving it in the grounds.

Hilary was making pastry in the kitchen. She looked round as he came through the door. 'Hello, Dad. How did it go? Will she do?'

'I think so.' He sat down at the table. He would never have sat in the kitchen in the old days, barely knew where it was, but then Isobel wouldn't have been in here making pastry then either. The war had changed a lot of things and he still hadn't got used to half of them. All the same, he had to admit that it was pleasant here with the Aga giving out a gentle warmth and Hilary standing there with her sleeves rolled up and her hands covered in flour. 'She seems a pleasant enough woman, and has had plenty of experience with children. We've given her the job, anyway. See how she goes on.'

'That's good. I met her in the church. She seems rather young.'

'Twenty-one. I just hope she doesn't up and get married when she's only been here five minutes. That's the trouble with young women.' He caught his daughter's eye and reached out hastily for the newspaper. You couldn't say anything in this house without putting your foot in it, but it was time Hilary found herself a husband. Twenty-eight and still not married! That was another effect of the war.

'Want a cup of tea, Dad?' she asked after a pause. 'The kettle's simmering. I'll just finish this first.'

He glanced at the pastry she was rolling out. 'What are you making?'

'Blackberry and apple pie. Your favourite.'

'Had pie at the vicarage,' he said before he could stop himself. Hilary stopped abruptly, the rolling pin poised above the flattened dough. 'Doesn't matter,' he added, knowing what she was thinking. 'Don't mind having it twice. As you said, it's my favourite.'

'Yes, but you need variety. It's not good for you to have pastry two meals running.' She looked at the bowl of blackberries and apples, sliced and ready to go into the dish. 'I'll just stew them and use the pastry tomorrow for a meat pie.'

'I'll still have pastry two *days* running,' he began, but she was already rolling it up and slapping it between two plates. She took it into the big larder without answering, and he sighed. I never used to have this problem with Isobel, he thought. I never knew what was for dinner until it was put in front of me, and it was always good. Of course, we had Mary to cook for us then and I wouldn't have been sitting at the kitchen table like a farmer, I'd have been in the drawing room or in my study, where a gentleman ought to be.

Hilary came back and tipped the fruit into a saucepan, ready to stew. They didn't have a permanent cook any more, but Dottie Friend came in and helped when they had guests or a dinner-party. Dottie was a village treasure – she cooked for the doctor's family occasionally, she worked at the pub and she helped out in the school if Mrs Dawe, who cooked the school meals, was ill. And since she sometimes took in paying guests, Basil Harvey had asked her if she would let her spare bedroom to the new teacher.

'Did you say you met Miss Simmons in the church?' he asked as Hilary came back into the kitchen and moved the kettle on to the hotplate of the Aga. 'What did you think of her?'

'I only spoke to her for a few minutes. She seemed just as you said – a pleasant person. We shan't know what sort of teacher she is until she starts at the school. Are her references all right? Or is this her first job?'

'It is, but she's worked as a pupil teacher in the Children's Home where she grew up. Got more experience than most in handling young children, I should think. They sent a good reference anyway.'

'A Children's Home?' Hilary turned from the Aga where the kettle had boiled almost at once. She swilled hot water in the teapot and tipped it into the sink, then put in two teaspoonsful of tea. 'You mean she's an orphan?'

'That's right. Parents killed in the war. Sad story, but only one of many. At least she's been looked after, given an education. And now she can earn her own living at a decent career, which is more than plenty of other young women can do.'

'Yes, it is.' Hilary heard the tinge of bitterness in her voice and glanced at her father, but his big, leonine head was bent over the newspaper and it seemed to have passed him by. She went back to the larder for the milk and poured a little into two cups, then stood gazing out of the window as she waited for the tea to brew.

I probably had a much better education than Stella Simmons, she thought, remembering her years at boarding school learning Latin, French and mathematics as well as English, history and geography. Yet there had never been any question of a career for her. When she left school, she would go to a 'finishing school', probably in Switzerland, be presented at Court and embark on a social whirl of parties and dances, then marry a wealthy and well-born young man and spend her life just as her mother had, having a family, running a home and, above all, being a good wife to her husband.

The war had changed all that. Aged seventeen when Mr Chamberlain had made the dreaded speech that announced that Britain was now at war with Germany, she had felt a great leap of excitement. Now women would come into their own, just as they had done during and after the Great War of 1914–18. Then, they had ridden motorbikes, driven buses, run farms and generally proved that they could do many of the jobs that men had always considered their own province. Hilary had seen her chance of escaping the chains that bound her, and leading her own life – a life of challenge and responsibility. She had applied to join the ATS, the women's branch of the Army, as soon as she left school. 'I won't accept any favours, though,' she'd warned her father. 'Whatever I do, I want to do on my own merit.'

To her delight, and because she could already drive her mother's little Austin and her father's Hillman Minx, she was given a job as a driver and found herself chauffering Generals, Brigadiers and – once – her father himself. By the time the war ended, she had the satisfaction of a job where she had authority and the respect of others, a job that was vital to her country.

But when she returned home to Burracombe Barton to consider what to do next, she had found herself chained all over again, first by her mother's long illness and then by her death. Hilary had taken over the running of the house and it seemed now as if it would be impossible for her ever to leave, unless it were by marriage. And that, she thought, was unlikely. Her years of independence had made her reluctant to hand her life over to any of the young men she was likely to meet in her circle.

'What's happened to that tea?' her father asked, jerking her out of her thoughts, and she turned quickly.

'Sorry. I was miles away.'

'I could see that.' He watched her pour the tea. 'Any word from Stephen, by the way?'

Hilary brought the cups over to the table and sat down. 'No. I imagine he's still in Italy. He was talking of going to Switzerland for some skiing when the snow starts, but that won't be for a few weeks yet. I dare say we'll get another postcard soon, when he remembers us again.'

'When he runs out of money, you mean.' Napier drew his brows together. 'Time that boy stopped gallivanting and came home to learn his job.'

'Well, it is supposed to be a cultural tour,' Hilary reminded him. 'And I think he feels he needs some time off after coming down from Cambridge.'

'Maybe he does. Doesn't mean he can gad about the

world like some rich playboy. There's work to be done at home – an estate to run – and as far as I can see, he hasn't the first idea how to go about it.'

Hilary bit her lip. 'I'm not sure whether Stephen will want to take over the estate,' she began, and the big head came up with a jerk.

'Not want to? Why the devil not? He ought to thank his lucky stars he's got such an opportunity. Fine estate, handed to him on a plate – all he has to do is learn to manage it. And it'll be a few years yet before he has to take on full responsibility. Of course he'll want to. Be a fool not to.'

'But do you think he's really suited to it?' Hilary said, feeling her way. There was no point in annoying her father unnecessarily, but she and her brother had had a long talk before he went off for his trip on the Continent, and she'd promised to pave the way for him if she could. 'I mean, he never expected to inherit, and—'

'You don't have to remind me of that,' Napier said harshly. He drained his cup and stood up. 'If it hadn't been for the damned war, I'd have had Baden here now, running the place with me. But since I haven't, it's up to young Stephen, and if you ask me, he's had more than enough time to come to terms with it. I dare say he *would* rather spend his time jaunting about Europe, but he's over twenty-one now and it's time to settle down to a job of work. And I don't know what other sort of work he might think he's capable of doing!'

'That's a bit unkind, isn't it?' Hilary said. 'He's capable of lots of things. He worked hard at Cambridge, after all, and got a good degree.'

'A good degree!' Napier snorted. 'In mathematics! What use is that going to be to him? Don't know why he wanted to bother about a degree anyway. The purpose of going to Cambridge was to get to know the right people, same as at

43

Harrow. Didn't want him to fail, naturally, but he wasn't supposed to spend all his time with his head in a book.'

Hilary suppressed a smile. She had been to visit Stephen a few times at Cambridge and knew that he hadn't by any means spent all his time with his 'head in a book'. He had played hard as well as worked hard, and was probably playing equally hard now, on his supposed 'cultural tour' of Europe. Well, she had done her best and would continue to support her brother in his desire to lead his own life, but it was going to be an uphill struggle.

Her father stamped out of the kitchen and she went back to her preparations for dinner that night. Dr Latimer and his wife were coming and she needed to get the meat into the oven to roast. They were having leg of lamb – the first of the year – with roast potatoes and vegetables from their own kitchen-garden. It was a pity about the fruit pie, but there was a piece of Stilton cheese that she'd managed to get from Creber's, in Tavistock, to go with the port. Like most dairy foods, cheese was still on ration but you could occasionally get a treat.

As she worked, she thought again of Stephen and his plans. He was going to have to come home and confront their father at some point. She wished that she could do the same.

I'm going to be here for the rest of my life, she thought, standing at the sink with a potato half-peeled in her hand. I'm never going to get away.

Val Tozer finished her jobs in the yard and decided to walk over to the Barton to see if Hilary had time for a cup of tea. Strictly speaking, she didn't have to work on the farm as she was a Sister at the Cottage Hospital in Tavistock, but she liked to occupy herself on her day off and enjoyed being with the animals. This afternoon, though, she needed to be away from the family.

44

Val and Hilary had known each other since childhood but had only been friends ever since they'd met, unexpectedly, in Egypt during the war. Val was an Army nurse at a military hospital and Hilary had been sent out with the regiment to which she was attached, as driver to the Brigadier. They'd encountered each other at a dance and stared in astonishment as they recognised each other. A meeting to catch up on village news and gossip had followed next day, and they'd discovered a rapport which had lasted ever since. Now they met at least once a week.

There were several ways to reach the Barton from the Tozers' farm. You could either go the short way, straight up the lane to where it joined the estate drive, or you could walk through the village past the shops and vicarage. Val chose to take a meandering way across the fields and through the trees to the top of Cuckoo Wood. From there, she could walk along the edge of the moor to drop down behind Barton House and walk through the grounds.

As she opened the gate into the meadow, she noticed a bent figure half in and half out of the ditch that ran beneath the hedge. It straightened as she came through and she saw Jacob Prout's weatherbeaten face. He was wearing the battered wax jacket that he was rarely seen without, his wispy hair stuck out at all angles round his head and she had the thought that he would only have had to stand in the middle of the field with his arms outstretched to be mistaken for a scarecrow. Scruff, his Jack Russell, emerged from a rabbit-hole and ran over to her, rubbing his muddy snout against her legs.

'Hello, Jacob. How are you?'

He squinted up at her against the afternoon sun, his eyes almost disappearing in a mass of wrinkles. Out in all weathers as he worked around the village, sweeping the lanes, clearing ditches, trimming and layering hedges, looking after the churchyard and digging graves, and doing any other odd jobs that might be asked of him, his face was the deep reddish-brown of cured leather. He lived alone in a tiny cottage at the end of the village street, keeping it as immaculate as he kept the village itself and maintaining a constant feud with his next-door neighbour Jed Fisher. Nobody knew quite how old he was, since nobody could remember exactly when he was born.

'Afternoon, Val. How be you?'

'I'm all right, thanks.' She leaned on the gate and watched as he swished at the brambles with his sickle. Scruff went back to the rabbit-hole and began to dig furiously. 'I expect you've been busy getting ready for the Harvest Festival. Are those your marrows I saw by the altar rail?'

Jacob snorted. 'One of 'em is. T'other's that Mrs Warren's. Took up vegetable gardening now, she has. Thinks because she've growed a marrow she'm an expert. I told her, "Wait till you can show me a basket of good red tomatoes with a proper flavour, then I'll take a bit o' notice".'

Val smiled. 'She's talking about starting up a Gardening Club.'

'Gardening Club!' he said contemptuously. 'What do us want a club for? Take up val'ble gardening time, that's all that'll do. I got too much to do in me own garden to be messing about with clubs.' He gave her a narrow look. 'Did I see you talking to that young artist feller down the lane this morning? Ferret, or something?'

'Ferris,' Val said, thinking that she might have known someone would have seen them. You couldn't sneeze in Burracombe without someone sending round beef tea. 'Yes, we did have a few words. He's renting the charcoal-burner's cottage, isn't he?'

'That's right.' Jacob wiped the back of his hand across

the end of his nose. 'Seems a decent enough young chap. Been in the Bell a time or two.'

Val was pretty sure that Jacob was hinting at something. It had probably been obvious that she and Luke weren't exchanging a few commonplace pleasantries; he might even have overheard them talking. 'Where were you, then? I didn't see you.'

'Oh, I were just over in the field,' he said vaguely and her suspicion grew stronger. He turned back to the ditch. 'Anyway, better get back to me work. If it comes on to rain before this lot's cleared we'll have a flood over the road, and I got me own garden to see to as well.'

Val walked on across the field, still thinking about Luke Ferris. She'd seen him speak to the young schoolteacher by the green and watched as she and the vicar went into the church. Luke might have turned towards the forge then, but instead he had wandered off along the lane and she'd hoped that he'd gone to do some sketching or painting. It had been a shock to hear his voice behind her, as she led Barley back along the farm track, and it had taken her a moment or two to gather her composure before she could turn and face him.

She climbed the footpath leading through Cuckoo Wood. The charcoal-burner's cottage where Luke was living was on the other side, but she was uncomfortably aware that she might run into him at any moment. At the top of the hill, she paused for breath and then looked around.

Luke was sitting on a rock at the edge of the wood. He was holding his sketchbook and talking to someone, and as she watched, Val realised that it was the young school-teacher, Stella Simmons.

She turned abruptly and plunged down the hill towards the Barton.

Chapter Five

Stella arrived in Burracombe a few days after Christmas. She had spent the holiday period with a friend she had made at college, after saying goodbye to the Children's Home and the local primary school where she'd worked as a pupil-teacher at the end of the term. Now, at last, she felt that she was beginning her own life.

The vicar had come to Tavistock in his rattling pre-war Ford Popular and packed her few possessions into the boot. It was early-closing day and the little town looked grey and quiet as he drove down the steep hill into the big square. Stella hadn't had time to look around on her visit in October, and she gazed about her with interest.

'It looks nice. Do they have markets in the square?'

'No, there's a pannier market – that's an enclosed market, in a big building – behind the Town Hall. That's the Town Hall there, opposite the church. This river we're crossing now is the Tavy. It starts up on the moor and joins the Tamar estuary above Plymouth. It's supposed to be the second fastest-filling river in the country, but don't ask me which the fastest is!'

They drove on through Whitchurch and then across open moorland. The sky was clear, with the cold paleness of winter, and the sun was sinking behind them, throwing a soft light across the coppery dead bracken. Sheep were grazing beside the road and the vicar had to slow down twice for ponies which lifted their heads and ambled across just in front of him.

'Wild ponies!' Stella exclaimed. 'They have those in the New Forest too. I was evacuated there for a while, when I was little.'

'Well, they're not quite wild – they belong to the farmers. But they roam like wild animals, except when they're gathered up in the autumn.' He slowed down for another one. 'Won't be long now, and you'll be in the warm. Dottie Friend will look after you – she's looking forward to having you as her lodger. You'll like her – a real Burracombe character. Of course, she's out a lot – works at the inn, and cooks for the Squire too – so you'll be a bit like ships that pass in the night. But she's a good soul. She'll make you very comfortable.'

He had been quite right. The sky was dark by the time the car nosed its way down the village street, but little squares of golden light spilled from all the cottage windows and there was a blaze of fire from the open door of the blacksmith's forge. The vicar drew up outside a cottage standing back from the lane, behind a picket fence and a tangle of wintry bushes, and as he did so the door flew open and a woman hurried out.

'Be that you, Vicar?' she called, peering out into the darkness, and then came down the path to the gate. 'Come you in, my dear. You must be wanting a cup of tea after all that journey.' She reached out and caught Stella's hands, rubbing them between her own. 'Why, you'm frozen stiff. Come and sit yourself down by the fire, do.'

'I've got some cases,' Stella began, but Dottie Friend was already urging her towards the door and she found herself pushed into a warm, square room with two chairs set on either side of a blazing fire. The stone-flagged floor was brightened by a mixture of coloured rag rugs and faded carpet runners, and there was a table to one side covered by a green baize cloth, with a ruby lustre glass bowl of oranges and small apples with wrinkled red skins in the centre. Festooned from the low wooden beams across the ceiling were strips of home-made paper-chains of scarlet, green and yellow paper, and a small Christmas tree stood in one corner.

'Come over to the fire,' Dottie urged hospitably. She was shorter than Stella, with a plump, rounded figure and a mass of yellow curls. Her eyes were brown and warm. 'Vicar and me'll bring in your bags. Kettle's on and there'll be a cup of tea ready in just a minute or two. I'll make a bit of toast as well. Nothing like a bit of toast when you'm cold and hungry. There's a nice casserole in the oven, for supper.'

Stella found herself pressed down into one of the armchairs while the vicar and Dottie brought in her shabby suitcase and shopping-bag. Basil Harvey carried the case straight upstairs and Dottie looked enquiringly at the shopping-bag.

'Oh, it's just a few things I couldn't get into the case,' Stella said hastily. 'And for the journey. Don't bother to take it up now.'

'Might as well get it out of the way,' Dottie said, and her round little bottom and stumpy legs disappeared up the narrow stairs.

The cottage was quite roomy, with three rooms down-stairs – one the parlour, kept for 'best', one the big, cosy living room and kitchen, and one the scullery with a lavatory tacked on to the back – and three bedrooms above. Stella's room had a colourful rag rug on the polished floorboards, a faded patchwork quilt on the iron-framed bed, and curtains patterned with spring flowers at the window. She had a bookcase, a dressing-table, a washstand, a cupboard let into the wall where she could hang her clothes, and a small table to serve as a desk. The room would have been cold, had it not been above the kitchen with the range that was kept stoked all night but, as it was, it was cosy enough for Stella to sit in, in the evenings, and prepare her lessons for the next day. Dottie made it clear, however, that she was to use the house as her home, and come downstairs whenever she pleased.

'You don't have to spend all your time in your room, my flower – I like a bit of company. In any case, I'm out most evenings, working at the pub, so it'd be a waste if nobody was here to enjoy the fire.' She beamed at Stella. 'I dare say you'll have schoolwork to do, so you can do it down here. Not that you look old enough to be out of school yourself, hardly!'

'I'm twenty-one,' Stella said. 'This is my first real post. I was a pupil-teacher at the Home and in the local infants' school, and during my training we went out to schools and did practice teaching. I haven't ever had a class all of my own, though.'

Dottie looked at her thoughtfully. 'They'm not so bad, Burracombe tackers, the little ones, anyway. Some of they bigger boys are little monkeys. And there's no more than a dozen in the Infants – just three or four babies, and three coming up to seven, and the rest are in between. You'll manage them well enough.'

'I think you'll be very comfortable,' the vicar said to Stella as Dottie bustled about making tea from a huge kettle which was whistling gently on the range. 'Now, if you'll forgive me, I'll be off – I've got a Parochial Church Council meeting this evening. We're starting to think about the Festival,' he said to Dottie. 'Mrs Warren's very keen for everyone in the village to become involved. I think she wants us to do something in the church.'

'I dare say I'll hear all about it in the pub,' Dottie said dryly as he departed. 'There's more decided there than in any of these blessed meetings. But there, they like to go through the motions, makes them feel important. Now, my dear,' she poured a cup of tea and handed it to Stella, 'you get that inside you and you'll soon feel better. You've come all the way from up-country, the vicar tells me.'

'Hampshire,' Stella said, raising the cup gratefully to her lips. It was too hot to take more than the tiniest sip but the warmth in her hands and the heat of the fire were already spreading through her body. 'It did take a long time. I started off quite early this morning. There were changes, you see, but the waiting rooms all had nice fires so it wasn't too bad.'

'Well, you'm here now.' Dottie sat down opposite. Her rosy face shone with goodwill, and as Stella looked at her she felt another kind of warmth spread through her body and her heart. She's really pleased to have me here, she thought in wonder. As if I weren't just a lodger but someone she already knows and likes.

She felt the prickle of sudden tears in her eyes, remembering the time when she'd been part of a family, with a mother, a father, a sister and a brother. Only when they were taken from her had she realised what she had lost; she felt as if half of herself had been wrenched away, leaving a gaping wound that had never properly healed; there always remained that aching loneliness.

Here, in Dottie Friend's cottage at Burracombe, where she had only been for a few minutes, her memory stirred with a glimmer of the warmth she had known as a child, and to her dismay, one of the tears that had pricked her eyes welled up and rolled down her cold cheek in a sizzling bead.

'There, you'm worn out!' Dottie exclaimed. 'Now, don't you worry about me, my pretty, I'll just get on with a few jobs while you drink your tea, and then we'll have supper all cosy together. And afterwards I thought you might like a bath.' She indicated the scullery door with her head. 'We'll bring it in and fill it up with nice hot water, and you can have it in front of the fire, which is the only way to have a bath, if you want my opinion. None of those nasty cold bathrooms like they got up at the Barton! And you needn't worry – I've got to go up to the pub about eight o'clock, so you can be nice and private and we'll empty it out in the morning.'

Stella had not had a bath in front of the fire since she was a small child. At the Children's Home they had had a large bathroom with two enormous baths in it, filled by a long tap from a large geyser. The children had had to queue up to have their turn at being dipped into the hot water, softened by gritty lumps of washing soda, and scrubbed with slabs of green carbolic soap. Girls were bathed on Fridays and boys on Saturdays so that they would be clean for church on Sunday.

Later that night, after a supper of rabbit casserole with floury jacket potatoes and mashed swede and carrots, Dottie had dragged in the long tin bath and set about filling it with buckets of hot water. It had taken some time to do this and Stella protested at the amount of water being used but Dottie shrugged her objections aside. 'Plenty of fuel hereabouts,' she said, nodding at the stack of logs in the big inglenook fireplace. 'And 'tis your first night. Us wants you to feel welcome here in Burracombe, Miss Simmons.'

Stella smiled at her, feeling the prick of tears again. 'I do. It's very kind of you, Miss Friend.' She hesitated, feeling sure that this comfortable little woman must have been married. 'Is that right? Should it be Mrs?'

'No, it's Miss, but if we're going to shake down here together we'd better get this straight from the beginning.' The little woman looked quite fierce as she shook a piece of wood at Stella. 'Dottie's my name, and everyone calls me by it, and you'd better do the same, maid. Otherwise us'll never be easy together, now.'

'All right,' Stella said, wishing that she wouldn't keep feeling like crying. It's because I'm so tired, she told herself, because I'm tired and cold and because she's so kind. It's a long time since anyone was as kind to me as this. 'And you must call me Stella. Please,' she added, seeing the objections already rising to the rosy lips. 'There – there aren't many people to call me by my name now, you see. I'd really like it if you would.'

Dottie gazed at her for a moment and there was an odd expression in her eyes. Then she nodded and stepped forward, putting one hand on Stella's shoulder and reaching up to give her a quick kiss.

'That's settled then,' she said rather gruffly, and turned away, reaching out for the coat that hung on the back door. 'Now I'd better be going. Don't you wait up for me, mind. The pub closes at ten but there's always the clearing-up and all to do, ready for tomorrow, so I won't be back much before eleven. You have your bath and make yourself a cup of cocoa if you want one – and there's a hot-water bottle in your bed already, so 'twill be warm for you to get into. I'll see you in the morning.'

'What time would you like me to get up?' Stella asked, and Dottie shook her head.

'Bless you, maid, you get up just whenever you want. 'Tis holidays, isn't it? Plenty of time for you to think about getting up early when school starts again.' She pulled on a shapeless grey coat and tied a belt round her middle. 'Now, you just help yourself to anything you need, and have a good rest. That's all you got to do.' And with a blast of cold air through the door, she was gone.

Stella did as she was told. Making sure the curtains were all securely pulled, she undressed and got into the bath, lying back and luxuriating in the feel of warm water and the heat of the fire on her bare skin. She stayed there a long time, half asleep, letting her mind wander over the events of the past days – her last Christmas term at the Home, the journey here, the nervousness of beginning her first job . . . and then drifting further back to the days when she had had a family. To memories of a warmth and cosiness just like this – baths in front of the fire, her mother's gentle hands as she soaped her body, herself and her sister wrapped in towels and sitting on the rug with an orange each, feeling cherished and safe.

They hadn't been safe, though, had they. The war had started and everything had changed. Everything had been spoiled. Daddy going away. The bombing – their house destroyed and everything lost – their clothes, their furniture, her little sister's favourite dolly Princess Marcia, and the little donkey with the straw panniers that Daddy had brought back from one of his sea-trips and which Mummy had kept on the mantelpiece. All gone. You could never really be safe.

The water felt suddenly cold. Stella shivered and got out of the bath, reaching for the towel Dottie had left hanging over a clothes-horse at the side of the fire. She dried herself and wished she could empty the bath. It didn't seem right to leave it for Dottie to find when she came home tired from her evening's work.

Forgetting about the cocoa, she lit a candle and went upstairs to the bedroom that Dottie had shown her before supper, and pulled on her long flannelette nightdress. The stone hot-water bottle made a lump in the middle of the bed. She got in and touched it cautiously with her feet, finding it wrapped in what appeared to be a specially knitted pullover of its own.

Stella blew out her candle and lay down. She felt almost too tired to sleep and her mind was a bewildered jumble of thankfulness and the sorrow that accompanied her every-where, sometimes dull enough to be ignored but sometimes sharply painful. The pain briefly touched her heart and then she fell asleep, and didn't stir again until morning.

In the two days that had passed since then, Stella had found herself settling down in Dottie's cottage almost as if she'd always lived there. Dottie was hospitable without being overpowering and because she had several jobs around the village, she was out as much as she was in, giving Stella plenty of the solitude that she craved. Living in a Children's Home, she had scarcely ever been alone, and she revelled in the quiet peace of the cottage when she had it to herself. Dottie's fat tabby cat, Alfred, kept her company, slumbering beside the range on an old brown cushion and occasionally waking to stroll ponderously over to his food bowl or go outside to fossick in the hedgerow and return with an air of satisfaction for a job well done. He rubbed himself against her legs when his bowl was empty, and clambered on to her lap when she sat in the armchair and picked up a book, settling into a large, furry mound and apparently growing heavier as the time went on, and when she eventually pushed him gently to the floor he turned and gave her a look of indignation.

'He thinks he's died and gone to heaven,' Dottie said when Stella apologised to him for her temerity in wanting her lap to herself. 'It's years since he had anyone to boss about like this. Don't you take no notice. You don't want to let him get the upper hand.'

Before she went to the pub in the evenings, Dottie made supper for them both. They listened to *Luscombes*, a radio serial about country families in Devon, to *Henry Hall's Guest Night*, and the six o'clock news; they chatted about the village, its inhabitants and their ways, and about their own lives. Dottie hadn't always lived in Burracombe; she'd gone off to London as a girl and worked in the theatre, backstage, as a dresser for a well-known actress.

'It started when she came to the village for a rest,' Dottie explained one evening. 'The doctor had told her she was overdoing it – always highly strung, she was, lots of those sort of people are – and she had to have peace and quiet. She was friendly with Mrs Gilbert – the Squire's wife, what died a few years ago, poor lady – they'd known each other at school – and she came to stay at the Barton. I was working as a maid there at the time, not long left school myself, and I did some sewing for her. She took a fancy to me and asked me to go with her when she started work again.'

'It must have been very strange for you,' Stella said, swallowing a piece of gravy-soaked dumpling. Dottie had made a stew and the dumplings were as light as balls of fluff. 'Going to London – not many young girls would have done that in those days.'

'No, and my mother and father weren't keen at all, to begin with. But she was a lovely lady, my actress, and she promised she'd look after me, and so she did. And I came home in between, when she was "resting" as they call it. But as time went on, she didn't rest very much. Always in demand, she was, you see. Some of her plays went on for years, and when one finished they were after her to do another one. But in the end I had to leave her.' Dottie's brown eyes were moist. 'My old mum died, you see, and I came back to Burracombe to look after my dad. But I always kept in touch with my actress and she used to come to Burracombe all through the war. Still does, from time to time, but she's getting on now, I don't see her so much these days.' The plump little woman got up and put their empty plates together, and went on briskly, 'I liked being in London, but it's no place to be now. I was glad to be out of it when the war started, I can tell you. And there was plenty for me to do down here. I started work at the pub and helped out at the Barton and the doctor's house, and that's what I've kept on doing. Now, there's some bottled plums for afters and some nice custard, will that be all right for you?'

'Yes, please.' Stella watched while Dottie spooned glistening purple plums from an enamel dish and poured custard on top. 'You're a wonderful cook, Dottie. And you do all that needlework too.' The patchwork quilt on her bed had, she had learned, been made by Dottie when she was a girl, and there were samples of her work all over the cottage – cushion covers, rag rugs, embroidered tablecloths, curtains – as well as the clothes she made herself. 'I don't know how you find the time, with all your other jobs.'

'Oh, I like to have something to pick up. Can't just sit doing nothing. Always got a bit of knitting or sewing to hand. If I'm not making something new or mending something old, I'm doing a bit of embroidery or knitting for the church bazaar.' Dottie leaned over and picked up a shapeless bundle of purple knitting from a chair. Stella gazed at it, wondering what it was. 'My favourite jumper, this was, but it was going under the arms so I unpicked it. I'm making a toy elephant.'

'A purple elephant?' Stella exclaimed, and they both laughed.

'Oh, I make all sorts of toys. The little uns don't care what colour they are.' Dottie finished her plums and jumped up again. 'Anyway, I can't sit here nattering all evening. I'll just get these few crocks washed and I'll be off to work.' She waved away Stella's efforts to help. 'No, you'm a guest. It'll only take me a few minutes and I know where everything goes.'

A little later, Dottie pulled on her old coat and woolly Fair Isle hat and whisked out into the night and Stella settled down by the fire with Alfred on her lap, feeling as if she had come home.

There was just one thing missing. That one person she

had longed for all through these past ten years. Where was she now? Where was her sister, torn from her side in the middle of a war that had wrenched apart so many lives. *Where was Muriel?*

Chapter Six

On the last day of the year, the old stone church of St Andrew, with its tall tower rising from the centre of the village, was filled with parishioners. Constance Bellamy sat in the pew immediately behind Grace Harvey and her daughter Erica. At seventy-six years old, Miss Bellamy was one of the longest and most regular attenders at St Andrew's, and took a proprietorial interest in all that went on. There had been a break during the First World War when she had volunteered her services as a VAD nurse and left the village to work in Service hospitals, spending nearly two years in Malta; but she had returned as soon as the war was over and resumed her life at the Grey House, on the edge of the village, almost as if nothing had happened. She had never married and never, as far as anyone knew, even had a sweetheart – although, as some murmured, you didn't know what might have happened out there in Malta – and when her parents died she had stayed on in the Grey House, where she lived with her dachshund Rupert and a cat called Malkin.

A tiny woman with a brown, weatherbeaten face, always bustling about the village, she made Basil Harvey think of a motor-powered walnut. In an earlier age, she would probably have been persecuted as a witch – although, as he'd remarked to Grace once, he wouldn't have given the persecutors much chance, faced with her energy and withering tongue. At the same time, he wouldn't have been very much surprised if it had turned out that she *was* a witch. 'The way she looks at me sometimes with those little black eyes of hers, I'm always thankful to find I haven't turned into a toad or a black beetle.'

'Don't talk such nonsense,' Grace had reproved him. 'Miss Bellamy's the salt of the earth. The village wouldn't be the same without her. And for goodness sake don't let anyone else hear you saying such things!'

Basil smiled. It was funny how people expected vicars to be innocent souls who had never heard a swear-word or made a joke in their lives – yet if a churchman were to be any use at all, he had to be fully aware of human nature in all its many shades.

Opposite Constance Bellamy, in the pew behind the Napiers, sat Henry Warren and his wife Joyce, who was President of the Women's Institute and also ran the Gardening Club and the drama group. Basil had heard that she was currently trying to set up a Bridge Club, which he thought would be a good idea, being a bridge-player himself, but if she went on like this, Joyce would need a village hall all to herself. The whist drives, Mother's Union, country-dancing group and Local History Society all held their meetings there too, and the diary was getting rather crowded. He'd had Edie Pettifer, from the newsagent's, round only a few days before Christmas, complaining that there hadn't been a date free for the kiddies' Christmas party until two days before New Year's Eve; and where Edie Pettifer went, Bert Foster, the butcher next door, was sure to follow.

They were into the second hymn now and Basil chided himself for letting his attention wander. It was easy enough to keep his mind on the prayers, but he knew all the village's favourite hymns so well by now that he could sing them without really thinking about them. If the villagers only realised, he thought, that their vicar's attention was as easily distracted as was theirs! And although he tried hard to make his sermons interesting, he couldn't really blame them for drifting off to thoughts of their own concerns while he was talking. Perhaps it even did them more good. That twenty minutes of peace and quiet might be all they got in their busy lives.

Still, it wasn't his job to preach today. He'd handed over that part of the service to his new curate, young Felix Copley. Rather more cynically than was suitable for a vicar, perhaps, he wondered if Felix's presence was part of the reason for the church being so full this morning. There were certainly plenty of young women in the congregation – Nathan Pettifer's two girls, Gillian and Angela, for a start, Ginnie Nethercott from the pub, and that pretty young schoolteacher Stella Simmons. Or was he being uncharitable? Miss Simmons would be bound to come, and the other girls were surely too young and lively to take much interest in a curate.

Basil watched Felix climb into the pulpit, tall and well-built, his hair gleaming like corn ripe for harvest, his mobile face full of warmth and humour. A bishop in the making, he thought. He's got the bearing and he's got the charisma and the personality. He'll have the women at his feet and the men on his side. Maybe he was, after all, the reason why the church was so full.

Felix stood still for a moment, looking down at the expectant faces of the congregation. Then he spoke the introduction and began to talk, and Basil listened attentively. The curate's voice was deep, smooth and musical, the kind of voice its owner might himself get rather too fond of hearing, but there seemed to be no danger of that at present, as Felix spoke simply and naturally about the welcome he had received in the village. He talked of a stranger's shyness at finding himself in a closely knit community, and the warmth of Devon hospitality that had

62

drawn him so swiftly to its heart, and he spoke of Jesus' words about entertaining angels unaware.

'I'm no angel,' he said with a grin that drew appreciative smiles from his listeners, 'but I can see that if ever angels do come amongst us, you will all be very well able to entertain them, for you've practised on many a lesser soul.' He paused, and his smile faded to leave his chiselled features suddenly grave. 'And I'm sure that angels *do* come amongst us. They may be here at this very moment. And I ask that you continue to extend, to all strangers, that same hospitality. For, angel or no, we are all God's beings and by doing so, we fulfil a part of God's own purpose. And now to God the Father, God the Son and God the Holy Ghost . . .'

Yes, the boy could preach a good sermon, Basil thought as the congregation rose to its feet for the last hymn and Felix came down from the pulpit. Not too long, not too short, lively enough to keep the people interested, and thoughtful enough to give them something to chew over. Basil gave him a nod of approval and went forward to receive the collection plates brought to him by Henry Warren and Dr Charles Latimer.

'Very nice service, Vicar,' Henry's wife Joyce said to him as they filed out through the south door. She looked at Felix, standing by Basil's side. 'Welcome to Burracombe. You did very well.'

The curate smiled his thanks. 'It's kind of you to say so. I'm looking forward to working here. It's a beautiful area.'

'Do you know Dartmoor well?' she asked, and he shook his head.

'I don't even know Devon well, I'm afraid. I grew up in Cambridgeshire. I hope the locals will accept a foreigner.' He crinkled another smile at her but Joyce Warren regarded him impassively.

'You must come to tea,' she commanded. 'Come on Tuesday. I have WI on Wednesday.' She spoke as if she intended to make a report on him at the meeting. 'Three o'clock at Tor House – the vicar will tell you where that is.'

She marched on through the door and Basil watched Felix having his hand shaken by a tiny woman with white curls and a birdlike face. The young man looked astonished when he saw that there were two of them – identical twins, each gazing up into his face with bright, eager eyes and nodding her head.

'Lovely sermon, Mr Copley.'

'Lovely sermon.' Their voices were like the twittering of sparrows in a hedge.

'Thank you,' Felix said, looking bemused. He glanced sideways at the vicar and Basil came to the rescue.

'These are the Misses Friend – Jeanie and Jessie. They run our Post Office and sell sweets and tobacco and stationery as well. And this is their brother, Billy, who lives with them.'

Felix turned to the rather podgy man standing just behind them; a smile of extraordinary sweetness broke out over the wide, flat face with its button nose and slanting eyes. The man held out his hand and Felix took it.

'I'm Billy,' the man said. 'I live at the Post Office. I help Mr Foster.'

'Mr Foster's the butcher,' Basil explained. 'He's a chapel man.'

Felix nodded. The vicar had already explained that the village had its own Methodist chapel, a sturdy grey building with a windswept graveyard overlooking the moor.

'I carry the meat,' Billy announced. 'Pigs and lambs and sides of beef. I carry things for Jeanie and Jessie too.' He lifted one arm. 'I'm strong, I am.'

'I'm sure you're very useful,' Felix said gently. 'It's good to be strong, and it's good to see you in church.'

'I like church. I like the music.'

'Come along, Billy,' one of his sisters said, taking his arm. 'Come along home, now. It's time for dinner.'

Billy nodded and smiled. 'Sunday dinner. I like Sunday dinner.' He ambled off down the church path, large and bulky between the two tiny women.

'Billy's a dear soul,' Basil said quietly. 'Quite a few years younger than his sisters. His parents were well into their forties when he was born, and they're both dead now.'

'He's lucky to have two good sisters to look after him,' Felix said, and turned to the next person who was waiting to greet him. Not all the parishioners had stopped to talk – many had hurried by with a smile and a greeting – and there were only a few left in the little group waiting to shake his and the vicar's hands.

'This is Miss Simmons who's come to take on the teacher's post,' Basil said, introducing Stella. 'Felix Copley, my curate. You remember, Felix – you met the headmistress, Miss Kemp, the other day. Miss Simmons lodges with Dottie Friend, whom you'll encounter all over the village and especially in the pub!'

'I keep encountering Friends wherever I go,' Felix said wryly. 'Friends and Pettifers seem to make up most of the village. Are they all related?'

'More or less,' Basil said vaguely. Even after five years, he had himself never quite got to grips with the ramifications of village relationships. 'But what a nice thing to be able to say – that you encounter friends wherever you go. And very true of Burracombe, I think you'll agree, Miss Simmons?'

'I certainly will,' she said, gently withdrawing her hand. 'I've only been here a few days, but it seems to be a lovely village to live in, Mr Copley.'

'Felix,' he said. 'I'd like everyone to call me Felix. I don't feel quite grown up enough to be called "Mr".'

'I'll be bringing our new curate round to the school as soon as term starts,' Basil said as Stella Simmons turned away. 'Sweet girl,' he added. 'Miss Kemp's very pleased with the appointment and I'm sure the children are going to love her.'

Constance Bellamy, the Latimers and Colonel Napier had all left the church, filing down the aisles immediately behind the vicar as he made his way towards the door. The last person to leave was George Sweet, the village baker, who always seemed to have a smudge of flour somewhere about his person. He stuck out a big, powerful hand and gave Felix a sharp look.

'Not a bad sermon, for a first time. Good to have you with us. Lodgings all right? Aggie looking after you?'

Felix nodded. He had already met George, who was one of the churchwardens and had found him lodgings with his widowed cousin Agatha Madge. He thought George looked more like a pugilist than a baker, but Basil had explained that kneading the huge amounts of dough that George Sweet made every night developed the muscles every bit as well as weight-lifting.

'Mrs Madge is like a mother to me,' he said. 'And we certainly don't lack the staff of life. Your bread's excellent.'

George nodded, as if this went without saying. 'Well, I dare say I'll be seeing you later on. I'm coming round to Aggie's for Sunday tea.'

'And he's coming to us for Sunday dinner,' Basil said, taking Felix by the arm. 'Come on, now. If you meet any more people today you'll be completely confused. That's one of the problems with this job,' he added as they went back to the vestry to remove their robes. 'Remembering all the new faces and being able to put the right name to them. It's not one of my strong points, which is one reason why I hope never to be moved from Burracombe. You'll meet them all again tonight, too, round the tree.'

'Round the tree?'

'Yes – to see in the New Year, you know. It's a tradition here – had to be stopped during the war, of course, but it was revived in 1945. The whole village gathers on the green. The bells are rung half-muffled to signify the death of the old year, and then the muffles are taken off and the tenor strikes the hour before they're rung out to celebrate the birth of the new year. And everyone dances round the tree – well, those who can – and there's a lot of hugging and kissing and good wishes. It's an excellent start, and I always hope that those who've spent the old year feuding will make up their differences then and be friends.'

'And do they?' Felix asked in amusement.

Basil Harvey sighed. 'Some of them do but I'm afraid most of them have slipped back by the end of the first week!' He hung his cassock on a hook and pulled on his overcoat. 'Anyway, we'd better get a move on or Grace will be worrying about the meal. Apparently it's very difficult to have everything ready at exactly the same moment, and if we're not there then it will be irrevocably spoilt.'

They closed the church door and set off along the path that led to the vicarage garden, each immersed in his own thoughts. On the whole, Basil thought, his new curate had shown up very well. The congregation seemed to have enjoyed his sermon and those who had stopped to talk had been pleasant and welcoming. The little exchange between the young man and the new schoolteacher had been interesting, but it was far too early in Felix's ministry for any complications of that sort.

Felix himself had no such reservations. He had had girlfriends before, but nobody serious. At almost thirty, he had begun to think it was time to settle down, and although he had no intention of rushing into romance on the promise of a pair of large hazel eyes, he was open to possibilities. He wondered if the new schoolteacher would come down to the village green that night and dance round the tree with everyone else.

As he followed the vicar through the front door of the vicarage and into the hallway, the smell of roast beef touched his nostrils and he drew in an appreciative breath.

He was going to enjoy this new year in Burracombe.

Chapter Seven

'Nineteen-fifty-one,' Alice Tozer said as the six church bells rang out their joyful peal in the frosty midnight air and the villagers burst into cheers. 'A new year's like a new start, that's what I always say.'

She gripped her mother-in-law Minnie's hand in one of hers, and her daughter Val's in the other as the crowd began to circle around the ancient oak tree, and hoped it wouldn't be too much for the old lady. Minnie was a marvel, you had to admit that, but she was eighty-one when all was said and done, and there was a limit to how much dancing round a tree at midnight she could do, even if it was New Year's Eve.

'Let's hope it is.' Minnie had lived through two world wars, not to mention the Boer War that had taken her own brother at the turn of the century. 'And so it would be, if they'd just let us ordinary folk live our own lives. It's all this argy-bargying in Parliament as causes all the trouble, and always will be.'

Val, on the other side of her mother, said nothing. It had taken all Alice's powers of persuasion to get her to come out at all, and she was still wishing she had stayed indoors by the fire or, better still, in bed with her memories. 'It's time you got over all that,' Alice had said to her earlier, standing in the warm farmhouse kitchen and winding a long green scarf round her neck. 'Nobody was more sorry than me when Eddie was killed, but it's six years ago now, Val, and you've got to look forward. We all have our troubles in this life, and it don't do no good to give way to them.'

Val had been shocked. Her mother had never spoken to her like that before. Ever since the news had come of Eddie's death, on New Year's Eve 1944, Alice had been unstinting in her support. Tears had come to Val's eyes as she stared at her, and Alice's face had softened. Quickly, she came across the big kitchen and laid her hand on her daughter's shoulder. 'I don't mean to be harsh, maid, you know that. But there's a time for grieving and a time to be happy, isn't that what we're told? And it seems to me that your time for grieving is over now, and if a new year isn't a cue to be happy, what is? I know what New Year's Eve means to you — I'll never forget the day we heard about Eddie — but that makes it all the more a time to put it all behind you and look forward. So won't you come out with us tonight? Listen to your dad and the others ring in the new year, and wish everyone a Happy New Year?' She looked pleadingly into Val's brown eyes. 'Nobody would want you to be unhappy all your life,' she said quietly. 'Eddie wouldn't, I know.'

Val twisted sharply away from her. Then she bit her lip, reproaching herself for her unkindness, and turned back. Alice was standing quite still, the scarf still not completely wrapped around her neck and her brown tweed coat still unbuttoned. Val took a deep breath and gave her a wavering smile.

'All right, Mum. I'll come. It won't make any difference to Eddie whether I dance round the old tree or not. He's gone, and that's all there is to it.' She lifted her head and squared her shoulders, but as she went to the cupboard to fetch her own coat, Alice watched her with troubled eyes. It would take a lot more than a few words from her and a dance round the village oak tree to bring Val out of the cocoon she had wrapped round herself for the past six years.

She sighed. She'd always thought that boys were harder to bring up, with their wild ways, but it seemed now that daughters were the ones that gave you more worry. Look at her youngest daughter, Jackie. She'd gone off earlier, saying she'd see her mother at the tree at midnight, and goodness only knew what she might be getting up to in the meantime. It was true she was only going to supper with the Pettifers, and Alice didn't doubt that Freda Pettifer, whom she'd known since she was a baby in a pram, would keep a strict eye on things, but there was a long time between eight o'clock and midnight, and no doubt Jackie and young Roy would find some way of slipping out into the darkness together. To Alice's mind, those two were altogether too keen on each other, and she shuddered to think what Ted would say if there was any trouble there.

As she watched Val slide her arms reluctantly into the sleeves of her winter coat, Minnie came into the kitchen with Joanna. Val started to take her coat off again. 'You go, Jo – I'll stay home with Robin. You'll have a much better time than I will.'

'Don't be silly!' Joanna had taken the situation in at a glance. 'I've been every New Year's Eve since the war ended. It's your turn now. Robin's my little boy, after all – I'm the one who ought to be staying at home. You go and let your hair down, Val.'

'Is this a conspiracy?' Val asked, her voice trembling a little. She looked at her tiny grandmother. 'Are you in it too?'

'I think it's time you started to go out and about a bit, if that's what you mean,' Minnie retorted smartly. 'And I'd offer to stay home myself if I didn't think this might be my last New Year's Eve. I don't suppose I'll see another at my age.'

'Go on, Mother,' Alice said automatically, holding up Val's coat. 'You've been saying that for the past five years and you're still here to make a nuisance of yourself . . . Come on now, Val, put this on and let's be off or we'll miss the peal and your father and our Tom'll never forgive us.'

Val allowed her mother to slip the coat back on to her shoulders and pulled the collar high around her neck. She felt in the pockets for the gloves Minnie had knitted her for Christmas and turned towards the door.

'Well, let's get it over with,' she said. 'Happy New Year, Jo. See you in the morning, if you've gone to bed by the time we come back.' A blast of cold air surged in as she stepped out into the yard, and she shivered and pulled her coat closer around her.

Minnie caught Alice's eye and shrugged. ''Tis no use worrying yourself about the maid. She'll get over it in her own good time.'

'Will she?' Alice murmured as they followed Val outside. 'It's been six years, Mother. I wonder sometimes if she's ever going to get over it. Not everybody does, do they? Look at Auntie Flo. She grieved over her Albert till the day she died.'

'Flo was always an obstinate piece,' Minnie said. 'I know she was my sister, and you shouldn't speak ill of the dead, but it's true. She got it into her head that it would be wrong to look at another man after she lost Albert and nothing would make her see any different. And what good did it do? She could have been a wife and mother, same as me, and brought a family into the world, but no, she had to wear it like a hump on her shoulder till the day she died . . . You don't want young Val going the same way, Alice. A waste, that'd be, a proper waste.'

They stopped for a moment, closing the door behind them and looking up at the sky, peppered with stars. The sound of the bells, softly muffled as they rang their last peal of 1950, accompanied them down the track between Devon banks that would in just a few weeks be thickly clustered with primroses, and when they reached the village green it was to find gathered there all the friends and neighbours they had grown up with and known all their lives. Then the peal stopped and there were a few moments of silence before they heard the sound of the tenor bell, tolling the notes of midnight for the death of the old year. The deep tone seemed to echo the sorrow in Val's heart, but just before the thirteenth stroke, the other bells joined in, pealing open and joyous to welcome the new year, and everyone broke into cheers.

'Nineteen-fifty-one,' Alice said in Val's ear. 'A new year. A new start.' And Val turned impulsively and kissed her mother's cheek.

'A new start,' she agreed shakily and made up her mind that, although she would never forget the boy she had loved, she would start now to make something worthwhile of her life.

She glanced round a little nervously, wondering if Luke Ferris was amongst the circle round the tree. She hadn't spoken to him since that day in late October when he'd caught her up in the lane. The hospital had been busy and she'd spent her days off helping on the farm or going to see Hilary at the Barton, and had avoided the wood where the charcoal-burner's cottage stood. There'd been Christmas shopping, too, and the usual debate about whether to go to Plymouth or Exeter for the day out that she, her mother and Joanna usually had, and all the preparations to do at home. This year, they'd shared out the work – Val had made the cake, Joanna the mincemeat and Alice the puddings, with Minnie chopping onions, the handle of a fork gripped firmly between her false teeth to stop her eyes watering. What with everything, she'd hardly been into the village except to go to church for the Carol Service, and it had been so full then that even if he had been there she could easily have missed him.

Still clasping her daughter's hand, Alice too glanced around the ring of faces, lit by the lanterns hung from the spreading branches of the old oak. Laughing faces, all filled with the same hope for the new year that she was feeling herself. It won't all go right though, she thought with a sudden prickle of fear. Some things are bound to go wrong – people will fall ill or die, there'll be accidents and sadness. That's life, after all. But at least, please God, let there be no more wars. Let us have peace now. And for goodness sake let's get rid of this blessed rationing!

'Now, where be that maid to?' she asked, searching the faces for her other daughter. 'Slipped off with young Roy Pettifer, I wouldn't mind betting. That girl's growing up too fast. Well, I'm not going home without her. I'll get Val to take you back, Mother.'

'You will not. I'm capable of finding my own way.' But Minnie was only arguing for the sake of it and didn't demur when Val took her arm to guide her along the rough track back to the Tozers' farm.

'Come on, Gran. Let's get you back in the warm while Mum finds our Jackie. I'm ready to go myself now, anyway.' They started to walk slowly back along the track, Val's torch throwing a pool of light to show Minnie the way.

Overhead, the stars seemed almost close enough to touch, a glittering sprinkle of light that seemed to reflect the frost already riming the hedgerows. It had been dry since Christmas and there were no puddles on the roads, no ice to slip on. Alice watched for a moment as the two women set off down the lane, then turned back to the green to look for her younger daughter.

'Jackie!' she called, peering into the darkness. 'Come on

– everyone's going home now. You've got to get up for work in the morning, remember.'

There was a pause and then, as the last few people moved away from the green, Jackie and Roy emerged from a hidden corner. It was too dark to see them properly, even by the light of the hurricane lamp Alice had unhooked from one of the branches of the oak tree, but Jackie's fair hair looked dishevelled and Alice could guess that her face was flushed. She gave them both a quizzical look and took Jackie's arm.

'Roy could've seen me home,' the girl said in an injured tone. 'You didn't have to go shouting out for me like that, Mum, in front of everyone.'

'It's too late for you to be out with a boy,' Alice told her. She nodded at Roy. 'I know you'd have looked after her, but her father's strict over times, even on New Year's Eve. And I can hear the ringers coming down the church path now, so we'd better be on our way. He won't be pleased to see us still hanging about here. Off you go now, Roy.'

The boy shrugged and grinned. 'All right, Mrs Tozer. I've got to be up at six anyway. I promised to help Dad with the milking since it's a Sunday.' He strolled off down the lane and disappeared in the darkness.

'He's a nice enough boy, Jackie,' Alice said after a short silence, 'but I don't want you getting serious. You're only seventeen and he'll be away doing his National Service before long. There's plenty of time before you need to think about all that sort of thing.'

'He might not go away yet,' Jackie said. 'He could finish his apprenticeship first.'

'Whenever he goes, it'll still be for two years. Anyway, you haven't had time to look around. You don't want to take the first chap that comes along.'

'Like you and Dad did, you mean? It don't seem to have

done you any harm.' Jackie's voice was sulky and Alice's heart sank.

'Come on, love, don't let's get the New Year off to a bad start,' she said. 'You know your father and me only want what's best for you. And there's a lot to look forward to this year. There's the trip to London to see the Festival—'

'Me and Roy've been talking about that,' Jackie said quickly. 'We don't want to go on the coach with everyone else. We want to go on the train, by ourselves, and stay for two or three days.'

Alice stopped abruptly. She held up the lamp and stared at her daughter's face. 'You want *what*? Stay up in London – by yourselves? Don't be so silly!'

'It's not silly. It's what we want to do.' Jackie faced her mother defiantly. 'Why shouldn't we?'

'You know very well why you shouldn't. A young maid going away with a boy, not even engaged! Whatever would people say?'

'I don't care what they say. Anyway, who says we're not engaged?' Jackie tossed her head.

'*I* say,' Alice said firmly. 'And so will your father, when he hears about it. Engaged, indeed! Why, Roy's never even asked your father – and neither will he, if I'm any judge. He knows what the answer would be!'

Jackie tossed her head again and her fair hair flew round her face. She'd worn it loose tonight, rather than tied back as she had to wear it for her work in the Barton. She spoke in a quick, nervous tone.

'He's asked *me*, and that's what matters. And I've said yes, so we're engaged. Nobody can stop that and I don't need to wear a ring, so there's nothing you or Dad can do about it.' She turned and began to march along the lane. 'And in four years' time we'll be able to get married whatever *anyone* says, so you may as well get used to the idea.'

'Jackie!' Alice hurried after her, shocked by the sudden turn the conversation had taken. 'Jackie, how dare you talk to me like that. And on New Year's Eve, too, when—'

'New Year's Day,' Jackie said, walking fast. 'It's New Year's *Day*. That's what we were all doing out here at midnight, remember?'

'And there's no call to be cheeky!' Alice said sharply. Then she caught her breath and spoke more gently, taking her daughter's arm as she did so. She felt it stiffen like a piece of wood under her hand. 'Jackie, don't let's have words over this. It's not a good way to start a new year, now is it?'

Jackie said nothing for a few moments. Then she stopped abruptly and turned towards her mother. Alice's arms went round her at once and they clung together in the dark lane. 'I do love him, Mum,' she whispered. 'I do! And he loves me. We can't help it that we're young, can we? We can't help it that we've fallen in love. And – you weren't much older when you and Dad started courting, were you? You've often said how you were childhood sweethearts. So don't be angry with us. Please don't be angry.'

Alice sighed. ''Tis all right, my dear. I do understand. I just don't want you to do anything you might be sorry for later on, that's all. I don't want you to rush into anything.' She paused, then said, 'Your dad and I were childhood sweethearts, it's true, but it don't always work out so well. Look at your Auntie Nell. That was never a happy marriage.'

Jackie lifted her wet face. 'Wasn't it? But she seemed so upset when Uncle Fred was killed.'

'Oh, she was upset, of course she was. He was her man, wasn't he? But she weren't never happy with him, never. It was a good day for her when he was called up. Anyway, we don't need to go into all that. All I'm saying is, you've got your whole life ahead of you, you and Roy, and things can change. People can change. Give it time, that's all, and don't go talking about engagements to your father. Not for a year or two, anyway.'

Jackie found a hanky and blew her nose. They began to walk on again and she said in a doleful voice, 'A year or two's a long time, Mum.'

'Not as long as a lifetime,' Alice replied. 'And these years are precious ones, Jackie. You want to enjoy them, not get tied down. I don't say you can't see Roy whenever you like, but just take it slowly, that's all. Like I said, there's a lot to look forward to now that the war's well and truly over and the country's getting back on its feet.' She hesitated and then said, 'But I can't see your father agreeing to let you go off to London with Roy, not to stay. You'll have to forget that.'

Jackie said nothing and it was too dark for Alice to see her face to know if she had accepted this or was still sulkily defiant. Jackie had always been strong-willed and determined to have her own way, and there was no reason to suppose she had changed now. It looked as if there were storms ahead.

I just wish our Val could find someone to fall in love with, Alice thought, turning her mind to her older daughter. Val was the sort of young woman who was cut out to be married. Warm and loving, she would make a good wife. But she seemed to have set her face against all ideas of marriage, and it looked as if she meant to stay at the farm for ever.

At least Tom and Joanna were settled and happy, and so were Ted and Alice's elder son, Brian, and his wife Peggy, over in Germany. Two out of four wasn't too bad, and the only real problem with Jackie was her wilfulness. And who knew what the year ahead would bring?

A new year, she thought as they came to the farmyard gate and Jackie unlatched it. A new year, with a Festival to give us heart. It's just what everyone needs.

Chapter Eight

Stella Simmons was hoping for a new start too.

Dottie had persuaded her to come to the midnight celebrations. 'You need to get to know village people,' she said, her rosy face beaming as she buttoned a cherry-red cardigan over her frilly blouse. 'And 'twill please them to see the new teacher joining in. That Miss Morgan was proper stand-offish – wouldn't even crack a smile. I don't think the children liked her much either. Good thing when she retired.'

'I hope they'll like me,' Stella said. As she'd said goodbye to the staff and children of the Children's Home before Christmas, she'd felt suddenly frightened at the thought of never going back again, except as a visitor. She knew they'd been good to her, allowing her to stay on during the holidays from college in return for working with the children, but now that was all over and she was on her own. Burracombe must be her home now.

'Why, my pretty, of course they'll like you!' Dottie found her Fair Isle hat and pulled it over her yellow curls. 'You don't have no call to worry about that. Now, you get your coat on sometime around ten o'clock or so, and come down to the Bell and I'll introduce you to a few folk. Us'll be having a little party there, see – Bernie and Rose always puts a few bits and pieces out for the regulars.' She scooped up a basket which Stella knew was filled with snacks prepared by her landlady earlier in the day – sausage rolls, mince pies, egg sandwiches wrapped in a clean teacloth, and an assortment of jam tarts. Dottie was a good cook and, as well as working as barmaid at the Bell Inn, made cakes and tarts for George Sweet's shop and helped out at the Barton House and at the doctor's house too, whenever they had guests. She had been baking all day and Stella had at last been allowed to help. She promised to come down to the pub later on.

Sitting by the fire, Stella hoped that Dottie was right about the children liking her. Despite having lived in an orphanage for so long and helping with the smaller children as she got older, she had found trying to control a room full of children she had never met before a daunting experience during her teaching practice. At the end of the first day, she was almost in tears.

'I'm not going to be any good at all. They won't do a thing I say.'

Miss Carter, the teacher whose class she was taking, had smiled sympathetically. 'They're trying you out. They always do it with a new teacher. I never intervene on the first day because you will come across children like these when you're qualified, and you need to know what they can be like. We'll sort them out tomorrow, don't worry.'

She had, too. The children had sat silent at their desks, some in tears, as Miss Carter had given them a tongue-lashing that almost had Stella weeping in sympathy. After that, she had had no further trouble with them; they'd even begun to enjoy the projects she had brought for them to do. At the end of the fortnight she was touched to receive a variety of posies of wildflowers, a small punnet of strawberries and even a jar of tadpoles, given her by the boy who had been her greatest torment in those first few days. His cheeky face split into a grin, he'd thrust them at her with the words, 'You're all right, miss. We wouldn't mind having you as our teacher all the time.' He'd nodded at the tadpoles. 'They're out of our pond, they are. Turn into toads, they will.'

'Thank you,' Stella said, wondering how she could transport them back to the college and what she could do with them there, but Miss Carter solved that problem as well.

'I've got a pond in my garden. I'll tip them in there. Toads are always useful – they eat slugs, you know.'

Stella looked at the clock and realised that it was already after eleven. She had sat too long over the fire and fallen asleep. She put another log on the embers; Dottie had asked her to keep it stoked up, since they'd both be coming home late. Not that Stella really felt like leaving her comfortable armchair in this cosy little room and going out into the night, but she knew that Dottie would be hurt if she didn't put in an appearance.

She wrapped herself in her coat and scarf. Pulling on gloves and the hat that her college friend Pat's mother had knitted her for Christmas, she stepped out into the frosty air and heard the bells already ringing their muffled peal for the dying of the year. As she came down the lane, she saw the villagers gathered round the tree, torches and lanterns dancing as they moved about, and she paused. The only people she knew were Dottie, the vicar, and the other school governors, and even if she had been able to see them in the darkness she would have hesitated to join them. She felt suddenly isolated and lonely.

'Why, it's Miss Simmons!'

She turned quickly and saw Felix Copley. He was bareheaded, his fair hair gleaming in the flickering light, his teeth glimmering in a wide smile. He held out his hand.

'Good to see you. I was hoping you'd come. Let's stick together, shall we? Two "furriners" together!'

Stella put her hand into his and he drew her into the circle. She felt warmed by the contact and grateful for his kindness in looking out for her. His hand was big and strong, more like a farmworker's than a clergyman's, she thought. But Basil Harvey was quite unlike the wispy little cleric who used to visit the Children's Home and take the services in the little chapel there. Then she remembered Mr Beckett, the vicar she'd been billeted with for a few months after the bomb had shattered her life, and tears filled her eyes.

The muffled peal faded into the darkness and the villagers fell silent, gripping each other's hands and waiting. It was as if, for a moment or two, the whole world held its breath. And then the tolling of the tenor bell struck the hour and they knew that another year had begun.

'Nineteen-fifty-one! Happy New Year!' someone called as the twelfth blow rang out, and then the rest of the bells pealed forth, their chimes as bright and clear as the stars above. The throng began to dance around the tree, skipping in a huge circle and then breaking away to greet each other and give their wishes for happiness and good luck in the coming months.

Stella and Felix found themselves standing together, a little apart as they had been at the beginning. They looked at each other and then he smiled again and shook her hand.

'Happy New Year, Miss Simmons.'

'Happy New Year, Mr Copley,' she said, and they both laughed, although Stella couldn't have said what they were laughing at. He was still holding her hand.

'A new year in a new place for both of us,' he said. 'When do you start school?'

'Not for another week, but I wanted to come early to settle in and get to know the village. And I've got to see Miss Kemp – we need to work out what I'm going to do. How I'm to organise my lessons and so on. I don't think there are any new children starting, so I need to find out how the little ones are getting on with their reading and writing. Miss Kemp says she expects them all to be able to read and ready to learn joined-up writing when they go up into her class.' She stopped. 'Sorry – this must be very boring.'

Felix laughed. 'It's not boring at all, but I think we ought to celebrate the New Year before you start to think too much about work. Come into the pub and I'll buy you a drink.' He grinned mischievously. 'I think the new curate and the new teacher can be allowed to be a little daring on New Year's Eve, don't you? There's just time before Bernie calls for last orders.'

He took Stella's hand again and pulled her across the green to the light spilling from the open doors of the Bell. Many of the villagers had gone back inside after midnight had been struck and were taking advantage of the extended licence to have another drink and finish up the supper that had been laid out on long tables. Felix pushed his way in and Stella caught sight of Dottie behind the bar, her yellow curls tumbling round her face and the frilly blouse she had put on 'for best' showing rather a lot of her plump chest as she leaned on the bar, laughing at something one of the farmers was saying.

'What'll you have?'

'Oh, I don't know.' Stella had been into very few pubs and the only drink she normally had at this hour of the night – if she were still awake and wanting a drink at all – would have been cocoa. You couldn't ask for cocoa in a pub though, especially not on New Year's Eve. Or New Year's Day, as she supposed it now was. 'A – a lemonade, please.'

'Really? It's rather a cold drink, isn't it? Why not have a ginger wine?'

'Yes, all right.' That didn't sound too alcoholic. She waited while Felix fought his way to the bar. People looked round at him, recognised who he was and made way, their eyebrows raised a little. He grinned back cheerfully and

Stella could see some of them pull down the corners of their mouths, as if to say 'he's all right', while others looked down their noses disapprovingly.

Dottie spotted her and waved cheerily, and several people turned to see who she was waving at. Stella felt her cheeks grow hot and was thankful when Felix battled his way back through the noisy throng and handed her a sherry glass filled with deep golden-brown liquid.

'Thank you.' She took a sip and gasped as the wine tingled against her lips, tongue and throat. 'Goodness me, it really is gingery!'

'It'll warm you up.' Felix was drinking beer. He glanced round and said, 'Look, there's a table and a couple of chairs – let's grab them.'

They made their way over to the corner which had just been vacated and sat down. Stella looked at Felix and felt a sudden sense of disbelief. I can't be doing this, she thought, sitting in a pub with a man I barely know. Whatever would Matron at the Home say? At the same time, she felt a warm pleasure that she had made a friend already, for she felt sure that Felix was going to be a friend. She smiled at him and when he lifted his glass to her, she raised hers in return.

'Happy New Year,' they said again, in unison; over at the bar, Dottie saw them and lifted the glass of stout that was standing by her side and shouted across, 'Happy New Year!'

'I don't think everyone approves of you being here,' Stella said, and Felix chuckled.

'They probably think clergymen shouldn't drink at all, and if they do they ought to do it privately, in their own homes and with the curtains drawn. But Mr Harvey comes in for a pint now and then, he told me, so they ought to be accustomed to it. And it's a good place to meet people – better than the church, in some ways.'

The bells had stopped ringing and there was a small commotion as the bellringers came in and good wishes were exchanged all over again. There was just time for one more drink and then Bernie, the tubby landlord, called 'time' and people began to head towards the door.

'Let me see you home now,' Felix said, putting his hand beneath Stella's elbow. 'It's the cottage just along the lane, isn't it?'

'That's right. But you don't need to bother – there are plenty of people walking that way. Besides, I can't imagine anything bad happening in Burracombe.'

'All the same,' he said, 'I can't let a lady walk home alone.' He kept his hand under her elbow, guiding her along the rough metalled road. As she had said, there were others going that way too, their torches making little pools of white light in front of them. The jubilation of the new year had quietened a little, and they were talking and joking. It was almost like a big family going home together, Stella thought, with sudden, sharp emotion that was half-pain and half-pleasure.

They came to Dottie's gate and Felix wished her goodnight. She gave him a final smile and stood for a moment looking up at the stars and listening to the silence.

Only once had she known the deep silence of the countryside at night. Her early childhood had been spent in cities, much of it under the roar of aircraft and what seemed, in memory, to be an incessant pandemonium of bombing. There had been that brief period in a small village, not so very different from Burracombe and sharing the same deep quiet under the starlit nights – and then the sudden wrench as she was torn away from the contented home she had found and taken to an orphanage on the other side of the county.

She stood now with her hand on the gate, looking up at

the stars. It was her first New Year's Eve away from the Home. 1951: a new year, a new start.

I haven't made a resolution, she thought suddenly, and closed her eyes. *Let me make a success of this job – of this whole year. And let me, somehow, find out what happened to my little sister.*

It wasn't a resolution so much as a prayer, but it said everything that was in her heart.

Chapter Nine

For Hilary Napier, that New Year's Eve had seemed to bring little promise of a new start. Even though her brother Stephen had come home just before Christmas, somewhat reluctantly and complaining that he hadn't done nearly enough skiing, nothing much seemed to have changed at the Barton. Her father was already beginning to make pointed remarks about 'still thinking you're on holiday' and 'work to do, even if it *is* Christmas', and Hilary could see that it was only a matter of time before the arguments began.

She had come in from walking the dogs to find her father already at breakfast with a copy of *The Sunday Times* beside him. 'Morning, my dear. Dogs behave themselves?'

She smiled at him and poured herself some coffee from the silver pot on the sideboard. Her father liked to have breakfast served in the old way, so Hilary prepared it all before she took the dogs out and left it ready in the breakfast room, for all the world as if they still had servants. 'Of course.' She glanced at the two black labradors, who had lumbered over to the fireplace and flung themselves down in front of it with huge sighs, as if this were all they had been waiting for. 'They're getting too old to do much else these days. They still enjoy their morning run, though.'

Napier nodded. 'I'll have to see how those youngsters Burley's been training are shaping up. Wouldn't do to be without the dogs. Selsey's showing signs of stiffness, and Bart was definitely tired after the last shoot.' He glanced at his newspaper.

Hilary helped herself to toast and a boiled egg. She sat down opposite him. 'What's the news?'

Napier frowned. 'It looks to me as if the Communists are going to take Seoul. This Korean War's a bad business. I thought we'd done with all that when we bombed the Japanese. Now here we are in the thick of it again.' He shook his head. 'And our own Government's no help. It's Churchill we want in charge now, not Attlee. That election last year was a complete shambles.'

Hilary had heard all this before. She remembered the election fever of a year ago, the campaigning and canvassing. Her father had been chairman of the selection committee for the local branch of the Conservative Party and, although their own candidate had won his seat, the return of Labour to Government had been a bitter blow.

He folded the paper and dropped it on a chair, then reached out for a slice of toast. 'Where's that boy? Still lolling about in bed?'

'I expect so. He was going to the Bouldings' party at Little Burracombe. I was invited too, but I'm going to the Latimers' tonight, so I passed.'

The Squire grunted. He'd been invited to the doctor's New Year's Eve party as well, but somehow he didn't have the heart for that sort of thing these days. The dogs stretched out in front of a smouldering log fire, a glass of malt and his memories would help him see in the new year, and then he'd shut the two labradors in the gunroom and gone to bed, hearing the last peal of the bells as he slipped between the sheets.

He glanced at his daughter, struck as he always was by her resemblance to her mother. Isobel had been just the same age as Hilary was now when he had inherited the estate in 1926, and Hilary had been four. Baden, the eldest of their three children, had been a sturdy boy of six, and young Stephen hadn't even been thought of yet. They'd had everything before them then, he thought – a growing family, a good, solid house and an estate to run which would take all his energies and give him the life he'd been bred for. They'd looked forward to a lifetime together, growing old in this place where he had been born, with Baden taking the reins when the time came and grandchildren playing round their feet.

And now both Isobel and Baden were gone. Stephen, the youngest, had only just finished with Cambridge and Hilary, still unmarried at twenty-eight, was old before her time. He still had the estate, of course, still had his positions as a magistrate and Master of the Hunt, still had his finger in all the appropriate pies – but life was an empty affair without his wife and the son who had seemed like another part of his own self. As for Stephen . . . He shook his big head.

'Time he stirred himself,' he said. 'Church at eleven, and then he could come round the estate with me, see what's what. He'll have to start taking an interest soon, make himself useful now he's finished with Cambridge. I'll need someone to hand over to eventually, and there's nobody else.' He looked down at his plate, frowning.

Hilary said nothing. She buttered her toast and cut it into narrow slices. Her father's eyes strayed back to the newspaper again.

'D'you think there'll be another election this year?' she asked. It had been talked of ever since Labour had got back in with their slim majority. A coalition was out of the question – the country had had six years of that during the war and, although it had worked well in those circumstances, neither of the main parties wanted it now. They wanted to work to their own policies.

'It's to be hoped so. Ridiculous, getting in with a majority like that – virtually a hung Parliament. Bad enough that they should have been brought in after the war. Gross ingratitude, that's what it was, after all Churchill had done for the country.'

'Well, Labour haven't been that bad,' Hilary said. 'They've brought in quite a few good measures – National Health insurance, pensions, better education for everyone. And I think people just wanted a change, after the war.'

'A *change*! For heaven's sake, Hilary, Government's not a suit of clothes or a strip of wallpaper, to be changed just because people are bored or there's a new fashion.' He folded his newspaper irritably. 'I dare say some of the steps they've taken – health and pensions – have been good enough, but they were on the cards before the war started. It was just a matter of waiting for the right time. As for education, I'm not so sure. What use would a grammar-school education be to a boy like Roy Pettifer, for instance, who's just going to take up an apprenticeship in a garage and work with his father? Or to a girl like young Jackie Tozer, working as a maid in our kitchen? It doesn't make sense.'

'It does if they've got the intelligence to pass the scholarship examination,' Hilary argued. 'If a bright boy like Roy had a grammar-school education he might not take up an apprenticeship. He could go on to college, even university. There's no knowing what he could do. And Jackie's intelligent enough to do something far better than kitchen work. She could become a teacher, or even a doctor like Felicity Latimer.'

Her father stared at her. 'Teacher? Doctor? What nonsense is that? Girl like Jackie will get married before she's twenty and settle down with half a dozen babies round her feet. What's the use of the country paying for an education for that, hey? And what's this about young

Felicity? I'd have thought her parents would have more sense. She's far too young to be thinking of a career, anyway.'

'Well, her father's a doctor,' Hilary pointed out. 'He might be pleased to have Felicity following in his footsteps. Women doctors aren't unknown, after all.'

Squire Napier grunted. 'Doesn't mean they're a good thing. Doesn't make any difference what class a young woman is, anyway – she's still going to get married and have children, and then she's got to stay at home and look after them, no matter who she is. Same for Felicity as it is for young Jackie.'

Hilary was silent for a moment or two. Then she said quietly, 'Not every young woman gets married.'

Napier drew in a deep breath. He coughed a little and said gruffly, 'I'm sorry, my dear. I wasn't thinking. Although you would have been married by now, and had a youngster or two as well, if it hadn't been for – for . . .'

'For Henry being killed?'

'I wasn't going to say that. I was going to say "if it hadn't been for the war".'

'It comes to the same thing, doesn't it,' Hilary said, and struck her egg with the back of her spoon.

The door opened and they both looked up with some relief, tempered in the Squire's case by an immediate irritation, as Stephen Napier came in, wearing his dressing-gown and with his fair hair rumpled. He gave his father an abstracted smile and touched his sister's shoulder lightly as he passed behind her. Hilary's features softened and she dipped her spoon into the yolk of her egg.

'Any coffee left?' Stephen cupped his palm around the pot to feel the temperature and then poured himself a cup. 'Mm, that's the stuff to give the troops.' He brought the cup to the table and sat down opposite Hilary.

'I'm not sure how you'd know that,' Napier said acidly,

helping himself to more bacon. 'Since you've never been in any of the Services.'

'Well, that's hardly my fault. I was only seventeen when the war ended and I've been up at Cambridge since I left school. I dare say my call-up papers will come through soon enough.' He winked at Hilary and put on a passable imitation of his father's voice. 'Few months' square-bashing, soon make a man of me.'

Napier raised his head abruptly. 'And that's enough of your impertinence, my boy! Not that it isn't true. Discipline's what you need, and discipline's what you'll get once you're in the Army. And while we're on the subject—'

'While we're on the subject,' Stephen said, reaching for the toast, 'I don't want to go into the Army. I'm hoping for the RAF.'

'The *RAF*?'

'Yes. Why not? Much better fun than tramping round muddy fields covered in leaves. In fact, I'm thinking of signing on as a Regular and training to be a pilot.'

'A Regular? A *pilot*?' Gilbert Napier stared at his son and snapped, 'Don't talk such nonsense! You'll do your two years in my old regiment – I've put in a word already – and then come back here and start learning to run the estate.' His face darkened a little and Hilary knew that he was thinking of Korea. Not all the British regiments were being sent to the Far East, but the way things were going there was a chance. There must be people all over Britain who had already lost one young man in the Second World War and were dreading losing another.

Stephen spread home-made marmalade thickly on his toast. 'I'd rather go into the RAF.'

'Rather? *Rather*? What in God's name does that have to do with it? You've got a job to do here, don't you understand? You're going to inherit. What use will you be

93

if you've spent all your time on an airfield? What sort of a job is a pilot anyway?'

'A pretty good one, I think. More comfortable than being in the Army, anyway. No mud, and you get back to your own bed every night.'

Napier stared at him. 'Is that all you can think about? Being *comfortable*?'

'No.' Stephen met his father's eye. 'I think about what I'd like to do with my life. And what I'd like to do, since I have to do National Service of some sort, is take the chance to be a pilot. I don't think I've got much chance of that by going as a squaddie for two years.'

'You wouldn't be a squaddie. You'd go in as an officer.'

'Jumping over the heads of other men. Sorry, Dad, I'd rather do things on my own merit than because of your influence.'

Napier stared at him, his face reddening with anger. Stephen continued to spread his toast but Hilary, watching them both, could see that his hand was trembling slightly.

'*My influence*? Don't you realise how fortunate you are to have the background you do? The family, the education, the *money*, behind you? I've never noticed you refusing any of these things before. Where do you think you'd have been without them, hey? D'you think you'd have gone to Cambridge, got that degree of yours, if you hadn't had *my influence* and all that goes with it?'

Stephen looked up. He too had noticed the tremble and laid his hand on the table. He spoke quietly, afraid that his voice would betray him as well. 'No, Dad, I don't suppose I would. And that's not fair, is it? As it happens, I do have a brain of sorts and I worked hard and got a First in Mathematics, but there were plenty of undergrads who didn't bother, men who were there because of *their* fathers' influence and would never have got to Cambridge otherwise. And there are people who ought to be there but don't have the chance, because their fathers *don't* have influence.' He paused, then said quietly, 'I'm grateful for everything I've had, Dad, but now I want to live my life on my own, without any help or influence. That's all.' He lifted his cup to his lips, his hand determinedly steady.

'It *isn't* all. Not as far as I'm concerned. You've got a job to do here, at Burracombe. You'll do your National Service, naturally, it's your patriotic duty, but once that's done you'll be needed here. Get that out of the way and you can come home and get on with your real job.'

'But that's just it!' Stephen exclaimed. 'It's *not* my real job. I was never intended to take over the estate. I never expected it – I'm not *suited* for it. Hilary would be better at it than me.'

Hilary opened her mouth quickly, but the Squire forestalled her. '*Hilary?* Don't be so ridiculous! She's got enough to do, running the house. As for not being suited to it, that's nonsense. Put your mind to it, you can do anything. And you don't have to remind me that you never expected to inherit.'

Napier's voice dropped on his last words and his eyes went to the mantelpiece where a portrait of his elder son hung. It had been painted when Baden had first joined the Army, at the beginning of the war, and showed him looking proud and smart in his uniform with the badge of the Devons on his lapels, his captain's three pips on his shoulder and his cap held under one arm. His ice-blue eyes, so like Gilbert Napier's, looked out steadily from beneath his smooth, dark hair and his lips were firm above a firmly set jaw. He had been killed in action less than six months after the portrait had been hung.

There was a silence. Hilary and Stephen stared at the portrait and then at each other. Stephen looked awkward, embarrassed and irritated. He put down his cup and said, a little too loudly, 'Father, you can't expect me to take on everything that Baden would have done. I can't *be* Baden.'

'Of course I know you can't "be" Baden – ridiculous suggestion. But you can be a very good substitute for him. You can do the job he would have done, if he'd been spared. It's what you *ought* to be doing – ought to be proud to do.'

Stephen shook his head violently. 'No! I'm not a substitute. I can't live his life for him. I keep telling you, I've got my own life to live – doesn't that count for anything?'

'Your *own* life? Isn't that just what I'm trying to tell you?' Gilbert Napier thumped his fist on the table. 'This *is* your life now. And you're damned lucky to have it, let me tell you.' The blue eyes, which could look like chips of ice, had darkened almost to black and his voice was low and tight. 'Your brother gave his life for his country – for this estate, this village. For me, for your mother, for you and your sister, for everything we've ever lived for. He gave his life so that our way of life could continue. So that England – oh yes, and Scotland and Wales and Ireland too, if you must have it – could go on being the England it's always been. And it's you, and men like you, who for one reason or another were fortunate enough to survive the war, who have to make sure that it does continue. Not by playing at being pilots. Not by messing about in punts up and down the Cam. But by getting your National Service done, learning a bit about what it means to be a man, and then coming back here and getting on with the job – the job of maintaining the style of living that made this country what it is. And you ought to think yourself privileged to do it,' he finished, his voice cracking a little. '*Damned* privileged.'

There was a short silence. Hilary and Stephen stared down at their plates. Then Hilary looked up at her father, but before she could speak, the Squire got up abruptly and strode towards the door.

'Going for a walk,' he announced, and the two black labradors scrambled to their feet from their place in front of the fire and dashed across the room. 'Be back in time for church.'

He shut the door hard behind him and Hilary met Stephen's eyes. 'You've really upset him, Steve.'

'I've upset *him*!' Stephen exclaimed. 'What about him upsetting me? It's my life he's trying to order, Hil. Look, I'm as sorry as anyone else about Baden, but it wasn't my fault he got killed. And it's not my fault it was him and not me,' he added in a lower tone, dropping his eyes again.

'Stephen! That's an awful thing to say. As if Daddy wished it had been you instead!'

'Well, doesn't he?' Stephen lifted his head. 'Don't you think he'd rather Baden had lived? If he'd been told he had to lose a son, which one d'you think he'd have chosen? Not Baden, that's for sure. Not the golden boy who never put a foot wrong – the son who was going to follow in his footsteps and be Squire one day. No, I'd have been the one he could do without – I've *always* been the one he could do without.'

'That's not fair, Steve.'

'Well, there's a lot of truth in it.' He looked squarely at his sister. 'You know that, Hil. And you know what it would be like for me if I had to stay at home and learn to run the estate. I'd hate it. I'd make a complete mess of it. And Dad would hate me for it.' He pushed his cup away and leaned his elbows on the table, resting his head between his palms. 'I'm just not suited for it.'

'Well, someone's going to have to do it,' she said.

'Why?' he demanded. 'Why does someone have to do it? Why, just because we happen to be born here, does it have to rule our lives? Look at you, Hil – you could be doing

97

something really interesting, something worthwhile, but you're trapped here, running the house for Dad just because Mother's not here. You could be married, have your own home and family—'

'No,' she said quietly. 'I don't think that's ever going to happen now.'

'Not while you're cooped up here, perhaps. But it could. And anyway, you could be doing something else with your life. It doesn't have to be given up for the estate. Same for me. Baden's not here, so I've got to give up my life. Why? What's so important about the estate that we have to sacrifice our whole lives to keep it going?'

'Because it's part of our family. Because it's been ours for generations.'

Stephen shook his head. 'That's no reason. Some other family could take it over if they wanted to. It could be sold. The farms could be sold – the tenants themselves might like the chance to buy them. It doesn't even have to be an estate.'

Hilary stared at him. 'Stephen, think what you're saying! That's exactly what Daddy *doesn't* want to happen – the estate being split up and sold. He wants it to stay as it is, as it's always been. He wants to preserve the English way of life. What you're saying would destroy it.'

'No,' he said. 'What I'm saying would change it. But it's changing anyway, Hil. It has to. The war's changed it. You know yourself, people aren't the same any more. I heard you and Dad talking just before I came in, about education. Girls being doctors, like Felicity. Boys like Roy Pettifer wanting to go to college. That's one of the things that the war has done – yes, and the Government too. The war showed ordinary people what they can do, given the opportunity, and the Government is giving them that opportunity. People don't want to be servants and slaves any more, they want to go further. And this Festival of

Britain that Dad's so keen on will change things even more.'

'How? How will it do that?'

'It'll show them what's out there,' he said. 'There'll be things at the Exhibition that will open your eyes, Hil. New scientific advances. Machines that can do all sorts of things. Factories are going to change. Homes will change. Farms will change. In a few years' time, we'll all be using tractors and machinery – there'll be no more horses on the land at all.'

'No more horses? But—'

'Not for work. There'll be horses for riding on, of course, and there'll still be hunting. But the carthorses and the big Shire and Clydesdale plough-horses – they'll be gone.' He reached out again for his coffee, sipped and wrinkled his nose. 'This has gone cold.'

'There's some more here.' Hilary reached absently for the pot and refilled her own cup as well. She stared into it for a minute or two. 'Steve, if you're right and there are all these changes, what d'you think will happen to the country? Will we lose our farms and countryside altogether? I don't think I could live here if that happened.'

'I don't know,' he said soberly. 'But it's not been much of a place to live since the war ended, has it? All the rebuilding, the shortages, the rationing . . . still going on years later. I tell you what, I'm not sure we're ever going to get over it all. This Festival, it's a good try. But will it work?'

'So, if you don't want to run the estate when you finish your National Service, what will you do?'

He looked up at her, his expression more serious than she had ever seen it. He seemed to consider for a moment, as if debating whether to tell her. Then he said, 'I meant it when I said I wanted to learn to fly, Hil. But after I've done my National Service, I'm thinking of emigrating. America,

Canada – somewhere like that. That's where the future is now. Not on some tinpot little estate, buried in Devon.' He nodded slowly, and then gave her his old, familiar grin. 'Tell you what, you could come with me. How'd you feel about that? Come and keep house for me if you like. It'd be a darned sight more interesting than keeping house for Dad.' He gripped her wrist and his eyes blazed suddenly into hers. 'Think about it, Hil! Just *think* about it.'

Chapter Ten

On New Year's Day the local Hunt assembled, as it did each year, in front of the Bell Inn. The shops were open, the scent of fresh bread issuing across the green from George Sweet's bakery, and hounds milled about, already eagerly sniffing the ground while members in both black and hunting-pink jackets sat tall and straight on their smartly clipped horses. Bernie Nethercott, his wife Rose and Dottie Friend were coming out of the inn bearing trays of glasses which they offered to the riders, and Constance Bellamy was standing by with a shovel and bucket ready to pick up any droppings.

'I pile 'em up in a corner and let 'em rot down, ready for the roses,' she explained to Stella Simmons, who was standing nearby. 'Best manure there is. Settling down all right, are you?'

'Yes, thank you.' Stella hesitated, not sure what to say next, but Constance was already speaking again.

'Time I came and had another look at the school,' she stated in the deep and forceful tones which seemed so incongruous in such a small woman. 'Grandfather endowed it, y'know. Take a personal interest, always have. Usually pop in sometime during the term – missed the Christmas party, touch of bronchitis.' She darted forward with her shovel as a large black horse deposited a heap of steaming dung on the road. 'Thank you, Sultan. Morning to you,

Gilbert,' she added, beaming up at the rider. 'Fine morning for it.'

Gilbert Napier nodded at her as his horse tossed its head and stamped one forefoot with impatience. 'Should have a good day.' The church clock struck eleven and he lifted one hand to the huntsman. 'Time to be off, Roger. Call 'em in.'

The huntsman, smart in his bright red coat and black hat, lifted his horn to his lips and blew. The scattered hounds immediately came together and set off along the lane, their tails like waving banners above a shifting kaleidoscope of black, yellow and cream bodies. The horses followed, their hooves clattering on the road and the riders lifting rhythmically up and down in the saddle. Stella, Constance Bellamy and the others stood watching and Dottie Friend heaved a sentimental sigh.

'Lovely, isn't it? I always like to see the Hunt. Real old country tradition, that is. Missed it during the war.'

'Foxes didn't though, did 'em!' Bernie Nethercott said. 'Anyway, it didn't stop altogether. Roger could still take hounds out.'

''Twasn't the same though, with no hunting pink and all the horses and riders.' Dottie turned to Stella. 'See, most of the younger men and women that were riding to hounds then were off serving somewhere. There were only Roger and a few farmers left, and they didn't have time for hunting. They kept the hounds and took 'em out when they could, but it were never like a real Hunt.'

Stella nodded and smiled, but in her heart she wasn't at all sure that she liked the idea of a fox being chased across fields and moorland by a pack of hounds, urged on by men and women on horseback. It seemed rather unfair – wouldn't just one or two dogs be enough? But there had been no fox-hunting in the village she'd lived in so briefly during the war and she was still learning about country ways. The first thing she had learned was not to question them, but simply to keep quiet and observe.

She turned and found Felix standing beside her, his corn-coloured hair shining in the January sunlight. He smiled down at her.

'Hello, Stella. We meet again. Happy New Year.'

'Happy New Year,' Stella said, feeling suddenly shy. It had taken her longer than she'd expected to get to sleep last night. The late hour, the gathering round the tree and the drink in the pub had all been unusual enough to keep her mind buzzing until after Dottie had come home, creeping about downstairs and tripping over the cat. She wasn't sure how to respond to the friendliness this young curate was showing her. He had to be friendly to everyone, it was his job, and he'd probably been as pleased to have her company as she'd been to have his. That was all it was.

'I'll be meeting you in a professional capacity soon,' he remarked. 'The vicar tells me we visit the school regularly to talk to the children.'

Stella nodded. 'It's hard *not* to meet people here anyway. I've only been here three or four days, and already I can't walk down the village street without running into half a dozen people I know.'

'And if you don't know them the first time, you will the second time,' he agreed with a grin. 'At least, they'll know you! Not that they wouldn't already. In my experience of villages, word gets round faster than lightning, and a new face stands out like a sore thumb. I don't mean that you look in the least like a sore thumb,' he added hastily.

Stella laughed. 'Did you grow up in a village?'

'Yes, in Cambridgeshire.' He glanced around the village green with its huge old oak tree, the cottages clustered around, the Bell Inn with its thatched roof and the church behind it. Beyond the fields and lanes the slopes of Dartmoor rose smooth and brown, frosted with white. 'It's rather different from this. You see, it's quite flat there, with the Fens and the ditches. The fields aren't hedged like they are here, so you can see for miles.'

'It sounds rather dull,' Stella observed, and immediately wished she hadn't. 'I mean, I'm sure it's very pretty really, but—'

Felix smiled. 'Actually, it is rather dull in comparison with Devon scenery, but the villages are attractive, and there's something about the wide expanse of sky . . . I suppose every part of the country has something to be said for it. Its own character.' They began to walk slowly along the lane, away from the green. 'Are you comfortable in your lodgings? You're living with Dottie Friend, aren't you, the barmaid at the pub?'

Stella nodded. 'That's right. She's a lovely person. I grew up in Hampshire.' She hesitated. There was nothing to be ashamed of in having been orphaned and grown up in a Children's Home, yet she knew that it sometimes embarrassed people when she spoke of it, and it was too complicated to explain anyway. 'I saw this job advertised and applied for it, and here I am.'

'And do you like it?'

'Well, I haven't started yet,' she said, raising bright eyes at him. 'The new term starts next week, remember. But I'm sure I will, once I can understand what the children say. The local dialect seems a bit like a foreign language at the moment.'

'The vicar keeps introducing me to people and I haven't the faintest idea what they're saying, either,' he confessed. 'I just wonder if they understand *me*.'

'Oh, they don't have any problem. They're used to listening to the radio, you see, so they hear ordinary speech all the time.' They arrived at the gate to Dottie Friend's cottage, and Stella laid her hand on the latch. 'It's been nice to meet you again, Mr Copley.'

'Felix,' he said, looking into her eyes. 'I told you yesterday, I'm hoping everyone will call me Felix.'

Stella looked back at him, a little nonplussed. She'd been taught that you called people by their surnames until you knew them well, and she'd been surprised when he'd called her Stella just now. She said doubtfully, 'I'm not sure that they will. Not till they know you better, anyway.'

Before Felix could reply, Dottie herself came panting up the lane, a laden shopping-basket hooked over her arm. She gave them both a beaming smile and Stella hastily opened the gate to let her through.

'What a morning! 'Tis always busy when the Hunt meets, but I think the world and his wife must have been there today. Bernie let me off to do a bit of shopping but I've got to go back straight away. I just thought I'd put some dinner up for you, my pretty, before I go, that's if you'm ready for it. 'Tis early, I know.' She gave Felix a quick, friendly nod. 'You'm the new curate. Heard you preach yesterday – not up to Vicar's standard, of course, but nice enough. Well, sorry I can't stop now, but I've to go up to the Barton when the inn closes, and I'm all behind like a duck's tail as it is. So if you'm ready for your dinner, Stella?'

'Oh – yes, of course.' Stella followed her through the gate and turned to smile at Felix. 'I'll see you again, Mr Copley. It's been nice to talk to you.' She followed Dottie into the cottage and the door closed behind them.

Felix turned away. It was his free day and he'd rather hoped to persuade the pretty young schoolteacher to join him for a walk. He might even have coaxed her into calling him Felix.

Never mind – there was plenty of time yet. All the time in the world, in fact.

It was gone three when Hilary clattered into the stableyard

on Beau, her bay gelding. She slipped off his back, rubbed his white nose in gratitude for a good day out, and fastened him to the ring outside the stable door, ready to wash him down. They were both exhausted and covered in mud, but Beau's needs came first. Once he was in his stall, munching at his feed, Hilary could go indoors and soak in a hot bath.

Her father had not yet come home, and she was grateful for the peace and quiet of the yard. She began her tasks of making Beau clean and comfortable, feeling the satisfaction of hard exercise.

They hadn't killed a fox; it didn't much matter whether they did or not, as far as Hilary was concerned, and she suspected that quite a few of the other Hunt members felt much the same. The unpredictability of the ride was what they enjoyed, the chase across fields and moorlands, never knowing where they would go next, taking hedges and ditches and streams as they came; the wildest way there was of riding horses in England these days, and the most exhilarating.

As she worked, she thought of her brother's outburst yesterday morning. He had gone off after breakfast and spent the day at Little Burracombe with his friend Jeremy Boulding. Their father had also been uncommunicative, coming home from church to shut himself up in his study, and Hilary had found herself alone, without even the company of Jackie Tozer, who came in every day except Sunday. Jackie and the gardener–cum–stableman Josh Crocker, with the occasional help of Dottie Friend, were all that remained of the staff of twelve kept before the war, and Hilary spent her days doing work her mother would never have dreamed of doing. Riding Beau was all the time she had off from the house.

How had this happened, she wondered as she rubbed down the horse's legs. How had she become what wasn't much more than a skivvy? She thought of her years in the

ATS – years when she'd had a responsible job, when she'd been expected to use her initiative, driving important people in a car that was better than any her father had ever owned, respected and accepted for who *she* was and what she could do, not who her father was or where she came from. I was myself during the war, Hilary thought, combing the mud from Beau's coat. I've never really been myself since.

Even Stephen, who had talked so excitedly about his plans to emigrate, who had seemed to want to include her in those plans, had seen her as no more than a housekeeper. In truth, he was no better than their father; whatever he wanted to do with his life, it hadn't occurred to him that Hilary might have a life as well, that she might want to spend it in her own way, be just as adventurous.

I meant to do something, she thought, brushing clots of mud from the horse's long black tail. When the war ended and I was demobbed from the ATS, I meant to look for something else, for some real work. The other girls had – her friend Rosemary, for instance, had become a stewardess on one of the new airlines and now flew all over Europe. I could have done that, Hilary thought. But when she thought honestly about it, she knew that most of the young women she had known during the war had simply done what was always expected of them – they'd got married, started families and settled down.

Perhaps they were happy with that. But a tiny worm of doubt moved in her mind. Would she really have enjoyed such a life? Or would she have come to feel just as frustrated and unfulfilled as she did now?

Beau whickered and she realised that she had been scrubbing the same flank for several minutes. She apologised and put her arm under his neck to hold his big warm head close to hers. They stood cheek to cheek for a moment, then she moved away and unhooked his rein to lead him into the stable. His feed – a mixture of oats, bran, maize and linseed – and haynet were already in place and he began to eat at once. Hilary closed the door to his stall and stood for a moment watching him and listening to his satisfied munching. Now for that hot bath, and then it would be time to think about dinner. And Val Tozer was coming over afterwards so they could have a good gossip over a glass of ginger wine or home-made sloe gin.

'I suppose I ought to be grateful that I've got a nice place to live and don't have to slave in a factory or an office,' she said later, when the dishes were cleared away – Val had arrived just in time to help, despite Hilary's insistence that she sit at the kitchen table and watch. Then Hilary got out the bottles and held them up enquiringly, and they settled down in two old armchairs by the Aga with a glass of sloe gin each.

'Or give farmers blanket baths,' Val said. 'You know Olly Sedge? He's just had his appendix out. Sometimes I think it would be better if I worked in Plymouth or Exeter in a hospital where I wasn't likely to know all the patients. It didn't bother me, I'm used to it, but the poor man didn't know where to look so he just shut his eyes and we pretended we'd never seen each other before.'

'Did you have to manage all by yourself?' Hilary asked. 'He must weigh twenty stone if he's an ounce.'

'He does. He nearly broke our scales when he came in. Well, he might lose a few pounds now. He's on a light diet and I can tell you, he doesn't like it much!'

Hilary smiled. 'That's another career I can cross off my list, then. I don't think I could give blanket baths to people like Olly Sedge. Or anyone else, for that matter.'

'What would you really like to do?' Val asked curiously. 'I mean, if you hadn't had to come home when you did, what would you have done?'

'I don't really know. That's part of the trouble. All my upbringing was aimed at fitting me for the sort of life I'm leading now – running a house, looking after men. Only I was supposed to be married and have my own family. Perhaps it would be all right if I had. If Henry hadn't been killed . . . What about you, Val? You lost your fiancé too. You wouldn't be nursing now if Eddie had lived.'

Val said nothing for a moment or two. She gazed at the purple liquid in her glass and finally said, 'I don't know, Hil. I don't know what I'd have been doing.'

Hilary glanced at her in surprise. There had been an odd note in Val's voice. She said, 'Well, you'd have been married, wouldn't you? And Eddie would have come out of the Army and gone back into farming, I suppose. That's what he was doing before the war, wasn't it?'

'Yes, but I don't think he'd have gone back to it. He was a mechanic in the Army, working on tanks, and I think he'd have stayed on. He liked the life. He liked seeing different places, and he liked working with engines. I don't think he would ever have gone back to farming.' She sipped her drink and added, 'There might not have been any jobs for him anyway. You know what an awful time farmers had during the war, with all those restrictions and everything. They couldn't make their own decisions any more, over their own land that they knew better than anyone.' Her voice rose in indignation. 'Look at Arnie Betterswell, he'd built up a lovely dairy herd and he was told to sell them all off and grow potatoes instead! Where was the sense in that? Didn't we need milk any more? Couldn't someone with decent arable grow potatoes?'

'I know.' Hilary had been away when most of this was happening although, like Val, she'd heard all about it. But Val went on as if she hadn't spoken.

'And there was that poor man over at Buckland. They told him he had to plough up two fields and put them down to wheat, and if he didn't do it he'd be evicted. He was *dying*, Hil, and Dad and some of the others wrote to tell them so, but did they take any notice? No, they didn't. They wrote back a pompous letter about their decision "not being reversible" or some such nonsense. It was cruel.'

'What did he do? Surely they didn't actually turn him out?'

'Oh yes, they did. I saw it myself – it was heartbreaking. He was out in the lane himself, looking as if he was at death's door, which he was, and his wife crying her eyes out. All their possessions were just dumped out in the lane and they had nowhere to go, nowhere. In the end the other farmers got together and brought their carts round to take the stuff to any barns where they had a bit of space, and the couple went to relatives in Plymouth. The man died a few weeks later. I don't know what happened to his wife but someone told me that some of their things are still in the barns; she just never came back to collect them.'

Hilary stared at her. 'That's awful. I didn't realise it had been that bad.'

'Oh, he wasn't the only one. Some people actually went and lived in shacks – *henhouses* – because they had nowhere to go. And they didn't get any compensation, you know, not a penny. It didn't make any difference whether they owned their farms or were tenants, or how much money they'd spent to improve them. They had nothing. And they couldn't even appeal. The "War Ag" – the Ministry of Agriculture – was above the law.' She leaned forward a little. 'And who do you think got the farms when the poor farmers were thrown out, Hil? I'll tell you. As often as not, it was friends of the War Ag men themselves. They put their sons in, some of them, so that they would be exempted from military service.'

'That's terrible,' Hilary said, shocked. 'It's corruption.' She thought for a moment, then said a little doubtfully,

'How do you know all this, Val? I mean, are you really sure it's true?'

'Oh yes! They formed a union, you see, and Dad went along to the meetings in London. Actually, the ones who owned their farms were offered them back at the end of the war, but a lot of them had lost heart by then. Some of them were dead, anyway. Some had even killed themselves. There was one poor man in Hampshire who refused to plough up four acres – four acres, Hil – and he ended up under siege in his house, surrounded by police. They put gas down his chimney but he had his gas-mask on so that was no good. And then he shot a policeman and injured him so they shot him dead. All over four acres!' She took a bigger sip of her drink and added bitterly, 'Who'd want to come back to farming? We kept the country fed during the war, but it was because people like Dad and the other farmers worked all the hours God sent – no thanks to stupid men from London who didn't know one end of a pitchfork from another. I'd soon have shown them which end was which, if I'd had the chance!'

Hilary laughed, and Val smiled a little unwillingly. 'It's true, though, isn't it,' she went on. 'It happened here as well. Your father had to plough up all those beautiful lawns and grow what he was told to grow, and they're only just getting back to what they were.'

'Well, Dad wasn't actually here much then,' Hilary said. 'He was away for most of the war and we had that estate manager looking after things, and the house was requisitioned. But you know, Eddie could still have worked in the country – farms are going to need mechanics when everyone stops using horses and goes over to tractors. Your sister told me the other day that young Roy Pettifer thinks there'll be more work than ever.'

'Yes, I suppose so,' Val said without much interest.

'Anyway, Eddie got killed, didn't he, so that was the end of that.'

Hilary looked at her. 'You do think you and Eddie would have got married, don't you?'

Val gave her a quick glance, then looked down at her drink again. 'Yes, of course. Why?'

'I don't know, it's just that sometimes when you talk about him – well, it's as if there's something else on your mind. And when we were in Egypt . . .'

'Well?' Val demanded when Hilary hesitated. 'What about when we were in Egypt?' She met Hilary's eyes, and Hilary saw something in them that disturbed her. 'What about it?' Val repeated. 'What do you mean? What are you hinting at?'

'Nothing! I didn't mean anything. Really I didn't. It's just that – well, sometimes I wondered if you were really as much in love with Eddie after all. Look, it *happens*,' Hilary went on desperately, trying to take that anger out of Val's face. 'It happened a lot then. Girls got engaged and their fiancés went away, and they realised they didn't really love them after all. Everything was so *hurried* in those days. And sometimes they met someone else, and—'

'Well, it didn't happen to me,' Val said tersely. She put down her glass, still with some sloe gin in it. 'I think I'd better be going. I've got an early start in the morning.'

'Val, no!' Hilary put out her hand. 'Don't go like that, please. I didn't mean anything by it. I wouldn't have blamed you anyway. But there were times when you – well, you just weren't around so much and I couldn't help wondering . . .'

'I was working. I was a *nurse*. We had busy times.'

'I know,' Hilary said. 'I'm sorry, Val. I shouldn't have said anything. Don't go, please.'

Val hesitated for a moment, then drew in a deep breath and picked up her glass. 'I could do with a drop more of this,' she said, and Hilary heaved a sigh of relief and poured more of the dark, glistening drink.

'You'd better not have too much. You won't be able to walk home.'

'I know. And I don't want a hangover in the morning.' Her tight face softened and she gave Hilary a wicked grin. 'You're a fine one to talk, anyway. Remember that night we went to a ball in the Officers' Mess? *I* saw you, with that blond Subaltern! If I'd had a camera with me, I could have blackmailed you for years.'

They laughed together and went off, as they often did, into a stream of reminiscence about their days in Egypt. Val relaxed and Hilary made a mental note not to suggest again that her friend hadn't loved the man she'd been engaged to marry. It was odd, though – they'd often talked just as frankly, and Val had never taken offence before. Her reaction had been quite unexpected.

But for the rest of the evening Val seemed cheerful enough, and it wasn't until after she had gone and Hilary was filling her hot-water bottle that her thoughts returned to her friend's moment of anger.

I was a tactless fool, she thought. How would I have felt if someone had suggested that I didn't love Henry? It would have been like suggesting I was glad he'd died and that I didn't have to marry him.

She stood for a moment, staring at her reflection in the dark, uncurtained window, and felt the chill of guilt creep into her heart.

Chapter Eleven

'Attention, everybody!'

Dr Latimer rapped the small wooden gavel that had been presented to the village hall by Gilbert Napier's father, the 'old Squire', and the hubbub died down a little. He waited until everyone had fallen silent and then began, in the pleasant voice that had asked most of them, at one time or another, to put out their tongue or say 'aah' or tell him how they felt this morning.

'Right. Good evening, everyone, and let me take this opportunity of wishing you all a rather belated Happy New Year. Thank you all very much for turning out on such a cold evening. I'm very pleased to see so many of you and hope you have lots of ideas for celebrating the Festival of Britain here in Burracombe.'

The audience, numbering about twenty, gazed back at him with stolid expressions. You would never have thought they'd been chatting with animation only minutes ago. The doctor waited for a moment, then said, 'Perhaps I should run through the official plans for the Festival. As you know, it was the King's idea, to give the country a chance to show the world that we're picking ourselves up after the war and are ready to build a new world in the peace. So some of us thought it would be a good idea to get together and decide what we want to do about it.'

He paused again and once more there was silence. Then Ernie Crocker, who was churchwarden and the oldest of

Ted Tozer's farmworkers, cleared his throat and said, 'Ah, but that be all happening up in London. 'Tain't nothing to do with us down here in Dev'n.'

'And I might point out,' said Joyce Warren, 'that we *are* doing something. We're running a coach trip to London to visit the Exhibition.'

'Yes, but you're not going to the Battersea Fun Fair, are you?' Jackie Tozer chipped in. She was sitting at the back with Roy Pettifer, their little fingers clasped under the cover of folded arms. 'I don't see much fun in going to a dreary old Exhibition.'

'Dreary? It won't be dreary!' Mrs Warren turned indignantly and her large felt hat swayed dangerously. 'It will be highly educational. The Festival is going to be filled with interesting exhibits. The Dome of Discovery itself—'

'Well, I don't mind going to see that,' Jackie admitted, 'and that Skylon they're talking about, but I don't see why we can't go to the Fun Fair as well. They're going to have a treetop walk and a Rotor, and all sorts of rides and roundabouts.'

'Roundabouts!' Ernie snorted. 'That's all you youngsters thinks about. Bain't Tavistock Goosey Fair enough for you? Plenty of roundabouts there. Mrs Warren's right – it's education you'm going to need in this brave new world they keeps telling us about. Anyway,' he added, 'what's a Rotor when it's at home? I've never even heard of it.'

'Oh, it's a new thing, Mr Crocker,' Roy Pettifer said eagerly. 'It works by centrifugal force, you see. People go in and stand against a wall built in a circle, and it suddenly starts to whirl round and they all get kind of stuck against it. They go right up in the air and the girls' skirts—' He caught Mrs Warren's eye and faltered into silence. 'Anyway,' he mumbled after a moment, 'there's all sorts of things there and I think Jackie's right. If we're going in a coach we ought to go to the Fun Fair as well.'

'It doesn't sound to me', Joyce Warren said after a frosty pause, 'at all the kind of thing Burracombe should be encouraging its young people to attend.'

Hilary, sitting beside Felix Copley, felt his elbow dig into her side. Her lips quivered and she slid him a reproving glance. With Basil and Grace Harvey, Felix had been invited to dinner at the Barton just after the New Year, and she had felt an immediate liking for the friendly, good-looking young curate. He had come into the church when she was arranging flowers and they had spent a pleasant quarter of an hour leaning against the ancient stone font, chatting and discovering a shared sense of humour. Rather a wicked one for a clerical gentleman, she had reproved him, but he'd only grinned and twinkled his blue eyes at her and told her that clergymen needed a sense of humour. 'I'm sure God has one,' he said. 'Who was it said that He must have had, to make ducks?'

'I've no idea,' she'd said, laughing, 'but I suppose you must be right. Think of donkeys and kangaroos!'

'And elephants,' he said. 'They've got a sense of humour too. And three-toed sloths – not that they've got one, but they always make me laugh just to think of them. And—'

Hilary brought her mind sharply back to the discussion. They were still arguing over the Fun Fair.

'But if it's the *King's* idea . . . ' little Jean Friend, who ran the village Post Office and sweetshop, began timidly, and her sister Jessie nodded her white head and joined in so that their voices sounded like the twittering of birds. 'I'm sure the King wouldn't agree to anything that wasn't quite suitable.'

Joyce Warren opened her mouth and then closed it again while the rest of the audience watched in fascination. It wasn't very often that they saw their WI President and doyenne of the Bridge Club, the Drama Group and the new Garden Society at a loss for words and the fact that it was the timid little twin sisters from the Post Office who had brought this about was something to treasure. There were a few chuckles, quickly muffled by gloved hands.

Charles Latimer decided that it was time to regain control of the meeting. 'Be that as it may, and it could well be a matter for discussion at another time, the purpose of this meeting is not to discuss what will be happening in London, but what will be happening here in Burracombe. Do we want to take part in the celebrations that will be taking place all over the country and put on some kind of event – or events – of our own here in the village? The Festival of Britain in Britain itself, rather than simply in the capital city.'

The small burst of animation caused by Jackie's complaint died away and once again the audience gazed at him with inscrutable expressions. He glanced towards Joyce Warren but she was looking straight ahead with her chin raised. He sighed.

'I'm sure some of you will have ideas. Some kind of village party, perhaps? A fête? The WI is always so good at putting on that kind of thing. A sports day for the children? The school might help there. Might the Drama Group perform an entertainment of some kind?' He glanced again at Mrs Warren, and this time she made a reluctant response, lifting one shoulder slightly and deigning to meet his eye. 'I was wondering about your idea of a pageant,' he said encouragingly.

Joyce Warren looked a little nonplussed for a moment and then rallied. 'A pageant? Well yes, I did mention the idea some time ago.' It had been two years ago, in fact, and nobody had shown the slightest enthusiasm. 'I'm sure it would be quite appropriate. Britain Through the Ages – the development of our nation. Yes, it has possibilities.'

'Especially as relating to Devon,' the doctor said gently. 'I think that was your idea, wasn't it? The people of our county who have done so much to put Britain in the forefront of the world. People like Drake – a local boy, indeed – and Raleigh. I'm sure there are many others.'

'I don't believe it was her idea at all,' Felix whispered to Hilary. 'He's just handing it to her on a plate.'

'What does it matter, so long as she takes it on?' Hilary murmured back, and blushed as Mrs Warren turned her head to see who was talking. She lowered her eyes quickly and stared at her clasped hands.

Dr Latimer was speaking again. 'Well, that's excellent, Mrs Warren. I'm sure we can leave that in your capable hands.' He moved on swiftly, before Joyce could make a protest. 'Now, what other ideas can we come up with, I wonder?'

The silence was even deeper this time. It was clear that nobody else was going to take the risk of being manoeuvred into taking on some project without having plenty of time to think about it. The doctor waited a few moments until the silence became embarrassing, and then smiled. 'You're all busy thinking of ideas, I know. Well, let's have another meeting in – let's say a fortnight from now, shall we? And then we can really begin to make plans. A sequence of events throughout the summer, I thought, with the pageant as a grand finale.' He looked round the gathering. 'Try to bring a few more people along to the next meeting, if you can. The whole village is going to be involved, so it's only proper that as many as possible should be here right from the very start.'

He tapped the gavel again and leaned over to speak to Miss Kemp, the school headmistress, who was in the front row. The rest of the company looked at each other and began to scrape their chairs as they got up. A low hum of conversation started as they put their chairs back against the walls and left the hall.

Dr Latimer and Miss Kemp smiled at each other. 'Well,

that's started the ball rolling,' he said, pulling on a pair of thick gloves. 'They'll talk about nothing else for the next fortnight.'

'That's right,' she agreed. 'The real meetings take place in the pub or the village shop or at field gates. It's as if the four walls of the village hall stifle them.'

Felix, walking through the village with Hilary, asked, 'Why do they seem so sure? I didn't think anyone appeared at all interested in doing anything at all.'

'That's villagers for you,' she said. 'Won't say a word at any meeting that seems at all official, but the seed's been sown and as Miss Kemp said, the real meetings will be taking place at this very moment.' She glanced at the warmly lit windows of the Bell Inn. 'Probably in there.'

'A much more comfortable venue,' he grinned. 'I don't suppose you would like to go in with me and see?'

Hilary shook her head. 'Not tonight, I'm afraid. I've got some things to do at home. You'd better go on your own.'

'Another time, perhaps,' he suggested, and she looked at him and said, 'Yes. Perhaps.' They had stopped and she put out her hand for him to shake. 'Goodnight, Felix.'

'Goodnight, Hilary,' he said, and watched as she walked through the big open gateway and up the Barton drive.

Stella had been to the meeting as well. She walked back along the lane to Dottie's cottage and slipped through the door into the warmth of the living room. The lamp had been left burning low and she turned it up and sank into the old armchair in front of the glowing range.

Her first week at the school seemed to have gone quite well. There had been no new children starting after Christmas, so even the youngest knew where everything was and what should be done. They'd been primed by Miss Kemp to be helpful, and were eager to guide Stella through her first few days.

'This is where we hangs our coats. We'm not allowed to wear our boots in the classroom.' A row of diminutive Wellington boots stood on the cold stone floor of the lobby. 'The lavvies are outside.' A small girl with red curls led her out into the playground and into a lean-to building round the corner, where there were three cubicles, each with a wooden seat over the earth closet. 'It stinks,' the redhead informed her cheerfully, 'but we'm used to it and the nightsoil cart comes round every week. The boys have got theirs the other side of the door. You and Miss Kemp have got your own; we're not allowed in there even when we can't wait.'

Next she was shown the classroom. The 'babies' who had started in September at the age of five had low tables and small wooden chairs in one corner, while the bigger children had desks and benches. Stella had six 'babies' and a dozen older children, some of whom would go up into Miss Kemp's class next door when they were seven or eight. Altogether, there were thirty-eight children in the school, coming from outlying farms and hamlets as well as from Little Burracombe and Burracombe itself. When they were eleven they would take the 'scholarship' exam which would determine whether they went on to the grammar school in Tavistock or to the secondary modern.

'There's the blackboard,' her self-appointed guide informed her. 'You has to write our lessons on there, see, only the babies can't read. They play with beads and things. And you got to watch out for the boys. They'm proper little terrors.'

'You'm a fine one to talk, Janet Crocker,' declared a big, rough-looking boy with black hair and eyebrows, who looked at least nine. 'You gets into more trouble than anyone.'

The red-haired girl poked out her tongue at him and he put both thumbs to his temples and waggled his fingers, screwing up his nose as he did so. She gave a yell of fury and dashed at him, and Stella found herself having to stop a fight even before the morning had properly begun.

Still, after that they had settled down quite well and, determined not to give self-important little Janet Crocker the satisfaction of seeing them with beads, she'd been able to start the babies off with some paper to draw on while she set the bigger children a writing exercise. Then she went back to the babies with a reading book, and having looked over the various standards of writing started to form a kind of teaching plan that would cover all abilities.

As the days went on, she'd got to know all the children by name and was beginning to get to know their personalities. On the whole, they were pleasant, easy children but by Wednesday she had identified three potential troublemakers – Brian Madge, the big, black-haired boy, who looked nine but was in fact not yet eight, his arch-enemy Janet Crocker, who was bossy and never stopped talking, and a small boy who looked exactly like a cherub. Not that he'd actually caused any trouble yet, but Stella had learned to be suspicious of little boys who looked like cherubs.

She had enjoyed her first week, but she was glad it was Friday. Two whole days to recover and relax, and plan her lessons for next week! After school today, she and Miss Kemp had had a cup of tea together in the headmistress's tiny office and the older woman had told Stella that she'd started well. 'I love to hear the little ones singing, and you've taught them two new songs already. They like you.'

'Well, it's early days yet,' Stella said. 'They're nice children. And I'm learning the dialect quite well – I only had to ask Barry Stacey to repeat himself twice today.'

'You're settling in very well,' the headmistress said. 'You'll be part of the village in no time.'

Stella wasn't too sure about that; she knew how long it

took for strangers to become 'part of' a village. But the meeting this evening had made her feel a little more as if she belonged. She put some more wood on the fire and sat back in her chair.

The room was full of memorabilia from Dottie's life as a dresser in the theatre. Photographs and playbills lined the walls, many of them featuring 'her' actress, but there were other pictures too – sepia prints of ancient ladies in thick coats, with sticks, or family groups with everyone sitting up very straight and stiff, looking as if they were held in clamps. Stella remembered reading once that the early photographs took so long to expose that the sitters really were clamped, to stop them moving and blurring the picture. She got up to take a closer look at some of them, wondering who the people were. Members of Dottie's family, she supposed – grandparents, cousins and so on.

Nearly all the photographs had been taken before the war. There hadn't been much film to be had during the war, and the family photos seemed to stop in the late 1930s. There were a few of Dottie herself, with 'her actress', and then no more. Stella sat down again, feeling a little sad.

She had no photographs of her own family. Everything like that had been lost when they were bombed out. Babies had been born, grown up a little and then died, without any pictorial record being made of them. Her own mother, father and sister, and her baby brother – all no more than memories. There would never be any pictures of them to hang on a cottage wall, fading as the years went by but still there for someone to gaze at and wonder about.

The one picture that had been saved was the wedding photo of her parents, which her mother had always taken to the air-raid shelter with her when there was a raid on. But after that awful night when that second, fatal bomb had fallen, it had disappeared and Stella had never seen it again. She felt suddenly lonely, the grief sweeping through her once more as it had done so often over the years, and she wished she had it now, to look at and hold and weep over. It seemed so cruel that she should lose so much and not even have that one small thing.

She got up, put the guard over the fire, and went to bed so that Dottie should not come in from the pub and find her crying.

The bellringers were at their usual table in the pub, slaking their thirst with a pint of ale each. As it was their practice night, they hadn't been at the meeting but had sent Ted Tozer's cousin, Norman, as their representative. Dottie Friend was there too, leaning her sturdy arms on the bar as she chatted with the regulars.

'Well into the new year now, aren't we? And just think, ten years ago those awful Blitzes were just starting. My stars, when you look back and remember all that's happened in that time!' Her face sobered. ''Tis a good job us didn't know what was to come. And a good job us can't know the future now, either.'

'Now then, Dottie, don't be so gloomy,' Bernie Nethercott chided her. 'That's not like you. Little ray of sunshine you are, as a rule, so no more of that long face. You'll turn the beer sour.'

'Oh, I'm not being gloomy – I'm just saying, that's all.' Dottie straightened up and began to draw Ted Tozer's pint. 'Live for the day, that's my motto, and be thankful for what you've got. That'll be a tanner, Ted, if you please.'

'No, I'm paying the full round tonight,' Ted said. The bellringers normally operated by their own agreed rule, each to pay for his own drinks. 'Being the first practice night of the new year and all. And to thank the team for being such a good 'un.' He turned, his pewter tankard in his hand, and lifted it high. 'Here's to all of you – to all the good ringing you've done this past year, and to more of the same in nineteen-fifty-one. Let's see a few more cups and trophies in the tower, shall us? Especially the Bill Barnaby Shield – let's make this the year we get it back from Little Burracombe.'

The others responded with cheers and nods. They were a keen competition band, going round to all the other towers in the area whenever there was a ringing contest and, as often as not, coming home with a cup, shield or First Certificate to pin proudly on the wall of the ringing chamber. But the William Barnaby Shield had eluded them for the past two years now – an especially bitter pill to swallow when the ringer in whose memory it had been presented had been a past captain of Burracombe itself.

The two villages, Burracombe and Little Burracombe, standing on opposite sides of the river, had been locked in conflict for longer than anyone could remember. The rivalry was often friendly – on the surface, at least – but sometimes went deep, and there had been times when real feuds had broken out. The ringers of both villages were always ready to help each other out, should a band be needed to ring for a wedding or some other event, but when it came to the competition they were deadly enemies. And the fact that Little Burracombe held a shield that Burracombe considered belonged rightly in Bill Barnaby's home tower, was a real bone of contention.

'They only won it by half a fault last time,' Norman Tozer remarked, sucking his beer noisily through his bristly grey moustache. 'Us'll get it back come May, see if us don't.'

The other ringers nodded their agreement. Nathan Pettifer, Ernie Crocker and George Sweet had all been in the team for years, getting back to the tower the minute they were allowed to after the war, for most of which the bells had remained silent. There were a few younger ones coming along now, too – Tom Tozer, Nathan's son Roy,

Vic Nethercott who was away doing his National Service at the moment, and a couple of boys from one of the outlying moorland farms on the edge of the parish – but none of them were yet considered good enough to take part in a competition. The older men were jealous of their position and not likely to give over a rope in favour of some youngster who had only been ringing for two or three years.

'Tell you what I've been thinking,' Norman Tozer said suddenly. 'This Festival the doctor was talking about at this meeting I just been to – we ought to be doing summat for that. A special peal, mebbe even a competition. Put on a bit of bowling on the village green, that sort o' thing. What d'you reckon?'

'I'm not sure about a competition,' Ted Tozer said at last, speaking in his habitual slow, thoughtful way. 'Didn't you say Mrs Warren's getting up a pageant? Us ought to ring for that, get the whole thing off to a good start. But a competition . . . that'd have to be on a different day. Us couldn't have it on Pageant Day, 'twouldn't do at all.'

'Well, there's plenty more days in the year,' his son Tom said, speaking up from the end of the long wooden table. 'And from what Norman's been telling us, seems the pageant's going to be on August Bank Holiday. Us could put on our competition on the Saturday. And I tell you what – why not have a novice competition as well, for ringers that haven't ever rung in one? That'd give some of the younger chaps a chance.'

Some of the older men looked down their noses at this suggestion, but Jimmy Sweet, who lived with his grand-father George, nodded enthusiastically. 'I reckon that's a good idea. Me and Roy've been ringing a few years now, it's time we had a crack at a competition but you chaps won't ever let us.'

'Well, and don't it make sense?' Ernie Crocker demanded.

As a farmworker, Ted Tozer was his boss and Tom very nearly so, but in the ringing chamber he was any man's equal. 'If us wants to win the competitions, us has to put our best chaps in, stands to reason. And me and your dad and Bob and Nathan and Norman here have all been ringers twenty years or more. You never even touched a rope till three years ago.'

'And whose fault was that?' Tom demanded quickly. 'Hitler's, weren't it? Had to go off to war, didn't we? But we're pretty good now and I reckon that with young Roy Nethercott and Vic, if he was back from the Army, we could make a decent fist of it. Have to have one of you older chaps in as well,' he added, 'unless we could teach someone else in the time.'

'And that us'll never do!' Norman Tozer slammed his tankard down and glared at him. 'There's nobody on this earth could learn to handle a bell well enough to ring in a competition by summer. Make us all a laughing stock, that would.'

'Well, all right, so we'd still need one of you,' Tom shrugged. 'But that could be in the rules – maybe up to two experienced ringers, to keep things steady like.' He turned to his father. 'What d'you think, Dad?'

Ted sucked in a deep breath and folded his lips together, thinking. Then he glanced at his cousin Norman, whose dark face was still glowering, and made up his mind. 'I reckon we could think about it,' he said at last. 'We'll have a talk next practice, when us have had time to turn it over in our minds. There's a lot to think about, see – who to have for judges, how many certificates we gives out, whether to go in for a trophy as well . . . it needs a lot of deciding. But it don't seem too bad an idea to me. Not too bad at all.' He slid another glance at Norman. 'Anyway, we'd better drink up now and be on our way. It's getting on for ten and Bernie's wanting to shut up shop. He called out for last orders five minutes ago.' He lifted his tankard again. 'And before we all goes our separate ways, I want to make another toast. A Happy New Year to all of us, and plenty of good ringing. Here's to the Fifties. Hope for the future.'

'That's right,' they agreed, and lifted their own tankards in response. 'The Fifties. Hope for the future.'

They stood up and took their tankards back to the bar, where Rose and Dottie would wash them and hang them on their hooks, to be kept for their owners' next visit. Then they made their way out into the frosty night and stood for a moment breathing the icy air and looking up at the stars.

'I tell you what,' Tom said to his father as they began to walk along the lane. 'I reckon things are going to start looking up a bit now. We've got over the war, almost, and this big Festival will show the world what Britain can do. Things are bound to be different now, Dad. There's going to be a lot of changes in the next few years.'

'Changes?' Ted said, stopping to light his pipe. 'Well, mebbe there will be up in London and places like that. But not down here in Burracombe. Nothing ever changes much in Burracombe.'

Chapter Twelve

'I've asked that young artist feller to tea,' Dottie announced one morning. 'Luke, his name is, Luke Ferris. I dare say you've seen him about the village.'

'Oh yes, I've met him,' Stella said, 'when I came for my interview. But I haven't seen him since then.'

'He've been away over Christmas and New Year – off to London, so I heard. He'll have friends there, being an artist. Anyway, he came into the pub a night or two ago and I thought he looked a bit lonely, so I asked him to come in this afternoon. You'll be here, won't you? I'll make some of my scones and there's still a piece of Christmas cake left in the tin.'

Stella looked forward to meeting Luke again. His welcome as she climbed off the bus on that October morning had given her a warm glow that had, she felt sure, carried her through the ordeal of the interview. Not that everyone else hadn't been welcoming too, but that first moment had been vital. And later, as she'd chatted to him at the top of the wood, she'd felt a sense of instant friendship – as if they'd known each other for years. She'd been vaguely disappointed not to run into him in the village during her first week or so back.

The infant class ended the afternoon at three-fifteen. Stella helped her small charges pull on their Wellingtons and wrap themselves in coats, scarves and gloves, and saw them through the door to their waiting mothers. She busied herself for a while straightening desks and tables and putting chairs neatly on top ready for Mrs Purdy to clean the floor, and wiped up some spilled water from the nature table, where someone had brought in a few early snowdrops and put them in a jar. The previous teacher hadn't been very interested in nature and there wasn't much to be put on the table in January, but Stella was determined that when spring came she would encourage the children to bring in any treasures they might discover. Miss Kemp had told her she could take her class out on walks too, on fine days, and she was looking forward to rambles along the lanes and through the fields and woods.

She heard the older children clattering their chairs and slamming down their desklids, oblivious of Miss Kemp's habitual instruction to do this quietly, and then they streamed along the corridor past her door. A few minutes later the whoops and cries of healthy young humans released into freedom after a whole hour and a half of incarceration sounded outside and then died away along the lane, and the headmistress's face, framed by its grey curls, appeared.

'Another day over. Really, to hear them you'd imagine they'd been tied up and chained to the walls for months! Not that I don't feel like that myself at times, especially on days like today.' She looked at the tall windows which were streaming with icy rain. 'I don't believe it's got light at all. Those clouds are sitting right on the rooftops.' She came into the classroom and settled down for a chat. 'How have you been? The little ones have been remarkably good, considering that they haven't been able to go out to play.'

'Oh, we've been doing all sorts of things. I read to the dinner children,' this was the way they referred to those who stayed at school for their midday meal, 'and when the others came back we did songs with actions, to give them some exercise. And then I let them do some painting, only it made a bit of a mess.' She glanced ruefully at the sheets of soaking paper she was gathering up as she spoke. 'They haven't quite got the idea of using just a *little* water.'

'So long as they were happy.' The headmistress gave her an approving nod. 'You've started well, Stella. The children have settled down and I can tell they like you. I think my class are quite jealous that they didn't have you when they were in the infants'!'

Stella blushed. 'I really do want to be a good teacher. I like children. I suppose it comes from being an older sister.'

'Are you?' Miss Kemp asked in surprise. 'I thought – the Home seemed to imply in their letter about you – that you were an only child.'

'I was, when I was there. But I used to have a sister, and a brother too, a baby brother. I lost them both in the war.'

'My dear, I'm so sorry! I didn't mean to pry.' The headmistress looked distressed. 'There are so many sad stories from that time. I still have a child in my top class who lost his father, and of course there are several whose uncles died. I didn't intend to bring back sad memories.'

'It's all right,' Stella began, but before she could say more, a clattering of galvanised buckets and brooms announced the arrival of Mrs Purdy in the lobby, and they heard an exasperated mutter.

'Just look at all this mud! I knew it'd be like this, with all this blessed rain, I knew it. A never-ending job this be, a never-ending job.' The cleaner, a thin, scrawny little woman with mousy hair scraped back from her pinched face and eyes like a sparrow's, appeared in the doorway, surveying the two teachers indignantly. 'I scrubbed that lobby clean yesterday and to see it now you wouldn't think it had been touched for a month. I don't like to question the Good Lord in all His ways, but 'tis almost as if He does it deliberate. Well, I suppose I'd better just clean it all over again.' She turned and stumped back into the lobby, muttering beneath her breath.

Miss Kemp looked at Stella and raised her eyebrows humorously. 'And we'd better make ourselves scarce, before we find ourselves being scrubbed clean as well! I'll see you in the morning, Stella.'

Stella smiled at her and pulled on her coat. She hurried through the village, hoping that nobody would stop her along the way, but the wet, darkening street was quiet. Lights were on in most of the windows and through some she could see children already sitting down to tea in a cameo of warm family life. A memory came back to her of her own childhood, before the first bomb had fallen – herself, her parents and sister in their pleasant home in Portsmouth and then, later, in the little terraced house where Thomas had been born.

She shook the memories away and opened the gate to Dottie's front garden. Through the small, square window she could see Dottie, setting out a plate of scones on to her round table and, already at the table, the figure of Luke Ferris with his lean dark face alight with laughter.

Stella pushed open the door and walked in.

'And then I had to come home,' Dottie said. She had been recounting stories of her time backstage in the London theatre with 'her actress' and the tea-table was strewn with photographs and playbills. 'Nearly broke my heart, that did, but family comes first and my dad needed me. She understood that, but I knew she didn't really want me to leave her, no more'n I wanted to go. We'd had such lovely times together. And she came back to Burracombe whenever she could, stayed at the Barton till the war started and it was taken over. She and Mrs Napier, the Colonel's wife, they were great friends, known each other since they were at school. She was a lady, you see, my actress was, a real lady, welcome in the best houses in the land. And then there was Maddy, of course. She came as often as she could to see Maddy.'

'Maddy?' Stella queried. 'Who was Maddy – a dog? I suppose it wouldn't be easy to keep a dog if you were in the theatre in London—'

'My stars, no!' Dottie rocked with laughter. 'Maddy weren't no dog! She was a little girl – my actress's little girl. Well, not hers exactly, but a pretty little thing that she took a fancy to and adopted. She brought her to me to look after. It wasn't safe in London, and she knew I'd love her like my own. And so I did.' Dottie took out a handkerchief and put it to one eye. 'The little girl I never had, she was. I knew I'd have to give her back in the end, of course. My actress would have liked me to go back to London with her and look after them both there, but I couldn't do that. I was settled here again by then, you see. I'd enjoyed being in London when I was younger, but after the war – well, I knew Burracombe was my place. I didn't want no more of the big city, especially not after all the bombing and such.'

'So Maddy lived here with you all through the war?'

'That's right, my pretty.' Dottie got up from the table. 'Now, I've chattered on long enough. Let's have some more tea, shall we? And look, there's more scones ready to go in the oven – take only a few minutes to bake, they will, and there's plenty more jam and cream to go with them.' She moved the kettle to the hotter part of the range and it began to sizzle at once. 'Don't tell me you'm not hungry – young folk are always hungry.'

'Well, I'm not going to deny that!' Luke said with a grin. 'Especially when it's your scones on offer. You're a marvellous cook, Dottie.'

'Go on with you, anyone can make a few scones.' But she looked pleased all the same, and Stella smiled at the young artist. He was looking better than the first time she'd seen him, she thought, his narrow face filled out a little and he wasn't quite so pale. He didn't seem to have had a haircut since they'd last met, but she supposed that was part of being an artist. They all seemed to want to appear unconventional in some way, as if ordinary clothes and hairstyles didn't go with artistic talent. Perhaps it was true.

Dottie went out to the scullery and Luke said, 'I've been looking forward to meeting you again. How have you been settling in? Do you like Burracombe?'

'Yes, I do. It feels like home already – even in the rain!' They could hear the wind in the trees outside, and the rain lashing at the windows. Darkness had fallen and Dottie had drawn the dark red curtains, enclosing them in a warm cocoon. Logs glowed in the range and Alfred was slumbering like a large mound of tabby fur in one of the armchairs. 'I'm so lucky to have a place like this to live, and the school's just the right size.'

'And what about the children? Are they little demons?'

'Some of them,' she acknowledged with a smile. 'But most of them are dears. And Miss Kemp's not at all like a headmistress – not the ones I remember, anyway. She seems to understand the children. She doesn't let them get away with anything, but she's very kind.'

'Sounds as if you've known some tartars!'

'One or two,' she agreed. 'The teachers at my school were very strict. And how about you? Are you comfortable in your cottage up in the woods?'

'Pretty well – as long as a tree doesn't fall on me!' He tilted his head towards the window as a particularly strong gust of wind rattled the pane. 'I've had a good look at all those near me, though, and they look pretty sturdy. I get plenty of fresh air, anyway, and that's important for me – I've had TB, you know.' Stella nodded, remembering that the vicar had told her this. 'And Uncle Basil and Aunt Grace make sure I get a good meal at least once a week.' He watched as Dottie opened the oven door and took out a tray of scones, risen to twice their size and golden-brown on top. 'And I sometimes get invited to the most delicious teas!'

'Go on with you, you'm nothing but a flatterer,' Dottie scolded, but she was flushed and smiling. 'Charm the birds out of the trees, you would.' She slid the scones on to a flowery china plate with fluted gold edging and put them on the table. 'Now, you help yourselves to cream and jam, and don't give none to Alfred, he's getting too fat as it is.'

'Never mind if *we* get fat, then!' Luke said, taking one of the scones and dropping it quickly on his plate. 'Ow! They're hot!'

'Come from a hot place, didn't 'em,' Dottie retorted. She seemed to enjoy bantering with the young artist. 'And you won't get fat, young things like you. Always on the go, the pair of you – you up there in the woods and Stella here with all those little tackers in the school keeping her on her toes. You need good food inside you.'

There were just three scones left when Luke finally announced that he thought it was time for him to go. He eyed them regretfully and Dottie found a bit of greasproof paper to wrap them in and put them into his hand as he stood at the door. He gave her his warm smile and then looked across at Stella.

'It's been good to meet you again. Why don't you come for a walk on Saturday? I'll show you some interesting bits of the moor.'

'Oh yes, I'd like that. Shall I bring some sandwiches?'

'I'll make some pasties for you both,' Dottie offered. 'And there's an old Thermos flask in the cupboard, so you can take some tea as well. You'll need a hot drink if you'm going on the moor.'

'I won't argue with that,' Luke said. 'If your pasties are

as good as your scones, they'll be worth walking for. Thanks, Dottie. But what about your meat ration?'

'Well, it'll only be a bit of mince and some potato and swede. But if you'm bothered about it, you can get a joint at Bertie Foster's one day and bring it round for me to cook for Sunday dinner for us all. Then us'll be square, see. Brisket makes a lovely pot roast.'

She saw Luke off into the darkness and came back to gather up her photographs. She replaced the framed ones on their hooks and put the albums back in the cupboard by the fireplace. Then she stood for a moment stroking the slumbering cat and looking into the glowing embers.

Stella was already clearing away the tea-things and didn't notice the satisfied smile on her face.

Val Tozer was walking down the farm lane when she heard the footsteps approaching. It had stopped raining but was too dark for her to make out who the other person was until they were face to face, and then she stopped abruptly.

'Val!' Luke exclaimed. 'What are you doing out here?'

'I suppose I'm allowed to walk along my own village street,' she retorted. 'What are *you* doing?'

'I've just been to tea with Dottie Friend.' He hesitated. 'Look, Val, I haven't been around because I spent Christmas in London . . .'

'Did you? I can't say I noticed.' She began to walk on. He fell into step beside her. 'Where are you going?'

'I'm going to work, not that it's anything to do with you.'

'To work? At this time of day? It's nearly six o'clock.'

'I'm on the night-shift at Tavistock Hospital. I'm a nurse, in case you've forgotten.'

'I haven't forgotten,' he said quietly. 'I haven't forgotten anything. Val, I want to talk to you—'

'And I've told you that *I* don't want to talk to *you*.'

'Maybe not,' he said, his tone hardening a little, 'but you

135

can't ignore the fact that I'm here. Look, can't we just talk to each other in a friendly manner? Why are you so angry with me? It's all a long time ago now, and I never understood what went wrong anyway.'

'I was *engaged*, Luke!'

'I know,' he said steadily. 'But that didn't seem to stop you falling in love with me.'

Val drew in a deep breath and quickened her pace. 'Go away, Luke.' Her voice was trembling with anger. 'Go away. Leave me alone. I've nothing to say to you. *Nothing.*'

He started to speak again, then stopped. They walked along side by side for a few moments. She said, 'It's no use, Luke. You might as well go back to your cottage.'

'But how are you getting to Tavistock? There's no bus now.'

'I'm walking to the main road. I can catch the bus there.'

'Couldn't someone have taken you? It's pitch dark and freezing cold. Your father's got a car, hasn't he?'

'Yes, and he's also got fifteen cows to milk. It's only a mile or so, for goodness sake. I've walked it more times than I've had hot dinners.'

'Well, I'll walk it with you if you don't mind.'

'I do mind!'

'I was brought up too much of a gentleman to let a lady walk along dark lanes on her own. You don't have to talk to me if you don't want to.' He waited but she said nothing and he sighed and said, 'I won't talk to you either. I'll just walk beside you. You can even pretend I'm not here, if you'd rather.'

'I shall,' she said shortly, and they marched along the lane together in silence.

Overhead, the clouds had rolled away, leaving a sky sprinkled with stars. The wind had dropped but the air was colder now and Val thrust her gloved hands deep into the pockets of her coat. Her heart was thumping uncomfortably and she was very aware of the man at her side. Pretend he wasn't there? It was no more possible than flying. She felt misery flood over her and tears sting her eyes.

They were almost at the main road. A few cars pricked the darkness with their headlights. The bus was due in a few minutes and she could escape him, but even a few minutes seemed too long.

'Please, Luke,' she said, her voice shaking, 'please leave me alone.'

He turned in the darkness and searched the pale oval of her face. The anguish of her tone hadn't escaped him and he felt a pang of sorrow. It was an anguish he knew so well, for it had kept him awake for many nights in those early months; and the unexpected sight of her in the village, on that October day when he had first met Stella Simmons, had brought it knifing back into his heart.

'Val,' he said gently, 'don't push me away. Please. I know you were hurt – we both were – but it's so long ago, and I've never forgotten you.' He laid his hand on her arm and she leaped away as if she had been bitten. 'Val, *please*!'

'I told you, Luke – leave me alone!' The lights of the big double-decker bus came into sight round the corner and she stepped out into the road, waving. 'I don't want to talk to you, I don't want to *see* you! Just keep out of my way!'

The bus drew up beside them and she jumped on to the platform. Without looking back, she ran up the stairs to the top deck and the bus rumbled away. Luke could just see the back of her head as she sat down.

He stood at the side of the road, watching as the lights disappeared into the distance. Then he turned and walked slowly back along the lane to Burracombe.

Chapter Thirteen

Joyce Warren lost no time in getting together a committee to arrange the Festival celebrations in Burracombe. She co-opted the vicar, Dr Latimer, Miss Kemp, Hilary and Ted Tozer. All protested that they were too busy, but their protests were ignored and on Thursday evening they found themselves gathered together in the vicarage drawing room and furnished with new notebooks and pencils.

'I've asked Felix to be present as well,' Basil Harvey said, indicating the curate. 'He ought to be involved in as many village affairs as possible, and it will be useful if I can't manage to attend all the meetings.'

Joyce looked slightly aggrieved, but nodded and said, 'I hope you've all brought your reading-glasses. It's so annoying when people come to meetings without them and can't make notes.' All except Hilary and Felix produced their spectacle cases. 'Now, we're here to discuss the Festival of Britain. As you know, I'm organising a coach trip to see the Exhibition itself – in fact, I'm organising several. The WI will be going, of course, and I dare say the church will want a trip as well; some of the same people would like to be with both groups, so I suggest we join together on the same date and I make the arrangements for both. And what about the school, Miss Kemp? Would you like me to—'

'That won't be necessary, thank you, Mrs Warren,' the headmistress said with a smile. 'Miss Simmons and I have already discussed this and we'd like to organise our own outing. We shall, of course, need a few mothers to come along as helpers, and we wouldn't want to impinge on your arrangements. And some people may like the chance to go more than once.'

Joyce Warren moved her shoulders slightly in acknowledgement. 'I'm sure you'll have a very successful day. Now, as to the—'

The doorbell rang and the vicar got up. 'That'll be Miss Bellamy. I'll let her in.'

'Miss Bellamy?' Joyce asked. 'I don't think she was on my list.'

'No, but she was on mine.' Basil opened the door and the little woman came through, unbuttoning her ancient tweed coat and puffing with cold. Her bright little eyes surveyed the gathering and she plumped down on a chair beside Felix Copley. Joyce stared at her with hostility.

'I'm sorry, I didn't think you'd wish to be involved.'

'Of course I "wish to be involved",' Constance said, slightly emphasising the repetition of Joyce's words. 'Get involved in everything in this village. Always have – see no reason to stop now. Don't often have a big Festival. Got to make our mark.'

The vicar sat down again. Joyce opened her mouth, but before she could speak Ted Tozer said, 'Before us gets under way, I'd like to make a proposal.' They all turned and looked at him. 'I'd like to propose that we asks the vicar to be chairman of this here committee. We'm meeting in his house and it seems only right and proper he should be in charge.'

There was a murmur of agreement from all except for Joyce, who said, 'But the vicar has already said he might not be able to attend all the meetings. How can he be chairman?'

'We could have a vice-chairman for when he can't come,' Hilary suggested. 'I propose Dr Latimer.'

'That's an excellent idea,' Constance said, but Joyce hadn't finished.

'The doctor is just as likely to be forced to miss meetings as the vicar. Suppose there's an emergency in the village? He might get called away at any time.'

'That's a good point,' Ted agreed. He turned to Dr Latimer. 'How many emergencies did you have last year, Doctor?'

'Let's think.' Charles Latimer stroked his chin solemnly. 'There was the new baby over at Walker's Farm – and that time when Ernie Crocker fell off a haystack and broke his collar-bone – no, that was the year before. Oh yes, and Bertie Foster cut his thumb quite badly when he was jointing a bullock, but I don't think that was really an emergency, I just happened to be passing at the time and—'

Ted turned back to Joyce. 'There you are. I don't reckon there'll be many times when neither the vicar nor the doctor could be here. So do I have a seconder for vicar being chairman?'

'I really don't think we can ask the vicar to shoulder any more burdens,' Joyce began, but Constance Bellamy had already raised her hand.

'And I'll second Charles as well,' she said in her gruff voice, and Joyce, seeing the hands raised all around her, fell into a dissatisfied silence.

'I think we can declare the meeting open, then,' the vicar said. 'Now, as we all know, the Festival of Britain—'

'Excuse me,' Joyce said loudly. 'Don't you think we need a secretary? There'll have to be notes taken – minutes of the meetings – and I imagine there'll be a certain amount of correspondence. In fact, we probably ought to appoint a treasurer as well. If we're going to have formal meetings, with a *chairman* and *vice-chairman*,' she lifted her chin and gave them all a challenging stare, 'then we must do the thing properly, and have all the usual officers.'

'I'm not sure that having a chairman necessarily means—'

'Oh, let her do it!' Ted Tozer, having got his way, lifted one hand and flapped it a little, as if brushing off a fly. 'Let's have Mrs Warren for secretary if that's what her wants. Might keep her quiet if she'm busy writing it all down,' he added, not quite sufficiently under his breath for Joyce not to hear him.

The potential secretary glared at him. 'Is that a formal proposal, Mr Tozer?' she enquired in a voice of ice.

'If you wants it to be,' he answered imperturbably.

'Are you willing to take on the post?' the vicar asked her. 'I'm sure we'd all be very grateful.' His voice faded to a murmur of '. . . clear handwriting . . . letters to write . . . nobody better . . .' and Joyce, her lips pursed sulkily, hesitated, then shrugged her shoulders in acquiescence.

'Since you've asked me yourself, Vicar, yes. I'll be glad to.' The others could almost see her thinking about headed notepaper. 'And the post of treasurer?'

'Don't see why we need one,' Constance Bellamy said. 'Not going to be fiddling about with money. This is just to think up a few ideas, isn't it?'

'Oh no!' Joyce was alight again at once. 'No, certainly not. This committee will be co-ordinating the entire village effort towards our part in the Festival. We shall be in a position to evaluate any ideas for events and make sure that the dates don't clash. I'm sure every active group in the area will be wanting to do something, and without efficient co-ordination it could so easily descend into chaos – absolute chaos. And that being so, it makes sense for us to handle the financial side as well.'

'But surely the different groups will handle their own finances,' Hilary said. 'I mean, if the Whist Club want to hold a special drive, it won't be anything to do with anyone else, will it? Why should they need to ask a special committee?'

'In case the dates clash,' Mrs Warren said with exaggerated patience. 'They'll want the village hall, won't they? Suppose someone else wants it the same day?'

'Well, they'll just ask Mrs Purdy,' Hilary said. 'She's caretaker, isn't she? Doesn't she have a list of dates? Don't people always ask her? Anyway, I don't see what that has to do with money. They'll just pay her in the normal way, and people will pay to go to the drive. And they'll organise their own prizes, just as they do when they have a Fur and Feather. So I really don't see why—'

'Oh, for goodness sake!' Joyce cried. 'I never said a word about the wretched Whist Club! I'm sorry, Basil,' she said, subsiding a little, her face pink, 'but really, if you can't keep some sort of order we're never going to get anywhere. Now, are we going to have a treasurer or not?'

'Let's have the question coming from the Chair, shall we?' Basil said mildly. He looked around at the committee members. 'What do you think? Are we going to need a treasurer?'

Nobody spoke for a moment, then Ted Tozer cleared his throat. 'It seems to me, Vicar, there be two ways of looking at this. Either we don't need one, so there's hardly any work to do and it might as well be lumped in with the secretary's job, or else we do need one, and it'd be better to sort that out now than wait and find out. And it often *is* lumped in with the secretary's job anyway, so why not do that now?' He paused and they gazed at him, waiting for more. 'I propose the two jobs go together and Mrs Warren does 'em both – and now can we please get on with whatever it is we'm here for?'

'We'll have to have a seconder,' Joyce began, and Charles Latimer cut in quickly, 'I'll second that!'

'All in favour?' Basil asked, and they all nodded. 'Carried

unanimously.' Everyone drew in a deep breath of relief. 'Now, shall we get on with the business of the day – er, evening.'

'Yes, let's do that,' Ted said, glancing at his wristwatch. 'Pub shuts at ten.'

Hilary caught Felix's eye and they glanced hastily away again. The vicar's mouth twitched and he looked at the sheet of paper in front of him.

'First, we must thank Mrs Warren for preparing this agenda for us. I can see you're going to make a very efficient secretary, Mrs Warren. Item One – oh, there's *only* an Item One – is "Events".'

'That's right,' Joyce began eagerly. 'As I said just now, it's most important that whatever events are to be held should be properly co-ordinated. We need to contact the organisers of all the different groups in the village and find out what they plan to do.'

'I don't think many of 'em have made any plans at all,' Ted Tozer said. 'Only the ringers, anyway. That's the only one I've heard anything about.'

'The ringers?' She stared at him. 'You mean the bellringers?'

'Well, I don't mean the clothes-wringers,' he said. 'Of course I mean the bellringers. Talking about it the other night, us was. Thought we might get up a competition.'

'A competition?'

'Yes. Like the one we has every year for the Barnaby Shield. And all the others round about as well. There's the Lydford Trophy and the Walkhampton Cup and the Devon Eight – us can't go in for that, of course, since us only got six bells here in Burracombe – but there's plenty of others.' He looked at her with a touch of impatience. 'You must know about the ringing competitions.'

'If that's when the village is full of men from all over the county and the bells never stop ringing all day and the

143

locals can't get into the pub, yes, I do,' she said disdainfully. 'I'm surprised the vicar allows it.'

'It's tradition, that's why! Good old Devon tradition. Used to ring for money and prizes, but that was stopped since it didn't seem fitting in a church, and now us just rings for the trophy or a certificate. And that's what us thought us'd do for this Festival. Set up a special competition, and have a bit of bowling for a pig while it's going on, that sort of thing. Maybe a race over the moor. And we thought we'd have one for novices as well – youngsters that have only been ringing two or three years and haven't had a chance at a proper competition. That'd bring some more in.'

Joyce looked unconvinced. She glanced round the little circle. Hilary, the doctor and Miss Kemp were looking interested, Felix enthusiastic, Constance engrossed in a worn patch in her baggy skirt. She looked at the vicar for support.

'I think that's an excellent suggestion,' he said promptly. 'And what a good example the ringers have set by coming up with such a splendid idea so early. I think we must give them the prize for being quick off the mark. Now, do we have any other suggestions?'

'Well, if you'd given me a chance to speak,' Joyce said huffily, 'I could have told you that the Drama Club is planning a pageant. In fact, it was mentioned at the meeting the other evening, so I hardly think the ringers can be said to be first off the mark. I'm sure their little competition will be very successsful, and I'll certainly put it on my list.' She wrote in her notebook. 'The pageant, however, will involve the whole village. The children will play a large part, of course,' she turned to Miss Kemp, 'and I'll need to discuss that with you – but there will also be parts for plenty of other people. It will portray the history of Burracombe from the earliest times to the present day and I shall be writing it myself. I see it as being the highlight of the celebrations.'

She gazed round triumphantly and the others looked faintly stunned. Basil said hastily, 'That sounds wonderful, Mrs Warren. You've discussed this with other groups, I expect?'

'Well – not as yet, no. I thought it more appropriate to apprise you of my intentions first.' Joyce looked slightly deflated.

Hilary bit her lip. She could feel Felix beside her, shaking slightly. 'I think it's a very good idea,' she said quickly. 'A real highlight, as Mrs Warren says. And it would be a good idea to have both these events quite close together – over a Bank Holiday weekend, for instance. The ringing competition on the Saturday and the pageant on the Monday, and something else in the church on Sunday. A flower display, perhaps.'

'August Bank Holiday,' Constance Bellamy interposed. 'Beginning of August. There'll still be plenty of blooms about. The Flower Club could look after that.'

'Certainly,' Charles Latimer said. He and his wife Marian were both keen gardeners. 'And if we put word round early enough, people will have time to make sure they plant appropriate flowers.'

Basil Harvey beamed. 'Excellent! We're getting on very well. A weekend of celebrations – our own Festival, in fact. And various coach parties, too – I think we could each look after our own, couldn't we? Or would it be more pleasant if all the various groups arranged to go on the same day? Quite a lot of people belong to more than one, and they won't all want to go more than once. Who would like to organise that?'

'Well, I was quite happy to do so, but if I'm to act as both secretary *and* treasurer, as well as writing and directing the pageant . . .' Joyce Warren said, as if she were bearing the entire world on her shoulders. She let her sentence trail away and put on a martyred expression.

'I'll do that,' Hilary said. 'I'll see which dates people would prefer and suggest we get together to fill the coaches. But if some want to do it on their own, I think they must be allowed to.'

'I agree. I'll certainly want to run the school trip separately,' Miss Kemp said firmly. 'As I said before, I'll need a few helpers and they'll be too busy with the children to look at the Exhibition on their own account. And we'll have to have some time at the Fun Fair as well.'

'Oh, do you really think—' Joyce began, but the headmistress squashed her protest before it was out of her mouth.

'The children will enjoy both the main Exhibition *and* the Fun Fair. There are going to be all kinds of interesting displays there as well as the usual rides. It will be something for them to remember all their lives.'

'That's settled then,' Basil said with a touch of relief. He looked at his agenda again. 'Well, that seems to be as far as we can go this evening. A most productive meeting. Thank you all for coming.'

'And the date for the next meeting?' Joyce prompted him.

'Let me see – it's still only January. I don't think we need be in too much of a hurry, do you? Unless there's anything urgent to discuss or some new ideas are put forward ... but to my mind, a pageant, a ringing competition, a flower display and coach trips are probably enough.'

'Us could have a sort o' fair as well as the pageant,' Ted Tozer said. 'Games and such for the kiddies, and teas, maybe a stall or two. Us'll have finished haymaking then so us could use my field, the one by the church.'

'Capital! And it's something that all the different groups

can join in with. Let's meet again in a month or two and see how far we've got with our plans.' The vicar folded his agenda as a signal that the meeting really was over and they all stood up and began to look for their coats.

Hilary and Felix walked away together, and this time she agreed when he invited her to go to the Bell for a drink. Dottie welcomed them and they stood with Ted Tozer at the bar, telling her about the plans for the Festival.

'Well, I reckon us ought to do summat about that too,' she said, her bright eyes sparkling at the thought of the celebrations. She turned and called through to the other side of the bar, where Bernie was serving customers in the snug. 'Listen to this, Bernie, there's going to be all sorts of shindigs going on in Burracombe for this Festival they'm getting up in London. A big pageant, games in Ted Tozer's field, a special ringing competition with bowling on the green as well, flowers on display in the church and goodness knows what else. Reckon we ought to put something on too, don't you?'

'I'll apply for a special licence anyway,' Bernie said, fishing a glass tankard out of the large bowl of hot water kept behind the bar, and drying it with a tea-towel. Bernie could never simply stand and talk, he always had to be doing something else as well. 'That's because there's always something else to be done,' he would say if anyone remarked on it. Now he said, 'All they ringers'll get a thirst on for a start.'

'Yes, but us ought to put on a bit of a show as well,' Dottie urged. 'Get out the flags, plant up a few of they barrels with some nice flowers. Pretty the place up, like.'

For months now, Dottie had had her eye on half a dozen old barrels that Bernie had stacked round the back of the pub. They would look lovely out the front with some bright flowers in them, she had told him, but Bernie, who barely knew the difference between a dandelion and a daffodil, had so far resisted. 'Who'd have to do all the work?' he asked now. 'Lug them round the front and fill 'em up with soil, and water 'em in the dry weather. Me, that's who, and I got enough on me plate already.'

'Look, I'd do all that,' Dottie promised. 'You just bring 'em round and I'll see to the rest.' To Ted, she said, 'You'll let me have some of Barley's dung, won't you, my handsome? I'll mix it up with a bit of good earth and the flowers'll grow a treat. I'll ask Miss Bellamy for some of her begonias, she always has a good show in her window-boxes. Make a nice bit of colour, they will.'

'Make it look like a flower-shop, more like,' Bernie grumbled. 'It's a *pub*, woman, a place where decent hardworking men can come and have a drink and a bit of a jaw. Who's going to want to come into a place that looks like Kew Gardens?'

'They'd go into Buckingham Palace if the beer was good enough,' Dottie retorted. 'Don't you think so, Miss Hilary?'

'I think it's a lovely idea,' Hilary said, finishing her shandy. 'Thank you, Felix, but I'd better be going now. I promised Father I wouldn't be late back. Not that there's any reason why I should be,' she added with a laugh. 'There's not exactly a lot of night-life in Burracombe!'

She shook her head at Felix's offer to see her home, and left him in the bar with Ted and some of the other regulars. It was a cold, clear night and she walked briskly, listening to the occasional bark of a fox and the shrieks of owls as they hunted across the fields.

I wonder if we can get Stephen interested in helping with the Festival, she thought. Her brother's call-up papers had still not arrived and he was at a loose end, roaming about the house, reluctantly accompanying the Colonel as he attended to estate business, or visiting his friend Jeremy Boulding at Little Burracombe. For the past few days, he had been in London, staying with friends from Cambridge, and had given no indication as to when he'd be home again. He hadn't said anything more about emigrating to America, but Hilary had seen some books about the country lying on his dressing-table and didn't think he'd forgotten the idea. She'd taken one back to her own room, to read in bed, and could see why Stephen was attracted to it. The wide open spaces, the lakes and mountains, the freedom . . .

It wouldn't be freedom for me, though, she reminded herself. Stephen just wants me to go and do the things I do here. Be a housekeeper. Do his cooking and washing and ironing, when what I really want is something interesting to do, something with responsibility. Something that will let me use my brain.

But whether she went with Stephen or made another attempt at leading her own life, there was still one question that loomed large in her mind. Who would look after her father? And how could she bring herself to leave him to his loneliness?

As Hilary stared at the alluring pictures in Stephen's book, she realised that she could not simply leave the man who depended on her so much. He's given his whole life to us, she thought – to his family and his estate. He never ran away from his duties. And neither can I.

Chapter Fourteen

Saturday was bright and cold, with frost casting a white blanket over the ground and riming the fronds of dead bracken with glitter. A robin was singing on Dottie's holly-bush as Luke and Stella pushed open the gate to set out on their walk, and the puddles along the lane cracked with thin ice.

'I'm glad it's cleared up – I was afraid it would rain,' Stella said. She had put on her Wellington boots, with an extra pair of socks inside. She wore a dark red jumper with a high neck that she had knitted herself, an old pair of navy slacks and a brown corduroy jacket that had been given to the Children's Home by a group of women who collected second-hand clothes for the children. Her knitted hat was pulled down over her dark curls and the cold air was stinging her cheeks into warm colour. She marched along at Luke's side, taking two strides to his one until he noticed and slowed down, apologising.

'Sorry – I forget that my legs are longer than other people's!' He hefted his old Army knapsack on to his shoulder. Dottie had filled it with pasties, still hot from the oven, the last of the Christmas cake and a Thermos of hot tea. 'You know, these pasties smell so good I think we should make a start on them now, before they go cold.'

Stella laughed. 'We'd better get out of sight of the cottage first! Which way are we going?'

Luke opened the gate leading into Ted Tozer's field. 'I

thought we'd go up the hill and on to the moor. There are some interesting standing stones up there – must have been a settlement thousands of years ago. There's a beehive hut as well – have you ever seen one of those?'

Stella shook her head doubtfully. 'I've seen beehives. Is that what you mean?'

'No. It's a stone hut shaped like a beehive. They're very old and there are only a few of them known on the moor. Some of them have roofs fallen in, so they're more like a shallow depression in the ground with stone walls round, but the one up here is complete. I don't think many people know about it – I found it one day when I was first here.'

Luke climbed the steep slope easily, talking as he went, but Stella was soon breathless and paused to look down at the village, tucked into its valley. Up here, the air was clear and fresh, and she drew a deep breath and held up her arms as if to embrace the rolling fields and woods and the moors above. She caught Luke's eyes on her and felt herself colour a little. 'It's so lovely, isn't it? I'm glad we came.'

'So am I,' he agreed, then said conspiratorially, 'Shall we have one of these pasties?'

She shook her head at him. 'I think we should at least wait until we're actually on the moor. Come on, I've got my breath back now.' She pulled off her hat and thrust it into her pocket, then plunged up the hill ahead of him, her dark curls springing out around her head. Luke watched her for a moment, then followed. After a few minutes, they emerged through a gateway on to the open hillside and paused again.

The moor stretched away before them, rolling towards the high tors. A rough track wide enough for a horse and cart ran along the contour, with sheep-tracks branching off to climb gently away through the bracken. A few sheep grazed nearby and in the distance Stella could see a group of Dartmoor ponies.

'Pasties!' Luke exclaimed, and they found a large, flat rock and sat down side by side, using their hats as cushions against the cold. Luke opened his knapsack and took out a tin box.

'Look how many she's given us. It's a good job we're starting early, we'd never manage them all otherwise.' He held the box towards Stella and she took one of the pasties. It was golden-brown, still warm, and when she bit into it she found that the crust was crisp and delicious, with just the right amount of rich gravy soaking into it from the meat and potato mixture inside. Luke closed the box and wrapped it in a spare jersey to keep the rest warm.

'I knew my old Army knapsack would be useful,' he remarked, biting the end of his pasty.

'You were in the Army? Was that during the war?'

'Mm.' He chewed for a moment before going on. 'I was a war artist. I wasn't painting pretty pictures – I had to go and draw things that were happening. Unpleasant, horrible things sometimes. It's a way of keeping a record, you see. Film can be damaged before it can be developed, or the photographer can run out, or something can happen to his camera, but an artist can usually keep his drawings safe. Or even do them again, if necessary.'

'You mean you couldn't actually *do* anything – you just had to draw what you saw, whatever it was.'

'That's right,' he said. 'It wasn't easy, at times. Seeing people being bombed or fighting battles – being wounded, dying even, and not being able to do a thing about it. But that was my job, you see. To draw. Make records of what went on. God knows what happened to all those drawings,' he added a trifle bitterly. 'I just handed them in and never saw them again. I suppose someone's got them, some-where.'

They sat in silence for a while, finishing their pasties. The village lay below them, a cluster of buildings with the church tower rising from their midst. The sun had melted most of the frost but here and there, in shady places, the ground was still white. High in the pale blue sky, a large bird hovered on outspread wings.

'A buzzard,' Luke said, tilting his head back to watch it. 'See how it soars higher and higher, in a spiral. It's using the thermals.'

'It hardly needs to use its wings at all,' Stella marvelled. 'Why does it go so high? It surely can't see its food from up there.'

'Ever heard the expression "eyes like a hawk"?' Luke asked, grinning. He stood up and took her hand to haul her to her feet and they began to walk on along the track. 'So what happened to you in the war, Stella? You must have been quite little when it started.'

'Yes, I was.' Stella thought for a minute or two before answering any further. It was a complicated story, and she didn't want Luke to feel sorry for her. 'We were bombed out,' she said finally.'Twice. The first time, we were in the shelter so we were all right, but our home was smashed to smithereens. The second time . . . ' She hesitated. It was still not easy to talk about what had happened. 'Well, we'd been in the shelter but we were going over to a neighbour. She'd come to fetch us – me and my mother and sister and baby brother. My mother went back to the house for something and the bomb fell while we were on our way across the road. Muriel and I were all right, more or less, but Mummy and Thomas were killed. Everybody said they couldn't have known a thing about it,' she hurried on, hearing Luke's intake of breath. 'They were trying to help, of course, but I don't think it did help all that much, not at the time. We were just little girls and we could only think about ourselves.'

'That's awful,' Luke said quietly. 'What happened to you

after that? Where was your father – or had he been killed before then?'

'No, he was in the Merchant Navy. He was away at sea. We went and stayed with another neighbour – Auntie Jess, we called her, she was a lovely person and she looked after us really well. And when Daddy came home, she suggested that we should go out and stay at the same place as her two boys. They were evacuated, you see, to a village in the country. And that's what we did.'

They walked on in silence. After his first reaction, Luke didn't attempt to express any further condolences, and she was grateful. Even after all this time, Stella still found it difficult to talk about her loss, and sympathy made it even harder. After a while, he said, 'Don't tell me if you'd rather not, but what happened after that? You said the other evening at Dottie's that you'd been in a Children's Home. That's an orphanage, isn't it? So was your father killed as well?'

'Yes,' she said. 'His ship was mined. So then there was nobody to look after Muriel and me – we had a granny but she was in hospital – and we were both taken away from the village. I went to one Children's Home and – and Muriel went to another one.'

He stared at her. 'You mean they *separated* you?'

'Yes. They thought it was best. They said we wouldn't get adopted if we were together – not many people wanted older children anyway, and nobody would want two sisters. And they said we'd settle down and forget more easily if we were apart.'

'But you must have seen each other sometimes – you must have written to each other.'

'No,' Stella said. 'I didn't know where Muriel had been taken and I don't suppose she knew where I was either. I never saw her again. I don't know where she is.' Her voice trembled suddenly and then broke. 'She could be dead too, for all I know,' she said, and burst into tears.

'*Stella!*' Luke stopped and pulled her into his arms. He held her against him, his long fingers stroking her shoulders and hair as she sobbed against his chest. 'I'm sorry,' he murmured. 'I'm so sorry. I shouldn't have asked – this was meant to be a happy day. Oh Stella, you poor little love. I'm sorry – I'm so, *so* sorry.'

'No, don't, it's just me. I didn't mean to do that – it just suddenly came over me.' She drew away from him a little and felt for a hanky. He kept his arms loosely around her as she wiped her eyes and blew her nose, then she smiled up at him rather shakily and said, 'I'm all right now. Sorry to make your jacket all wet.'

'It doesn't matter.' He looked down at her gravely. 'Look, if you'd rather go back . . .'

'Oh no! No, let's go on. I'm all right. Really.' She pushed her hanky into her pocket and brushed back her hair with a determined gesture. 'I didn't want to spoil the day, I'm sorry.'

'You haven't. And I'm the one who ought to be sorry.' He smiled his wide, slightly wicked smile and added, 'Now that we've both said sorry more than once, we'll leave it at that, shall we? And I promise I won't ask any more questions.'

They began to walk on along the track. The air was still, and on a holly tree nearby a robin was singing, as if spring had already arrived. The sheep moved across the ground to the side of the track, their heads down as they munched the short winter grass. After a bit, Stella said, 'Actually, I think I'd like to talk about it. I never have much, you see – they didn't want me to at the Home. I suppose it was all part of their idea that if nobody mentioned it I'd forget. But you don't forget having a family, even if most of them have been killed. And you don't forget you've got a sister somewhere.' Her voice shook once more and Luke took her hand and held it warmly in his.

'I'd like to find her,' Stella said. 'I think about it a lot, especially now that I've finally left the Home. I don't know where she is or where to start, but it would be so lovely to find her again. I want to know she's all right.'

'Was she older or younger than you?'

'Two years younger. I used to look after her – well, I thought I did.' She laughed a little. 'The big sister, you know! I was so upset when they took her away. I knew she'd be missing me, and I didn't think anyone could look after her as well as I did.' She was silent for a moment, then said, 'I hope she found nice people to adopt her. I hope she's been happy all these years.'

'Are you sure she was adopted? After all, you weren't, were you? If you could just find out which Home she went to—'

'Oh, I was adopted,' Stella said quickly. 'At least, I was fostered first, but they wanted to adopt me. And then she died suddenly, the woman who would have been my mother. And the man didn't think he could manage on his own. I don't think he wanted a child as much as she did, anyway. So I went back to the Home and that was that.' She paused, then said, 'They were very good to me there, you know. It was a good place to be – I mean, if you have to be in an orphanage at all. We used to go to a local school and I did well there, and they let me go to the local grammar school and stay on after I was fourteen. Even when I was too old to be in the Home, they let me stay on, in return for helping with the little ones. I was an assistant nurse then, but Matron knew I wanted to be a teacher and she helped me to go to college and let me go back during the holidays. Otherwise I'd have had nowhere to go. I couldn't have done any of it without her.'

'I suppose you were lucky in that respect,' Luke said.

'Oh, I was. I know that. If anyone could be said to have been a mother to me, after I lost my real one, it would be Matron.'

'Wouldn't she help you find Muriel, then,' he asked, 'if she's so helpful and so concerned? She must know how hard it's been for you, to be separated from your sister like this.'

'I did ask her once, just before I left to go to college. I knew her better then, you see, she'd taken an interest in me and helped me. But she just said all those records were confidential and after this amount of time it would be impossible to find out where Muriel had gone. She didn't know herself where Muriel went. When I was first sent there, all she knew was that I'd lost my family in the war. Nobody even told her I had a sister. And I wasn't old enough then to do anything about it.' She tried to explain to Luke what it had been like to be in a Children's Home during the war. 'We never got much chance to talk to people, you see. The nurses were all so busy and a lot of the children there were in just the same position as me. It wasn't at all unusual to separate families.' Once again, she paused and then added very quietly, 'Muriel might even be dead. I don't think I'd want to find that out.'

Luke was still holding her hand. He tightened his fingers around hers but remained silent. After a long time, he said, 'I've never lost anyone in that way, Stella, but I do know what it is to lose contact with someone you love. You never stop wondering. If there's anything I can do – if you'd like to try again to find her – well, I'd really like to help. I mean that.'

Stella stopped and looked up at him. The bright blue of his eyes was no more than a rim around the darkness of his pupils. His wide, smiling mouth was serious, the lips pressed together in a firm line. She felt the tears come to her eyes again and stepped forward to lay her head against his chest. He put his arms around her and they stood close and quiet.

'Thank you,' Stella said at last. 'I'll remember that. I'm not sure if I'm ready to try again, or how to go about it, but when I do, I'll talk to you. It would be good to have a friend to help.'

'And two heads are always better than one,' he said with a touch of humour back in his voice. He held her away from him and dropped a quick kiss on her hair. 'Now let's go on and find these standing stones. And then I think it'll be time to broach this flask of tea and maybe try another pasty!'

Chapter Fifteen

Val had come off night-duty and decided to do some shopping in Tavistock before going home to the farm. She had the weekend off and could go to bed for a few hours to keep herself going until her normal bedtime. Next week, she was on days again and would be able to come home every evening.

She walked down the hill to the town, feeling her heart lift at the view down West Street towards the church, with the moors rising beyond. The air was clear and bright, and she heard the mellow tone of the tenor bell chiming the hour. The streets were quiet at this time, with the shops just beginning to open, and Val went to the greengrocer for some fruit, and then to Pillar's, the newsagent, for the *Radio Times* and her mother's *Woman's Own* magazine. By then, Perraton's was open and she decided to have a cup of coffee before catching the bus back to the village.

It was gone ten when she got off the bus at the corner of the lane which led from the main Plymouth road to Burracombe. The local bus ran less often than the Plymouth bus, and Val enjoyed the walk on a morning such as this, after a night spent on the ward. She would be ready for bed when she arrived home, but would sleep all the better for the fresh air and exercise.

She strolled along, swinging her bag of shopping and letting her gaze wander over the rolling moors. The road sloped up gently before dropping over the rim of the hollow in which Burracombe lay, and as she came within sight of the village she paused for a moment, leaning on a stone wall and enjoying the view of the cottages straggling between winding lanes, the church and pub, her father's farm and the Barton where her friend Hilary lived. She looked at the fields, still frosted after the clear, cold night, and the woods where the charcoal-burner's cottage was just visible through the leafless trees, smoke rising from its chimney.

Luke was there. Val felt a tightness in her chest and her pleasure evaporated. The thought that she might meet him at any time in the village brought a sharp pain to her heart; she wished that he had not come, or that he would go away. Why had he come here, to Burracombe of all places? Was it on purpose to torment her? It was possible, she reluctantly acknowledged, that he hadn't known she lived here – and even if he had, he would have thought she was married by now. But once he had realised it, shouldn't he have moved away? Shouldn't he, if he'd had a shred of decency, have left the village – left her in peace? I don't want him here! she thought furiously. I don't want him reminding me of everything that happened. I just want him to go away, so that I'll never have to see him again.

As she stood gazing towards the wood and the sloping fields, her mind swirling with bitter thoughts, she saw two people sitting on the edge of the moor. Her eyes narrowed as she realised who they were.

One was the new schoolteacher, Stella Simmons. And the other was Luke.

Val stared at them. A strange mixture of emotions struggled within her as she watched. There was the pain that always came with the thought of Luke, and the desire to push him from her thoughts; yet at the same time there was an unexpected annoyance at seeing him with Stella. So that's the man who says he still loves me! she thought scornfully, but followed this with a swift reminder to herself that Luke could not be expected not to make other friends, especially when she had told him so clearly that there could never be anything between them again. And he was only going for a walk, for heaven's sake! It didn't have to mean that he and Stella were anything but friends. The young teacher had only been in the village for a week or two, anyway – they hadn't had time to develop anything more.

She watched as they stood up and began to walk on. Luke was carrying a knapsack, as if they planned a long hike. They were looking at each other, obviously talking with some animation – and then, to her amazement, they stopped suddenly and Luke pulled his companion into his arms. She leaned against him, her face buried against his chest, and he stroked her back and her hair with both hands.

Val shrank back against the wall, her heart thumping uncomfortably in her chest. She wanted to look away, but couldn't. She could only watch as the two distant figures stayed still and close for several minutes and then, at last, broke away and walked on. They were holding hands as they walked.

Val pushed herself away from the wall. She felt sick and near to tears. I'll have to tell her, she thought. I'll have to tell that poor girl how dangerous he is. I can't let what happened to me happen to her as well.

She walked slowly down the hill, her pleasure in the morning gone. She felt tired and depressed, and wanted nothing more than to get into bed and pull the covers over her head.

Church flowers were always a problem during January, but Hilary had become an expert at making interesting arrangements. Today, she and Constance Bellamy had raided Constance's garden and entered the church armed with sheaves of evergreen foliage, hellebores and a few early camellias.

Felix was in the vestry. He peered out to see who was coming in and hurried out, beaming. 'Goodness, you look like the march of Macduff – I can hardly see you behind all that greenery. And flowers, too! I didn't think there were any about at this time of year.'

'They're Christmas roses,' Hilary told him as she laid bunches down on the chancel steps. 'And camellias from Miss Bellamy's garden – she's got an early bush. I'm going to put some on the altar and some more here and there to brighten up the foliage. And here's a bunch of snowdrops for the pulpit.'

'I'd offer to help,' he said, 'but my idea of arranging flowers is to stuff them into a jam jar and hope they're the right way up!'

'You'd better leave us to it, then,' Constance Bellamy said. She was already heading towards the vestry with the containers from last Sunday. She put the dying flowers into a galvanised bucket and tipped the stale water into the sink, then refilled the vases. All her movements were brisk and energetic. She brushed past Felix as they met in the vestry doorway and began to sort out the foliage, clipping it to the required length with secateurs.

'What did you think of the meeting the other evening?' she enquired as Felix hovered about, trying to help by picking up the bits and dropping them into another bucket. 'Your first experience of a village committee, was it?'

'Yes. I'd already met Mrs Warren, of course – she asked me to tea the other day. She's certainly very active in village life.'

Constance snorted. 'Likes to think she is! Got her finger in all the pies, that woman has. Ted Tozer's got her measure, though. *He* wasn't going to let her take charge.'

Hilary said, 'She will be more or less in charge, all the same. The secretary usually ends up running things, especially when the secretary is Mrs Warren!'

'Oh, that's all right,' Constance said. 'Nobody minds her doing all the work. We just don't want her swanning about the village as if she owned the place. Not that she won't do that anyway, whatever she's called.' She carried the vase of bright pink camellias to the altar and set them in the middle, where they glowed like June roses.

Hilary made a face at Felix. 'Miss Bellamy and Mrs Warren are sworn enemies,' she whispered. 'Miss Bellamy's family's been here for centuries, but Mrs Warren only came here when she got married. Her husband's a solicitor in Tavistock.'

'Well, we mustn't criticise. Her sort are often the backbone of the village. Love to spend their time organising things.'

Hilary laughed. 'Mrs Warren was her husband's secretary before they got married. I expect she organised him too. Still does,' she added. 'I shouldn't say this, but I've heard that he only goes to work to get some peace!'

They giggled together and Constance came back and looked at them suspiciously. 'What are you two finding so funny? Have I got my skirt tucked up at the back?'

'No, no,' Hilary assured her. 'It's nothing to do with you, really, Miss Bellamy. We were being rather naughty about Mrs Warren, I'm afraid.'

'That's all right, then. Mind you, it wouldn't be the first time. Went up to take Communion once and knelt down in front of everyone with my skirt tucked into the back of my knickers!' Constance picked up another armful of foliage and began to stuff it into the pedestal that stood in front of the pulpit. 'Good thing I'm not easily embarrassed.'

'I can't imagine that ever happening to Mrs Warren,' Hilary said, laughing. 'She always looks as if she's off to a wedding, even when she's only going down to the butcher's shop for a few chops.'

Constance sniffed. 'Puts too much importance on appearances, she does. You don't see me spending an hour every morning titivating! Too much to do.'

Felix and Hilary looked at each other again. Constance certainly didn't appear to have spent an hour on her appearance today. She was wearing a shapeless skirt and jacket of a rather murky green tweed and a bright yellow handknitted jumper that hung almost to her knees. On her head, as usual, was something that looked very like a tea-cosy.

'She once did wear a tea-cosy to church,' Hilary said to Felix after Constance had finished the flowers and stumped away, bearing the remnants to be added to the compost heap Jacob Prout kept in the corner under the yew trees. 'You could see the holes for the spout and handle. She knits them herself and I think she uses the same pattern for both.'

'She's a very good soul, though. Although I feel rather ashamed of the way we laughed at Mrs Warren. A man of the cloth shouldn't behave like that.' He gave her a sidelong glance. 'I'm afraid you're a bad influence on me, Hilary.'

'*I'm* a bad influence!' she exclaimed. 'Who was it who kept trying to make me giggle at the meeting the other evening? I'm surprised Basil didn't tell us he'd split us up.'

'I'm afraid my sense of humour does get the better of me at times,' Felix admitted, 'especially when someone's being pompous or self-important. But you're right, I really must learn to behave. I'll never be a bishop if I keep laughing at the parishioners.'

'Is that what you'd like to be?' Hilary asked curiously as she wrapped her scarf round her neck. 'A bishop?'

'It's what my father would like me to be. He *is* a bishop.' Felix disappeared into the vestry and came out without his cassock on. He was wearing a tweed jacket and grey flannels, and although his dog-collar proclaimed his status, he looked like any other lively young man out for a jaunt on a Saturday afternoon with his girl.

As soon as the thought entered Hilary's head, she felt herself blush. She turned away quickly and walked out through the old oak door into the January sunshine. Felix followed her and they stood for a moment looking out across the churchyard towards the green.

'How are you spending the rest of the day?' he enquired after a moment.

Hilary shrugged. 'I'm going home now to get my father's lunch ready. Then I'll probably go for a ride. What about you?'

'Got a few things to prepare for tomorrow, as I'm preaching at Evensong. Apart from that . . . '

Hilary turned and looked up at him. 'Don't you have any friends here? People you can spend your spare time with?'

'Not yet,' he said cheerfully, 'but I'm sure I shall have. Friends come to you wherever you live, but you do have to be willing to go halfway to meet them. You and I, for instance – I think we could be friends.'

'Yes,' Hilary said thoughtfully, 'I believe we could.' She smiled at him. 'Let's start now. Do you ride?' He nodded. 'Why don't you come for a ride with me this afternoon? And then you could stay for supper. We haven't got any other guests, I'm afraid. It might be boring for you with just my father and me.'

'It won't be boring at all.' He looked pleased. 'I'd like that very much. Thank you, Hilary.'

'I could ask a few others if you like,' she said. 'The new schoolteacher – that young artist who's living in the old charcoal-burner's cottage. I saw them going up on the moor earlier when I was on my way to the church. They looked quite friendly.' She thought for a moment, then said, 'On second thoughts, it might be a better idea to arrange something a bit further in advance – they've probably already got plans for this evening. I might get up a little supper-party next week, perhaps. I could ask Val Tozer as well – she's Ted Tozer's daughter and we're great friends, but she nurses in Tavistock so I'd have to find out when she's got an evening off. We'll soon get your social life going, Felix!'

'I'll look forward to it,' he said. 'But today, I'm happy just to go riding with you and come over to supper this evening. Thank you, Hilary.'

'I'll see you about two o'clock,' she said and walked away down the church path.

'I don't know about our Val,' Alice said as the family sat down to their midday meal. On Saturdays they always had sausages and mash with whatever vegetable was available from Alice's kitchen garden. Today, it was cabbage. The sausages came from Bert Foster, who made them himself at the back of his shop, and were meaty and full of flavour.

'Why, what's wrong with her?' Joanna asked, cutting Robin's sausage into small pieces. 'She seemed a bit tired when she came in, but she's been on night-duty, after all.'

Alice shook her head. 'She seemed more than tired to me. She was looking downright miserable – as if something had happened to upset her. I wondered if it was something at the hospital but she said no, everything was all right, nobody died sudden or nothing like that. And then she just brushed me off and went upstairs to bed. Wouldn't even stop for a cup of tea. And she wouldn't look me in the eye, neither. That's what worried me most.'

'Why d'you suppose that was, then?' Minnie asked. 'There's nothing she's ashamed of, is there? I can't imagine our Val doing anything she'd not want to tell us about.'

'No, of course she wouldn't. She didn't want me to see

how upset she was, that's why.' Alice offered the last sausage to Tom and he speared it with his fork. 'There's something eating her, and I just wish I knew what it was.'

'Well, you can't ask her,' Minnie said. 'She'm a grown woman now, Alice. She'll tell us soon enough if there's anything really wrong.'

'I don't know so much. I don't think she will.' Alice went on with her own meal, looking dissatisfied. After a moment or two, Jackie spoke in an injured voice.

'Well, if you've finished worrying about our Val, maybe you could think about me a bit. *I'm* upset too, and I don't mind telling you why!'

'Go on, then,' Tom said in a resigned tone. 'Tell us why. You've been dying to do it ever since we sat down.'

'Thanks very much! You're sure you don't mind listening, just for a minute?' Jackie looked round the table to make sure she'd got their attention. 'All right, then – I'm upset because Roy's got his papers.'

There was a brief silence. Then Alice said, 'His papers? You mean his call-up papers?'

'Yes, of course I do. His National Service call-up papers, just to make it absolutely clear.' Jackie's voice trembled a little. 'I wanted to tell you straight away, but you were too interested in our Val. He's going away, Mum.' Tears sprang to her eyes and began to trickle down her cheeks. 'Roy's going away.'

The family sat staring at her in silence. Tom rolled his eyes at his wife, who frowned at him. Ted looked faintly exasperated and Alice concerned. Robin, fastened into his high-chair beside Joanna, pointed his small fork at his young aunt and said, 'Jackie crying. Kiss her better.'

'It's not us she wants to kiss her better,' Tom muttered, and Joanna kicked him under the table.

'You see!' Jackie accused them all. 'You don't care. None of you cares about me.'

'Jackie, don't be silly,' Alice said. 'Of course we care about you. But you knew this would happen. You knew Roy'd be called up soon.'

'I didn't think it would be this soon,' she sniffed. 'I thought it'd be after the summer. We wanted to do all sorts of things together. We wanted to go to London and see the Festival.'

'Well, I expect you'll still be able to do that. He'll get leave. When does he have to go?' To be honest, Alice wasn't sorry to hear this news. To her mind, Jackie and young Roy had been getting altogether too serious. All that talk of an engagement, for instance! Alice hadn't even dared mention it to Ted. He'd have hit the roof. It would be a good thing if Roy was removed for a while, to let things calm down a bit.

'Next month,' Jackie said sullenly, obviously still disgruntled by the reception of her news. 'Less than three weeks. It isn't fair, Mum. The war's been over for years, I don't even see why men have to do this horrible National Service.'

'Because it's their patriotic duty, that's why,' Ted said sharply. 'Because we don't want to be caught napping like we were last time. We need our Armed Services, ready to go wherever they're needed. And you might remember, young woman, that there *is* a war going on – the Korean War. And our chaps are going out there just the same as—' He caught his wife's eye on him and trailed off into silence, while Jackie stared at him in dismay.

'Korea? You don't think he'd be sent there, do you? Oh Mum,' she turned to her mother, her face white with real distress, 'Mum, he could be killed!'

Thank you, Ted, Alice said silently, giving her husband a look before she turned back to her daughter. 'Now, don't you worry your head about that, my flower,' she said as comfortingly as she could. 'I don't suppose young Roy'll be sent out there, not for a minute. Why, it stands to reason he'll need to be trained proper and that takes time. He'll be safe enough, don't you fret.'

'Well, they sent blokes out in the last lot with only a few weeks' training,' Tom said, cheerfully oblivious of the effect of his words. 'Some of the young 'uns who joined our lot were barely out of school. At least Roy can handle a gun – quite a good shot, he is.'

Jackie stared at him and then burst into tears and jumped up from the table. She ran from the kitchen and they heard her feet on the stairs. Alice looked at both her husband and her son with vexation.

'You two! Don't you have no feeling at all? Upsetting the poor maid like that. Now we've got both of them crying their eyes out. I don't know why you men don't have more sense.'

'Come on, Mum,' Tom said. 'You've been worrying that she and Roy were getting too thick ever since New Year's Eve. I'd have thought you'd be pleased he was called up.'

'I am, but you didn't have to go talking about Korea, and what they did last time. It's your fault too, Ted. You brought it up. She was bound to be upset about him going away but she didn't have to have ideas like that put into her head. Next thing we know, she'll be asking to get married.'

'Get *married*?' Ted threw down his knife and fork. 'Now, that *is* a stupid idea! She'm nothing but a little maid still.'

'She's old enough to get married, all the same. She's already told me that she and Roy reckon they're engaged.'

'Engaged? I've heard nothing about this.'

'No, because I told her there was no point in mentioning it. I said you wouldn't hear of it for another two or three years at least. And what do you think she told me? She said that she and Roy had promised to marry each other, and that made them engaged, whether we like it or not. I wouldn't be a bit surprised if he hasn't bought her a ring and all. She's probably got it on round her neck now, on a bit of ribbon.'

Ted looked at her. 'You ought to have told me this, Alice. I'm her father. I've got a right to know.'

'Well, maybe I should have, but I was hoping it would all come to nothing – especially if Roy got his call-up. But now you've gone and put ideas into her head about Korea there's no knowing what those two silly children will do. We don't want no trouble brought to this house, Ted.'

'Hold on a minute,' Tom said. 'She's only just told you that Roy's been called up, and you've got her halfway down the aisle already, or else left holding the baby—'

'Tom!' Alice said sharply. 'We'll have none of that sort of talk, if you don't mind.'

'Well, that's what you meant. And it wasn't me who started all this.' Tom pushed away his empty plate. 'Are we getting any afters today, or shall I just go out and start work again?'

'Of course there's afters. It's roly-poly pudding, same as it is every Saturday.' Alice got up and began to collect plates together while Minnie went to the pan that had been simmering all morning. 'Now, don't you do that, Mother, it's too heavy for you. I don't want you scalding yourself.' She took the pan over to the sink and fished the pudding out carefully with two large wooden spoons. It was wrapped in a cloth and she untied the strings quickly from each end and tipped it on to a large plate. Red jam oozed from either end and Tom smacked his lips appreciatively.

'That's the stuff to give the troops – oh, suppose I shouldn't have said that! Us'll be walking on eggs now, till we know young Roy's going nowhere further than Crown-hill Fort, down in Plymouth. Come on, Mum, give us a smile,' he cajoled her. 'You know she'll get over it. She's only a kid – it's a nine-days' wonder, this "engagement".'

'I hope you'm right,' Alice said as she brought the suet pudding to the table and began to serve it into bowls. 'I just hope you'm right.'

Chapter Sixteen

Roy Nethercott wasn't the only one to receive his call-up papers. Stephen Napier's came at the beginning of February and he was pleased to find that he'd got his wish and would be going into the Royal Air Force.

His father was not so pleased, and made his feelings known as he and Stephen were on their daily walk round the fields. It was the first step in Napier's plans for Stephen to take over the estate when the time came, and although Stephen was well aware of this, he could think of no real reason not to accompany him.

'Thought you'd forgotten that nonsense. Still, I dare say I could pull a few strings, get you back into the Regiment—'

'*No*, Father! I want to go into the RAF. I've told you, I want to learn to fly. What chance would I have to do that in the Army? I'd be better off in the Navy – at least they've got the Fleet Air Arm. But I've been put into the RAF and that's where I want to be, so let's leave it at that.' His face was flushed. Sent to his father's school and then on to Cambridge, never wanting for anything that could be given him, he had never had to defend his own desires, and Gilbert Napier was a hard man to oppose.

Napier's face was reddening too. He glared at his son. 'Leave it at that? No, I will not leave it at that! I want to know what other ridiculous notions you've got in your head. For a start, what's all this about America?'

'America?'

'Yes, America! All those books I saw lying around in your room the other day when I went in to find that cigarette case you borrowed. Brochures about emigration.' The big, silver head lowered, like that of a bull about to charge. 'Don't trouble to deny it.'

'All right, I won't,' Stephen said after a pause. He opened the gate into the next field and waited for his father to go through before closing it again. 'I have been thinking about it. Some men at Cambridge have been talking about it. They want people like us over there, Dad. Mathematicians and scientists. They want people for all kinds of research – the sort of research I could do. It would be a new life for me – a worthwhile life.' He looked at his father, willing him to understand, knowing that he wouldn't.

Napier responded exactly as his son had known he would.

'You've got a worthwhile life here! You've got an estate to run!'

Stephen shook his head. 'No, Father. *You've* got an estate to run. I didn't ask for it and you never expected me to have to do it. Baden would have made a good job of it, but I—'

'Baden's not here,' his father said harshly. 'If he were, then maybe I'd think about this crackbrained notion of yours – only *think* about it, mind you – but since he's not . . .'

'Since he's not,' Stephen said in a quiet voice, 'I'm to give up any ideas I might have had about using my own talents. I'm to be a substitute – and not even a very good one.' He bent to pick up a stick that was lying close to the hedge.

Napier made a sound of exasperation. 'That's ridiculous. You've got a perfectly adequate brain, or so your professors seem to think – they gave you a first-class degree. Of course you wouldn't be a poor substitute. You're quite capable of learning the job. You've grown up with it, after all.'

Stephen brushed his fair hair back from his eyes. 'But I don't want to do it. Doesn't that make any difference? You do it well because you love the estate and the life, and so did Baden. But I don't. Oh, I don't mean I don't love it in my own way – it's my home, after all.' He flung his arm out and gestured at the fields and the moors above. 'I think it's one of the best places on earth. But then, I haven't seen many other places, have I?'

'You've seen most of Europe! Spent the last six months gadding about when you could have been at home learning your job.'

'But it *isn't* my job! And Europe's still a pretty dismal place. There's a lot to do before it's back to how it was before the war.'

'And don't you think it's people like you who should be working to put it back?' the Squire demanded. 'Instead of running off to America, reneging on your responsibilities?'

'The responsibilities *you* think I have.' Stephen's own anger was beginning to show in his voice. 'Father, you never took the slightest interest in me until Baden died! I was the second son, the *spare* – bit odd, a bit wet, a disappointment. More interested in my books than in the estate. Not much good on a horse, not interested in going out hunting foxes and coming back plastered in mud, talking about the kill. You never, ever took any trouble to find out what I *was* interested in. You never bothered about what I did.'

'That's quite untrue! I always read your reports – and good reports they were, too. I gave you credit for that.'

'Except that you'd rather I'd been good at sport than maths. You'd have been better pleased if I'd been rugby and cricket captain like Baden than got the maths prize.'

'I accepted the fact that you weren't any good at sport—'

'I didn't like it! I liked different things.' Stephen shook his head and swished his stick at some grass growing from the bank. 'Oh, what's the use? You'll never understand – we just go round and round in circles. Look, the fact is that you knew perfectly well then that I wouldn't be any good at running the estate. It didn't matter because you had Baden, and he wanted to do it. And the only thing that's changed is that—' he saw his father's face and bit back his next words, then said more quietly, '—we haven't got Baden any more. And I'm as sorry about it as you are. He was my hero.'

'So why not do his job for him?' Napier asked passionately. 'Why not take it on as – as a *memorial*, if you like? It would be the finest thing you could do with your life, Stephen, can't you see that?'

Stephen shook his head. 'No, I can't. I can't see it as being that important. Father, the big estates have had their day. Oh, it may take years – decades – for it to happen, but they just won't be practical any more. Families like us are dying out. Elder sons have been lost and younger sons don't want to take their place. The expense alone is going to drive us into the ground. Maintaining these big houses, keeping armies of servants – it's just not going to be possible. People don't want to do that sort of work any more. Look at us – think of how many indoor servants we used to have, and how many we have now. Two or three, and none of them live in. And outdoors too – the gardens and stables, they're all getting run down. You know it's true.'

'We're still getting on our feet after the war,' Napier began, but Stephen shook his head.

'It's been five years now. Things have changed, Father. People won't go into service any more. Women aren't content to spend their time in the kitchen. Look at Hilary – she's miserable because she hasn't got a life of her own. She wants a career, but since Mother died she's been trapped here, looking after you.'

'Trapped – Hilary? How can you say such a thing! She has more freedom than most young women of her age. It's marriage Hilary wants, not a career – a husband and children to look after. That'd soon put all these ideas about a career out of her head.'

Stephen said nothing. He walked along at his father's side, wondering if things would have been different if he'd been able to do this as a child. If Baden had never existed, or if he'd been the elder son, groomed for his inheritance, would he have felt differently then? Would he still have wanted to take a degree in mathematics and go into some kind of research? Or would he have accepted his fate, accepted the grooming that Baden had been given, and taken on his inheritance without ever knowing that he might have had a different life?

But it wasn't any use wondering all this. Things hadn't been like that, and he did want a different life. He'd been hoping that his National Service would open the door to it, that by the time he'd done three years, as a Regular, and become a pilot, his father would have realised and accepted the fact that he was never going to come back to the estate, and turned his attention to someone else.

Hilary, for instance.

Hilary was busy preparing for a supper-party that evening.

She didn't want to call it anything as formal as a 'dinner-party'. Her father had been invited to dinner at the doctor's house that night and it seemed a good opportunity to bring together a group of the younger people in the village for a relaxed evening. She'd asked her friend Val Tozer, and Stella Simmons and the artist Luke Ferris, whom she had seen together several times. Stephen would be there, of course, and his friend Jeremy. Three men and three women. It should be fun, she thought as she went about her preparations.

They were having pheasant casserole with mashed potato and greens, followed by stewed dried fruits and cream. It was easy to prepare, with little last-minute cooking, and they could relax over a couple of bottles of wine from her father's cellar. She'd asked his advice and he'd recommended a claret and gone down to fetch it himself.

'Are you sure?' she'd asked doubtfully. 'I remember you saying this was a specially good one.'

'Of course I'm sure. There to be drunk, isn't it? Good for young Stephen to play host once in a while – got to have something worth giving his guests.' He'd put the bottles on the sideboard and gone off, leaving Hilary looking after him rather wryly. So it had become Stephen's party, had it? Well, no doubt it was all part of her father's plan to entice his younger son to take over the mantle of the estate, but she had a strong feeling it wasn't going to work.

She laid the table in the breakfast room, which was nearer to the kitchen and cosier than the big, formal dining room with its vast table and silver candelabra, and the portraits of grim-featured past Napiers looking down. Enough to put anyone off their food, she thought, lighting the fire.

Stephen came into the kitchen as she was peeling potatoes, and sniffed appreciatively. 'Smells good. Anything I can do?'

'You can fill the log-basket.' He went off to do so and came back after a few minutes to sit at the kitchen table, looking pensive. Hilary glanced at him.

'What's the matter?'

'Oh, the usual. Father wants me to become the next Squire and I don't. And he's found out about America.'

'Well, he had to know about it sometime. The rest of the world found out when Columbus did.'

Stephen looked at her for a moment and then slowly screwed up a ball of newspaper and threw it at her. 'Very funny, I don't think.'

'Well, come on,' Hilary said, grinning. 'It's not the end of the world, is it? Columbus thought it was, of course, but we know—'

'*Hil!*'

'All right,' she said, coming over to the table and sitting opposite him. 'I'm probably over-excited at having friends round for the evening. Is he upset?'

'Well, what do you think? Of course he's upset. He thinks the estate's going to be broken up into little bits and sold the minute he's dead, and the Napier name will be lost and forgotten, and all because I won't give up my life to looking after it. Honestly, he reckons that just because the war's been over for five years we're going to go back to the old feudal ways, with serfs touching their forelocks and dozens of servants keeping everything spick and span. You wouldn't have to peel potatoes then, Hil. You'd be in the drawing room eating chocolates and reading ladies' magazines.'

'What an awful idea,' Hilary said. 'I may not enjoy peeling potatoes, but it's better than being bored out of my mind, which I would be if that's all I had to do.' She paused for a moment, her hands pressed together, and gazed out of the window. 'He's living in the past, isn't he? None of that's ever going to come back.'

'No, it's not. The trouble is, I don't think we've really decided what's going to happen instead. This Festival – it's a step in the right direction, showing people what *can* be done. It'll make a lot of people sit up and open their eyes. But there are still a lot who won't move forward, and I think it's people in places like this – farmers and old families with estates – who will be the slowest of all. They want everything to stay the same, but it can't. Not after something like a world war.' He drew in a deep sigh and gave her a hunted look. 'I never expected to end up running the Burracombe estate and I don't want to. I'd be no good at it. I'd ruin the whole place.'

'Of course you wouldn't! You've got a good brain and you know the way things are done. You could do it easily.'

'All right, I could. I could forget all the plans I've been making since I was a kid – all the ideas I had about making my own way in life – and just settle down to running the home farm and collecting rents from the tenant farms. And be a magistrate, like Dad, and Master of the Hunt when I don't even like riding, and stride around the village as if I owned it . . . *No.*' He thumped his fist on the table. 'It's not for me, Hilary. It wouldn't be right.'

His sister said nothing for a few moments. Then she stood up and went back to the sink.

'Well, it'll sort itself out one way or the other, I'm sure. In the meantime, we've got guests coming this evening and I want time to have a bath and get myself ready before they come. And Dad'll be wanting one too, before he goes to the Latimers', so if you're not to sit at the table smelling like a farmyard, you'd better go and have yours now. And don't use all the hot water.'

'All right,' he said, getting up. 'I know when I'm being told to shut up and go away.' He came over to his sister and leaned back against the draining-board. 'I meant what I said the other day, you know. I've got to do this National Service first, and I'm going to do three years so that I can be a pilot. But after that, I'm going to America – and if you want to come with me, I'd like to have you.'

'We'll wait and see, shall we,' Hilary said, poking the eyes out of a potato. 'Three years is a long time, Steve. A lot could happen before we have to think about that.'

Chapter Seventeen

The party gathered at about seven. Felix was coming in place of Jeremy Boulding, who had telephoned full of apologies to say he couldn't come after all. Hilary had shrugged off Stephen's disappointment and asked the curate. 'He's not at all stuffy,' she'd told her brother. 'Anyway, we've got to have another man.'

Val was first to arrive, wearing a new plaid skirt in soft heather colours and a pale blue jumper. She came into the kitchen through the back door, looking tired but determined to enjoy herself.

'I'm glad you could come,' Hilary said, testing the potatoes to see if they were cooked. 'When I rang to invite you, you seemed a bit flustered. I wondered if there was anything wrong.'

'No, nothing's wrong. We're quite busy at work, that's all. I'll take my coat through to the hall, shall I?' She disappeared, leaving Hilary looking after her thoughtfully. She knew her friend too well not to notice that brisk, over-casual tone.

'Sorry it was all rather sudden,' she said as Val came back. 'I didn't realise till this morning that Dad was going out and it seemed a good chance for a few of us to get together. Not that I can't have friends round when he's here, but he always wants everything so formal, and it seemed a bit hard on Stella to subject her to an evening with one of the school governors.'

'Stella?' Val paused with her hand on the door. 'You mean the new schoolteacher?'

'Mm.' Hilary opened the oven door and checked the casserole. The pheasant had been jointed and was simmering gently in a rich gravy with mushrooms, chicken stock and a glass of her father's port wine. 'I ran into her in the village the other day and we had quite a chat. She seems very nice and she hasn't met a lot of people yet. And I've asked Felix as well – the new curate, you know. And—' The doorbell rang and she shut the oven door. 'That's someone now. I'll go and let them in. Go in the little sitting room and sit by the fire, Val, and we'll all have a drink. Stephen's around somewhere.'

Val did as she was told. The sitting room was smaller than the main drawing room, and comfortably shabby. It was the room that had always been used for the family when they were on their own, and the furniture was big and old-fashioned, with sagging leather sofas and armchairs. Blankets were thrown over them, and the dogs had their baskets in one corner. Newspapers and copies of *Horse and Hound* littered a side table, and a small bookcase was filled with books on hunting, horse management and Dartmoor ponies. A copy of Crossing's *Dartmoor* lay open and face down on the top, and a map had been folded up beside it.

Stephen was in one of the armchairs. He looked up and grinned when Val came in, then jumped to his feet. 'Hello, Val. Sherry?' He went over to a trolley on which stood two or three bottles. 'Dry or sticky brown?'

'Dry, please.' Val had learned to enjoy sherry when she'd been in Egypt. At home, it would have been sweet or nothing. She thought briefly of those days, then pushed the memory away. She sank into one of the other armchairs and accepted the glass that Stephen handed her.

In the hall, she could hear voices – a woman's, light and eager, and the deeper tones of a man. Her skin tingled.

Hilary had said she'd invited Felix, but this didn't sound like the curate's well-modulated light tenor. The woman's voice must be Stella's. And the man's . . . ?

Oh no, Val thought in dismay. Please, no. I've managed to avoid him all these weeks. I can't spend a whole evening being polite to him here.

Stephen was saying something, but she barely heard him. She sat tensely in her chair and watched the door. In another moment it was open and Hilary was ushering the schoolteacher Stella Simmons into the room. And behind her, as Val had known he would, came Luke Ferris.

'Here we are,' Hilary said cheerfully. 'And Felix is coming too, he arrived just as I was shutting the door. So that's all of us. Steve, give everyone a sherry, will you, while I see to the potatoes.' She whisked out of the room, leaving the door open for Felix to come in. The little group stood awkwardly for a moment, and then Stephen broke the ice by moving over to the trolley.

'You all know each other, don't you,' he said. 'No need for introductions. Val, have you met Luke before? He lives in the old charcoal-burner's cottage.'

'I know.' Her voice sounded as dry as a dead leaf. 'Hello, Luke.'

'Hello, Val.' His look was questioning, as if to ask if they should acknowledge that they already knew each other, but she returned it blankly. *Just don't mention Egypt*, she begged him silently. *Just pretend we're strangers*.

She turned to Stella. 'How are you settling in, Miss Simmons? Do you like the school? Are the children behaving?'

'Oh, let's use first names,' Stephen broke in, handing Stella the sweet sherry she had asked for. 'I can't be bothered with all this Miss Something and Mr Something Else. Anyway, Stella's too pretty a name to be kept under wraps. It means star, doesn't it? A bright, twinkling star.'

'I think it does,' she said, blushing. 'I'm not sure if my parents knew that, though. I can't have looked much like a star when I was born.'

'Didn't Winston Churchill say that all newborn babies looked like him?' Stephen asked. 'I'm sure he was wrong in your case, Stella. Not that I've seen all that many newborn babies. None at all, come to think about it. Have you, Val?'

'Well, there was Robin,' Val said rather shortly. 'My brother's little boy. But he looked more like a coconut.'

'Is he in the school?' Stella asked. 'There's a Robin in Miss Kemp's class. I wouldn't say he looked like a coconut, but he's got ginger hair!'

'No, he's only two. It'll be three years before you have him. And he doesn't look like a coconut now. It was just when he was born.' She caught Luke's eyes on her and turned away. 'Come and sit down on the sofa, Stella, and tell me how you like Burracombe. Did you know the area before you came here?'

'No, I'd never been to Devon, although I lived in the country for a while when I was little. I was evacuated to a small village near Southampton. I lived in a vicarage, as a matter of fact,' she added, smiling at Felix who had taken the armchair nearby.

'A lot of big houses were taken over for evacuation,' Stephen remarked. 'This one was. It became a school of some sort – I know we had to move out to one of the bigger cottages. I didn't mind too much as I was only home during the holidays, but it must have been hard for my mother.'

'The vicarage I was in hadn't been taken over,' Stella said. 'The vicar still lived there, with a housekeeper. He had four children billeted on him – two boys, and my sister and me.' She stopped abruptly, then went on, 'He was a lovely man. He used to play games with us, and we used to sell him our sugar.'

'Sell him your sugar?' Val echoed, thankful that the subject had been changed. 'Whatever do you mean?'

'They had a black-market operation going,' Stephen said with a grin. 'Did he flog it round the village? Was it "brandy for the parson, baccy for the clerk" like in the poem we learned at school?'

'No, it was nothing like that,' Stella said, laughing. 'It was just that we all had our sugar ration and he gave us a penny for every teaspoonful he put in his tea. He had a very sweet tooth,' she added thoughtfully. 'In fact, looking back, I can't believe that anyone *could* like that much sugar in their tea. I think he probably did it just to give us some extra pocket-money.'

'He sounds a very kind man,' Felix remarked. 'As of course, he should be, considering his calling!'

They all laughed at this. Felix had left off his dog-collar tonight and was wearing a plain white shirt and dark blue jacket, with a maroon silk tie. His fair hair glinted almost gold in the soft light. He sat back in his armchair, sipping his sherry, looking like any other young man out for an evening with friends.

'I've never known another vicar like him,' Stella said. 'He was more like a little boy who'd never grown up. He'd make snowmen and have snowball fights, and play cricket or collect conkers – and the housekeeper used to tell him off for getting his feet wet, just as much as the rest of us!'

The door opened and Hilary came in. 'Supper's ready,' she announced. 'I hope you're all nice and hungry. We're having it in the breakfast room – I know that sounds ridiculous, but it's cosier in there.'

They followed her. Stella, who had never been in the Barton before, was somewhat over-awed by the spacious rooms and comfortable furniture. Having spent years in an orphanage, she was accustomed to large buildings and plenty of rooms, but she was also more used to utilitarian furniture, linoleum floors and bare walls or, at best, a series of notices, mostly admonishing. Here, the floors were of polished wood with Persian rugs, and on the walls were pictures – portraits or landscapes. Those in the hall were mostly oils, but when she went into the breakfast room she saw that the pictures here were water-colours, softer and more gentle.

The room was looking warm and cosy, with a good fire burning and the lamps casting a soft light. Deep red velvet curtains were drawn across the French windows that led into the garden. The square table was laid for six, with a large candelabra in the middle, and on the sideboard was an array of vegetable dishes and two bottles of wine.

Stella took her seat nervously. When Hilary had invited her to supper, she'd expected something more like her evening meal in Dottie's cottage – fish pie, perhaps, or cauliflower cheese. This looked like a smart meal, and she hoped she would use the right cutlery. She glanced at Luke, who had sat beside her, and he gave her a reassuring smile.

To Val, accustomed to meals round the kitchen table at the farm, it also looked formal, but she had been in the Barton dining room and knew that from Hilary's point of view this bordered on the casual. She saw Luke smile at Stella and wished again that Hilary hadn't invited him. Of course, Hilary didn't know that they'd met before – she had left Egypt before Luke had arrived. She was just being kind to a newcomer to the village. For the first time, Val wished she had confided more deeply in her friend. But I thought I'd put all that behind me, she thought miserably. I never expected to have to face it all over again . . .

Stephen was handing her a warm plate with two pheasant joints on it, bathed in dark, rich gravy. 'Is that all right for you, Val? There's more if you'd like it.'

'No, this will be plenty.' She began to help herself to

mashed potatoes and cabbage. 'Hilary, this looks lovely. You must have been slaving away all afternoon.'

'Well, I'm used to cooking a meal every evening,' Hilary said a trifle ruefully. 'At least it's a bit more productive than some of the other things I have to do.' Stephen began to make violin-playing gestures and hum 'Tell Me, the Old, Old Story', and she made a face at him across the table. 'It's all right for you. You're a man – you can do as you like.'

'Oh, can I! Not if Father has anything to do with it. If he has his way, I'll be trapped here in Burracombe for the rest of my life.'

'And aren't I already?' she asked with a sudden twinge of bitterness.

'You could leave,' he said. 'You could just walk out, the same as I'm going to do.' And as she hesitated, he added, 'Give me one good reason why not.'

'I had to come home when Mother was ill. You know that. You were still at school, Baden was dead – there was nobody but me to do everything. She needed me.'

'I know,' he said more gently, 'but she doesn't need you now, does she? And all Dad wants you for is a housekeeper. Why don't you do it, Hil? Why don't you tell him you want to live your own life, and just walk out?'

Hilary stared at him. Then she said in a low tone, 'I can't. You know I can't. He has to have someone, doesn't he? And it's not going to be you, is it – so what else can I do but stay?'

The others sat silent, listening to this exchange. Stella, embarrassed, stared at her plate. Luke's lips twitched. Felix said, 'Are you sure you want us to hear this?'

Hilary glanced round, as if startled to find that there were other people in the room. Stephen shrugged. 'Doesn't bother me. We're not talking family secrets. Anyway, it's practically all Hilary and I do talk about these days. I'm leaving – I got my call-up papers today. I'm going into the RAF.'

An excited babble of conversation broke out at once, as if everyone was relieved at the change of subject. Patiently, Stephen answered questions on whether he actually wanted to go into the RAF and what his father thought about it. 'He hates the whole idea – wanted to get me into his old Regiment. But I want to learn to fly, so I've told him there's no go. I expect he's grumbling about it to the Latimers at this very minute, but he can grumble till the cows come home. I won't change my mind.'

'Well, there you are, then,' Hilary said. 'Isn't that just what I've been saying? You've got your National Service to do, and you can make up your own mind what to do after that. But I left my chance of a career behind when I came home to look after Mother. By the time she died, I was running everything here. What would Dad do if I left him now?'

'Well, he could employ a housekeeper. And a few maids, like we used to have.'

'Stephen, don't be silly! Why do you think we don't have them now? People don't want to do those kinds of jobs any more. We have Jackie to come in every day, and Dottie Friend when I need help with some cooking, and we're lucky to have them, but proper, live-in housekeepers are like gold dust. You can still get them, but some are better than others and then they don't always stay, and Dad would hate having to get used to a series of strange women. And with neither of us here, he'd be so lonely. How could I go off and leave him here all by himself, with just a housekeeper?'

'Well, I still can't see why you shouldn't be able to lead your own life, the same as I can,' Stephen said, and Val nodded.

'I agree with Stephen,' she said. 'It's not really fair, is it?

I mean, look at me – I'm nursing, I could be a senior Sister, even a Matron. And Stella here could end up as a headmistress. Look at the things you did in the war, Hil – there must be heaps of jobs you could do.'

Hilary shrugged. 'Well, maybe. Anyway, let's change the subject. It's horribly bad manners to go on about our problems in front of guests.'

When everyone had finished their casserole, commenting how tasty it had been, Hilary gathered up their empty plates and Val helped her carry them out to the kitchen. They brought in the stewed fruits and cream and as Hilary was serving them out she turned to Luke. 'How have you settled down in the charcoal-burner's cottage? Are you comfortable there?'

'Very,' he said, smiling at her. 'I've got a woodburning stove that I can keep going all night, and plenty of kindling just outside the door. I get my water from a spring in the woods, and I've even dug over a little patch to grow a few vegetables. With those and the odd rabbit that I find on my doorstep, I can be quite self-sufficient.'

'Better be careful what you say about rabbits,' Stephen warned him with a grin. 'Father'll have you up for poaching, and since he's the local magistrate I wouldn't give much for your chances!'

Luke chuckled. 'I meant it literally. I find them on my doorstep, neatly skinned and – er – emptied out. I'm pretty sure I know who puts them there, but I wouldn't want to get him into trouble.'

'Jacob Prout!' Hilary said. 'It's all right, Luke, old Jacob can do as he likes. He's immune from prosecution.' She turned to Stella. 'Jacob's the old man you see doing all the hard work around the village – hedging and ditching, sweeping leaves, clearing culverts . . . '

'Mending roofs and drainpipes,' Stephen said.

'Building sheds –'

'Mowing lawns –'

'Digging his garden –'

'Looking after the churchyard –'

'Digging graves –'

'Ringing the church bells –'

'And anything else that anyone wants doing!' Hilary finished with a laugh. 'Burracombe simply couldn't afford anything to happen to Jacob.'

'Oh yes, I've seen him,' Stella piped up. 'He's nice. I took the children out for a walk the other day and he was showing them all kinds of things in the hedgerow – the tiny leaves of primroses starting to come up, and some old birds' nests from last year, and even some frogspawn in the pond. They all know him.'

'Everyone knows Jacob,' Hilary said, and Felix nodded.

'He showed me the bells the other day. We went up the little spiral staircase into the bell-chamber and he told me how he has to keep an eye on the frames and the wheels, and grease the bearings so that they'll ring smoothly. He says the ringers are going to get up a special competition for the Festival.'

'Oh, the Festival!' Hilary exclaimed. 'Do you know, if I've had Mrs Warren round here or on the telephone once this past month, I've had her a hundred times. If she has her way, it'll be Burracombe that everyone comes to, not London! We'll put their Exhibition right into the shade.'

'What's being planned?' Luke asked. He turned to Stella. 'You mentioned something about the children.'

'Yes, they're going to be in the pageant. Mrs Warren wants all the different groups in the village to take part, and each one will represent some event in local history.' She spoke a little shyly at first, then more eagerly as she gained confidence. 'The children are planning to do Queen Victoria's Jubilee. We're going to borrow two horses and a farm-cart from your father,' she looked at Val, 'and dress it all over like a golden carriage, with some of the children in the costume of courtiers, and the others will be outriders on ponies or part of the procession. It's a lovely idea because they can all join in and they don't have to remember any words!'

'And who's going to be Queen Victoria?' Stephen asked curiously. 'Miss Kemp? She's not really the right size – Victoria was tiny, wasn't she?'

'No, it's going to be Miss Bellamy.'

Stephen spluttered with laughter. 'Constance Bellamy? You're not serious!'

'Yes, I am. She's ideal. She'll look just like the Queen when she's dressed in the right clothes. I don't know what you find so funny about it,' Stella told him severely.

'Neither do I, now I come to think of it,' he admitted. 'You're right, she's ideal. Especially when she's got that "We are not amused" look on her face!' Stephen chuckled again. 'I'm looking forward to this pageant more than I expected. Oh, damn! I probably won't be here.'

'You'll have to ask for special leave,' his sister told him dryly. She turned to Luke. 'We're putting on a craftwork exhibition in the village hall. Things people make, that sort of thing. The big Exhibition is all about what Britain is making and doing, so we thought we'd do the same. I wondered whether you might like to put in some of your paintings.'

'Oh, but he probably won't be here then either!' Val blurted out. They all turned and looked at her, and she flushed scarlet and looked down at her plate. 'I mean, I don't suppose he will be. He's only rented the cottage for six months. Or so someone told me,' she finished, wishing she had never opened her mouth. For the first time in the entire evening she looked across the table and met Luke's eye. 'You'll be going back to London soon, won't you?' It sounded almost like a plea.

Luke didn't answer for a moment. Then he said, 'Actually, no, I don't think I will. I've already talked to Colonel Napier about renting for a further six months. Possibly even longer. I like Burracombe and there's so much to paint, I don't know when I'll be ready to move on.' The words *if ever* hung in the air.

'There you are, you see,' Hilary said in a pleased voice. 'So would you let us have some of your paintings in our exhibition? They'd be such a wonderful addition to our other crafts.'

'What else will there be?' Felix enquired.

'Oh, heaps of things. A lot of the women do needlework – embroidery, making clothes, that sort of thing – or knitting. And some of the men do very good woodwork.'

'Jacob Prout makes walking sticks,' Val contributed, her voice still a little tense. 'He marks them out in the hedges when he's layering and grows them into the right shape. They take two or three years to be ready, and then he cuts them out and carves them and polishes them up. Sometimes he puts a sheep's horn on top for a handle. They're real works of art.'

'And Bert Foster – you know, Felix, the butcher – does wood-turning in his spare time. He makes lovely fruit-bowls. We've got one here, see, on the sideboard.'

'Yes. If anyone cuts down a tree he goes round to get some of the wood.'

'Well, Burracombe never ceases to amaze me,' Felix said. 'So much talent in one small village!'

'I think it's going to be quite an event,' Hilary said. 'And on the day itself, as well as the pageant, there'll be games and races for the children and a few stalls and sideshows – someone's got a coconut shy somewhere, and there'll be bowling and guessing the weight of the sheep, and all that sort of thing. On the Saturday there'll be the bellringing competition, of course. It's going to be a really big weekend.'

'All we have to hope for', Val said, 'is good weather.'

Luke glanced across the table and she met his eye again. She looked away quickly, but not before he said, 'I think I hope for even more than that. Don't you, Val?'

There was a tiny silence. She looked down, furious with him and hoping that nobody else had noticed. Then Hilary got to her feet and began to collect their plates.

'If everyone's had enough, I think we'll go back into the sitting room and have coffee. Unless you gentlemen want us ladies to be traditonal and retire while you sit over your port.'

'Good grief, no!' Stephen exclaimed. 'Much rather be in comfortable chairs with you girls.'

Val and Stella helped Hilary to carry the dishes out to the kitchen. Hilary gave Stella the coffee-pot to carry and then touched Val's arm.

'What's the matter?' she asked in a low voice. 'I've been watching you all evening. Something's upset you. Is it Steve?'

'Stephen?' Val looked at her in surprise and shook her head. 'No, it's not him. It's – oh well, I just wish you hadn't invited Luke Ferris, that's all. I don't like him.'

'Don't you?' Hilary asked in amazement. 'Why, he seems a really nice person. What don't you like about him?'

'I don't know. I don't trust him, that's all. The way he looks at people.' Val was floundering and took refuge in irritation. 'I just don't *like* him, Hilary – isn't that good enough?'

She walked stiffly through the kitchen door and back to the sitting room, leaving her friend staring after her. For a moment, Hilary felt at a loss. She had never known Val to behave like this. She had never known her to take an instant dislike to someone, especially someone as pleasant and likeable as Luke Ferris.

Shaking her head, she picked up the jug of cream and went to join the others.

Chapter Eighteen

Easter, coming towards the end of March, was a cold weekend and, to make matters worse, it was also the weekend on which Summer Time started and the clocks were put forward by an hour. On Easter Sunday, Stella woke to a damp, gloomy morning and heard the bells ringing for early service. She sat up and looked out of the window.

Dottie's garden was filled with spring flowers. Primroses clustered on the bank in a carpet of gold, spangled with purple violets. Daffodils filled the borders and there were still some nodding white hellebores beneath the bushes of azalea and rhododendron. Soon these would be out too in a glory of colour, but Stella hadn't been here last spring, so she didn't yet know what colour they would be.

She slipped down under the covers again. She and Dottie were going to the mid-morning service together, and then Luke was coming for Sunday dinner. Luke didn't go to church services but he had painted the grey stone building from a number of different viewpoints around the village. He had even got Basil Harvey's permission to paint inside, and had told Stella that this was one of the pictures he would show at the exhibition.

It had become accepted now that Luke and Stella would go for a walk most weekends, either on Saturday or Sunday, and that Luke would also come for dinner or supper on one of those days. Stella felt easy and comfortable in his company, and he was the one person she could talk to about her sister Muriel. After a few attempts to find out about her when she had been in the Children's Home, she had given up. Everybody there had lost their family one way or another, and the staff had made it clear to her that they expected her to forget. One had told her that sisters weren't anything to write home about anyway (a remark that had baffled Stella for a long time) and she hated her own sister and hadn't spoken to her for five years. After that, Stella had kept her sadness to herself and even Matron, who had become a friend, didn't know how much she still thought about and grieved for her little Muriel.

She won't be so little now, she thought, looking past the garden and over the roofs of the cottages opposite to the field and moors beyond. She'll be nearly nineteen. A young woman. I probably wouldn't even recognise her if I saw her. If she walked down the lane and knocked on Dottie's door, I wouldn't know her. The thought was such a sad one that tears came to her eyes and trickled down her cheeks on to her pillow.

Just then, Dottie knocked on the door and came into the room bearing a tray. 'Morning, Stella. I've brought you your breakfast in bed for a special treat. Why, whatever be the matter, my flower? You'm crying!'

'Not really,' Stella said, sitting up. 'Oh Dottie, you shouldn't have! I'm the one who ought to be bringing you breakfast in bed. You spoil me.'

'Well, 'tis time someone did.' Dottie arranged the tray on Stella's lap. There was a bowl of cornflakes, a pot of tea, a little jug of milk and two slices of toast with a small dish each of butter and honey. 'I don't suppose you can remember the last time you had breakfast in bed.'

'No, I can't, except when I was ill. And you had to be really ill in the Children's Home to be brought breakfast in bed. You had to be in the Sick Bay, and nobody wanted to go there – Sister was a real tyrant.'

Dottie's eyes softened. 'You poor little soul. Well, 'tis all over now and if I think you need a bit of pampering, I'll give it to you. Been looking tired lately. I reckon they children have been playing you up a bit.'

'No, they haven't. They're very good. It's nice to have a couple of weeks' holiday, though. Next term's going to be very busy, getting ready for the pageant and everything.'

'Oh yes, the whole village is getting excited about that. I will say that for Mrs Warren, she do get things going, though Miss Bellamy don't see eye to eye with her.' Dottie chuckled and moved towards the door. 'Now, us'll need to leave for the church about twenty to eleven, 'tis always full of an Easter Day. I've got a nice shoulder of lamb to cook for our dinner. I'll put it in the oven before we go and the potatoes are all ready to pop in soon as us gets back . . . You take your time now, have a nice lie-in.'

She closed the door and Stella ate her breakfast, gazing out of the cottage window and thinking how different her life was now. She only had a few memories from before the war – mostly a warm blur of the house in Portsmouth, she and her sister playing on the hearthrug in front of the fire while their parents sat in their armchairs listening to the wireless Mike Simmons had built, or chatting. Her father hadn't been there all the time, of course – as a Merchant Seaman he'd been away more than he'd been at home – but in Stella's memories he was always there. And so was Muriel, her younger sister, with her toy animals and the doll Princess Marcia from which she had never been parted, until the night of the bombing.

She and Luke had discussed endlessly how they could set about finding Muriel. Up by the standing stones that first Saturday, they'd talked about it and he'd offered to help. 'I know a lot of people in London. They might know where records are kept.' Stella had felt a warm rush of gratitude towards him then. And he'd been as good as his word and had come back from his next visit to London with a list of names and addresses. Stella had written letters, explaining her problem, and they'd been sent off. Some had written back, regretfully apologising for not being able to help, but one had thought he might know a way of finding out which orphanage Muriel had been sent to. Some children, like Stella, had gone to local council homes, some to church orphanages, others to Dr Barnardos. Using Portsmouth and Southampton as starting-points, it might be possible to find out where she'd gone.

Stella finished her breakfast and got out of bed. She took the tray down to the scullery and had her morning wash there. Dottie had already prepared all the vegetables and they were in their pans, ready to be cooked when she came back from church.

What a lucky little girl Maddy had been to stay here with Dottie during the war, Stella thought. What a shame it couldn't have been Muriel.

'I've had a letter from my friend,' Luke said after dinner. After doing the washing-up, he and Stella had gone out for a walk, leaving Dottie to have her Sunday-afternoon nap by the fire. Alfred was curled up on her lap, the picture of contentment, a knitted yellow mouse with purple stripes resting under one paw. The little room was cosy and warm, and Luke had remarked that the best thing about going out on such a day was knowing you could come back in again.

'A letter? You mean from the man I wrote to about Children's Homes?' Stella's face flushed with excitement. 'What does he say?'

'Well, it's not quite as encouraging as I'd hoped.' He saw her face fall and added hastily, 'But it's not all bad news. He says that a lot of records got lost in one of the bombing raids – the building they were kept in was destroyed. And if Muriel was adopted, they might not tell you anything anyway. I think it's kept secret.'

'Oh.' They walked on in silence and Luke glanced down at her and laid his arm across her shoulders. 'Oh,' she said again in a small, disappointed voice.

'It doesn't mean there's no hope,' he said gently. 'We can still keep writing to the different authorities to see if they have records of Muriel. And I thought we might put a notice in one of the newspapers too. The big ones, like *The Times* or *Daily Telegraph*, often have notices in them asking people to get in touch.'

'You mean, "where they will hear something to their advantage",' Stella said. 'I don't know, Luke. Anyone could answer that, pretending to be Muriel. I was thinking only this morning, she will have changed so much by now I might not even know her.'

'You could soon find out. There must be lots of things you would both remember from when you were little.'

'Yes, but Muriel's two years younger than me – she won't remember as much. And anyone who wanted to pretend to be her would only have to say they'd forgotten all that. People do, you know. If they've had horrible times they just push the memories away.' She thought for a moment and then said, 'I'll do it if there's nothing else left, but let's try writing to the authorities first.'

They were walking slowly, Luke with his arm still laid lightly across her shoulders, when Val Tozer came round the bend in the lane, mounted on her father's riding horse Tricker. They were face to face almost before any of them realised it, and they all stopped, Luke quickly removing his arm.

'Hello, Val,' he said pleasantly. 'Nice to see you. Where have you been hiding yourself? I haven't seen you since we had that wonderful pheasant casserole at the Barton.'

'I've been busy,' she said shortly. She glanced down at Stella. 'I hope you're well.'

'Yes, thank you.' Stella felt embarrassed, without knowing quite why. There was no reason why she and Luke shouldn't walk along the lane together, and his arm had only been laid across her shoulders in a friendly way. Perhaps Val felt it was unseemly behaviour for an assistant teacher even so. 'It was a lovely evening,' she added.

'Goodness me, I'd almost forgotten it,' Val said carelessly. 'I'm surprised you haven't gone away for the Easter holidays. You must need a break from Burracombe.'

'No, not really. It's nice to have a chance to get to know the area, and Luke's been showing me around.' For some reason, Stella still felt the need to explain their being together. 'We've been to all sorts of places.'

'Nice for you,' Val said coolly. 'Well, I mustn't keep this fellow standing.' She patted her horse's neck. 'Walk on, Tricker.'

They stood looking after her. 'How funny,' Stella said. 'She didn't seem very pleased to see us, did she? I thought she was such a nice, friendly person.'

'She is,' Luke said absently, and then turned to continue along the lane. Stella glanced at his face. He wore a strange, shuttered expression as if he didn't want to talk and, although she still had questions to ask about their search for her sister, she decided to remain silent for the time being. Luke too had moods, she'd discovered, and although he was never unpleasant, there could be a chill in his voice which she found upsetting. It was best to wait until he got over whatever it was that had disturbed him.

They were through the fields and out on the open moorland before either of them spoke. And neither Val nor Muriel were mentioned again that afternoon.

Val was rubbing down Tricker, watched by the Shires, who

had just enjoyed their Sunday off, when Luke came into the stableyard. She felt his presence before she saw him, and her skin prickled. Slowly, she straightened, turned and faced him.

'What are you doing here?'

'Val,' he said, 'I need to talk to you.'

'I don't see why. We've said all we need to say to each other.' She turned back to the horse.

'No, we haven't.' He moved a step nearer. 'Val, we've got to sort this out. We can't live in the same village, running into each other all the time—'

'So go somewhere else.'

'Val!'

'Well, why not? Burracombe's not your home. You're only renting the cottage. You could move away, easily. I wish you would.'

'But why?' he asked. He spread out his hands. 'Val, we never quarrelled in Egypt. I know we did wrong – we went too far – but it was because we loved each other. I thought so, anyway. I know I loved you.'

Val flushed and glanced round, but the yard was empty. The afternoon chores of feeding chickens and shutting them in the barn had been done, and her father and Tom were in the milking parlour. Alice and Joanna were indoors and Jackie was out somewhere with Roy Pettifer, who would be going away next week. 'Don't say such things,' she hissed. 'Go away!'

He stared at her and sighed. 'Val, what is it? Why won't you talk to me?'

'I've told you. I told you in Egypt that it was over. I should never have let it happen. And when Eddie was killed . . .'

'Yes,' he said. 'I'm sorry about that, I really am. Please believe me, Val, if he'd still been alive, if you'd been married to him, I'd never have—'

'What do you mean, *if* we'd been married? Of course we'd have been married!'

'I'm only saying that for one thing, I didn't even know you lived here, and for another that if you'd been married to Eddie I'd never have said a word. I mean that, Val. But you're not married. He isn't here. And you've still got your own life to live.' He paused and Val, her colour high, scrubbed hard at Tricker's sides. 'Hasn't there been anyone else at all?'

'That's none of your business!'

'Perhaps not. But don't you think I have any rights at all, Val? I love you. I've loved you all these years, and I'll probably love you for the rest of my life. Doesn't that give me the right at least to know if there's a chance for me? If there *is* anyone else, if you really don't have any feeling for me at all, then I'll leave you alone. Otherwise—'

'Leave me alone anyway,' Val said. 'Go back to your little schoolteacher.' She faced him again. 'Do you really expect me to believe you, when I've *seen* you with her? Why, even this afternoon, not two hours ago, you were walking through the village with your arm round her, for all to see! You're always together. You go walking on the moors every weekend – she told me that herself. And it's quite obvious that she's in love with you.'

'Don't be ridiculous! There's nothing between Stella and me – nothing at all. We're friends, that's all.'

'So why were you kissing her then?' Val demanded.

Luke stared at her. '*Kissing* her? I've never kissed Stella in my life!'

'I saw you!' Val cried. 'Up on the moor – the first Saturday in January. I'd been on night-duty and I was walking back from the main road, and I saw you going up towards the standing stones. You put your arms round her and kissed her. I *saw* you, Luke.'

There was a small silence. Then he said quietly, 'All

right. You did see what you obviously thought was a kiss. But it wasn't like that.'

'Oh no? So just what was it like, then? Tell me, Luke.'

He sighed. 'I can't tell you. It's Stella's business.'

'Oh, so you've got secrets!' Val knew she was sounding childish now, but she couldn't help it. She felt confused, upset, angry and let down. And she didn't know why she felt like this. I don't care about him any more, she thought, rubbing the curry comb hard over Tricker's side so that he whickered in surprise. I don't even like him. I wish he'd go away.

'Val,' Luke said patiently, 'Stella and I are friends, that's all. There are no *secrets* – not the sort you mean. It's just something I'm helping her with, but it's her business and I don't think I can tell you about it.' He reached out towards her. 'Look, Val, what's this all about? What *is* this idea you've got into your head about Stella, and why does it matter so much?'

'It matters because you keep saying you love me and I don't know why!' Tears streamed down her face and she shook her head angrily. 'Why do you keep saying it if it's not true? What are you doing to me, Luke? Why are you tormenting me like this?'

'Val!' He reached out and tried to grip her hands, but she lashed out at him, and turned away. He dropped his hands back to his sides. 'Val, I'm not tormenting you, I'm telling you the truth. I do love you. I always have. I imagine I always will.' He spoke a little bitterly. 'Do you think I *want* to feel like this? Seeing you, looking just as lovely as you ever did, wanting you so much and knowing that it's never going to come right between us. I know we did wrong in Egypt, but it all seemed so different out there, we were thousands of miles from home, and we fell in love. Don't shake your head like that – we *did*. I know you loved me just as much as I loved you. But you were going to be married and we couldn't do anything about it. I knew you couldn't let Eddie down. I knew you had to keep faith with him.'

'I didn't though, did I?' she said tonelessly. 'I *didn't* keep faith, and I *did* let him down.'

'It was only the once,' he said, and reached out again for her hand. This time, she didn't reject him and he took it in his and turned it over, stroking the palm with his fingertips. Val shivered but made no other response and after a moment he went on, 'It was something I'll never forget, Val, that one night. It was all I'd ever dreamed of. It's in all my paintings, you know. They might be of fields and woods and moorland, but the feeling behind them all is the feeling you gave me that night. The love and the joy. I've never regretted it. I never will.'

'You're lucky then,' she said bitterly. 'I've regretted it a million times.'

Luke looked at her. Her eyes were dark with anger and remorse. A sense of futility and despair flooded into his heart and he let go of her hand and stepped back.

'I'm sorry, Val. I didn't realise you felt so strongly. I won't bother you again.'

Val said nothing. She turned back to the horse and laid her face against his neck. Luke hesitated, wanting nothing more than to take her in his arms and comfort her, but he knew that she would rebuff him. After a moment, he turned away and walked slowly out of the yard.

Val heard him go. She didn't lift her head until she was sure he had gone. When she did, Tricker's neck was soaked with her tears.

Jackie was also out walking, with Roy Pettifer. They had roamed for miles across the moors, golden now with gorse in full flower, and were at the standing stones, high above the village. As the afternoon drew towards evening, the clouds had drifted away and the sun came out low in the west, throwing long shadows behind the great rocks.

'When gorse is out of season, kissing's out of reason,' Roy quoted, proving that kissing was by no means out of reason today. 'Oh Jackie, I do love you.'

'I love you too. I'm going to miss you so much.'

'I know. How am I ever going to be able to bear being away from you?' He nuzzled her neck. 'You'll write to me, won't you?'

'Every day. I just hope they don't send you to Korea. I couldn't bear it if you had to go and fight. Our Tom says they sent people to the Front after only a few weeks' training in the war.'

'I don't suppose they do that now,' he said. He ran his hand down her neck and touched her breast with his fingers. 'Jackie . . .'

'Oh Roy,' she said longingly. 'Roy, I don't know . . .'

'Please,' he said. 'Please, Jackie. We won't get another chance before I go. It'll be weeks before I get home again – months. Please.'

'I don't know,' she said again. 'Suppose something happens? If my mum found out, she'd kill me – and suppose I had a baby? They'd send me away, I know they would, and you wouldn't be here. We wouldn't even be able to get married. I don't know what would happen to me.'

'You won't have a baby, I'll make sure of that. It'll be all right, Jackie, honest. Please.' He drew her down into the shadow of the stones, his hands and lips urgent. Jackie could feel her body melting. Roy's pleas had been growing ever more insistent over the past weeks and she knew that she wouldn't be able to resist for much longer. Almost, she wished that the next few days were over and the decision out of her hands. I'd be safe then, she thought. I wouldn't have to worry any more.

Jackie's desire for Roy was just as strong as his for her, but always in her mind was the fear of pregnancy. Alice and Ted had told their daughters often enough that they must never 'bring trouble to the doorstep' and Jackie knew very well what that meant. The 'little bundle of joy' would be a bundle of misery and pain if it came out of wedlock, and it was the girl who suffered, especially if the boy didn't 'stand by her' and marry her. The whole thing could be smoothed over then and people would forget in time, but if Roy were far away in the Army – perhaps even in Korea – Jackie would have to face it all on her own.

'Nothing'll go wrong, maid,' he whispered, stretching out beside her and stroking her from neck to thigh. His hand strayed a little further, and she shivered and felt her last few shreds of resistance slip away. 'Please, Jackie. I love you so much. Please . . .'

Jackie lay beside him, her heart thumping. His body was warm and hard against her and she seemed to have no strength other than to return his kisses. The sky wheeled above them and the shadows of the standing stones were flung like blankets of darkness on the close-cropped turf. I can't stop him, she thought. I can't. I don't want to stop him. Oh Roy, Roy, *Roy* . . .

Both were quiet and a little subdued as they came down the hill half an hour or so later. Roy held Jackie's hand tightly in his and when they reached the farmgate they stopped and turned to face each other.

'Jackie,' he said, 'you know I love you, don't you?'

'Yes,' she whispered, her eyes meeting his for a second. 'I love you too, Roy.'

'You're not sorry, are you?'

'No. I don't think so.' But the fear was there again and he heard it in her voice.

'Nothing will happen, Jackie. It really won't. You'll be all right.'

'Yes,' she whispered again, her voice almost too small to be heard.

He hesitated. 'It was good, wasn't it? You liked it?'

'Yes.'

There was a slight pause. Then Jackie reached over to unlatch the gate. 'I'd better go in now. Mum likes us all to have supper together of a Sunday night.'

'I'll see you again, won't I, before I go away?'

'Oh yes, of course you will. It's not till Friday, is it?'

'No,' he said. 'Not till Friday.'

A few hours ago, Friday had seemed unbearably close. Now the week stretched ahead like a desert, and neither of them knew how to cross it. Jackie slipped through the gate and closed it. They stood on either side, looking at each other.

'Oh Jackie,' he said again, 'I do love you. I love you even more now. And when I come back again we'll get married. I'll bring you an engagement ring, whatever your dad says, and they'll have to let us get married. They'll *have to*.'

Jackie looked at him. He could see the fear in her eyes, the dread that they might have to get married before that, if only he weren't going to be too far away. He felt a great, heavy load on his shoulders and he didn't know how to shed it.

'Goodnight, Jackie,' he said at last, and reached across the gate to put his arms round her shoulders. 'Goodnight, my flower.'

'Goodnight, Roy.' She leaned closer and let him kiss her. They drew apart, looking at each other with a sadness that they hardly understood, and then Jackie turned and walked across the farmyard to the back door.

Roy watched as she went inside. He saw her figure silhouetted against the light, and presently he too turned away and walked slowly back to his own home.

Chapter Nineteen

With Easter over, preparations for the pageant began in earnest. Joyce Warren and Miss Kemp had been busy during the holidays, planning the schedule, and the committee met in the vicar's drawing room on the first Wednesday in April to discuss their progress. As secretary, Joyce read a detailed account of the discussion at the first meeting, most of which the others had forgotten and would rather not have been reminded of, and gave a brief report of the state of the finances. Since there were so far neither income nor outgoings, this didn't take long. She then prepared to reveal the plans that had been made so far.

'Perhaps Miss Kemp would like to tell us about that,' the vicar suggested. He had been quite grateful to Joyce for her lengthy note-taking, since it had given him a chance to recover his breath after dashing through the door at the last minute, explaining that he'd had to slip over to lock up the church. Joyce, however, had been displeased by his lateness and had given him a severe frown. He smiled back affably and turned a benign gaze on the headmistress.

'Well,' Miss Kemp said, unfolding a sheet of paper, 'Mrs Warren and I have been roughing out a few ideas. We thought it would be nice if Burracombe's part in the Festival were to stretch over the whole of the Bank Holiday weekend – that's the first weekend in August. I believe the bellringers are happy to hold their competition on the Saturday?' She glanced at Ted Tozer, who nodded. 'We thought the Craft Exhibition could be open in the village hall every afternoon – except Sunday, of course – and serving teas as well. And we could have the flower displays in the church all over the weekend, with a special service on the Sunday, and then the Pageant and Summer Fair, with games and races and so forth, on Monday.'

'That sounds very exciting,' Basil said. 'Plenty going on. Are we going to be able to man the village hall every day? There'll have to be someone on each stall, and a regular army of people serving teas.'

'That's no problem. Each group that has a stall will provide helpers, and the WI will look after the teas. We'll need some of the men to organise the field for the games and races. Oh, and we'll need prizes, of course.'

'The villagers are usually very generous with that sort of thing,' the vicar observed. He turned to Hilary. 'Will you be loaning your donkey for rides?'

'I should think so. He rather enjoys it. He loves the children and they give him far too much to eat. Could you suggest carrots, rather than sugar lumps, Miss Kemp?'

'I'll try. The mothers will certainly be pleased not to have to provide a donkey with sugar out of their rations.' She went back to her papers. 'We've been planning the pageant itself, too. Burracombe Through the Ages – from the Standing Stones through the Bronze and Iron Ages, medieval times, the Elizabethan Age, the Civil War, right through Victorian times to the present day. The children are very excited about it.'

'Will there be enough of them to do all that?' Felix asked. 'Stella – Miss Simmons – was telling us about your plans for the Victorian Jubilee scene, and I got the impression that the whole school was going to be involved. How will they manage the rest of the scenes?'

'They won't,' Joyce said before the headmistress could answer. 'Other village groups will be taking care of the rest.

It will be like a carnival, with a procession through the village, starting at the ford and ending on the village green where there will be country dancing and a maypole. I shall be in charge of the country dancing, of course.'

'Why "of course"?' Felix murmured to Hilary and she gave him a reproving frown. 'Because she runs the village folk-dance group,' she whispered back. 'Surely you knew that.'

Mrs Warren coughed irritably. '*If* I could have everyone's attention—' she began, but Basil Harvey interrupted her gently.

'Actually, I think it was Miss Kemp who was telling us about this. Are all the groups willing to be involved in this, Miss Kemp? There's a lot of work in organising these fancy-dress affairs.'

'Costume,' Joyce corrected him. 'Fancy-dress is for parties.'

'Costume, then.' He raised his eyebrows enquiringly at the headmistress.

'Mrs Warren and I are working together on this,' she said. 'We've approached the Whist Club, the Scouts, Cubs, Guides and Brownies – most of them are in the school anyway – the Gardening Club and the Young Farmers. Let's see, who else ... oh yes, the Drama Club, the bellringers – that's right, isn't it, Mr Tozer? – the Mother's Union and the WI. We're hoping to portray seven ages or events, and there'll be famous personalities too, like Sir Francis Drake who lived so near here and did so many wonderful things for us, Queen Elizabeth herself, and some other famous Devonians like Sir Walter Raleigh, Captain Scott, the Pilgrim Fathers and Sherlock Holmes.'

'Sherlock Holmes?' Felix echoed in surprise. 'Was he a Devonian?'

'We were thinking of the *Hound of the Baskervilles*,' Joyce told him reprovingly. 'One of Conan Doyle's most famous stories. We're hoping that someone will loan us a dog.'

'Well, you can't have my Rupert,' Constance Bellamy said at once, and they all laughed at the idea of Miss Bellamy's dachshund trotting along beside Sherlock Holmes and trying to look like a ferocious hound. Although, as Charles Latimer remarked, he had once given the postman a nasty nip on the ankle.

'I'm sure you'll be able to have one of the foxhounds,' Hilary said. 'I'll ask my father.'

'And then there's a Queen,' Joyce continued. 'We'll have to have a Queen.'

'A Queen?' Felix queried.

'Like a May Queen,' Hilary told him. 'One of the little girls, with a couple of Princesses. They love it. And it isn't just for the day itself – they'll be Queen and Princesses for the whole year. They'll give prizes at the Christmas party – that sort of thing.'

'Oh yes, I see. So how are they chosen? A beauty competition?'

'Oh no,' Miss Kemp said, horrified. 'That gives the children quite the wrong idea. No, we choose in various different ways, sometimes by ballot with the whole village voting, sometimes by fund-raising – the girls all have tickets to sell, and the one who sells the most becomes Queen – but for myself, I favour choosing on character. The other ways depend too much on families and favouritism. I think being appointed Queen should be an honour that can be achieved only by the child herself.'

'I agree,' Basil said, and Constance and Charles Latimer both nodded in concurrence. Joyce Warren looked doubtful.

'Presumably that means that you would have the choice, or at least, the casting vote, since you know the children best. Don't you think that could be construed as favouritism as well?'

Miss Kemp looked annoyed. 'I don't think so. I try to run my school fairly in all respects.'

'Yes, but Mrs Warren does have a point,' Basil said. '*We* all know that favouritism wouldn't enter into it, but you know what parents can be like. Perhaps it would be better if we appointed a small sub-committee of judges – people who know the children well. You would be on it, naturally, and if I might suggest myself, since most of the village children come to church and Sunday School, and perhaps the doctor? He sees them all at one time or another.'

Miss Kemp inclined her head. 'I think that would be excellent.' She allowed herself a small glance at Joyce Warren, who didn't seem to know whether to be pleased or irritated. She had gained a point, but since she had no children herself and as little contact as possible with those who lived in the village, she could hardly propose herself as a judge of character.

The meeting ended after another hour, and they all went out into the twilight. The evenings were getting longer now and it wasn't dark until after nine. Felix and Hilary sauntered along the lane together and walked out to the end of the village, where the Burra Brook ran under a narrow stone bridge and made a shallow ford. There were a few trees there, scattered over a small green, and they sat on a fallen trunk and watched the water. Since their ride together in early January they had developed a pleasant friendship, and Hilary often invited Felix over to the Barton to help exercise the horses. A few times they had gone into Tavistock for dinner at the Bedford Hotel or to go to the cinema. They'd laughed at *Father of the Bride*, thrilled to *King Solomon's Mines* and wept at *Sunset Boulevarde*. At least, Hilary had wept. It had been too dark to see if Felix had as well.

'You can see a kingfisher here sometimes,' Hilary murmured. 'Just a flash of colour, like a jewelled necklace going by. And a dipper, too, bobbing on a rock in the middle of the stream.'

'It's a beautiful area,' Felix said. 'I've really fallen in love with it.' He paused, then said, 'This Festival's going to be rather fun, isn't it?'

Hilary nodded. 'Yes. It'll be a busy summer but I love these village events. They bring everyone together. Not that it all goes smoothly, mind you – there are usually a few tears before bedtime! – but generally it all works out pretty well, and we're glad we made the effort.'

'Will you be going on one of the coach trips?' he asked. 'There seem to be quite a few being arranged – the WI, the church, and the school outing for a start. I'm not sure which I'll be able to go on. Mr Harvey will be expected to go with the church group, of course, and we can't both be away at the same time – certainly not on a Saturday in the middle of the summer. Someone might want to get married!'

'Not with half the village away in London, surely. Still, it wouldn't do if the coach broke down on the way back and neither of you could be here for Sunday services.' She stretched her arms above her head. 'You're a bit like the Royal Family, aren't you – you can never go anywhere together in case something goes wrong.'

'And I should think that's the only resemblance you're likely to find.' They were both silent for a few minutes and then Felix said, 'Are you still wondering what to do with your life, Hilary? Now that Stephen's gone into the RAF and there's just you and your father, it must be rather lonely for you.'

She shrugged. 'I don't know what to do. Sometimes I feel as if I'll go mad if I have to stay here much longer, and then I realise how involved I am with the village and I don't

213

see how I can ever leave. Look at tonight, for example – all those arrangements for the Festival. I really do enjoy all that, but do I want to be doing it for the next forty years? It would be different if I were married to someone who was involved in the village as well, but I'm not.'

'Well . . .' Felix began, but she went on without hearing him.

'I mean, like my mother, or Grace Harvey. Being married to the Squire or the vicar is a career in itself – there are things it's traditional for the wife to do. She's a person in her own right. But me, I'm just the Squire's daughter – the *spinster* daughter – with no real place of my own.'

'Is that what you'd like to be?' Felix asked. 'Married to a man who was involved? I rather thought you wanted a career of your own, something like the one you had when you were in the ATS.'

'Well, yes. That probably is what I'd really like. I know it's an awful thing to say, Felix, but I *enjoyed* the war. I enjoyed having responsibility and authority. It showed me all kinds of things I'd never dreamed of – things I could do, things I was capable of. It was like stepping out from the shade into the sunshine.'

'I expect a lot of young women found that too,' Felix said.

'I expect they did. And some of them were able to go on and discover even more about themselves.' She got up restlessly and wandered down to the brook. 'Well, there's nothing I can do about it. Father would have a heart attack if I suggested leaving now. And he's lonely too, you know, Felix. He's lost the two people who mattered most to him in the world – Mother and Baden. He's disappointed in Stephen, and there's only me left. I can't walk out on him now, can I?'

'No,' Felix said, coming down to join her. 'I don't think you can.' He stood for a moment as if lost in thought, then caught at her arm. 'Come on! Let's go back over the stepping-stones. First one to fall in's a sissy!'

Hilary laughed and followed him across the big, flat rocks that had been placed at the side of the ford. It was a game that children had played for centuries. Halfway across, her foot slipped and she gave a little shriek. Felix turned and caught her, holding her steady as she regained her balance. They stood still for a moment, close together on the stones, and then he let her go and stepped across to the bank.

They walked back along the lane in silence and said goodnight at the entrance to the Barton drive.

Stephen Napier and Roy Pettifer had departed for their National Service within a week of each other. Hilary, expecting Jackie to mope for a while and then cheer up, was concerned when the young housemaid seemed to grow more miserable. She decided to broach the subject one morning while they were polishing the dining-room silver.

'We had a letter from Stephen today,' she said cheerfully. 'He seems to be quite enjoying the RAF, even though they haven't let him anywhere near an aeroplane yet. How's Roy getting on in the Army?'

'All right,' Jackie said listlessly. She was pale and there were dark rings under her eyes.

'Does he write to you much, or doesn't he get a lot of time?'

'Oh, he writes two or three times a week. I write every night. He's got his mum to write to as well,' she said a little defensively, as if Hilary might think this not enough. 'Anyway, he's not much of a hand at writing letters, Roy isn't.'

'Neither's Stephen,' Hilary said with a smile. 'A few lines was all we ever got while he was at school, and we were lucky to hear at all when he was at Cambridge. I don't think men are very good at putting their thoughts on paper.' She waited for a moment, then said gently, 'You mustn't let it stop you enjoying your life, Jackie. You ought to be going out with your friends, not sitting at home every evening.'

'I don't feel much like going out. Anyway, there's not all that much to do.' She rubbed half-heartedly at one of Baden's rowing cups.

'There's the Country-Dance Club. There's usually a dance to go to somewhere on Saturday evenings. And aren't you in the Rangers?'

'I suppose so. I haven't been to a meeting for a while.'

Hilary looked at her more closely. 'You are all right, aren't you, Jackie? You're not worried about anything?'

The girl's head came up and she flushed. 'No. Why should I be?'

'No reason. I just wondered.' Hilary took the cup from her hands. 'Look, I'll finish this. Why don't you make some coffee? My father will be wanting one soon and I'm sure I'm ready. We'll have that and then do the vegetables.'

Jackie said nothing but went to put the kettle on. Hilary watched her and sighed a little. I hope they didn't do anything silly before Roy went away, she thought. It would be a dreadful pity if Jackie were to spoil her life at this stage.

Jackie knew all too well that she and Roy had been silly, and was even more anxious than Hilary that her life shouldn't be spoiled. She finished her chores in silence, and left as usual at four o'clock, but instead of going straight back to the farm, she walked in the other direction, along the lane and into the woods, where she found a log to sit on and buried her face in her hands.

We shouldn't have done it, she thought. It wasn't all that special anyway – it was cold and uncomfortable and there was a rock digging into my back. And I just felt like crying afterwards. It wasn't a bit like I expected.

And now there was this awful, nagging worry that, whatever Roy had said, she might find herself having a baby. She didn't know what he'd done to prevent it. He hadn't used anything – just pulled away from her rather quickly and roughly. She didn't know if he'd been in time or not. It had all been so hurried; they'd both been afraid they'd be seen, and they'd both felt guilty afterwards. She thought he might have been almost as disappointed as she was.

She didn't even know if he still loved her. Could he, after that? It didn't seem to matter now whether she loved him or not; all that mattered was whether she was pregnant, and whether he'd be able to marry her quickly if she was. Whether her mother and father would let them marry – and the thought of telling them brought her out in a cold sweat of terror – and whether Roy would even want to marry her.

Oh, it's such a mess, she thought. It's such an awful, awful mess, and no one can help me. Whatever am I going to do?

Chapter Twenty

'We need to choose the Festival Queen and Princesses as soon as possible,' Miss Kemp said to Basil as she came out of church the following Sunday. 'We may have to make new frocks for her and her attendants. There are two or three in the school dressing-up box, but they're beginning to look a little worn now.'

'Yes, and that means extra expense,' Joyce Warren chimed in. She had come out just behind the headmistress. 'Where is the money going to come from for all this? We didn't discuss that at all at the last meeting. In my opinion, it should have been at the top of the agenda.'

'I rather fear you may be right,' the vicar admitted. 'I suppose we'd better organise some fund-raising. I'd hoped that each of the different groups would finance themselves, and we could repay them from money raised at the Fair itself.'

'And there's another thing we haven't discussed,' Joyce said triumphantly. 'Entrance fees – charges for the side-shows. It all has to be taken into account.'

'Yes, yes, I realise that.' He glanced past her at the queue of churchgoers waiting to shake his hand and tell him what a lovely sermon he had preached. 'Perhaps we can foregather at some other time and go over all this. Meanwhile, I think Miss Kemp is right and the choosing of the Queen and Princesses is our first priority.'

'Excellent,' Miss Kemp said. 'I'll give it some thought and let you and the doctor have a list of my suggestions.'

She walked on. Joyce, who could think of no reason to insist on being involved in this, moved away as well, and Maggie Culliford, who lived with her husband and five children in a ramshackle cottage at the end of the village, took her place.

'Did I hear you say there's going to be a Festival Queen?' she asked eagerly. 'I'll enter my Shirley. Her'd look a real picture in a nice frock. Blue satin, that's what would suit her best. Would her be able to keep it after?'

'I don't think so. Miss Kemp's hoping that one of the dresses already in the school box will do. If not, new ones will be made but I expect they'll go in with the others afterwards. Unless the Queen provides her own,' he added without much hope.

Maggie's face fell. 'Oh, if it's Teacher has the choosing of 'em there'll be no chance for my Shirley. Miss Kemp don't like her, never has. Always picked on my Shirley, she has. Do you know what she said the other day?' Her voice was beginning to rise with indignation and Basil's heart sank. The Cullifords were known all over the village for their quickness to take offence and their ability to make trouble. Their cottage was an eyesore, the garden a heap of rubble and thick with weeds. Jim Culliford hadn't had a regular job for years but eked out a living by doing casual labour on farms all over the area. The children were dirty and poorly clothed, and Miss Kemp was at her wits' end trying to teach them to read and write, when they came to school at all. They only attended Sunday School just before the summer picnic and the Christmas party, and Maggie herself was only seen in church when there was something to be gained from it. He'd wondered why she was here this morning, and now he understood. News of the Festival

Queen had leaked out. Miss Kemp was right – the sooner the choice was made, the better.

Alice Tozer came out next, with her daughter Jackie. Basil smiled at Alice and looked thoughtfully at Jackie. She seemed pale, and quieter than usual. She caught his eye, gave him a wan smile and looked away again.

'Ted asked me to tell you he and the other ringers are going up to Lydford next Saturday, for the Barnaby Shield competition,' Alice said. 'There'll be a service in St Petrock's, of course, and tea in the Nicholls Hall. You'd be welcome to go along and hear the ringing and have a cup of tea.'

'That sounds very interesting. I'll try to go. Lydford hold the Shield at the moment, do they?'

'No, 'tis Little Burracombe, but you know they got woodworm in the frames and the deacon says they got to be repaired before they can do a lot of ringing there. They'm all right for Sunday services and practices, like, but 'twouldn't do for the bells to be rung all day. So they decided to have it at Lydford.'

'Well, it will be a nice day out,' Basil said. 'I'll make a note of it. And how are you, Jackie?' The girl was standing there with her head drooping, taking no interest in the conversation – quite unlike her normal bright self, he thought. 'I hope you haven't caught this nasty cold that's been going round?'

'I'm all right, thanks, Vicar,' she said lifelessly, and looked at her mother. 'Can I go home now? I feel a bit tired.'

'Yes, I'm coming now anyway.'

Alice waited as her daughter moved away and Basil said quietly, 'Are you sure she's all right, Mrs Tozer? She seems very downhearted. I suppose she must be missing Roy. They're very fond of each other, aren't they?'

'A bit too fond, if you ask me,' Alice said grimly. 'And if

there's anything wrong, she hasn't told me about it – but to tell you the truth, Vicar, I've been a bit worried this past week or more. She don't seem to have no energy and no interest. It's not like her. I just hope—' She caught herself up and shook her head. 'I dare say she's just moping, that's all, but the sooner she gets over it the better. She's too young to be mooning over one boy.'

'Girls, eh!' the vicar said with a laugh. 'I know all about it – I've got two of my own, don't forget. Right, everyone seems to have gone now – I'll go and tidy up in the vestry, if young Felix hasn't already done so, and then we can all go home for our Sunday dinner. Will I see you and Ted at Evensong, Mrs Tozer?'

'I expect so.' Alice said goodbye and then walked down the church path after her daughter. I'm going to have to talk to that young woman, she thought resignedly. If even the vicar's noticed how she looks, everybody else must have done so as well. But it's too soon for anything to be showing up yet, surely. When was it Roy had gone away – just after Easter. And it was only the middle of April now.

It wasn't too soon to be worried, though. And if ever a girl looked worried to death, young Jackie certainly did.

The William Barnaby ringing competition was a big event, drawing teams from miles around; this year, there were eighteen entries. Some came in the morning and some not until the afternoon, and ringing would begin at 10 a.m., when the judges were safely ensconced in their upstairs room at the Castle Inn, close enough to the church for the ringing to be heard, and after the times had been drawn from Bill Barnaby's old trilby hat, kept specially for this task. Each team would go into the church, sound three notes on the tenor to warn the judges that they were ready, then raise the bells from their resting position, ring the required changes, and lower them again. The whole thing took about twenty minutes and the judges would be listening for every tiny fault – such as two bells striking too close together, or too far apart. The rhythm had to be kept perfectly all the way through, so that the ringing sounded almost mechanical, and it was difficult to believe that there were men pulling the ropes and listening for the calls.

Little Burracombe, as last year's winners, got first pick from the hat in the afternoon and were to ring at four o'clock, immediately before service. Peter Tavy, Meavy and Walkhampton went before them, and the first team to ring would be Whitchurch, followed by Lamerton. After the service, and a tea of pasties and cake, would come Bere Ferrers, Lydford itself and Kelly. Burracombe drew the last time.

'Separated you two all right, then, boys,' the captain of the Walkhampton ringers said to Ted Tozer. 'One before tay, t'other last of all. Well, there'll be some good ringing to listen to the rest of the time, sure enough!'

'I'll have a pint off you for that,' Ted retorted. 'We'm taking the Barnaby Shield back home with us, where he belong, aren't we, boys?' The others laughed and nodded their agreement, and then fell silent as the first three notes were struck to announce that Whitchurch were ready to begin.

There wasn't much to do except listen while the ringing was going on, but as they stood around the churchyard and on the knoll of the old castle ruins, the ringers took the opportunity to catch up with all the gossip from the various villages. A new vicar at one, a new baby at another, the death of a respected ringer and farmer at a third. Several were planning their own celebrations of the Festival of Britain, and they were all interested in the Burracombe ringing competition. 'Us'll be along for that,' one grizzled old farmer said, leaning on his stick, 'but you could've had

222

it on a better date – right in the middle of haymaking, us'll be.'

'Well, you can nip back home to carry on once you've rung,' said Ted Tozer, who had the same objection but couldn't see any way round it. 'So long as you'm here for the judging at the end.'

'Oh, us'll manage that,' the old man said with a wink. 'Got to be here to collect our prize, ain't us? And have a pint in the Bell to celebrate.'

'Don't count your chickens,' Ted warned, but just then the Whitchurch ringers came down the path and the Lamerton team went in for their session. All the teams had been practising the special peal – Kilkhampton Queen's – which had been chosen by the previous year's winners, and they'd also been allowed one practice at Lydford itself. A good many of the villagers had come out to hear the ringing as well, including one couple who were complaining loudly.

'Is this going on all day?' the man demanded furiously in a nasal accent. He had recently moved from a large city 'up-country' and ran a men's tailor's shop in Tavistock. 'I never heard anything so ridiculous! They've been at it since ten o'clock. We came here for peace and quiet, not to be hounded out of our own house by wretched church bells.'

'Nobody's hounding you out,' Ted Tozer said. 'And the bells were here before you come. Didn't you think to ask if they was ever rung?'

The man glared at him. He wore a new-looking tweed jacket, an open-necked shirt and a yellow cravat. 'Of course we knew they'd ring – on Sundays. We're even prepared to accept them ringing on Tuesday evenings, to practise, if they've absolutely got to. But we did *not* expect to have this noise inflicted on us all day Saturday. And that's not all. They've been ringing on other evenings as well, for the past three weeks. It's out of all reason.'

'It's a competition,' Ted told him. 'Us've all had the right to come here once and practise. It's in the rules.'

'Your rules, perhaps! Nobody gave *me* these rules. Why do bellringers have competitions, anyway? It's not a sport!'

''Tis our sport,' someone else joined in. ''Tis the finest way us knows of spending our spare time. Ringing one night a week, and twice on Sundays – why, you couldn't have a finer hobby. Good for your body, good for your brain, and you won't find a better fellowship nowhere than in the tower. And *most* people appreciates listening to it, too.'

'But not all,' the tailor's-shop manager said nastily. 'And not all the bloody day long.'

'Now, look here,' Jacob Prout said angrily. 'There's no call for that sort o' language. Bells is Church business and we'm all decent Christian churchgoers.'

'Well, you wouldn't think so,' the man said. 'Disturbing the peace like this. And I still don't see why you have to have competitions. I don't call that Christian.'

'Christians can have competitions, same as anyone else—' Nathan Pettifer began, but Ted interrupted him.

'There be a good reason for ringing competitions. Keeps the standard up. Keeps people interested. Devon ringing be the finest in all England,' he went on proudly. 'None of that "scientific" stuff they goes in for up-country, we sticks to good old call-changes. Devonshire as clotted cream, they be, the finest bell-music there is.' He lifted his hand towards the church tower, where the bells were just coming down at the end of their peal. A few of the listening ringers were looking at each other and nodding appreciatively.

The shop manager was unimpressed. '*You* obviously think so. Not everyone agrees with you. How long is all this going on, anyway?'

'Should be finished by eight-thirty,' Ted told him cheerfully. 'Nine at the latest.'

'Eight-thirty? Nine? You mean it's going on all evening as well?' The man's jaw dropped. 'Well, we'll see about that! I'm going straight round to the vicarage to complain.'

'Why not wait till the vicar comes here?' the Lydford captain suggested. 'He'll be along at half-four to conduct the service.'

'Service? What service?'

'Why, the one us always has at a competition. You know what a service is – a few hymns, some prayers and a bit of a sermon. Vicar's been looking forward to it. Learned to ring hisself once, he did, only he don't get much time for it these days. You come along then, I'll introduce you to him meself.'

The shop manager scowled at him, then turned on his heel and marched away, stiff with indignation. The ringers laughed.

'How long's he been in the village, then?' Nathan asked the Lydford captain.

'About six or seven months, and he's been nothing but trouble since the minute he arrived. First it was old Mrs Barrow's cockerel crowing early in the morning. "Well, when d'you expect them to crow?" she asked him. Then it was my cows, after I'd turned 'em out in the spring. Said they was snuffling and snorting round his back window all night long. "So why did you buy a house with fields right up to the wall?" I asked him. Now it's the bells. I dunno why people like him comes to live in a village, I don't really.'

'Don't reckon he'll live here long,' Nathan said, and the others laughed again. Townies who came to live in the country and then complained about country life got short shrift.

Towards the end of the afternoon, Felix arrived. The crowd was making its way into the church, ready for the service, but the Burracombe ringers were still outside, listening intently and flicking their eyebrows at each tiny fault.

''Tis Little Burracombe ringing now,' Ted told him. 'And they ain't doing too bad neither, though it hurt me to say so. Best so far, any road.'

'They're the ones holding the Shield now, aren't they?' Felix asked. 'Mr Harvey sent his apologies, by the way. He's had to go and see Mrs Jessop, who lost her husband last week. I say,' he moved away a little, gazing down at the big, flat tombstone against which they were all leaning, 'look at this!'

The others glanced at him. 'Oh, that be the clockmaker's tomb. Well known, that be.'

'It's wonderful,' Felix said. He read the long inscription, cleverly likening the life of the watchmaker, George Routleigh, to that of one of his clocks or watches, and ending with the words:

> *He departed this life*
> *Nov 14 1802*
> *Wound up*
> *In hopes of being taken in hand*
> *By his Maker*
> *And of being thoroughly cleaned,*
> *repaired*
> *And set a-going*
> *In the world to come.*

'What a beautiful inscription,' he marvelled. 'I wonder who wrote it.'

'George hisself, likely as not,' Nathan Pettifer said. 'Don't suppose no one else had the book-learning.'

'No, probably not. I wonder how much business a clockmaker would have in Lydford. It seems an odd sort of trade for a country area.'

'Not at all. Think of all they wonderful old grandfather clocks they made in Callington.' The bells sounded their final round and Ted turned to go into the church. 'Better get inside. Service'll be starting any minute.'

Lydford had been an important place in medieval times, Felix realised as he talked to the ringers over their tea of pasties and sponge cake provided by the Lydford ringers' wives. The castle, whose ruins stood next to the church, had been a substantial courthouse and prison, and the infamous Judge Jeffries had sat here. There had once been a mint, where silver pennies were made, and the Castle Inn had some on show. Although it was now a mile or more away from the main road, the village used to be on the main stagecoach route and had originally been built by King Alfred.

'What – the one who burned the cakes?' Felix asked, at that moment in the act of taking a slice of Victoria sponge from a passing plate.

'That's right.' The wife of the Lydford ringing captain paused and smiled at him. 'Us don't use his recipe here, though!'

The competition ended at last, with an almost perfect peal from Burracombe. When they emerged from the ringing chamber at the back of the church, all the others were seated in the pews, waiting for the three judges to bring their results. It had been a long day for them, locked into their little room above the bar, and they looked pleased to be outside again. They traipsed up the aisle and stood facing the churchful of ringers. The tension, which had been growing all day, tightened its hold on them all.

'Well, boys, you all know what we'm here for,' Bill Brimacombe said in his deep, gravelly voice. He was one of the most respected ringers in the whole diocese. ''Tis the Barnaby Shield, and before us tells the results I'd like to take a minute or two to remember one of the finest ringers and the finest gentlemen any of us is ever likely to know. Old Bill Barnaby were an institution in these parts. He started ringing when he was no more'n ten year old, far too young some folk might say, but he were a strong little tacker and determined to do well, and he had a good ear. That be vital for a bellringer, a good ear. He picked it up quick as you like, and by the time he were sixteen he were in the village team, and ringing treble as well. And didn't they win some competitions, back then! Well, boys, I won't go all through his life or we'll be here all night, and you knows it as well as I do, but let's just say he rung the bells every Sunday, come rain or shine, and 'twas only the war that stopped un, when no bells was allowed. But who was it struck the first note as soon as VE Day was declared? It were Bill Barnaby, that's who, even though he were eighty-five year old if he were a day. And he rung till he were eighty-seven, and darn near – beg pardon, Vicar – *pretty* near died with a rope in his hand. So that's why this Shield was give in his honour and that's why the team that takes it home can be proud to put it on their wall.'

He paused for breath and his audience gazed stolidly back at him. If applauding had been allowed in church they would all have clapped heartily, but such displays were frowned on and there was no other way, apart from a few throat-clearings and low murmurs of agreement, that they could show their appreciation. In any case, they had done that this afternoon and evening, by ringing to the best of their ability.

Bill Brimacombe, having regained his breath, looked down at the sheet of paper in his hand and continued, 'Well, boys, with no further ado as they say, I'll tell you the results . . .' He read the list in reverse order, giving the number of faults counted and any other remarks made by the judges. 'Tenor was too slow, spoiled the whole rhythm . . .'; 'Second clipped the bigger bells every time . . .'; 'A beautiful peal once they was up, but the rise let 'em down . . .' Finally, he came to the top three.

'Fourth team: rung a fine peal, we didn't think 'twould be beat, thirty-four faults. Sixth team: like clockwork, pleasure to listen to, twenty-nine faults. But the best of all was the last team of all – hard put to it to make any marks at all on our papers but it come out at twenty-one faults.' Bill looked up over his glasses and beamed, and his fellow judge Lès Wonnacombe stepped forward and announced what everyone knew by then: 'The winners of the William Barnaby Shield are Burracombe, with Little Burracombe second and Meavy third.'

They did clap then. Church or not, you couldn't not clap the winners, especially when they'd all rung such grand peals. Ted Tozer, red with pleasure, collected the First Certificate and Shield, thrilled to the marrow to be taking it back to what he and the others considered its rightful place, while the Little Burracombe captain conceded defeat with a shake of his hand before going up for the Second Certificate. Every team received a certificate, signed by the judges and with a picture of St Petrock's Church on it, which would be pinned on the ringing-chamber walls with all the others. Those who hadn't won were only slightly disappointed; they all knew the best teams deserved their honours, and there was always a next time. Practice made perfect – or, as Jacob Prout remarked, as near perfect as you could ever be, being human. And there was the Burracombe Festival competition to look forward to, and still time for a pint in the Castle Inn.

The only person who hadn't enjoyed the day was the manager of the gentlemen's outfitter's. But he was nowhere to be seen.

Chapter Twenty-One

'Well, who do *you* think would be the best choice for the Festival Queen?' Miss Kemp asked with more than a tinge of exasperation in her tone. She, the vicar and Charles Latimer had met in her small living room in the school-house to discuss the problem, and so far had not been able to come to any agreement.

'I know you don't like the idea of Shirley Culliford,' Basil said ruefully, 'but she's really a sweet little girl and it would give her such a boost. That family always seems to be at the end of the queue when anything good is being given out.'

'That's hardly fair! They don't take advantage of what's offered them. If Shirley came to school in a clean frock once in a while, or even if she came to school at *all*! She misses at least one day a week, you know, and there's always some excuse – her mother's ill, or one of the little ones has to go to the doctor and there's no one else to take her – it's endless. If we did make her Queen, there would be no guarantee that she'd turn up to the events.'

'Well, would that be so very dreadful?' Basil asked mildly. 'There aren't really very many, are there? The Christmas party and the Carol Service – and perhaps one or two other children's occasions. And I'm sure she would come, if only for the party itself and the chance to wear a pretty dress.'

'That's just what I mean. They're only out for what they

can get, the Cullifords. You must know that, Vicar. How often do they come to Sunday School? Only when there's a party or outing in the offing.'

'I know. But I'm always hopeful that with encouragement . . .' He looked at the doctor. 'What do you think, Charles?'

'I can see both sides. Miss Kemp naturally wants the honour to go to a child who really deserves it by her behaviour and natural comportment, while you would like to give encouragement to a child who really doesn't get very much and – who knows – might really blossom if she only had some trust shown in her. Of course a little girl like, say, Jenny Pettifer would make an excellent Queen. And the Nethercott twins would be delightful as her attendants. But I have to confess to a soft spot for Shirley Culliford. I don't think she's ever had a really pretty frock in her life, or one that wasn't handed on to her or bought at a jumble sale. It does seem a shame, somehow . . .' He let his voice trail off, pensively.

'Oh all right,' Miss Kemp said. 'I know when I'm beaten! Shirley Culliford it is, and when her mother starts to complain about the dress and the rehearsals – if the child ever turns up for them at all – I'll send her to you. Along with all the other parents who think it should have been *their* child,' she added with bitter emphasis.

'Dear me, Miss Kemp,' Basil said, 'I would never have thought you a vindictive woman.' The doctor laughed and Miss Kemp shook her head in an I-give-up gesture. 'Now, who do you suggest as Princesses?'

'The Nethercott twins,' the other two said in unison, and the headmistress added, 'At least we can make two dresses from a single pattern and know they'll fit. And you must admit they'll look charming.'

'I think they'll *all* look charming,' Basil said. 'Do you

think you've got dresses in the school box that will do, Miss Kemp?'

'There are those bridesmaids' dresses from Margaret Courtenay's wedding two years ago,' Miss Kemp said thoughtfully. 'They might fit the twins – but there's another thing: Shirley Culliford's a year older than they are but she's no bigger. If anything, I'd say she's smaller. Don't you think that it's going to look rather foolish, having a Queen smaller than—'

'No, I don't,' Basil said firmly. 'Remember Queen Victoria. She must have been smaller than almost everyone in Court. And Constance Bellamy is going to look exactly right, taking her part in the pageant. Our own dear Queen herself is quite petite, you know.'

'Yes, of course,' Miss Kemp said meekly. In truth, she was beginning to feel rather ashamed of herself. She had been so pleased at the thought of Jenny Pettifer – top girl in the school, clever, well-behaved and pretty as well – being Festival Queen that she had rather lost sight of other aspects. The vicar was right. Shirley had none of the advantages that the Pettifers, humble though they were, had given their children, and you never knew what miracles a little encouragement might work. Even if nothing came of it, it might be the only time in her life when that little girl had a chance to shine.

'I'll find a nice dress for Shirley,' she said. 'Dottie Friend may run something up – she's a marvel with a sewing-machine. It'll be all right, Vicar. Shirley will make a lovely little Queen.'

'Excellent,' he beamed at her, and the matter was settled. They discussed a few other items, and then the two men departed, leaving Miss Kemp alone in the schoolhouse with her ginger cat Dundee, wondering just how it had come about that she had been persuaded to give up her choice of neat, pretty little Jenny Pettifer in favour of the dirtiest little ragamuffin in the school.

And what are the Pettifers going to say? she wondered, fondling Dundee's ears before getting up to make her bedtime Ovaltine. They were as sure as I was that Jenny would be chosen.

The life of a village schoolmistress was not easy at times.

Shirley Culliford could not believe her luck when she was told that she was to be Festival Queen. Miss Kemp had, as usual, called the whole school together for morning prayers and after 'Our Father' and a rendering of 'All People That On Earth Do Dwell', with Stella at the piano, she asked them to sit quietly while she gave out the notices.

'As you all know, we're going to London soon to see the Festival of Britain.' The children wriggled and grinned at each other excitedly. 'We'll be going on a charabanc from Tavistock and some of your mothers are coming too.'

'My daddy's coming,' Ernest Crocker said loudly from the back of the room, and two or three others joined in. 'Mine is, too.' 'And mine.' 'Mine says he wants to but he'll be too busy on the farm—'

'Yes, and some fathers are coming as well,' Miss Kemp said, raising her voice against the hubbub that threatened to break out as the children explained to each other which of their parents was coming and why the other wasn't. 'And it's going to be a lovely day for everyone, but you must remember that London's a very big place and we've got to be careful not to lose each other. We'll all need to keep together.'

'Will we be going to the Tower of London?' Micky Crocker, Ernest's brother, asked. 'They cut off people's heads there. I'd like to see someone have their head cut off.'

'Micky!' Miss Kemp exclaimed, as some of the girls cried out in horror and the smallest Culliford burst into tears. 'Of course we shan't see anyone have their head cut off. We're not going to the Tower – and anyway, they don't cut people's heads off now. Stop crying, Betty, he was only teasing. He's a very silly boy. Lend Betty your hanky, Shirley . . . Because she's your sister, that's why . . . Well, why haven't you got a hanky? Silly question,' she muttered beneath her breath. 'When did any of the Cullifords have a hanky? Here you are, you can have one out of the box.' She opened the shoebox which contained various articles of property lost and never claimed, including a few small and tattered handkerchiefs which she had washed and ironed for just such an emergency. 'Here you are – now, blow. Good girl.'

Order restored, she resumed her lecture on staying together while at the Festival of Britain. 'Now, we'll leave here at half past seven in the morning. I know that's rather early but London's a long—'

'We'm always up by six,' remarked Brian Madge. 'My dad has to be up for milking and my mum works for the doctor, so she has to get all the housework—'

'Yes, well, it's not as early as all that. I'm sure you can all be on the green by seven-thirty, with clean clothes on and your faces washed. We won't be taking any dirty children,' she could barely prevent her eyes from straying to the Cullifords, all present this morning for a wonder, but in their usual grubby state, 'and remember you'll need to bring sandwiches. And some money for ice creams.' She remembered the outing they had gone on to Exmouth once, when Pamela Briggs had taken a pound note and lost it the minute she got off the bus, spending the rest of the day in tears. 'No more than a shilling each, mind. That will be quite enough.'

'Us won't be able to take a shilling each, miss,' Shirley Culliford said. She had finished wiping her sister's face and returned to her own seat. 'My mum can't afford a shilling for us, not with having to pay to go on the charabanc as well.'

'I don't expect everyone will take a shilling,' Miss Kemp said. 'I just mean that nobody's to take more than that.' She looked at the little girl in front of her. Her frock was dingy, the colours faded from much use and washing. Her fair hair was tangled and looked as if it could do with a good shampooing. She quite possibly had headlice – it was some time since the school nurse had been to inspect them. Yet there was a wistfulness in her large grey eyes that Miss Kemp suddenly longed to take away. She wanted to see the child smile. I don't think I have ever seen her look really happy, the teacher thought.

'And now,' she said, 'I've got some very special news to tell you all. News that you've all been waiting to hear, about our own celebrations here in Burracombe.' The childen buzzed with excitement. We'd better take them out for a walk after this, she thought, to let off some of this steam. And drill in the playground wouldn't be a bad idea, either. 'You all know that the vicar, Mr Harvey, and Doctor Latimer and I have been talking about who should be Festival Queen. Well, we had a meeting last night and we thought very, very hard, and we've made up our minds.' She paused. Jenny Pettifer was already swelling slightly with pride and the others were looking at her. Oh dear, Miss Kemp thought, and went on rather quickly, 'And we've decided that the Burracombe Festival Queen shall be – Shirley Culliford!'

There was complete silence. The headmistress sneaked a swift glance at Jenny and saw her face pale, then flush bright red. Her friends turned to her and there was a confused mutter of, 'It's not fair – it should have been you! You're prettier than Shirley Culliford. It's not fair. Not fair – not *fair*!'

Shirley was sitting very still. Her face too had turned

scarlet. To her astonishment, Miss Kemp saw tears in the big grey eyes. They ran down her cheeks, making streaks on her dirty face. Her lips quivered.

'No, Miss,' she said. 'That's a mistake. I can't be Queen.'

'Why not?' Miss Kemp forgot the indignant mutterings of the other children and beckoned the trembling child out to her. Reluctantly, Shirley came, and the others fell quiet and stared at her.

'Now then,' Miss Kemp said, 'tell me why you think you can't be Queen.'

'Because I'm not pretty enough, miss. Jenny's much prettier than I am. Everyone says so. And nothing nice like that ever happens to us. Cullifords don't get good luck, my dad's always saying that.' She lifted the hem of her frock to wipe her eyes and remembered that she had a handkerchief tucked into her knickers. She fished it out and scrubbed at her face.

Miss Kemp glanced at Stella and saw the compassion in the assistant teacher's eyes. Stella would sympathise more than most, the headmistress thought, remembering the tumultuous childhood she'd been told about. There must have been times when she thought that luck never came her way. She had a brief sense of what it must be like to live without hope, and turned back to the piteous figure before her.

'Shirley,' she said, 'you must never, never think like that. Good luck can come to any of us, and nice things can happen to you just as much as to anyone else. And being Festival Queen is nothing to do with being pretty – although I happen to think that you're every bit as pretty as . . . as any little girl in the school.' It would never do to make a direct comparison with Jenny, and it wouldn't be true – Jenny was a particularly attractive child. 'We all have different ways of being pretty,' she went on, 'so we'll hear no more about that. And today, you'll be able to go home

236

and tell your mother and father that nice things *do* happen to Cullifords. Because today, you've been told that you are to be Festival Queen.'

She looked down into the small, grubby face. Joy shone through the tears, lighting the large grey eyes like opals, and the trembling mouth had widened into the first real smile Miss Kemp had ever seen. Why, she thought, I do believe the child will look really lovely, dressed in a pretty satin frock and with a little tiara on her head. Or maybe flowers in her hair. And for Christmas we could . . . She pulled her thoughts back quickly to the present. There were still the two Princesses to announce, and the rest of the children to pacify, not to mention Jenny Pettifer's disappointment to deal with.

'We'll talk about it later,' she said gently to Shirley. 'Go back to your place now, and come and see me at playtime.' She might take the opportunity to persuade the child to wash her face in the mornings, and perhaps they could find her a clean, tidy frock to wear, just for school. 'Now, the rest of you, settle down and stop that chattering. I've already told you that the Festival Queen is a very special appointment – yes, I know your mum had an appointment at the doctor's, Henry, but that's a different kind of appointment – what I was saying is that the Festival Queen is nothing to do with being pretty, or all the girls would be Festival Queens. We had to choose just one. And because the Festival of Britain is all about showing the world how wonderful Britain is and how everybody has such a good chance of having nice things happen, we had to be very careful in our choice. And that's why we chose Shirley.' She paused, not at all sure that she'd made it clear, even to herself, but the children were nodding wisely. It seemed to appeal to their logic, anyway. Only Jenny Pettifer was still looking upset.

She continued briskly: 'Now, we have three more

appointments to make this morning – the two Festival Princesses, and one very special one indeed. An important position that we've never had in this school before.' She smiled at Jenny, so that she would know that this was something for her, then announced: 'The two Festival Princesses, who will attend the Queen at our pageant and on lots of other important occasions as well, will be . . .' she paused dramatically '. . . June and Helen Nethercott!'

The children burst into loud cheers. The twins, identical with their dark curls clustered over their heads and their bright brown eyes, were popular with everyone. This was largely because they were always into mischief and had the enormous and much-envied advantage of being able to pass themselves off as each other; this meant that their popularity didn't always extend to their teachers, but as the headmistress often remarked, there was no real malice in them, and which of us wouldn't have taken such a wonderful advantage? 'I know there have been plenty of times when I'd have liked to have a twin to share the blame!' she'd said once to Stella.

'And just before we start our lessons,' she said now, aware that they'd spent rather a long time on their morning assembly, 'I want to tell you about the other very special and important post. With such a busy and exciting term ahead of us, Miss Simmons and I are going to need a lot of help. Now, I know you'll all do your best, but we felt,' she glanced at Stella, who hadn't the faintest idea what was coming, since Miss Kemp had only just thought of it herself, 'we felt that it would be a good idea to have one of you as a special helper. Someone we can trust to take on some of the little tasks that we would have to do. We're going to have a Head Girl! And the Head Girl is going to be none other than Jenny Pettifer!'

'When did you think of that?' Stella asked later, as they

drank a welcome cup of coffee while watching the children dash madly about the playground. 'I had no idea!'

'Neither did I,' the headmistress confessed. 'It was only when I saw Jenny's face and realised how disappointed she was – but more than that, I knew the children would never accept Shirley unless I did something to mollify them. The idea of a Head Girl just popped into my mind, and thank goodness it did,' she added feelingly.

'You realise you're going to have to have one every year now,' Stella told her. 'And what about a Head Boy? I'm surprised nobody's thought of that.'

'Well, I expect they will, and I dare say we ought to have one anyway. I'd probably choose Ernest Crocker, he's a willing little boy and quite bright. As for having one every year, why not? It's another thing the children can strive for and another challenge to their skills. We'll give Jenny – and Ernest, of course – real things to do – some of the simpler tasks we would have done ourselves. And Shirley's so pleased to be Festival Queen. She really couldn't believe it, you know. Her little face lit up like a lamp.'

'I know.' Stella's own face grew pensive. 'What is she really like, Miss Kemp? It's a problem for me, not knowing the older children. The ones I have in my class now will be familiar all the way through school, but I hardly know yours, and I'd like to. I wondered if I could take them for lessons sometimes, or for nature walks?'

'That's a good idea. You need to know all the children, even though you're just teaching the infants. I was thinking this morning that a nature walk would be a good idea. We'll take the whole school out together.'

As the crocodile of children trudged through the village half an hour later, Stella looked about her at the high Devon banks, studded now with thick clusters of primroses and scattered with violets, and at the hawthorn hedges with their soft green leaves now fully broken from their buds.

They turned off the lane and into the woods, already touched with a sheen of azure from the bluebells that would be the next flowers to carpet the ground, and then went into Ted Tozer's meadow and gathered round the pond that lay in one corner.

'Them's tadpoles, miss,' Ernest Coker informed her. 'See, they've come out their jelly stuff – spawn, it's called – and they'll get legs soon and turn into frogs.'

'Or toads,' Henry Bennetts added. 'They might be toads, just as easy.'

Stella crouched down and peered into the pond. The water was full of tiny creatures – tadpoles, water boatmen, skaters, snails – and she wondered if the school had a microscope. At the training college, they'd looked at pondwater and she would like to show these children that there were even more fascinating plants and animals to wonder at than could be seen with the naked eye.

They moved on after a while and Stella heard the full-throated song of a blackbird in a nearby tree and the high, sweet notes of a skylark soaring far overhead.

'I don't know why they need to build an Exhibition in London to tell the world how great Britain is,' she said to her headmistress. 'All they need do is come to Burracombe. There can't be a better place on earth.'

Only one more thing would make her life perfect now – to find her sister, Muriel. But any hope of that seemed as far away as it ever had.

Chapter Twenty-Two

The Festival Is Yours Today.

Dottie put down her newspaper and beamed at Stella. It was 4 May 1951 and the King was to open the Festival of Britain. The day before, riding through cheering crowds in his carriage, flanked by trumpeters in silver, horsemen in scarlet and blue, and accompanied by his wife and daughters, the Duke of Edinburgh and Mr Attlee the Prime Minister, he had gone to St Paul's Cathedral for a service of dedication.

'There's pictures, look,' Dottie said, moving the milk jug and honeypot to spread the paper out on the breakfast table. 'All of them sitting in the front pew. The Princess Royal, the Duchess of Gloucester and Prince William, Princess Margaret – she's ever so tiny, you know, I saw her once close to, at the theatre – and the Duke of Edinburgh and Princess Elizabeth. She'll be Queen one day – it do seem funny, don't it! And there's old Queen Mary, Queen Mother she is properly, only they don't say so here, and the King and Queen themselves. Don't they look lovely!'

'The King made a speech, too,' Stella said, reading the report. '"*One hundred years ago, Queen Victoria opened the Great Exhibition in Hyde Park . . .*"'

'That was the Crystal Palace,' Dottie nodded. 'They moved it afterwards. I saw it burned down before the war – terrible sight, it were.'

'"*This Festival has been planned, like its great predecessor, as a visible sign of national achievement and confidence",'* Stella continued, running her eye down the column and reading out scraps here and there. *'"Dark clouds still overhang the world . . . yet this is no time for despondency . . . I see this Festival as a symbol of Britain's abiding courage and vitality . . ."'*

'Oh, what lovely words!' Dottie cried, wiping her eye with the corner of her apron. 'Oh, he do talk lovely. They say he's ever so shy, you know, and stammers, but I always listen to him at Christmas and I think he sounds a real nice man.'

'"We look back with pride and forward with resolution . . . I have been told of the pageants and displays which have been prepared throughout our countryside—"'

'That's us! Someone's told him about us! Oh, suppose he comes down to see our pageant! The King hisself, here in Burracombe!' Dottie clasped her hands with excitement.

'Well, it doesn't actually say he'll go to visit the pageants,' Stella said. 'I don't expect he'll have time to go round them all, but it's nice that he knows about them, isn't it? Look, it tells you here what they're doing today – they're opening the Exhibition on the South Bank at eleven and they're going to be there an hour and a half. The public will be able to go in at half-past two.' She turned the page. 'Here are some more pictures of them. A nice one of the King and Queen, and one of Princess Elizabeth and Prince Philip. And – oh, look at this one of the little boys – Prince Charles and Prince Richard. I wonder where Princess Anne was?'

'Home in her pram, I should think.' Dottie took back the newspaper. 'She's only nine months old, dear little blossom. Look at this – pictures of what it looked like on television. My stars, that'd be something, wouldn't it – to be able to sit indoors and watch it on your own television. I don't know that anyone's got one in Burracombe, do you?

They haven't even got one up at the Barton. Let's see what's on the wireless tonight.'

Dottie and Stella had fallen into the habit of scanning the newspaper each morning to decide what they would listen to that evening, if Dottie wasn't working at the pub. *The Archers* was a firm favourite now, although Stella was aware that the children at school – especially the boys – still missed *Dick Barton*. Tonight, on the Home Service, there was a programme about the Exhibition as well as the first concert from the new Festival Hall. Then there was *Letter From America*, which they didn't usually bother with since they preferred programmes such as *Family Favourites* or *Palace of Varieties* on the Light Programme. Dottie said the latter reminded her of her days in the theatre.

'Well, it do look lovely,' Dottie said at last, folding the newspaper. 'I'm looking forward to the outing, aren't you?' She had offered to come on the school coach to help with the children, and was going to bake a huge number of rock cakes to take with them.

The outing had been fixed for a fortnight's time, and the children were so excited they could scarcely contain themselves. Stella had set up a table in the corner of the infants' classroom and they had made cardboard models of the Dome of Discovery and Skylon, covered with silver paper carefully saved from bars of chocolate. The Thames was represented by a winding snake of grey paint on the hardboard base, and a start had been made on the Battersea Pleasure Gardens. Ernest and Henry had brought in some leafy twigs and stuck them around like trees, with a woollen cat's cradle slung between them for the Treetop Walk, and two of the other boys were trying to make a model of the Guinness Clock out of plasticine.

'We really needs to see it to make a decent job of it, miss,' Micky told Stella solemnly. 'We will be able to go there on the outing, won't we?'

243

'I'll talk to Miss Kemp about it,' Stella promised. 'The model's looking very good. You're clever with your hands.'

'Well, me dad's the blacksmith, miss. He lets me help him.' Micky brushed his hands together. 'I want to make a proper model of the clock – one that works. It does all sorts of things, miss. It's got the toucans and pelicans and lions and the seal with the bottle of Guinness on his nose, and a kangaroo and a crocodile, and the Mad Hatter from that story about the girl that fell down a rabbit-hole –'

'*Alice in Wonderland*,' Stella said automatically.

'That's right, her's only a girl but it's a good story just the same. Anyway, this clock comes to life every quarter of an hour, miss, and all these birds and animals goes round in a circle and does things, and I thought if I could get a good look at it I could see how it works and make one. My dad'll help with the iron bits.'

'Will he? I'm not sure you'll be able to make one that works,' Stella began doubtfully, but he nodded his head vigorously.

'We will, miss, you'll see. My dad does clocks as well, see, he knows all about them. So I needs to get there in good time to have a proper look at it. I might need to stop there all day.'

'I'm afraid you won't be able to do that,' Stella said firmly. 'There's a lot to see, and we'll be going to the Exhibition itself first. But I'll make sure we see the clock as well. If it's as good as you say, everyone will want to see it.'

Micky sighed and shrugged. He hadn't really expected that he would be allowed to stay and watch the clock all day. There would probably be other interesting things to see, anyway. The Emmett Railway – that was something else he'd heard about. Perhaps if he could get a good look at that, he and his father could build one of their own, right here in Burracombe. What a fine sight that would be, chuffing round the village green . . .

He went off to find some paper, his head filled with ideas he wanted to jot down.

'Val, tell me to mind my own business,' Hilary said, 'but is there anything wrong in your family? I wouldn't ask, but you and Jackie both seem so miserable lately. If there's anything I can do to help . . . ?'

They were sitting on the terrace at the Barton, large cups of coffee on the table between them. Val had brought over a few of her mother's flapjacks and Hilary had put them on a plate. They were made to Alice's own recipe, with peanut butter as well as the more ordinary ingredients, and were deliciously chewy. But despite this and the view of the gardens, burgeoning now with life and spring colour, Val was looking pale and unhappy.

'No, there's nothing the matter,' she said listlessly. 'I'm just a bit tired, that's all. Too much night-duty. And Jackie's still upset over Roy going away.'

'Are you sure that's all it is?' Hilary asked gently. 'It seems to me like more than just missing her boyfriend. She seems worried over something.'

'Worried? Why, what could she be worried about?' Val was staring down the expanse of lawn towards a stand of tall beech trees, tinged with the salmon pink of uncurling new leaves. Then Hilary's meaning seemed to strike her and she turned her head, her eyes widening.

'You don't think she could be *expecting*? Our Jackie?'

'I hope not, but it did cross my mind. She seemed upset as soon as he went away. Oh, I know she would be, but I thought then there was more to it than just saying goodbye to her boyfriend. Most girls have to do that anyway. They drift around the house in tears for a few days, and then they get used to it and start writing letters and going out with their friends again. But Jackie didn't seem to do that.'

'She was talking about getting engaged before he went

245

away,' Val said. 'In fact, she told Mum that they *were* engaged. She didn't say anything to Dad, mind – she knew he'd hit the roof at the very idea. My goodness, Hil, if you're right he'll blow the roof right off! What are we going to do?'

'I don't know that I am right. I just wondered – I'm probably being very unfair.'

'I hope you are.' Val shook her head. 'It certainly puts my problems into the shade.' She stopped abruptly and Hilary gave her a curious glance.

'There *is* something the matter, isn't there?' she said after a moment or two. 'Why don't you tell me about it, Val? You know it won't go any further.'

Val looked at her indecisively, then seemed to make up her mind. 'Oh, I don't know, Hil – I'm just feeling restless, I suppose. I don't seem to be going anywhere with my life. I mean, it's the same thing, day in, day out – going into Tavistock, coming home again. Night-duty, day-duty. It's a worthwhile job, I know, and it's better than working in a factory or a shop, but where is it taking me? Am I going to do the same thing until I'm old? Isn't there anything else?'

'What else do you want?' Hilary asked quietly.

'What I *had*!' Val cried, thumping the little table so that the cups and saucers rattled. 'Or what I *thought* I had – what I thought it would lead to. Marriage, my own home – children.' Her eyes filled with tears and she brushed them away angrily. 'I didn't want to do this, Hil. It's so selfish. I'm not the only one to have lost her sweetheart in the war. Look at you, you were just the same – never got as far as being married.'

Hilary was silent for a moment. Then she said, 'I'm not sure that I wanted it all that much.'

'What do you mean?' Val stared at her. 'Didn't you want to marry Henry?'

'I'm not sure. I thought I did, but in those days we just

did what we were expected to do, didn't we? Girls were expected to get engaged and married; if you were still single at twenty-four, you were on the shelf. Too old to get a man. And Henry was around at the right time – our families knew each other ... we were sort of thrown together. Everywhere I went, he was there too. I sometimes wonder whether it wasn't all arranged. It all seemed so suitable – his father and Daddy being such friends and having the same kind of estates and everything. To tell you the truth, Val, I don't even remember him actually proposing; we just seemed to drift into it.'

'But you must remember him proposing!' Val exclaimed. 'No girl could forget her proposal.'

'Well, there you are then. I *have* forgotten – so he can't have done.' Hilary frowned, as if racking her brains. 'There was a day when we were out riding – it was a hunt meet – and Henry took a bank too fast and fell off. I went over to see if he was all right and when he'd got up and brushed himself down he said something about taking care not to do anything like that just before the wedding. And when I asked him what wedding, he just said, "Ours, of course!" And I think that was the nearest he ever got to a proposal. I went home and told Mummy about it, and she was so thrilled, she wanted to announce it at once. She sent in notices to *The Times* and the *Daily Telegraph* and Henry gave me his grandmother's engagement ring – I gave it back to his parents after he was killed, it didn't seem right to keep it – and that was that. I never even accepted him, not properly; it was all taken out of my hands and I went along with it. I couldn't see what else to do. It was the way things were done, you see. People like me married people like Henry, and that was that. We were just thinking about starting the wedding preparations when he went off and got killed.'

'But you must have loved him, surely?' Val asked doubtfully. 'You must have been upset when he was killed.'

'I was upset, yes, of course I was. But not heartbroken. Not like other girls were. I could see the difference between them and me. It was then that I began to wonder if I really did love him. I never really thought about it, you see. I just assumed that I did. I'd never been "in love" so I didn't know what it meant. And I never have been,' she added with a touch of wistfulness in her voice.

Val reached across and touched her hand. 'Oh Hil, I'm sorry.'

'There's no need to be. At least I've never had my heart broken.' She shrugged. 'Maybe I'm not the sort to fall in love. But I can tell you something, Val: I feel the same as you do about life. What are we supposed to do with it, we single women? We can't just sit about and wait for some man to take pity on us and give us a "life". We need a life of our own – something to do that we can be proud of. At least you have that, with your nursing.'

'I suppose so. But I *was* heartbroken when Eddie was killed.' Val paused, then added in a lower tone, 'And I have been in love.'

Something in her voice made Hilary glance at her sharply. 'Well, of course you were. You were engaged to Eddie.'

'Yes,' Val said, staring at her hands. 'Yes, I was.'

They sat quietly together for a few minutes and then she got to her feet. 'I'd better go now. I promised Mum I'd help her in the garden – she's planting out a lot of seedlings. Are you going on any of the charabanc outings to the Festival?'

Hilary nodded. 'I'm helping Felix with the church one. Why don't you come as well, Val? There are still a few seats. See if you can have your day off then.'

Val nodded and walked off round the corner of the

house. A trip to London to see all the wonders of the Festival that the newspapers had been talking so much about would be something to look forward to. But as she strolled down the drive, thoughts of days out and trips to London faded from her mind as she recalled their conversation.

Hilary didn't seem to mind that she hadn't married or had children. But I do, Val thought. I mind a lot. I don't like being single. It doesn't suit me. And yet, with Eddie gone, and never having the opportunity of meeting anyone else, what hope do I have?

She thrust away unwelcome thoughts of a lean, pale face and dark blue eyes beneath a mane of black hair, and turned her mind instead to her sister Jackie. Suppose Hilary was right! Suppose Jackie was worried and frightened about having a baby. Too frightened to tell anyone about it; too frightened to ask for help.

I'll have to talk to her, Val decided, pushing her own anxieties out of her mind. I'll have to find out if it's true.

'I don't know,' Jackie said. She twisted away from her sister, but Val gripped her arm and pulled her back to face her. 'I don't *know*, Val – I wish I did! How can you tell? And how soon can you tell? I don't know about people, only about cows and sheep and pigs.' Her lips trembled and her voice broke into sobs. 'Oh, Val, I'm so frightened! I don't know what to do!'

'So you could be,' Val said flatly. All the way home, she had hoped against hope that Hilary was wrong – that Jackie would tell her there was no chance of her being pregnant, that she and Roy hadn't done anything wrong. It had been a relief to find her sister at home by herself and Val had made sure they wouldn't be interrupted by asking Jackie to come up to her bedroom. Then she'd asked her straight out what was the matter, and whether she thought she might be pregnant. She'd thought that Jackie would be furious with her for even suggesting such a thing. I wish she *was* angry, she thought now, looking at Jackie's terrified face. It would be better than this. 'You could be expecting a baby.'

'Don't say it! Don't say it out loud! I've been trying not to think of it. I thought if I didn't say it, it might go away.' Jackie caught the expression on her sister's face. 'I know it's stupid, Val, but you don't know what it's like. It's never happened to you.'

'That's got nothing to do with it!' Val said sharply, and then softened her tone. 'Look, Jackie, it's not going to go away but first of all we've got to be sure that there *is* a baby. When did you and Roy – I mean, when do you think it could have happened?'

'Just after Easter,' Jackie said dully. 'Just before he went away.' She sat on the edge of Val's bed, plaiting the hem of the bedspread between her fingers.

'So that's, let's see . . . about five weeks ago. Well, that's not long. Much too soon to panic, anyway. What makes you so sure? Didn't you take any precautions?'

'We didn't know it was going to happen, did we? *I* didn't, anyway. And I wished we hadn't, straight away.' Jackie's eyes filled with tears again. 'I thought it was supposed to be wonderful, but it wasn't at all – it was just uncomfortable and peculiar. I felt as if everything had gone, somehow. And I was worried all the time that this might happen.' She started to cry again.

'Jackie, we don't know that anything *has* happened. When should you have come on?'

'Three weeks ago. I've been hoping every day – but it's never happened. So I must be, mustn't I. But how could it have happened so quickly? We only did it once!'

'Once is all it takes,' Val said grimly. 'It doesn't happen gradually, you know. It doesn't matter if you take risks once or a hundred times, it's still only once that you fall.'

'Well, I wish we hadn't done it at all,' Jackie said miserably. She dropped the edge of the bedspread and looked at her sister. 'Val, you're a nurse, isn't there anything I can do? Something I could take? You know – to bring things on. I'm sure I've heard—'

'*No!*' Val surprised herself with the sharpness of her voice. 'Don't even think about it. It's a baby, a human being. You can't kill it.'

'It's not a baby, not really. Not yet. It's just a speck, that's all.' Jackie grabbed at her sister's arm and shook it desperately. 'Please, Val, there must be something! Don't you remember when I missed three times once, a couple of years ago, and Mum took me to the doctor and he gave me some pills and they brought on my period? Couldn't you get me some of those?'

'No, I couldn't.' Val could barely speak for the surge of emotions welling up inside her. Anger, bitterness, regret – and yet, beneath those, a deep compassion for her young sister, so frantic and bewildered. She must have been going through absolute hell over the past few weeks, Val thought, and fought down her anger.

'Jackie, I can't just steal medicines from the hospital. And it's dangerous, anyway. Women have died trying to do what you're suggesting.' She paused, then added, 'And besides, it's murder. It isn't just a speck, Jackie, it's a baby, and it's growing all the time. It's going to be a person and there's nothing you can do to stop it.'

Jackie stared at her. Her face was as white as a paper mask, and her eyes like huge black holes. 'I'll have to kill myself then,' she said hopelessly. 'Because if I don't, Mum and Dad will.'

'*Jackie!* That's a terrible thing to say. A *wicked* thing. You mustn't ever, *ever* say such things again, do you hear me?' Val took her by the shoulders and shook her angrily. Then she caught herself up again and held her sister more gently. 'It won't be as bad as that. I'll stand by you. These things happen, you know they do. It's awful at the time, but people get over it. And once the baby's born – well, you know what they say. Babies bring their love with them.' Her voice shook and she turned away so that Jackie wouldn't see her own tears. 'Anyway,' she added, 'I expect Roy will marry you. You wanted to get engaged, didn't you?'

'Yes, but Mum told me there was no chance that they'd let us get married before I was twenty-one. And Roy's only nineteen. Suppose *his* mum and dad won't give permission? Oh, it's all such a *mess!*' Her tears began to flow again. 'It's not fair. There's you been engaged but never got married, and me having a baby I don't want. Why does everything have to go wrong?'

'I don't know,' Val said quietly. 'I just don't know, but it's the way it is and what we've got to do now is face up to it. Now look, it's still early days – if you've been worrying yourself sick over what happened, that might easily have stopped your period coming. When would you be due again?'

'Next week, I suppose.' The girl looked at her with sudden hope. 'D'you really think I might be all right?'

'We'll just have to wait and see, but it can happen. And you're more likely to come on if you stop worrying like this. Try to put it out of your mind for a few days and see what happens.'

'*Put it out of my mind?*' Jackie stared at her sister as if she'd suddenly grown two heads. 'Well, it's easy to see *you've* never had to worry about anything like this, Val! It's on my mind all the time. I can't think of anything else. I've been *trying* not to think about it all these weeks and it just gets worse and worse.' She picked up Val's pillow and thumped it back on the bed. 'It's like being in a horrible trap all the time, and there's no way out. There's no way out at all.'

Val bit her lip. 'Jackie, if there was anything I could do . . .'

'There is. But you won't, will you.'

'I've already told you, I can't. Do you want us both to end up in prison? Look, I've promised I'll stand by you. If it has happened, you'll have to tell Mum and Dad sometime, and I'll help you. And then there's Roy.'

'What about him?' Jackie asked with a return to her old, listless manner.

'Well, he'll have to know as well, won't he! Isn't he due some leave sometime soon? Don't they get a weekend or something after the first six weeks? Hilary says Stephen's coming back the week after next.'

'Yes, he's coming back then too. But I don't even know if I want to see him again. I don't know what I feel about him now.'

'I expect you feel just the same,' Val said gently. 'You've had a nasty shock and you're worried and frightened. I expect you love him just as much, underneath.'

Jackie was silent for a few minutes. She picked at the bedspread again. 'Do I have to tell Mum and Dad yet?' she asked at last. 'Can't I wait a bit longer?'

'Well, I certainly wouldn't tell them until you know for sure. There's no point in upsetting them unnecessarily. But you do have to tell Roy. If you two have to get married in a hurry, he'll need to arrange leave. You don't want him being sent off to Germany or Korea or somewhere before you've had a chance to have a wedding.'

'Korea! You don't really think they'll send him there, do you?' A new fear sharpened Jackie's voice and Val cursed herself.

'No, of course they won't. I don't suppose he'll ever

leave the country. Now look, I can hear someone down-stairs — it's probably Mum, back from Tavistock. Go and wash your face and then have a lie-down on your bed. I'll bring you a cup of tea — I'll tell Mum you've got a headache. You don't want her to see you've been crying.'

She went downstairs. Alice had gone out again to feed the hens so Val was able to make the tea without answering questions. She stood in the big kitchen, waiting for the kettle to boil, thinking of what Jackie had said.

There's you, been engaged and never got married, and me having a baby I don't want. And: *It's easy to see you've never had to worry about anything like this.* And then the age-old cry: *It isn't fair!*

She's right, Val thought sadly, unable to stop her own tears overflowing and rolling slowly down her cheeks. It isn't fair.

Chapter Twenty-Three

The school outing was fixed for Whit Monday, halfway through May. It was a Bank Holiday and half-term as well. Burracombe School being a church school, the children had Ascension Day off too, but the vicar had vetoed any suggestion that they should go to the Festival then.

'We always have a service in the morning,' he told Shirley Culliford's mother. The Cullifords weren't church-goers and had little idea of the significance of the various dates, apart from Christmas and Easter which seemed to have more to do with presents and chocolate eggs than anything spiritual. 'It would be much too late to think of going to London after that.'

'A service?' It happened every year, and every year Mrs Culliford seemed equally surprised. 'Do my youngsters hev to go as well?'

'Those who go to school, yes. They must come to school just as usual in the morning and they'll all walk to the church together. Everyone else is welcome too. You could bring the little ones,' he added without much hope.

As expected, Mrs Culliford shook her head vigorously. 'I ent been inside the church since my Joe were christened. Makes me go all funny, it do. Well, never mind. Shirley can help with a few jobs round the place in the afternoon, look after the little 'uns while I goes to Tavi on the bus to get me hair done.' She touched her brassy yellow curls self-consciously. 'Need a new perm, I do.'

She went on her way, leaving the vicar reflecting that there always seemed to be enough money in the Culliford household for hairstyles and cigarettes, if not for clean, tidy clothes for the children. Still, young Shirley seemed to be taking more care of herself these days. Ever since being appointed Festival Queen she had come to school every day with a clean face and a not too dirty dress. She had made an apron in the weekly sewing class, with three strips of coloured bias binding sewn on to it, and her stitches were really neat. Mr Harvey seemed to have been right about her after all, Miss Kemp had admitted to Stella.

The day of the outing dawned fine and warm, with just a faint hazy mist to promise good weather. The children were on the green by seven-fifteen, clutching their lunchboxes and the macintoshes that Miss Kemp had insisted upon, and hopping with excitement. The mothers and fathers who had agreed to come and help were there as well, trying to keep their own children under control, and Hilary and Val had managed to persuade Jackie to come along.

'It'll do you good to have a day out,' Val had said. 'And you know how much you wanted to go to the Exhibition.'

Jackie looked at her dolefully but said nothing, and Val remembered that the Festival had been a bone of contention between Jackie and their mother. She'd wanted to go with Roy – and stay overnight. She and Alice had quarrelled about it on New Year's Eve. What a long time ago that seemed.

Still, Jackie had agreed to come on the outing, although she didn't look as if she expected to enjoy it. Her face was paler than ever, her eyes smudged with dark shadows, and she was looking thinner. Val glanced at her anxiously. I hope she's not going to faint on us, she thought. Maybe I shouldn't have persuaded her to come after all.

The charabanc arrived and everyone scrambled aboard. Miss Kemp had a list and stood at the front, by the driver, checking off all the names. The driver was from a neighbouring village and often drove the bus into Tavistock as well; he was a cheerful man who seemed to have an inexhaustible supply of jokes to entertain his passengers, but wasn't quite so good at finding his way on long journeys. Stella had been deputed to sit behind him with the road map and make sure they didn't end up in Glasgow.

'He can't be that bad,' she'd protested, laughing, but Basil Harvey had given her a wry look.

'He can. He took the Mother's Union on a summer outing to Castle Combe once and they finished up in Castle Cary! They enjoyed themselves, but the Castle Combe Mother's Union wasn't too pleased. They'd prepared tea in the church hall and had to take it all home again.'

'Well, I don't think he could miss London quite so easily,' she said, 'but I'll make sure he doesn't go wrong.'

Felix was coming too; he sat down next to Hilary in the other front seat. Val and Jackie sat behind Stella. Stella gave them both a friendly smile, surprised when Val returned it rather coldly.

The charabanc set off and the children immediately began to investigate their lunch packets. Miss Kemp, well used to this, walked down the aisle telling them to put the food away again. 'We'll eat it when we arrive. There's a long day ahead and you'll be hungry if you eat it now.'

'Please, miss, when will us be there?' one small girl asked. 'Only I forgot to go to the lavvy before us came out.'

Miss Kemp gave her a look of exasperation. 'I asked you all if you'd been. You could have gone to the school lavatories.'

'I don't like the school lavvies,' the little girl said. 'There's germs there.'

'There are germs everywhere, but Mrs Purdy keeps the lavatories nice and clean.' The headmistress realised that there was no point in argument and sighed. 'We'll stop at Moretonhampstead. You can all go to the lavatories there. Well, those of you that *want* to, then,' she added, forestalling further objections. 'You don't have to go, but we shan't be stopping again for a long time. You'd better make sure all the little ones go,' she added to Stella. 'It's excitement more than anything else. Most of them have never been so far on an outing before, let alone to London.'

The journey continued, with the usual brief stops for children who felt sick, and a few traffic hold-ups. Stella was almost as excited as the children. I wish Luke could have come, she thought, but he doesn't really have much to do with the village, and nothing at all with the school. I must get him to come in and give them a painting lesson one day.

Felix, sitting across the aisle, gave her a warm grin. 'Are you all right with that map?'

'I think so. I've never been to London myself, so I won't be much use when we actually get there. I just hope everything's signposted.'

'I might be able to help you there. I know London pretty well – my grandparents live there and I visit them a lot. They used to take me about quite a bit when I was a child. There've been a few changes since then, with the bombing, but I can still find my way about.'

'You'd better take over then,' Stella said gratefully. 'I was dreading sending the driver the wrong way.'

Felix came and sat beside her. 'It's quite easy, really. It's right in the middle of London, on the South Bank of the Thames, and the Battersea Pleasure Gardens are a bit further down.' They put their heads together over the maps, and Val took the opportunity to go and sit with Hilary.

'How's Jackie?' Hilary murmured, glancing back at the girl who was staring dully out of the window. 'Did you get a chance to talk to her?'

Val nodded. 'You were right. She's scared stiff she's – you know.' She glanced around, aware that some of the villagers and children had sharp ears. 'Hasn't she said anything to you this week?'

'I've hardly seen her, to tell the truth. I've been away most of the week. I went to see one of my VAD friends – the girl who became a stewardess on one of the airlines.'

'Oh yes?' Val said with interest. 'Is she enjoying it?'

'Yes, she is. She goes all over Europe – to Paris and Rome, places like that – and she has a lovely flat in London. She's been sharing it with two other girls.' Hilary hesitated, then said, 'One of them's leaving soon, as a matter of fact, and she's asked me if I'd like to take her place.'

Val turned her head and stared at her. 'You? Go and live in London?'

'Ssh!' Hilary begged her. 'Yes, why not? I might apply to the airline for a job, too. Or find something else to do. There must be plenty of jobs in London – in one of the big stores, for instance.'

Val was silent for a while, taking in the idea of Hilary going to live and work in London. 'I'd miss you,' she said at last. 'And what about your father? He'd be pretty upset, wouldn't he?'

'Yes, he would.' Hilary frowned a little, then added with a touch of defiance, 'But I can't spend my whole life looking after him, Val. I came home when Mummy was ill, but that was years ago now. It's not as if he lets me do anything interesting. I could do more to help him with the estate, but you know what he's like – thinks a woman's place is in the home. In the kitchen, in fact,' she added bitterly. 'But I want more than that.'

'I know you do. So are you really going to London? When d'you think it will be?'

'Soon, I think. Now I've made up my mind, I don't want to wait. I feel I've waited long enough already. In fact, I'm planning to tell him tonight, when we get back. It'll be a good opportunity, don't you think? He'll ask how the day went, and I can lead into it from there.' She looked at her friend, flushed and bright-eyed, more excited and happy than Val had seen her for a long time.

It's the right thing for her, Val thought. She really needs something more than running a house for her father. But what about me? All I've ever wanted is to run a house for a man I love, and have his children. And it doesn't look as if it's ever going to happen. Hilary's getting the life she wants. Jackie might be having a baby she *doesn't* want. And me?

She thought of the hot, bright days in Egypt; the star-studded nights; the work on the wards, nursing soldiers who had been brought in suffering wounds that seemed almost unimaginable now. And the young war artist with his dark blue eyes and wild black hair, that even Army discipline couldn't tame.

And then, as always, she thought of Eddie.

The Exhibition was everything that they had expected. From the moment they entered the seemingly endless streets of London and first saw the shape of Big Ben, familiar from the pictures Stella and Miss Kemp had been showing the children, it seemed as if the little ones would blow the bus apart with their excitement. They made their way slowly, following a long line of coaches and charabancs, with Stella and Felix giving the driver directions and the children chattering like sparrows. When they finally reached the big coach park, Miss Kemp had difficulty making herself heard.

'Nobody will be allowed off this bus until you've all quietened down and listened to me,' she said, raising her voice so that it penetrated to the back of the bus. 'That's better. Now, this is a big place and we don't want to lose anyone. Every helper has four children to look after. We shall keep in our group, but there are a lot of people about and we may get separated, so stay with each other and don't wander off on your own.' She paused and looked at her map of the Exhibition. 'First of all, we'll go to the Dome of Discovery and the Skylon. They're easy to see.' She pointed out of the window and everyone twisted and craned their necks. 'If anyone does get lost, go to the Skylon and wait for someone to come and fetch you. After that, we'll find somewhere to have our sandwiches and then we'll go to the Battersea Pleasure Gardens.' The children cheered. 'We'll have two hours there and I've arranged for you to have tickets for some of the rides. You'll be able to go on the Emmett Train and the Treetop Walk, and the Caterpillar. And you'll be able to see the—'

'What about the Rotor?' Henry asked in an aggrieved voice. 'I wants to go on the Rotor.'

'They don't allow children on the Rotor,' Miss Kemp said firmly, making up her mind not to go anywhere near it, 'but you will be able to see the—'

'What about the Big Dipper, then?' he persisted. 'My brother knows someone who's been on it and he says it's 'andsome.'

'You can go on the Cake Walk and into the Hall of Mirrors. And you can—'

'There's an 'Aunted 'Ouse as well,' her tormentor said. 'I wants to go in that. Full of ghosts and skellytons, it is.' He put both hands to the sides of his head and waggled his fingers, pursing his lips to make the eerie noise he believed ghosts and skeletons to make. 'Whooh. Whoo-ooh.'

'Henry, will you please be quiet!' Miss Kemp snapped, losing patience. 'You'll have tickets for some of the rides and you'll have to ask your helpers if you can go on any of the others.' Having neatly passed the responsibility to Henry's own mother, she went on, 'We'll be leaving at five o'clock sharp, and I'll tell you where we're to meet when we get to the Pleasure Gardens. Now—'

'Ain't us going to see the Guinness Clock?' came the disappointed voice of Micky, the blacksmith's son. 'I wanted to see that. It goes every quarter of an hour and there's all these animals—'

'Yes, of course we'll see the Guinness Clock,' Miss Kemp said. Micky had been drawing the clock and trying to work out its intricate movements in every spare moment for the past three weeks. 'That's what I was going to tell you when Henry kept interrupting me. We'll go to see that together, and then you'll be able to choose which rides you want to go on – with your helpers, of course. And it'll probably be a good place for us to meet at the end of the afternoon.'

'Please, miss,' said a little girl anxiously, 'will there be any lavvies here, only I don't think I can wait much—'

'Yes, of course there'll be lavatories. We'll find one now and everyone can go before we visit the Dome of Discovery.' The headmistress climbed out of the bus and there was a rush for the door. 'One at a time, *please*! Remember that people will be looking at you and thinking that Burracombe people don't know how to behave themselves. Show them what lovely manners you all have.'

The children obediently got off the bus one by one and formed themselves into a crocodile. Miss Kemp heaved a sigh of relief and said to Stella, 'They should be all right. We've got enough mothers here, and a couple of fathers as well. Nothing should go wrong.'

'Provided Henry doesn't go on the Rotor or the Big Dipper,' Stella said with a grin. 'He's the sort of boy who'd be right at the top when it got stuck. Trouble seems to stick to him like grass.'

'Well, his mother's come along as one of the helpers so it's up to her,' the headmistress said. 'So long as she gets him out of whatever scrape he manages to get into before five o'clock ... Now, if you've all made yourselves comfortable,' she announced to the children who were returning from the lavatories, 'we'll start.'

From then on, the day was nothing but wonder, and the children would remember it all their lives. They filed into the darkness of the Dome and progressed through all the Zones, from Land, Earth and Sea through the Living World and Polar Zones with the Captain Scott displays and husky dogs, ending at Outer Space where they could see radio signals being sent to the Moon and a huge screen showing their return. The wheeling display in the roof of the Stars and Planets didn't impress them so much, since they could see a similar display on any clear night in Burracombe, but by the time they emerged blinking into the sunlight half the boys had made up their minds to be spacemen and the other half explorers.

The tall, silver cigar shape of the Skylon rose into the air just outside the Dome and they took turns to stand on the spot exactly underneath and stare upwards. Then they went down to the seats all along the riverside and ate their lunch.

'There's so much to see,' Hilary remarked to Felix, who had escaped from the Cullifords to come and sit beside her. 'It seems a shame to leave it and go to a Fun Fair.'

'Well, it is the children's outing,' he said. 'I expect the others will be more worthy – the Mother's Union and the WI. And then there's Mrs Warren's village outing, for anyone who wants to go again or didn't go on the others. I can't imagine that she'll allow us to ride on the Caterpillar or the Big Dipper!'

Hilary laughed. 'She might find herself over-ruled about that. Anyway, once we're here we can do as we like. Will you be coming up again, Felix?'

'Oh yes. Mr Harvey and I will both come on the Mother's Union trip, and so will Mrs Harvey, of course.

But it would be nice to come independently too, don't you think? It would be easy enough to come by train.' He looked at her.

Hilary knew she was blushing. She said, 'Yes, I suppose it would.'

'Would you like to do that too?' he asked. 'Come with me, for a day out by ourselves? No villagers around to watch what we're doing and start any gossip?' He grinned and one of his eyelids flickered.

Hilary felt confused. She liked Felix and knew that he liked her, but she wasn't at all sure that it went any further than that. She didn't even know whether this suggestion meant that he wanted it to. What's more, she wasn't even sure how much longer she would be in Burracombe, if she took up her friend's offer of a place in the flat . . . On the other hand, if she had moved to London, she could always meet him here.

'It depends when it is,' she said at last. 'I'm quite busy just now. Let's think about it after we get home.' By the time Felix suggested it again, she would have told her father that she was leaving. She quaked at the thought of the fury and disappointment that this announcement would create, and knew that she couldn't make any plans until things had at least begun to settle down.

'All right,' he said cheerfully. 'We'll look at our diaries . . . It looks as though the headmistress is getting the children rounded up now. It must be time to make for the Fair.' He gathered up the debris of their lunch and crammed it into his tin. 'I'm looking forward to this. It's years since I've been on a roundabout.'

'Now, that I don't believe,' Hilary retorted, screwing up her own paper bags. 'Didn't you go to the Goosey Fair in Tavistock last October?'

'Yes, I did, but I didn't have the nerve to go on anything. I'd only just arrived then, hadn't I, and I didn't want to shock the local populace too much. But this is different. This is the King's Festival and if he and the Queen approve, I think Burracombe should approve as well.'

'Even Mrs Warren?' Hilary asked wickedly, and he put his head on one side and pretended to consider.

'Well, perhaps not Mrs Warren. But she's not here today, is she? Today is just for the kids!' He gripped her hand and pulled her up beside him. 'Tell you what, let's escape Miss Kemp's eagle eye and go on the Big Dipper. We might even get stuck on the top!'

Hilary followed him, laughing. Felix was a nice man, she thought, dropping her rubbish into a litter-bin. And although he was a curate, he wasn't nervous or obsequious as some she had met, trying too hard to make a good impression. He behaved with an easy confidence, as if sure that everyone would like him. And most people did.

All the same, she wasn't sure that she wanted their relationship to go further than friendship. As she'd told Val, she'd never felt herself to be really 'in love' and didn't know if she would recognise it if it came along. Nor was she convinced that it even existed, except as a romantic dream.

I don't want to end up as a vicar's wife, she thought. I want a life of my own. I want to *do* something, before it's too late.

Val and Jackie had agreed to help look after the Nethercott twins and two other little girls. 'At least if we lose one of the twins, we'll have the other one to show people,' Val said with a grin, but her sister responded only with a small, dismal smile.

Val sighed and shook her head. If only Jackie could relax for a little while. Even if her fears came true, there was no point in being miserable all the time. Hang on, you're a fine one to talk, she told herself ruefully. You've been mooning about like a lost weekend for the past six years now.

As she sat in the charabanc, gazing out of the window at the countryside, at orchards full of apple trees in blossom and gardens filled with late spring flowers, she realised that her mood had begun to lift just lately. Ever since New Year's Eve, when her mother had persuaded her to go down to the village green to hear the bells and dance round the oak tree, she had felt less oppressed by her memories. It was as if a heavy black shadow had begun to shift from her heart.

Yet her remorse over Eddie hadn't changed. She felt as guilty as ever about the way she had treated him. The fact that he had never known about Luke didn't make any difference. Val had been unfaithful to him, and nothing could change that. And Luke's return to her life should have made it worse. It *had* made things worse, she told herself fiercely. Seeing him had brought it all back – the anguish of saying goodbye to Eddie, knowing that she might never see him again; the misery of living through the days, the months, the years of separation; the sudden rapture of a forbidden love, coming out of the blue when she was in Egypt, and the inevitable guilt. And, most crushing of all, the terrible remorse when she heard that Eddie had died of his wounds.

None of that had changed, and the few encounters she had had with Luke had all been angry ones. Yet they were the only times when she had been able to express her anger – anger that she felt with both him and herself. Never, until now, had she been able to speak of what had happened. It was like the release of a volcano, dormant for months and then suddenly allowed to erupt.

'Val, wake up,' Jackie said suddenly, and Val shook herself and turned, disorientated for a moment. 'I've asked you three times now if you want a toffee.'

'Sorry – I was miles away.' She took the sweet that her

sister was offering her. 'How are you feeling now? You haven't been sick or anything, have you?'

'No. When's that supposed to happen?'

'At about six weeks, I think.' They were talking in low voices, wary of being overheard even though everyone else on the bus was talking at the tops of their voices. 'It doesn't happen to everyone, though. I don't think it's much of a sign if you don't get it.'

'Thanks, that's cheered me up a lot.' Jackie stuffed the bag of toffees back into her pocket. 'Val, you haven't thought any more about what I asked you, have you? You know – about medicines and things?'

'No, I haven't!' Val's voice was sharp and she lowered it quickly. 'I've told you, it's dangerous and it's illegal. And don't go asking anyone else.' A sudden fear gripped her. 'You haven't done that, have you? You haven't mentioned it to anyone else?'

'No, I haven't, you don't need to fuss.' Jackie sat back and stared out of the window. In front of them, Felix was moving over to sit beside Stella to look at the map, and Hilary glanced round at Val. 'Go and sit beside Miss Napier,' Jackie said. 'I'll be all right. I just don't feel like talking any more.'

Val hesitated and then shrugged. 'All right, then.' She did as Jackie had suggested and settled down beside her friend.

Jackie leaned her head against the window and wished she hadn't come. She felt tired and uncomfortable and had a headache coming on. I ought to have stayed at home, she thought. This was supposed to be such fun. Me and Roy were planning to come up to the Festival together and see all the sights. And now he's gone away and it's all been spoiled. My whole life's been spoiled. And all for the sake of a few minutes that were just a big disappointment anyway.

I wish I'd never done it. I don't think I'll ever do it again.

Stella was enjoying herself. She knew all the children now and liked the way they clustered round her, peppering her with questions about London. They ignored her when she told them she'd never lived there – anyone from 'up-country' must know about London, they believed – and continued to ask her about the Tower, Buckingham Palace, Big Ben and whether she had ever met any of the Royal Family, especially the dashing Prince Philip.

'I think he's proper handsome,' one of the older girls said as they walked down to the lunch-spot beside the river. 'Princess Elizabeth's lucky. Just think, he'll be King one day – King Philip.'

'No, he won't,' Stella said. 'Princess Elizabeth will be Queen, but he won't be King.'

They stared at her. 'Why not, miss? Why won't he be King?'

'Because it's Princess Elizabeth who will inherit the throne. Don't you remember the lesson Miss Kemp gave us all about it a little while ago? She'll be Queen, because she's the King's daughter, but Prince Philip won't be King.'

'So who will be King?' one of the boys asked.

'Nobody. We won't have one.'

'Won't *have* one?' he demanded, outraged. 'How be us going to manage without a King?'

'I've told you, we'll have a Queen,' Stella said, suspecting that they were about to go round in circles.

'Well, I don't think that's fair. If a girl can be Queen, a boy oughter be able to be King, didn't un?' He turned to his friends but they had reached the picnic tables now and were more interested in their lunch-tins. Stella heaved a sigh of relief. The rules of accession were more than she could cope with today.

Felix and Hilary were sitting together, and the children had rushed for the wooden benches. Stella hesitated, looking for a space, and noticed one beside Val Tozer. Rather unsure of her welcome, after the cool smile Val had given her in the morning, she slipped into it.

'Hullo,' she said, opening her packet of sandwiches. 'It's a wonderful Exhibition, isn't it? And the children are having a lovely time.'

'Yes, they seem to be.'

Stella took a bite from a Marmite sandwich. Val was staring across the river towards the Houses of Parliament. Not far away, the Festival Hall was beginning a lunchtime concert, and in the Riverside Theatre Leo Sachs was presenting a 'Song Saloon'. The whole area was filled with life and colour, and the sights and sounds of people enjoying themselves.

'They're going to enjoy the Fun Fair too,' she said. 'Are you going to go on any of the rides?'

'Haven't decided,' Val said crisply, and got up. 'Excuse me.' She walked away briskly, leaving Stella looking after her blankly. Whatever did I say to offend her, she wondered. She seemed quite annoyed – almost angry. Is it because Felix Copley came to sit beside me? Yet as far as Stella knew, Val had no special friendship with the young curate. Perhaps she wanted one, and was jealous of anyone else who had his attention. Yet she didn't seem jealous of Hilary Napier, who had more of Felix's attention than anyone else.

I suppose the truth is that she just doesn't like me, Stella decided, and shrugged her shoulders. There was nothing to be done about that. She finished her sandwiches and turned to the little girl who had come to sit beside her. It was Shirley Culliford.

'Are you having a nice time, Shirley?'

'Oh miss,' the child said, her eyes shining. 'It's like heaven!'

Val felt irritated with herself for the way she had treated Stella. The girl had done nothing to her, and had gone out of her way to be pleasant. It was just that whenever Val saw her, yet another emotion stirred amongst all the other complicated feelings she was experiencing lately, and she didn't want to give it a name.

I know Luke said there's nothing between them, she thought crossly, leaning on the low wall to look down at the river, and it doesn't matter to me if there is. So why does it annoy me so much? *I* don't want him.

And you don't want anyone else to have him either, a small voice whispered inside her. *Ever heard of dogs in mangers?*

I just wish he'd told me what this stupid secret is that she's got, Val argued. If I knew that, I'd know if he was telling me the truth. What can it be that he's helping her with? Why can't he tell me?

And why, asked the little voice inside her, *don't you tell Luke your little secret?*

Angrily, Val turned away from the river. It wasn't a nice river, anyway – too wide, too turbid, too deep. She preferred the rivers of Devon, like the Tavy, rushing over rocks and between heather-covered banks and through woods and fields towards the Tamar, or the Walkham, dancing to meet the Tavy at Double Waters. Or the Meavy as it cascaded into the Plym at Shaugh Prior. Clear, sparkling streams where fish could breathe and you could see the dipper flirting its brown tail on a rock or diving into the water to run along the riverbed. I don't like London at all, really, she thought. This Exhibition's all very well, but I'd hate to live here, and I had enough of travelling during the war. I'd rather be at home where I belong.

She thought of Hilary's plans to leave Burracombe and

start a new, independent life. Could her friend really be doing the right thing? Whatever Hilary believed, she had been brought up to live in the country, on an estate. She liked that way of life. She enjoyed the hunting, the daily routine of the countryside, the rhythm of the seasons, the social life. Could she really adapt to living in a place like London?

Someone touched her arm and she turned to find her sister standing beside her, a strange look on her face. 'Val . . .'

'What? What is it?' She felt a spurt of alarm. 'You're not feeling ill, are you? You haven't got pains or anything?'

'No. *Yes*!' Jackie shook her head, half-laughing, half in tears. 'Oh Val, it's all right! *It's all right*! I'm not going to have a baby after all.' She buried her face against her sister's shoulder. 'There isn't anything to worry about. It was all a false alarm! Oh Val!'

At last the outing came to an end and the charabanc set off for home. It had been a long day and there was still a lengthy drive ahead of them, but most of the children were so worn out with the excitement of it all that they would probably sleep a lot of the way. Miss Kemp had arranged to stop for fish and chips, which would revive them a little, and then they would doze again. She just hoped they hadn't eaten too much ice cream and wouldn't start feeling sick.

'I shouldn't think so,' Stella remarked. 'Did you see the cost of those Eldorado Neapolitans? *Three shillings*! I didn't know an ice cream *could* cost that much.'

'There were cheaper cornets, but I agree they couldn't have afforded much, and I don't think any of them brought sweet coupons. I did see Shirley Culliford almost obliterated by an enormous stick of candy floss, but really that's not much more than sugary air. Anyway, they all seem to have enjoyed themselves, and that's the main thing.'

'They'll never forget it,' Stella said. 'It's been a wonderful day.'

The children were talking about it too as they slumped in their seats, almost overwhelmed by the wonders they had seen. They had all been on the Emmett Train and along the Treetop Walk, and most of them had been on the Caterpillar. Micky had had to be dragged away from the Guinness Clock, and Henry and Ernest had given their mothers the slip and were next seen on the Rotor, glued upside down to the wall as the centrifugal force whirled them around. They had then managed to get on to the Big Dipper, where Henry had been sick and ordered off by the man running it, and after that, more subdued, they had done more or less as they were told.

'I liked the Cake Walk best,' Helen Nethercott informed Stella. 'June and me couldn't walk properly – the floor kept breaking up. It were ever so funny.'

'And in the Hall of Mirrors we went all funny shapes,' her twin said. 'I were all long and thin, and Helen were short and fat with bendy legs.'

'Those were two different mirrors,' Helen added. 'But there was all sorts, and us didn't know which way to go some of the time.'

'I'm not sure I know which way to go now,' the driver remarked, overhearing this. 'Is anyone looking at the map? It was all right coming into London, everything was signposted, but there's nothing to tell us how to get back to Burracombe.'

Stella and Felix grinned at each other and returned to their duties. With only a few wrong turnings and views of some unexpected parts of London, they finally found their way out and on to the right road to Devon. They settled back in their seats and relaxed.

'It's been a good day,' Felix said quietly. He had gone

back across the aisle to sit beside Hilary. He glanced sideways at her. 'You've enjoyed it, haven't you, Hilary?'

'Yes, I have. It's done me good. Helped me to come to a decision.' She was sitting with her head back and her eyes closed, a small smile touching her lips, and Felix looked at her curiously.

'A decision? An important one?'

'I think so. Important to me, anyway.' She opened her eyes and smiled at him. 'I can't tell you yet. I can't tell anyone yet. I have to talk to my father first. But when I have, I'll tell you all about it.'

She looked out of the window. They were leaving London behind now and trundling through the green countryside of Berkshire. She thought of the life she wanted to lead, the responsibilities she yearned to take on, the skills and abilities she knew she possessed and so desperately wanted to use.

Dad will be furious, she thought. He'll hate it. He'll rant and rave and tell me I'm letting him down, especially now that Stephen's gone. I couldn't even have done this if Stephen had still been at home – it would have been like condemning him to a life he didn't want, just as I've been.

But she was sure that her father would come round eventually. He wouldn't want to alienate his children for ever. He would have to accept that life had changed, that Hilary didn't want to stay at home cooking his meals and running his house. That she deserved more.

I'll tell him tomorrow, she thought. I'll tell him first thing in the morning.

But by then, everything had changed.

Chapter Twenty-Four

'And you don't know how long he's been like this?' Charles Latimer asked. He let go of the Squire's wrist and looked gravely at the distraught young woman beside him. 'You didn't see him last night, when you came home?'

'No. He left a note saying he was tired and had gone up early. And I didn't wake up until after eight. I thought when I came downstairs that he must have gone out – then I saw the dogs were still there and obviously hadn't been fed, and I began to worry. But I didn't actually come up to see for another half-hour. The first one down sees to them and I thought he must have heard me open the door . . . It wasn't until nine o'clock that I really started to worry. He's always down by then. And then I heard him call out.'

The doctor moved away from the bed and Hilary followed him, still casting anxious glances over her shoulder. She lowered her voice. 'He was obviously in awful pain and he seemed so frightened – I've never seen him like that before. What's happened to him, Charles?' She looked at her father, propped up on a pile of pillows and slipping into a doze. 'What's the matter with him? He – he's not dying, is he?'

'No, no, certainly not. But I'm afraid he's had a heart attack.' He laid his hand on Hilary's shoulder. 'I don't think it's a serious one – more a warning.'

'A warning?'

'Try to understand,' the doctor said. 'The heart's a

muscle, like any other, but if it's made to work too hard it will be overstrained. Your father's heart obviously can't cope with the amount of work he's been asking it to do. He needs to cut down in several ways – on the amount of work he does, the burden of running the estate, and also perhaps in the way he eats and drinks. He needs to lose some of that weight,' he glanced at the big body, 'just to give his heart less to do. Pumping blood round a heavy body and forcing the muscles to carry extra weight is a strain in itself.'

'I thought he ate well,' she said remorsefully. 'He enjoys his food so much. And he's very active.'

'It's not your fault. And activity is good, it keeps the heart strong, just as it keeps any muscle strong. But as I said, this must be treated as a warning that he's doing too much. If you don't want it to happen again, things have to change.' He paused, then said gently, 'It doesn't have to be the end, you know. People do recover from heart attacks and live many more years. Try not to worry too much.'

'But how do they live?' Hilary asked drearily. 'As invalids, needing help for the rest of their lives. Father would hate that.'

'Not by any means. Let's not worry about that.' He glanced out of the window. 'I can see Val Tozer running up the drive. She'll be a help.'

'I rang her as soon as I'd rung you. I rang Stephen as well, at Coltishall. He's coming straight home. I was so frightened, Charles.'

'I know. It is frightening, when it happens. But you did all the right things, and he's going to be all right.'

'Does he have to go to hospital?'

'No, he can stay at home. I'll leave you these pills – if he has any pain you just slip one under his tongue and let it dissolve. I'll see that you get a supply, but it's mostly rest that he needs. It's vital that he has bed-rest for at least two weeks and then takes it very easy – and I really do mean *very* easy, just getting up for an hour or two at most to sit in a chair by the window for instance, not even coming downstairs for some time after that. You'll need help. I can let you have the names of some excellent nurses. Diet's important too.' They heard quick footsteps on the stairs. 'Ah, that sounds like Val now.'

Val came in and went straight to the bed, casting a professional eye over the Squire. Hilary caught at her hand.

'It's a heart attack, Val. Dad's had a heart attack.'

Val squeezed her fingers. 'I know. Don't worry, Hilary. He's a strong man. He'll get over this, I'm sure.'

'I hope so,' Hilary said. 'Oh Val, I do hope so.'

Val looked at her friend. In Hilary's eyes she saw nothing but anxiety and love for her father. There was no sign that she had even considered the implications to herself of a long illness.

She'll never get away now, Val thought.

Stephen arrived at teatime. He was stationed at RAF Coltishall in Norfolk, and came by train through London to Tavistock. Val went to meet him in her father's farm-truck and was waiting on the platform as he jumped off the train, looking unfamiliar in his RAF uniform and dragging a grey canvas kitbag.

'Val! How is he?'

'Not too bad. The pain's under control now but he's very tired. Sleeping quite a lot, which is a good thing.' She marched briskly across the station yard and climbed into the driver's seat. Stephen tossed his kitbag into the back.

'Thanks for coming to meet me. What about Hilary – how's she coping?'

'As well as she copes with everything else. Doctor Latimer's arranging for a nurse to come in. Your dad has got to stay in bed for at least a fortnight, for a start. And there's the estate business, too. Pity you can't be here.'

'Well, I can't, can I?' he said defensively. 'I'm on National Service now. Can't get a discharge just because my father's got to stay in bed for a few weeks. I had to make a pretty strong case for getting these few days off now – make out he was virtually at death's door. Mind you, the way Hilary was carrying on this morning, I thought he was.'

'So did she. A heart attack's not funny, Stephen.'

'No,' he said after a pause, 'I know it isn't. Sorry, Val. I didn't mean that to sound the way it did. Of course I'm worried about the old man. Look, what are his chances? You're a nurse, you must know.'

Val drove in silence for a few moments. They were on their way through Whitchurch before she said, 'I don't think it was a really bad one, Stephen. Doctor Latimer called it a "warning". That means he could have another one, and it would probably be more serious. They leave scars on the heart, you see. And if you carry on doing the things that caused the first one, you're obviously in danger.'

'What sort of things? What do you mean?'

'Just generally doing too much, I suppose, in lots of different ways. Your father's not a young man, Stephen, and he's been through two wars. I know he didn't actually fight in the last one, but he was there, taking decisions, having to see his Regiment go into action. And he's lost his wife and his eldest son—'

'All right, you don't have to remind me about that,' Stephen cut in. He frowned and then said, 'So you're saying that it's what he's done and what's happened to him that's caused this, as much as any actual disease.'

'Partly, yes. He needs to take things more quietly. Get some help running the estate – that sort of thing. And cut down on what he eats and drinks as well,' she added. 'Really, he's got to do all he can to take some of the load off his heart.'

Stephen stared gloomily out of the window. They were out of the village now and running through farmland before crossing the moor to Burracombe. The afternoon light was so clear that the rocky tors stood out in sharp relief. A buzzard soared high above and a crowd of lambs raced from one end of a field to the other.

'I don't know what I can do,' he said at last. 'I've already had my Service postponed because of going to Cambridge. I don't think I can get exemption now.'

'And you don't want to, do you?' Val said quietly.

Stephen sighed. 'I'm a selfish swine, aren't I.'

'No, I don't think so, not really. You've got your life to live too.'

'Yes, but Dad thinks I ought to live it in Burracombe. Run the estate, be Squire like he is – like Baden would have been.' He sighed again. 'This would probably never have happened if Baden hadn't been killed.'

'A lot of things would never have happened if people hadn't been killed. But other things would have happened instead. It's no good thinking like that, Stephen. What you have to think about is what happens next. If you don't want to – or can't – run the estate, who will? Not that it's any of my business,' she added. 'It's Hilary you've got to talk to.'

They drove on, not speaking again, and Val dropped Stephen off at the Barton. He hauled his kitbag out of the truck and stared up for a moment at his father's bedroom window. Once again, he thought, their lives were about to change. Already *had* changed.

He heaved his kitbag on to his shoulder and started up the steps to the front door.

Stephen wasn't the only one to come home that week. The day after the Squire's heart attack, Roy Pettifer arrived on his first week's leave and astonished his mother with his polished shoes and sudden ability to iron his own trousers.

Without even waiting to change out of his uniform, he hurried round to the Tozers' farm and asked to see Jackie.

'Why, hello, Roy,' Alice said, a slightly reserved note in her voice. Jackie seemed to have cheered up a lot since the outing to London and she had a very good idea why. 'My stars, you do look smart! And how d'you like being a soldier?'

'It's all right. It's been all square-bashing so far.' He didn't tell her about the misery of those first weeks, the shouting and swearing, the continual hard graft and the apparently stupid things they'd had to do, just to learn to obey orders. That was more or less over now, he hoped, and they'd go on to more interesting things. He liked using firearms, and he was hoping that his skill with engines would be recognised and he'd be put on to tank maintenance. The massive vehicles fascinated him and he longed to get at their insides.

'I'm afraid Jackie's gone up to the Barton. They've got trouble there – Squire's had a heart attack. Had to get a nurse in, and Jackie's working extra time to help out. Mr Stephen's home too. You'd better go home again, boy, and I'll tell Jackie you'm back when she comes home.'

'You don't know when that'll be?'

'No, I don't. She said she might even stop the night. Dottie Friend's round there too, helping with the cooking. But I dare say her'll have a few hours off sometime. I'll tell her, don't you fret.'

Roy turned away and trudged off through the yard. He felt disappointed and vaguely hurt by Alice Tozer's manner. He'd expected a welcome, an invitation to come in and have a scone or something fresh from the oven – someone was always baking at the Tozers' farm – but instead she'd been quite cool and given him no idea as to when he might see Jackie. It was a funny thing, but he'd noticed a coolness in Jackie's letters too, just recently, and they hadn't been quite so frequent. He wondered what was going on and hoped her parents weren't putting her off him. He'd hoped they might get officially engaged during this leave.

He thought of their last proper meeting. The hour they'd spent up at the standing stones. It had been his first time as well as Jackie's and he thought he'd done pretty well. The memory of it had warmed him during the cold, lonely nights in Army camp, and it was all he'd thought about on the journey home. He wanted to do it again. He'd thought they'd do it again the first night he was home. And now he didn't even know when he'd see her.

Briefly, he remembered the Squire's heart attack. I suppose that means the old man will die, he speculated. Wonder what'll happen then. Anyway, whoever takes over, they'll still want housemaids. Jackie would still have a job.

When he reached home, his mother had a plate of scones ready, straight from the oven. He sat down and piled them with strawberry jam and cream, and ate four without stopping.

'We're going to have to have a talk, Steve,' Hilary said. She was pale and had huge dark rings under her eyes. Since discovering her father on the floor of his bedroom, gasping with pain, his eyes filled with fear, she had barely left his side. The nurse sent by Charles Latimer had urged her to get some rest, but she'd been unable to stay away for more than an hour or so and had then come back to sit beside him, holding his hand and watching his face. Even though he seemed to be sleeping peacefully, she'd been afraid to leave him.

Stephen's return had helped. Napier had been awake when he crept into the room, and his lips had moved in a weak smile. He'd lifted one hand and Stephen had gripped it in both of his. 'Hello, Dad.'

'Stephen.' The strong voice was barely a thread of sound. 'Glad you could make it.'

'You gave us a scare. But you're going to be fine now, Dad. And I can stay for a few days – enough to see you on the mend.'

A small shadow of disappointment crossed the white face. 'Only a few days? I thought—'

'Got to do my National Service, Dad – patriotic duty, you know,' Stephen reminded him, a lump in his throat as he remembered the arguments they'd had over his call-up. 'Can't get out of it now, I'm afraid.'

'Hm.' The grunt sounded almost like the Squire's normal sceptical reaction to one of his son's remarks. But the tired eyes were closing again and Stephen glanced across at his sister. She nodded slightly and motioned to him to join her by the window.

'He's just drifting in and out of sleep. Charles gave him some sedatives and I've got pills for if he has more pain. The nurse he sent seems very good – Pat Smith, she's called. She's having the Pink Room, so that she's nice and near. She's in there now, unpacking.'

Stephen nodded. He glanced again at his father, now sleeping, and hesitated. 'I might as well do the same, if that's all right with you.'

'Yes, of course. And go down to the kitchen – Dottie's there with Jackie; they're getting dinner ready but she'll give you something to be going on with. I think there's some cake in the tin . . .' Her voice trailed away as she sat down again by the bed and Stephen stood irresolute for a moment or two, then left the room. I don't really know what I should be doing, he thought, running down the stairs for his kitbag. What *does* one do at times like this? I'm not needed for the nursing or anything like that, and it sounds as though the kitchen's pretty well organised – not that I'd be much use if it wasn't! And I can't take over the estate because I've never been here long enough to know what's going on, and when I have been home I refused to take any interest.

In fact, he thought as he bent to heave the long, cumbersome bag on to his shoulder, I'm pretty useless all round, really. And as he climbed the stairs and went to his bedroom, he felt as if a cloud of gloom had descended upon him, crushing all the pleasure and satisfaction he'd felt during the past few weeks, and bringing with it a dread that the bright new world that had opened up before him was going to be taken away after all.

When Hilary told him again the next day that they needed to talk, he looked at her warily, noting the weariness in her face and feeling the dread sweep over him again. Yet he knew she was right. Baden, who would have kept everything together, was gone and it was up to them to decide what to do. Neither of them could escape the responsibilities that had been dropped on their shoulders.

'I know,' he said, 'and we'd better start now. The nurse is up there, isn't she?'

'Yes, and he's asleep again. She'll call us if she needs anything, so we'd better stay close by. Shall we go into the drawing room?'

They settled into two armchairs and Stephen handed her a glass of sherry. Hilary sipped it and leaned her head back against the cushions.

'You look worn out,' Stephen said.

'I'm all right. Just didn't get much sleep last night. And we had a pretty long day the day before, as well – at the Festival. Goodness, it seems years ago now.' Her voice quivered a little. 'I suppose it's shock too. It was so horrible, finding him on the floor like that. I thought he was dead, Steve.'

'I know. It must have been awful.'

'Then he started to gasp and cry out. He was clutching at

his chest with both hands, so I knew it must be a heart attack. I didn't know what to do, so I just pulled the pillows off the bed and wrapped the blankets around him and tried to make him more comfortable. Then I rang Charles and Val. Charles came straight away and gave him a pill, and we managed to get him back into bed.' She sat up, putting the sherry glass on to a small table and wiped her eyes. 'Sorry, managed to keep it back till now, but talking about it . . .'

'It's all right, Hil.' Stephen hadn't seen his sister cry for years, not even when she'd heard that her fiancé Henry had been killed. He got up and went over to pat her awkwardly on the shoulder. 'I expect it's good for you to cry. Let it out.'

Hilary sobbed for a few minutes, then pulled herself together. 'Sorry. I'll be all right now, I think. What are we going to do, Steve?'

'About Dad, you mean? Or about the estate?'

'Both. I know you can't come home, but something's got to be done. He's going to need nursing for quite a long time. Charles won't say how long – I suppose he can't. It's too early. But Dad's got to stay in bed for at least two weeks, and even after that he'll only be able to get up for short periods. It'll be months before he can do anything much at all. And Charles says he must never go back to doing everything he's been doing.'

'Things are going to have to change, aren't they,' Stephen said after a pause.

'Yes, they are. And we're the ones who are going to have to change them.'

'Don't ask me to be the one to tell Dad that,' he said wryly. 'It'll put his blood pressure straight up again. He's the one who makes the decisions round here, and a few weeks in bed aren't going to change that.'

Hilary sighed. 'I know, but surely we can do it gradually. If we can get things organised, so that he can see we're coping with it all, it'll be better for him than letting him start worrying. Because that's what he's going to do, and that's one of the things that Charles says are so bad for him.'

'All right,' Stephen said. 'So what's he going to worry about most? The house or the estate?'

'Well, the estate, of course. He knows I've got things in the house under control.'

'And you could have the estate under control as well.' He saw her startled look. 'You know you could, Hil! You go round with Dad, you know all the tenant farmers and they know you. They respect you, too, and they'd all rally round. I've always said you could run this place with one hand tied behind your back. Far better than I could, anyway.' He grinned. 'Mind you, even the dogs could run it better than I could!'

Hilary smiled faintly and picked up her glass again. 'That doesn't mean I could do it – or that Dad would let me. I can't just effect a *coup*, you know. It's still his estate.'

Stephen leaned forward. 'No, but now's probably the only chance you'll ever get to show him what you can do. Wouldn't it be better than just going on as you are, without any real life of your own? Well, wouldn't it?'

Hilary looked at him for a long moment. She took another drink of sherry. Then she said, 'I hadn't intended going on without any life of my own, Steve. I've been thinking a lot about that and I'd come to a decision. As a matter of fact, I was going to tell Dad about it yesterday.'

He stared at her. 'What? What decision?'

'I've been planning to leave home,' she said. 'I've been offered a room in a flat in London. I'd just decided to leave Burracombe and live my own life at last.'

Chapter Twenty-Five

Roy was waiting at the end of the Barton drive when Jackie walked home that evening. He stepped out from under the beech trees and she stopped abruptly. 'Roy!'

'Hello, Jackie.' He made to take her in his arms but she backed away. 'What's the matter, maid? Aren't you pleased to see me?'

'I don't know – I mean, it's a surprise, that's all. What are you doing here? I didn't know you were coming home this week.'

'You knew it was going to be soon.' He sounded sulky. 'Come on, Jackie, give us a kiss. I've been looking forward to seeing you again.'

'Sorry.' She lifted her face and let him kiss her, but drew away again as his lips grew more urgent. 'Don't do that! Not here – anyone could see.'

'You weren't so fussy last time,' he grumbled, dropping his arms. 'What's got into you, Jackie?'

'Nothing. I'm just tired, that's all.' She began to walk on. 'We've got trouble here. Squire's ill.'

'I know, your mum told me. But that don't make no difference to you and me, does it?'

'No, I suppose not.' But her voice was listless and he gave her a sharp look.

'What is it? What's the matter? You've gone cold. Don't you love me no more, is that it? Have you started going out with someone else, the minute me back's turned?'

'No! I haven't been out with anyone else. If you want to know, I've hardly been out at all since you went away. I've been too busy sitting at home writing you letters.'

Roy stared at her. This wasn't at all the homecoming he'd expected. All the way home, he'd pictured Jackie running into his arms, letting him kiss her, kissing him back. He'd imagined them walking along the lane together, their arms round each other's waists, climbing through the woods to the standing stones, making love again in the very same grassy hollow with the stars wheeling above and the scent of gorse and heather all about them.

He quickened his step so that he was in front of her, then turned to block her way. 'So what's all this about, then?' he demanded. 'What have I done to upset you? You're treating me like something the cat dragged in.'

To his dismay, Jackie burst into tears. She stopped, right in the middle of the lane, and put both hands over her face. He stood helplessly before her, feeling angry and hurt. '*Now* what's the matter?'

'You don't understand!' she wept. 'You don't understand at all, Roy Pettifer. There's poor Squire laying up there in his bed and nobody knows whether he's going to live or die, and I've been there all day doing whatever I could, and Doctor's been three times, and there's this nurse come from Plymouth wanting this, that and the other, and Miss Hilary all upset and getting Mr Stephen home from Norfolk, and only me and Dottie Friend to see to everything, and you turn up and expect me to be all pleased and excited and just as if I've had nothing to think about but you coming home. And I can't, that's all. I just can't.' She burst into fresh sobs and Roy put his arms round her awkwardly.

'I'm sorry, Jackie. I really am. I never thought of it like that.'

'You never think at all, that's your trouble,' she sniffed,

but she didn't push him away. 'Look, I just want to go home and go to bed, Roy. I'm tired out.'

'Well, will I see you tomorrow, then?'

'I dunno,' she said wearily. 'I promised to go back as early as I could. There's ever so much to do there.'

'I haven't got all that long,' he said. 'Only a few days.' His suspicions returned. 'You do want to see me, don't you?'

There was a lengthy pause. They were walking along the lane now, and approaching the farm gate. Jackie sighed and turned to him.

'I don't know what I want, Roy. I'm too tired to think about it. Look – I'll try to get out sometime tomorrow. I'll come round to your house, shall I? That'll be best.'

'All right,' he said doubtfully, and watched as she unlatched the gate. She went through and turned to say goodnight, and he said, 'Aren't you even going to give us a kiss then, maid?'

Jackie hesitated, then leaned across the rail and gave him a brief peck on the lips. 'Goodnight, Roy.'

'Goodnight, Jackie,' he said, and stood there while she crossed the yard and opened the farmhouse door. Then he turned away and walked off down the lane towards the pub. If there was nothing else to do, he might as well go and have a drink. There were bound to be a few old mates there.

Perhaps it was just that she was tired and upset. Girls were funny like that.

It was true that Jackie was upset, but it wasn't just about the Squire. It had certainly been a shock to answer the phone yesterday morning and hear Hilary's frantic voice asking for Val, and she'd gulped the rest of her breakfast down hurriedly and arrived at the Barton close behind her sister. She'd been on the go ever since, doing her best to keep things going without Hilary's instructions, deciding for herself what ought to be cooked for lunch and dinner, letting people in as news of the Squire's illness had permeated round the village. It had been a relief when Dottie Friend arrived to lend a hand, but Dottie had other commitments too, at the pub and in the doctor's house. She'd been a big help, but Jackie was the only one who was there all the time.

Yet, despite the anxiety and the rush of it all, Jackie had found herself – in a strange, scarcely acknowledged way – enjoying it. She had never had full responsibility before, never been expected to make decisions, and although just deciding what to cook for dinner wasn't exactly world-shaking, it made her feel grown-up and competent. She liked it.

What had really upset her was seeing Roy waiting for her at the end of the drive.

It's daft, she thought as she went through the kitchen with barely a nod to her mother and grandmother. I knew he'd be coming back soon. And now that I know I'm not going to have a baby, I ought to be pleased to see him. I love him, don't I? We were going to get engaged . . .

She stood at the window, gazing out at the twilit fields and the dark bulk of the moors, and repeated the words over to herself. *I love him . . . We were going to get engaged* . . . They sounded strange, like a foreign language she only half understood.

'Jackie! *Jackie!*'

The girl went to the bedroom door. Her mother was standing at the foot of the stairs, calling up to her. 'Jackie, come down here. Me and your granny want to know how the Squire is. You came in with such a rush, we wondered . . .' She looked closely at her daughter as she came slowly back to the kitchen. 'He'm not worse, is he?'

Minnie was in her chair by the stove. She looked

288

anxious, her eyes wide and her wrinkled lips shaking. Jackie felt ashamed; she should have known they'd be waiting for news.

'No, he's not worse. Miss Hilary says it'll be a few days before they know for certain he's going to get properly better, but she told me the doctor's pleased with him. And the nurse is looking after him, and Mr Stephen's there as well.' She paused. 'It do seem funny though,' she said, her own voice quivering suddenly. 'I've never known him ill before, and to think he could have died all on his own up there, laying on the floor . . .'

Her voice broke and she sat down suddenly at the table and started to cry again. Alice came over quickly and laid her arm across her shoulders, murmuring comfortingly. She looked at Minnie.

'I knew she were more upset than she let on. 'Tis a shock for a young girl. And they've been asking a lot of her too, these past couple of days.'

'I don't mind working extra time,' Jackie said tearfully. 'Miss Hilary's been good to me. I didn't even know I was upset!'

'Poor Mr Gilbert,' Minnie said sadly. 'Knowed him since he were a little tacker, I have. I used to be his nursemaid when he were a babby, pushed him in his pram many a time. I never thought he'd go before me—'

'Mother!' Alice said sharply. 'He hasn't gone at all yet, nor's he going to. Didn't you hear our Jackie just say he weren't no worse and the doctor's pleased with him? Don't upset her any more than she is already.'

Jackie lifted her head and wiped her eyes. 'I'm all right, Mum. It just came over me a bit sudden. I'll help you get supper ready, shall I?'

'No, you won't.' Alice looked at her carefully. 'You'm looking worn out. You go and have a lay-down while me and your granny sees to it. Oh, and there was something else I meant to tell you. Young Roy was round here an hour or two ago. Home on leave, he is – come to ask for you. I dare say he'll be back sometime this evening.'

'I know. I saw him. He met me as I was coming home.' Jackie's voice was dreary as she got up from the table, and her mother and grandmother raised their eyebrows at each other. 'I told him I was too tired. I expect I'll see him tomorrow, sometime.' She went up the stairs and they heard the creak of her bed overhead as she lay down.

'Well!' Alice said in a low voice, lifting a pan of potatoes on to the top of the stove. 'And what do you make of that?'

'Same as you, I dare say,' Minnie said. 'She's had a fright. I think young Roy Pettifer's the next one due for a shock – and serve him right!'

Stephen Napier had had a shock too. He stared at his sister and then got up and poured himself a second sherry.

'You're not serious,' he said at last. 'Leave Burracombe? Go to live in London? *You?*'

'Why not?' she asked defensively. 'Don't tell me you just see me as a substitute for a wife and housekeeper too, because that's all Dad sees me as now – and I'm tired of it, Steve. I'm really, really tired of it.' Her voice shook a little and she held out her glass. 'I'll have another one too, please.'

He did as she requested, still looking stunned. 'But you're such a country girl, Hilary. You like everything about it – the farms, the moors, the hunting, everything. And you love Burracombe. How can you think of going to live in a place like London?'

'I haven't always lived in the country though,' she pointed out. 'Don't forget, I was in the Army. I had a high rank and a responsible job. I worked with some of the most important men in the war. I miss it. I miss the company, the responsibility, all of it. I miss being someone people think is capable. I suppose I miss the respect.'

'People respect you here,' he said.

'Do they? Do they really? Oh, I'm the Squire's daughter so some of the older ones still touch their forelocks or lift their caps as I pass by, but I'm not sure that's the sort of respect I want. It isn't the sort I've earned, is it? Apart from that I'm quite good at arranging the flowers in the church, and being secretary of the Mother's Union and WI, and I can't think of much else. It's not exactly what they'll put on my tombstone, is it, Steve?' She drank again. 'I'll have one of those fulsome tributes that you see on church walls – *She was a dutiful daughter, wise and gentle in her ways, and loved by all who met her*. Well, is that how *you'd* like to be remembered?'

'Well, since I'm not a daughter . . .' Stephen began, then caught her eye. 'Sorry, Hil. I know it's not funny. But there could be worse ways to be remembered, you know.'

'Worse than being a dutiful daughter? I don't think so.' She put down her glass. 'I'd better not drink any more of this. I'll have to go and sit with Dad again soon. Nurse Smith's being very good but she's got to have some time off.'

'I know. I'll do my share as well, while I'm here. I'm only sorry I've got to go back the day after tomorrow.'

'Oh, that's all right.' Hilary leaned back against the cushions. 'I suppose I'll just have to set my own plans aside until we see what's going to happen.'

Stephen looked at her and, for the first time, saw Hilary as a person rather than just the girl he'd grown up with and known all his life as his big sister. He saw a tall, slim young woman with fair hair worn in a loose page-boy style and tired grey eyes. She was nearly thirty, he realised, and had lost her chance of marriage when her fiancé had been killed

– yet why shouldn't she have another chance? Why hadn't some lucky man snapped her up long before this?

Perhaps she was right – she needed to get away from Burracombe, start a new life, find another circle of friends. It wasn't right that a woman like Hilary should moulder away in the country, doing all the things a married woman would do, yet not being married. It might not have been so bad if she'd never known anything different, but she had. She'd had a very different life during the war, and he wasn't surprised she missed it.

'Don't forget what I said about emigrating,' he said at last. 'It's still on the cards, you know.'

'And how long do I have to wait for that? Two years – three – while you finish your National Service? You might decide to stay in the RAF even longer. You might make it *your* career. And I'll still be stuck here, arranging flowers and asking Dad what he wants for supper.' She bit her lip and added more quietly, 'That's if *he's* still here.'

'Of course he will be!' There was an edge of panic in Stephen's voice. 'Charles Latimer says he'll be fine in a few months. He's just not got to do so much. He'll be all right, Hil.'

'This time, yes. But what if it happens again?' She met her brother's eyes. 'One of these days, it's going to be the last time.'

'I know. But—'

'And who do you think is going to have to take over?'

He stirred uncomfortably and didn't speak.

'How do you think Dad will have made out his Will? You know what he's like. He won't leave this place to me, that's for certain.'

Panic flared in his eyes now. 'I don't want it – he knows I don't!'

'You'll get it all the same. He believes it should be left to the eldest son and now that Baden's gone, that's you.' She stood up and brushed down her skirt. 'But you've got plenty of time to play at aeroplanes before then, because it's not going to happen for a long time. Now I'd better go and take over from Nurse Smith. You'll come up when you've had your dinner, will you?'

'Yes,' he said in a deflated tone, sitting back in his chair. 'Yes, I'll come up then.'

Hilary left the room and Stephen sat and stared at the empty fireplace. He felt vaguely ashamed of his part in the conversation. It didn't seem fitting to be talking about what would happen when their father died, yet Hilary was right – it would have to be faced eventually. Neither of them could drift along as if Gilbert Napier would live for ever.

Some day, someone was going to inherit the estate, and it was almost certain to be himself. It wasn't something that could be tossed aside like an unwanted keepsake. He could stay in the RAF, he could emigrate, he could fly to the moon, but it would still have to be dealt with. The Barton was a major part of his life, whether he wanted it or not.

Stephen buried his face in his hands and groaned.

By the time Jackie came home from work the next evening, Roy was almost in flames with impatience. Once again, he was waiting at the Barton gates, and this time he wouldn't take no for an answer.

'I've only got a couple of days, Jackie. You've got to come with me.'

'Why?' She saw the look on his face and shrugged. 'Oh, all right, then. Where d'you want to go?'

'Anywhere, so long as it's with you. Anywhere nobody can see us.' He gripped her hand tightly and began to walk along the lane. 'I want to be with you. I want to kiss you properly. Don't you want to kiss me?'

'Yes,' she said without enthusiasm. 'Of course I want to, Roy.'

'Well, you might sound as if you meant it,' he grumbled. There was a short silence, then he said, 'How's the Squire, then?'

'A bit better, I think. No worse, anyway. I took a cup of tea in for the nurse today and he's all propped up on pillows. They're not letting him lay down at all. I don't see how he gets any sleep – I know I couldn't, if I was sitting up all night.' She waited as Roy opened the gate into the woods. 'I don't want to be too long, Roy, Mum's expecting me back for supper.'

'She'll know you'm with me.' He closed the gate again and glanced at her. 'You never used to be so particular about your mother, Jackie.'

'Well, maybe I've grown up a bit since then.' They began to climb the narrow path, twisting its way up the hill between the trees and moss–clad rocks. 'A lot's happened since you went away, Roy.'

'And what's that supposed to mean?' He stopped and looked at her. 'You *have* met someone else! You've been two–timing me!'

'I haven't! I told you, I stayed in every night and wrote to you. You know that.' She tried to pull her hand away but he gripped it even more tightly. 'Let me go, Roy. You're hurting me.'

'Well, you're hurting me, too. I thought you'd be real pleased to see me again and you've treated me like dirt. Like *dirt*. And you say you've been writing to me every evening – well, all I can say is, you must have been doing something else as well, because the last week or so you haven't written more than a line or two any night. What's been going on, Jackie? Don't you think I got a right to know?'

Jackie looked around. They were well above the village now, almost at the edge of the moor. Not far above them were the standing stones, encircling their grassy hollow. If there was one place she didn't want to go, it was to the standing stones.

'All right,' she said, sitting down on a rock cushioned with moss. 'I'll tell you.' She waited as Roy sat down beside her and then turned to look at his face. 'I thought I was going to have a baby.'

There was a long silence. She saw Roy's face change — first with shock, then with dismay, a shiver of fear, and finally with a puzzled kind of relief. 'You *thought* you were? So you're not, then?'

'No. But I didn't know that until this week — when we were in London. It's been awful, Roy. I didn't know what to do. And I couldn't tell anyone — not till Val asked me, anyway.'

'Val? Your sister? You mean she knows?'

'Yes, and I think Miss Hilary does as well. But never mind that, it was you I ought to have been able to tell and I couldn't because you weren't here. I didn't know what to do,' she said again, reliving the terror of those weeks. 'You don't know how awful it was.'

'Well, it must have been. But if you're not — well, everything's all right, isn't it? And I promise it won't happen again.' He stroked her arm. 'I've got some rubbers — you know, French letters. We can get them on the station so I brought some with me. It'll be all right next time, Jackie.'

'Next time?' She turned her head and stared at him. 'What are you talking about? There isn't going to be a next time, Roy! I'm never going to go through that again, never.'

'But if we use—'

'*No!*' She was on her feet, tearing her hand from his grasp. 'I've told you, Roy, I'm never going through it again, never. I don't care what you use, I'm not taking any more chances.' She stared down at him. 'D'you know what would have happened to me if it had been true? My dad would

295

have turned me out and my mum would probably have died of shame. Nobody would ever have spoken to me again. I'd have had to leave the village and I'd probably have had to give the baby away. And what could *you* have done about it?'

Roy jumped up too. 'I could have married you, of course! That's what we want to do anyway, isn't it? I know our families wouldn't have been best pleased, but they'd have got over it, and they'd have had to let us get married.' He gripped her hand again, his eyes shining. 'Jackie, think of it! We could get married – we could just tell them—'

'No!' she shouted again. 'No, we couldn't! I'm not telling lies and having everyone look at me and waiting for me to get fat. And what about when I *don't* get fat? What are we supposed to say then? And anyway,' she turned her face away, then turned back and looked him in the eye, 'I don't want to marry you, Roy. I wouldn't marry you if you were the last man on earth.'

The silence this time was so intense that Roy felt as if he could hear the moss growing on the rocks at his feet. He kept his eyes on Jackie's face, unable to believe what he had just heard. The world seemed to sway about him and he heard his blood roar in his ears; then it steadied and he realised that he felt sick.

'What do you mean?' he whispered at last.

Jackie took her hand out of his. His fingers seemed to have no strength in them. 'What I say. I don't want to marry you.' Her voice was quiet too, and tired, as if by shouting at him she had used up all her energy.

Roy shook his head. 'I don't understand. Why not? What have I done wrong? Jackie, we love each other. You don't mean it – you can't.'

'I do. I don't want to marry anyone. Not if it's going to be like this – all this trouble. I'd rather be single, like our Val.'

'All what trouble? I told you, it won't happen again.' He reached for her hand once more. 'Jackie, you said you loved me.'

'I thought I did.'

'You mean you don't any more? But I still love you!'

'I can't help it,' she said. 'It's not just the baby, anyway.'

'So what is it? What have I done?' He returned once more to his old suspicions. 'There *is* somebody else!'

'There's *not*! How many times do I have to tell you? There's nobody else and I don't suppose there ever will be.' She started to walk back down the path and he grabbed her arm again. 'Let go of me, Roy!'

'Not until you tell me what this is all about.' All his anxiety and disappointment came together in a flash of real anger. 'I got a right to know, Jackie! If it's not somebody else, and it's not anything I've done, and it's not the baby that never was, what the hell *is* it?'

'There's no need to swear,' she said. She stopped again and drew in a heavy sigh. 'All right, then, if you must know, it's what we done. You and me. What you wants to do again.'

'What we . . .' For a moment, he didn't understand what she meant. Then a painful flush swept up his neck. 'You mean when us went all the way? Up at the stones?'

'Yes.'

'But – but what's wrong with that? Oh, I know us shouldn't have, and I know you've been worried and upset – but there weren't nothing *wrong* about it, not really. It's just doing what comes naturally. Everyone does it. Even your mum and dad must have done it, or you wouldn't be here now.'

'Don't talk like that!' she flared. 'I know all that – I'm not a kid. But I didn't like it, that's all. I didn't like it and I don't want to do it again, and that's all there is to it.' She began to walk down the hill again.

Roy stood bewildered for a moment, then caught her up. 'What do you mean, you didn't like it? You wanted to do it as much as I did.'

'So I might have done, but I didn't know what it was like, did I? Now I do.'

'But it was marvellous. I thought so, anyway.' His voice was bemused, the anger gone. 'You don't really mean that, do you?'

'Yes, I do.' She turned and faced him again. 'It was uncomfortable. There was a rock sticking into my back, and it hurt. And you hurt me too. I didn't like it and I don't want to do it again, and if that's what being married is all about, I'll stay single.' She walked on again.

This time, Roy didn't follow her. He stood very still, rejected and humiliated. He thought of the times he'd relived that magical experience by the standing stones, under a twilit sky. He thought of the promises he and Jackie had made to each other, the plans they'd made, the life they'd meant to lead. He thought of the excitement he had felt on his way home.

She couldn't mean it. It didn't seem possible that she no longer loved him. It didn't seem possible that she hadn't felt that magic too, that it had been something uncomfortable and even painful for her.

He watched her go down the path and through the gate. He waited for her to turn and look up at him, but she didn't. He put his hand into his pocket and felt the little packet there, the packet that should have enabled them to love each other safely, without any of the worries Jackie had suffered over the past few weeks.

Then he turned and walked up the hill again. He found his way through the gathering darkness to the standing stones and their hollow, and he lay down on the grass alone and stared up at the wheeling stars.

Chapter Twenty-Six

Val spent as much time as she could at the Barton, but her duties meant that she could spare only an hour or so each evening. About a week after the Squire's heart attack, she hurried up the drive to find Hilary walking on the terrace. She ran up the steps and Hilary turned to look at her.

'Hilary! Whatever's the matter? You look as if you've been crying.'

'Oh, nothing.' Hilary shrugged and her mouth twisted. 'Or everything. Nothing new, anyway.'

Val stared at her. 'You're not making sense. What is it? Is your father worse?'

'No, he's still making good progress. Charles says if he goes on like this he'll be able to get out of bed and sit in a chair next week. Can you imagine, Val? Dad, sitting in a chair! It's as if he's become an old man all of a sudden.'

'Well, he's not a young one, is he?' Val said quietly. 'And he will get stronger, you know. The heart takes a long time to heal but in a few months . . .'

'A few months!' Hilary echoed. 'In a few months he'll be back to normal. And what about me, Val? Where will *I* be in a few months? What will *I* be doing?'

Val gazed at her helplessly.

'I'll tell you,' Hilary said bitterly. 'I'll be stuck here, the same as before. I'll be running the house and arranging the church flowers and doing all the things I've been doing ever since Mother died. I'm going to be doing them for ever,

Val. For the rest of my life. I'm *trapped*. I'm trapped all over again.'

'Oh Hilary . . .'

'It's true. I've known it all along really. I knew I'd never be able to leave and go to London. It was just a dream.' Hilary sat down on a bench and stared out across the wide lawn. Tonelessly, she said, 'I was a fool to think things could change.'

Val sat beside her and took her hand. 'What's happened? Tell me.'

Hilary sat without speaking for a few minutes. Then she heaved a sigh and turned to her friend. Her face was sad, as if she had just given up something that meant a great deal. She said, 'Stephen's gone back to Coltishall.'

'Oh.' Val didn't know what to say. 'But you knew he was going back. He only had a few days' compassionate leave, didn't he?'

'Oh yes, I knew he'd be going. But now that he has . . . We had a long talk about things – several talks, in fact. I don't think we came to any fresh conclusion but at least we've thrashed it all out between us. He's never going to come and take over the estate, Val.'

'No, I don't think he is. You knew that too, didn't you?'

'Yes, of course. He's made it clear often enough. But I suppose I thought, when Dad was taken ill . . . well, that it might have changed Steve's mind, made him think a bit more about it. Made him look at the place with fresh eyes.' She sighed again.

Val said, 'But it didn't.'

'No. It didn't make any difference at all. He really doesn't want to have anything to do with it. And he's right, I suppose – he wouldn't be much good at it. But would that really matter? There've been other Squires who weren't very good – look at our great-grandfather! He was terrible – wasted money, lost several farms gambling, let the house and gardens run down, but when Grandad took over everything improved again, and by the time he died, the estate was back to where it had been before. It's keeping it in the family that's important, and Stephen wouldn't have been as bad as that. He wouldn't even have to do the work himself – he could just put in a good manager, like we had when Daddy was away during the war.'

'Who would cost a lot of money.'

'Well, yes, there is that. But it would be better than letting it all be split up, which is what he's talking about doing.'

'So what's the answer?' Val asked.

Hilary shrugged. 'We'll just go on as we are. I'll stay here and look after Dad and do whatever I can. At least I know enough about the estate to be able to take over most of the work he used to do. We won't need to think about getting a manager just yet. But I suppose that's what we'll have to do in the end.'

'And London?' Val ventured, hardly daring to ask.

'Oh, that's gone by the board. I've written to Katharine telling her it's off. She'll be able to find someone else for the flat easily enough.' Hilary looked up at the sky. 'So much for my dream of becoming an air stewardess and flying all over Europe. America, too. Oh Val, I'm sorry. You come to see me in your time off and all you get is moans and groans. I'm a selfish, self-pitying wreck!'

'You're not at all.' Val put her arm round Hilary's shoulders. 'What are friends for if you can't let off steam to them? Oh Hil, I'm really sorry about all this. I know I didn't want you to go away – that was *me* being selfish – but I'm sorry you can't. I know how much you wanted to have your own life.'

'Mm. Well, I suppose I just have to accept the fact that this *is* my life. At least I did have those few years when I saw something more. If it hadn't been for the war, I'd never have had even that.'

'If it hadn't been for the war, a lot of things would have been different,' Val said quietly, and they sat together in silence for a while, looking at the lawns sweeping away to the beech wood and the moors above. 'Everyone's lives have been changed by the war, one way or another. But it doesn't necessarily mean they'd have been better.'

'We just can't tell.' There was a pause, then Hilary laughed and jumped to her feet. 'Listen to us, getting all philosophical! Come on, let's go indoors. Dottie's left a nice cold supper for us and Stephen brought up a bottle of wine from Dad's cellar last night. We never opened it, and I was going to put it back today, but I think we'll have it instead, don't you? Drown our sorrows?'

'Sounds a good idea.' Val got up and followed her into the house. But before she went in, she cast a last look at the view of the fields, the woods and moors, and wondered just how different her life would have been if it hadn't been for the war.

Eddie would still be alive, for a start. And she would never have met Luke Ferris.

Luke was sitting with Stella in the little orchard behind Dottie's cottage. The cherry-blossom was over but the apple trees were as white as snow, gently tinged with pink as if touched by the sunset. There were a few bluebells nodding their azure heads in the grass, and birds were busy dashing to and fro with their beaks laden with small worms and insects for fledglings or nesting partners. Stella followed their flight with her eyes, but she felt dispirited and watched them without her usual joy.

Once again, the search for Muriel seemed to have hit a brick wall. With Luke's help, she had written to everyone they could think of, but nobody had been able to come up with anything. The records of any orphanage that Muriel might have been sent to had been lost. There weren't even any records of where Stella herself had gone, and if anyone had been searching for her they would have reached the same impasse.

'So if Muriel's been looking for me, she'd be having just the same problems,' she said despairingly. 'I don't see what else we can do, Luke.'

'There may still be some way,' Luke said. He leaned back in the old wooden seat and closed his eyes, letting the warmth of the sun stroke his face. 'We could advertise in a newspaper.'

'Well, perhaps.' She turned her head and looked at him. His face had lost some of its winter pallor and was lightly tanned by the sun. Long dark lashes lay on his cheeks and she thought of the dark-blue depths of the eyes hidden beneath their lids. He was still thin, but not so gaunt as he had been when she had first met him last October. Burracombe suited him, she thought, just as it did her. The outdoor life, with so much of his time spent in the open air, walking the moors and painting, had completed his cure and he looked in perfect health. She wondered suddenly if he had any plans to go back to London, and felt a twinge of dismay.

Luke opened his eyes suddenly and stared at her. Stella felt her cheeks colour and turned hastily away. 'I was just going to ask you something,' she said at random, 'but I thought you were asleep.'

'No, just enjoying the warmth. What was it?'

'Nothing – I can't remember now.' Her colour deepened. 'It was probably about the newspaper idea. I don't know, Luke, I just can't see it working. We don't know which newspaper she reads or if she even looks at the Personal columns, or if she'd realise it was meant for her anyway. I mean, what are we going to say? "Have you lost a sister?" It sounds silly.'

'I do have another idea,' he said thoughtfully. 'I've heard that the Salvation Army looks for missing people.'

'I tried that, while I was still at college. They don't look for people who might have been adopted, and I'm sure she must have been, otherwise we would have found each other. I just can't think of anything else, Luke. I don't think I'm ever going to know what happened to her.'

At the desolate note in her voice, Luke turned and slipped his arm around her shoulders. 'Stella, don't give up. She must be out there somewhere. There must be some way of finding her. What about the woman you stayed with in Portsmouth – didn't you say she kept in touch with you?'

'Yes, until we were taken away from Bridge End. After that, we weren't allowed to write letters. At least, I wasn't . . .' She turned to him with a flash of hope. 'But *Muriel* might have been able to. Luke, you're a genius! All I need do is write to Auntie Jess! Muriel might have been going to see her all these years. I can't think why it never occurred to me before!'

'Hold on a minute,' he said, half-laughing, half-anxious. 'It's only a guess. It might not have happened that way at all. This "Auntie Jess" might never have heard from Muriel again. She might not even live there any more. All sorts of things might have happened.'

'Yes, I suppose so,' Stella said, feeling a bit flattened. 'But it's worth a try, isn't it. I can write to her. If she answered straight away, I might know by the end of the week. I'll do that, Luke. I'll write this evening and post the letter first thing tomorrow. Oh, wouldn't it be wonderful!'

Luke looked at her. Her face was bright and happy again, her eyes sparkling with excitement. He felt a rush of tenderness towards her and tightened his arm around her shoulders. She turned her face towards him and her lips parted in a smile of joyfulness. Without even thinking about it, he bent towards her and kissed her mouth.

'Oh,' Stella said faintly as he drew back again. 'Luke—'

'I'm sorry,' he said hastily. 'I didn't mean to do that. Don't be upset.'

'I'm not upset. I just didn't expect . . .'

'Neither did I,' he said. He hesitated, then withdrew his arm. His heart was thumping a little and he felt confused and uncertain. He said again, 'I'm sorry.'

'You don't have to be sorry,' she said. 'I – I didn't mind.'

Luke looked at her more carefully. Stella had never mentioned any boyfriends to him, never given any hint that she had ever had a relationship. For all he knew, this might be the first kiss she had ever had. He didn't know what she might make of it. Plenty of girls would treat it lightly, as no more than a kiss, a friendly gesture or something that might lead to more. He had a feeling that Stella was not like those girls. Stella would take it seriously.

He disengaged himself and stood up. 'I'm sorry – I'd better be going. I promised to start sorting out paintings for the exhibition. Mrs Warren's coming up to the cottage tomorrow to look at them.' He looked down at her and said gently, 'Don't worry about it, Stella. It was just that I felt so pleased for you – pleased that there's still a chance. Let me know when you hear from your Auntie Jess, won't you?'

He opened the gate and Stella heard his footsteps receding up the lane. She sat motionless, still feeling the touch of his lips on hers, and then she lifted one hand and touched her mouth with her fingers. The sun seemed suddenly to have grown very warm, the song of the birds was sweeter, and the colours of the garden much more vivid.

She got up and wandered slowly into the cottage to write her letter.

Luke walked down the lane, his hands in his pockets, his head down. He was angry with himself for kissing Stella Simmons. She was hardly more than a child, for all that she was a teacher. She had lived almost all her life in a Children's Home, leaving it only to go to college, which had probably been all women anyway. Not only was he almost certainly the first man to kiss her, he was probably the first man she'd ever had as a friend. He knew all too well how easily a girl like that could be swept off her feet.

And yet . . . And yet . . . He felt again that strange, warm tenderness and knew that he too had enjoyed the kiss. Her lips were soft and gentle, her body yielding towards his. And they were friends, with a pleasant, easy companionship that had comforted him through the cold, dark days of winter and through the bleakness of his relationship with Val Tozer.

Perhaps, he thought, he had loved Val long enough. She'd made it clear that she wanted nothing to do with him. He could live the rest of his life alone, wishing for something he could never have. Or he could turn his back and walk into a different future.

He was aware of standing on the brink of an abyss. He could let himself fall in love with Stella Simmons, or he could draw back.

What he could not do, *must* not do, was let Stella fall in love with him if he didn't mean to return her love. He could not ruin the lives of two women. Rather than that, he would have to leave Burracombe and disappear from both their lives.

The thought was a cold and lonely one, and he knew that it would not be simply the two women he would miss. He would miss Burracombe itself – the clustered cottages, the inhabitants with their different characters, some friendly like Dottie, others wary like Jacob Prout – and even he was beginning to come round, Luke thought with a smile. He would miss the companionship in the pub, the welcome he had been given at some of the farms, the solitude of the fields and moorland with its rolling hills, its rocky tors and hidden combes. He would miss the chime of the bells as they rang throughout the valley, and the mew of the buzzard as it soared into the sky, and the high, sweet singing of the lark.

All this was a part of him now. It was in his heart and his mind, and it went into his paintings. He did not know what he would paint if he left the village now.

He came to the gate to the woods and climbed the path to the charcoal-burner's cottage. In half an hour or so, Joyce Warren would be there with her ebullient presence, sweeping him along, commandeering his pictures for her exhibition, taking him over as she took everybody over.

Even she was a part of Burracombe. Even she was a part of what he didn't want to leave.

Chapter Twenty-Seven

Gilbert Napier continued to make slow but steady progress, and by the middle of June he was able to sit in an easy chair by his bedroom window, looking out over the wide lawns towards the beech trees and the moor. His first shock over, he was insistent that he felt well again, and Hilary was hard put to it to prevent him from getting up altogether.

'You've still got to go very carefully, Dad. You know what Charles said. As long as you're resting, you will feel better, but you mustn't put any strain on your heart. You mustn't even climb the stairs, so what would be the point of you coming down?'

'We could have a bedroom made up for me. What about the breakfast room?'

'Well, I'm using it quite a lot – it's cosier than the dining room.'

'The dining room, then.'

'Dad, you know we can't do that! That huge table – where would it go? And all the silver and everything.'

'So start eating there and let me have the breakfast room!' he barked, and Hilary stifled a sigh. There was no point in keeping her father upstairs to save him strain, if he were simply going to get himself all worked up about it. As well as physical rest, Charles Latimer had told her he must be spared any worry or anxiety. Yet she knew exactly what would happen if he came downstairs too soon.

'The next thing he'll be wanting to do is go to the estate

office,' she told the doctor next time he came. 'And then he'll start worrying about how things are being run there, and wanting to interfere. He'll want me to take him round in the Land Rover and before we know it, he'll be back working as hard as ever.'

'I rather expected this,' Charles said. 'He's used to being active – boredom will be his biggest enemy. I'll talk to him, anyway.' He went up to the bedroom, where Gilbert greeted him with a scowl.

'I hope you're going to make that girl of mine see sense. I'm perfectly all right now. What harm could it possibly do to make me up a bed downstairs? I could go outside – sit on the terrace, get some fresh air.'

'You seem to be getting plenty of fresh air here,' the doctor said, looking at the open window. 'I know it's frustrating, Gilbert, but you've got to follow the rules. You don't want another attack, do you?'

'Of course not! But—'

Charles sat down in the other chair. 'Believe me, Gilbert, this is the best way. Hilary's quite right when she says that if you come downstairs too soon you'll start wanting to go outside – which would be fine if you just stuck to the terrace, but you wouldn't, would you? You'd be wheedling or, more likely, bullying the poor girl into taking you to the office. Then it would be a trip round the estate in the Land Rover, perhaps dropping in to see some of the farmers. And you'll naturally want to discuss their farms with them, ask if they've got any problems – and before anyone can say Jack Robinson, you'll be back at work and heading for another attack. And the next one might not be a warning.'

The Squire sat silent for a moment or two, frowning. Then he said grudgingly, 'Well, maybe I would. But dammit, Charles, the work's got to be done. Can't let the place go to rack and ruin.'

'Is it going to? Hilary tells me she's putting in quite a bit of time in the office, and I saw her over at Whitstone yesterday when I looked in to see the old lady. She seemed to be getting along quite well with Stan Hodge and his son.'

'Hilary's got the house to run.'

'Dottie's helping out there, and young Jackie. You could always get more help in if you feel it's too much for her.' He paused. 'You trust your daughter, don't you?'

'Trust her? Of course I do! What sort of a question's that?'

'So why not give her her head? Let her take over the estate work for a while, just until you're fit again, and leave her to it. You can work your way back in gradually after a couple of months and take over again when you're completely fit. Mind you, you mustn't ever take on as much as you've been doing – that's what led to this first attack. But you and Hilary could work together.'

'And what about the house? I was thinking of getting a manager in for the estate, just for the time being. Then the girl wouldn't have to worry herself about it.'

'And where would you get a manager good enough to take over at a moment's notice but willing to leave again in a few months?' the doctor asked. 'It would be much easier for Hilary to find a housekeeper. And the business would be safe in her hands. It would still be in the family.'

Gilbert Napier sat silent, his face set in a heavy frown. Charles waited quietly, knowing that his old friend needed time to readjust his thinking. The idea of Hilary taking his place in managing the estate might need quite a lot of time.

'Think about it, Gilbert,' he said at last. 'At the very least, it means that you needn't make any big decisions just yet. Take the time to rest and get your strength back. But I do think Hilary needs a bit of help somewhere. She's rather a one-man band at the moment.'

'We've got this nurse woman. She does quite a bit.'

'She does the nursing work you need. That still leaves

the house, which Hilary was running before, and the estate which she's taken on. She's doing her work *and* yours, Gilbert. For heaven's sake, man,' he exclaimed, allowing his voice to become more emphatic. 'You can afford someone, can't you? And a housekeeper would be cheaper than an estate manager!'

'That's true.' The heavy face settled once again into a corrugation of frowns. 'Oh, all right, Charles, you win. I'll tell her to get a woman in for the time being. Maybe that'll stop you bullying a sick old man!'

Charles laughed. 'Sick old man indeed. You'll outlive us all – but only if you're careful.' His voice grew serious again. 'I mean that, Gilbert. You've got to take things slowly. It's too easy, when you feel well, to forget that there's a pump inside you which has been badly hurt and needs time to heal. You'll get tired anyway, and that'll tell you to slow down, but you've got to stop worrying about things as well. That's just as harmful.'

Napier nodded. 'All right. Point taken. I'll stay up here and play the invalid for as long as you think it's necessary. And maybe you'll come round and entertain the invalid now and then. Give me a game of chess, that sort of thing.'

'I'll be glad to.' The doctor got to his feet. 'Now I'd better be going. I've got other patients to see as well, you know, and most of them aren't so cantankerous as you. They do as they're told. Now, I'll drop in again tomorrow but remember – no going downstairs, and tell young Hilary to fix herself up with a housekeeper. It'll give Dottie Friend a break too – she's on the go all the time these days, either here or at the school or in the pub. I sometimes think there must be three of her.'

'She's a good woman.' Gilbert watched him go, then turned back to the window. So he was to be kept up here like a naughty child for another week or two, and Hilary was to take over the job he'd always thought he'd be handing over to Baden. He sighed and then picked up a book the doctor had brought him. Reading in the morning seemed like the ultimate in decadence, but at least it took his mind off things.

When Hilary looked in an hour or so later, he was fast asleep in his chair.

'. . . And so Charles has persuaded Daddy to let me get a housekeeper so that I can concentrate on the estate,' Hilary told Felix as she arranged a huge bunch of roses on the altar. '*And* he's got him to agree to stay upstairs for at least another two weeks. He'll be allowed to do more and more – walk around, go from room to room – until Charles thinks he's ready for the stairs. And then he'll probably only be allowed on to the terrace. Charles is being terribly careful.'

'That's good,' Felix said, leaning back against the front pew. 'So you'll have a bit more time to yourself, then?'

'I don't think that's very likely,' she said with a grin. 'There are quite a few things that haven't been done since Dad had his attack. I'll need to go round all the tenant farms, for a start, and let them know what's happening and see if they've got any problems. And I haven't got the housekeeper yet – I suppose I'll have to advertise.'

'Perhaps someone will hear of it through the grapevine,' he suggested. 'You've only got to tell someone a piece of news before breakfast and everybody for miles around knows by lunchtime. I don't know how they do it.'

Hilary laughed. 'There's a lot more communication in the countryside than people think. We don't need telephones out here. Why, there's the man who collects the milk churns from the farm gates, there's the shepherd out looking over his sheep, the cowman in the fields, old Jacob Prout working in the lanes – it's a real network.'

Felix smiled, then glanced down at his hands before looking up again. 'I was hoping you'd be able to take a day off, now that your father's out of danger. I thought we might go out somewhere.'

'Oh.' Hilary didn't know what to say. She knew that he was growing fond of her but she still didn't really know what she felt about him. 'Well, that sounds nice,' she said doubtfully. 'But I'm not sure I can afford the time just now.'

'Can't you? It would do you good to get away for a day. You need a change. You're looking tired.'

'I am,' she admitted. 'And it would be nice . . . Tell you what, I have to go to Exeter one day – why don't you come with me? It's estate business, I'm afraid, but it won't take long and it's a nice drive across the moor.'

'Friday's my day off,' he said. 'Would that do?'

'It'll be fine.' They smiled at each other and Felix went off to the vestry while Hilary finished her arrangements. This was one job she had decided not to hand over, even though both Joyce Warren and Constance Bellamy had offered to take an extra turn. But Hilary enjoyed being in the dim, quiet church. Above her, the trusses of the vaulted roof ended in carvings of winged angels and at certain times of day the sun slanted through the stained-glass windows to light them with bright, jewelled colour. The ends of the pews were carved too, with animals and flowers which she loved to touch as she moved by them, passing her hand over the smooth wood and thinking of all the people who had done the same down the centuries. Members of her own family, many of them, for the Napiers had been in Burracombe since Norman times. This is why it's all so important to Dad, she thought. His own family, part of the village and the valley, part of Burracombe for as long as this church has been standing. This is why he doesn't want it to go.

She gathered up the debris and took the old flowers out to the compost heap in the corner of the churchyard. Jacob

Prout was there, tidying some of the graves. He straightened up as he saw her and gave her a nod.

'Mornin', Miss Hilary. How be Squire today?'

'Getting better, thanks, Jacob. It's a long job, though. Doctor Latimer says he needs to rest for some weeks yet.'

The old man nodded. He'd looked just the same all the years she'd known him, Hilary reflected, as sturdy as an oak tree and with a face that looked as if it had been carved from its trunk. It struck her that he could have been a model for the old Jack-in-the-Green figures one sometimes saw in old churches or on pub signs.

He said, 'My grandad were the same. Went down like a stone one December afternoon and spent the rest of his days in a chair. He liked being out in the sunshine, mind. Us used to put him outside of a nice morning and bring him in come evening.'

'You make him sound like a line of washing,' Hilary said. 'What did you do with him the rest of the time?'

'Sat in his chair by the fire, o' course,' Jacob said. 'He were an institution. Whole village knowed he were there and they used to beat a path to the door. Never short of company, my grandad, right up to the last.'

Hilary looked at him and thought of her father. He hadn't been short of visitors – as well as Charles, there had been Basil and Grace Harvey, Constance Bellamy, Miss Kemp and a few others – but she couldn't say that the whole village had beaten a path to his door.

'I don't think I remember your grandfather, Jacob,' she said doubtfully. 'When did he die?'

'My stars, you wouldn't remember my old grandad!' Jacob exclaimed, showing a mouthful of unlikely looking teeth as he laughed. 'Us lost he when I were a liddle tacker – why, I couldn't have been more than eight or nine, knee-high to a grasshopper, I were when we buried un. He'm over there now,' he said, nodding towards the far corner of the churchyard in such a manner that Hilary turned sharply, almost expecting to see the old man rise from his grave. 'Jacob Prout, same as me. Been there this sixty year or more. Ninety-five when he died. Ninety-five.'

'Goodness me,' Hilary said, trying to work it out. 'So he'd have been born – let's see, in about 1795! Good heavens!' She stared at Jacob. 'That's incredible. Why, who was on the throne then?' She racked her brains for long-ago history lessons. 'It must have been George the Third! Your grandfather must have been able to remember Queen Victoria's Coronation.'

'Went up to London to see it,' Jacob nodded proudly. 'Mind you, there was two more before that – George the Fourth and William the Fourth. Four different monarchs, my old grandad knowed. Four different monarchs. There can't be many as can say that.'

'My goodness,' Hilary marvelled. 'Just think of all the things he lived through. All the Napoleonic wars – why, he could only have been ten years old at the time of Trafalgar. Then there was the Industrial Revolution, the Crimea – the Boer War ... he must have been like a walking history book by the time he died.'

'Not walking,' Jacob corrected her. 'He were in his chair by then, see.'

'I wonder if he could remember the Great Exhibition in 1851,' Hilary mused. 'The one that gave them the idea of having the Festival of Britain this year.'

'Oh, ah. He took my dad to see that,' Jacob said in a matter-of-fact tone, and bent to carry on with his work. Hilary stared at him.

'He took your father to London to see the Great Exhibition?'

'That's what I said, maid.'

'And you've never mentioned this to anyone?' Hilary demanded in an outraged tone. 'You knew we were getting up a pageant and all sorts of things and you never said a word about it?'

He straightened up. 'But that were a hundred years ago. Nobody's interested in all that now.'

'I think you'll find we are,' Hilary said. 'I don't suppose you've got any souvenirs – pictures, books, that sort of thing?'

'Might have.' His mouth had tightened and she wondered if she'd offended him.

'I'd really like to see them,' she coaxed. 'We might be able to put them on display at the Fair.'

He said nothing for a moment, then shrugged. 'S'pose I could have a look.'

'Oh, thank you, Jacob. Shall I come round and see you in a day or two, when you've had time to look them out?' She had a sudden brainwave. 'Or maybe you'd like to bring them up to the Barton. I'm sure my father would like to see them too.'

'Squire?' He looked incredulous. 'What would he want to be looking at old stuff like that for?'

'Because it matters to him,' Hilary said. 'He loves Burracombe just as much as you do, Jacob. Don't forget, our family's been here for hundreds of years too, and he wants it to go on like that. Why, his grandfather – my great-grandfather – must have known yours. Our families have known each other for centuries. Think of that!'

Jacob gazed at her. She saw his face change as he grappled with the idea. The carved features seemed to soften and he nodded slowly.

'I dare say you'm right, maid. I dare say they did. In fact, one of my uncles worked in your gardens. I've heard un tell about it many a time.'

'There you are, then.' Another thought struck her. 'Jacob, there must be old pictures and letters and all sorts of things lying about in some of the cottages around here.

Wouldn't it be wonderful if we could collect them all together and make an exhibition of them. A Village History corner.'

'I thought this here pageant was supposed to be about history,' he objected, but she shook her head.

'That's *big* history. Things like Sir Francis Drake making the leats that supplied water to Plymouth, and the building of Dartmoor Prison for the Napoleonic prisoners-of-war, all that kind of thing . . . and I bet your grandfather remembered that too, but what I'm talking about is history right here in the village. Ordinary people and families who have lived here for generations. Trips to London to see the Coronation or the Great Exhibition, just as we're getting up trips to see the Festival now. I expect we've got some old photos too.' She was beginning to feel really excited. 'Jacob, it's a wonderful idea!'

He scratched his nose. 'Well, I dunno as I could put all that together, Miss Hilary. I mean, I ain't got the book-learning for that kind of thing.'

'No, but I know someone who has. And if you could just talk to people – get them to dig out their old keepsakes and photos and things . . .' She gazed at him. 'Would you do that, Jacob?'

He looked back at her and sighed. He'd always had a soft spot for Miss Hilary. She looked a lot like her mother, who had been, in Jacob's opinion, the loveliest lady who'd ever walked the village green. A crying shame it had been, someone like that dying so young.

'All right, then,' he said, bending to his work again. 'Won't do no harm to try, I suppose.'

Hilary threw her bundle of flowers on to the heap and went on her way. She was sure that Jacob would find sufficient memorabilia for a good display and she was equally sure that there would be plenty of old photographs and documents in her father's possession. She just hoped that he would agree to her suggestion.

Boredom, Charles had said, would be his biggest enemy. Perhaps sorting out old village papers and pictures would give him an interest, and perhaps when the villagers realised what he was doing they would beat a path to his door, just as their fathers and grandfathers had beaten a path to old Jacob Prout's cottage.

Chapter Twenty-Eight

Jess Budd, over in Portsmouth, didn't know where Muriel was. She wrote back to Stella at once, so delighted to have heard from her that Stella felt guilty at not having written before, and gave her some of her own family news. Rose was married and had a baby boy, Tim had done his National Service in the RAF and then joined the Merchant Navy, Keith was in the Royal Navy and Maureen was at the local Girls' Grammar School. Stella tried to imagine them all grown so much older, and gave up. I can't even imagine my own sister grown up, she thought sadly, and felt as if another door had been slammed in her face.

Dottie and Miss Kemp both knew of her search by now, and were sympathetic. 'It's such a pity when families are broken up like that,' the headmistress said. 'I don't know why they do it. Couldn't they have taken you both to the same Home?'

'Couldn't they have left us where we were?' Stella said. 'We had a lovely billet at Bridge End with Mr Beckett, and Tim and Keith Budd. We were as happy as anyone could be who'd lost both their parents and their baby brother. There was no need at all to take us away like that. It was cruel.'

'Yes, I think it was. And I'm really sorry you're having such trouble in finding your sister.'

Stella twisted her lips together and shrugged. 'Well, I don't know what else I can do. I think I'd better give up for the time being. We've got too much to do at school, what with the pageant as well. Have you seen the frock Dottie's making for Shirley Culliford? She's going to look really sweet.'

'A Culliford looking sweet?' The headmistress raised her eyebrows. 'Well, I must admit she's improved tremendously since she was chosen. The vicar was right. And she's quite a bright child as well, you know. I've never expected much from her before but she's doing really well in her writing and arithmetic.'

'Let's hope the others follow her example.' Stella had two smaller Cullifords in her class, each as tattered and grubby as Shirley had been. 'It looks as if Shirley finds keeping herself clean and tidy as much as she can cope with.'

'And her mother doesn't seem to have taken the hint, does she,' Miss Kemp agreed. 'Still, it's a big leap forward to have Shirley doing so well. We must be thankful for whatever mercies come our way.'

Hilary had been into the school to tell them about the exhibition of old village memorabilia, and the children were all pestering their parents and grandparents to turn out cupboards and unpack boxes of fading photographs. A few bits and pieces had already been brought in – Coronation mugs showing the faces of the King and Queen, and older ones with Edward VII. One boy had even brought in a mug with Edward VIII's face painted on.

'But he was never crowned!' Stella exclaimed when she saw it. 'We can't put that out.'

'How strange,' Miss Kemp said. 'They must have sold a few before he abdicated. I wonder if it's valuable, like the threepenny bits they minted.'

'You'd better take it home again,' Stella said to the disappointed boy. 'But look after it, won't you.'

The children had all gone home and Stella was tidying

the nature table when Luke popped his head round the door. She looked up with pleasure.

'There you are! I haven't seen you for days. I was beginning to think you'd left us.'

He came in a little awkwardly. 'I've been busy sorting out pictures with Mrs Warren, amongst other things. I wondered if you'd had a reply from your Auntie Jess?'

Stella's face clouded. 'Yes, but she hasn't heard anything. I'm not going to try any more, Luke. Not for a while anyway. It's just making me miserable.' She looked up at him. 'I've decided that this is where my life is and I've got to put the past behind me and make the most of it.'

He looked down at her and felt the tenderness sweep over him again. He wanted to pull her into his arms and kiss away the tears that were already filling her eyes. But that was all it was – a tenderness, a sorrow for what she had lost – and he was afraid that Stella would think it meant something more. He wasn't ready yet to let that happen and so he drew back slightly. As he did so, he caught the tiny change in her expression and cursed himself.

'I came to tell you I've got to go away,' he said with a rush. 'Oh, not permanently,' as her face dropped, 'just for a couple of weeks, that's all. I've got the chance of a space in an exhibition in London.'

Her face lit up. 'Oh, that's good. It's just what you've been wanting. You mustn't miss that. When will you be going? Can I help you pack up your paintings?'

'No, I've done that. I'm off tomorrow, first thing – catching an early train. Just popped in to tell you and say goodbye.' He hesitated, knowing that if their relationship had progressed as Stella thought it had, this would be the moment to kiss her. Damn it, he thought, I *want* to kiss her! But not in the way she'd like.

He stepped back a little. 'Sorry to be in such a rush – still quite a lot to do. As I said, I'll be back in a fortnight. I

321

want to see some friends while I'm there too, and catch up with my family.'

He saw the look in her eyes and knew that she understood. I feel a cad, he thought miserably, yet all I wanted was to be friends. I still want that. I just don't want to hurt her.

'Yes, of course you must.' Stella turned back to the nature table and examined the glass accumulator tank which was full of tadpoles. 'Look, they're getting their legs now. We'll have to take them outside soon and put some stones nearby for them to climb out on.' She turned back and smiled at him, her eyes bright. 'I'll miss you. But I'm really pleased about the exhibition.'

'Thanks. I'll miss you too, of course, but I expect you'll be busy getting ready for the pageant. Jacob Prout was telling me about this history corner at the Fair. It sounds a good idea.'

'I think it is. We're getting all sorts of items from the children, and Dottie said she'd look out some old things as well. It's amazing how far back some of the families go, and they all seem to be absolute magpies, never throw anything away.'

He laughed, feeling more relaxed. The difficult corner seemed to have been turned. 'That's useful!' He settled himself on a corner of one of the desks. 'But you know, it really is amazing to think that if we could walk out into the village street and go back, say, three hundred years, we'd see dozens of people we recognised, just because the family likenesses go down through the generations. There'd be a Squire Napier trotting by on his horse, a Dottie Friend working at the village inn, a Bertie Foster in the butcher's shop, a George Sweet baking bread, and a Constance Bellamy living at the Grey House.'

'You're probably right. And there'd be Cullifords living in the end cottage, and a Jacob Prout keeping everything tidy – well, we know that because he started all this! – and a Ted Tozer farming the land with his horses. We're the strangers here, Luke.'

'Yes.' He looked thoughtful. 'And how long is it before we're part of the village? Of course, we need to get married first and have a family to start a new dynasty!' He caught her expression and slid quickly off the desk. 'Look, I'm sorry but I've got to go. Got a lot to do before I set off for the big city.'

'Yes,' Stella said. 'Well, have a good time, Luke, and I hope the exhibition goes well.'

'Thanks.' He paused for a moment, but Stella had turned back to the tadpoles. 'I'll see you when I get back, then.'

Stella murmured something and he hesitated again, then slipped quietly out of the door. Outside, he stood irresolute. Then he walked quickly away.

Stella stood very still, staring at the tadpoles. After a while, she straightened up and went to fetch her coat.

I made a mess of that, Luke thought as he walked along the lane. She's upset and disappointed. But it's better to do it now than let things go further and hurt her more. If only she hadn't been so hurt in the past. He thought of the big, sad eyes and the loneliness he sensed in her heart, and wished that he could be the one to take away her sorrow. If only they could have found her sister . . .

He was so deep in thought that he didn't even see Val Tozer when he turned a bend in the lane. They were almost face to face when he raised his head and saw her coming towards him. Involuntarily, he put out his hand and she immediately veered away.

'Val!'

She didn't stop. She was marching briskly, her eyes straight ahead. He tried again.

'Val, don't ignore me. Please.'

She stopped and faced him. 'What do you want me to say?'

He shrugged helplessly. 'I don't know. Anything. "Hello" would do, for a start. Val, I haven't seen you for weeks.'

'I've been busy. I've been helping Hilary – you know her father's ill, I suppose.'

'Yes. I went up there myself to see if there was anything I could do.' He looked at her and knew why he couldn't give Stella the kind of love she yearned for. 'Oh God, Val. We can't go on like this.'

'Like what?' Her voice was stony.

'Please,' he said. 'Come up to the cottage and talk to me. I'm going away tomorrow – I've got to go to London. I can't go without sorting things out between us.'

'There's nothing to sort out.'

'There *is*!' he cried. 'Val, you can't hide it from me. You're as miserable as I am. All right, I accept that we're never going to be together, you don't want that – but I will *not* accept that you've got no feeling for me. I know you have. I can see it in your face – it's in your eyes. It's all over you. Val, I know you as well as I know myself. Let's at least be honest with each other.'

'Honest!' she exclaimed, and turned her face towards him. He saw in her eyes a depth of pain that made him gasp, and he put out his hand again and laid it on her arm. This time, she didn't flinch away and he saw her eyes fill with tears.

'Come with me, my darling,' he said gently. 'Please. And then I promise I'll never bother you again.'

Val's head and body drooped. As if she had lost the will to resist any further, she let him lead her through the gate into the wood. Together, silently, they climbed the twisting path between the mossy rocks and the tall trees with their canopy of leaves, and came to the charcoal-burner's hut. Luke opened the door and they went inside.

'I haven't been in here for years,' Val said tonelessly, looking around. 'It hasn't changed much, except for the paintings.'

Luke's canvases and water-colours were everywhere, some hung on the walls, some stacked on the floor. There were two old armchairs by the fireplace and bookcases in the alcove. Oil lamps stood on the table and the wide windowsill. A bright rag rug – one of Dottie's – lay on the stone floor.

'Sit down.' He pressed her lightly into one of the armchairs. 'Would you like a drink? I could make tea.'

She shook her head. She seemed deflated, without spirit, and he knelt before her, looking up into her face, and took both her hands in his. She met his eyes and said wearily, 'Well? What do you want to talk about?'

'Us! What else? Val, we've got to get things clear between us. Why do you hate me so much? I know what we did was wrong, but we can't turn the clock back and we can't pretend it didn't happen. All we can do is put it into the past.' He stroked her hands. 'I told you last time that I still love you,' he said quietly. 'It's true. But if you want me to go away, I will. I don't want to make you unhappy.'

Val's head jerked up. Her eyes had lost their dead, dull look and were sparking with anger. 'You don't want to make me unhappy? It's a bit late for that, isn't it?'

'You weren't unhappy that night,' he said. 'You loved me then as much as I loved you. And ever since then . . .'

'Ever since then,' she said, 'you've been able to live your own life. You could forget about me if you wanted to. You probably did forget about me, until you came to Burracombe and we met again. Why did you have to come *here*?' she cried. 'Why here, of all the places in England you could have gone?'

'I don't know,' he said. 'Maybe we were meant to meet again. Maybe we're meant to be together.' His voice shook a little and he stopped, then went on steadily, 'I didn't forget you, though. What happened was something I'll always remember.'

'Oh yes,' she said savagely, snatching her hands away. 'You'll *remember*. But that's all you had to do, wasn't it – remember! I was the one who had to live with what I'd done. I'm the one who's had to live with the consequences.'

Luke looked at her. She had turned her face away and her expression was hidden beneath a fall of hair. A terrible suspicion began to dawn within his mind.

'Did – did Eddie find out about us?' he asked at last. 'Did you tell him?'

'Oh no! No, he never knew. He never had time to find out.' Almost inaudibly, she added, 'Thank God.' And then she whipped round, her face twisted with pain, saying, 'Don't you think that's a wicked thing, Luke? Don't you think it's terrible that I should be thanking God that my fiancé was killed?'

'Val—'

'But I do,' she whispered. 'I do thank God that he was killed before he found out. I even thanked God that my baby died too.' And she began to cry.

Luke stared at her, horrified, unable at first to take in the full meaning of what she had just said. Her crying tore at his heart. Great, painful sobs of anguish seemed to be forcing their way up from her throat, wrenching at her body, so violently that he was afraid they would tear her apart. He reached out again, then drew back, knowing that his touch was the last thing she wanted. Distractedly, he rubbed the back of his neck, unable to decide what to do. He couldn't torment her with more questions, yet now that she had begun to tell him the truth of what had happened, he needed to hear the rest. He thought that she probably needed just as badly to tell him.

Val's sobs diminished at last, leaving her exhausted. Luke found a hanky and wiped her face tenderly, and she submitted to his touch. When her eyes were dry, he cupped her cheeks in both hands and said gently, 'Tell me about it, Val.'

'It was on the way home,' she said in a voice still thick with tears. 'Coming home from Egypt. It took us weeks and weeks, you know – we had to sail all the way round South Africa. I began to suspect after we'd been at sea for a fortnight. At first, I thought it was just the voyage, I thought it was sea-sickness. But I hadn't been sick on the way out, and besides it wasn't even rough. And then I realised what it was.' She raised her eyes and looked at him. 'I was scared stiff. I didn't know what to do. I couldn't keep it from Eddie and the family – everyone would know. Mum and Dad might not even let me stay at home. There was Jackie too, she was only ten years old. I didn't think I could even *go* home. But what would I tell them if I didn't? I'd been away nearly three years. How could I say I wasn't going home?'

'Oh Val,' he said. 'And I didn't even know.'

'There was nothing you could do. And we'd agreed it was over.'

'It wasn't, though, was it?' he said. 'It was never over for me. And with a baby on the way – our baby . . .'

'I never thought of it as "our baby",' she said. 'It was mine – and I was frightened to death of it. Oh Luke!' She began to cry again. 'It was my baby and I would have loved it, but I was *frightened* of it!'

'You were frightened of other people,' he said. 'Not of the baby. It was what other people would do or say that frightened you, and I ought to have been there to help.'

'Well, you weren't.' The anguish had gone from her voice again, leaving it flat and toneless once more. 'Nobody was there to help.'

Very gently, he drew her close. He felt the resistance in her body and then suddenly it vanished and she rested against him. He stroked her hair and shoulders and was suddenly reminded of the way he had held Stella, just like this, when she had told him about her sister. He would explain to Val, but not now. This moment was too important.

'What happened?' he asked at last. 'You said the baby died. Can you tell me about it, Val? What happened to our baby?'

'It was never born,' she said. 'I had a miscarriage. I didn't bring it on,' she added quickly. 'I was frightened and I didn't know what I was going to do about Eddie and the family, but I didn't do anything. I swear I didn't!' Her voice rose in panic and he soothed her again.

'It's all right, darling. I know you didn't. Were you ill – or hurt in some way? Tell me.'

'I don't know why it happened,' she said. 'I just woke up one night and I was bleeding. I told Mary – you remember her – and the other girls; you'd probably remember them too, there were half a dozen of us, all good friends, who'd been together in Egypt. They did their best but it wouldn't stop, and then the baby was born.' Her voice trembled and broke again. 'He was so tiny – like a little doll. I could hold him in the palm of one hand.'

'A boy?'

'I thought so. You couldn't really tell, he was so small, but I somehow knew it was a boy. I called him John. Little John.' She drew in a ragged breath. 'Nobody else knew. We – we gave him a burial at sea. We found a bit of flag and wrapped him in it, and the six of us went up on deck one night – they had to help me – and we said some prayers and put him over the side.' Once again, the tears came and the sobs shook her body. 'Oh Luke, it was like throwing a piece of rubbish over the side! We tried so hard not to make it seem like that, but that's what it was. Just a little piece of rubbish that nobody wanted.'

'It's not true,' he said. The tears were in his own eyes too, and his throat ached. 'He wasn't rubbish. He was our baby and we would both have wanted him. Oh Val, what a terrible time you've had. No wonder you didn't want to see me again.' He caught her against him. 'Oh Val, Val, can you ever forgive me for what I did to you?'

'We did it together,' she admitted. 'It wasn't your fault. I wanted it as much as you.' She paused, as if the admission had surprised her; as if she had never made it before. 'I felt so guilty. And it was all the worse that you didn't know – I had to feel guilty for you as well. And then, when I heard that Eddie had been killed, it was like a punishment. The worst punishment I could ever have had.'

'It was war,' he said quietly.

'I know. But he'd survived all those years, and to be killed then, when we would soon have been together again . . . oh, it seemed so cruel. And I really did believe it was my fault. I really did.'

'It wasn't your fault. He could have been killed at any time – you know that.' He was silent for a few moments, holding her against him, then he said, 'Do you think you'll ever be able to get over it, Val? Do you think there's any chance for us?'

'I don't know,' she said. 'I just don't know.'

'About Stella—' he began, but she cut him short with a gesture.

'Not now. I can't think about anything else now.' She moved away from him. 'I think I'd like to go home now.'

'I'll take you,' he said, and lifted her to her feet. They

walked down the hill together without speaking, and when he left her at the farm gate he felt as if dark clouds had gathered in his heart.

Chapter Twenty-Nine

'Well, that's a piece of good news!' Dottie laid down her letter and beamed at Stella over the breakfast table. 'My actress is coming to the Fair. She'm going to open it for us. Miss Bellamy suggested I might ask her, so I did, and she'm coming. Oh, it'll be good to see her again, her and little Maddy!'

'That's lovely.' Stella was pleased for her. 'How long is it since you've seen her?'

'Why, it must be two year or more. She used to come here a lot, you know, specially during the war. If ever she got a bit of spare time, she'd be down here to see us all, and Maddy of course when she were here too, and she'd have a rest. Everyone in the village knew her. They'll be thrilled to bits to hear she'm coming again.'

'Where will she stay? D'you want me to move out? I expect someone would give me a room, so long as it's not the Cullifords!'

Dottie laughed. 'No, my flower, there'll be no need for that. She'll stop at the Barton, likely as not. She knew the Squire and Miss Hilary as well, you see – a family friend she were. It'll do him good to see her again, too. She won't be here till the day of the Fair, more's the pity – she'm in Spain, making a film – but she'll be here in time to make her speech and all that.' She got up and began to bustle about clearing the table. 'I'm going up to the Barton this morning, to help Miss Hilary sort out some of they old papers and things Squire's been keeping all these years. She wants to make sure there's nothing that can upset the poor man, like pictures of Mrs Napier or Mr Baden. Then they'm going to make displays for the exhibition.'

'That'll be interesting.' Mention of the exhibition reminded Stella of Luke. She hadn't seen him since he'd called in at the school, and assumed that he must have left for London now. She sighed, wondering what had gone wrong between them. They'd been such friends and he'd been so helpful in her search for Muriel, that she'd begun to think it all meant something more. Obviously I was wrong, she thought, and now I've frightened him away and lost his friendship as well.

She set off for school. Preparations for the Festival were taking up a lot of time now and the children were getting very excited. Some of them had been to London again and come back with stories of the other exhibits they'd seen, or the rides they'd enjoyed at the Fun Fair. Micky was still working on making a clock like the Guinness one and had made several cardboard models. Shirley Culliford had started to wear her hair in plaits and continued to wash her face every day.

'If it encourages just one child to raise her standards, it could all be worthwhile,' Miss Kemp remarked dryly. 'Especially if it's a Culliford.'

Stella was teaching her infants' class some country dances. Jacob Prout had promised to make a maypole and Miss Kemp had said she could take two of the biggest girls into Tavistock one day to buy ribbons. They were making costumes out of existing garments – coloured skirts and blouses with puff sleeves for the girls, breeches and white shirts for the boys. Meanwhile, the bigger children were to act two short scenes about Francis Drake – one showing the famous incident on Plymouth Hoe, when he refused to break off from a game of bowls to go and fight the Spanish

Armada, and the other showing his return to Plymouth and being knighted by Queen Elizabeth. This had caused some dispute amongst some of the younger children.

'Can't us do when he threw down his cloak so the Queen could walk over a puddle?' Ernest asked. 'I wouldn't mind doing that. My mum's got some stripey curtains that would do for a cloak.'

'That was Sir Walter Raleigh,' Miss Kemp told him. 'And we've already got Geoffrey Martin to play Francis Drake.'

'Well, can't us do when Walter Raleigh threw down his cloak, then?' Ernest persisted. 'I've seen pictures of un. And there's bound to be plenty of puddles.'

'Well, thank you for being so optimistic about the weather, Ernest,' the headmistress said. 'Although I expect you're right. But I don't think we can do Raleigh as well as Drake. There are going to be lots of other things happening and we only have a little bit of time.' She saw his disappointment and said, 'I don't see why you can't dress as Raleigh in the procession, though, Ernest, if your mother doesn't mind making a cloak out of the curtains. Are they old ones?'

'Oh no, miss,' he said, cheering up. 'They're our best ones, in the front window. I'll go and tell her, miss.' He ran off and Miss Kemp turned to Stella with a wry expression.

'We'll be getting a visit from an irate parent any minute, asking why I sent Ernest home to say that she'd got to cut up her best curtains for fancy-dress costumes! Oh well, I dare say worse will happen before the whole thing's over. How are the dancers coming along?'

'Quite well, I think. I just hope they come for the last few rehearsals, after term ends.'

'Yes, that's the snag with putting on things in the holidays. Luckily, none of them are going away – not many do, in fact. What about you? Are you planning a holiday?'

333

'I'm going to stay with a college friend for a week,' Stella said, brightening at the thought of it, 'but not until after the Fair. I won't be leaving you in the lurch.'

'Good. Now, I want to discuss the plans for the Sports Day . . .' And the Fair was temporarily forgotten in plans for races involving sacks, eggs and spoons, and people with three legs.

Dottie arrived at the Barton to find Hilary sitting at the dining table surrounded by documents and photographs. The new housekeeper, Mrs Ellis, was now in command in the kitchen, with Jackie to help her, Pat Smith was still coming in during the day to look after the Squire, and Hilary was free to manage the estate and continue her part in village affairs.

'I don't want to give up too much,' she'd told Val. 'I like arranging the church flowers and helping with the Fair, but it's *so* good to be able to do something that demands a bit more initiative.'

She looked up and smiled as Dottie came in. 'I'm glad you're here. You'll know more of these people than I do. Look, I've sorted them into some sort of order – school photos, the football and cricket teams, WI outings and things like that. And there are quite a lot of the farms, look, with people sitting outside them. Do you know any of the names?'

'My stars,' Dottie said, running her eye over the fading pictures. 'You've got a collection here, and no mistake. Why, surely that's old Mrs Tozer, Ted Tozer's granny. She's been gone these past forty years – I remember her when she used to sit at the door with her spinning-wheel. Used to spin her own yarn, she did, from a fleece that Ted's grandad would give her, and she made all their jerseys from it. Dyed it, too.'

'Well, that's a nice piece of history, for a start,' Hilary

said, making a note on a piece of paper and putting it with the photograph. 'And who's this?'

'I don't know who that be,' Dottie said, staring at it. 'Don't look like none of the villagers to me ... Wait a minute, though. Isn't that the travelling salesman that come here a time or two, and put up at the Berrows' farm? Got a bit too friendly with their youngest girl, he did, and got her into trouble. They never saw him no more after that and the babby were born and grew up a bit wanting. They'm dead now, all of 'em.'

'Oh. Well, maybe we'd better not put that one in the Exhibition,' Hilary said, making another note. 'Now, here's an interesting one. It was taken here, you see – at the Barton. Outside on the terrace.' She handed over a larger print, less faded than the others, and Dottie took it and scanned it eagerly.

'Why, you know what that be, don't you?' 'Tis that school that was evacuated here during the war. Why, I knew every one of they little tackers. See that boy? Red hair, he had, and I never saw such a boy for getting into mischief, but a nicer little chap you'd never wish to meet. Now that one, the big one, he was different, a nasty piece of work, he was – and this one here, you'd think he was an angel straight from heaven, butter wouldn't melt in his mouth, but I wouldn't trust un further than I could throw un! And look, here's my little Maddy.'

'Really?' Hilary took the photograph back. 'My goodness, she changed, didn't she. She's quite a plain little thing there. I never really saw her as a child, I was away for most of the war. I only met her when she was about fourteen or fifteen.'

'Grew up a real beauty,' Dottie said with satisfaction. 'A real bit of village history, that be. I suppose you know my actress is coming to open the Fair?'

'Yes, I meant to mention it to you – we had a letter

335

asking if she could stay with us. It'll be good to see them again.' She looked at the picture once more and put it with the photograph of old Mrs Tozer. 'Yes, that must definitely go into the display. Now, Father's coming downstairs in a minute and he'll go through the rest with you. I've taken out all those I don't think he should see. Don't let him do too much, will you? An hour or so will be quite long enough, to start with.'

'Don't you worry about that, my flower,' Dottie said. 'Us'll have a high old time, looking through all these old pictures. Bring back a few memories, they will.'

'Yes, I'm sure they will. It's going to be one of the highlights of the Exhibition.' Hilary stood up. 'I'll go and bring him downstairs now. It's very good of you to do this, Dottie.'

'Bless you, 'tis a pleasure. I'll enjoy it. And I'll look after your father, don't you worry. You go off and do whatever you got to do. He'll be all right with me.'

Hilary smiled at her. 'I know he will,' she said. 'Everyone's all right with you, Dottie.'

Jackie Tozer was another one who felt all right these days. Her relief that she wasn't pregnant after all was so great that she had a smile on her face for everyone she met, and went about her work singing. It was her sister Val who seemed cast down.

'It's just like being on a blessed see-saw,' Alice complained to her mother-in-law. 'If it's not one, it's the other. There was our Jackie going about with her chin down to her knees – and you 'n' me have got our own ideas about why that was, Mother – and now she's bucked up and it's Val who looks as if she's lost a shilling and found sixpence. Between the pair of them, I don't know where I am.'

'I thought Val was picking up a bit,' Minnie said. She was sitting just outside the door, shelling peas, and Alice was scrubbing a bowlful of new potatoes. 'After you persuaded her to go down the village with us on New Year's Eve, she seemed to be making a real effort. I thought she must have made a resolution.'

'If she did, she's broken it. She goes off to work in the morning without hardly a word and when she comes back it's straight up to the Barton to see Hilary. I don't begrudge her that, mind,' Alice added quickly. 'They'm good friends and Hilary needs a bit of company, what with her father being ill and her having to do all the work round the estate. But it don't seem to be doing our Val no good. She'm looking proper peaky.'

'Well, there's not much you can do about it, flower,' Minnie said. 'Her's a grown woman and got to make her own way. I've finished these peas now, if you wants to take them in.'

Alice took the pods over to the compost heap and then came back for the bowl. 'D'you know what I reckon, Mother? I reckon something's happened, and it happened all of a sudden. She were doing all right, looking a lot brighter, and then something changed. I'd dearly like to know what it is.'

She went indoors and Minnie closed her eyes and basked in the warmth of the late June sunshine. She understood Alice's worries – she'd felt the same way at times about her own children, Ted and his sisters Florrie and Maud. You could see there was something amiss, but unless they told you what it was, there was nothing you could do about it. You probably wouldn't be able to do anything if they did tell you. You couldn't sort out your own troubles, half the time, let alone anyone else's.

Grown-up children had grown-up problems, that was the top and bottom of it, and there was no sense in worrying yourself over it all. It would either come right or it wouldn't.

337

That was life.

Joyce Warren's problems also seemed to be getting worse. She was accustomed to things not going quite to plan, but there were moments when she thought the Fair and Exhibition were never going to happen. First, the boiler in the memorial hall had broken down, which meant that nobody could make tea. A few large kettles had been brought but they could only be boiled one at a time on the little stove and Joyce was frantic in case the boiler could not be repaired in time for the Fair.

'We'll be serving at least two hundred teas on the day,' she said after the next parish council meeting. The others had gone but she had managed to corner the vicar and was determined to make him listen. 'Probably twice that number. However are we going to manage?'

'It'll come in time, I'm sure,' Basil Harvey said soothingly. He had already suffered similar complaints from the Mother's Union, the WI, the Whist Club and the Drama Group. 'I don't know why people can't bring a Thermos flask if they can't get through a couple of hours without tea,' he went on. 'There really isn't any need to struggle with stoves and kettles.'

'That's not the point. It's the Fair I'm worried about. Have you actually sent for the engineer, Vicar?'

'Of course I have,' he replied a little indignantly. 'At least, I think I have. I rang him on Monday . . .' He stared at her anxiously. 'I meant to ring him, anyway. I can't actually remember . . .'

Joyce tutted and rolled her eyes. 'I knew I should have done it myself! I'll ring him as soon as I get home.' She looked round the hall. 'And those chairs could do with renewing. I suppose it's too late to do that now?'

'It certainly is,' he said firmly. 'Anyway, if we're lucky enough to have fine weather I dare say everyone will want

338

to be outside, and Miss Kemp says we can borrow the forms from the school. They're rather low, but at least everyone will be able to see what's going on.'

'And if we *don't* get fine weather?' she enquired, and he sighed.

'Then I don't suppose many people will bother to turn up, and the problem won't arise.'

'And what about the Exhibition itself? I'll need the hall for at least three days beforehand to set it up. Nobody will be able to use it during that time, and we must have the boiler in operation by then. I can't have men tramping in and out with muddy boots and spanners while I'm trying to organise the tables and the Art display. There's the bellringing competition on the Saturday as well. We've got to feed all those ringers. Where are we going to put them? Mr Tozer thinks there'll be at least sixty.'

'We could give them their tea in the church,' Basil suggested. 'There's plenty of room to sit there.'

'In the *church*? Did I really hear you say in the *church*?' She stared at him, scandalised.

'Why not? We can sweep up the crumbs afterwards. They have the announcement of their results in the church, after all. And we do break bread and drink wine there, you know,' he added with a twinkle.

Joyce was not impressed. 'I must say, Vicar,' she said in a tone so acid it could have dissolved metal, 'I never expected to hear you, a man of the cloth, speak in such a facetious way about your own church. I think it would be best if we forgot that this conversation ever took place. Do you know what they *eat* at these affairs?' she demanded, breaking her rule the moment she'd made it. 'Cornish pasties! The church would smell of them for days. Besides, we're having the Flower Festival in the church. We can't have a lot of great, clodhopping, muddy-booted bellringers stamping about amongst all our floral displays. Most of them are farmers, you know.'

'Most of them are churchgoers, too,' he murmured. 'And they do wear their best clothes for competitions.'

'Pubgoers, more like,' she retorted, ignoring the second part of his remark. '*I've* seen them in the Bell on practice nights.'

'Have you?' He looked at her with such innocence that she blushed and hastily changed the subject.

'Have you heard anything from that godson of yours? I wanted to go and have another look at his paintings, to make a final choice, and what do I hear but he's gone dashing off to London. Is he coming back, or is he going to let us down?'

'I'm sure Luke would never let anyone down—'

'Well, I hope you're right,' she snapped. 'Now, I'm sorry, Vicar, but I really don't have time to stand here gossiping. Some of us have things to do, you know! I'd better go straight home and ring up that boiler-man for a start – it's nearly nine o'clock, he should be at home, unless *he's* in the pub as well – and then I'll need to talk to Mr Tozer about the catering for the ringing competition. He told me his wife would see to it, but I haven't heard a word from her. I'd better go up to the farm first thing in the morning and see what she's arranging, if anything. Honestly, it sometimes seems as if I'm the only one who does anything at all around here!'

She marched out of the hall, leaving Basil Harvey staring after her, his mouth open. If only I were more quick-witted, he thought, I'd have reminded her that the ringing competition is none of her business and that Alice Tozer is sure to have everything well in hand. But no doubt Alice would make that clear herself. She could have quite a sharp tongue on her when she liked, could Alice.

Well, never mind, he told himself as he put away the

chairs. There were people like Mrs Warren in most villages and you had to admit that without them not much would get done. Bossy, impatient and high-handed, they nevertheless got things organised and, as a rule, quite successfully. He had no doubt that the Fair and all its attendant events would go off very well.

And do you know, he thought, standing in the middle of the floor with a chair in one hand, I do believe I did ring up the boiler-man. He said he would be here first thing tomorrow morning. Well, that will show Mrs Warren that she's not the only one who can get things done!

Gloating wasn't at all a suitable thing for a vicar to be doing, he chided himself as he closed the door, but even vicars are human.

Chapter Thirty

'Jackie!' Alice called up the stairs. There's someone down here to see you. It's Roy,' she added as her daughter emerged from her bedroom and started down the stairs.

'Roy!' Jackie stopped and half-turned to go back upstairs, but Alice's sharp voice stopped her in her tracks.

'Yes, Roy. And don't go dashing off upstairs and expect me to say you're not in. He's heard me call you, anyway. Whatever's the matter with you, maid? You used to be so thick!'

'Well, we're not now.' Slowly, Jackie came down the rest of the stairs. 'We just lost interest, that's all. Cooled off. I'd have thought you'd be pleased – you went on at me enough when I said we wanted to get engaged.'

'Yes, well, never mind that now.' Alice didn't really want to discuss the reasons why Jackie and Roy had apparently cooled off. 'He's here and he wants to see you. He's in the garden, wouldn't come in.'

Jackie went reluctantly through the kitchen and found Roy sitting outside on the bench where her grandmother often sat. He stood up when she came out of the house and she saw that he was in uniform. She looked at him.

'What are you doing home, then? There's nothing wrong, is there?'

'Depends what you call wrong,' he said. 'Come for a bit of a walk, Jackie.'

She opened her mouth to object, but the look on his face

stopped her and she followed him through the gate. They walked along the track for a short distance in silence and then she said, 'Well, come on then, Roy. How far do we have to go before you'll tell me?'

'I'm being drafted away,' he said briefly, and stopped to lean on a gate. His face was tight, his eyes shuttered. 'I'm being sent to Korea, Jackie.'

'*Korea?* But you've only been in the Army five minutes – and you're only National Service. Why are they sending you to Korea?'

'It's not just me,' he said impatiently. 'We're all going. You knew I might go there. We talked about it, remember? We wanted to get married before I went,' he added bitterly.

Jackie moved closer to him. 'Roy, I'm really sorry. You don't want to go, do you?'

'Of course I want to go! I might get killed – save me the trouble of doing it meself.'

'*Roy!* Don't say such things! It's wicked.' She put her hand on his arm. 'You won't get killed, Roy. You'll be all right.'

'Oh yes, and you know that, do you? There's a *war* going on out there, Jackie, a proper war. Just because we're not getting bombed over here doesn't mean it's not just as real as the last one. People are getting killed all the time – why should I be special?' He turned to her and she saw the tautness in his face. He looked thinner, she thought, and older too. Something had changed him from the bright apprentice and the eager lover to a man who feared what lay ahead.

'I didn't ask to be a soldier,' he said. 'I just wanted to be a mechanic. I'd like to work on tanks, I wouldn't mind doing my National Service on that sort of work, but instead they're going to make me fight. If I'd joined up as a Regular because I wanted to fight, I wouldn't mind, but I didn't. I don't even know what it's all about. I didn't know where Korea was till I looked it up in my school atlas.'

'Oh Roy,' Jackie said. 'I'm sorry. I really am.'

'And if that wasn't bad enough,' he said miserably, 'everything's gone wrong between you and me, and I don't know why that's happened either. I never meant to get you into trouble, Jackie. I just wanted to love you. I still do,' he added in a low voice.

She looked at him and felt her heart move. The tenderness she had felt a few moments before strengthened and she tightened her hand on his arm.

'Roy . . . I don't know what to say.'

'Just tell me it's not all finished,' he pleaded. 'Tell me we've still got a chance. You don't have to let me make love to you, if you don't want to. You don't have to be engaged to me. Just say you'll write to me, and let me write to you.' He looked into her face. 'Please, Jackie. Please.'

'Of course I'll write to you,' she said, her voice filled with tears. 'Not every night, like I did before, and I'm not promising to wait for you, but I'll write every week. I'll do that.'

'And I'll write to you.' He moved uncertainly towards her. 'Look, I know you'll probably meet someone else, but if you don't – if you haven't by the time I come home – well, d'you think there'll be another chance for us? Do you?'

'How do I know that? You could be gone two years!' Panic gripped her again, then she caught herself up and gave him a wavering smile. 'Look, I'm sorry, Roy, but what with everything that's happened I don't know what I think or feel any more. I just know that Mum was right – it's too soon. I'm too young. *You're* too young. I don't want to think about that sort of thing any more – not for a long time, anyway.'

'You might think different in two years' time,' Roy said.

'Well, we'll just have to wait and see, won't we. I've said I'll write to you, and that's all I'm going to say.' She looked into his face. 'It wasn't just your fault, I know,' she said more gently. 'I wanted to do it too. But it was all wrong and I don't want to do it again. Not yet.'

'All right.' He gave her a doubtful glance. 'Can I – would you give me a kiss, then, Jackie? Just one, to send me on my way? Please?'

'All right.' She reached up and touched his lips with hers, as lightly as a butterfly. He put his arms around her and held her loosely, and kissed her back. They stayed very still for a few moments and then he let her go and moved away.

'I'd better be going. I'm off in the morning. Goodbye, Jackie. Take care of yourself, won't you.'

'And you, Roy,' she said softly. 'You take care.'

He hesitated for one more moment, then turned and walked away. Jackie watched him, thinking that even from behind he looked different – more upright, more sure of himself. And yet he hadn't been at all sure of himself with her.

She felt a sudden fierce desire to call him back, to pull him tightly into her arms, to kiss him with all the passion that she'd learned with him during the long winter nights. And then he turned the corner and was gone.

When Jackie went indoors again, her eyes were damp and red. Alice and Minnie looked at her and then at each other as she went slowly back up the stairs to her bedroom.

'I do think her looks better for it, all the same,' Minnie said. 'They've patched it up, and it'll be a fair long time before anything else can happen. Got time to grow up, both of 'em.'

'And I can't say I'm sorry,' Alice remarked, sliding a tray of lamb chops into the oven. 'I can't say I'm sorry at all.'

Hilary started up the estate car her father had finally agreed to buy her only a month before his illness. Since taking over the estate management, she had been visiting all the tenant farmers in turn, telling them what was happening and talking over any problems they might have. They had all known her since childhood and welcomed her so heartily that sometimes she had difficulty getting away.

'You'll take a glass of my sloe gin, now,' one apple-cheeked farmer's wife urged her.' 'Tis full of goodness, won't do you no harm at all. Put heart into you, that will.'

'Gin, at ten o'clock in the morning? I don't think I'd better!' Hilary said. 'Thank you very much, all the same, but if everyone offers me alcohol I'll be rolling drunk by the time I get home.'

'A glass of home-made lemonade, then?' the woman suggested, and Hilary nodded gratefully. She followed her hostess into the kitchen and sat at the big, scrubbed table. 'And how's the Squire, then?'

'He's getting along very well, thank you, Mrs Barrow. Doctor Latimer's allowing him downstairs now and he's going through some old photographs and things for the Exhibition. I don't suppose you've got anything, have you?'

Hilda Barrow pursed her lips and shook her head. 'No, I wouldn't have anything of interest like that. Only a few old photograph albums and some old papers about the farm-house. I suppose by rights they should be yours, but your grandfather gave them to my man's father when he took over the tenancy, and we've always kept them. 'Twouldn't be right to throw them away. They'm nothing to look at, though – all yellow and tattered.'

'Old papers?' Hilary echoed. 'Papers about the farm?'

'That's right. In an old envelope in our tin box. I haven't looked at them for years.'

'Do you think I could see them?' Hilary asked tentatively, scarcely able to believe her luck.

'Well, if you want to.' Hilda Barrow clearly thought this a strange idea. 'I'll fetch them down.'

Half an hour later Hilary left the farmhouse, her head reeling more than it would have done had she accepted the sloe gin, a large bundle of photograph albums and a packet of documents clutched under her arm. She had been almost afraid to ask if she could borrow them, but Hilda Barrow had pressed them into her arms.

'You take 'em, my blossom, if you think they'd be any good in that old Exhibition. 'Tis only some old maps and ledgers, and the ink's so faded you can hardly read them anyway. And there's nobody left now who even knows who the people be in those photographs.'

'But *you* know,' Hilary said.

'Oh, *I* knows, all right. They'm all my man's grand-parents and uncles and aunties, that's who they be. But there's nobody else to be interested.'

'But that's just the point,' Hilary said, gathering them together. 'People *are* interested. This is exactly the kind of thing we want for the Exhibition.'

Carefully, she put the packages on the back seat of the car and drove off. If she were to find such a treasure-trove in every farm she visited, they'd need the entire hall for the History part of the Exhibition alone. She hugged herself, thinking of her father's face when he saw them. Basil Harvey and Miss Kemp would be excited too, and even Mrs Warren. Nothing else as old had yet been found.

She was on her way home an hour or so later when she noticed Felix walking along the lane in front of her. She drew up beside him and leaned across to open the door. 'Like a lift?'

'Hilary!' His face lit up. 'What a nice surprise.' He ducked his head and folded himself through the door. 'I'm really out for the good of my health, but I'd rather ride with you. Where have you been?'

347

'Touring the tenant farms. I thought they ought to have a visit, to let them know what's happening. And I've found treasure!'

'Treasure?'

'Yes. Wonderful old photographs, and documents showing all the old field boundaries, with their names. "Twelve acre", "Holly Meadow", "Sticky Bottom" –'

'I don't believe the last one!' he protested, laughing.

'It's true – I'll show you. It refers to a rather muddy field low down in the valley. Really, Felix,' she added primly, 'for a curate you have a very naughty sense of humour.'

'Most curates have a naughty sense of humour,' he said. 'Vicars too, and probably even bishops. We're only human, you know.'

'Well, most of them don't let it show. And you should be more careful too. Suppose Mrs Warren heard you.'

'Ah, but Mrs Warren's not here, is she? Thank the Lord,' he added piously.

'Felix! Stop it.' Hilary tried to stifle her laughter, but failed. She gave him a wry look. 'You know, you're a bad influence on me – and you shouldn't be. I may complain to the vicar.'

'Oh, he knows what I'm like already,' Felix said, 'and he has quite a sense of humour himself, you know. Well, where shall we go now?'

'Nowhere. I've got to go home and see how Dad is. I left Dottie going through old photos with him. You can come with me if you like, and have a bit of lunch.'

'Do you think I should? I wouldn't like to intrude. And I've been very remiss, I should have asked after your father. How is he?'

'He's doing very well. Please come, Felix. It does him so much good to see a different face, and kind and pleasant as Dottie is, he doesn't really have much in common with her.'

'All right, then. If you put it that way. But I'll ask a favour in return.'

'What's that?' she asked cautiously.

'That you come for a walk with me afterwards. It's my day off and we haven't spent any time together since we had that day in Exeter. Which I enjoyed very much indeed,' he added, turning to look at her.

'So did I. All right, I'll come for a walk, but we can't go far. I'll need to be back by four, when the nurse goes off-duty.'

'And so you shall be, Cinderella. I shall make sure of it. So long as you don't want me to turn into a white mouse or something, to draw your carriage along. I don't think I could manage that.'

'You wouldn't have to. It was the white mice who changed into footmen. And we're going for a walk, remember. I won't even wear my glass slippers.'

'I can't imagine why anyone would want to,' he said thoughtfully. 'Most uncomfortable, I'd have thought, not to mention being rather dangerous.'

'I've heard somewhere that it was a mistranslation from the French for "fur". Not that I'd wear my fur slippers to a ball, either.' She turned the car through the gateway. 'Really, this is a very silly conversation. I hope you're not going to twitter on like this at lunch.'

'Not if you don't either,' he said solemnly, and they were still laughing when Hilary drew the car to a halt in front of the steps and they got out.

''Tis all in hand, Mrs Warren,' Alice said. 'You don't need to be worrying yourself about the bellringers' tea. I always sees to that, along with some of the other ringers' wives. 'Tidn't nothing to do with the Fair, anyway.'

'Of course it's to do with the Fair!' Joyce's patience was being stretched thin and it showed in her voice. 'It's a special competition, isn't it? A Festival shield? Well, then, of course it's to do with the Fair, and as principal organiser I ought to know what's going on.'

'Well, that's as may be,' Alice said. She didn't like Mrs Warren much at the best of times, and she especially didn't like her poking her nose into things Alice had been doing for years with one hand tied behind her back. 'As far as I'm concerned, 'tis just a competition, same as all the others, and as Ringing Captain's wife I does the tea, and that's all there is to it.'

'Yes, but you don't understand,' Joyce insisted. 'The point is that you won't be able to use the village hall. We'll have the Exhibition in there. And handing out sixty Cornish pasties in the church is out of the question. You'll need to think about it and let me know what you're planning to do.'

'Oh, that's what you'm making all this song and dance about, is it?' Alice folded her arms. 'Well, that's all right, then. 'Tis all fixed up. We'll be using the tent.'

'Tent?' Joyce stared at her. 'What tent?'

'Why, the tent we'm putting up in Ted's field, of course. Didn't no one mention it to you? 'Tis a proper marquee. Miss Hilary offered it to us. Left over from when they had that Army camp over at the Barton. Nobody never come to collect it, so they've had it stored in one of their barns ever since. She mentioned it to Ted and he thought it would be a good idea, in case it rains. I thought you'd be pleased,' she finished, giving Joyce Warren a bland smile.

'Of course I'm pleased. It'll be a wonderful asset. But I'm rather surprised that no one thought to mention it to *me*. I'm only the one who's trying to see that everything's co-ordinated and works well on the day. Over the whole weekend, in fact. It would have been common courtesy, if nothing else.'

'Well, we knows that, and if you'd give me a chance

when you first come, instead of starting on at me about ringers' teas the minute you were over the doorstep, I'd have told you then and saved all this argy-bargying. It were only this dinner-time that Ted told me. He saw Miss Hilary this morning. So nobody else has heard about it, and you'm the first to know.' Alice met her eye and Joyce found herself stared out. She flushed and looked away.

'I see. In that case I owe you an apology. I'm glad it's all been sorted out. How will you boil the water?'

'Big camping stoves. The Army left them as well.' Alice caught the gleam in Joyce's eye and added quickly, 'They wouldn't be no use for the village hall. Got to be used outdoors, see, in case of fumes. Anyway, the boiler's getting repaired tomorrow, so you should be all right there.'

'Tomorrow?' Joyce felt as if she were completely losing grip. 'How on earth do you know that? I haven't been able to get through to the repairman myself yet.'

'Saw un this morning, when I were in Tavi. He said the vicar had been on to him and that he'd be out tomorrow.' Alice smiled again and took pity on the other woman. She might be irritating – a pain in the backside, her Ted said – but her heart was in the right place, and you had to admit she put in a lot of work on things like this. 'Now, why don't you sit yourself down for a minute, Mrs Warren, and have a cup of tea with me and Ted's mother? Just made some scones, she have, and there's our strawberry jam and cream to go with 'em. You looks a bit fraught, if you don't mind me saying so.'

'Well, I've got a lot of things to do, but – yes, a cup of tea would be very nice, thank you, Mrs Tozer.' She smiled at Minnie, who was sitting in her chair and watching all that went on. 'These scones look delicious. Will you be making some for the Fair and Exhibition?'

'I dare say I will. And for the ringers' tea, of course. It looks like being a busy weekend.'

'It does.' Joyce felt slightly faint as she thought of all that was to happen – the bellringing competition, even though that did seem to be under control, the pageant, the Exhibition and the displays on the green and in the field. And heaven knew how many scones and pasties and sandwiches and cakes were going to be required. 'I just hope it all goes well,' she said with feeling.

'Oh, it will.' Alice brought the big brown teapot to the table and set it down. 'We'm all looking forward to it, Mrs Warren. 'Tis going to be a good day. And nothing's going to go wrong.' She smiled again. 'There might be a few surprises, but nothing will go really wrong.'

Chapter Thirty-One

Term ended and Stella spent the last few days with her class, taking down drawings and maps from the walls, tidying desks and clearing the nature table. The tadpoles had long turned into tiny frogs and been set free near the village pond; the water from the accumulator tank had been tipped into the pond as well, so that the snails and any other pondlife in the weed could return to their proper home. The puss-moth caterpillars had pupated and could be left in their tin until it was time for the moths themselves to emerge. There were several discarded skins, which were borne off as treasures by Micky and Ernest.

Miss Kemp came in just as Stella was finishing the last of the clearing-up. The children had rushed out into the sunshine, shrieking with excitement at the prospect of six weeks with no school, and Stella felt rather like shrieking with them.

'Well, that's that until September,' the headmistress said. 'Except for the Festival weekend, of course. But that's only just over a week away, so we'll have a nice long stretch after that. You said you were going away, didn't you?'

'Yes, but not until the last week of August. I'll be back in time to think about the new term, and I'm hoping my friend might give me some ideas. She's teaching at a school in Oxfordshire.'

'That's good. You'll be able to swap experiences.' Miss

Kemp settled herself against Stella's desk. 'You are happy here, aren't you? You seem to have settled in very well.'

'I love it, I really do. The children, the school, the village – it's all I've ever wanted.' She gazed out of her window at the view of Dartmoor sweeping away above the village. 'I'd like to stay here for ever.'

'I can understand that,' the headmistress said, 'but you won't want to remain an assistant mistress all your life. And I'm afraid you've a few years yet to wait for my shoes.'

'Oh, goodness no, I didn't mean that!' Stella felt her colour rise. 'I suppose I'll have to move on at some time, if only to get more experience. It would be interesting to work in a bigger school, too. But not yet. I want to stay in Burracombe as long as I can.'

'I hope you do. You've fitted in very well – the children love you and the parents seem very happy. Now, I don't want to start talking about next term yet, but we will need to get together a few days beforehand to talk about the new intake. There'll be some new children starting, and amongst them are the Crocker twins.'

'Oh yes, the vicar mentioned them when I came to see the school and have my interview. I've seen them around the village too. They look rather sweet.'

'They do indeed,' the headmistress said a trifle grimly. 'But so do their older brothers. You won't know Joseph and Sam Crocker. They're quite a few years older – the twins were an "afterthought". Sam's doing his National Service now, and Joseph – well, the less said about him the better, perhaps. Anyway, we shall have to hope for the best. I believe there will be three other new infants as well, so you'll have your hands full.'

'There are five going up into your class,' Stella pointed out, and the headmistress nodded.

'That's right. But as I said, we don't need to discuss this now.' As she glanced around the classroom they heard the shuffling and muttering sounds that accompanied Mrs Purdy's arrival. 'If you're all finished here, why not come over to the schoolhouse for a cup of tea? I think we deserve it, don't you?'

Stella agreed, and they opened the door to find the school cleaner already getting out her brooms and mops. She looked round as they came into the lobby and gave a nod of bitter satisfaction.

'So that's another term finished with, then. At least I'll be able to get on with me cleaning in peace and quiet, and know that when I comes in things'll be same as I left 'em yesterday. I know children have to come to school, but I just wish sometimes they could bring a bit less mud and dirt with 'em. Well, you go off and enjoy your holidays. Some of us don't get the luxury. Six weeks!' they heard her say indignantly as she shuffled into the main classroom. 'And they say teaching's a hard job . . .'

The two teachers looked at each other and Stella laughed. Miss Kemp smiled too and said, 'I think school cleaners are a breed apart. They either love the children or hate them. But under all that grumbling, Mrs Purdy's got a heart of gold. And she's an excellent cleaner.'

They walked across the playground together. It was mid-afternoon and the sun was still high in the sky. Stella could hear the sound of children's voices, playing on the green or in cottage gardens. She heard the clip–clop of hooves and glanced over the fence to see Val Tozer passing by with her father's Shire horse, Barley. She remembered seeing them on her first day here, as she got off the bus and heard Luke Ferris ask if she were the new teacher, and she waved, then remembered Val's coolness towards her and was pleasantly surprised when she waved back.

Miss Kemp paused as she opened the door and glanced over her shoulder. She waved as well.

'Val Tozer. A nice girl. One of my first pupils when I

came here. Such a sad thing that her fiancé was killed. I hope she'll find someone else some day.'

They went inside and Miss Kemp put the kettle on. Stella looked out at the tiny back garden and sighed a little. The bright summer sunshine seemed suddenly dimmed.

We all seem to have lost something, she thought. Hilary and Val lost their sweethearts and I lost my family. And millions of other people lost their loved ones as well, and their homes and all they owned. But we all have to go on living. Some of them are lost for ever, and we can't go on searching all our lives.

Val had surprised herself by waving at Stella. She walked on down the lane, with Barley's nose rubbing at her sleeve as he plodded at her side, and thought about the young teacher. I don't know why I felt so jealous of her, she thought. Luke told me there was nothing between them. Yet that sight she'd had of them, standing so close together on the edge of the moor, had been easy to misconstrue, and even though Val had tried hard to put Luke Ferris out of her mind, his arrival in the village had been more disturbing than she would have expected.

You can't stop loving someone just like switching off a light, she thought. I had a terrible time after Luke and I gave each other up, but it wasn't fair to blame him for that. He didn't even know. She thought of the comfort she had found in his arms, as he held her when she told him about the baby. The sensation of coming home. And she knew that she still loved him; that she had never really stopped.

She hadn't been able to let Luke go to London without seeing him again. She had got up early next morning and caught the first bus to Tavistock, walking quickly up the hill to the railway station. Basil Harvey would be bringing Luke and the paintings in his car, and she wanted to be on the platform before they arrived. I hope to goodness the vicar manages to get him here in time, she thought anxiously. I hope they don't arrive at the last minute . . . And just in case, instead of a platform ticket she bought a return to Okehampton and then ran across the bridge to wait behind a pillar on the opposite platform.

It was only a few minutes before the train was due, and she had begun to fear that Basil was going to live up to his reputation, when she saw the two men hurry on to the station, laden with their packages. I hope Luke's got a taxi waiting for him in London, she thought, watching as they scrabbled for money and bought tickets, then panted up the steps and across the bridge. By the time they reached the platform the train was pulling in and the two men said a hurried goodbye before Luke scrambled aboard. Val, thankful for her foresight in buying a full ticket, climbed aboard too and as the train drew out again she made her way down the corridor to where Luke was struggling with his paintings.

'Here,' she said as he almost dropped one, 'let me give you a hand.'

Luke straightened up and stared at her. The thin package fell from his hand. '*Val*!'

'Yes,' she said, and bent to retrieve the picture. But as she too straightened up she felt his arms around her, and found herself drawn tightly against his lean, hard body. The painting fell to the floor once more as they clung together. 'Oh Luke, I had to come. I couldn't let you go away again, not knowing. Oh *Luke* . . .'

Dottie Friend was standing at her gate as Val passed. Now that they had a full-time housekeeper at the Barton, she was able to spend more time at home, and she was busy in the garden, dead-heading roses and threading honeysuckle through a trellis arbour that Nathan Pettifer had put up for her. She gave Barley a fallen apple and stroked his broad, smooth nose as he munched it.

'I was going to come up to the farm to see you,' she said to Val. 'Saved me a journey, you have. Squire and me have finished going through all they old photos and things, and Mrs Warren's asked me to pin them all up on some screens for the Exhibition. I wondered if you'd give me and Stella a hand with it.'

'Yes, all right.' It'll be a good chance for us to get together, Val thought. I know I've been unwelcoming towards her. 'When d'you want to do it?'

'Well, us can't get into the village hall till next Tuesday, so us had better do it as soon as possible after that. When be you off-duty next week?'

'Wednesday should be all right. Morning or afternoon?'

'Let's make it the morning, then. That'll be a proper job.'

'I'll be there about ten.' Val smiled at her and walked on. Luke would probably be home again by then, she thought. And she felt a lightening of her heart, as though spring had made a return visit and life was about to begin once more.

The whole village was geared towards the last-minute preparations for the Festival Fair and Exhibition. In Ted Tozer's field, the big Army tent was erected and trestle tables brought down from the village hall. This caused Joyce Warren some consternation, as nobody had thought to mention this to her and the first she knew of it was when she met Nathan Pettifer and Norman Tozer hauling them up on to Ted's cart, with Barley waiting patiently in the shafts.

'What do you think you're doing with those?'

The men looked down at her. 'We'm taking them down to the field. We needs 'em there for the ringers, tea.'

'But I need them in the hall! What do you think we're going to display our exhibits on? Put them back at once!'

Nathan climbed down slowly and faced her. 'Can't do that, missus. Boss'll have us guts for garters.'

'And I'll have your guts for garters if you don't! Put them *back*.' She looked round helplessly and saw Dottie Friend coming down the lane with Stella. 'Dottie, do you have any influence on these people? Can't you explain to them that we need the tables for our exhibits?'

Dottie looked at the two men. 'How many are you taking?'

'Dozen or so. We'm leaving a dozen there – Miss Val said that'd be all you'd need.' He gave Joyce an aggrieved look. 'I were going to tell you, but you never give me a chance.'

'Oh. Oh well, that's all right, then.' The woman turned to Dottie and Stella. 'We'd better go inside and get started. I gather Val Tozer's already here. I hope that young artist's going to be back in time to set out his paintings. I can't understand why he had to go rushing off to London at an important time like this. They've got exhibitions going on up there all the time . . .' She bustled into the hall, leaving Dottie and Stella to follow her and the men to finish their loading.

As Nathan had promised, there were trestle tables already up around the sides of the hall and Val was standing at one, sorting out a pile of photographs. Beside her was a small enclosure made of rather wobbly canvas screens. She looked up as the women came in and gave Stella a friendly smile.

'These are fascinating. Look, this is the Army camp that was in the Barton grounds, and here are some of the evacuees at the school that took over the house itself. And look at these, from the Barrows' farm! I'm amazed anyone even had a camera as long ago as that. This one must be

359

from the turn of the century, at least. Look at the women's dresses!'

They picked through the photos, exclaiming over them and deciding where to display them. Stella started to read some of the tattered documents.

'You know, someone ought to put all these into a book,' she said. 'It would be a lovely record to have. *The Book of Burracombe*, with lots of photos and documents, and people's stories written down – all the things we've been hearing while this has been going on.' She looked up, bright-eyed and excited. 'Don't you think so?'

'I do,' Val said. 'It's a wonderful idea. You ought to do it, Stella. You're the one with the education.'

'Oh, I couldn't! People don't know me well enough – I'm still a stranger here. It would have to be someone they'd trust and could talk to. You'd be the one.'

'Well, perhaps we could do it together. I could collect the stories and you could write them down.' They looked at each other with enthusiasm. 'Look, when all this is over, why don't you—'

A sudden commotion interrupted her words and she turned to see what was happening. The door was open and someone was struggling in backwards, evidently trying to get a large, flat bundle through without dropping it. Val stared and then put down the document she was holding and ran across the hall.

'*Luke*!'

He turned, and as he saw her coming towards him, he laid his bundle of paintings down on the nearest table. Then he held out his arms and she ran straight into them.

'*Well*!' Joyce Warren exclaimed, and drew herself up very straight.

'Oh, look at that,' Dottie Friend said, her round face beaming with pleasure. 'Isn't that lovely!'

Stella stared at them. Then she turned away and picked

up a photograph at random, studying it intently. Her face paled.

'Stella, my flower! Are you all right?' Dottie was at her elbow, her face anxious. 'You're not upset, are you, maid? He's a lovely man, I know, and you're good friends, but you can see there's something proper special there. You mustn't take it to heart.' She looked more closely at Stella's white face. 'Stella?'

'It's not that,' Stella said breathlessly. 'It's this photograph.' She held it up so that Dottie could see. 'Where is it? Who are all these children?'

Dottie fumbled for her glasses. She held the photo up to catch the light from the window, and then a smile broke out over her face. 'Why, it's the little evacuee children that were up at the Barton. It were taken over by a school, you know – well, us always called it a school, but it were more of a Home, really. Poor little tackers that had lost their mums and dads in the war. And look, here's Maddy – the little girl my actress adopted and brought to live with me.'

'Maddy?' Stella almost snatched the photograph away and stared at the child Dottie was pointing at. '*That's* Maddy?'

'Yes,' Dottie said, beaming at the photograph as if the sight of it brought back happy memories. 'That's her. It must be almost the only photograph there is, because you know we couldn't get much film during the war. Why?' She looked at Stella again. 'What is it? You look as if you've seen a ghost.'

'Not a ghost,' Stella said, and her eyes filled with tears. They spilled down her cheeks and as Dottie stared at her in dismay she shook her head, laughing and crying at the same time. 'Not a ghost at all. Dottie, it's Muriel – my sister! That little girl is my *sister*! My sister, that I've been looking for for years and thought I'd lost for ever. Oh Dottie, I've been searching so hard, and you knew her all the time. *She lived with you during the war.*' She sat down suddenly on one of the hard wooden chairs and put her face into her hands. The others noticed what was happening and came over in concern, Luke and Val still holding each other's hands.

'What is it? What's the matter?' Val asked. She looked at the others, bewildered and concerned. 'She seemed so happy a few minutes ago. What's happened to upset her?'

Dottie turned her head and looked at them.

'She's not upset,' she said. 'She's not upset at all. She's just found her sister, the one Luke's been helping her look for all these months.' She put her hand on Stella's shoulder and spoke directly to her. 'And what's more, my blossom, you'll be able to meet her soon, because when my actress is coming to open the Fair, she's bringing Maddy with her!'

Chapter Thirty-Two

The day of the Fair dawned at last. Stella woke and stared at her bedroom ceiling, hardly able to believe that it was finally here. She stretched under her sheets and thought over all that had happened since she had seen the photograph of her sister in the village hall.

She still found it amazing that she was actually living in the same cottage that Muriel had lived in. It seemed incredible that Dottie had known her and looked after her and yet, even though she had known Stella was looking for her sister, never realised there could be a connection. Yet it was understandable. There had been hundreds, perhaps thousands, of children orphaned during the war, and many more put in Children's Homes. And for some reason, although the village had known that the children at the Barton were in a Home, they always referred to it as a 'school'.

And then there was the change of name. By the time Dottie met her, Muriel had been known as Maddy for two years. They had changed her name at the Home because there was another Muriel of the same age, and when the actress had adopted her, she had decided to keep it. She told everyone that the little girl's name was Madelaine, Maddy for short, and Muriel herself had never corrected her.

'Didn't she ever say she had a sister?' Stella had asked wistfully, and Dottie shook her head. They were back in the cottage then, for Dottie had said Stella had had a shock and needed a rest and a nice cup of tea. What she had really meant was that Stella needed to get used to finding her sister at last and to ask questions and, now that they were home and the tea was made, she settled in the armchair facing Stella and prepared to answer those questions.

'I'm afraid she didn't, my flower. I did ask her once about her family and she said they were all dead.' She saw the pain cross Stella's face and added, 'Maybe they told her that at the Home – who knows? They did some funny things during the war, but they usually thought they were doing them for the best.'

'How could they believe that?' Stella burst out. 'How could they think that telling a little girl that her whole family was dead could be for the best, when it wasn't true? It was cruel! Separating us at all was cruel.'

'I know, my pretty, but we don't know their reasons, do we? Maybe she was grieving so much that they had to tell her that. You can get over a death – eventually – but 'tis hard to get over losing someone when you know they're still alive somewhere.'

'You don't have to tell me that,' Stella said bitterly. 'I've spent all these years grieving for Muriel, but I wouldn't rather have thought she was dead.' She looked at Dottie. 'Did – did she seem to grieve?'

Dottie sighed a little. 'I couldn't really say that, flower. She was just a little girl, wasn't she? She were only ten year old when she come to me, not quite eleven, and she'd been in the Home for two years then. I never knew exactly what had happened to her before that. We all thought it were best not to ask her too much – remind her, like. It was best that she put it all behind her.' She looked apologetically at Stella and Stella reached over and patted her hand.

'It's all right, Dottie. You did what you thought best, and you didn't know about me. And I know you'll have given her a good home. She couldn't have been with anyone better than you.'

Dottie's eyes filled with tears. She sniffed and rubbed her nose, and said gruffly, 'I only did what were right. And she were a sweet little maid, Maddy – still is.'

Stella was longing to see her sister. They were in France now, the actress and Muriel, but on the day of the Fair itself, they would be here in Burracombe. After all her desperate searching, Muriel was coming to Burracombe – and she would have been coming even without my searching, Stella realised. All I had to do was wait, and she would have come to me.

'Can we let them know?' she asked Dottie. 'Can you get in touch with your actress and tell Muriel about me?'

'I can't, maid. I don't know where they be. I had an address to write to before, so I could ask her about the Fair, but since then they've been travelling about, and I don't know where. Us shan't hear no more from them until they arrive.'

'So Muriel won't know I'm here? I'll be a complete shock to her.'

'A surprise,' Dottie said gently. 'A lovely, lovely surprise.'

'A shock, just the same, if she thinks I'm dead. We'll have to be very careful, Dottie.'

They sat quietly for a while, drinking their tea and thinking about what had happened. I need time to take it all in, Stella thought, and if I need time after just seeing a photograph, how is Muriel going to feel meeting me in the flesh, with no warning at all?

'She might not even believe me!' she said suddenly. 'She might not recognise me. Oh, *Dottie*!'

'Now, don't you start worrying yourself about that. She'll know you all right, and if she don't recognise you straight away, there'll be lots you can talk about, things you did when you were little, that only you'd know about. Anyway, we only see the differences in people for the first few minutes, when we meet them again. After that, we just see the things that are the same.'

'I hope you're right,' Stella said. And I hope Muriel likes me too, she thought. We've lived such different lives – me in the Home and now teaching in a tiny village, and her living with an actress in London and going abroad . . . What is she going to be like after all that? What changes will there be?

She tried to keep her mind off the coming meeting by immersing herself in the Festival preparations. Almost everyone in the village was involved in one way or another, and she and Miss Kemp had arranged several last-minute rehearsals for the children. Jacob had put up the maypole, and they practised their dances, getting their ribbons so tangled at times that, as Constance Bellamy remarked, pausing to watch them as she gave Rupert his afternoon walk, you could have knitted yourself a Fair Isle jumper from them.

'I think they have,' Stella said, trying to unravel the brilliantly coloured strands. 'Honestly, there are more knots here than there are in a Boy Scouts' competition!'

The Drama Group was busy rehearsing too, and with the village hall now closed to everyone except those still putting up their Exhibition displays, the big tent in Ted Tozer's field was coming in very useful. On Friday night, however, everything had to be cleared out and the tables set up for the bellringers' tea. Alice Tozer and the rest of the ringers' wives were busy all morning, baking pasties, scones and rock cakes and setting the tables, while on the green Ted and Nathan were setting out bales of straw for the bowling.

The competition was to start at ten in the morning. It had been agreed that it would end with the last team at six, after the tea, and then the Burracombe ringers, who were not taking part in the competition itself, would ring a final peal. There were three novice teams as well, and Burracombe had been permitted to enter theirs, since it was their idea to set this up, although they would not be placed. The novices went first and the older ringers had to admit that they made a pretty fair job of it.

'Might let young Tom ring in the Barnaby next year,' Ted observed. 'He did all right on the treble. And young Jimmy, too, he rung that tenor as steady as a rock. Maybe they're right – us ought to give them a chance in one or two competitions.'

News was exchanged as usual, and everyone wanted to know how the men's outfitter's manager was getting on at Lydford. The captain laughed. 'Oh, he be leaving! Couldn't stand it no longer. Didn't you hear how he come into the church one day when us was ringing for a wedding, and started all his shouting and carrying on? Vicar told un a few home truths, I tell you! Told un he was never to come near the church again unless it were to pray at a proper service. I reckon that were enough for him. House went up for sale very next week.'

'Well, let's hope he don't come to Burracombe,' Ted said. 'Us don't want his sort here. Plymouth'd be the best place for he. City man, he is – likes the sound of traffic better than the sounds of cockerels and cows and good church bells.'

The new Shield was finally won by Little Burracombe. Ted Tozer presented it to his rival captain and they shook hands heartily in front of everyone. 'I'm pleased it's stopping at a Burracombe, if 'tis only the Little un,' he said, and they all laughed. 'But us'll get it back next year, see if us don't!'

By the time the ringers had all drifted away from the village after visiting the pub, and the women had cleared up in the tent, it was getting late. Val and Luke, who had been putting the final touches to his display in the village hall, walked home together under the pale twilight sky. They paused by the gate to the woods and leaned on it, watching the moon rise over the swell of the moor.

'It's all right between us now, isn't it?' he said at last. 'We've found each other again.'

Val nodded. 'I think so. But I still need time – it was such a shock to see you again after all these years. And then, thinking that you were in love with Stella . . .'

'I never was,' he said quietly. 'I like her very much – I suppose, in a way, I do love her – but more like a little sister than anything else. It seemed so sad, the way she'd been looking for her own sister all these years, and I wanted to help her. And all the time, she was going to find her anyway! It's so incredible.'

'I know. But I think she was falling in love with you, all the same.'

'That's why I went away,' he said. 'I couldn't let that happen. I'd already done so much damage to you. I couldn't have forgiven myself if I'd hurt another woman.'

Val leaned her head on his shoulder. 'You didn't hurt me, Luke. Everything we did, we did together. It wasn't your fault that Eddie died, or that I lost the baby, and it wasn't your fault I felt so guilty. I just couldn't face it all, and I took it out on you. Somehow, during the last few months, I've learned to take my own responsibility for it all.' She paused, then said quietly, 'Jackie thought she was pregnant a few weeks ago.'

'Jackie?' He turned and looked at her in astonishment. 'Your sister Jackie?'

'Yes. You know she's been going out with Roy Nethercott for a year or so now. They wanted to get engaged but Mum wouldn't have it, said they were both too young – and so they are. But then Roy got his call-up papers and was going away and – well, we can understand, can't we? It was all too much for them.'

Luke was silent for a moment. Then he said, 'Yes, we can understand. It's so powerful, isn't it? It puts everything else into the shade and nothing else seems important.'

'She told me she regretted it the minute it was over,' Val said. 'I don't think she even enjoyed it much. It was the first time for both of them, and they hardly knew what they were doing.'

Luke tightened his arm about her shoulders. 'I didn't regret making love to you,' he said quietly. 'It was the most wonderful thing that ever happened to me.'

'For me, too,' she said. 'I only regretted it because of Eddie. I never meant to let him down, Luke. I did fall in love with you, but I was engaged to Eddie, and I loved him too. I shouldn't have let it happen.'

'It's in the past,' he said gently. 'We can't alter that. But we can make the most of the rest of our lives.' They were quiet for a moment, then he said, 'But what about Jackie? You said she "thought" she was pregnant. Does that mean the same thing happened to her as it did to you? Is she all right?'

'Yes, she's all right. It was a false alarm. She realised it the day she went to London.' Val remembered something and added, 'I was so mean to Stella that day, you know. Jackie'd gone to the Ladies' – that's when she realised she was all right – and Stella came to sit beside me. I was rude to her. I still thought then that she and you . . . Honestly, I've treated her very badly.'

'Well, that's over now, too,' Luke said. 'You've made up for it in the past few days, and on Monday she'll have her sister back. And she's so excited about that, that she seems to have forgotten she might be falling for me, so that's OK! But is Jackie really all right? She must have had a bad fright.'

'She did. She told me about it in the end, and I felt so sorry for her – I could understand how she felt. Not that I could tell her that, of course.' Val was silent for a moment. 'I think she's got over it, though, and it's put paid to any ideas she might have had about getting engaged to Roy. She wouldn't even speak to him when he first came home, but she says now that she's agreed to write to him while he's away. He's going to Korea, you know.'

'So I heard. It's a bad business out there.' Luke shook his head. 'We've lost a lot of men, and some of them have been National Servicemen like Roy. We all thought that once the last war was over we could put that behind us, but it hasn't happened, has it? God knows where it will end.'

They stood very quietly for a while, watching the moon lift its head above the hills, and then he drew her closer and turned his face to hers. Their lips met in a long, tender kiss. He stroked her hair and face and kissed her again. Then he said huskily, 'You will give me another chance, won't you, Val? I know we've got a lot to talk about, and we need to get to know each other a lot better – we mustn't rush into things like we did before. But there's more time now. We can take it slowly.' He paused. 'If we can just be friends – that'll be enough, to start with.'

'Yes,' she whispered, and he saw the stars reflected in her eyes as she looked up at him. 'Yes, Luke, we can be friends. To start with.'

The sun was streaming through the yellow flowered curtains in Stella's room, casting stripes of golden light across her bed as she lay thinking over the past. Her memories had drifted further back now – to the dark days of the war, when she and Muriel and their mother had emerged from their shelter to find their house destroyed by bombs, the misery and confusion of the church hall where they'd slept until they'd been allocated the dismal little house in October Street, and the work their mother had done to turn it into a home. The birth of their brother Thomas during an air-raid, and then the second bomb, which had robbed her and Muriel of him and their mother.

There had been happier times, even then – the months they had spent with the Budd brothers, Tim and Keith, at the vicarage in the country, the visits their father had made to them there. And then he too was gone, and they had been swept up and parted. Why were people so cruel, Stella wondered, even when they meant to be kind? Why had it been considered better to separate her from her little sister? And why ever had they told Muriel that Stella was dead?

I'll never understand it, she thought.

It was time to get up. Dottie was cooking breakfast downstairs in the sunny kitchen, and Stella had promised to be at the village hall by ten, when the Exhibition was to open again. They had had a good many visitors on Saturday, when the bellringers had all taken the oppor-tunity of some entertainment while the other teams were competing, and a lot of them had brought their wives too. Yesterday being Sunday, the Exhibition had been closed and the focus was on the church, with its flower displays. Both services had been full, and Hilary and her helpers had been congratulated over and over again on their arrange-ments.

Even when Felix had come to lock the church, Hilary had still been busy, checking over each urn and vase for dying leaves or petals beginning to turn brown. The last of the sunset was slanting through the windows as he came in, and she turned to smile at him.

'You must have finished by now,' he said, coming to stand beside her. 'They're perfect.'

'I want them to be perfect,' she said. 'Everyone's worked

so hard for the Festival, Felix, and it's all gone so well so far, but tomorrow's going to be the big day.'

'The big day for everyone,' he said softly. 'And I was hoping . . . I want to ask you something, Hilary.'

'What's that?' Her eyes were still on the flowers, but something in his voice caught her attention and she turned to face him. 'Felix?'

'I'd like you to make it a big day for me too,' he said. 'These last few months, Hilary, you've made such a difference to me. Coming into a village like Burracombe, a stranger from the other side of the country, well, it could have been so difficult. But you've eased my path. You've been a friend to me, a really good friend. And I wondered – is there any possibility that you might be more than that?' He paused as she gazed at him, and then said, 'I'm asking you to be my wife, Hilary.'

'Oh,' she said.

There was a long silence. Then she took his hand and led him to the front pew. They sat down and she turned towards him.

'Felix, I don't know how to say this.' She saw his face fall and added quickly, 'I've enjoyed spending time with you – showing you around, going riding sometimes, the day we spent in Exeter. It's been lovely. But with Dad being ill, and with my feeling so restless and dissatisfied with my life, I've never thought of anything else. I've been selfish, I suppose. I've never thought at all about how it might be for you.'

'But that doesn't mean there's no chance—' he began eagerly.

Hilary lifted one hand, and he fell silent again. 'I'm sorry, Felix, I think it does. I've been thinking a lot during these past weeks, since Dad had his heart attack. You see, what I've always wanted was something to *do* – something real and solid and satisfying. I thought I'd have to go away to find it – I even planned to leave home and go to London. But now, I think I've found it at home after all.' She paused and he saw the light in her eyes. 'Dad and I have talked about it and he's accepted at last that he's never going to be able to do all he used to do. He needs someone to help him run the estate – to take over from him – and I'm going to do it! He's going to hand over the reins to me. Burracombe Barton will stay in the family and a Napier will still be running it. And I know I'll be good at it – it's what I've always wanted.'

'But that doesn't mean you can't marry if you want to,' Felix said, and she shook her head.

'No, but you see, I don't think I do. I don't think I ever did, really.' She looked into his eyes. 'There *are* people like me, Felix, who stay single. It doesn't mean they don't want friends, though. I hope we'll always be friends. And that you'll find someone else – someone who'll make you a far better wife than I would.'

'I don't know,' he said a little sadly. 'I don't know if I will, Hilary.'

Hilary touched his cheek with her fingertips. 'You will,' she said. Then she got up and walked out of the church.

Felix sat for a long while in the front pew, with the colours of the flowers fading in the gathering dusk and their scent all around him. Then he too got up and walked out, locking the door behind him.

He felt as if he were locking away his heart.

Chapter Thirty-Three

By two o'clock, everyone was ready. The stallholders and those running sideshows were all at their posts, with coconut-shies, bowling for a pig, plant and bric-à-brac stalls, a plywood cut-out of a clown with holes for faces and hands, where you could choose a grinning Boy Scout to throw wet sponges at, and a display of woodcarving with Jacob Prout red in the face with pride and embarrassment behind a forest of walking sticks. Willy's, the local ice-cream maker, had sent a van to stand at one side of the field, and the ladies of the WI were all ready to serve teas in the big tent. There was a stage for the Drama Group and the Sunny Side Up children's dancing troupe to give their show, and a big arena fenced off in the middle for the Hunt Puppies and a demonstration of sheepdog skills. Over in another corner, Norman Tozer was preparing to shear a ewe, once everyone had had a go at guessing her weight.

Stella was in a fever of nervous impatience but was too caught up in the last-minute panics of the children to let herself worry any further. While Miss Kemp was making sure the older children were in their costumes and ready for the procession, she was dealing with a flurry of elves, fairies and pixies who were to accompany Shirley Culliford on her grand parade from the school playground to the village green, where she would be crowned Festival Queen. The Nethercott twins, in their Princesses' gowns and tiaras and clutching posies of flowers, looked as delightful and pretty

374

as everyone had expected them to, but nobody was quite sure about Shirley.

'I know she's improved a lot over the past term,' Miss Kemp murmured to Stella, 'but you never know with that family. Suppose her mother's decided to dye her hair and it's turned green? Or she put her frock on at home and fell in a cowpat!'

'Dottie will see that she's looking lovely,' Stella said. Dottie, having made the dress, had insisted on being the one to get Shirley ready. 'She'll be out any minute anyway, and then we'll see for ourselves.'

The rest of the grand parade had assembled as well. Ernest, wrapped in a cloak made (Miss Kemp was thankful to see) from an old curtain instead of his mother's best pair, made a splendid Walter Raleigh walking beside tow-headed Geoffrey Martin as Francis Drake. There were half a dozen Stone Age children clad in hessian sacks and carrying a large cardboard standing stone between them, and Micky and Henry had manufactured a very creditable replica of the Guinness Clock, which gave some of the other children the opportunity to dress as Mad Hatters, toucans and unicorns as they capered around the proud clockmakers. In the middle of all this was Constance Bellamy as Queen Victoria, her small sturdy figure clad in black, a stern expression on her face and with the burly figure of George Sweet in his best black suit and top hat as Prince Albert at her side.

The smallest children looked like a scattering of flowers, blowing in the wind, as they ran about ignoring Stella's instructions to stay together in one corner. Ted Tozer's trap was standing in the middle, covered in decorations, with Barley in the shafts wearing a large straw sunhat festooned with honeysuckle and rambling roses. In a few moments, the trap would lead the parade through the village, with Shirley in the place of honour on her throne (a kitchen chair wrapped in a red velvet curtain).

The school door opened and everyone stopped what they were doing to see the Festival Queen come out.

Shirley Culliford emerged. Her usually stringy hair was shining with cleanliness and hung in ringlets on each side of her glowing face. Her eyes were huge with excitement, and her face beamed with the biggest smile Stella had ever seen. She wore a dress of shimmering gold taffeta, and she carried a bouquet of summer flowers as proudly as if she were a bride – or, indeed, a royal Queen.

'Oh, my dear,' Miss Kemp said quietly. 'She looks perfectly lovely. Basil was absolutely right.'

The bells began to ring as the procession moved off, and all through the village the people gathered to cheer their very own Festival Queen. Stella, trying to keep her fairies and elves in order, found herself looking up at the clock and then searching the crowd with increasing anxiety. Dottie's actress still hadn't arrived. Suppose she was late. Suppose she didn't come at all.

Suppose there had been an accident on the way.

I can't lose Muriel again, she thought, with wings of panic beating in her breast. Not when she's so close. Oh, suppose she's decided not to come! Suppose she doesn't recognise me. Suppose she doesn't *like* me . . .

She felt someone grip her hand and turned her head to see Luke beside her, with Val on his other side. He smiled down at her reassuringly and her lips quivered as she tried to smile back. 'It's all right,' he murmured. 'It will be all right, you'll see.'

'Oh Luke,' she whispered. 'I can't believe it. I can't believe it's really going to happen.'

'I think it is,' he said, and nodded towards the end of the lane. 'I think this is her coming now.'

Stella felt her heart shake. The procession had reached the green now and Shirley was being lifted down, throne and all, and placed beneath the ancient oak tree. At the end of the lane, a large black car was nosing its way through the crowd. It stopped in the space reserved for it by the church gate, and a woman climbed out.

It was Dottie's actress – the famous Fenella Forsyth, who had entertained the Forces all through the war, who was a star of the London stage, her voice and beauty renowned throughout the world. Tall, slender and lovely, she had never married but she had once adopted a little girl and treated her like a princess. And that little girl had lived here in Burracombe; and she was Stella's sister Muriel.

As Muriel followed Fenella Forsyth from the car, Stella stood frozen to the spot. She could scarcely breathe. She watched, helpless, as her sister, dressed in the latest fashion and yet still, unmistakably, her little Muriel, smiled and waved at the people she knew so well. And then Dottie went forward and embraced them both, and murmured something in Muriel's ear, and Muriel looked past her and met Stella's eyes.

For a moment or two, they seemed to be enclosed in a bubble of silence. Even the bells had stopped, as if waiting. Then the cheers of the crowd, as Shirley Culliford was crowned Festival Queen, broke out and surged around them, and the two sisters ran across the green and fell into each other's arms. And, as they did so, the bells of Burracombe rang out once more, with joy in every note.

'Muriel!' Stella cried, feeling the years slip away as she hugged her sister against her. 'Oh *Muriel*!'

A Stranger *in*
Burracombe

All my Australian family —
especially Roy, Linda and Meghan.

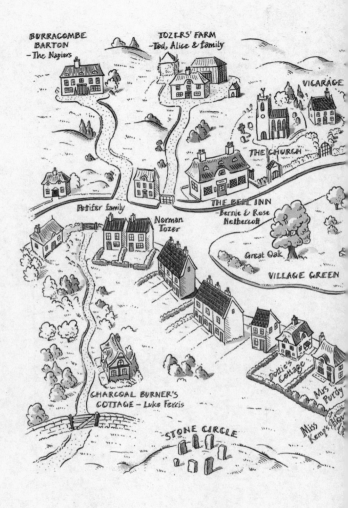

Chapter One

Burracombe, South Devon, 1952

The stranger came to Burracombe on the day the King died.

It was a cold, dry February morning in 1952, with grey skies and no wind. Basil Harvey, the vicar of Burracombe, had just heard the news on the radio and hurried over to the church at once, to find Alice Tozer at the altar, clearing away the flowers from last Sunday's service. Her round, cheerful face beamed as she turned to see him marching up the shadowy aisle, and then, as he came closer, she saw the expression on his face and her smile faded.

'Why, whatever be the matter, Vicar? You look as if you've seen a ghost.'

He stopped at the chancel steps. 'I've just heard the most dreadful news, Alice. I can hardly believe it. The King's died.'

She stared at him. Dead flowers dropped from her hands and scattered themselves over the flagstones. Her mouth worked for a moment or two, and then she said, in a strange, creaking voice, 'Died? The *King*? Are you sure?'

'It was on the wireless. They broke into the programmes. You know how they announce really serious news – "This is London". Grace and I stopped what we were doing at once to listen.' He shook his head. 'I don't quite know what we expected, but it wasn't that.'

'The King dead,' Alice said slowly, and tears spilled from her eyes. 'And with poor young Princess Elizabeth away in

1

Africa, too. My stars! That means she'm Queen now, don't it! Oh, that poor young lady.'

'I know. I suppose they must have told her already. She'll have to come home straight away. At least she'll have her husband to support her. Well, I'll need to see Ted as soon as possible – the bells must be rung muffled. And there'll be services to arrange.' He turned as they both heard a sound at the back of the church. 'Oh, I'm so sorry. Were you looking for me?'

The woman walking up the aisle looked to be in her early thirties. She was of medium height, rather slight, with a pale, oval face. Her eyes were an almost luminous grey, fringed with thick, black lashes, and her lips were touched with pale pink. She wore a dark green coat, fitted to her slim waist, and a green beret over her chestnut hair.

'I didn't mean to disturb you,' she said hesitantly. She spoke with a Devonshire accent, though not exactly local. 'I was just looking round the church. And then I heard what you were saying. Is it true? Has the King really died?'

'I'm afraid so,' Basil said. He glanced round at Alice again, not wanting to leave her out of the conversation. 'In his sleep, they said. At least we can be thankful that it was peaceful.'

'And he'd been very poorly,' Alice added, lowering her voice to murmur the word, '*Cancer.* And I'll tell you something else, Vicar, now I come to think of it. Me and Ted went into Tavistock last week, to the pictures, and we saw him on the Pathé Pictorial News saying goodbye to the Princess. I said to Ted then, he looked proper grey, and I reckon he knew he'd never see her again. He had such a sad look in his eyes.'

'Well, that's something we shall never know,' Basil said as Alice bent to pick up the flowers that had fallen to the floor. He saw that she was in tears again, and turned back to the stranger. 'Is there anything I can show you? The church is

2

very old – it dates back to Norman times – and we've some interesting features. The font—'

'Oh no,' the woman said hastily. 'I won't bother you now. I just wanted . . .' Her voice faded as she glanced round the dim church. 'Perhaps I'll come back another day. I . . .' Once again, she didn't seem to know how to finish her sentence. 'I'll just go and look outside – there's a bus soon.'

Alice straightened up, her arms filled with dead and dripping stalks, and came down the chancel to where they stood. She stared at the young woman and opened her mouth to speak, but the stranger was already turning away. Basil accompanied her down the aisle.

'I don't want to drive you away. The news has come as rather a shock – as of course it will to everyone. You're very welcome to stay and look around – perhaps say a prayer. And of course you can come back at any time. The door's always open.'

'Thank you.' They stood in the porch, looking out at the village green with its ancient oak tree, the cottages clustered around and the more distant view of meadows rising to the brown, rock-cluttered moors above. 'I wondered—' She broke off again, hesitated, then turned, gave him an uncertain smile and said, 'I think I can hear the bus coming. I'd better go. Goodbye.' And before he could speak again, she was gone, walking quickly down the path to the lychgate and across the green to the bus stop.

Basil watched her go, puzzled and anxious. He knew that the bus wouldn't be along for another five minutes at least and had a strong sense that the visitor was troubled by something. He felt inadequate, as if there ought to have been something he could have done for her. Perhaps if he and Alice hadn't been absorbed by the news of the King's death, she would have confided in him. There must be some reason why she was here in our church, he thought, and for a brief moment he toyed with the idea of following her. Then he shook his

3

head. He could hardly pursue the woman across the green and insist she talk to him. And he might be quite wrong, anyway. He turned to go back into the church.

Alice was at the door, the dead flowers now in a bucket ready to be taken to Jacob Prout's compost heap. She had wiped away her tears, but her eyes were still watering. She followed his glance across the green.

'Who do you think she were, Vicar? Nobody from round here. Sounded as if she come from Plymouth, I'd say.'

'You may be right. She must have come on the bus, anyway. I wonder what she wanted. She hadn't come into the church before I arrived, had she?'

Alice shook her head. 'I did see someone up in the top corner of the churchyard when I arrived, behind the big tomb. It could have been her. As a matter of fact, when I came down the chancel and saw her in a better light, she did remind me of someone, just for a minute, like.' A small frown touched her face. 'But no – 'twas just a trick of the light, that's all.' She looked at Basil and indicated the bucket of flowers. 'What should I be doing about Sunday, Vicar? There's not much about in February. I were going to go down the riverbank and pick some snowdrops, there's always a big patch down there, but would they be right now? Or shouldn't we have no flowers at all, till after the funeral?' Her mouth quivered and her eyes brimmed with tears again. 'I still can't believe it. The King dead! And him such a lovely man – we always listen to his speech on Christmas Day, you know. Remember that one where he said that bit of poetry about the man at the gate of the year? I wrote it down and our Val copied it out in her best writing so we could put it up on the wall. And now he'm gone. It's too soon, Vicar. It's too soon.'

'I know.' Basil laid his hand on her shoulder for a moment. 'We're all going to feel it very much. Well, I think I'll go back to the vicarage and see if I can get in touch with the Bishop. I'll let you know about the flowers as soon as I can, Alice, and

4

you might ask Ted to slip up to the vicarage so that we can decide about the bells. They ought to be rung today, muffled of course, and I think Friday's practice must be cancelled. There'll be a good deal to do, even down here in Devon. Heaven knows what they'll be going through at Sandringham and in London and Windsor! It'll mean a state funeral, you know.'

'And to think that this time last year we were making plans for the Festival of Britain,' she said sadly. 'Whoever would have thought it?'

She carried the dead flowers up to the compost heap in the corner of the churchyard. It was near here that she had seen the stranger, half concealed behind the big family tomb of the Napiers, peering at the headstones. When Alice had thrown the dead flowers on the heap, she paused and then walked round to see what the visitor had been looking at, but the faded lettering gave no clues.

Alice gazed past the church and towards the green. The bus was there now, and she could see the woman climbing aboard. Once again, she was touched by a faint tremor of distant memory, but it was gone before she could catch it, like gossamer on a breeze.

The thought of the King came to her mind again. She felt the ache of grief in her throat, and as she walked back down the churchyard, her eyes were blurred with tears.

By dinnertime the news was all over the village. As usual, it seemed to spread almost on the air. When Dottie Friend, washing glasses and polishing tables ready for lunchtime opening at the Bell Inn, heard it from the landlord, Bernie Nethercott, she immediately went outside to see if anyone was crossing the village green. Jacob Prout was there, sweeping the road and having a look at the ditches to see if they needed clearing, and after he'd shared Dottie's shock, he passed the news on to George Sweet, the village baker, who told Bert

5

Foster, the butcher, and then Edie Pettifer at the village shop. Edie scurried into the post office to tell Jean and Jessie Friend, and by the time they had all gathered in the road to discuss it, Jacob had reached the blacksmith's forge where Alf Coker came out to stand at his door, wiping his hands on some cotton waste and shaking his big head.

Nobody could quite believe it.

'I know he was poorly,' George Sweet said. 'Had that operation on his lungs, didn't he? But I thought he were getting over it. Reckon his doctors must've thought so, too, or they wouldn't never have let Princess Elizabeth go off to Africa like that. Here, do you suppose they'll be able to find her, out in that jungle?'

'Well, I don't suppose her's camping out with lions and tigers,' Edie Pettifer said sharply. 'Gone to some nice hotel built up in the trees, so I read in the *Daily Express*. I dare say they'll be able to get a message out to her pretty quick.' She took out her handkerchief and wiped her eyes.

All the women had shed tears, and even the men looked stricken. The King – who had never been meant to be King but had been forced into it by his brother's abdication – had been such a stalwart figure all through the war, staying determinedly at Windsor and Buckingham Palace, visiting the most severely bombed areas during the Blitz, seeming to share in all his people's troubles, and he had earned a deep affection in the hearts of his subjects. Like Alice Tozer, everyone had listened to his Christmas broadcasts and drawn strength and comfort from the slightly hesitant voice that had seemed to make him all the more human. They'd felt almost a part of his own family – the pretty, gentle Queen Elizabeth and the two Princesses, Elizabeth and Margaret Rose – and when the governess, 'Crawfie', had published the story of her years with them in *Woman's Weekly*, it had sold out week after week as readers enjoyed the tale of their growing-up: their schoolroom days, their Guide company, the pantomimes they had

6

performed at Windsor. Everyone had celebrated Elizabeth's marriage to Philip Mountbatten and thrilled to the birth of her two children, Charles and Anne.

And now the King was gone and she was Queen. It was hard to take in.

Ted Tozer, who had been out in the fields all morning, heard it from Alice when he came in for his dinner. He saw her red-rimmed eyes and looked from her to his mother, Minnie, sitting in her usual chair by the fire with a handkerchief pressed to her face, and thought at first that something must have happened to one of the family – Val, perhaps, or Jackie. His son, Tom, was all right – he knew that because they'd been together all morning – and Tom's wife, Joanna, was in the kitchen, too, looking equally subdued as she strapped young Robin in his high-chair. He opened his mouth to ask what was wrong, but before he could speak, Alice told him.

Ted sat down heavily in his chair at the table. 'My stars, that's a bad job. He were a good man.'

'Vicar wants to see you about the bells.' Alice set a huge bowl in the middle of the table. 'He says they ought to be rung muffled tonight.'

'So they should, and so they will be.' Ted watched as she ladled meat and vegetables on to the plates. Shock hadn't prevented her from making dumplings as light and fluffy as snowballs, or from boiling a large pan of potatoes to go with the rich golden-brown stew. He helped himself to cabbage and began to eat. 'Us'll need to ring muffled on Sunday, too, and maybe for the funeral. I'd better get word to the ringers.'

'I'll do that,' Joanna offered. 'I'll walk round with Robin this afternoon and call in on everyone. If there's no one at home, I'll drop a note through the door. What time will you be ringing?'

'Better make it half seven, same as on a practice night. And that's another thing, us'll have to put off the practice this

7

week. Wouldn't be fitting.' He laid down his fork suddenly and shook his head, staring down at his plate. 'I dunno – I can't hardly take it in. The King dead! Seems like the end of an era.'

'It is,' Joanna said quietly. 'But it's the beginning of another one.' She looked at the sombre faces round the table. 'A new Elizabethan era.'

At the village school, the two teachers didn't hear the news until the children were either on their way home for their dinner or settling down to the shepherd's pie that Mrs Dawe had made. Basil Harvey came to tell them and sat down in the small classroom to discuss how they should break the news to the children.

'A lot of them will hear it at home,' Miss Kemp observed. 'We'll have to assemble them all in the big schoolroom as soon as they come back and tell the others, or heaven knows what stories they'll be spreading. You know what gruesome imaginations some of them have.' She looked at the vicar. 'Will you stay and have a talk with them?'

'I was going to suggest that myself.' He nodded. 'I expect they'll be upset. And they'll have quite a lot of questions, too. We might make a little service of it – we ought to say a prayer at the very least.'

Stella Simmons, the young assistant teacher, got up and went over to a cupboard, taking out a sheaf of sheet music. 'Perhaps you'd like to have a hymn, too,' she suggested. '"There's a Friend for Little Children", perhaps, or "Around the Throne of God a Band of Glorious Angels Ever Stand". Just to remind them that the King's in Heaven now and we don't need to worry about him.'

'An excellent idea,' Basil approved. 'And singing always seems to relieve the mind. I'm sure that's one of the reasons why we have hymns in church.' They all looked up at the

8

sound of a minor stampede outside. 'There they are now. Let's get them in as quickly as possible.'

Stella went outside to ring the bell and the children rushed chattering into the two schoolrooms. She ushered the little ones into the larger room and had just managed to quieten them down as the headmistress and vicar came through. She then went to the piano in the corner. Miss Kemp took up her position at the big desk, and the children stared at her, their faces taut with anxious excitement.

'Now, some of you have heard the sad news that our beloved King has died,' she began gravely, and one or two of the girls began to cry. 'Of course we're all upset about this – he wasn't a very old man, and although he'd been ill, we all hoped he would get better. I expect you remember saying prayers for him in the church, don't you?' There were a few assenting sniffles. 'Our vicar, Mr Harvey, thought you might like to say a prayer for him now, and for the rest of the Royal Family, who must be so upset at this time. And then he's going to talk to you about the King and about what it means to Christians to die, and then we're going to sing one of your favourite hymns. All bend your heads now and put your hands together like steeples.'

The little service was soon over, and as Basil Harvey had predicted, the children had a number of questions to ask. They accepted the idea that the King was now safe and well in Heaven, but wanted to know about the family he had left behind, and especially about the young Princess who was already Queen and on her way home from Africa. Would she be wearing her crown, Shirley Culliford wanted to know, and looked disappointed but resigned when Miss Kemp explained that she wouldn't have taken it with her. It was always kept at the Tower of London. In any case, the crown was only worn on big state occasions and couldn't be worn at all until after the Coronation. This led to more questions about what happened when a king or queen was crowned, which she and

9

the vicar did their best to answer from their memories of George the Sixth's own Coronation in 1937. Stella, who had been a small girl herself at the time, listened with as much interest as the children and thought how exciting it would be when the new Queen was crowned.

'That won't be for quite a long time yet, though,' Basil finished up. 'It'll probably be sometime next year. There's such a lot to arrange, you see.'

'And I think we've talked about it enough for now,' Miss Kemp said, realising that he must have a dozen other things to do. 'Let's all say thank you to Mr Harvey for coming to talk to us this afternoon, and then we'll go back to our lessons. Except that I don't think we'll have our usual lesson this afternoon,' she added. 'I'll read a chapter or two from *Little Christian's Pilgrimage* to the older children, and perhaps Miss Simmons will find a nice Bible story for the babies.'

The vicar then led them all in a recitation of the Lord's Prayer, and, with the bigger children sitting more quietly now at their desks, Stella took the little ones into their own room next door and did as the headmistress had suggested. All the children loved being read to, although the youngest ones often fell asleep, their heads pillowed on their arms, and nobody was in the mood for ordinary lessons. By the time the bell was rung for the end of the afternoon, they were all much calmer and went out in unaccustomed silence to collect their coats and Wellingtons from the lobby.

'Not that it'll last,' Miss Kemp observed ruefully, watching as they made their way along the village street to their various homes. 'Within a quarter of an hour, they'll be rushing about and making as much noise as ever. But I think the quiet afternoon did them good.'

'It did me good, too,' Stella confessed. 'I was only about six years old when the old King died, and then of course there was all the fuss about the abdication. I never really understood all that then, but we had a book with pictures of the

Coronation and I used to look at the pictures for hours. I always thought he was such a handsome man.'

She said goodbye to the headmistress and walked home through the grey February afternoon to Dottie Friend's cottage, where she lodged. Dottie, who worked for the Napiers and the doctor's wife as well as at the inn, had just taken a tray of scones out of the oven as Stella walked in, and she looked round, her rosy face sad. The kettle was coming to the boil, and while she made tea, Stella buttered some of the scones. They sat on either side of the fire and talked about the only topic of conversation that was in anybody's mind that day.

'The wireless has shut down for three days in mourning,' Dottie said. 'So there's no *Mrs Dale's Diary* this afternoon, and no *Archers* after tea.'

'And no *Children's Hour* at five o'clock!' Stella said. 'The children won't like that. Isn't there anything on at all?'

'Not a thing. Daft, I call it. How are we supposed to know what's going on, with no wireless to tell us? Still, I suppose it's only right and proper that us should show our respect. I mean, it wouldn't seem right to sit laughing at *Take It From Here* or *The Charlie Chester Show*, would it? Not that you and me would do that, we've got more of a sense of what's right, but there's some that haven't got the manners they were born with.' Dottie finished her tea and stretched out a hand to pick up her knitting. 'Oh – do you think I ought to be doing this, maid? I mean, if us can't listen to the wireless, what did we ought to be doing?'

'I don't think knitting a jumper is disrespectful,' Stella said. 'You'd do it if it was someone close to you that had died – someone in the village. It's useful, after all, not just for enjoyment.'

Dottie nodded, and they sat talking quietly, reminding each other of the little things they knew of the King and his family, of the scandal of his brother's abdication and the wonderful way he and his wife had conducted themselves during the war. It seemed almost a relief that there was nothing on the wireless so that they didn't have to decide for themselves if it would be right to listen to their favourite programmes. After a while, Stella cleared away the tea things and worked on her next day's lessons while Dottie got the supper ready, and they both went to bed early.

As she drew the curtains against the dark February night, Stella found the same words in her mind as Joanna Tozer had spoken earlier that day; words that must have been echoed up and down the land.

It was the end of an era. And the beginning of a new one.

Chapter Two

Even after the death of a king, ordinary life must still go on.

Val Tozer and Luke Ferris were thinking about their wedding. It couldn't be just yet – they'd only announced their engagement at Christmas and weren't really planning to marry until the end of the year. But it was nice to dream.

'I really wouldn't mind coming to live in the charcoal-burner's cottage,' Val said as they walked along the lane, hoping to spot some early snowdrops. 'It's cosy enough.'

'Cosy enough for me. I don't think your dad would consider it good enough for his daughter. He's not all that happy about me as it is.' Luke swung his stick at the dead, blackening stalks of a clump of nettles. 'You don't have to pretend, Val. You saw his face when we told the family on Christmas Day.'

'Oh, Dad'll come round,' Val said with a dismissive shrug. 'You know what fathers are like. He'll be just the same when it's our Jackie. And Mum thinks you're the bee's knees – she'll soon bring him round. It's mainly because you're not a farmer.'

'And even worse, I'm an *artist*!' Luke said wryly. 'He just can't believe that's a proper job at all. I don't think he actually thinks I'm a pansy now, but he did look at me a bit sideways at first!'

Val laughed. 'Of course he doesn't think that, you idiot! He likes you, anyway – he's just not sure whether painting pretty pictures is going to keep me in the luxury I'm accustomed to!'

'Which the charcoal-burner's cottage isn't,' Luke said. 'And I'm not sure I'll ever be able to keep you in luxury, anyway, Val. In fact, I've been thinking maybe your dad's right – I ought to get a proper job.'

Val stopped and stared at him. 'What sort of job?'

'Well, it would have to be to do with art – that's what I'm trained for. Teaching, I suppose, or something like that. I might get something in Tavistock, or Plymouth.'

'I wouldn't want to live in Plymouth,' Val said at once, and Luke shook his head.

'Neither would I. But we've got to find somewhere to live, and it's got to be something we can afford. And if I'm going to be teaching, I need to be able to get to the school, which means either living close by or near a bus route. Or within cycling distance.'

'I'm earning—' Val began, but he shook his head again.

'You know you won't be able to go on working for long after we're married – we'll be starting a family as soon as we can, won't we? And that's another reason why we can't live in the cottage,' he added. 'It's certainly no place for a baby.'

Val nodded regretfully. 'I know. But we could live there for a little while – just to start with – couldn't we? It's so romantic.'

'Only if we know for certain there's something better coming along soon,' he said firmly.

They strolled along in silence for a few minutes. It was a cold, grey afternoon with a threat of light snow damping the air. Val was working morning shifts at the hospital in Tavistock, where she was a nurse, and Luke had met her from the bus at the main road, a mile or so away from the village. Val thought about what Luke had been saying.

'I'll go on working for as long as possible after we're married, though. There's no point in staying at home with nothing much to do.'

14

'So long as it's just day shifts,' Luke said with a grin. 'You don't imagine I'm going to let you work nights, do you?'

Val blushed and laughed. 'No, and I wouldn't want to, either.' They gripped each other's hands tightly for a moment. 'It's a pity we can't live at the farm, like Tom and Joanna. But my room really isn't big enough. And there's Robin as well – he's going to need his own room soon.' She hesitated, then said, 'I've got a feeling Joanna's expecting another baby.'

'Really? Has she said anything?'

'No, but I've noticed one or two things. And she went to see Dr Latimer last week without mentioning it at home. I happened to spot her coming out of his surgery, but she didn't see me so I didn't say anything. She'll tell us in her own time.'

Luke grinned. 'If you saw her, I'm surprised nobody else did. It would have been all over the village by now if they had.'

'Well, it was dark and she had her hood up so probably nobody else would have recognised her. Anyway, back to our own plans . . .'

'I wouldn't really want to live at the farm, anyway,' Luke said. 'I mean, your family are all very nice, but I want us to be on our own. It's different for Tom and Joanna – Tom works on the farm, they'll take over one day. But we're going to have a different sort of life.'

They were coming close to the village now. There were few people about; most of the women would have done their shopping in the morning and be at home now, baking or preparing the family meal, and it was too cold for many strollers. As Luke and Val came round the last bend in the lane the only person in sight was Jacob Prout, who did all the jobs around the village such as clearing ditches, keeping hedges tidy and digging graves. He was raking leaves and other debris out of a culvert and straightened up as he saw them. His rough-haired Jack Russell terrier, Scruff, ran over and sniffed their legs.

'Cold enough for you?'

'Plenty,' Val said, rubbing her arms. She was wearing a thick brown coat, but the wind had seemed to slice through it as they walked down from the road, which crossed the open moorland. It was much more sheltered in the lanes that approached the village, tucked away in its little valley. All the same, the ice covering the puddles and turning mud to stone showed that the temperature was still below freezing.

'Ah, it's a lazy wind today,' Jacob agreed. 'Goes straight through you instead of taking the long way round. It'll be cold for them as have gone to London, queueing up for hours to see the King lying in state.'

'Hilary Napier was saying that her father wanted to go,' Val said. 'She won't let him, though. It's not all that long since he had his heart attack.'

'Asking for trouble, that'd be,' Jacob concurred. 'Mind you, I can understand him wanting it, seeing as he was a colonel and served King and country through the war. "Tis only patriotic to want to pay his respects.'

'I don't think the King would want anyone to catch pneumonia on his account, though.' Val and Luke made to walk on, then she stopped and turned back. 'I meant to ask you, Jacob – did you notice a strange woman in the village on Wednesday morning?'

'The day the King died? Can't say as I did, maid. Why?'

'Oh, nothing really. She came into the church while Mum was there clearing away the flowers. It was just as the vicar came in to tell her the news. They both got the feeling she was looking for something, or someone, but when they asked her she wouldn't say – just said she'd got to catch the bus and hurried off. Mother said she thought she'd seen her up in the corner of the churchyard just before, looking at the graves.

16

We wondered if she might be looking for a family grave — someone you'd recognise.'

Jacob shook his head. 'Never saw hide nor hair of her, maid. Mind you, we do get folk poking about now and then, but they'd usually ask the vicar. Happen she didn't like to, when she heard about the King.'

'Probably. Perhaps she'll come back sometime. Only Mum thought there was something familiar about her — she couldn't put her finger on it. As if she might be related to one of the village families.'

Jacob shook his head. 'Dunno who that might be. Us knows most of the families who moved away since the war. Before that, there were one or two emigrated to America or Australia, but I don't suppose it were one of they.'

'No, I don't think so. Mum said she sounded as if she came from Plymouth. Oh well, I expect she'll come back if she really wants to find anything.' Val began to walk on again, with Luke beside her. 'She might just have come out for a bit of an outing.'

'Mm. Odd sort of day to do that, though — at the beginning of February. It would be interesting if she really was looking for a family connection.' Luke had spent some time the previous year helping the young schoolteacher, Stella Simmons, to look for her sister, Muriel, separated from her during the war. 'Pity she didn't say anything to Uncle Basil.'

They parted at the farm gate. Val had asked Luke to come up for tea and some of her mother's rock cakes, but he'd shaken his head and said he wanted to go up to the Standing Stones to catch the last of the chilly afternoon light for the painting he was working on. He'd painted the stones in many of their moods, and this was the most sombre yet, with the grey granite monoliths etched starkly against the pewter sky. He was hoping to catch their mystery and even, with the addition of some subtle shadows, the old tradition that the stones couldn't be counted. Today's conditions were ideal.

He walked up the twisting path through the woods to the cottage where he had come to live the year before, after his slow recovery from the TB that had nearly killed him. If it hadn't been for that, he thought, he would have stayed in London and his godfather, Basil Harvey, would never have suggested his coming to Burracombe. And he would never have met Val Tozer again – the girl he had fallen in love with in Egypt during the war, and never forgotten.

Not that their meeting had been an easy one – there was too much that he hadn't known and that Val hadn't wanted to tell him. But eventually all the secrets had been told. All the tender passion, locked away for so many years, had been allowed to flower again, and their engagement had been announced at Christmas.

It hadn't turned out to be quite the joyful moment that they'd anticipated. Alice and Minnie had been delighted, hugging them both with pleasure, and Joanna had obviously been pleased, while Tom had shaken Luke's hand in congratulation and given his sister an affectionate push. But Ted had taken a moment or two to add his good wishes, and Luke had caught the brief darkening of his face as Val and her mother turned away.

After the dinner of turkey and all the trimmings, followed by a rich Christmas pudding made back in October, the farmer had suggested that he and Luke take a walk outside before it got dark. Tom was doing the milking, along with one of the farmhands, and Alice and Val would see to the hens.

'We'll see to the pigs,' Ted announced. 'And maybe take a turn round some of the fields, see how they ewes are getting on.'

They'd looked at the ewes only that morning, but Luke understood that the outing wasn't really to do with farming matters and he wasn't surprised when, after the pigs had been fed, Ted turned to the matter of the engagement.

'I know you think a lot of our Val,' he began rather

ponderously, 'and she thinks a lot of you, too. But you might have said summat to me before making it an official engagement.'

'I'm sorry if you feel offended, Mr Tozer,' Luke said. 'I think Val considered she was too old to need her father's permission.'

'Well, maybe she is, but it would have been manners all the same. However, 'tisn't that that I wants to talk about. 'Tis only a small matter, after all.' He paused and leaned on a gate, staring into the dusk that was creeping across the meadows. 'I'd like to know what you means to do about supporting her.'

Luke felt his face flush. 'Naturally I want to look after her, Mr Tozer . . .'

'Yes, I dare say you do, but how? That's the question. You can't say you've got a steady job, now, can you? Living from hand to mouth, that's how it seems to me, and what sort of a place is that old shack in the woods to take a decent young woman? Nothing more than a hovel, that be. Ought to have been burned down years ago.'

Luke stared at him, shaken by this outburst. He'd known Ted might find the situation a little difficult, but he'd been unprepared for such strong feelings. As he searched for words, Ted started again.

'Our Val's not had an easy time of it, you know. Should have been married years since, if her young chap hadn't been killed in the war.' He turned his head and Luke saw the glimmer of his eyes. 'You didn't do no fighting yourself, as I understand it.'

'No,' Luke said quietly. 'I was a war artist.'

'War artist!' Ted echoed, although he'd already known that. 'And what's that, when it's at home? Drawing pretty pictures while other boys—'

'No, I'm sorry, Mr Tozer,' Luke said more forcefully. 'The pictures I was drawing weren't pretty at all. They were pictures of what was going on – men fighting, men being killed. And not just men – women and children, too.' He looked at Ted. 'You were in the First World War, weren't you? You know as well as I do that there's nothing pretty about it.'

'All right,' Ted said after a moment. 'Maybe I spoke out of turn there. But I still don't see what use it was drawing pictures instead of getting on with what had to be done.'

Luke sighed. 'I don't really know what use any of it was, Mr Tozer, but we all have to do what we're best at. And it's important to *show* people at home what happens – it's not always easy for them to realise what it was like, without pictures. There were others taking photographs, too, and filming, but sometimes it's not possible to do that – your camera might get damaged, or you might run out of film. It's usually possible to find a pencil and a bit of paper.' He paused, thinking back to some of the situations he'd been in when he'd longed to put down his sketching materials and take part in whatever was going on, when his own life had been in danger yet he had continued to draw the horrors that were before his eyes. 'If I hadn't thought it was important, I wouldn't have done it,' he finished quietly. 'I was trained to fight as well, you know. I could handle a rifle as well as any man.'

'Well, it's all in the past now,' Ted said after another pause, 'and maybe us should leave it there. But it don't answer my question – how be you going to provide for her? Our Val deserves better than a shack in the woods with no running water or proper kitchen. And I don't suppose you'd want to pack into the farmhouse with the rest of us.' He turned his head again, and even though it was almost dark by now, Luke could see the frown on his face. 'Let's put our cards on the table. What sort of an income does your painting bring in?'

Luke hesitated, then said simply, 'It's erratic, Mr Tozer. I can earn quite a good sum from one painting – the exhibition in London last summer brought me in enough to live on for several months. But then I might not sell anything else for quite a while. As my name builds up, things should improve – but it all depends on whether people like my pictures.'

'You'm not likely to get asked to paint portraits and such?'

'Not really. I'm a landscape painter, you see – that's what I enjoy doing and—'

'Now wait a minute,' Ted broke in. 'Who said anything about *enjoyment*? It's earning a living I'm talking about, not playing games.'

'So am I. Don't think I look on painting as a game, Mr Tozer – I don't. I'm as serious about it as you are about farming. I know you may not think it's as useful – and perhaps you're right. But people do like pictures on their walls, and it's what I can *do*. That's what I mean when I say I enjoy it. Just as you must enjoy your farming.'

'Not all the time, I don't,' Ted retorted. 'Not at five o'clock on an icy-cold winter's morning when there's forty cows waiting to be milked. Or when I'm up all night with a difficult calving and then loses the beast anyway. Or sees a field of taters go down with blight. Or any of the other hundred and one things that can go wrong. I'm sorry, Luke, but if you think a farmer's life is all making hay in the sunshine, you got no idea. No idea at all.'

'No,' Luke said with a sigh. 'I don't suppose I have.' There was another short silence, then he said, 'Look, Mr Tozer, I know how you feel about me and what I do. It doesn't seem like work to you at all, and you're worried that Val's going to be spending all her time working to keep me playing games with my time. Looking at it that way, I'd feel exactly the same. And I've got to be honest and tell you that at the moment, my painting won't bring in a living wage – not to support two of us, and maybe a family. So I've decided to look for a job.'

Ted turned his head. 'A job? What sort of a job, then?'

'Anything I can do,' Luke said. 'Something to do with

21

pictures and painting, if I can find it. Teaching, perhaps. But if not – well, I'm not a bad hand with a saw and a piece of wood. I can turn my hand to a bit of carpentry or joinery, if it comes to it.'

Ted stared at him and then turned back to gaze into the darkened field. 'It's not that I wants you to give up whatever you'm good at,' he said at last, his voice sounding different now. 'I might not be an arty sort, but I can understand when summat's in a man's blood. You'm right, I *am* like that with farming – there might be plenty of times when I wish I had some nice job indoors in the warm, but I'd never really give it up. If it's the same with you—'

'It is,' Luke said. 'I won't ever give up painting, but I can put it to one side if it makes life better for Val. And we won't get married until I can offer her a decent home. I promise you that, Mr Tozer.'

Ted's shoulders moved as he drew in a deep breath. Then he turned back and put out his hand.

'No man could say fairer than that,' he said gruffly. 'And now I reckon us'd better go back indoors, before they sends out a search party. 'Tis Christmas night, and the womenfolk likes a bit of a party. I hope you'm up to joining in a few games, Luke, now you'm one of the family.'

Luke had never told Val exactly what he and Ted had said to each other that afternoon, but he meant to hold firm to his promise not to marry until he could offer her a proper home. Today, as he walked up the twisting path to the cottage, he faced the fact that it wasn't really enough for him to make such a promise – Val expected a say in the matter, too. Gone were the days, as in Ted Tozer's youth, when the man would have made the important decisions in a marriage – that's if he ever did, Luke thought, remembering times when his father had apparently come to a decision already made quietly by his mother – and now women assumed a right at least to

22

consultation. The independence they'd discovered during the war had left them stronger.

Some day soon, Luke thought as he opened the door of the tiny cottage and collected his painting gear, I'll take her to London to meet my own folks. But perhaps not just yet. Not until the King's funeral is over, anyway. I'd like everyone to be feeling happy when they first meet my future wife.

After Val and Luke had gone on, Jacob Prout finished clearing the culvert and gathered the cold, muddy leaves into his wheelbarrow. He wheeled it along the lane and took them just inside the wood, where he had collected a large pile, which were slowly composting down. Then he stowed the barrow in a shed by the bank and went home. He was looking forward to a good meal of Bert Foster's beef sausages with fried onions and mashed potatoes, with a big pot of tea to wash it all down, and maybe a baked apple for afters. You needed something hot and tasty after working outdoors in this weather.

With his hand on his front gate, he paused, frowning. His own cottage looked as immaculate as ever, the garden tidy and ready for spring, the hedges neatly trimmed and the path clear. But the cottage next door, where Jed Fisher lived, was a shambles. Old net curtains, grey with age and grime, sagging at the windows, moss growing on the slate roof, a tangle of weeds in the sour earth, paint peeling off the front door. Inside, Jed had lit a lamp and you could see past the pile of old newspapers on the windowsill (harbouring God knew what vermin) to the battered furniture inside. You could almost smell it.

Jacob turned his eyes away and went up the path to his own front door, stained and varnished to within an inch of its life. He was proud of that door, as he was proud of everything else in his home. He'd learned in the Navy during the First World War how important it was to keep everything spick and span, and he looked after himself and his own cottage as well as he looked after the village. It was a pity Jed had never gone into the Forces, he thought. He'd have learned a bit about what was what. He'd never have gone downhill the way he had.

Inside, Jacob closed the door and switched on the light, driving away the late-afternoon shadows to cast a bright glow on the faded but clean chintz cover on his own old armchair, the round table covered with a green baize cloth, the dresser with his mother's china gleaming on the shelves. His tortoiseshell cat, Flossie, curled up on one of the straight-backed kitchen chairs, raised her head and stretched out a paw as Scruff ran over to sniff at her.

'You've been asleep all day on that cushion, I'll be bound,' he said. 'Reckon I'll be a cat, next time around. Nearest thing to Heaven there be, on this earth. Either that or a swallow and fly off to Africa every winter.'

Flossie gave him a reproachful look at the idea of becoming a bird, and stood up, stretching each leg separately and arching her back before jumping down to walk into the tiny scullery where Jacob kept her saucers. They were all empty and she turned to give him an accusing stare. Scruff went, too, pushing the saucers about with his nose in the hope that some scrap or other might have been forgotten.

'All right,' Jacob said, stooping to open the lower door of the Rayburn and riddle the ashes through. There were just enough embers left to catch on the kindling and sticks that he kept in the basket close by, and, once they were burning well, he'd add a couple of logs. The Rayburn kept the whole cottage snug, and the wood ash was good for the garden. 'You'll get your suppers soon enough.'

Jacob had lived alone ever since his wife, Sarah, had died ten years before. She'd been a few years older than him and it had been a late marriage, so they'd never had children, but they'd been good companions and he had missed her when she'd gone. Now, he was accustomed to living alone again in the cottage where he'd been born and brought up, with just

24

Flossie and Scruff to keep him company. There were times when he sat quietly, with Flossie on his knee and Scruff at his feet, thinking of days gone by and wondering how it would have been if things had turned out differently, but he wasn't the sort to bemoan the past. Not until the sight of his neighbour Jed reminded him, anyway. Then it took only a word or a look to bring the old bitterness welling up inside him, and he was hard put at times to keep his anger in check. It was funny how it could still boil up, hot and strong as ever, after all this time.

Mostly, though, he could push his thoughts away, and he did this now as he opened the back door to fetch the sausages in from the meat safe outside. Bert's delivery boy had brought them round that morning, and Jacob was pleased to see that they were good thick ones, as big as Alf Coker's fingers. The blacksmith had huge hands, and it was commonly believed that Bert Foster used them as a measure for his sausages. Some people even asked for 'half a pound of Cokers' when they went into the butcher's shop.

Jacob laid the sausages in an old enamel dish, pricked their skins with a skewer and put them in the oven. Then he peeled a few potatoes and set them on the hotplate to boil while he fried an onion to go with them. He made gravy out of the onion juices, with an Oxo cube crumbled in and half a cup of hot water poured over it, and within half an hour his supper was ready. Just before he put it all on a plate, he took the core out of a big cooking apple with his potato peeler, filled the hole with currants and sultanas, and slid that into the oven. He'd make the custard last so that it was hot when the apple was ready.

You didn't have to eat rubbish just because you were on your own, he thought, sitting down at the scrubbed kitchen table while the animals took up their positions on either side of his chair. A man on his own could feed himself as well as any woman. There weren't many weeks when Jacob didn't have a rabbit in his big roasting-pan, stewing gently through the day with an onion and some turnips and carrots beside it, and he always had fish on Fridays, like a Christian should, off the van that came round the villages. He liked a bit of liver, too – pigs' fry was the tastiest, to his mind, especially with a bit of bacon thrown in – and a slice or two of good fatty pork belly was a treat. With his own vegetables, grown in the back garden, Jacob reckoned he lived pretty well.

Not like that Jed Fisher next door, who got his vegetables out of tins if the mess in his back garden was anything to go by, and more than likely lived on bread and jam most of the time. No wonder he was a surly old cuss. You couldn't be cheerful if your stomach wasn't looked after proper.

Jacob turned his thoughts away from his old enemy and reached out to switch on the wireless. Then he remembered that there was nothing on tonight, out of respect for the King, and looked for something else to occupy his thoughts. His eye caught the row of photographs on the mantelpiece.

They were old photographs, most of them – snaps taken of village outings long ago – with a few more recent including one the vicar had taken of the bellringers when they'd won the Burracombe competition last year. There was also one of his parents, taken at their wedding nearly seventy years ago, and another of himself in his naval uniform, when he'd enlisted in 1914.

He stared at it, chewing his sausage and thinking of those days so long ago. Two world wars, there had been since then. Two terrible wars, killing millions of people and changing the whole world. Changing lives everywhere.

Changing his own life.

Chapter Three

After supper, Val took the big torch down from the shelf and announced that she was going up to the Barton to see Hilary Napier.

'That's a good idea, maid,' her mother said. 'I dare say she'll be glad of some company. Not having the wireless makes you wonder how us managed before us had it!'

'Pretty well, from what I remember,' Ted said. He liked the radio as much as anyone, but he spent as much time reading his *Farmer's Weekly* as he did listening and always complained that there wasn't enough about farming. *The Archers*, which was supposed to be a kind of farmers' *Dick Barton*, did give you a bit of information, but it stood to reason it couldn't give much, what with having to have all those stories about Dan and Doris and their family, and that old Walter Gabriel, who set such a bad example and didn't ought to have been in a decent farming programme, to Ted's mind. Not that he wasn't a typical old village character – you only had to look at Jed Fisher to know that every village had one – but you had to remember that town folk listened to the programme as well. Mind you, Walter Gabriel was a lot funnier than Jed Fisher.

'Us could always play a game of cards,' he suggested now, but Alice frowned and shook her head and he recollected the reason why there was no wireless at the moment. 'No, 'twouldn't be fitting, not with the King dead. Got to show proper respect. Reckon I might get that book out, the one I got for Christmas about old Devonshire traditions. Never had time for a proper read of that, I haven't.'

'And me and Mother will get on with that new rug,' Alice said. This was another Christmas present, given by Ted to his wife, and consisted of a half-moon-shaped piece of canvas marked with a pattern of roses, and a set of coloured wools. Alice and Minnie had started it soon after the New Year and it was almost finished. It would look lovely down in front of the fire, they thought.

They settled down for the evening. Jackie was up in her bedroom, writing a letter to Roy Pettifer in Korea, and Tom and Joanna had put Robin to bed and then gone to their own sitting-room. The family got on well, but everyone agreed you had to have your own space as well, to be private. They'd join Ted and Alice in the big, warm kitchen again later on for a bit of supper. Val pulled on her thick coat, wrapped her new purple scarf (knitted for her for Christmas by her grand-mother) round her neck and stepped out into the cold, dark night. It wasn't far to the Barton, and she was soon shucking off her Wellington boots on the doormat of the Napiers' kitchen.

'Oh, there you are,' Hilary said, turning, with her hands sticky with bread dough. 'We'll never train you to come to the front door, will we? Leave your boots near the Aga: they'll keep warm for when you go back.'

'That's why I come to the back door,' Val said. 'I'm always too muddy to come in the posh way.'

'Father's in the drawing-room,' Hilary said, going back to her kneading. 'We'll go in and say hello to him in a minute, but we'll have a chinwag out here first. It's Mrs Ellis's night off so I'm doing the chores. He'll be pleased to see you – he needs cheering up, poor dear. And you can help me convince him that it isn't a good idea for a man in his condition to go and queue for hours in the London streets to see the King.'

'Of course it's not,' Val said. 'I thought Dr Latimer had told him that already.'

'He has, but you know what Dad's like. Even a heart attack isn't enough to convince him he's not immortal. It scared him at the time, but now he's feeling better he's trying to pretend it never happened.' She set two loaves on the side of the Aga and covered them with a clean tea-towel. 'It's all I can do to stop him coming round the estate with me. It wouldn't be so bad if he'd stay in the Land Rover, but he keeps wanting to get out and look at things. It's just too cold at the moment.'

'It must be very hard, when you've been used to being active and in charge all your life,' Val commented as Hilary washed her hands at the sink. 'Not very easy for you, either, when you're trying to do his job.'

'Oh, I dare say we'll shake down eventually,' Hilary said, getting a bottle of ginger wine and two glasses out of a cupboard. 'He's had nearly six months to get used to the idea, after all. Let's have a drink here before we go in to him. He'll probably like a game of cards – pity you didn't bring Luke with you, we could have had a rubber of bridge.'

'I'll bring him another time.' Val sat down at the big table and waited while Hilary poured out the wine and handed her a glass. 'Cheers. Actually, there's something I wanted to ask you.'

'What's that, then?'

'I wondered if you had any cottages coming vacant soon on the estate. Luke and I are going to need somewhere to live, and I can't think of anywhere in the village. All the farm cottages are tied, and anyway, they're all occupied, and we can't live in the charcoal-burner's cottage. And I really don't want to move away.'

'Surely you're not thinking of that?' Hilary stared at her friend in dismay. 'Where would you go?'

'Well, it would depend where Luke got a job. He's thinking of trying for an art teacher's post – he's well qualified for it, you know. He'd try the Tavistock schools at first, of course, and then Plymouth, but if he couldn't find anything there . . .' She shrugged and left the words hanging as she took a sip of ginger wine.

'He wouldn't go back to London, surely?' Hilary said. 'You wouldn't want to go there, would you?'

'Why not? *You* nearly did! You were really keen, as I remember it.' There was a short silence as both recalled the day of the village outing to the Festival of Britain last May, and their return to find that Gilbert Napier had suffered a heart attack. Hilary had been on the point of leaving Burracombe then, to take up an appointment as an air hostess and share a flat with a friend. She still had moments of regret as she wondered what her life would have been, had she gone on with her plans instead of giving them up and staying at home to take over the management of the family estate. 'Mind you,' Val added, 'I'm glad you didn't!'

'And I feel just the same about you,' Hilary said. 'Except that I think you'd hate living in London. Or even Plymouth.' She sighed. 'Has Luke really got to look for a job? Isn't he earning enough with his painting? I thought he was doing quite well since he had that exhibition.'

'He is, but it's so uncertain, Hil. It's all right for a single man who doesn't need much money – except for paints and canvases and things, which cost a lot – but he couldn't support a wife and family.'

Hilary sipped her drink thoughtfully. 'It's difficult, isn't it? There's nothing at all wrong with being an artist – Luke's got real talent, and he ought to be able to use it – but unless you're lucky and get recognised, you just can't make any money at it. And why *shouldn't* married women be able to work – at least until they start a family? The country was pleased enough to have us during the war.'

'Oh, you know what men are like – it's all to do with their pride. Wanting to be the providers and all that. And despite

30

what we did during the war, most of them still don't really think we can do as good a job as they can. Look at the struggle you had persuading your father that you could run the estate.'

'I know. And in his heart, I believe he'd still rather have Stephen in charge, even though we all know he'd make a mess of it. Dad won't admit that, of course – Stephen's a man and his son, therefore he ought to take over. Never mind that he was never intended to run the estate – that was always going to be Baden's job, as eldest son, and he'd have done it well. But Dad just can't see it that way. Thank goodness Steve's got the sense to see it wouldn't work.'

'How's he getting on in the RAF?' Val asked.

'Oh, he loves it. He's just got promotion. I wouldn't be surprised if he decides to make it his career instead of just doing it as National Service. He thinks he'll be going to Germany soon.' Hilary chewed her lip thoughtfully. 'I'm just thinking . . . There's the estate house we lived in during the war, when the Barton was requisitioned for that children's home. It's always been meant for an estate manager, but since Dad came home and took over it's been rented out. The lease will be coming up sometime this year and I've a feeling the present tenants might not want to renew it. Would that do for you and Luke?'

Val stared at her. 'It would be marvellous! I know the place you mean – up beside the coppice, near the gamekeeper's house. It's a lovely spot.'

'The house might need a bit of attention. I was waiting to see if the Cherrimans wanted to stay before doing any work there. I couldn't evict them, mind,' she added hastily. 'They're friends of Father's and if they want to renew . . .'

'Oh, I understand that. I wouldn't want anyone put out on the street on my account. All the same –' Val put her chin in her hands and looked wistful '– it would be lovely if we could have it. And if not, maybe you might find some other cottage lying about that we could use!'

'Who knows?' Hilary said, laughing. She sipped her ginger wine and rose to her feet. 'Come on, let's take this into the drawing-room. Dad's there all on his own with a bottle of port and you know he's not supposed to have too much of that. I don't want him getting gout on top of his other troubles!'

Val picked up her glass and followed her friend into the drawing-room, with its comfortable, shabby armchairs and sofas, and its roaring fire almost obliterated by the two black Labradors stretched out in front of it. Gilbert Napier, ensconced in his own armchair with *The Times* folded into a pad on his knee so that he could work on the crossword, raised his leonine head.

'And about time, too. I was just thinking of coming out to see if you'd drowned in the washing-up water. Evening, young Val – I suppose Hilary's been keeping you out there gossiping. Never mind her poor old father, left in here all alone with his sorrow.'

'Hello, Mr Napier,' Val said, bending to give him a kiss. Since her help when he had had his heart attack, he had been firmly convinced that she had saved his life and now looked on her almost as another daughter. 'It's sad news about the King, isn't it? You must be very upset.'

'Fine man,' he said gruffly. 'Fine man. Took over a difficult job, even though he was only the second son, and made a better fist of it than his brother ever would have done. Showed his true colours during the war – ought to have had years ahead of him.' He paused, staring into the fire. 'Feel I'm letting him down, not going to pay my respects.'

'He wouldn't have wanted you to make yourself ill,' Val said gently. 'He'd have wanted you to stay here and get your own health back so that you can carry on looking after his countryside. And serving the Queen.'

'Yes,' he said, looking up at her. 'Yes, I think you may be right. Pity nobody else has been able to put it like that. Yes . . .'

There was a short silence, and then he repeated quietly to himself, 'It just shows what a second son can do.'

And the two women looked at each other, knowing that he was no longer thinking of the King.

Chapter Four

Slowly, the country began to look forward to the new Elizabethan era. The new Queen was young and pretty, and had a handsome prince at her side as well as two small children. Her mother now became the Queen Mother, and Mary, the former Queen Mother, was the Dowager Queen Mother. With the state funeral over, attention turned to the future.

'The Coronation won't be until next year,' Basil Harvey said at the next meeting of the Parish Council. 'So we needn't think about that for a while. We can concentrate on this year, instead.'

It was customary, early in the year, to consider the plans for village events until the autumn. Last year, Burracombe had held a pageant in celebration of the Festival of Britain, and a number of other events as well. The bellringers had put on a special competition, there had been a craft exhibition in the village hall, little Shirley Culliford had astonished everyone by her blossoming as Festival Queen, and the games and teas in Ted Tozer's field had been enjoyed by everyone.

'To my mind,' Ted Tozer said now, 'us'd be best to take things a bit quiet this year. Last year was a big effort, right in the middle of harvest and all, and if we'm going to make a splash for the Coronation next year, it don't make no sort of sense to do anything too much this year. Anyway, 'tidden fitting, not with the King still warm in his grave.'

'That won't be the case by summer, though,' Joyce Warren

pointed out. She was the wife of a Tavistock solicitor and had her finger in most of the village pies. 'With all respect, we don't have to be in mourning for the whole year. I'm sure there are lots of people who will want the usual village events – the Summer Fair, the Flower Show and so on.'

'I'm not saying nothing about those,' Ted said. 'They always goes on. I'm just saying, us didn't ought to be breaking our backs over nothing special.'

Miss Kemp, the headmistress of the village school, nodded. 'I'm inclined to agree with Mr Tozer,' she said. 'We're bound to want to do something special next year. I suggest that we confine ourselves to the usual annual events such as those Mrs Warren has already mentioned. Next year's obviously going to be a busy one, and we ought to save our energies for that.'

Joyce Warren looked put out. 'But it does seem a shame not to follow up last year's success. Quite a lot of people came to the village especially for the fair, you know. It brought in a good deal of extra money.'

'And I'm afraid it's money we're going to need,' Basil said apologetically. 'I don't know if any of you have noticed the sounds the church organ's been making just lately?'

The others turned to look at him. His round, cherubic face was pink, and his halo of silver hair seemed to stand out around his head. He glanced down at the papers that lay on the table before him and shuffled them awkwardly.

'It seems all right to me,' George Sweet said dubiously, but since he was well known for being tone-deaf nobody took any notice. Ted, who had a fine baritone voice and would have been in the choir if he weren't already captain of the bellringers, nodded.

'I have, Vicar, now you mention it. I was going to say something to Edie Pettifer about it, as a matter of fact. I wondered if a mouse or summat had got stuck in one of the pipes.'

35

'I think it's worse than that,' Basil said. 'It's a very old instrument, you know, and probably needs a thorough overhaul. And heaven knows what expense that might involve.'

'Once you starts to look at things like that, you don't know what you might find,' Ted agreed. 'I remember when our thresher went wrong, right in the middle of—'

'Well, never mind that,' Joyce said impatiently. 'It's the organ we seem to be discussing now, not your thresher. Do you really think it needs attention, Vicar? Have you taken advice, for instance?' Her tone made it clear that she didn't think his opinion would carry much weight without the back-up of a professional opinion.

'Not yet,' he admitted. 'I thought I should apprise the Parish Council of it first. The Parochial Church Council has already discussed it, of course. We had a little meeting last night –' he glanced at Ted Tozer, who hadn't been present '– and agreed that it should be brought up here as well.'

'I'm sorry I weren't there, Vicar,' Ted began. 'I had a problem with one of my cows, as young Jackie would have told you when I sent her round with a message.'

'Oh, I know, that's quite understood,' the vicar said hastily. 'I didn't mean to reproach you in any way. I would have let you know before, but I've been busy myself and—'

'Be that as it may,' Joyce interrupted, 'I'm not sure why you think it's a parish matter anyway, Vicar. St Andrew's isn't the only church in the village, after all – there's the Methodist Chapel and the Baptist. I think they'd have something to say if the Summer Fair were only to raise money for the church organ.'

'Don't you think that's a rather narrow point of view?' Charles Latimer suggested mildly. As chairman, he was generally content to let discussions take their course until he felt it time for an intervention. 'We raised quite a substantial

36

amount for the chapel roof not so long ago. This has always been a village where we all pull together, after all.'

'Up to a point, yes,' said Joyce, who had clearly forgotten the chapel roof but didn't want to admit it. 'And I suppose it would be all right to give *some* of the proceeds to the church organ. So long as the rest goes to other village causes.'

'Exactly,' Dr Latimer said, and the others nodded their agreement. 'Just as we've done in the past . . . In any case, there's nothing we can do until the vicar has taken the appropriate advice and knows just how serious the problem is and what will have to be done. As Ted says, once you look into these things, you can find all kinds of problems, and church organs are expensive items. I'm sure everyone in the village, whatever their persuasion, would be willing to contribute. It will probably take us a year or two at least to raise the money.'

'Anyway,' said Bert Foster, speaking for the first time, 'most folk who comes to the fair don't care what the money goes to so long as they has a good time.'

Joyce opened her mouth to say that this was not the point, but Charles Latimer was already moving on to the next item on the agenda – the men's lavatory at the village hall. Since this was a perennial point of discussion and had never yet been satisfactorily resolved, everyone settled back for another ten minutes of tedious argument.

The meeting was over at last and they all filed out into the dark February night. Joyce Warren fell into step beside Miss Kemp.

'Quite a good meeting, don't you think? The Summer Fair as usual and the Flower and Produce Show to look forward to as well as all your usual school events. And I dare say the bellringers will be putting on a competition.' She sighed a little. Living not far from the church, she was well aware of the amount of use the bells received and usually tried to be out of the village on competition days, when the ringing went

37

on all day long. 'What do *you* think about raising money for the church organ, Miss Kemp?'

'I think it's essential,' the head teacher said promptly. 'It's a lovely organ, with a beautiful tone, and Miss Pettifer plays it so well. It would be a tragedy if we lost it.'

'Oh, I quite agree,' Joyce said hastily. 'As a regular churchgoer myself, I'm sure I appreciate the organ as much as anyone else. But I'm not convinced that the villagers will all agree. I know money went towards the chapel roof, but that was something that had to be done to stop the building deteriorating. It would have become an eyesore in no time and affected everybody. I don't know if the chapel people, for instance, will feel the same about a musical instrument they never hear.'

'We'll find out soon enough,' Miss Kemp said peaceably. 'I don't think it's urgent at the moment, anyway, although it would certainly be a good thing to have any repairs done in time for it to be at its best for the Coronation. I think there are vague plans for a music festival as part of the celebrations.'

'*Are* there?' Joyce asked in an outraged tone. '*I've* heard nothing about them! And I thought we weren't supposed to be thinking about next year, just yet.'

'No, we're not,' Miss Kemp said hastily. 'And they're really very vague – I may have got the wrong idea entirely.' In fact, she had been in the vicar's drawing-room only the night before, when she, the vicar and his wife, Charles Latimer and Gilbert Napier had been enjoying a glass of sherry after the meeting of the Parochial Council. Without actually conspiring to keep their ideas secret from the busy WI president, and organiser of both the Bridge Club and the Gardening Club (all in the person of Joyce Warren), there had been a tacit agreement that the less said, the better, at least for the time being. Gilbert Napier, indeed, had gone so far as to say that it would be a good thing if that interfering old busybody could be kept completely out of it.

38

'She doesn't know a quaver from a roll on the drums,' he'd declared. 'Let her organise the roses and marrows, and keep away from the music.'

'Can I rely on you to help me with some kind of dramatic production with the children for the fair?' Miss Kemp asked now, ruefully discarding her earlier resolution not to let Joyce anywhere near her own plans but realising she had to do something to distract the other woman's attention. 'Last year's pageant was such a success.'

Joyce Warren's voice softened. 'But of course. I shall be delighted. We must get together and discuss what we're to do. I've always had a fancy for putting on some Shakespeare. That lovely scene from *A Midsummer Night's Dream*, for instance, with the fairies . . .'

Miss Kemp opened her mouth to say that she thought Shakespeare might be a little beyond her charges, and then closed it again. 'Actually, that's not a bad idea. Not a bad idea at all. There's a lot of comedy in that, and some nice parts for the boys as well.' Her enthusiasm grew, and as they stopped to go their separate ways, she turned to look into Joyce's face, pale and round in the moonlight. 'Yes, we'll think about it. Thank you, Mrs Warren.'

If it had been less dark, she might have seen the blush of pleasure that suffused the pale face. Joyce Warren wasn't accustomed to enthusiasm for her ideas. Not that she ever allowed any lack of it to dissuade her; she had enough enthusiasm of her own for the rest of the villagers put together.

Still, it was pleasant to hear that note in the headmistress's voice, and the pleasure warmed her all the way home.

The brightest spot on Stella Simmons's horizon these days was the prospect of a visit from her sister, Muriel, whom she was now learning to call Maddy.

'It still seems funny, thinking of her by a different name,' she told Dottie Friend as they sat by the fire one evening. Dottie was knitting a dark blue balaclava for Felix Copley, the young curate, who had acquired an elderly sports car, which he had named Mirabelle and drove with the hood down all the time unless it was actually raining. Dottie had stopped to admire it one day, and he'd told her his grandfather had given it to him for Christmas and he loved it, but his ears got very cold, and Dottie had immediately made up her mind to do something about it.

While Dottie knitted, Stella was working on her lessons for the next day, and Dottie's cat, Alfred, who had feasted on bread soaked in the juice of two leftover pilchards for his tea, was slumbering on the rug like a shaggy black cushion. 'I suppose Madelaine is a more glamorous name than Muriel, but I feel sad that she isn't still called by the name our mother and father chose for her. But she doesn't want to go back to it. She's too used to being Maddy now.'

'It don't really matter what name we call her,' Dottie said comfortably. 'She's a sweet little maid whatever her name be. It'll be good to have her here again for Easter. Not long now.'

'Nearly eight weeks,' Stella said. 'It seems a long time to me! It's that long since Christmas, and that seems ages ago.'

'Spring's on its way, though,' Dottie said, reaching for another ball of wool. 'There's snowdrops out down by the ford – have you seen them? And the primroses'll be along soon after, and the hedges will start to green up a bit, too. And tomorrow's St Valentine's Day, and you know what they say about that.'

'They say a lot of things about St Valentine's Day,' Stella said with a smile, and Dottie laughed.

'You don't have to tell me that, maid! But what I had in mind was the one about birds finding their mates that day. Seen it myself, I have – little bluetits fluttering about, flirting with each other, pretty as you like. And there's a bit of nest-building going on already. I saw a magpie fly over only this morning with a girt big stick in his beak.'

'I hope you said good morning to him, then,' Stella said, joining in with her own bit of folklore. 'I wouldn't like to think he was one for sorrow.'

Dottie laughed again. 'And how many Valentines d'you reckon will come popping through the door for you?'

'Me? Oh, I shan't get any Valentines,' Stella said at once. 'I've only ever had one and that was in the home – one of the boys sent it for a joke.' She thought a little wistfully of Luke Ferris, whom she'd begun to grow fond of a year ago. 'I don't think many men are interested in country schoolteachers.'

'Now, that's just silly. I know Miss Kemp's never been married, but I don't think it's for want of chances. She were engaged once, so I heard tell, but the chap died in the First World War. That were a cruel time for women, you know – so many of them lost their menfolk, and there just weren't enough to go round when it were all over. But you'm a pretty girl, Stella, and there's plenty of time for you to find a nice young man. I dare say there's more than one in this very village interested in you, only they'm too shy to say so.'

'Well, we won't get very far at that rate,' Stella said with a laugh. 'But honestly, Dottie, I'm quite happy as I am, living here with you and Alfred and getting to know the children and the rest of the village.'

'You've settled in real well.' Dottie nodded. 'And young Maddy turning out to be your sister has helped a lot. Folk are proper fond of her.'

'I know.' Stella gazed into the fire thoughtfully. Finding her sister again after so many years had seemed like a miracle, but she couldn't help realising that those years had had an effect on them both. They had lived such different lives – herself in an orphanage, Maddy adopted by a famous actress – that getting to know each other, once they'd gone through the initial stage of shared reminiscences, had proved more

41

difficult than she'd expected. If only they could have spent more time together . . . but Maddy had gone away with her adopted mother almost as soon as they'd first met again, and had only managed a few days in October and then a week or so after Christmas. It seemed as if Stella's dream of being as close to her as they'd been in childhood was doomed to disappointment.

'It's early days yet,' Dottie said, guessing what was on her mind. 'It takes a long time to catch up on missed years. Why, it even took me a while to settle down again after I'd been in London all those years with Miss Forsyth. It was a bit different living there than down here in Devon, I can tell you. But I know Maddy's as pleased to have you back as you are to have her. All you need is a bit of time together, to catch up.'

'Which is what we don't seem to be able to have,' Stella said. 'A week or two at Christmas and then again at Easter – it's just not long enough to get to know each other. We have to start all over again every time.'

'Well, perhaps her'll come down for longer in the summer, when you have your long holiday. Or you could go away together. I dare say she'd be pleased to have you with her if Miss Forsyth goes abroad again.'

'Miss Forsyth might not be so pleased, though,' Stella observed. Fenella Forsyth was the actress who had adopted Maddy, believing her to be alone in the world, and although she'd been very gracious and welcoming towards Stella, the young schoolteacher had been very aware of the gulf between their worlds and the fact that both felt an equal claim on Maddy's attention.

'It'll all come out in the wash,' Dottie observed, casting off her stitches. 'There, that's done. I'll just sew it up, and maybe you could pop it round to Aggie Madge's on your way to school in the morning. 'Tidden far out of your way. Curate'll be wanting it in this cold weather.'

'All right.' Stella had almost finished her work. 'How about a game of crib when you've done that?'

'That'll be nice, maid.' Dottie sewed industriously for a few minutes and then held up the completed garment. 'That should keep his ears cosy. He's a nice young man, Mr Copley. We've got to look after him.'

Stella smiled. Dottie, who worked as a barmaid as well as helping at the Barton and standing in for Mrs Dawe, the school cook, when she had one of her attacks of bronchitis, seemed to look after most of the village at one time or another. She had often wondered why the plump, comfortable woman had never married; she seemed cut out to be a wife and mother.

Perhaps she was another of those women who had lost a sweetheart in the First World War. There must be so many similarly tragic stories from that time, she thought as she put away her work and fetched the cribbage board and cards. Just as there were, in her own experience, from the Second.

Even now, there was a war raging on the other side of the world, in Korea, and young men like Roy Pettifer fighting it. If only this could be the year when all the conflict might come to an end and the world find peace at last.

Felix Copley was just finishing his breakfast at Aggie Madge's cottage when Stella arrived with the balaclava. He took it out of the paper bag with delight and immediately tried it on.

'That's marvellous! I'll be warm as toast. How do I look?'

'Like a bank robber,' Stella said with a laugh. 'Or Biggles when you've got your goggles on. But I don't suppose that'll matter. You'd better take it off when you visit your parishioners, though.'

He pulled the helmet off and his fair hair stuck out all round his head. Stella smiled at him. The young curate had arrived in Burracombe at more or less the same time as herself and they'd shared a sense of fellow feeling. But Felix had

43

become friendly with Hilary Napier, and Stella had begun to search for her sister, with Luke Ferris's help, so their friendship hadn't progressed. Perhaps now, with Luke engaged to Val Tozer and Hilary occupied with managing the estate, they would find themselves thrown together a little more.

Felix was looking at her oddly. She felt herself colour, and then her blush deepened as he said, 'D'you realise, you must be my Valentine!' He saw her embarrassment and added hastily, 'It's all right, I'm only joking. Only, you know what they say – the first person you see on St Valentine's Day and all that!'

'I didn't think clergymen were supposed to be superstitious,' Stella said, rather more tartly than she'd meant to, but Felix just grinned.

'Is it a superstition when it's applied to a saint? I suppose it is, really – but it's a nice one, isn't it? And I must admit I'd rather it was you than, say, Mrs Warren. Or even Miss Bellamy!' They both laughed, and Stella made a move towards the door.

'I'd better be going. It's nearly time for school.'

'Yes, of course. And thank you for bringing this in.' He picked up the balaclava again. 'Dottie really is a treasure. You're quite comfortable, living in her cottage, are you?'

'Oh yes. She's so kind; she looks after me like a mother.' Stella looked around the living-room, not so very different from Dottie's own. 'You seem snug enough here, too.'

'I am. Aggie's a wonderful landlady. And a very good cook.' He lowered his voice conspiratorially. 'But she can't knit balaclavas!'

Stella laughed again. 'Dottie can knit anything. Jumpers, cardigans, socks, toys – you must have seen her work at church bazaars. In fact, when I first saw her cat, I thought she'd knitted him! He looks exactly like a woolly cushion when he's asleep.' Feeling more at ease now that they were off

44

the subject of Valentines, she opened the door and an icy draught swept in. 'Brr, it's cold out there. I'll shut the door quickly. Goodbye, Felix.'

'Goodbye,' he said. 'And thank you again for bringing the balaclava round for me.'

He moved over to the window and watched Stella step away along the village street. Her dark hair was covered by a scarlet beret, and her blue coat swung round her slim figure. Her hands were encased in warm gloves, exactly the same shade as her hat and probably knitted by Dottie.

He watched until she was out of sight and then returned to the breakfast table. The balaclava lay on the back of the armchair, and he glanced at it once or twice. I must go and thank Dottie properly, he thought. Perhaps later on, around teatime. Stella would be back from school by then . . .

Chapter Five

The stranger came to the village again at the beginning of March.

Once again, she made her way to the church, but this time there was no one there. She opened the door and slipped into the dim interior, moving slowly between the pews, trying to make out the lettering on the tablets that adorned the walls. 'An Excellent Gentleman in All Respects ...' 'A Virtuous and Faithful Wife, Most Loving and Affectionate Mother to Her Eight Children ...' 'A Most Beloved Squire ...' The village seemed to have been filled with illustrious inhabitants, or perhaps it was just that they were the only ones who had memorials erected to them. Or maybe because you only spoke good of the dead, especially on church tablets.

For a few minutes, she explored the church, looking at the worn, faded hassocks and standing at the chancel steps to raise her eyes to the stained-glass window behind the altar. The centre panel depicted the church's patron saint, St Andrew, standing with his cross held before his body. The colours were rich and deep, a blue robe picked out in crimson, with a paler blue sky behind, and the saint's halo shining with golden light as the sun poured through.

The dank chill of February had been replaced, first by blustery March winds and then a softer calm, with no more than a few drifting clouds and a hint of warmth in the pale sunshine. The snowdrops sprinkled along the Devon banks like icing on a cake were already beginning to give way to a golden cloak of primroses and wild daffodils, and birds chased each other from branch to branch. The hedgerows were dripping with yellow catkins, like a shower of golden rain, and there were even a few early lambs in the more sheltered fields.

The woman laid her hand on the ancient stonework as she peered through the squint, through which congregations in the smaller north wing of the church could have seen the Elevation of the Host in bygone days, when the church was Roman Catholic. She looked up at the pulpit, touched the polished wood of the lectern with her fingertips, then moved again to the back of the church to examine the old stone font, plain and uncarved, in which so many babies of the parish had been baptised. Lastly, she sat down in one of the pews.

Basil Harvey found her there when he came in about fifteen minutes later. He saw her at once, her back straight as she gazed towards the east window, and hesitated, not wishing to disturb her contemplation. But as he closed the door softly behind him, she turned and he saw that she was the person who had come to the church the day the King had died. He moved nearer.

'Good morning. We've met before, haven't we? It's good to see you here again.'

She nodded. 'I came about a month ago. I was looking . . .' She paused, as if searching for words. 'I wondered . . .'

'Is there something you want to know?' Basil asked. 'Something about the church? Or the village, perhaps?'

She looked at him, as if wishing he could read her mind. Once again, he was struck by the luminous quality of her grey eyes, fringed by their thick, dark lashes. Her chestnut hair gleamed in the sunlight that filtered through the coloured glass, and her face had a soft, creamy pallor. She wore a light grey coat with a blue scarf tucked into the neck.

'If there's anything I can do . . .' he suggested gently, and saw her chew her lip, as if trying to make up her mind, or perhaps to pluck up courage. Not wanting to press her, he

47

half turned away. 'Shall I leave you in peace for a while? I'll be in the vestry if you need me.'

As he turned, she made a small gesture, quickly withdrawn, as if to ask him to stay. As before, he had a sense that she was troubled in some way, and felt convinced that she had come to the church for a reason and wanted to ask his help. Yet something was holding her back, and he knew that if he made the wrong move he might frighten her away completely. Whatever it was, he must tread delicately.

'You know that you can talk to me in complete confidence,' he said quietly and waited, still half turned.

'It's just—' she began and then caught herself, frowning a little as if inwardly scolding herself. 'It sounds so silly. But I think I might come from here.'

Basil considered her words, several ideas as to what she might mean passing through his mind. He waited for a moment, and she went on, her voice stumbling a little as the words tumbled out, in a hurry now to be spoken.

'I've never *lived* here, I don't mean that. I'd never even *been* here until that day – when the King died. But I think my – my parents came from here. I was wondering if – if I could find out. If anyone would know.'

'It's quite possible,' he said, sitting down beside her. 'What were their names? And when did they move away?'

The woman's eyes fell, and she stared at her hands, clasped together in her lap. She didn't answer for a moment, and then she said, 'Well, that's just it, you see, Vicar. They didn't move away. At least, my mother did. I don't really know whether my father did or not.' She looked up at him again. 'They weren't married, you see.'

'Ah.' He thought for a moment, then asked, 'Do you know his name?'

'No. I don't know who he was. I only know that he had the same initial as me. I found a piece of paper.' She felt in her coat pocket and handed it to him. It was cheap lined writing-

48

paper, yellowing with age, with a few words written on it in the copperplate hand that all children had learned during the early part of the century. It was obviously the end of a letter and was signed 'J'.

'J. That could be any number of names,' Basil said thoughtfully. 'John, James, Jeremy . . . And this is the only clue you have?' She nodded. 'And has your mother never told you any more?'

'My mother never mentioned him at all,' she said. 'I didn't even know I had a different father until a few weeks ago, when she died and I looked through her papers. She married, you see, when I was two years old. I've got two younger sisters – I always thought I was just the eldest of the family. And our father – *their* father – died in the war. So there's nobody to ask at all.'

'I see. And you want to find your real father.' He paused again, wondering how best to deal with the situation. 'You realise he might not want to be found?'

'But I wouldn't actually need to tell him, would I? I'd just like to *know*, that's all. I'd like to see him – to be able to think of him and my mother. Like other people can think of their parents together.'

Basil looked at her. He judged her to be in her early or mid-thirties. There were no rings on her twisting fingers, and she was neatly but plainly dressed. He guessed that the family had not had an easy time and wondered if she might be hoping to find a father who was well off. But she didn't strike him as mercenary.

'Perhaps it would be better if we went across to the vicarage to talk about this,' he suggested. 'That's if you'd like to. It's rather public in the church – anyone might come in. And I have the parish records there as well, if you want to look at them.'

The woman didn't answer immediately. She stared down at

her hands. Then a sound from outside caused her to raise her head again, and she nodded.

'Yes, please. I'd like that – if you've got time.' Uncertainty crept into her eyes. 'You must be very busy – perhaps it would be better if I came back another day.'

'No, not at all.' He didn't want her to go away again, rebuffed for a second time. 'I can always find something to do, of course – what vicar can't? – but I can also always find time for someone who needs my help. That's the most important part of my job.' He smiled at her and got to his feet. 'It's only a few steps across the churchyard, and I wouldn't be surprised if my wife isn't making some coffee at this very moment. I can offer you refreshment, and we'll be quite private in my study.' He held out his hand. 'My name's Basil Harvey, by the way.'

The woman stood up as well and took his hand. Her grave, pale face softened as she smiled back, and a glow lit her luminous grey eyes.

'If you're sure you don't mind, then . . . And my name's Jennifer Tucker. That was my mother's married name – Tucker.'

'I see. Well, it's a pleasure to meet you, Miss Tucker, and I hope I can help you.' He ushered her towards the door and opened it for her. Outside, the sun was flooding the churchyard and the sound of birdsong filled the air. One or two people were crossing the green; Alf Coker was standing at the door of his forge, and he could see Jacob Prout wheeling his barrow towards Constance Bellamy's house.

He hoped that he was not about to uncover a family tragedy, or some old secret best left untold. But that was not for him to judge, he thought a little ruefully. He could only assist Jennifer Tucker with her quest, counsel her if she requested it, and hope that she dealt with her discoveries – if she made any – with wisdom.

He guided her across the churchyard to the gate that led to the vicarage garden.

*

Alice Tozer had just come out of the post office, her shopping-basket over one arm, when she saw the vicar leading his visitor across the churchyard. She paused, visited by a fleeting sense of familiarity, of *déjà vu*, as if the little scene had taken place before. She almost felt, for a moment, as if she knew exactly what would happen next.

Then the two figures were gone, and she shook herself and rubbed her eyes with her free hand. You'm getting fanciful, she told herself. Seeing things. Getting old.

She walked along the lane to the farm track and through the yard. Ted and Tom were both out in the fields somewhere, and Val was at work in Tavistock Hospital. Joanna had taken Robin over the river to Little Burracombe to visit her friend, so only Minnie was at home, preparing the vegetables for their midday meal. She turned as Alice came through the back door, her birdlike eyes bright.

'What's the matter with you, maid? Look as if you've seen a ghost.'

'I feel as if I have.' Alice set her basket on the kitchen table and began to unpack it. She shivered suddenly and said, 'Goose walking over my grave.'

'Why, what's happened?' Minnie dried her hands on a tea-towel, looking concerned, but Alice smiled and shook her head.

'Nothing's happened, Mother. It's just that I saw someone in the churchyard with the vicar and for a minute it took me back—' She stopped, frowning a little. 'The funny thing is, I don't really know *where* it took me back! It was like that feeling you get sometimes, as if it's all happened before, you know? It's gone before you can get hold of it, like a shred of gossamer.'

'Who was it, then?' Minnie tipped some peeled potatoes into a saucepan of water. 'You'll have to lift these over for me, my flower – the pan's too heavy for me.'

'I don't know who it was, that's the funny thing. Not

51

someone from the village, I can tell you that. But I have seen her before – at least, I think I have.' Alice paused, thinking. 'There was a young woman came into the church the day the King died. She spoke to us then, but she seemed upset – well, us all were – and went straight off to catch the bus. I only saw her back view today, but I think it was the same one.'

'Come to see the vicar, you reckon?' Minnie started to take the outer leaves from a large cabbage. 'Wonder what that be about. But I don't see why it should give you a funny turn, Alice.'

'Neither do I,' Alice said thoughtfully. 'But it was the same feeling as I got the first time I saw her. As if there were something about her – something I ought to know.' She stood staring at the groceries on the table, her brows drawn down, and her lips folded inwards over her teeth. Then she shrugged her shoulders and chided herself again. 'No. There's nothing – nothing I can put my finger on, anyway. Getting fanciful, that's all it is.'

'It's spring,' her mother-in-law said, giving her a nudge. 'Getting your blood up. It gives people all sorts of funny ideas, spring does.'

Alice gave her a dry look. 'Yes, maybe it does. But I'd have thought I was old enough to know better.'

'Go on!' Minnie said. 'You'm not old. You wait till you're eighty-four, like me, then you'll be able to think about getting old. Only *think* about it, mind – I've still got a few years left in me yet, and so have you. Plenty of time for us both to get funny ideas!'

They laughed together, and Alice began to put away the groceries. By the time the water was boiling for the cabbage, they had both forgotten all about the stranger in the churchyard.

Chapter Six

Since calling round to Dottie's cottage to thank her for the balaclava, Felix had dropped in again two or three times, usually late in the afternoon when Stella had come home from school. There was usually a tray of scones or biscuits coming out of the oven just about then, and a pot of tea brewing. Dottie welcomed him with her usual comfortable smile, and the three of them would settle down to tea and a gossip about village affairs.

'Mrs Warren seems to have got plans for the village fair under way already,' Felix observed, spreading a scone with some of Dottie's blackcurrant jam. 'She's a very energetic lady, isn't she?'

'That's one way of putting it,' Dottie replied dryly. 'Busy as a bee, that one is, and got her finger in all the village pies. Still, someone has to do the work, and she don't seem to mind badgering others to pull their weight.'

'Has anything happened about the organ yet?' Stella enquired. 'I saw someone coming out of the church with Mr Harvey the other day – I wondered if it was the person he was getting to examine it and say what was wrong.'

Dottie shook her head. 'No, that were a young woman, at least if you mean the one I saw last week. They went through the churchyard towards the vicarage. Alice Tozer saw her, too.'

'I suppose they might send a woman to look at the organ,'

Felix said doubtfully. 'Women do play church organs quite a lot, after all.'

'I don't see why it shouldn't be a woman,' Stella said. 'Women are perfectly capable of looking at church organs.'

'It could be pretty heavy work—' Felix began, but it was Dottie who interrupted him this time.

'So's rolling out beer barrels, but that don't stop Bernie Nethercott leaving it to me to do round at the Bell. And women did all sorts of men's jobs during the war.'

'All right!' Felix exclaimed, holding up his hands. 'I give in! Of *course* a woman could advise on what needs doing to the church organ, but I don't think anyone's been to look at it yet. I don't know who it was who came to see Mr Harvey last week, but I'm sure that wasn't why she came.'

'Didn't he tell you about her, then?' Dottie asked innocently, and he gave her what she termed an 'old-fashioned' look.

'Now, you know I can't discuss that, Dottie. Anyway, he didn't.' He turned towards Stella. 'What I can discuss is the new film they're showing in Tavistock next week. I wondered if you were thinking of going to see it.'

'I'd like to,' Stella said, 'but it's getting there and back that's the problem. I could catch a bus, but I don't like walking back from the main road in the dark.'

'Well, why don't we go together?' he suggested, and she looked at him in surprise.

'In your car, you mean?'

'Of course. Or we could go on the bus, if you'd rather – so long as you don't mind walking in the dark with me!'

Stella laughed. 'Oh, I think I'd feel safe enough with you. Well – yes – that would be very nice. Thank you. Which evening were you thinking of?'

'What about Thursday?' he asked, and she nodded. 'We'll make it a date, then. We'll sort out a time later on – I'll drop in again one day.' He glanced at Dottie, who was watching them both with a smile on her face. 'That's if it's all right with you, Dottie. I don't want to take advantage of your hospitality.'

'Bless your heart, my handsome, 'tis no trouble to give you a cup of tea and a bite to eat,' she said. 'I know Aggie Madge feeds you proper, but a young chap like you, out and about all the time, needs regular feeding, 'specially in this cold weather. You'm always welcome to pop in here of an afternoon.'

'You've got a heart of gold,' he said. 'But then, so have so many people in Burracombe. This is the friendliest village I've ever known.'

'We're not a bad lot,' Dottie said. 'Most of us, anyway. There's one or two I could mention who could do with a few lessons in manners, but every village has got a few like that. Arthur Culliford, for one – how that poor wife of his puts up with him, I do not know. Not that she's all that much better herself, and those boys of theirs are turning into proper little hooligans. And then there's Jed Fisher, but he's always been a bad-tempered old misery, and his cottage is nothing but a slum.'

'Unfortunately, I can't offer him much comfort,' Felix said regretfully. 'He's Chapel and we can't interfere.'

'It's not comfort he needs!' Dottie retorted. 'It's fumigating!'

The other two laughed, but Felix shook his head as well. 'There must be some reason why he's always miserable. Perhaps he had a bad time in the First World War. Has he always lived alone? Was he ever married?'

Dottie shook her head. 'No girl in her senses would ever have taken Jed Fisher. Though he weren't bad-looking as a young chap, believe it or not. And it weren't his war experiences, neither, not like with some poor fellows who came back with shell-shock and weren't never the same again. Jed Fisher never went to war at all. Got exemption on account of some medical condition, though you'd never have knowed

55

there was anything wrong, while others went off and did his fighting for him. You can see some of their names on the war memorial on the green.' Her voice was suddenly edged with bitterness and Stella remembered how she had wondered if Dottie had been one of those who had lost her sweetheart during that war. 'No, Jed's just that sort and there's nothing anyone can do about it. You can be thankful he'm Methodist, Mr Copley, and no burden of yours.'

Felix smiled. 'I'm sure he's in good hands, anyway, Dottie. The Methodist minister is a good man.' He finished his tea and rose to his feet, stooping slightly under the low ceiling. 'Thank you very much for the tea and scones. I still feel guilty at taking so much of your rations. I'll bring you something in return, next time I come.'

'Go on with you,' the countrywoman said, fetching his coat from where she had hung it behind the door. 'A cup of tea and a scone don't leave the cupboard bare. Mind, you'd think all this rationing would have come to an end by now – who'd have thought us'd still be using coupons nearly seven years after the war finished? At least we'm better favoured out here in the country – we can have a few eggs and a drop of milk and that sort of thing. What it can be like in the towns, I don't hardly like to think.'

Felix departed, promising to call by and make arrangements with Stella for their trip to the cinema the following week, and Dottie began to bustle about clearing away the teacups and making preparations for their supper, smiling to herself as she did so.

Stella gave her a sideways glance. 'What are you laughing at?'

'Oh, nothing. I'm just pleased to see you going out with a young man, that's all.'

'I'm not "going out with a young man"!' Stella exclaimed. 'Not the way you mean, anyway. I'm just going to the

56

pictures with Felix, that's all. It's very kind of him to suggest it, knowing I don't like walking along that road in the dark.'

'If you think that's all it is,' Dottie said, 'you'll believe anything, my dear.'

'Dottie, he's the *curate*.'

'He's a man,' Dottie said. 'A healthy young man. Just because he's a clergyman don't make no difference to that. They're just the same as any other man. Except for Catholics, of course,' she added thoughtfully. 'They're not allowed to be the same. But Mr Copley's not Catholic, he's Church of England, so you don't have to worry about that. And a very nice young chap he is, too,' she added. 'You don't have no call to worry about him not behaving hisself.'

'I'm not,' Stella said with dignity, unpacking her school bag. 'And there's nothing like that in it, nothing at all. We're just going to the pictures together because it's a convenient evening for us both and it's nice to go in company. That's all.'

Dottie's lips twitched, but she said no more. Instead, she went out to the kitchen and began to scrub potatoes. After a little while, she began to sing to herself, and Stella, recognising the tune of 'I'll Take You Home Again, Kathleen', sighed and shook her head.

'And my name's *not* Kathleen!' she called, laughing.

Felix walked back to his lodgings, thinking how pleasant it was to have the evenings drawing out. It was light now until six o'clock; in a few weeks, when the clocks went forward for Summer Time, it would be light until after seven, and from then on the days would lengthen until darkness wasn't falling until after ten.

There could be disadvantages to this, of course. Stella Simmons wouldn't be afraid to walk along the mile of road from the main bus stop to the village and wouldn't need an escort from an evening out at the cinema. But by then, perhaps they would have made a habit of such weekly outings.

Felix had liked the young schoolteacher from their first meeting, soon after they'd both arrived in Burracombe, and they'd met at various village events, but he had been attracted by Hilary Napier, too, and it wasn't until she'd gently turned down his proposal of marriage that he'd really begun to see Stella as a possible companion. He'd also been aware that she and Luke Ferris were spending a lot of time together, although it wasn't until later that he'd realised that Luke's interest lay with Val Tozer.

Being a young clergyman made it difficult to make female friendships. You had to be so careful, especially with parishioners. But Felix liked women's company and wanted someone special in his life. He wanted, eventually, to marry and have the kind of home life that Basil Harvey had, with a wife and family.

Aggie Madge's cottage stood almost opposite the pair occupied by Jed Fisher and Jacob Prout. As Felix came closer, he saw that Jacob was in his front garden, cutting down some bushy twigs.

'They're rather nice,' Felix said, stopping. 'A lovely red colour. Why are you cutting them down? Don't you like them?'

'Won't get no colour next winter if I don't,' Jacob said, snipping another crimson twig off at the base. 'Dogwoods, these be, and you only gets the colour on the young wood. They'll soon grow up again, you don't need to worry about that.' He straightened up and gathered the twigs into a bundle. 'Doctor's wife likes a few of these in a pot in her hallway. I said I'd pass some on to the vicar's wife, too. They makes a pretty decoration.'

'Yes, I've seen them, now you mention it. I thought they were artificial. I'm not much of a gardener, I'm afraid,' Felix said apologetically, catching Jacob's look. 'Mrs Madge asked me to help her last summer, but I pulled up more plants than weeds.'

'Ah, well, there be a secret to that,' Jacob said solemnly. 'Weeds be the ones that are hard to pull out.' He waited a moment while Felix worked this out, then jerked his head towards the fence separating his garden from Jed Fisher's. 'You could do your apprenticeship on that mess next door. Wouldn't matter what you pulled out there, it's all weeds.'

'It does look rather untidy,' Felix agreed, looking at the blackened, soggy mass of last year's foliage. Jacob snorted.

'Untidy! That's all nettles and ground elder and convulsions, and God knows what else – pardon my language, but He'm the only one who does know what's there. Not that weeding would make much difference. Wants a good digging over and all the roots pulling out and a cartload of muck put in before you could grow anything in there. And it used to be a nice little patch, too, full of colour in the summer. Crying shame it is, letting it run wild like that.'

'Well, we can't all be good gardeners like you,' Felix said diplomatically, but Jacob snorted again.

'Us can all keep our own place tidy. 'Tidden much to ask, is it – little bit of ground like this? 'Tis a responsibility to the Good Lord's earth, that's what I say. But there, some folk are nothing more than heathens, and that's the top and bottom of it.'

'I don't think you ought—' Felix was beginning, when the door of the other cottage flew open and Jed Fisher's face appeared, red and angry under his thatch of straggly grey hair.

'What be you two staring at? You been standing there for the past ten minutes looking in at my bit of ground and chewing the fat – what's it all about, eh?'

'Why, nothing, Mr Fisher,' Felix said hastily, taking a step back, but Jacob was made of sterner stuff.

'We'm allowed to look where us likes. It's a free country, or 'twas last time I heard. Not that your rubbishy old garden's

59

anything to look at – nothing but an eyesore, that ain't, and Curate agrees with me, don't you, Mr Copley?'

Felix opened his mouth, but Jed was marching down the path, waving his walking-stick, and he took another step back. 'So you *was* looking at my garden, then? I thought so when I looked out of the winder. They'm talking about my patch of ground, I says to meself. I'm not having that. 'Tis my own business what I does with it, so you get back to your own side of the fence, Jacob Prout, and mind your own. As for you, Curate, you can go back to your church. I'm Chapel, I am, and nothing to do with you.'

'Does the minister know that, then?' Jacob asked. 'I'd bet good money he don't see you inside that building from one year's end to the other.'

'I went in at Christmas, for your information!' Jed retorted. 'And I looks after the graveyard, too, same as you do at the church. Anyway, Chapel folk don't bet,' he added, as an afterthought.

'Don't drink neither, from what I hear,' Jacob said. 'Don't stop you propping up the bar at the Bell, though, do it!' He regarded his neighbour thoughtfully and then said, 'I'll say one thing for you, Jed, you got darn good eyesight.'

The other man looked nonplussed for a moment, then said suspiciously, 'What d'you mean by that?'

'Why, being able to see out through your window,' Jacob replied innocently, glancing towards the grimy panes of glass with their piles of newspapers and oddments on the sills inside. 'I wouldn't have thought you could see anything through that filth. Must have X-ray eyes.'

Jed glared at him, his face reddening and his chest swelling with fury. For a moment, Felix was afraid he was about to strike out with his walking-stick. Then, making a sound rather like a car tyre going down suddenly, he turned on his heel and stamped back to his door. As he went inside, he looked back for one parting shot.

60

"'Tis just your way, Jacob Prout, to make nasty remarks when you'm in the wrong. 'Tis just your way. And it ain't a Christian way, neither – I hope you realises that, Curate. I hope you realises just what sort of a man you got looking after your churchyard and digging graves there. Sooner he digs his own grave, the better for us all, that's what I say!'

The door slammed, and Jacob laughed. 'Silly old fool. Always got to have the last word. Always been the same, ever since he were a little tacker. Never did like no one to get the better of him.'

'You've known him a long time?' Felix said, feeling that he ought to try to mend matters.

'Knowed him since he were a babby in his pram. Grew up together, us did, in these two very cottages. His mum and dad and mine were good friends in those days.'

'And didn't you and Jed get on even then?'

'Oh, ah,' Jacob said, turning away. 'Us got on all right as boys.' His voice was terse, as if he didn't want to pursue the subject, and Felix sighed. He glanced towards Jed's window and, seeing the other man's face peering malevolently at them, decided it was probably better to move away. He didn't want Jed complaining to Mr Harvey that the curate was gossiping about him at his own gate.

'I'd better be getting along,' he said, as Jacob began to snip at the last few twigs. 'Mrs Madge will be getting my supper ready, and I've got Sunday's sermon to prepare. Perhaps we can have another talk, sometime.'

'If it's *him* you wants to talk about, you needn't waste your breath,' Jacob said, obviously still ruffled. 'He ain't worth it. I know you might say that's not a Christian way to talk about him, but I've knowed him for the past sixty years and more, and I can tell you this – when the Good Lord told us to love thy neighbour, he didn't live next door to Jed Fisher. *Nobody* could love that man, and there ain't nothing more to say about it. Nothing.'

61

He loaded his twigs into his barrow and began to push them up the path, too irritated even to wish Felix goodbye. The curate watched him go and then turned away, rather dispirited, towards the cottage across the lane. He could see smoke drifting up from the chimney. Aggie Madge had lit the fire; the front room where he sat in the evening, working, reading, or listening to the radio, would be warm and cosy. It would be clean and tidy – or as tidy as it ever could be with his papers cluttering the table and his books piled on the shelves. Like Jacob Prout's spotlessly kept cottage, it would feel comfortable and homely.

He wondered what it was like inside Jed Fisher's house. He would probably never know, for Jed was unlikely ever to invite him in, but he had been inside other cottages that were poorly kept and had seen and smelled the dirt and the damp of neglect; of rotting plaster walls, scrappy meals and unwashed clothes and bodies. It was a depressing way to live and something he always found hard to come to terms with. He felt sad that, even in this pretty Dartmoor village, there were people who lived in this way.

With a sigh, he opened the gate to Mrs Madge's garden and walked up the path to her door.

Chapter Seven

Basil Harvey was thinking about villages, too.

Not that this was unusual – most of his time was taken up with thinking about villages, and Burracombe in particular. But his thoughts this evening were taken up with the hidden life of a village – the things that went on behind closed doors. The long-held grudges and the family feuds whose cause had been either forgotten or distorted out of all recognition. The secrets that were perhaps never revealed to anyone else and were taken to the grave.

'It was obviously a very loving letter,' he said to his wife as they sat by the window of their drawing-room, having tea. They didn't often get the chance to have tea quietly together – there would either be a parishioner or two with them or Basil would be at one of the farms or cottages. They were now discussing the woman who had come to Burracombe searching for her father. 'It was the end of it – there were only a few lines at the top of the sheet of paper – but it was so fondly expressed. *"With All my Love, my Dearest Girl, from Your Own J."* Nearly every word had a capital letter – the way they used to write in those days.'

'And that would have been when?' Grace asked, pouring him a second cup of tea. 'You think the woman was in her early thirties?'

'Oh yes – she told me she'd been born in June 1917. So she's now coming up to her thirty-fifth birthday.'

'And she knew nothing about this until her mother died?'

'Not a thing, apparently.' He stirred his tea pensively. They had both given up sugar during the war and never used saccharin, but it still didn't seem to taste the same without being stirred. 'She always believed she was the eldest child of a perfectly ordinary family. The father – her stepfather, as it turns out – was in the Navy and lost at sea during the war. Jennifer Tucker herself was in the Wrens and overseas, so couldn't get back, and by the time she came home, both her younger sisters – half-sisters, really – had married as well and left home, and Jennifer went back to live with her mother. Plymouth was still in ruins, of course, but she managed to get work in a shop, and they rented a small house, somewhere in Devonport. She was never very strong – the mother, I mean – and Jennifer looked after her until she went into hospital a few months ago, and eventually died there.'

'What a sad little story,' Grace said after a moment. 'And what about the two sisters? I suppose they know no more than Jennifer does?'

'No, they're both several years younger. Neither of them lives in Plymouth now, so distance is another problem.'

'So she feels rather alone in the world.'

He nodded. 'I think that's why she wants to find out something about her father. She thinks he may still be alive – he'd probably only be about fifty-five or sixty, after all.'

'But would he be pleased to have a long-lost and unknown daughter turning up on his doorstep?' Grace asked dubiously. 'He's probably got a family of his own by now. He may not even have known there was to be a baby all those years ago. She could cause a lot more problems.'

'I know. I discussed this with her. I think she realises all that, and wouldn't want to impose herself on him – but who knows how she would feel once she'd discovered his name? She might be so desperate to have someone of her own that she'd ignore the consequences and make herself known to him.'

64

'It's a tricky situation,' Grace said thoughtfully. 'How has it been left?'

'Well, she's asked me to make cautious enquiries, and she says she doesn't mind my discussing it with anyone who might know the truth, or who can be relied on to be discreet. The thing is, she doesn't even know for certain which village the man came from – or if her mother lived there, too. She's given me her birth certificate – the shortened form, showing her date of birth, sex and place of registration, which is Plymouth, so there's no help there. And I've also got her mother's marriage certificate to Arthur Tucker, the man Jennifer believed to have been her own father. This does at least give the name of her mother's father, which is Hannaford, and his job. He was a farm labourer.'

'Hannaford . . . Well, it's a Devon name, but I don't know of any in this area, do you? Not in the village, anyway.'

'No, I don't. I've looked through all our records of baptisms and deaths for the period we might be interested in, and there are none mentioned.'

'So doesn't that mean the mother didn't come from Burracombe after all? What makes Miss Tucker think she did?'

'I don't quite know. Certain references – the occasional mention of childhood games, the school she attended, that kind of thing. The odd local name dropped into a conversation – Cuckoo Wood and the Standing Stones in particular. She's looked at the Ordnance Survey maps in some detail, and although this isn't the only village it could be, from the few clues she has, it does seem to be a possibility. And she says that the first time she came here – back in February – she had a feeling that it was the right one. It felt almost familiar to her.'

'But how could it have done? If she'd never been here before . . . ?'

'We don't know that she hadn't,' he pointed out. 'It's quite possible that her mother brought her here when she was a child. She might have been too young to remember in any detail, yet still have a faint memory of it.'

Grace sighed and shook her head. 'I don't know, Basil. It seems an impossible quest to me. I feel sorry for her – she seems to be a lonely person – but I can't really think that it's going to help her, to search for a father who may not be alive now, or who may have a family of his own and not welcome her. That would only leave her feeling all the more hurt and alone. Is she coming back to see you again?'

'Probably. I suggested she leave it for two or three weeks first.'

'Well, when she does, I think you ought to suggest that she try to make her own life from now on. Looking into the past can turn up all kinds of things that are better left alone.'

'I'm inclined to agree, dear, but I can't make her give up, and if she asks my help, I'm duty-bound to give it to her. And if I'm helpful, she may be more likely to take notice of my counsel if we do find out anything.' He picked up the last of Grace's homemade biscuits. 'I thought I might start by talking to Miss Bellamy. She knows everyone for miles around and she would have been in her twenties at the time Jennifer was born – she might remember something. And I can rely on her not to say anything to anyone else.'

Grace held up the teapot, but he shook his head. 'Well, I can see that you feel you have to help, but I have to say I rather hope it all comes to nothing. If the mother's died only recently, this young woman's probably feeling unhappy and unsettled – in a few months' time, she may have thought it over and decided not to search any further. She might even get married herself. It's a little unusual that she hasn't already.'

'Perhaps there was someone in the war,' Basil said. 'So many young men were killed . . . And I rather gathered that the mother was ill for a long time. Jennifer probably didn't have much chance to meet anyone, what with looking after her and working as well. As you say, that may change now that she hasn't got that responsibility any more.' He got to his feet and stood gazing out through the French windows. 'Look at all those little daffodils! They're like a bright patch of sunshine fallen into the garden. A promise of brighter days to come.' He turned to his wife, his round, pink face smiling a little sadly. 'I'd like to think that there will be brighter days for Jennifer Tucker. I really would like to think that.'

There was certainly a promise of brighter days to come at the Tozers' farm, where Joanna and Tom had just announced that there was indeed a new baby on the way.

'I thought so!' Val exclaimed, laughing and kissing her brother and sister-in-law. 'I didn't say anything, but when you went to see Dr Latimer . . . '

'I wondered, too,' Alice agreed, her face flushed with pleasure. 'I said to Mother – didn't I, Mother? – I wouldn't be at all surprised if our Joanna wasn't expecting again.'

'She did,' Minnie confirmed, nodding from her chair by the range. 'And I said I thought so, too. We've just been waiting for you to give the word so we could start knitting.'

'Honestly!' Joanna said, pretending to be exasperated. 'You can't keep anything a secret round here. It seems as if you all knew even before we did.'

'Well, we'm not farmers for nothing,' Alice remarked. 'And with our Val being a nurse as well . . . Did you hear that, Jackie?' she asked as her younger daughter came through the back door. 'You'm going to be an auntie again.'

'Am I?' Jackie looked at her sister-in-law. 'When?'

'Not until September. Plenty of time for all that knitting,' Joanna replied, giving Minnie a smile. 'And we've still got lots of Robin's things, anyway, so we won't need all that much.'

'But they'm blue!' Minnie said, outraged. 'Supposing it's a girl.'

'That's something we won't know until the day it arrives. We're not going through all that palaver with a wedding-ring again.' At Minnie's insistence, while Joanna was expecting Robin, the women had conducted several experiments with a wedding-ring suspended over her stomach on a length of cotton. If it swung back and forth, the baby would be a girl; if it went in circles, it would be a boy. Or possibly the other way round – they had all differed on which it was meant to be, and since it performed both actions at different times, depending on who was holding it, it didn't seem to matter, anyway. 'We'll dress it in white for the first few weeks and you can knit coloured things then.'

The family continued to discuss the news, with Tom coming in for a good deal of teasing and Ted pretending to be put out that he was to be a grandfather again. 'Making me old before my time,' he grumbled. 'Still, we'll be needing a few more pairs of hands around the place before too long. Maybe then I can look forward to a bit of retirement.'

'Go on, Dad, you'll never retire,' Tom told him. 'You'll be out there in the yard, sticking your oar in, when you're a hundred. We'll have to tie you to your chair to get any peace.'

'I dare say I'll still have me uses,' Ted retorted. 'Look at your grandmother – place'd fall apart if 'twasn't for her keeping us all on our toes.'

They laughed, but they knew there was a grain of truth in his words. Minnie, whose main task now was to prepare the vegetables for the family's dinner, had been a mainstay during the difficult years of two world wars. In the Great War of 1914–18, she had been the one to keep the farm going while Ted and his brother, George, had gone off to war, especially after her husband, William, had been killed in a farm accident. And during the more recent conflict, although Ted had been able to stay at home, when their sons, Tom and Brian, had been called up and their places had been taken by Land Girls – one of them Joanna – it had fallen to Minnie and Alice to help out on the farm and to look after the city girls while they found their feet. Alice had often said that she didn't know how she would have managed without her mother-in-law.

After a while, Val slipped out and made her way across the fields and up through the wood to the charcoal-burner's cottage. She found Luke working on a frame for his latest picture.

'Val! I didn't think you were coming tonight.' He kissed her, then held her away from him for a moment and looked into her eyes quizzically. 'Is anything wrong?'

'No, not wrong at all. In fact, it's lovely. You remember I said I thought Joanna might be expecting again? Well, she is – the baby's due in September. They're thrilled about it, and so are the rest of the family.'

'Including you?' he asked quietly, knowing that the idea of another baby on the way might bring its own small pang to Val's heart.

'Including me. That's all over now, Luke. I'm just looking forward to the future – our future. That's really why I came to see you.' She brushed a few strands of brown hair from her eyes. 'We really do need to find somewhere to live, especially with another baby on the way.'

'It won't need a room of its own straight away, will it?' he asked. 'Or will they need your room for Robin? Has Joanna said anything to you about it?'

'No, of course not. And it'll be a while before they need my room – but they will, eventually. And babies need an awful lot of space for all their stuff. Joanna's still got a lot of Robin's things, of course, but there'll be other things – they'll have to get the cot down from the roof again and the pram and so on. It would be better all round if they had the space.' She looked up at him again. 'I wish we could get married soon. I feel as if we're just treading water at the moment.'

'I know.' He led her over to the fallen log he used as a garden bench, and they sat down, gazing over the rolling

69

meadows towards the sunset. 'But we can't until we find somewhere to live. This place is no good for two. It was only meant for a couple of men working in the woods. It's not much better than camping out.'

'I sometimes think I'd be happy to do that,' Val said moodily, and he laughed and squeezed her waist.

'So would I – you know that. But I don't think your parents would be too pleased about it. And I really don't want to start off on the wrong foot with them. What about that house on the estate that Hilary mentioned? Has anything happened about that?'

Val shook her head. 'The lease is due for renewal in May or June, but nothing's been said about them moving out. And there doesn't appear to be anywhere else. The trouble is, so many of the cottages around here are tied – you have to be working on the land to be allowed to rent them.'

'Oh well,' he said, 'I expect something will turn up.' He glanced down at her hand and played with her fingers. 'I saw an advertisement for a job today.'

'A job!' She turned and looked up into his face. 'A teacher's job, you mean?'

'Well, not exactly. It's a picture-framing business in Plymouth. They're just getting started again in new premises – they were bombed out during the war and have been working in an old garage until now. They're looking for experienced frame-makers.'

'But you're an artist, Luke!'

'I'm also quite good at making frames. I do all my own, after all.'

'I know you do. You're very good at it. But how could you paint if you were working full-time?'

'I could paint at weekends.'

'A weekend painter!' she said. 'That's no good. You need to be free to paint whenever you want to. All day. Or when you see something with just the right light on it. How many times have you dashed out at a moment's notice because the light's just right for some picture you want to paint? How could you do that if you were working in Plymouth? And when would we ever have time to spend together?' she added forlornly.

Luke gripped both her hands. 'That's the important thing, Val. Us being together. I don't care what I do so long as I've got you. At least I'd be working with pictures—'

'Other people's pictures!' she interposed bitterly.

'—and I'd have you to come home to. We'd be together. We'd be married and in our own home. *That*'s what's important to me. We've wasted enough time,' he added quietly. 'After Egypt – well, I thought I'd lost you for good. I didn't think we'd ever see each other again. And then, when I found you were living here, in this very village, it was as if all my dreams had come true. But even then, it was a long time before we'd sorted everything out.' He gripped her hands so tightly she squeaked. 'Sorry. I didn't mean to hurt you.' He stroked her fingers and kissed them, then went on with the same intensity in his voice, 'I don't want to wait any longer, Val, my darling. I want you to be my wife as soon as possible. And if it means working in Plymouth, and only painting at weekends, then so be it. That's what I want.'

Val was silent for a few moments. Then she said, 'But it isn't what *I* want, Luke. I don't think it would be enough for you, either, after a while. You're an *artist*. It's different from me being a nurse – I love it, but I could give it up without any problem. I don't think you could give up painting. It's like – well, it's like asking Dad to give up farming. Only today, he was talking about retiring and Tom said he'd never retire, he'd still be out in the yard, poking his nose in, when he was a hundred years old! And he was right. It's in his blood, just as painting is in your blood.'

'I know which I'd rather give up if it came to a choice between painting and you,' he said, and put his hand beneath her chin so that she was forced to meet his eyes. 'I mean it,

Val. As long as I can earn an honest living, doing something I'd be good at, and paint at least part of the time, being with you is the most important thing in my life. I've known what it's like *not* to be with you, you see. I don't want to go back to that.'

Their glances held for a long moment, and then she said, 'We're not going back to that, Luke. Whatever happens, we're never going back to that.' And she raised both hands to his head and drew him down to her, their lips meeting in a long kiss.

'We'll find somewhere to live,' she whispered. 'We'll find somewhere soon.'

Chapter Eight

Stella was in her classroom, tidying the Nature table, when Felix popped his head round the door a week or so after their outing to the cinema.

'Hello. You look busy.'

'Oh, there's always something to do. They love this corner and bring all kinds of things in. See, we've got some frogspawn from the village pond, and these horse-chestnut buds – stickybuds, the children call them – to watch breaking into leaf, and we're hoping to get some silkworms. Miss Kemp says she always does that, and the children are fascinated by them. They do actually make silk, you know – they wind it round themselves in their cocoons, and then the children can unwind it on to spools and use it for sewing! After the moths have emerged, of course.'

Felix came to stand beside her. 'Perhaps I ought to talk about that instead of what I'd planned. It's a lot easier to understand!' He had taken to calling in at the school on one or two days a month, to talk to the children. It was something the vicar did regularly, and he approved of his curate following his example. Felix had never had much to do with children, other than his older sister's two, but he enjoyed the talks and didn't mind where they led.

Often, they seemed to lead in directions where his own interests lay. At Christmas, the conversations had centred around the Star of Bethlehem, and he had told the children how some people believed that this was a comet, which would appear only very occasionally. This had led to an explanation of comets and what they were, and a description of Halley's comet, which his grandmother had seen in 1910.

'It comes round every seventy-six years,' he said, drawing a diagram on the blackboard of a comet orbiting the Earth. 'It was seen in 1066 just before the Battle of Hastings – we know this because it's shown on the Bayeux Tapestry.' He paused. 'Do you know what that is?'

'Miss Kemp told us about it the other day. Us drew pictures of it,' Micky Coker said, pointing a grubby finger at the gallery around the classroom walls. 'I done King Harold with the arrow sticking out of his eye, see, and Henry Bennetts did a picture of him burning the cakes.'

'But that wasn't Harold,' Felix said, diverted from comets for a moment. 'That was Alfred, and it was a long time before—'

'I knows that,' Micky said in a tone of contempt. 'Henry Bennetts is always getting mixed up between kings. But Miss Kemp said it was a good picture so she'd let him put it up just the same.' From the tone of his voice, it seemed that Micky didn't approve of this departure from accuracy and Felix decided not to pursue the matter.

'Well, anyway, a man called Edmund Halley worked out that this comet came round every seventy-six years, and—'

'And it was called Halley as well, just like him! That's a *coincidence*, that is.' This time, it was Brian Madge who interrupted. 'Miss Kemp told us about coincidences yesterday. It's when two—'

'Yes, that's right, but this wasn't a coincidence,' Felix said, wondering if they would ever get to the end of the story of Halley and his comet. 'They called this comet after Halley because he was the one who found it. He said it would come round again in 1758, and so it did, but unfortunately he died in 1742, so he never knew that his prediction came true. But it's always borne his name, and it's probably the most famous comet there has ever been.'

'Will it come round again?' Jenny Pettifer asked. She was one of the brightest children in the school and had been made head girl last year. After the summer, she and some of the other older children would be going to one of the senior schools in Tavistock. Jenny herself, along with Ernest Coker and Helen Nethercott, had passed the examination for the grammar school.

'Yes, it'll come round again in 1986,' Felix said, and the children drew in their breath. 'So you'll all be lucky enough to see it. How old will you be then?'

There was a babble of noise as the children all worked out their age in that far-off time. 'I'll be forty-five.' 'No, you won't, you'll be forty-four.' 'Forty-*five*. My birthday's in February. Yours ain't till July.' 'All right, then, I'll be forty-five, too. When's it coming?' Aggrieved eyes were turned upon Felix. 'Will it be coming before my birthday?' This caused further agitation as the rest of the children began to wonder if the comet would arrive before or after their own birthdays. Felix raised his hands and called out for quiet, and Miss Kemp, who had been sitting with Stella on chairs at the side of the room, added her voice to his.

'I'm not sure exactly which month the comet will arrive,' he said. 'But it won't just flash through the sky and be gone, all in one night. You'll be able to see it for several weeks.'

'Will you still be alive then, Mr Copley?' asked Shirley Culliford, looking up at him with big grey eyes. Shirley was one of a large family living in a run-down cottage at the end of the village. Her feckless father, Arthur Culliford, scraped a living doing odd jobs and spent as much of it as he could in the pub before his ineffectual wife could get her hands on it and use it for cigarettes or hairdos. As little as possible, it seemed, went on clothes for the children, and most of their food came either from poaching or from payments in kind – a dozen eggs for a morning's hedging, a jug of milk for helping out with the milking.

'I hope I'll still be alive,' Felix said, smiling at her. He had a soft spot for Shirley, who had been chosen as Festival Queen the year before and had unexpectedly blossomed through the honour. She always brushed her hair and washed her face now before coming to school and had started to do the same for her younger sister, Betty. Sometimes they even had quite clean handkerchiefs.

'You'll be ever so old, though,' Betty said doubtfully. 'You'll be nearly a hundred.'

'Well, not quite.' How old did they think he was now? Felix wondered. He glanced at Stella, who was smiling with amusement. 'Not much more than sixty, really.'

'Well, that's old,' Micky Coker said authoritatively. 'My grandad's sixty.'

'So's mine,' came a chorus. 'Mine's sixty-*two*.' They then began to compete with each other. 'Mine's sixty-five.' 'Mine's *seventy*.'

'Yes, well, that's all been very interesting,' Miss Kemp said, rising to her feet. 'I'm sure we'd all like to say a big thank-you to Mr Copley for coming in and telling us about comets and the Star of Bethlehem.' Having reminded them all of the actual purpose of his visit, she raised her hands again for quiet and added, 'We'd all like the curate to come and talk to us again, wouldn't we?' There was a chorus of agreement, and then the head teacher picked up the school bell and rang it to signify that lessons were at an end for the day.

Since then, Felix had found himself giving regular lessons in such subjects as astronomy and other branches of science, though always with an emphasis that it was God who had created these marvels as well as the other wonders of Nature that they could see about them every day. It didn't matter whether it was a star in the sky or a daisy in the field, he told them, they all belonged to God.

'So what are you planning to tell them today?' Stella asked now, as they stood beside the Nature table.

He grinned a little. 'Splitting the atom! A bit more complicated than silk. Although I'm not sure anyone knows exactly how the silkworms make it, so maybe it's not after all.'

'Splitting the atom?' exclaimed Miss Kemp, who had just come into the room. 'Don't you think that's a little advanced for the children? I'm not sure I understand it myself.'

'I'm not sure anyone does,' Felix said cheerfully. 'But doesn't that make it all the more important to help them think about it? It's their world, too, and they'll be the ones to take us even further into the future.'

'We saw something about it on Pathé Pictorial last week,' Stella said. 'I expect some of the children saw it, too, and they might have heard about Mr Churchill announcing that we'd got the atomic bomb a couple of weeks ago. It could be a good idea to see if they've got any questions about it – you know how confused they get if things aren't properly explained.'

'Well, if you think you can do it,' Miss Kemp said. 'I just hope you have better luck than I did over the differences between King Harold and King Alfred!'

Felix grinned, and they went into the large classroom. This time, the subject had been deemed too difficult for the younger children, so Stella kept her class in the smaller room, and while Felix described the principles behind nuclear fission, in the simplest terms he could think of, she let them draw pictures of dinosaurs. This was a perennially popular subject amongst all the children and would prevent any gloating by the older children about their lesson; she just hoped they wouldn't be jealous of the younger ones!

When the afternoon was over, Felix came in to wait for her while she tidied the classroom.

'They do enjoy their painting, don't they?' he observed as she emptied coloured water out of a batch of fishpaste jars and began to wipe the tables. Most of the pictures were too wet to pin on the wall, but Betty Culliford had done quite a good one of an ichthyosaur and another of a plesiosaur. Stella held them up.

'Betty's fascinated by the idea of a little girl only a year or two older than herself finding these fossils in the cliffs at Lyme Regis. In fact, I'm not at all sure that the idea of a *girl* making the discoveries doesn't enthrall her even more than the dinosaurs themselves. Betty suffers rather a lot of teasing by her brothers. She'd probably have been a suffragette if she'd been around during Mrs Pankhurst's time.'

Felix laughed. 'You'd better give them a lesson on women's rights and see what happens. She could be our first woman prime minister.'

'I think that should wait until she gets into Miss Kemp's class,' Stella said. 'I'm only supposed to teach them the three Rs, some Nature, a bit of simple history and geography, and how to say their prayers. Although that's more your department, really.' She gave him a mischievous glance. 'When you can spare time from your science lessons, that is!'

'I *always* teach them their prayers,' he said. 'And science is just a clever way of saying Nature. I'm trying to show them the wonders of the world and how we can use them for good, that's all.'

'And evil,' Stella said, thinking of the atomic bomb. 'I know it won the war for us, but it was horrible, what we did to the Japanese.'

'I know,' Felix agreed more seriously. 'I didn't go into details, of course – even the older children are a bit young for that – but I think they understand that killing on such a scale must be wrong. If the same principles could be used for peace. . . ' He folded his lips and nodded. 'And I'm sure they will be. That's what makes science so wonderful. It can always be used for good.'

Stella finished tidying the classroom and collected her coat from the tiny staffroom. Mrs Purdy had just arrived and was collecting her cleaning materials from the cupboard. She wrapped her crossover pinafore around her thin body, tied a scarf turban-wise round her straggling grey hair and stood for a moment leaning on her mop.

'I hear Jessie Friend's not so well. In bed with her chest again, so Dottie told me.'

'That's right,' Stella said. 'Jean sent Billy round this morning to ask if Dottie would go and see her. Dr Latimer was going in this afternoon, so Mrs Dawe told me when she came to do the dinners.'

Felix nodded. 'And Mr Harvey said he'd pop in as well, just to make sure they had everything they needed.' He smiled. 'The grapevine's been working overtime – expect everyone in the village knows by now.'

'Well, of course they do,' the cleaner said with a touch of indignation. 'Jean and Jessie Friend are important people here, apart from running the post office. Of course us is all interested.' She made a pass or two at the floor with her mop. 'I'll look in myself on my way home – knocked up a batch of scones this afternoon, may as well drop half a dozen in for them while they'm fresh.'

'They'll have more cakes and biscuits than they can eat,' Stella said to Felix as they walked along the lane. 'Dottie never goes to see anyone without a cake in her basket. I hope Jessie's not really ill, though. She's had bronchitis twice already this winter.'

The Friend sisters, who were vaguely related to Dottie in the way that many of the villagers were related to each other without knowing to quite what degree, were identical twins – tiny, birdlike women with halos of snow-white hair and twittering voices. Their younger brother, Billy, lived with them; he was a short, rather tubby man with a flat nose and small mouth. His eyes slanted upwards at the outer corners, and he had been slower than the other children at school, never going on to Tavistock and eventually leaving when he was thirteen. He worked for Bert Foster, the butcher, helping to carry sides of meat and make sausages, and he made deliveries with Bert's horse and cart.

'I hope Billy doesn't get it, too,' Stella said. 'He has a weak chest, you know, and he always takes longer to get over things, for all he likes to boast about how strong he is.'

'I know. People like him don't often live into old age. He's a very sweet-natured person – so are his sisters, of course, but Billy's special. All the villagers seem fond of him.' Felix walked in silence for a moment or two, then added, 'I'll slip into the post office and see how they are.'

'I'll come, too,' Stella said. 'I need some envelopes and stamps anyway. I want to write to Maddy tonight.'

The post office was next door to Aggie Madge's cottage. They went in together, to find Jean Friend behind the counter, working out the postage on a parcel Constance Bellamy was sending to her cousin in America. Her dachshund, Rupert, sat at her feet, taking up most of the floor in the tiny office.

'I suppose we'll be getting stamps with the Queen's head on soon,' Miss Bellamy said, looking at the small portraits of George the Sixth that the postmistress was sticking on to the brown paper. 'If it hadn't been so unexpected, they'd probably have had them ready, but with the King being still a young man . . .'

'I'd like you to come and tell the schoolchildren that,' Felix said, thinking of his talk about Halley's comet. 'They're not at all sure that many of us will survive until sixty!'

Constance snorted. 'I intend to live to at least ninety. Both my parents did, and I shall, too. We're a long-lived family.'

'I don't think I'd want to live that long,' Jean said doubtfully. 'Grandmother was ninety-two when she passed on, and the last few years were misery for her and everyone around her. She was bedridden by the time she was eighty-eight, and I know I shouldn't speak ill of the dead but it's the honest truth, she were a real trial. Poor Mother was up and down stairs all day long, looking after her – 'twas no wonder that her turn came so soon: she were worn out with it all.'

'I shan't be bedridden,' Constance said stoutly. 'Keep myself healthy with plenty of exercise. Don't I, Rupert?' she added, looking down at the dachshund who had stretched himself out to his full length on the floor and was snoring peacefully. She twitched his lead and he opened one eye and looked at her, as if wondering what she wanted him to do. 'Come on, you lazy creature. Get up.'

Rupert staggered reluctantly to his feet, not much taller standing up than when he was lying down, and Constance towed him out of the post office. Felix and Stella grinned at each other and then turned to the little woman behind the counter.

'We were wondering how your sister is,' Stella said. 'We were sorry to hear she's not well.'

'Oh, she's not too bad,' Jean Friend said in her soft voice. 'She caught a cold last week and it went straight to her chest. Doctor's given her some medicine and it's doing her good already.'

'Well, don't let her come back to work too soon,' Felix told her. 'Although I suppose you could do with her help. Is there anyone else who can help you?'

'Not really. You see, it's only Jessie and me who are allowed to do the post office work, and there's not much else apart from the bit of stationery and sweets and so on that we sell. If we were both ill, they'd send someone from Head Office, but I can manage on my own for a few days. And Billy helps with any carrying. He's a good boy.'

The good boy came in at that moment, a smile beaming all over his wide, flat face as he saw Felix and Stella. 'Hello, Mr Copley. Hello, Miss Simmons.' He was always scrupulously polite. 'I'm helping Jean in the shop.'

'So you are.' Felix smiled back at him. 'Could you weigh

me out some toffees, please, Billy? I've got my coupons here.'
He handed his ration book across the counter and Jean took it
and began to snip out the tiny squares.

'How many do you want, Mr Copley?'

'Oh, the whole week's worth, I think – a quarter of a
pound. Two ounces don't get me through an evening!'

They watched as Billy took the big jar down from the shelf,
unscrewed its lid and then carefully tilted it over the scales.
When enough toffees had dropped in to make the balance
equal, he screwed back the lid and returned the jar to the
shelf. Then he tipped the sweets on to a square of blue paper,
rolled it into a cone and tucked in the end. Finally, with a
beaming smile, he handed it over.

'Thank you very much, Billy.' Felix counted out six
pennies and put them on the counter. Stella produced her
book, too. Normally, both books would have been held by the
two landladies, Aggie and Dottie, but they were needed for
the purchase of sweets and, like small children spending their
pocket money, Stella and Felix were allowed to have them
back one afternoon a week.

'Are you having anything, Miss Simmons?' Miss Friend
enquired and Stella asked for a tube of Spangles. The brightly
striped packet was put into her hand, and she bought her
envelopes and stamps as well.

'Is there anything I can do for you and your sister?' Felix
asked. 'I expect the vicar's been in already, but if there's
anything you need from town, it would be no trouble for me
to slip into Tavistock.'

'Bless you, we've got all we need here in the village,' the
little postmistress said, smiling at him. ''Tis kind of you to
offer, though.'

'Well, just remember the offer's there if you think of
anything,' he told her, and they turned to go. As they reached
the door, it opened and Jed Fisher came in. He scowled at
them both and pushed past.

''Bout time you got yourself a bigger place than this, missus,' he said in a hectoring tone to Jean Friend. 'Not enough room to swing a cat. I wants ten Woodbine.'

Felix, already halfway through the door, stopped and turned back. His face was pale with anger. 'Excuse me, Mr Fisher, but do you really think that's the way to address Miss Friend? Couldn't you at least say please?'

The man stared at him. As usual, he looked scruffy and unkempt, his dark-grey hair greasy on his collarless shirt, and he smelled of old sweat and dirt. His jaw was black with stubble, and his fingernails rimmed with grime. He opened his mouth and Felix caught a whiff of onions and bad breath.

'What's it got to do with you?' Jed demanded belligerently. 'I ain't nothing to do with you. I be a chapel man.'

'And I'm sure the minister would want you to use a little common politeness just as much as I do,' Felix responded quietly. Miss Friend was looking nervous and Stella anxious. 'If you'll just apologise and ask for your cigarettes in a civilised manner, I'm sure she'll be willing to serve you.'

'Her'll serve me anyway. That's what her be here for.'

'She has no obligation—'

'Oh, shut yer mouth!' Jed broke in. 'I ain't got time to stand here all day argufying with pansies like you.' He turned back to the postmistress. 'Ten Woodbine, *please*, if that be good enough for you.'

He threw the money on the counter and the little woman handed him the green packet. He grabbed it without a word and thrust his way past Felix and Stella again, deliberately knocking Felix against the wall as he did so, and slammed the door behind him.

'Well!' Stella exclaimed, staring after him. 'What a horrible man! Are you all right, Miss Friend?'

'Bless you, my dear, I'm all right. I've known Jed Fisher since we were all youngsters together. I don't argue with him.

83

I just serve him and let him get out as quick as he can. That be the best way with folk like him.'

'Well, I don't think he ought to be allowed to get away with it,' Felix said, still annoyed. 'Didn't anyone teach him manners when he was a child?'

Jean Friend shrugged. 'I'm sure his mother and father tried their best. Good, God-fearing people, they were. And Jed himself wasn't a bad chap when he was a boy, just a bit wild, that's all. It was only when he got older . . . 'Twould have been better if he'd gone for a soldier, like some of the other lads in the village, perhaps, though maybe I shouldn't say that since some of 'em never came home again. But 'twould have taught him a bit of discipline.'

'Why didn't he go?' Stella enquired. 'Was he too young?'

'No, he was just the right age. Went along to the office in Tavistock, if I remember rightly, but they turned him down. Some sort of health problem, though I never heard what 'twas. Flat feet, my dad reckoned. Couldn't have been anything serious because look at him now, hale and hearty – or would be if he looked after himself proper and didn't smoke so much. There was a lot of feeling about it in the village, you know – folk whose own boys had had to go, and maybe got killed or wounded. They didn't like seeing Jed Fisher walking about free as air.'

At that moment, someone else came into the post office and Stella and Felix said goodbye and went outside. They stood for a moment in the street, both looking across at Jed Fisher's cottage and not sure what to do next.

'How about a short walk before going home?' Felix suggested, and they turned and strolled along the lane towards the ford. There had been quite a lot of rain recently and the Burra Brook was flowing briskly, almost covering the stepping-stones. They leaned over the little stone bridge and gazed down at the peaty water, foaming white as it broke over the rocks. Wild daffodils and primroses patterned the mossy banks with gold, and the trees that hung over the water were a silvery drift of soft, furry pussy willow.

'Spring,' Stella said dreamily. 'I think it's my favourite season. And this is my second spring in Burracombe – I can hardly believe I've been here over a year.'

'Do you think you'll stay a long time?' he asked. 'Or will you want to move on – to a bigger school, perhaps?'

'Oh no, I'm not even thinking about moving. Not yet, anyway.' Stella lifted her head and gazed about her. 'I don't think I'll ever want to leave Burracombe, anyway. It's so lovely, and I've made such good friends. And besides, there's Maddy. She lived here as a child. It makes it feel even more like my home.'

'I remember seeing your sister at the pageant last summer,' he remarked. 'She's very pretty, isn't she?' He reverted to their previous topic. 'Still, you might not want to remain an assistant teacher all your life. Don't you think you might want a more senior job – as a headmistress, for instance? You'd have to move away then – it'll be some time before Miss Kemp retires.'

'Listen,' Stella said firmly, 'I've only been here a year or so. This is my first post. I'm still settling in – I don't even want to think about moving on for ages yet.'

'And by that time,' he said, 'you'll probably have found some nice young man to marry you and you won't want to work at all.'

Stella blushed a little. 'Well, that's something we don't know, isn't it?' She gazed pensively down into the water again.

Felix watched her for a moment, then said, 'I thought for a while last year that you and Luke Ferris were very friendly.'

She looked up at once. 'That's all it was! Luke was a good friend – he still is. He helped me try to find Maddy. But it was always Val Tozer he was really fond of – they knew each other during the war, you know.'

'Yes, so I gather.' They were quiet for a minute or two, then he said, 'I really enjoyed our trip to the cinema last week.'

'Yes, so did I. It was lovely, and I enjoyed the drive as well.'

'Shall we do it again? There's quite a good film on this week – we could go on Thursday or Friday, if you like. What do you think?'

Stella turned and smiled up into his eyes. 'I'd like it very much. Friday would be best for me. Thank you.'

'And maybe,' he went on, 'during the Easter holidays, we could go out in Mirabelle for a day, over the moor. Take a picnic. Or will your sister be here then?'

'She'll be here over Easter itself, and for part of the holiday, but I don't know exactly how long for.'

'Well, when you know, we'll see if we can fit in a day to ourselves.' He grinned at her. 'Well away from Burracombe! The trouble with these small places is that everyone knows you, and in my job – yours, too, I suppose – you daren't do anything to cause gossip.'

'Are we likely to do anything to cause gossip?' Stella asked demurely, still gazing down into the stream, and he burst out laughing.

'I don't expect so, but you never know, do you! For one thing, I shan't be wearing my dog-collar – and in these parts, that's as bad as going naked.' He put his hand on her arm and turned her to face him again. 'Not that I'd do anything to embarrass you, Stella, ever,' he said more quietly. 'You can be quite sure of that.'

They stood very still for a moment, their eyes locked. Stella could feel her heart beating fast. Felix was very close. Her lips parted as she drew in a small breath and she saw his glance drop to her mouth.

The silence was broken by a flurry of footsteps and the calling of childish voices. As Felix and Stella moved abruptly apart, half a dozen children appeared round the corner of the lane, chattering like sparrows. They stopped as they saw the two figures on the bridge.

'Coo, look, it's Miss Simmons and Mr Copley. They'm holding hands!' The words were meant to be spoken in a whisper, but the voice of Henry Bennetts, who uttered them, was already beginning to break and they came out in a squeaky croak. The others shushed him, their faces scarlet, and Felix laughed.

'Hello, you lot,' he called cheerfully. 'We've just been playing Pooh sticks. Want to have a game with us?'

The children approached warily. Playing games with the teacher and the curate out of school-time was a new idea and not one they entirely approved of. Stella took pity on them.

'I'm afraid I've got to get back home,' she said briskly, moving away. 'I promised to help Dottie with a frock she's making for Val Tozer, and I've got some letters to write. We'll come out for a Nature walk one day, children, and play the game then, shall we?'

The natural order of things restored, the children looked more at ease and clattered on over the bridge, on their way to round up some cows for Ted Tozer. Stella and Felix looked at each other again.

'Well,' she said a little awkwardly, 'I really had better go. Dottie wants me to put the frock on so that she can make sure the hem's level. It's been nice to have a walk, though.'

'We'll do it again one day,' he said, looking as if he wanted to hold her hand again. 'And you won't forget we're going to the pictures on Friday, will you?'

'No,' Stella said, smiling at him. 'I won't forget.'

She walked along the lane, back to the village street. A robin trilled from a holly bush, and from a taller tree she could hear the liquid song of a blackbird. The wild daffodils and primroses looked even brighter now and the hedges greener. Even the sun seemed more golden as it dipped towards the horizon.

Spring, she thought. The best season of the year. A season of promise.

Chapter Nine

Hilary and Gilbert Napier were also feeling the promise of spring.

'You can let me take over some of the work now,' Gilbert said to his daughter at breakfast. 'I'm perfectly well again. There's no reason why I can't do as much as I ever did.'

'And have another heart attack,' Hilary answered, buttering her toast. 'You know what Charles Latimer said. It was working too hard that caused the first one. If you go back to your old ways, you risk another – and it could be worse.'

'Oh, fiddlesticks. It wasn't as bad as all that. I just got overtired, that's all—'

'Because you were doing too much and working yourself up over Stephen. You must take notice of what Charles says, Father. And I'm managing very well – I enjoy doing it.'

That had been the wrong thing to say. The big, heavy face took on a glowering look. 'So would I enjoy it. I always did enjoy managing the estate. Why take it away from me?'

He sounded like a petulant child, deprived of a toy, Hilary thought. And yet, he had reason to feel aggrieved. The estate was his, after all. It had been his life. And he really did look well – she had no doubt that he *felt* well. You just couldn't see the damaged heart, beating less strongly now.

'Nobody wants to take anything away from you, Dad,' she said more gently. 'We just don't want to risk losing you. And it's not all that long since your attack—'

'It's nearly a year! Whit Monday – that's nine months.'

'Charles wants you to take things easy for a little while longer. Maybe after Easter—'

'I know what it is,' he said suddenly. '*You* don't want to give it up. You've got your head now – you're in control, and you don't want to hand anything back.'

Hilary opened her mouth indignantly, then closed it again. Getting her father excited and upset, Charles Latimer had told her, was as bad as letting him overwork. She'd managed to avoid argument as much as possible until now. She clamped her lips firmly together and tried to think of a less provocative way of refuting his accusation.

'You see,' he said, watching her. 'You can't deny it. You know it's true.'

'I—' Hilary began, and caught herself up once more.

Before she could speak again, he said, 'We're too alike, you and I. Like to be in charge. That's why you did so well in the war, driving generals about. Felt you were in control.'

His fierce eyes met hers and she sighed. Perhaps he was right; perhaps she did like to be in charge of things.

'I don't think I'm trying to hang on to the estate, though, honestly,' she said, trying not to feel a twinge of doubt. 'I just don't want you overdoing things.' She hesitated, not wanting to say anything that would hurt him, then went on carefully, 'Suppose it were Baden who was taking over now, instead of me.' She saw him flinch and went on quickly, 'I'm not trying to upset you, Dad, but just think about it. Would you be so anxious to get back to work if he were in charge? Wouldn't you trust him to manage the estate properly?'

He scowled and she was afraid she had gone too far. All the same, she reminded herself, he had never been averse to bringing his dead son's name into the conversation when it suited him – when he was trying to compel Stephen to taking over, for instance. She saw him look away, out through the window towards the sunlight sloping across the lawn, and then he turned back to her.

'Of course I'd trust Baden if he were in your position now,' he said quietly. 'And he'd trust me, too. He'd discuss things with me – ask my advice, and take it. He wouldn't shut me out.'

Hilary stared at him. 'Is that what you think I've been doing, Dad? Shutting you out?'

'It's what you have been doing,' he answered, and rose to his feet to leave the room. '*You* think about it.'

He walked out, more slowly and heavily than he had done a year ago, but still upright, his big frame still powerful, and closed the door behind him. The dogs got up and padded across the room, but were too late to go through and sat down, facing the door, their thick tails like rudders behind them. One of them looked round, as if to ask to be let out after their master.

Hilary sat quite still, staring towards the garden. Beyond the trees at the far end of the lawn, she could see the rise of ground towards Dartmoor. A sheen of gold lay on the gorse, lit by the March sunlight. A cluster of ponies moved slowly across the grass, nibbling it to a fine sward.

Is he right? she wondered. Have I really shut him out? Only a few moments ago, she had likened him to a child whose toy had been taken away; now she saw herself suddenly as the bigger child, the bully who had snatched it. Surely that couldn't be true! She had acted in his best interests – setting aside her own plans to leave Burracombe to make a new life for herself, taking over the management of the estate so that her brother, Stephen, could follow his own career in the RAF, keeping the house and its lands in the family when her father was taken ill . . . Had it really been so selfish of her?

She got up, leaving her coffee unfinished, and opened the door. The dogs were through it immediately, their claws scrabbling on the wooden floor of the hall as they scuttled to find their master. The front door stood open, letting in the cool March air, and they raced outside and disappeared round the corner. Probably he'd gone round to the stables, Hilary thought. That was the first place he'd gone when he was allowed outside again after his heart attack, the place where he seemed to find most comfort. She half turned, meaning to follow him, then paused, aware that she was too shaken herself to be able to offer comfort to her father – not even sure she could offer reassurance. She needed time to come to terms with this unsettling view of herself.

Jackie Tozer came out of the kitchen carrying a tray to collect the breakfast things. She had been working at the Barton since leaving school, but Hilary thought she was capable of something better than domestic service and had been trying to persuade her to take training for some sort of career – cooking, or hotel work, perhaps. Jackie was a bright girl, and since her boyfriend, Roy Pettifer, had been called up for his National Service and sent to Korea, she'd seemed rather at a loose end.

'Is there anything wrong, Miss Napier?' Jackie asked, seeing Hilary hesitating in the doorway. 'I saw Mr Napier go by the window just now. He's all right, isn't he?'

'Yes, I think so.' Hilary came back into the hall, still feeling troubled. 'He's just fed up with not being able to do much.'

'I expect he is, poor man.' Jackie paused, the tray held against her hip. 'I remember when Dad had pleurisy one winter, he were like a bear with a sore head because he couldn't go out on the yard. It's worst when they're on the mend, you know,' she went on, sounding like her grandmother, Minnie. 'They start to feel a bit stronger and they just want to be *doing*. Especially when they've been used to being outside. It don't seem right to them to be stuck indoors all the time.'

'That's exactly right,' Hilary said, amused to find herself having this discussion with her eighteen-year-old housemaid. 'What did your mother do about it?'

'She got our Tom to sort it out. Doctor said Dad could go

out for a bit every day so long as he was wrapped up proper, and Tom asked him to help him out with a few jobs round the place – feeding the calves, things like that, mostly in the sheds and barns so he wasn't out in the cold in all weathers. He made out he couldn't manage without Dad, see. Mind you, I reckon Dad knew what he was up to, but he never said nothing, and he gradually stopped outside a bit longer until he were back working as usual. But it made him feel he could still be a bit of use while he couldn't do too much.'

'Yes, I see,' Hilary said thoughtfully. 'But I've already done that. There was all that work my father did for the pageant last year – sorting out those papers and photographs for the history display. That kept him busy for quite a while. And Dr Latimer absolutely forbade him to do any outside work during the winter. But now, with spring coming, he's getting restless, and I really don't want to ask too much of him.'

'I thought he was going to make a book of all them papers,' Jackie said. 'Lots of folk'd be interested in that.'

'Yes, he did talk about it.' But Hilary knew that even this wouldn't be enough to satisfy her father. It was the estate he wanted. It was control.

And I don't want to give it up, she thought as Jackie went into the breakfast room. I'm afraid that if I let him start doing even the smallest things, he'll gradually take over again, as Ted Tozer did with the farm. Except that the Tozers were happy with the situation – and Hilary wasn't. Ted and Tom worked well together, but she wasn't at all convinced that she and her father could.

I really am selfish, she thought miserably, going upstairs to get ready for the day's work. I'm like a dog in the manger, snapping at Dad whenever he tries to get too close. And I have the nerve to tell myself I'm trying to make things easier for him, when what I'm really doing is making them worse.

Yet if he took over the estate again, Hilary would be back where she started, running the house. Her one bid for

93

freedom, which she had been just about to make when he had his heart attack, had had to be abandoned. She could never make it again. She could never leave him now and risk causing another attack.

I've made this my career, she thought, staring from her bedroom window at the meadows and farmland that ran up to the moor. And I enjoy it. I want to go on doing it. But it's still Dad's property, and somehow I've got to learn to share it with him. We've both got to learn.

She moved to her dressing-table and looked at the photograph that stood in its frame beside the mirror. It was a family photograph, taken before her mother had died – the five of them together; her parents, her elder brother, Baden, herself and Stephen, the youngest. Even at that age, Baden looked like his father – the same strong build, the same thick mane of hair over strong brows, the same fierce, uncompromising stare.

I'm not like that, she thought. I'm not like Father at all. And yet . . . Maybe he was right. Maybe she did like to feel in control. But did that really mean she was stopping him from getting properly better?

The thought came as an unpleasant shock.

Dottie had finished Val Tozer's frock, and Val came to collect it one afternoon after she had finished her shift at Tavistock Hospital. She tried it on and admired herself in the long mirror that had been taken off an old wardrobe door. Dottie and Stella looked on approvingly.

'It looks proper handsome on you,' Dottie said with satisfaction. 'That green suits your colouring.'

'You're a good dressmaker, Dottie,' Val said, twisting round to examine the back view. 'I'd never get anything to fit as well as this in a shop.'

'Oh, shop clothes!' Dottie said scornfully. 'All the same, they be. You can tell in a minute where they come from, and

94

the quality's not there these days. Better off with a nice piece of fabric and a good Butterworth pattern.' She narrowed her eyes as she considered her workmanship. 'I'm still not happy about that back seam . . .'

'It's perfect, Dottie. I'm not letting you change a stitch.' Val began to take the dress off and Dottie laughed.

'Well, if you say so. Now, my flower, when be you going to let me make your wedding-dress? Set the date yet, have you?'

Val made a face as she pulled on her old skirt and jumper. 'We can't until we know where we're going to live, and there doesn't seem to be anywhere around here. Luke's talking about getting a job in Plymouth. Well, between ourselves, he's actually applied for one. He's waiting for an answer now.'

Dottie and Stella stared at her.

'In *Plymouth*?' Dottie said at last, as if it were somewhere on the moon. 'But do that mean you'd be leaving Burracombe?'

'Not unless we've got to. He could go on the bus. But if we can't find anywhere to live in the village . . . ' She shrugged.

'Oh, Val,' Dottie said in the same tone, 'do you think you'd really like that? All them streets – and no fields for miles and miles. And all them strangers everywhere.'

'I don't know why you're talking like that,' Val said with some amusement. 'You lived in London long enough.'

'Only because I had to, and we weren't in London all the time. Miss Forsyth took me on tour with her. Anyway, that was different. It were my job.'

'Well, being married to Luke will be my job,' Val said. 'I might even get work in the hospital – Freedom Fields, perhaps.'

Dottie shook her head dubiously. 'I thought the two of you were settled here. He always seemed so happy in the village.' She looked at Stella. 'When he used to come round here of an afternoon for tea, or go off with you for walks on a Sunday after a bit of dinner, I was sure he'd want to stay.'

Stella blushed and glanced sideways at Val, embarrassed by the reference to the time when she and Luke had spent a lot of time together. But Val was folding the new dress and laying it in her basket and didn't seem to have noticed. Stella felt a small pang of envy for the other girl. She'd obviously had sadness in her life – she'd lost her fiancé in the war and had grieved for him for years, so Dottie had said – but now she'd found happiness with Luke, and there was a serenity about her that Stella longed for in her own life. A certainty that as long as she was with Luke, nothing else mattered too much.

'When's Maddy coming again?' Val enquired.

'Easter. Not long now.' It still seemed strange to Stella that people in Burracombe knew her own sister better than she did. 'I can't wait to see her again.'

'They'm in Paris now,' Dottie said. 'Miss Forsyth spends a lot of time there. She's very popular in France – speaks the language like a native, and she's got a lovely voice. Sings like an angel, she do.'

'But is Maddy going to spend the rest of her life going about with her?' Val asked. 'Doesn't she want a career of her own? Although I suppose she'll be getting married before long. She must meet all kinds of interesting people, travelling about like that. I don't suppose she'll ever want to settle in Burracombe.'

'No,' Stella said, feeling suddenly miserable. 'I don't suppose she will.'

Dottie glanced at her sharply, and after Val had gone, she said, 'You don't want to worry too much about your sister, maid. I know she'm enjoying her life now, but she always seemed to me to be a little homebird at heart. I don't think her'll ever want to settle down abroad permanent.'

'But Val's right. She must meet all kinds of people. And she's so lovely to look at – there must be men falling in love with her all the time. I should hate to think that she'd stay abroad and hardly ever come back. I've missed her so much, all these years.'

'I know, flower,' Dottie said softly. 'But I still think her heart's here in Burracombe. And if it turns out different, well, there's nothing us can do about it. And you'd want her to be happy, wouldn't you?'

'Yes, of course I would. I'm being selfish, Dottie. It should be enough for me to know that she's alive and well and that she's been so happy all this time. And a lot of that is because of you!'

She hugged the plump little body and gave the round cheek a kiss. Dottie stayed still for a moment or two and then moved away. Her face was pink, and her voice shook a little as she said, 'Well, that's as may be. I only did what anyone would have done for the poor little mite. Now, let's get all this clutter out of the way and you can get on with your school work while I thinks about supper. I got a nice piece of lamb's liver from Bert Foster this morning – how do you fancy that with a bit of bacon and an onion and some mashed potatoes?'

'Lovely,' Stella said, starting to pick up scraps of coloured fabric from the rag rug in front of the fire. 'Oh, Dottie, look at Alfred! He's made a bed for himself out of your sewing.'

'Alfred!' Dottie exclaimed, picking the big cat up unceremoniously and dumping him on the floor. 'You bad cat! I shan't let you in again, if you don't behave. My stars, if you sits on Val Tozer's wedding-dress and leaves black hairs all over it, nobody'll never trust me again to make their clothes. And that'll mean no more fish-head suppers for you, my boy!'

Alfred sat on the rug, his fur tousled, blinking indignantly. Then he got up and stalked out of the room, his thick tail held erect and offence in every line of his body. The two women laughed.

'He's a star turn, that one,' Dottie said. 'Mind you, it's my fault, really. I ought to know what he'm like by this time. And he's been good company while I've been by meself. You can't beat an animal for company when you'm on your own.'

She went out to the kitchen, and Stella settled down with her preparations for the next day's lessons. She thought briefly of her sister, possibly marrying and living abroad, and of Val Tozer, ready to go anywhere with Luke, and wondered how she herself would end up.

Married, with a family of her own? Or alone, like Dottie, with just a cat or a dog for company?

Chapter Ten

'I think I've made an enemy of Jed Fisher,' Felix said ruefully. He was in the vestry with Basil Harvey slotting numbered cards into the hymn board for the next day's service. Normally, one of the churchwardens would have done this, but Ernie Crocker was busy on Ted Tozer's farm, and George Sweet had been kept busy baking for a wedding in Little Burracombe. 'He was so rude to poor little Miss Friend when I was in the post office the other day, and I couldn't help being sharp with him. This morning, when I met him in the village, I said good morning, but he just looked the other way.' He hesitated, then said, 'He *spat*.'

'At you?' Basil asked, but Felix shook his head.

'Not directly at me, no. He'd turned his head away by then. But it was meant for me, all the same.'

'He's an unpleasant person,' Basil said thoughtfully. 'And not one of our parishioners. All the same . . .'

'. . . it's not a good idea to have bad blood between us,' Felix finished. 'I know. I'm sorry.'

Basil sighed. 'It's not your fault. If it hadn't happened then, it would have done some other time. He sets out to create it, I'm afraid, and it's hard to resist. However determined you are not to fall into the traps he sets, a time will come when he's just too clever for you. He seems to take a perverse sort of pleasure in it.'

'So in the end, nobody likes him,' Felix said. 'Poor man.'

'I know. Even though it's by his own doing, it's still rather sad.' Basil finished sorting out the notes for his sermon and laid them on the rickety wooden table. He placed a large pebble on them to stop them blowing away in the draught that came through the open doorway. 'It's difficult to imagine what it must be like to be such a person – what it's like inside his head. And his heart.' He shook his own head, and the sunlight slanting through the narrow window gleamed on his halo of silver hair. 'Very lonely, I should think.'

'Does he get any help from the Chapel? Any comfort, I mean?' Felix went through to the church to hang up the board. He glanced around before coming back, taking his own comfort from the stone walls, the sturdy round pillars, the barrel-shaped roof. Lozenges of brilliant, jewel-coloured light lay flung on the stone-flagged floor from the east window, and the altarcloth glowed deep purple. He went back into the vestry. 'The minister must know him pretty well.'

'As well as anyone, I imagine. But I don't think Jed goes through the door very often. He looks after the graveyard – in a fashion.' Basil walked to the door and looked out at his own churchyard, immaculately kept by Jacob Prout. 'And he knows a good many Bible texts, learned in his childhood at Sunday school, I've no doubt. He's not above quoting them at you if it suits him. But I don't think religion figures very large in his life these days.'

'What about his family? Does he have any?'

'Not that I know of. He lived with his parents until they died some years ago. I don't think there were any brothers or sisters, and there don't seem to be any other Fishers hereabouts, or any other relatives at all.' He sighed. 'If there are, they don't have anything to do with Jed – and quite honestly, who could blame them?'

'And never married, I suppose.'

'I've never heard of a wife, but of course I've only been in the village twenty years or so. But don't take it too much to heart, Felix. There's someone like Jed in almost every community, and we can't win every heart and soul.'

'I certainly don't seem to have won this one!' Felix said wryly, and Basil slapped him on the shoulder.

'Think of those hearts you *have* won, Felix. The young schoolmistress's for a start, or so I've heard.'

Felix's fair skin flushed. 'I don't know about that. We've just been out a few times, that's all – to the cinema, or for a walk. Nothing more.'

'Well, perhaps not. But she's an attractive young woman, Felix – you need to keep your head. She also strikes me as being rather innocent, especially with her upbringing. And she *is* a parishioner.'

'It's all right,' Felix said soberly. 'I'm not going to do anything foolish. She's safe with me.'

'And are you safe with her?' Basil asked, and the young curate laughed.

'That's something we'll have to wait to find out! Honestly, Mr Harvey, you don't need to worry. We're friends, that's all. If it turns into something else, I'll let you know. But I won't do anything to cause gossip in the village.'

'I'm sure you won't. Just remember that in a village, you don't actually have to *do* anything at all to cause gossip. It causes itself! It's usually kindly gossip, and we don't need to worry about that, but in our position . . .'

'I know,' Felix said. 'My father's a vicar, and my grandfather's a bishop, so I've grown up with it. I'll be careful – but I've got to be allowed to have friends. Even girlfriends.'

'Of course you have,' Basil said as he looked round the vestry to see that everything was tidy. They went out into the churchyard together. Primroses clustered at the foot of the stone wall surrounding the graves, and the blue saucers of periwinkles brightened the tumble of green leaves that spilled over one corner. 'After all, you'll be wanting to marry one day, so of course you must be allowed to make friends. But it's not an easy path to tread.'

'A nice one, all the same,' Felix said with a grin, and they both laughed.

'I think,' Basil said to his wife at lunch, 'that I ought to make a few enquiries about Miss Tucker. She's written to me again, asking if I've made any progress, and I'm rather ashamed that I haven't tried harder.'

'You were going to ask Miss Bellamy if she knew anything,' Grace said, serving him a fillet of haddock. The fish van had been round that morning and half the village would be eating fish of some kind for their main meal. She spooned out some mashed potato as well and brightened the plate with a helping of broccoli and some sliced carrots.

Basil took some parsley sauce. 'Yes, I think that's a good place to start. She knows everyone for miles around, and she won't gossip. I think my enquiries should be discreet.'

'Certainly they should.' Grace served herself, and they began to eat. 'It's sad to think of someone so lonely that they have to search for relatives who may not even be here any more. She has sisters, doesn't she?'

'Half-sisters, yes. But there's still a need to find out about where her mother and father came from. A gap in her history. She seems to have grown up believing that Tucker was her father and that they were a Plymouth family, and suddenly she's found herself with a completely different background, and possibly relatives she's never known about. Relatives who would in all probability have known her mother. She might even find her real father.'

'Which might not be such a good thing,' Grace observed. 'But we've been through all this before, and it's not for us to judge. I think you're right, Basil – you ought to make some enquiries. Go and see Miss Bellamy this afternoon.'

Basil agreed, and set out as soon as they had finished lunch.

The clear skies of the morning had clouded over, and a spiteful wind had sprung up, rattling the still bare branches of the trees and cutting through the gateways of the fields. He walked past the village hall, the shop and Alf Coker's forge to Constance Bellamy's house opposite the school. The children were still in the playground, making the most of their freedom before afternoon lessons started, and they waved and called out to him.

'Be you coming to see us, Vicar?'

'Not today,' he answered, pausing by the fence. They clustered round, voices babbling eagerly as they vied to tell him their latest news.

'My cousin's got a new babby!' Henry said importantly, then added in less exultant tones, ''Tis only a girl, though.'

'What's the matter with girls?' demanded Brenda Pellow, who lived on a farm at Little Burracombe. 'Us had a new calf in the night and it's a heifer. My dad says heifers is much better than bull calves, and heifers is girls!'

'*Are* girls,' Basil murmured, and they stared at him blankly. 'Heifers *are* girls.'

'Well, I knows that,' Brenda said. 'That's just what I said.' The children looked at each other with resignation at the obtuseness of grown-ups, but before the discussion could continue, the headmistress came into the playground to ring the school bell and they ran to line up and file into school. Basil caught Miss Kemp's eye and she came over to him.

'Do you think we'll ever get them to understand the difference between *is* and *are*?' he asked. 'I know you try, but it never seems to sink in.'

'Oh, I think they do understand it,' she said. 'They just don't think it's worth bothering about. They hear their parents and other adults using the local dialect, and everyone seems to manage perfectly well, so why bother to change? And in some ways, I sympathise with them – after all, it is the old way of speaking. Remnants of an earlier language. Who are we to say it's wrong?' She gave him a mischievous look, then added, 'But don't let anyone else know I said that. It's far too radical for a head teacher!'

Basil smiled, and as she turned away to follow the children into the school, he crossed the road to the Grey House, where Constance Bellamy lived. It was larger than the cottages that stood near it, set back a little from the road and surrounded by a sprawling garden in which Constance spent a good deal of her time. As well as lawns, there were shrubs and a number of trees, and Basil was surprised at the colour that greeted him as he came through the gate. Several large camellia bushes were smothered with a variety of red, pink and white blooms, an early cherry tree was a froth of blushing-pink blossom, and the ground beneath the trees was covered with the nodding cup-like flowers of white and purple hellebores, while the grassy Devon banks were spattered with primroses. Even the lawns were a carpet of gold and white crocuses, with the chequered heads of fritillaries swaying above them in a mosaic of colour.

An old wooden wheelbarrow was standing on the path, half filled with twigs and dead stalks, and as he pushed open the gate Constance herself came round the corner of the house, wearing a baggy tweed skirt that sagged halfway to her ankles, muddy Wellingtons and a baggy brown jumper with threads pulled out. Her black-and-tan dachshund was following her and he stopped and barked when he saw Basil.

'Oh, hello, Basil. Quiet, Rupert!' She dumped another armful of foliage into the barrow and started to push it across to the far corner of the garden. 'I'll just get rid of this.' As she tipped the barrow up, the dachshund came over and sniffed Basil's shoes. 'Leave the vicar alone, you bad dog. You know him well enough. It's more out of duty than anything else,' she added, leaving the barrow upturned over the heap and brushing her hands together as she came back. 'Anyone who comes through the gate must have the statutory couple of barks. After that, he shuts up. Coming in for a cup of tea?'

'Well, I've only just had lunch,' he said, following her round the cottage to the back door. 'But I'd like to—'

'Lunch? Good heavens, is it that time already? I lose all sense of time when I'm out in the garden,' she added, pushing open the back door and leaning on the jamb while she trod on the heel of one boot and pulled it off. The second one dumped beside the first, she led the way through an untidy area, not much more than a corridor, with coats hung on one side and shelves along the other, laden with bags of dog biscuits, chicken feed, gardening tools and other paraphernalia. Two or three steps at the end led into another small hallway with doors to left and right, and Basil followed his hostess to the left, into a large kitchen with an Aga taking up much of one wall. Rupert pushed past his legs and flung himself down on an old rug.

'Trust a dog to pinch the best spot,' Constance remarked, leaning over him to slide a big kettle on to the hotplate, where it immediately began to sing. She took the lid off a fat brown teapot and peered in, then carried it over to a bin in the corner and tipped out the tea leaves. 'Find yourself somewhere to sit, Basil.'

The vicar looked around. There was a big table in the middle of the kitchen, with chairs around it, and a battered sofa at the end of the room, occupied by a large ginger cat, which had evidently been woken by their arrival and had raised its head and fixed the newcomer with a suspicious stare. Basil decided not to disturb it further – he had tried to stroke it once, and had to go to Charles Latimer afterwards with a badly swollen hand – and took one of the chairs at the table. Constance shifted a heap of papers with one hand and dumped a cup of tea in front of him with the other.

'I'll have a cheese sandwich in a minute,' she said. 'Do you know, a cheese sandwich with some watercress will give you all the nourishment you need. You could live on that. Better still with some Marmite,' she added.

Basil, who had loathed Marmite ever since he was a small boy and his older sister had encouraged him to spread it thickly on his toast in the belief that it was chocolate, shuddered slightly. He shook his head at the sugar bowl Constance proffered, but stirred his tea anyway. She sat opposite him and gave him a sharp look. The cat, evidently deciding that the vicar wasn't worth bothering about, put his head down again and went back to sleep.

'Well, what did you want to see me about? Not to talk about the weather or cheese sandwiches, I can tell. There's something on your mind.'

Once again, Basil marvelled at the old lady's perception. He'd hardly said a word, yet she knew that this wasn't purely a social call. He stared thoughtfully at his tea, trying to arrange his thoughts, then said, 'I need your help, Constance. Well, to be specific, I need your memory. You see, a young woman has come to see me recently – well, not *so* young, perhaps, in her mid-thirties—'

'*That*'s young!' Miss Bellamy interrupted. 'Anyone under fifty's young to me these days.'

'To me as well,' Basil said with a smile. 'Anyway, this young woman is searching for her family. For her parents, to be exact. She thinks they came from Burracombe.'

'She *thinks*? What happened to them, then? Were they killed in the war?' She thought for a minute. 'No, it couldn't be that, could it? If she's in her thirties now, she'd have been a young woman when the war broke out. Did they die when she was very young?'

'No. At least, her mother didn't – she died only a few months ago.' Basil recounted the story Jennifer Tucker had told him. 'So, you see, she doesn't really know for certain that it was Burracombe her mother came from, and she knows nothing at all about her father. He might have been a

Plymouth man, or come from anywhere in the country. He might not even have been English,' he added with sudden realisation.

'Didn't you say she had a letter? That was written in English, wasn't it?'

'Yes, although that doesn't mean he couldn't have been foreign.' Basil tried to remember the wording of the few phrases at the end of the letter. 'No, I don't think he was foreign. It *felt* English somehow. But he still needn't have been local.'

'She did think her mother had come from here, though?' Constance asked, and he nodded. 'So that's where we need to start looking. And she would have been born – when? Around the time of the Great War?'

'In 1917.' The vicar looked at her. 'Do you remember anything from that time? A young woman, unmarried but expecting a baby? Or leaving home on some pretext? There would surely have been some scandal.'

'There certainly would. It would have been the talk of the village. But I wasn't here then, Basil. I was a VAD nurse in Malta. By the time I came home after the war, everyone was too busy trying to get back on their feet again to worry about telling me old news. And no sooner was the Armistice signed than we had that 'flu epidemic. I went to help out in Plymouth. It took us a long time to settle down, and the world was never the same again. People were trying to look forward, not back – not that they had much to look forward to, what with the General Strike and the Depression and then another war coming.'

'No, I can see that,' he said thoughtfully. 'So you remember nothing that might help?'

'Sorry, I can't.' She sipped her tea, her weathered face, walnut-brown even in March, screwed up in concentration. 'There must be plenty of people here who would, though. Anyone over fifty would be the right age – probably know the girl well, might even know the man involved. You could ask anyone.'

'I was asked to make *discreet* enquiries,' Basil said mildly, and she laughed.

'Yes, see your point. Need to be careful who you approach or it'll be all over the village by teatime.'

'That's why I came to you first. Whom do you think I should ask next?'

She thought for a moment. 'What about Alice Tozer? She's the right age, and her mother might know even more. They won't spread gossip.'

'You're right. I need to go and see Ted soon about the Easter bellringing. Perhaps I'll ask them then, if the rest of the family aren't around. Not that I wouldn't trust them all just as much,' he added hastily, 'but somehow, once you start to talk about things like this, they seem to spread through the air, with no need of human assistance. I really don't want poor Miss Tucker to find herself a subject of general interest next time she comes to Burracombe.'

'And yet, if she does find anything out, she's bound to become one,' Constance pointed out. 'You can't have long-lost relatives turning up and people not notice. Look at young Maddy Forsyth and her sister. That caused plenty of excitement when they found each other.'

'Nice excitement, though,' he said. 'Everyone was so pleased for them, having known Maddy since she was a child and Stella being such a popular teacher.' He thought for a moment. 'I see what you mean, though. One of the village men suddenly discovering he has a daughter he knew nothing about might not be such a pleasant surprise.'

'If you ask me,' Constance said in her forthright voice, 'she'd be better off forgetting all about it. She might find out things she'd rather not know. Why did the mother have to go to Plymouth, for instance? Did the man refuse to stand by her? He might not be at all pleased by this. He might even refuse to acknowledge her. I don't see how this Miss Tucker can hope to prove anything, anyway.' She shook her head. 'No, I'm sorry, but I think some things are best forgotten. Let sleeping dogs lie.'

They both looked down at Rupert, stretched out on the rug, and Basil, who knew that the dachshund had an uncertain temper and could suddenly decide to nip unwary ankles, couldn't help agreeing. 'But I can't stop this young woman making her enquiries,' he said. 'And if she asks my help, I don't see how I can refuse it.'

'No, don't suppose you can. But you might put in the odd word – a little bit of guidance here and there. Anyway, I'm afraid I can't help you. I'll give it some thought, though,' she added as Basil put his cup back on the saucer. 'See if I can call anything to mind – any scrap of conversation when I came home, any young girls not being around the village, that sort of thing.' She furrowed her brow so that her wrinkled face looked as if it might crumple into pieces. 'But I can't say anything strikes me at the moment.'

'Oh well.' Basil stood up, one eye on the dachshund, the other on the cat. Both opened an eye at his movement and either could have been ready to spring. He edged towards the door. 'I'll try the Tozers. If anyone is likely to remember, I should think it would be them. But you know, I don't think the answer lies in Burracombe at all. I can find no mention of any Hannafords in the church records.'

'They might have been Chapel people,' Constance said thoughtfully. 'But if she came to you, that doesn't seem likely.'

'She was definitely brought up as Church of England.' He nodded. 'But it could have been in any of the villages hereabouts – Little Burracombe, or Meavy, perhaps, or Walkhampton. Or even the other side of Tavistock – Peter Tavy or Mary Tavy. It could have been anywhere.' He reached the door unmolested. 'Well, all I can do is try, and if I don't find anything, that'll be an end of it, as far as we're concerned. I don't mind telling you, Miss Bellamy, that would be a relief to me. I'm very much inclined to agree with you – some stones are best left unturned.'

Constance Bellamy saw him to the door and began to pull on her boots again. He looked at her.

'You never had your sandwich.'

'So I didn't,' she said. She turned her head to see the time on the clock that hung on the wall of the inner hallway. 'Bit late for it now. It'll be teatime before we know where we are, and I've got a few jobs I want to do outside before the sun goes down. At least the evenings are drawing out a bit now, and the clocks'll be going forward in a week or two.' She hauled on an old waistcoat that looked as if it had once belonged to a man. 'Not that it really makes any difference to the amount of daylight we get! It just means that people make better use of what we do have, for a while at any rate.'

Basil knew that Constance was up with the sun at any time of year. She worked like a beaver in her garden, though she kept a large part of it wild, to encourage birds, and could always be relied upon to find something for the church decorations. She had a vegetable patch, too, and was an enthusiastic member of the village Gardening Club – even though it had been started by her arch-enemy Joyce Warren. This year, they were to hold the Flower and Produce Show in June, when everything would be at its peak.

'Well, don't forget to eat entirely,' Basil said as he departed, and she gave a snort of laughter.

'Not much chance of that! Rupert and Tibby will remind me when it's suppertime. And then there's the hens as well.' As if on cue, three brown chickens came stepping round the side of the house. 'Got too many other mouths to feed to forget my own.' She picked up a pair of secateurs from the old wooden bench just outside the door and waved them at him. 'Nice to see you, Basil. And good luck with your search – I just hope turning over these old stones doesn't bring out too many worms.'

He smiled and waved to her from the gate, then set off back along the lane, his brow furrowed in thought. Constance was right – this investigation might not produce the results Jennifer Tucker wanted. But it was not for him to tell the young woman to abandon her search, and he knew from the wistful way in which she talked that if she didn't find out who her father was, the mystery would haunt her all her life. Perhaps it really was better to know, even if the knowledge itself brought more sadness.

All I can do, he thought as he waved to the children, out in the playground again, is help her in whatever way she asks, and be there in case she needs something more.

Chapter Eleven

Minnie Tozer was sitting in the garden by the kitchen door, cutting the purple heads off some stalks of sprouting broccoli while her daughter-in-law, Alice, planted out pea seedlings. She had been growing them in a cold frame in a corner of the kitchen garden, but the weather had turned so mild that she'd decided it was safe now to put them in the ground.

'I won't do the broad beans, though,' she observed as she knelt on the grassy path. 'You know what Ted's like, always puts them in himself on Good Friday. He says that be the proper day to plant them.'

'And so 'tis,' Minnie said. 'Just coming up to full moon, see? Plants always do better if you put them in near the full moon. It draws up the water – just like the tides.'

'Well, I think these little chaps will do all right,' Alice said, straightening up and dusting off the front of her skirt. She looked down at the row of seedlings and gave a little nod of satisfaction. ''Tis nice and sheltered here, and I've got they old cloches handy in case there's a frost. I'll just get the can and water them in.'

She fetched the galvanised watering-can and sprinkled water over the plants. She had already furnished them with twiggy sticks, gleaned from the hedge Jacob Prout had been cutting in the lane, and as she sat down next to Minnie both women looked forward to the day when the first peas would be harvested. 'A nice leg of lamb and some new potatoes and spring greens,' Minnie said. 'Go down a treat, that will. With some rhubarb and custard for afters.'

Alice laughed. 'You'll never stop enjoying your food, will you, Mother!'

'When you stop enjoying your food, you might as well go,' Minnie said. 'Not much else to live for, when you'm my age.'

'Don't talk so mazed! You've got years ahead of you yet, and there's plenty to look forward to. Joanna's new baby, our Val's wedding – though heaven knows when that'll be, at the rate they'm going. They've still not found anywhere to live.'

'Nor likely to,' Minnie observed. 'All the farm cottages for miles around be spoken for, and some of the ones that were took over in the war haven't been given back yet. And there's city folk still living in some of 'em – look at the Cherrimans, over in that estate house. Val said Hilary told her the lease would be coming up for renewal soon, but it seems as if they might want to stay on.'

'You'd think they'd want to go back to Plymouth, where they came from, wouldn't you?' Alice said.

'I don't see why,' Minnie argued. 'I mean, who in their senses'd want to go back to a city that was bombed to bits and still isn't properly rebuilt?' 'Tis like a bombsite still, Plymouth is – I wouldn't want to go back, not when I had a place like that estate house to live in.'

'It's not theirs, though, is it? That makes a difference. And their house in Plymouth's a lovely one, from what I've heard. Big place, down in Mannamead, with a good garden. It were took over for offices or summat for the Government during the war. But you'd think they'd have given it back by now, wouldn't you?'

'Maybe the Cherrimans don't want it back. They know when they'm well off – must be getting a good rent for it, and they can stop out here in the country. Still, it don't seem fair, not when there's proper country folk like our Val needing somewhere to settle down and raise a family. And didn't her say young Luke's thinking about getting a job in Plymouth? Us don't want them moving down there, Alice.'

'No,' Alice agreed. 'Us don't. But I don't know what us can do about it, Mother, I really don't.' She got to her feet. 'I'll put the kettle on for a cup of tea, then I'll get on with a bit more gardening before it turns cold. There's a heap of weeding wants doing in that front flowerbed; the seeds must have been waiting all winter, and now they'm sprouting up like I don't know what.'

She went indoors, and Minnie turned her face to the sun and closed her eyes. Whatever she might say about getting old, there was still plenty to enjoy in life apart from good food. The family, the life of the village, the sunshine and the song of the birds. Her mind drifted back to her younger days, when it had seemed impossible to believe that she would ever be an old woman. Queen Victoria had been on the throne then, and life had been slower. Wars were fought in far-off places such as Africa, and the village had been full of young people and families, none of whom ever ventured far. Even a trip to Plymouth was only undertaken by the more adventurous, and Minnie knew many people who lived out their entire lives without going any further than to Tavistock Goosey Fair.

It hadn't been all good, of course. There was plenty of poverty and families, like the Cullifords today, who filled their tumbledown cottages with children, many of whom died young. But most of the cottagers had enough garden to grow a few vegetables, as Alice was still doing today, and there were enough rabbits in the fields to be able to snare one for the pot now and then. Looking back, it seemed a good enough life, and Minnie felt thankful that she'd had her youth then, and not known of the terrible wars that were to come.

It would be a shame if Val and Luke were to be forced to move to Plymouth, away from the family and from the peace and good fresh air of the countryside.

*

As it happened, Hilary had gone out that very day to see the Cherrimans. The estate house was some distance away, and although you could reach it via several field paths and a pleasant walk through a beech wood, she drove round by the road in the Land Rover and went up the long, narrow track to park in the gravelled forecourt. She parked next to the smart, silver-grey Austin Somerset already standing there, stopped the engine and sat for a few moments, looking at the house her family had lived in during the war.

It was nearly as old as the Barton itself, and had been built originally to house the head forester. Over time, many of the trees had been felled and the head gamekeeper had been put there instead. At some point, the squire – probably Hilary's grandfather – had decided that the gamekeeper, being a single man at that time, didn't need so much space and had moved him to the smaller house known now as Keeper's Cottage, leaving this one free for someone he considered more deserving. A succession of farm managers, Napier relatives who needed housing and various other tenants had followed, and the house had somehow lost its 'tied' status, so that now it could be let to anyone, not just agricultural workers.

The Cherrimans had come at the end of the war. When Plymouth was suffering its Blitz and the Government was requisitioning houses for its offices, Arnold Cherriman, who had been Gilbert Napier's friend since their schooldays and had become an eye specialist, had moved out of the house in Mannamead, where he had his own surgery, and taken a house in Tavistock. After hostilities ceased, the owners had returned, and as his own house was still under Government control, he had had to find somewhere else to live. It was then that the Napiers were about to return to the Barton, which had been occupied by a children's home, and Gilbert had offered the estate house to the Cherrimans.

It was like a game of 'musical houses', Hilary thought. But it really was time that it came to an end, and she wondered why the Cherrimans had stayed so long, and whether, when the lease ran out, they would be wanting to go back to Plymouth. It would certainly be the answer to Val and Luke's problems if they did.

Arnold Cherriman was waiting for her at the front door. He was a tall, broad-shouldered man with black hair combed smoothly back from his high forehead and dark, rather intimidating eyebrows. Hilary climbed down from the Land Rover and walked across the gravel to greet him. The front of the house had trellis fixed to its walls, which she knew would be covered in pink roses during the summer. Evelyn Cherriman was a keen gardener and had worked hard in the patch of ground surrounding the house, turning it from a practical vegetable patch to a blaze of colour. There were still vegetables and soft fruits hidden away behind the house, but flowering shrubs were Evelyn's joy, and here at the edge of the woods she had created a small arboretum of camellias, azaleas and even one or two magnolias. The camellias were already covered with glowing pink and scarlet blooms, their petals unfurling like roses.

She isn't going to want to leave this, Hilary thought with a sinking heart. She's put too much of herself into it.

Arnold reached out to shake her hand. 'Good afternoon, Hilary. Nice to see you. Father not with you?'

'No, he generally rests in the afternoon.' Hilary didn't tell him that she hadn't actually mentioned this visit to her father, knowing that he would immediately take over the discussion and she would be left to make pleasant but fruitless conversation with Evelyn Cherriman. Moreover, if the Cherrimans wanted to renew the lease, her father would agree at once and Val's hopes would be dashed.

She pushed away the guilt that she couldn't help feeling, and followed Arnold Cherriman indoors, aware that he was probably disinclined to talk business with her, but determined to do so anyway. She had grown accustomed to being greeted with suspicion, but she'd found that it could usually be dispelled by a firm manner and obvious knowledge of estate business. The tenant farmers all knew her, anyway, and although some of them seemed to find it difficult to accept that she was now a grown woman and in charge, they were slowly coming round to the idea.

Arnold Cherriman wasn't a tenant farmer, though. He was an educated man, accustomed to doing business with other men, and almost certainly believed that a woman's place was in the home.

Evelyn Cherriman came out of the sitting-room. She was a slender woman with brown hair drawn back from her face and rolled loosely on her neck. She had rather pale blue eyes behind glasses with tortoiseshell rims and a soft, almost whispering voice.

'Hilary, how nice to see you. I've made tea.' Hilary followed her into the room, which looked out to the front of the house. A fire burned in the grate, with a sofa and two armchairs drawn up around it, and a low table was laid with a china teapot and a plate of buttered scones. Arnold Cherriman took one of the armchairs by the fire, and Hilary and her hostess sat on the sofa.

'How do you like your tea?'

'Milk and no sugar, thank you.' Saccharin tablets were offered as well, but Hilary shook her head. 'I've always preferred it unsweetened.' She accepted a scone, wondering how to introduce the subject of the lease. The Cherrimans must know why she was here, but they seemed to be determined to treat it as a social visit. 'You've made this room very comfortable,' she said, looking round at the newly papered walls and the pretty curtains.

'Oh, we're very happy here,' Evelyn said at once. 'It's a delightful little house.'

Hilary seized on the word. 'It is, isn't it? But it must seem rather small after your house in Plymouth. I remember coming to see you there before the war – it seemed almost as big as the Barton.'

Arnold laughed a little patronisingly. 'Not quite up to that standard, I'm afraid. But yes, it's a good size. Room for me to have my surgery and offices there.'

'But you do still have your practice in Plymouth, don't you?'

'Certainly. It was a little inconvenient when we had to live in Tavistock, but there was no scope there so I had to keep it on. And of course the Eye Infirmary is in Plymouth, too. I used to go in by train.' He looked proudly out of the window, where his highly polished Austin stood beside Hilary's rather muddy Land Rover. 'Don't need to do that now. I can be in Plymouth within half an hour.'

Hilary turned to his wife. 'Don't you find it rather lonely out here, though, Mrs Cherriman? Especially if you have no transport of your own.'

Evelyn's hands fluttered a little and she glanced quickly at her husband, then away again. 'I have my garden—'

'Yes, you've done wonderfully with that. It was nothing much at all while we were here, though Mother did grow quite a lot of vegetables. Your camellias are a picture.'

'Well, the larger ones were here before we came,' Evelyn admitted. 'But I did put in some more. I love flowering shrubs, don't you?'

Hilary nodded. 'We're lucky to have the right soil for things like camellias and azaleas. I expect you had a nice garden in Plymouth, too, didn't you?'

Evelyn looked wistful. 'It was lovely. I spent a lot of my time there. I had a gardener, too, of course, and a boy who came in to help with the heavy work, but I did all the design and a lot of the planting. I often wonder . . .' Her voice trailed away, and Hilary spoke quickly, seeing that Arnold was beginning to look impatient and afraid that he was about to change the subject.

'Have you seen it since the war? Do you know how it's being looked after?'

'I don't suppose it's being looked after at all,' Evelyn said sadly. 'It's still Government offices, you know.' Her voice brightening a little, she looked at her husband and said, 'But there's a chance we may be able to move back soon, isn't there?' She turned back to Hilary. 'Arnold had a letter only the other day – they'll be moving out sometime this year and we can have the house back. I'll be able to see it then. It'll need a lot of work, I know, but . . .' She was clearly looking forward to it and Hilary's spirits rose.

Arnold Cherriman, however, was not looking so pleased. 'I'm afraid Evelyn's jumping the gun a little,' he said to Hilary, and frowned at his wife. 'I've already told you, my dear, it won't be as easy as that. We have no idea what condition the house is in – it's been used as offices for years now, it'll be quite unfit to live in. It'll need complete renovation before we can even think of moving back. And I'm not at all sure that I want to. It might be better to sell.'

'*Sell?*' Evelyn repeated faintly, and Hilary realised that this was the first she had heard of it. 'But Arnold—'

He shook his head at her, the black brows drawn heavily over his eyes, and lifted one hand, palm outwards, so that she fell silent. Hilary waited, biting her lip, her heart sinking. At last, having apparently considered his words carefully, he turned to her and spoke again, making it very clear that not only was his wife not included in the discussion but he would have preferred it if Hilary hadn't been either.

'I've been thinking this over very carefully, and of course I'll need to talk to your father as soon as I come to a decision. But you might be kind enough to tell him, my dear, that we shall almost certainly be renewing the lease on this house. Obviously, we shall be looking to move back to the city at some point, but whether we renovate the old house and go back there or look for somewhere different has yet to be decided. I've been thinking of building something new, and that would take some time. There's position to be considered, architects and so on – I needn't trouble you with all that now, but you'll realise that it can't be done in a moment.' He paused, ignoring his wife, who was clearly completely taken aback by all this, and suddenly produced a charming smile. 'But you don't want to be worrying your head over all this. You didn't come to talk about such tedious subjects as leases, I'm sure. Have another of these delicious scones, my dear – Evelyn, pour Hilary some more tea – and then you must look at the garden. It's my wife's pride and joy and there's a surprising amount of colour, even at this time of year. It's going to be a big wrench for her to leave it when we eventually do go, I know.'

Dazed and feeling as if she'd been neatly manoeuvred into a corner, Hilary took the scone he offered and gave her hostess a sympathetic smile as she poured the tea. After a few more moments, and before she had time to gather her thoughts, Arnold Cherriman rose to his feet and declared that he must be off.

'One or two patients to see. The working man's job is never done!' He waggled his palm to show that she shouldn't get up, and leaned down to shake her hand. 'Very pleasant to see you again, Hilary. Give my regards to your father and tell him I'll be glad to see him at any time. We can discuss things more fully then. Evelyn, don't forget to show Hilary that new magnolia you planted last year, and remember we've got the chairman of the Rotary Club coming to dinner on Wednesday.' He dropped a kiss on his wife's hair and was at the door before either of the women could speak. 'Goodbye, then.'

Hilary drew in a deep breath. She stole a look at the other woman and saw that she was looking distressed and embarrassed. It wouldn't be fair to say anything more, Hilary thought, even though she was screaming inside and wanted nothing more than to pick up the pretty china teapot and throw it at the door her host had gone through. Her host? He was her *tenant*, for heaven's sake! It was for her to say whether or not he could take on the lease of the house again, yet somehow he'd ridden roughshod over her, treating her as if she were the supplicant. While making it perfectly clear that he didn't consider her an appropriate person to negotiate, he would have no hesitation in telling her father that she'd agreed to their staying on. He'd patronised her, talked over her and outmanoeuvred her, and she was furious.

There was no use in taking it out on his wife, however, and Hilary had heard enough to know that Evelyn wanted nothing more than to return to her own home and garden. She could be an ally, even if not a very strong one. At any rate, she was the only one Hilary had at the moment.

She finished the scone and drained her cup, grateful for the soothing heat of the tea. Then she wiped her lips with the dainty lawn napkin she had been given, and said, 'Let's go and look at the garden, Mrs Cherriman. You can tell me about the one you had in Plymouth as well. Perhaps I could take you to have a look at it sometime. I'm sure the people there wouldn't mind.'

Evelyn gazed at her. Her eyes were suddenly moist and Hilary felt guilty again, at using this pleasant, rather mousy little woman for her own ends. But not entirely mine, she thought. Mrs Cherriman really did want to go back. If Hilary could help her to do that, while at the same time securing this house for Val and Luke, who could possibly object?

Apart from Arnold Cherriman, that is.

Chapter Twelve

'He more or less told me to go away and play with my dolls,' Hilary told Val indignantly as they sat in the Barton kitchen with a bottle of sherry between them. 'He practically said I wasn't to worry my pretty little head about it! Honestly, I could have thrown the teapot at him. I would have done, if it had been my own old brown one instead of Evelyn Cherriman's rather nice Wedgwood bone china.'

Val smiled, but her smile faded quickly and she sighed. 'Oh well, thanks for trying anyway, Hil. It looks as if we'll just have to start thinking about Plymouth.'

'I hate the thought of you going to live in Plymouth,' Hilary said morosely. 'Especially when we've got that dear little house that would be just right for you and Luke. And the thing is, I know Mrs Cherriman would like to move back to Plymouth. She's longing to get back to her own garden.'

'I thought you said she'd done a lot with this garden, though,' Val said doubtfully. 'Are you sure she'd want to leave it?'

'I'm sure she'd be quite sorry to leave it, but she'll be more pleased to have her own garden again. And I think she misses being in the town – she's not really a country person. She must be awfully lonely out here. There's not another house within half a mile. Have a drop more of this.' She poured some more sherry into Val's glass.

'Maybe she'll be able to persuade her husband to move back, then.'

'I don't think so,' Hilary said grimly. 'Arnold Cherriman doesn't strike me as the sort of person who could be persuaded to do anything.'

The two women sat in silence for a few moments, then Val said with an obvious determination to look on the bright side, 'Still, you did say he's talking of looking for somewhere else to live. Or even building a new house.'

'And how long will that take? You know what it's like in Plymouth now. All that rebuilding – the entire city centre was flattened during the war, and they're only just getting to grips with it now. They need shops, new streets and thousands of houses. Every builder in Plymouth will be employed for years to come – getting a house built of the sort Arnold Cherriman would want is going to be almost impossible.' Hilary drew in a breath of exasperation. 'I don't know why he can't be satisfied with the house he's got! It wouldn't take nearly as long to renovate it. Using it as offices can't have done it that much damage.'

'Well, we can't force him to go back if he doesn't want to,' Val said. 'Unless you refuse to renew the lease. And you can't really do that, can you, since he and your father are friends.'

'It would give Dad another heart attack,' Hilary agreed. 'But it makes me so cross, Val. *I'm* running the estate now, yet men like Arnold Cherriman just don't seem to believe I'm capable of it. You should have seen the way he looked at me, and heard his voice! I might have been three years old.' She thumped the bottle on the table, gripping its neck so tightly that her knuckles turned white.

'Well, don't strangle the poor thing,' Val remarked mildly. 'It's not Mr Cherriman's neck you've got there. Honestly, Hilary, you don't need to get so worked up – it's not the end of the world. Something will turn up, and even if it doesn't and we have to go to Plymouth, I dare say we'll still be able to mount the odd expedition back to Burracombe.'

Hilary stared at her, then relaxed. She grinned reluctantly and let go of the bottle.

'Sorry. I just get so fed up with it. And you're right, it doesn't really matter. It's finding you somewhere to live that's important, not how pompous old fools like Arnold Cherriman treat me.'

'The rest of the tenants accept you, don't they?' Val asked. 'And the other people you have to deal with?'

'Most of them, I suppose. A lot of them still think I'm only *helping* Father – that I report everything back to him and take his advice, like a messenger, and that when he's better we'll go back to the way things were before.' Hilary sighed and looked down at the table, tracing a pattern with her forefinger on the wood. 'Sometimes I think Dad thinks that, too. And maybe he's right. Maybe I *am* just a temporary substitute.'

'Of course you're not!' Val reached across to touch her friend's hand. 'Surely that's all been agreed. He knows he can't ever do all the things he used to do. He knows you're perfectly capable of running things.'

'He also knows that *he's* capable of running quite a lot,' Hilary said. 'I know I'm being selfish – trying to take it all over for myself. But I'm so afraid that if I let him start to take control again, I'll be back here in the kitchen—' she waved her hand '—and my one chance to make something of my life will be gone for ever.' She thought for a moment. 'Well, not for ever. Just until he has another heart attack and kills himself. And I don't want that to happen, Val.'

'Of course you don't.' Val regarded her friend with sympathy. Her own problems seemed small when set beside Hilary's. She had Luke, and although they had nowhere to live just yet and didn't know whether their future lay in Burracombe or Plymouth – or somewhere else entirely – she did at least know they had a future together. Hilary's life, centred round her father and the estate, seemed bleak in comparison. It's a shame she lost her fiancé in the war, Val thought. And a shame she's never found anyone else to love.

'Stop worrying about Luke and me,' she said. 'You've got enough on your plate without trying to find a home for us. We'll find somewhere eventually. And if all else fails, I *will* go and live with him in the charcoal-burner's cottage. It's not that bad.'

Hilary laughed, although her laughter sounded a little wobbly. 'I suppose you could always build on another room or two.' She looked at the sherry bottle. 'I'd better not have any more of this. I've got to have a clear head in the morning – the accountant's coming and we're going to go over last year's figures. It's coming up to the end of the tax year, and I need to get everything right or I'll have yet another man telling me not to worry my pretty little head over it!'

'I've got to go, too.' Val stood up and then reached over and patted Hilary's shoulder. 'Don't let them get you down, Hil. You're proving you can do it. They wouldn't be getting so worried otherwise. That's what all this is about, you know – they're scared women are going to take over the world. We showed them during the war that we could do all their jobs just as well as they could and they're terrified!'

'Arnold Cherriman didn't look very terrified,' Hilary said ruefully. 'He wound me right round his little finger. And I'll tell you something else, Val – he's a bully. That poor little wife of his is scared stiff of him.'

'Well, that's a shame, but there's nothing much we can do about it.' Val pulled on her green tweed jacket. 'Just don't let him bully you.'

She grinned at Hilary and let herself out of the back door. The evening was drawing in now, the sun gone and dusk creeping over the meadows like a soft brown fuzz. From the hedges came a busy twittering as the birds settled down for the night, and she heard the first soft hoot of an owl. Val walked down the drive and along the lane to the track leading to the farm and paused for a moment, her hand on the gate, looking up into the velvet sky.

I really don't want to leave here, she thought. I was away long enough during the war to learn to appreciate all that we have in Burracombe, and I want to make it my home for ever. But if Luke and I can't find anywhere to live, we'll have to leave.

She had lost Luke once, years ago. She didn't intend to lose him again.

Basil was already in the kitchen of the Tozers' farm when Val arrived home. He'd come round after supper, knowing that Ted would be there and the family settling down for the evening. Alice and Joanna were just clearing away the dishes when he knocked on the back door, and Jackie let him in.

'Jackie, how nice to see you, my dear. How are you these days? And how's that boyfriend of yours? Any news of him coming home from Korea yet?'

Jackie blushed and shook her head. 'Doesn't seem like it, Mr Harvey. But he's not really my boyfriend, you know. We stopped being serious when – well, before he went away. I just write to him as a friend now, that's all.'

'Ah, I see. Very sensible.' He wiped his feet on the doormat and came into the kitchen, pulling off his woolly gloves. They were the ones that Minnie had knitted him as a Christmas present and he'd been careful to wear them this evening, just as he always tried to wear the various gloves, mittens and scarves his parishioners had given him whenever he visited their houses. Sometimes he got it wrong and had to endure quizzical glances and queries as to whether the gifts had fitted or been the wrong colour (not very likely, since they were invariably black, dark blue or grey), but on the whole he thought the donors were satisfied that their gifts were appreciated. He looked around the big kitchen and thought for the hundredth time how warm and cosy it seemed.

'I hope it's not inconvenient, my calling round now,' he said apologetically. 'You weren't planning to listen to anything on the radio, were you? I looked in the *Radio Times* to make sure *Take It From Here* or *PC 49* weren't on.'

Alice laughed. 'Bless you, Vicar, 'twouldn't matter if they were. Us have always got time for our friends. Now, I dare say you wants to talk to Ted about Easter bellringing, is that it? I'll give him a call. He's just popped outside for a minute.' She indicated the wheel-back chair by the range. 'Sit you down, flower.'

Basil sat down opposite Minnie. Joanna had taken Robin upstairs to put him to bed, and Jackie had disappeared as well. Tom was evidently out in the barn; probably he and Ted were busy with lambing. Basil half turned, meaning to tell Alice not to bother her husband now, he would come back later, but she had already gone.

''Tis all right,' Minnie said comfortably. 'Ted won't mind coming back in. He's owed a rest, anyway, been travelling ever since six o'clock milking this morning, he has, and only sat down for his meals. Tom can look after things outside for a bit.'

Basil knew that 'travelling' simply meant that Ted had been busy, not that he'd been away from the farm. The first time he'd heard this expression, he'd enquired innocently where the person had been, expecting to be told Plymouth, Exeter or even London, only to be met with a blank stare. It had been his first introduction to the local dialect, and he sometimes felt he was still learning.

'And how be you, Vicar?' Minnie asked. She was busy knitting something in fine, white wool, and Basil wondered if Joanna was expecting another baby. Nothing had been said officially yet, but he'd heard one or two speculative murmurs around the village, and young Tom had had an air of suppressed pride and excitement about him lately. Minnie's knitting seemed to confirm it, and when she caught him looking, she smiled and said, 'That's right, Vicar. Us got another little one on the way. 'Tisn't common knowledge yet, but I dare say there's a few keeping watch on our Joanna's shape. You can't keep news like that secret for long in Burracombe.'

·'You can't keep anything secret for long in Burracombe,' Basil said, thinking of Jennifer Tucker. Surely if her parents really had come from this village, someone would know. Minnie herself was one of the most likely ones – she would have been almost fifty in 1917 and would surely have been aware of any scandal. Alice herself would have been about seventeen or eighteen, and Ted only a few years older. But Ted had been away during the First World War, in the Army, and might have missed any goings-on in the village.

Basil realised that his thoughts had led him away from the kitchen and from Minnie and her news. Belatedly, he congratulated her on being about to become a great-grandmother again. 'I expect they'd like a girl this time.'

'I don't think they'll mind, so long as it's healthy,' Minnie replied. 'Mind you, most folk like to have their pigeon pair. Then it don't matter so much what the next one is, though I thinks meself that two of each is the best family. Everyone gets a brother and a sister that way.'

'Goodness me, you *are* in a hurry!' Basil said, laughing. 'This is only Joanna and Tom's second – it'll be quite a while before they think about a third and fourth.'

Minnie wagged one of her knitting-needles at him. 'That's for the Good Lord to decide,' she said severely. 'If He wants our Tom and Joanna to have a big quiverful, then that's what they'll have. Still, maybe we'm looking ahead a bit there. We've got to get our Val settled next. She don't have too much time ahead of her for starting a family.'

The door opened before they could say any more, and Ted and Alice came in, bringing a gust of March night air with them. Since dusk, the warmth that the sun had brought had disappeared and a thin, cold wind had sprung up. Ted closed the door quickly, and shucked off his boots on the mat.

'Evening, Vicar. Turning cold out there again.'

'It is, Ted. You're busy, I dare say. Everything going well?'

'Mustn't grumble.' Ted came over to the range, rubbing his hands and holding them out to the glowing fire. 'Got a few twin lambs coming along. Lost a couple last night, but that's always the way of it. What can I do for you, now? Easter bellringing, is it?'

'That's right.' Basil glanced up at the ceiling. It was criss-crossed with dark oak beams, and from each one hung a row of handbells, their leather straps as highly polished as a pair of undertaker's shoes and their metal gleaming. 'I was wondering if we might bring these little fellows into the service this year, for a change. I often think they're not used enough, except at Christmas.'

Ted looked up, too. The handbells had come down through his family and he'd collected more over the years. Nearly every church had their own set, some well used and others packed away in their cases and hardly ever touched, and occasionally a privately owned set was sold by a family who had no use for them. Ted's father had been an enthusiastic handbell-ringer, making up his own changes for them to ring, and Minnie had arranged the notation for several carols. During the war, when the church bells couldn't be rung, Ted had kept interest going by having a handbell practice one evening a week.

''Twould be nice to use 'em a bit more,' he admitted. 'It seems fitting at Christmas, somehow, but I don't see why us couldn't do summat with 'em the rest of the year. What was it you were thinking of, Vicar?'

'Well, not Christmas carols, of course. Do you have any other music?' He glanced at Minnie, who had laid down her knitting and was looking interested. 'I know you're a talented musician, Mrs Tozer – could you do some arrangements for us?'

'My stars, Vicar, that be laying it on a bit thick,' Minnie exclaimed, laughing. ''Tis a few years since I put me hand to anything like that. Isn't there no one else could do it?'

'I really don't think there is. You're the one who understands the bells, you see. And you used to play the church organ, so I know you're a musician – why, you still play that harmonium you've got in your parlour, don't you?'

'Yes, she does,' Alice said quickly, before Minnie could deny it. 'We often has a bit of a sing-song of a Sunday evening – starts off with a few hymns, of course, and then goes on to some of the old tunes – and Mother plays as well as ever. There are all sorts of tunes we could play on the bells, if she did the notes for us.' She looked at her mother-in-law. 'What about "All On the April Evening"? That's a lovely tune, and just right for Easter.'

'Well, I might be able to do it,' Minnie said, her sparkling eyes belying any reluctance in her voice. ''Twould be nice to hear it on the bells, I can't say it wouldn't.' She nodded her head. 'I'll think about it.'

'That's very good of you, Mrs Tozer,' Basil said warmly, knowing that this was virtually a 'yes'. 'And perhaps one or two hymns. I thought "All Things Bright and Beautiful" might be appropriate, and perhaps "Jesus Lives!" But I'll leave it to you to decide what would sound best on handbells.' He turned back to Ted. 'The band's ready for the normal ringing, I expect? Early, for eight o'clock Communion, and then again for matins? And there'll be no ringing during Holy Week, of course.'

'No, Palm Sunday'll be the last time the bells is heard until Easter Day,' Ted confirmed. ''Tis always a quiet week, then.' He didn't mention his plan to plant broad beans on Good Friday. 'Let's hope for a nice spring day and a good attendance in church, eh, Vicar?'

Basil agreed a little self-consciously, aware that the collection on Easter Day was, by tradition, his to keep. He then glanced at the three Tozers and cleared his throat.

'Now that we're here together, with nobody else around, there's another matter I wanted to discuss with you. It's a little delicate, and I know you won't mention it to anyone else, but I think you might be the best ones to help. You see—'

The door opened and Val came in. The three heads, which had bent nearer to the vicar as he began to make his interesting statement, turned in some frustration and she looked at them with surprise.

'Whatever's going on? You look like conspirators! Not planning to rob a bank, are you?'

'Don't be silly,' Alice said with a touch of asperity. 'We've just been having a talk about the handbells, that's all. Vicar wants 'em used in the Easter service this year. And how are things over at the Barton?'

'Oh, all right.' Val took off her coat and hung it with the others on the row of hooks inside the door. 'Hilary's a bit fed up. She went over to see the Cherrimans today and Mr Cherriman treated her like a kid. And they don't look as if they're going to move out of the house in a hurry, either.' She came over to the fire. 'It's getting really cold out there. I wouldn't be surprised if we get a frost tonight.'

'My peas!' Alice jumped up. 'I meant to cover 'em up . . . I'd better do it now, while I'm thinking of it. I'm sorry, Vicar,' she added, turning to Basil. 'If you don't mind waiting a bit, I'll make you a cup of cocoa before you goes. But if I don't do this now, I'll forget and then we'll have nothing to go with our roast lamb.'

'No, I'd better be going,' he said, standing up. 'I promised Grace I wouldn't be late, and I've got another call to make first.' He nodded towards Minnie and Ted. 'I'll look forward to hearing what you do with the handbell music. I think it will make a delightful addition to our Easter Day service. Now, I

131

really must be on my way – Grace will think I've absconded with the offertory box!'

He pulled on his coat and gloves, gave them all a little wave and went out of the door that Ted was holding open for him. Alice, who was still looking for the old net curtains she used to cover her plants when a frost threatened, looked after him thoughtfully.

'I wonder what it was he wanted to talk to us about,' she mused. 'Something *delicate*, he said. Whatever do you think it could be? I wondered if it might be about old Jem Squires, over at Little Burracombe. 'Tis his funeral on Monday.'

'I shouldn't have thought so,' Ted said, shaking his head. 'That's not much to do with us, although I'll be going along, of course. Old Jem was a good old boy, and a fine bellringer in his day.' He shrugged. 'No, if 'twas anything important Vicar wanted to say, he'll get round to it again sometime. And there can't be anything going on in the village that one of us don't know about. One way or another, all the news gets to the Tozers sooner or later.'

Alice nodded. But as she found her curtains and went out to the kitchen garden to tuck up her peas, she was still looking thoughtful. Whatever it was, the vicar had obviously not wanted to discuss it once Val had arrived. What could be so 'delicate' that it couldn't be mentioned in front of her?

As Ted had said, however, if it were at all important, the vicar would find some other opportunity to broach the subject. Alice, her curiosity now aroused, just hoped he wouldn't take too long.

Chapter Thirteen

Basil's next call was at the village inn, where Bernie Nethercott presided behind the bar, helped by his wife and, on busy nights, Dottie Friend. It wasn't so much that the vicar wanted a drink – although he wasn't at all averse to the odd pint and often joined the villagers in a game of darts or dominoes – but he knew that Jacob Prout was likely to be there at this time, and it was Jacob that Basil wanted to talk to.

'It's about Jem Squires's funeral,' he said, finding the odd-job man sitting in his favourite corner nursing his own pewter tankard, kept specially for him on a hook over the bar. 'The vicar over at Little Burracombe is ill with bronchitis so I'll be taking the service, and now I've heard that their gravedigger's had an accident and broken a rib. Do you think you'd be able to dig the grave for them?'

Jacob took a swallow of his beer and nodded. 'Reckon so. I could make a start on Friday, get young Billy Friend to give me a hand, and if us don't finish it, then us can have another crack on Saturday. I dare say they'll be ringing the bells, too, seeing as old Jem were a ringer.'

'I believe so. Will you be going to the funeral, too?'

'Oh, ah, Ted's already had a word with us about that. Us'll all be going along, and tower captain's said us can ring a special peal for him after the burial. Give him a proper send-off, like. Why, when you comes to think of it, he must have rung those bells for Queen Victoria herself, God bless her.'

'So he must. Just think of all the changes he must have

witnessed.' Both men were silent for a few moments, their minds roaming back through almost a century of history. 'Aeroplanes, cars – why, there probably weren't even bicycles when he was a boy.'

'Just about coming in, I reckon,' Jacob said. 'He told I once, he saw a couple of penny-farthings at Tavistock Goosey Fair when he were a young chap. Two young chaps rode 'em all the way out from Plymouth. Cars didn't come in till after the turn of the century, though – and it were a while even then before one were seen in Burracombe. I reckon Jem must've been well over forty before he saw one with his own eyes.'

Basil shook his head wonderingly. 'And now there are cars everywhere, and jet aircraft flying across the sky. So much change in just one lifetime. And what will happen next, I wonder. People are even talking about going to the moon.'

Jacob gave a scornful grunt. 'That'll never happen, not in my lifetime nor yours, Vicar. Stands to reason, don't it? I mean, how many millions of miles is it? And you can't even go to London without wanting more petrol, so they tell me. No, there'll never be anyone going to the moon – that's just for far-fetched stories in boys' comics, like that *Eagle* they all reads now.' He took another long swallow of his ale. 'Reckon I'd better go over to Little Burracombe tomorrow and have a look at where they wants this grave dug. The ground's going to be pretty hard, with all this frost we been having lately. Better sharpen up my old mattock.' He looked down into his tankard. 'Can I get you another pint, Vicar?'

'No, no, let me get this. I only want a half, anyway – have to be going soon.' Basil went back to the bar. A few more men had come in, and he saw his godson, Luke, among them, and then Jed Fisher. Basil nodded to them both and went back to his seat beside Jacob. After a few minutes, Luke came over and joined them on the settle.

'Jed's in a nasty mood tonight,' he murmured. 'Got a bee in

his bonnet about incomers. Apparently, he went over to the Cherrimans in the estate house to look for some work and they gave him a flea in his ear.'

'So they should,' Jacob said indignantly. 'He ought to know I does their gardening for them. He'd no right to go there, pestering.'

'I suppose he has a right to ask,' Basil said mildly. 'And he doesn't get as much work around the village as you do, Jacob.'

'And why's that?' the old man demanded. 'It's because he don't do as good a job, that's why! Scamps his work and leaves it all at odds, always has done. He only gets chapel work because his old dad did their graveyard for them and the minister's got a kind heart. *Too* kind, if you asks me.' He snorted.

'We all have to live,' Basil began, but Jacob's indignation was taking a hold on him now, especially when he saw Jed coming towards them, his own tankard in his hand.

'I knows that, Vicar. I knows the Good Lord put us all on this earth for a purpose. We all got our place, human beings, cows and sheep, dogs and cats, the lot of us. But that don't stop some of us being vermin, all the same!' He raised his eyes and stared defiantly at the man who now stood opposite him.

'I suppose you means me,' Jed exclaimed angrily. 'That's slander, that is!'

'I never said a word about you. Not a single word. I was talking about everything being for a purpose, even rats. If you thought I meant you, maybe that's because you—'

'Gentlemen, gentlemen,' Basil interposed hurriedly. 'I'm sure there's no need for this. Jacob, sit down again, and Jed, why don't you join us here for a while? We were just talking about old Jem Squires. It's his funeral on Monday.'

'I knows that. I knowed old Jem, too, and his sister. Good friends to me, they was.' He glowered at Jacob, who bristled at Basil's side. 'Better than some others I could mention. I won't join you, Vicar, thanks all the same. No offence, but I don't like the company you keeps.' He turned and made his way to the other side of the room.

Basil sighed. 'I wish you and Jed could get along better, Jacob. It makes it so difficult for you both, living next door to each other. Have you always been such enemies?'

Jacob scowled into his beer. ''Tis too far back to mend matters now, Vicar, and best not talked about. Jed and me'll never get on, and that's all there is to it. Now, what about a game of darts before you goes?'

Basil shook his head. 'I'm afraid I'll have to be going now. Perhaps Luke will give you a game – although he's better at dominoes.' He half feared that in Jacob's present mood, one of the darts might go astray, even as far as the corner where Jed was sitting now. He rose to his feet and laid his hand on Luke's shoulder for a moment. 'Good to see you, my boy. Bring Val over to the vicarage for supper one evening. You'll be wanting to make arrangements for your wedding before long.'

'Got to find somewhere to live first,' Luke said ruefully. 'Val's beginning to get a bit downhearted, I think. But somewhere will turn up, eventually.'

'And don't you worry about old Jem's grave,' Jacob said. 'I'll see that's done proper. Be a pleasure to me, that will, doing something for Jem. Last of the family, he was. There be no more Squireses now, over at Little Burracombe.'

Basil left the warmth of the inn and walked back to the vicarage. The sky was thick with stars, shining down on the dark streets of the village, and the only lights were those that glowed behind curtained windows. He felt in sombre, reflective mood, saddened by the bitter enmity between the two old men, and still humbled by the long stretch of memories that had died with Jem Squires. He would probably have known Jennifer Tucker's family, if they really did come from round here, he thought suddenly. People like him and Minnie Tozer had lived all their lives in this small corner of the country, and seen so many changes, yet their main interest had been the doings of their own families and neighbours.

He'd meant to ask Ted, Alice and Minnie if they had known of a young woman forced to leave the village through her pregnancy during the First World War, but Val had interrupted them and the moment had passed. I must do it soon, he thought. Minnie herself is over eighty, and although she seems hale enough, you never know when the Lord might decide her time is up. I really must do something about it soon.

He opened the front door of the vicarage, still thinking of all the changes that had taken place during the lifetime that had just ended. Not even bicycles on the road when Jem Squires was born – and now look at the world. And yet people were much the same. They still took more interest in their families and neighbours than in anything else. Look at Jennifer Tucker, searching for the father she had never known.

He felt suddenly ashamed. It's important to her, he thought, and I haven't tried hard enough. I'll go and see Minnie again.

Stella Simmons, too, was thinking about family matters.

'I just can't wait to see Muriel again,' she said to Dottie, as she enjoyed a cup of tea after school the next afternoon. 'Sorry – I mean Maddy. I suppose I'll get used to it eventually.'

'When is she coming, maid?' Dottie asked. She was making pastry at the kitchen table, her strong fingers rubbing the fat and flour together so that the mixture was as fine as tiny breadcrumbs. 'Easter, isn't it?'

'The week before, on the Wednesday before – the ninth. We break up on Friday, so that'll be just right. And she's staying two whole weeks! Isn't that lovely, Dottie? – we'll really have time to get to know each other.'

137

Dottie made a hollow in the middle of the mixture and poured cold water into it. She began to stir, gently drawing the dry flour and fat into the liquid until it became a stiff lump. 'I've been wondering where she means to stay. Usually, when she comes down with Miss Forsyth, they stop up at the Barton, with the Napiers, but when she's on her own she comes to me. And then, of course, she has your room. Well, 'twas hers when she lived here, so naturally—'

'Of course it was. Do you know, I hadn't really thought about it.' Stella looked at her in dismay. 'I suppose because they stayed at the Barton last time . . . It would be much nicer if she could be here, though.'

'It would,' Dottie said, sprinkling flour on the board and turning the lump on to it. 'But there's not room for another bed in that room, and you can't sleep in that single one together for two weeks, 'twouldn't be comfortable. And mine's not much better, or I'd say have that. But it's something us ought to be thinking about.'

'You're right. I can't think why it never occurred to me before.'

Stella looked around the living-room, which did duty as part of the kitchen as well. It was furnished with a couple of armchairs, the table where Dottie was working and where they ate their meals, and some kitchen chairs. There was a small footstool made of woven seagrass and Dottie's sewing-box, which was also a footstool, and in one corner, near the window, stood her treadle sewing-machine.

'I suppose there's room here to put a mattress on the floor, or a camp bed if we could borrow one,' she said doubtfully. 'I could sleep down here then and Mur— *Maddy* could have my bed.'

'If the worst comes to the worst, that's what us'll do,' Dottie declared, rolling the pastry out with her wooden rolling-pin. 'Better if I sleep down here, though, then Maddy can have my bed and you can stop where you are. It's handier

138

for me coming in late from the pub, too – I'd only be disturbing you if 'twas you down here.'

'Oh no, we can't turn you out of your bed!' Stella exclaimed, horrified. 'I'm sure Maddy wouldn't want that. There, I did it,' she added with a pleased smile. 'Called her Maddy, I mean.'

'You'll soon get used to it once she'm here again,' Dottie said comfortably. She folded the strip of pastry into thirds and rolled it out again, gently so as not to push the air out. 'I wonder if there's anyone else nearby might let her have a bed. There's the Bell, of course – Bernie's always talking about letting rooms for a bit more income, only I don't know if he'd be able to get it ready in time. And a pub's not really the place for a young lady like Maddy. Not saying anything against it, mind, a better village inn than the Bell you'd go a long day's march to find, but it don't seem right for a young lady on her own.'

'No, I wouldn't want her staying at the pub.' Stella watched as Dottie fetched an enamel pie dish from the scullery. It was already filled with the blushing pink stems of chopped rhubarb, sprinkled with sugar and scattered with a few pieces of chopped crystallised ginger. 'Is that for our supper?'

'It is, and there's some nice clotted cream to go with it, made from the top of our own milk.' Dottie laid the pastry over the rhubarb, where it settled into a knobbly blanket, and cut round the overlapping edges, crimping them together in a pattern with the back of her knife. She gathered the scraps into another lump, rolled it out and cut it into strips, which she twisted into ropes and laid across the top of the pie. Then she dipped her pastry-brush into a cup of beaten egg and stroked it swiftly across. 'There,' she said, opening the oven door and sliding the dish inside. 'A feast for a king, though I says so meself. You can't beat the first rhubarb pie of the season. A real treat, that is.'

Stella agreed. Although she'd been living with Dottie for over a year now, she still hadn't got used to the meals Dottie seemed to make out of almost nothing. The rhubarb had been grown in their own garden, forced under galvanised buckets with holes in the top; the cream had been made from the milk of Ted Tozer's cows, simmered in a bowl on top of the range until it formed a thick crust; and the butter had been made by Nathan Pettifer's wife, Iris. Only the flour had come from a shop in Tavistock, and a few years ago even that could have been obtained from the mill, just along the valley.

Maddy had been so lucky to live with Dottie during those last years of the war, she thought. Her own years in the children's home, kind though the staff had been, seemed bleak in comparison. All the same, she was glad it had been that way round – she could never have felt completely happy, even if living in complete luxury, while she had no idea where her little sister was.

All those years lost to us both, she thought wistfully. But it was no good mourning them now. The main thing was that she and Muriel – *Maddy* – had found each other and would soon have a whole fortnight with nothing to do but get to know each other again.

We must find her somewhere really nice to stay, she thought. Somewhere close by, if she can't be here in the cottage with Dottie and me. I don't want her even as far away as the Barton.

'But it's simple,' Felix said when he and Stella went for a walk the next evening. They were following the brook through the woods, picking their way along a narrow footpath that wound between moss-covered rocks and gorse bushes yellow with flowers. 'Aggie's got another room. She lets it to visitors in the summer sometimes. Maddy could stay there and be just across the road from you.'

Stella paused and looked at him. 'I never thought of that.

But would it be all right, do you think – her and you staying in the same house? You know how people gossip.'

Felix burst out laughing. 'Oh, come on, Stella – she's your sister! Everyone must know by now that we – well, that we're friends. They couldn't possibly find anything to gossip about in Maddy staying at Aggie's. Why, there was quite often a single woman staying there last summer. Don't you remember the birdwatcher lady, with her binoculars and boots and haversack?'

Stella smiled. 'Yes, I do, but she was about sixty-five and looked like a tortoise. That's a bit different from Maddy, who's only just over twenty and looks like a film star.'

'I hope you're not suggesting that I wouldn't behave like a perfect gentleman,' Felix said, pretending to be offended, and she laughed and took his arm.

'Of course not. But not everyone knows you as well as I do. And some people can be quite spiteful.'

'How sad,' he said more seriously, 'that you should know that already. I hope it's not from personal experience.'

Stella hesitated. 'Children can be very cruel, you know. The children's home where I lived had all kinds of children in it, most of us orphans, so you'd think we'd have some sympathy for each other, but there were still some who could make some very unpleasant remarks about you and your parents. And outside, in the local school, children who had ordinary home lives seemed to think there was something peculiar about us – almost as if we weren't quite right in the head. It was better at college, but it wasn't really until I came to Burracombe that I began to feel normal.'

He stared at her. 'Stella, that's dreadful. I had no idea.'

'I don't talk about it much,' she said with a shrug. 'It's all behind me now, and I feel as if I've come home. Especially now that I've found Maddy and know she lived here, too, as a little girl.' She gazed about her, at the tall chestnut trees with their rough bark and the leaves just beginning to come out, at the green, furry humps of the moss-covered rocks, at the tumbling waters of the brook. 'I don't think I'll ever want to leave Burracombe,' she said softly.

Felix took her hand. 'Never? Even if you found a better job, say, in another place? Or – or fell in love and got married?'

Stella gave him a quick glance and then looked away again. 'I don't know. I can't say how I'd feel then, can I? We talked about this before, remember? I still don't think I'd want to move to another job.' She glanced at him again and then went on, a faint blush touching her skin, 'And if I ever did get married, it might be to someone in Burracombe.'

There was a short silence. They were standing very still, and the only sounds were the babble of the water and the singing of the birds as they went to their roosts. The setting sun was spreading a haze of apricot across the sky, laced with a delicate pattern of filigree branches. The air was as soft as silk against their faces.

Felix laid his hand on her cheek and turned her head gently so that she was looking up at him. His dark blue eyes were very intent and she felt her colour rise again, warming her cheeks. Her heart quickened.

'You're a lovely girl, Stella,' he said quietly. 'I hope you do fall in love.' And he bent his head and touched his lips against hers.

Chapter Fourteen

There was a good turn-out for Jem Squires's funeral. The rivalry between the two villages didn't mean that there wasn't plenty of friendship as well, and on Monday afternoon, a steady stream of people from Burracombe itself could be seen taking the path down the valley to cross the old wooden footbridge and climb the track on the other side to the smaller village. Once, both had been mining villages and there were still several remains to be seen – the old engine house of Wheal Freda, with its chimney pointing like a stark finger towards the sky from the broken ground, the fences around the adits that led down to the abandoned lead and copper mines, the tumbled walls of a few buildings where miners had once scoured a living from the harshness of the moor. There had been a large community in Little Burracombe then, with several inns and cottages, and both a church and chapel, but now much of it was gone and there was just one inn, a handful of cottages, one or two larger houses and some more scattered farms and dwellings in hidden combes and valleys.

Both church and chapel still retained their congregations, however, and before going to the church for the funeral, Basil called at the vicarage. Mrs Berry, the vicar's wife, showed him up to the bedroom where her husband was sitting up in bed, propped up by several pillows and looking frail.

John Berry was growing old now, and Basil suspected that when he finally gave up, the living would be merged with his own, and his parish enlarged. He shook the thin, bony hand and sat down beside the bed.

'Sorry you're not feeling well, John. But you're in the best place – there's a nasty chill in the air today. I just hope the mourners won't all go down with colds as well.'

'There'll be plenty of them,' John Berry said, his voice wheezy. 'Jem was well known and well liked in the parish. I'm sorry I can't take his funeral.'

Basil nodded. 'I'm sure you'll be missed,' he said. 'But I'll do my best.' He looked at John's grey face. He seemed very tired and fragile, and Basil hoped that there wouldn't be another funeral in Little Burracombe in the near future. They talked quietly for a few minutes and then shared a short prayer before Basil rose to take his leave.

'I'll come again when it's over,' he promised, holding his friend's hand. 'And I know you'll be with us in your thoughts.'

The old man nodded weakly. Each breath he took rattled in his chest, and as Basil went down the stairs, he felt anxious. He found Mrs Berry waiting for him in the hall.

'What does the doctor say?'

The vicar's wife lifted one shoulder. She was as old as her husband, and looked nearly as frail. Why ever hadn't they retired long ago? Basil wondered. But he knew the answer. Like many clergymen, John Berry had never been able to buy a home of his own, and once he gave up working, he would have to leave the vicarage. There were houses available for people in his position, but they usually meant moving away from the community where you had spent so many years and had so many friends, and for a couple like the Berrys, who had no family of their own, such a move would mean a lonely old age.

'He says if John gets any worse, he'll have to go to hospital. And if he does that . . .' She left the sentence unfinished, but again Basil knew what she was thinking. If John went into hospital now, he would probably never come home again. They would both rather he stayed at home, and either get better or die in his own bed.

And then what would happen to this poor old lady, who had given so much to the community and would be left quite alone?

With a heavy heart, Basil left the house and walked round to the church. There were already a few mourners there, their black clothes making them look like dark birds of sorrow amongst the gravestones, and as Basil stood at the door, welcoming them quietly, he saw the hearse approach. It had taken the long way round the village, passing every point of which Jem Squires might have had fond memories – the cottage where he had been born, the school where he had learned to read and write, the old mines where his grandfathers had worked, the farm where his father had tended the tough moorland sheep and cattle after the mines had closed during the 1870s. Jem had been a boy then, and had often talked of the hardship this had brought to the area, with families breaking up as the younger men were forced to leave the area and look for work elsewhere. Like the Cornish tin miners, many of them had gone to the Americas or Australia and lost communication perhaps for ever.

As the hearse came to a stop, the mourners made their way into the little church. The bells were already ringing, their clappers muffled so that only every other round sounded clearly, the others soft and sad. The bearers – all friends of the old man – carried his coffin slowly up the path, and Basil preceded it into the church, while the chief mourners – Jem's nephew and his wife, their family and two or three more distant cousins – came after it. There was just one bunch of flowers on the coffin: a posy of spring flowers gathered that morning from Jem's own garden.

As Basil came to the chancel steps and turned to face the

congregation, he saw a last mourner slip quietly into the church and take a place in the pew at the very back.

It was Jennifer Tucker.

'I saw it in the newspaper,' she said afterwards. 'Jeremiah Squires. And since the name began with "J" . . .'

'My dear, I owe you an apology,' Basil said. 'I've begun to make enquiries, but I haven't got very far. And it never occurred to me that old Jem might have anything to do with you – he'd have been nearly sixty when you were born.'

'It doesn't mean he couldn't have been the one, though, does it?' she said. She had waited after the service and they'd arranged to meet in the churchyard, after everyone had gone. Basil had made a brief visit to Jem's nephew's house, where the mourners were being given sherry and sandwiches, and had then come back to find her wandering among the gravestones. They sat on an old bench in a sheltered spot and talked. Over in the far corner, a mound of fresh earth spread with a few flowers showed where Jem had been laid to rest. Basil saw Jennifer Tucker looking at it. 'Men of sixty have become fathers before now.'

'That's true,' he admitted. 'But even so . . . I can't believe that Jem . . .' He thought for a few moments, then looked at her seriously. 'I know this is really none of my business, Miss Tucker, but do you really want to go on with this? You might find out things you'd really rather not know. You might even upset other people.'

Jennifer Tucker was silent for a while. He watched her anxiously, noting the delicacy of her profile and the warm chestnut of her hair against the pale, oval face. She closed her smoke-grey eyes and he saw the thick, dark lashes lying on the creamy skin and wondered again why she had never married.

At last she said, 'I've thought of that, too – that it might be painful to find out the truth. And I don't want to cause any trouble – if it looks like that, I'll stop. At least, I think I will.'

She turned her head and gave him a rueful smile. 'I can't know for sure. I feel so driven, you see – driven to find out something about my family, about *myself*. I thought I knew, until my mother died, and now I feel as if I've lost her in more ways than just by her dying. I feel as if I didn't even know her – not fully. And until I find my father, I *can't* know her.' She shrugged. 'Maybe I'll never find him. I may be looking in the wrong place, or he may be dead.' Her eyes went to the mound of fresh earth. 'But there might still be people who knew him – and who knew my mother. There might still be people who can fill in the gaps.' She paused again. 'I suppose I just want to find my family. People of my own.'

'But you have a family,' Basil said kindly. 'You have sisters.'

'Half-sisters. And the other half – well, that's nothing to do with me. The funny thing is, they don't seem to want to know any more about our mother. They'll be interested if I find anything out, but it's not the same for them as it is for me, because they have their father's family. I feel I have no one.'

'And has there never been anyone else?' he asked. 'You've never married?'

Jennifer sighed. 'It's a familiar enough story. We were engaged during the war, but he never came home. I've never felt the same for anyone else.'

'So what would you like to do now?' Basil asked. 'As you saw at the funeral, Jem's only close relative was a nephew, and he's in his seventies. All the others have died or moved away. If you make enquiries now, you'll have to rely on gossip, and ancient gossip at that. Jem was a well-respected man, and a very old man, too.'

'And if I start to ask questions, when he's no longer alive to answer them, I'll be besmirching his reputation,' she said. 'I can see that. Well, it probably wasn't him, anyway – as you say, he would have been quite old to have fathered a baby. Especially an illegitimate one.'

'I've never heard that he had a reputation in that area,' Basil said delicately. 'He was married years ago, and widowed in his fifties. After that, he lived with his sister, who died a year or two ago. I suppose it's possible that in the early years of his widowhood . . .' He sighed. 'I really think it's something we'll never know for sure. It might be better to look for people who knew your mother – they might know something.'

'Yes, I think you're right. And you've found out nothing?'

'No.' He told her about his conversation with Constance Bellamy. 'As she says, life was very uncertain in those last months of the Great War, and then with the 'flu epidemic and the upheavals of the 1920s – there was so much change going on, even in Burracombe. I'm sure there would have been gossip at the time, but whether anyone still remembers it . . .' He glanced up as a figure came round the corner of the church. 'Here comes Ted Tozer. He's one of the farmers in Burracombe itself – he came over to ring the bells for the funeral, with the Burracombe team. He would be the right age to ask, and he's utterly trustworthy.' He stood up and hailed the sturdy figure. 'Ted! That was a fine peal you rang.'

'Well, 'twas the least us could do for old Jem.' Ted came up to them and looked at the woman standing beside the vicar. 'Be you a relative, miss?'

'No. I thought I might have known him – or his family – but now I'm not so sure.' She hesitated, glancing at the vicar, and Basil said, 'Miss Tucker thinks she might have relatives in the area, Ted. I wondered if you or Alice might be able to help her. I was going to suggest she might come and see you at some time.'

'No time like the present,' Ted said cheerfully. 'Look, I be going home now and I know my Alice'll have the kettle on the hob and a few scones or something in the oven – why not walk back with me and have a chat? 'Tis no distance over the Clam.'

'The Clam?' she asked, and Basil smiled.

'It's the word for the footbridge over the river. Ted's right, it's only about ten minutes' walk that way, and you can catch the bus back to Plymouth in the village, as you know. I'd come with you, but I promised to go and see John Berry – the vicar here – before I go home. He's in a poor way,' he added to Ted. 'I was shocked when I saw him earlier.'

Ted nodded soberly. 'Always suffered with his chest, he has, and he's not getting any younger. Well, 'tis the same road for us all, and not always an easy one. I reckon old Jem had the best of it. Hale and hearty up to the last week or two, and then just drifted away. A good end to a good life.'

They stood for a moment or two in respectful memory of the man whose funeral they had just attended, and then gave each other a nod, Basil turning towards the vicarage and Ted setting off down the path towards the river, with Jennifer Tucker following him.

The church of Little Burracombe cast its shadow on the graveyard surrounding it, and the mound of fresh earth faded into the deep shade of the tower itself as old Jem Squires settled down into his last long rest.

Alice and Minnie were in the kitchen as usual, waiting for *Mrs Dale's Diary* to start with its signature tune of harp music and the pleasant, slightly anxious tones of the doctor's wife whose family doings were recounted each day on the radio. The fact that, unlike the farming programme *The Archers*, it depicted a life that was quite different from their own only added to their enjoyment. Joanna often listened to it, too, but Val was indifferent, and Jackie openly scornful.

Minnie was working on the tunes the vicar had asked her to arrange for the handbells. Spread all over the kitchen table, she had sheet music for the hymns he had suggested and a large pad of paper for writing down the notes of the handbells. Each one had its note embossed on its leather strap, and Minnie was writing the notes in columns so that several bells could be chimed together to create a chord. Sometimes only one bell would sound, its clear note striking a different sound amongst the harmonies, and this too was indicated in the columns. Once Minnie had finished the arrangements, Joanna, who had the best handwriting, would put them all on to large pieces of card and the handbell team would stand in front of it, striking their bells as the conductor pointed at the columns.

'We can use these old changes as well,' she said. 'My William did these years ago. Pretty little tunes they be, too. It'll be good to hear they again.'

Alice came and looked over her shoulder. The changes were in a small, yellowing notebook, written in a copperplate hand that was fading with age. She took the book, unhooked the small, wooden-headed hammer that could be used to strike the handbells, and picked out some of the changes on the bells hanging from the beams overhead.

'That's really pretty. I think us ought to do some of them as well. Is that what they call scientific ringing?'

Minnie shook her head. 'I don't think so. That's what they do on tower bells up-country. Makes a terrible noise, it do, all the bells clashing against each other all the time instead of changing decently one at a time. My William wouldn't have no truck with that.' She went on with her notation, carefully drawing straight lines with her ruler so that the columns of figures would stay in their place. 'I think while our Joanna's doing this, she might as well make some new cards for the Christmas carols and the tunes us've already got. Be nice to have them all new and fresh now we'm getting the team together again.'

Mrs Dale's Diary had just begun when Ted opened the kitchen door. As soon as she saw that he was ushering in a visitor, Alice turned off the radio and moved the kettle on to the hotplate. She came forward, holding out her hand in welcome.

'This is Miss Tucker, Alice,' Ted said. 'This is my wife, and this is my mother. She lives with us – keeps us all in order. I met Miss Tucker over at the funeral,' he added to Alice.

'Oh, I see,' Alice said. 'A relative of old Jem, are you?'

Jennifer shook her head. 'I don't think so. I don't really know – that's why I came today. I've been telling Mr Tozer—' she glanced at Ted '—I've been looking for relatives I think might have lived in the area. I came a few weeks ago and talked to the vicar, and he was wondering if you might be able to help me.'

Alice looked at her, frowning slightly. 'I've seen you before, haven't I? Didn't you come to the church once?' She moved back to the stove and poured hot water into the teapot, swilling it round and tipping it into the sink before going back to make the tea. 'I know when it was! 'Twas the day the dear King died. I was clearing out the flowers when the vicar came to tell me, and you were there then. That's it, isn't it?'

'You're right.' Jennifer sat down in the seat indicated by Ted. 'It didn't seem the right time to ask questions then, so I just went away again, but I came back to see Mr Harvey and we had a long talk. And then we met again at Mr Squires's funeral. I'd seen it was today in the paper, and I wondered . . . But I don't think it was him.'

'I'm sorry, maid,' Alice said, leaving the tea to stand for a few minutes while she got an extra cup and saucer from the dresser and brought a plate of fresh scones from the larder. 'I don't understand what you'm saying. You don't think *what* was him? And who d'you mean by "him"?'

'Sorry. I'm not making any sense, am I? The trouble is, I don't really know what does make sense.' Jennifer looked round at them all. 'The vicar says I can trust you not to talk about it if I tell you.'

'And so you can,' Alice said. She poured milk and tea into the cups and brought them to the table, where Minnie had swept all her papers into a pile. 'If you asks us not to talk about it, we won't. But you don't have to tell us if you don't want to,' she added. 'Every family has its secrets and there's no reason why you should tell us yours.'

Jennifer smiled. 'Thank you, Mrs Tozer. But I won't get very far if I don't tell someone, and Mr Harvey thinks you might be the best people. He's talked to Miss Bellamy, but she was away during the war and doesn't know anything—'

'No, that's not right,' Ted broke in. 'I don't know why he should say that – Constance Bellamy hasn't been out of the village for years, except for the odd week when her goes to stay with a cousin somewhere up north – Bristol, or Gloucester, or some such place. And she was certainly here during the war, because—'

'No,' Jennifer said, 'I don't mean the last war. I mean the first one – the 1914–18 war. She was in Malta then, as a nurse.'

'That's right,' Minnie said. She had been gazing at Jennifer in silence until that moment. 'What they called a VAD, she were. But why be you asking about that time, Miss Tucker? What are you trying to find out?'

Jennifer looked at their faces, puzzled yet kindly, and took a deep breath. Alice pushed her cup of tea a little nearer. She split and buttered a warm scone and put it on a plate at Jennifer's elbow. Sudden tears swam in the grey eyes.

'I'm trying to find my family,' she said. 'I don't even know if there's anyone left now, and I don't know for sure that they came from Burracombe. But I *feel* that they did. I feel as if this is somehow my home – the place where my mother and father grew up. There must be someone who knew them. There must be *someone* who knew that I was going to be born.'

Briefly, she told them the story of her mother's life in Plymouth, the stepfather she had believed to be her own father and the sisters who now seemed to have stepped away from her. As her voice broke and she put her hand to her eyes, Alice came over and put an arm round the young woman's shoulder.

'There, my bird, don't you upset yourself. We all understand how you must feel. And if there's anything we can do, we'll do it. Now, dry your eyes and have a sip of that tea while it's hot, and tell us if there's anything you know. Anything at all. For one thing, is there any names that might help?'

'Yes,' Jennifer said, doing as she was told. The hot tea warmed her chilled body, and she cradled the cup in her palms and closed her eyes. 'I know my mother's name. It was Hannaford. But the vicar says he can't find any record in the church papers of any Hannafords at all.'

'No more he would,' Minnie said unexpectedly. 'They were chapel folk.'

Jennifer stared at her. 'Chapel? But my mother was Church of England – she had me christened at St Budeaux—'

'So her might have done,' Minnie said. 'But her was Chapel when her lived here.' She turned to Alice. 'You must remember the Hannafords, over to Whinberry Cross. You knew young Susan. Disappeared off to Plymouth when she were about eighteen years old.' She tilted her head towards Jennifer. 'And now, us knows why!' To Jennifer herself, she added, 'I knowed it the minute you walked in. Like seeing a ghost, it were.'

Alice turned her eyes first to her mother-in-law and then to Jennifer. 'You mean you think this is Susan Hannaford's child? But how could you know, Mother? She don't look a bit like Susan.'

'No, she don't,' Minnie agreed. 'But she'm the spitten image of her grandmother. And I ought to know – Liza Lilliman were my best friend when us were girls, right up to when she wed Abraham Hannaford. And afterwards, too, whenever the poor soul were allowed off the farm.' She turned back to Jennifer. 'I know who your mother was, my maid, and I got a good idea who your father was, too. And I reckon you'd better stop here for supper, because us has got a lot to talk about.'

Chapter Fifteen

'Liza Lilliman come from t'other side of Tavistock,' Minnie said as they sat round the kitchen table.

They had eaten shepherd's pie and carrots, followed by a bottle of plums Alice had taken from her store cupboard and a bowl of junket, and now the dishes had been cleared away and Joanna and Val were tackling the washing-up while the others talked, a large brown pot of tea on the table in front of them.

'Over Horndon way, that's where her lived. So of course us didn't know each other as little uns, but us both went into service together up at the Barton, for old General Napier. Took to each other straight away, us did. She were a nice little body, and it were a proper shame when she wed Abraham Hannaford.'

'Why? What was he like?' Val asked, hovering nearby with a pie dish and tea-cloth in her hands.

'He were a bully,' Minnie said tersely. 'A lot older than her for a start – he'd been wed before and his first wife died, of overwork and misery, I dare say – and he just wanted a strong young woman to do the work around the farm and give him children. Oh, he were smooth enough when it come to courting – good-looking man, in his way – and poor Liza was proper taken in by him. Like a fly walking into a spider's web, she were, and by the time she realised what he was really like, 'twas too late. She were out there on that farm, miles from anywhere, nobody nearby to know what was going on, and the only time she were allowed out was on Sunday to go to

Chapel. Hardly saw her after that. I saw the baby, of course – little Susan – but she were just as downtrodden as her mother. Well, you'll remember that yourself,' she added, turning to Alice. 'You knowed her well enough.'

'I remember her at school,' Alice said. 'Her father used to bring her in on the trap. But she was such a quiet girl, none of us really knew her very well, and she was never allowed to stay after school, to go to tea with anyone, and she never came on picnics or the Whit Monday outings. He was always there after school, waiting for her, and she had to go straight home.'

'But what about after she left school?' Val came and sat down at the table. 'Didn't you have village dances and things like that? Wasn't she allowed to come to any of those?'

'Yes, she did, whenever she could. There wasn't no village hall then, that was built as a memorial after the Great War, but Dad used to let us use the big barn when it was empty. I got quite friendly with her then. She told me once she used to slip out when her father was busy in the barn of an evening, or reading – he used to read the Bible a lot, so she said, not that you'd know it from the way he carried on – and one of the farmhands would give her a lift into the village. And that was where she met . . .' Alice drew in a sharp breath and stared at Jennifer, her eyes growing large and her mouth opening wide. She put up her hand to cover her lips. 'But that don't mean anything. It couldn't have been him. It could have been any of the boys there – she were a pretty girl, they were all after her, and there was plenty to give her a lift home again. It *couldn't* have been him!'

The others stared at her. Jennifer was pale and tense, the rest of them leaning forward. At last, as Alice sat gazing at them, clearly picturing scenes from years ago in her head, Val burst out, 'Who are you talking about, Mum? Is it someone we know? Someone still living in the village? Come on – you can't leave us like this! You've got to tell us!'

Ted slapped his hand on the table.

'Now just you wait a minute, our Val! This isn't some party game, you know. It's people's lives we'm talking about. *This* young lady's life in particular.' He laid his hand on Jennifer's arm. ''Tis for her to say if she wants us to go on talking about it between ourselves. 'Tis for her to say if your mother mentions any names, and who she mentions them to. Us can't know the truth of it, anyway, and bringing names into this without knowing that could cause a lot of trouble.'

Val bit her lip and sat back in her chair, abashed, and Joanna, who was standing behind her, put a hand on her shoulder. There was a short pause, and then Ted turned to Jennifer Tucker.

'Well, what do you think, maid? Would you rather go in the parlour with my mother and Alice here, and talk it over quiet together? Nobody'll bother you, if that's what you wants. None of us'll talk out of turn, anyway – you needn't worry about that.'

'No, I know you won't, Mr Tozer.' She thought for a moment or two, then looked round the ring of faces. 'I think I'd rather stay here, actually. You've all been so kind – I feel almost as if you're part of my own family, especially now I know you knew my mother.' She looked at Minnie. 'And if you were my grandmother's best friend – it seems to bring them both so close. I want to hear as much as you can tell me about them. But – but I would like to find out who my father was as well, if there's any chance.'

'Well, as to that,' Alice said slowly, 'I don't know if we'll ever know, not without going and asking straight out. And that's not an easy thing to do, is it? We don't know what the chap I'm thinking about might say. We don't know for *certain* you're his daughter, you see. All I know is, he was sweet on Susan. He might be proper upset to think that there were somebody else she thought more of than him. And I don't see as that would do anyone any good.'

There was another silence. Then Jennifer said, 'Tell me

about my mother. What happened to her? When did she leave the village – and why? Or at least, why did people *think* she left?'

Alice frowned at the table, and Val reached out and lifted the big brown teapot to refill their cups. They waited while Alice got her thoughts into order.

'I'm just trying to cast my mind back,' she said slowly. 'I know I said I was friendly with Susan, but I didn't know her all that well – none of us did, even though we'd been at school with her and all that. But when we all come to leave school, she didn't go into service or nothing, like her mother did, she just stopped at home on the farm. There weren't no more children, you see, and her mother always seemed a bit frail and poorly—'

'Anyone would be, married to that old termagant,' Minnie said grimly.

'—but I always liked her,' Alice went on. 'She were a sweet little soul, for all she grew up in such a miserable household. Like a flower, she were. Must have been a real comfort to her poor mother.'

'I'm glad she was,' Jennifer said quietly, and they remembered that this was her own mother that Alice was talking about. Her mother, her grandmother and her grandfather. Val wondered suddenly what it was like to discover that your own grandfather had been a bully and a tyrant at home.

'And the boys liked her, too,' Alice said, a little apologetically. 'I don't mean she were a flirt or nothing. Well—' she glanced with a trace of a smile at Ted '—no more than the rest of us! She didn't encourage them. But she were sweet and pretty, 'twould have been a wonder if they *hadn't* gathered round her like bees round a honeypot. And there were always a few wanting to see her home.'

'And was there one in particular?' Jennifer asked. 'One she seemed to like better than all the rest?'

Alice flicked a look at her and seemed to debate with herself for a moment. Then she went on, firmly, 'I'll tell you about Susan first. Then us'll think about that. Well, 'twas wartime soon enough – the First War, this was, that they called the Great War and was supposed to make England a land fit for heroes to live in. The war to end all wars – only we all knows what happened to *that* idea! And a lot of the young men went off to fight, those that could be spared from the farms, and a lot that couldn't. You went yourself.' She looked at Ted again. 'In the Army, you were, and never said a word about it all once you come back.'

'Nor ever want to, neither,' Ted said sombrely. 'It were a bad time, and those of us who came home safe and sound just wanted to get back to our ordinary lives and forget it ever happened.'

Alice touched his hand. 'The women went, too, some of 'em – like Miss Bellamy, who volunteered as a nurse and went to Malta. And some went into the towns and cities to take over the men's jobs there, and some stopped on the farms to do that work, and some even come out *from* the cities, like our Joanna in the last lot. It were a proper musical chairs. Anyway, top and bottom of it was that you hardly knew where anyone was, and goodness knows what happened in all the muddle. And a lot of the young men never come home – you can see their names on the war memorial down on the green – and some of the women didn't neither. And us'd hardly got ourselves shaken down and sorted out when it all started all over again.' She shook her head.

'And my mother?' Jennifer asked. 'She went away from the village, didn't she? But was it because of me, or because of the war?' She stared at Alice and then at Minnie. 'Perhaps it wasn't someone from Burracombe at all. Perhaps it was someone she met in Plymouth.' She glanced round the table in sudden dismay. 'If that's what happened, I'll *never* be able to find him!'

'No,' Minnie said before Alice could speak again. 'It didn't happen like that. You see, me and your grandmother, poor Liza, we still managed to have a word now and then, when they came into the village of a Sunday for Chapel, and other times, too. I used to walk out to the farm sometimes when I thought Abraham might have gone to market in Tavistock. She told me how her Susan were fond of a boy in the village. She hoped that in time Abraham might see his way to letting the maid get married. She'd get away from the farm then, see, and have a proper life. 'Twas all poor Liza wanted by that time – she'd given up hopes of any decent life for herself.'

'Poor Grandma,' Jennifer said softly, her eyes filled with tears.

'Then the war started,' Minnie went on. 'The boy went away – joined the Navy. Poor Susan were heartbroken, and so was Liza.' She paused.

'Didn't he ever come home?' Val asked. 'Is his name one of those on the memorial?'

'It couldn't be,' Jennifer objected. 'I wasn't born until 1917. He *must* have come home again. Unless he was killed later on,' she added.

'No, maid, he weren't killed. He were one of the lucky ones – he got through the war, though it took him hard, like it did a lot of the poor souls. He come home on leave once or twice, wounded, and that's when him and Susan started seeing each other again.'

'He used to write to her, mind,' Alice put in. 'And she wrote back, but of course he couldn't ever send the letters to Whinberry. He sent 'em to me, as a matter of fact, and I used to pass them on.'

'Mum!' Val exclaimed. 'Why, that's really romantic!' She caught her father's eye and subsided again.

Alice sighed. 'I suppose 'twas, when you come to think about it, but it didn't seem so then. It just seemed to be the only way . . . Anyway, 'twasn't long after he come home that time that Susan went off. Took a job in one of the hotels in

Plymouth, so us was told, and the next thing us heard was that her'd caught that pesky 'flu and died.'

Jennifer gasped and Minnie turned to her quickly. ''Twasn't true, though, maid. Liza told me on her deathbed, but she made me promise not to tell anyone else, except for Alice here.'

'That's right,' Alice confirmed. 'I was that upset to think of poor Susan sick and dying all by herself in Plymouth. I used to think if only I'd known about it, I could have gone and found her and brought her back here. But us didn't know where she was, and by the time I knew the truth it was too late.'

'In the family way, she was, poor little flower,' Minnie said, 'and sent off the farm in disgrace. 'Twas Abraham who put the story about, and threatened his wife with all sorts if she ever let out the truth. She couldn't live with the secret, though. It killed her. Went downhill from that very day, her did, and died herself eighteen months later. Crying out for her Susan till the last, she was, and crying for the poor little babby as well.'

All the women were in tears as she finished her tale, and even Ted's eyes were moist. There was a silence, and then, while they fumbled for handkerchiefs and blew their noses, he cleared his throat and turned to the young woman who was sitting with Val's arms about her, tears streaming down her cheeks.

'It's a sad story,' he said gruffly, 'but I reckon you knew there'd be sorrow in it when you first decided to come looking. Now, what you got to make up your mind about is this: do you want Alice here to tell you the rest of it, and who the young feller was, or do you want to let it rest? Once you knows, there's no going back, and until she tells us who it might be, us don't know what trouble might be heaping up. And come to that,' he added, 'us still won't know for certain.

161

It could still have been some other chap, took advantage of her, like. You got to remember that as well.'

'I know,' Jennifer said quietly. 'But whatever happened, at least I know there was someone who really loved her. I'd like to know who that was – whether I'm his child or not.' She turned back to Alice and gave her a steady look. 'Who was it, Mrs Tozer? Who was the man who loved my mother?'

Once again, the faces round the table were tense, all watching the two women who knew the secret of this stranger's birth. Without taking her eyes from her mother's face, Val laid her hand on Jennifer's, pressing it gently in reassurance.

Alice and Minnie looked at each other and Minnie gave a tiny nod. Even then, it took a moment or two for Alice to find the words, but at last she spoke and a soft breath of relief sounded in the room.

'All right,' she said. 'I'll tell you. The man who was sweet on your mother, and had to leave her to go to war – the man I think must be your father – was Jacob Prout.'

Chapter Sixteen

The silence this time was stunned. The family stared at her and then at Minnie. Then Val said in shocked, unbelieving tones, '*Jacob Prout*? Do you really mean it?'

'Would your mother say so if she didn't?' Ted demanded, but his voice was rough with amazement. He looked from Val to his wife and mother in turn. 'Old *Jacob*?'

'Not so very old,' Minnie retorted. 'Only in his sixties – not that much older than you, Ted Tozer. And he was young enough back in 1914 or so, and proper handsome, too. There was more young girls than Susan Hannaford taking a shine to him, I can tell you.'

Jennifer reached down and picked up her shabby handbag. They watched as she took out a brown envelope and looked at the faded snaps and scrap of paper she laid on the table.

'Is that him?'

Minnie reached across and picked up one of the yellowing photographs. She fumbled for her glasses and rested them on her nose, then peered at the young sailor in the picture. For a moment, she seemed undecided, then she nodded slowly.

'That's Jacob Prout all right, as a young man. And look at those rocks – they'm up by the Standing Stones. That's where all the courting couples go, in Burracombe,' she added to Jennifer. 'I reckon this must've been took just before he went away the first time.'

She passed it to Alice, who stared at it as Ted leaned over her shoulder. They both nodded their agreement, too.

'I'd forgotten he ever looked like that,' Alice said a little ruefully. 'But you're right, Mother, 'tis Jacob. It just shows how we all change over the years ... And what's this?' she added as Jennifer handed her the fragment of writing-paper. 'A bit of a letter?'

'It's the only piece I've got. It was with the photographs – I think she must have kept it because of what it said.' Jennifer's voice was shaking and Val patted her arm comfortingly. 'It's signed "J". And if you say that's Jacob Prout in the photograph, that must be him, mustn't it! He *must* be my father!'

'It do look a bit like it,' Ted agreed, although his voice was still cautious. 'But it's still not really proof, is it?'

'But surely,' Val began 'if Mum and Grandma both know that Jacob and Susan were courting, and Jennifer's got this photo and this bit of letter – surely that's proof enough. They were in love – they wanted to get married. Who else could it have been?' She stopped abruptly, then stood up and said, 'I'll make some more tea,' and went over to the sink, standing with her back to them.

Alice glanced at her curiously, but Minnie was speaking again. 'There's some funny things happen in wartime, maid – any other time, come to that – and there's many a slip 'twixt cup and lip. It do look as if the babby could have been Jacob's, but if 'twas, why didn't he marry the maid? He'm a decent sort of chap, he'd have stood by her. Even if he were away at the time, he'd have done the right thing when he come home again.' She shook her head and looked at the photograph again. 'Seems to me there's more to this than meets the eye.'

'Well, there's only one person who can answer those questions,' Ted observed. 'And that's Jacob himself. And that's a tricky sort of a question to ask, you got to admit that. If 'twasn't him, he might be mortally offended or upset – and whether it was or wasn't, it could open up all sorts of old wounds.'

They sat in silence for a few minutes. Val made a fresh pot of tea and came back to the table with it. Alice glanced at her and thought she looked upset, though what about she had no idea. All the same, it triggered a memory in her mind – a remark she'd once made, either to Minnie or Ted, about how Val had never seemed quite the same since she'd come home from Egypt during the war. But that was years ago now, and it had been understandable. Val had lost her own fiancé at that time. Perhaps all this had reminded her of her own grief.

'I don't know what to do,' Jennifer said at last. 'It seems so cruel, to find the man I think must have been my father and yet not see him and talk to him. I can see that it might upset him to be reminded of it all – but mightn't he be pleased to find he's got a daughter? What sort of man is he? Is he married? Does he have any other family?' She paused, and then added in a small voice, 'Other children?'

The family looked at each other. Joanna, who had said nothing until now, asked, 'How would you feel about that? Would you like to find some more brothers and sisters?'

'I don't know—' Jennifer began, but Alice spoke quickly.

'No, maid, you don't have to even think about that, because Jacob never had no family. He did get wed in the end, mind – married Sarah Foster, over from Walkhampton. Widow, she were, lost her first in an accident with the thresher, nasty business, took her a long time to get over it. She didn't have any children, and by the time she and Jacob got wed 'twere too late so Jacob never had none neither. Not as far as anyone knew, anyway,' she added, looking at Jennifer.

'And Sarah died a good few years back now,' Minnie supplied. 'Don't think they were together much more than ten years, all told. Jacob's lived on his own ever since, in the cottage he was born in.'

'He must be lonely,' Jennifer said, her eyes filling with tears. 'And the way you talk about him – you like him, don't you? He's a nice man?'

'Oh, everyone likes old Jacob,' Val said. 'The village wouldn't be the same without him.'

'It wouldn't be as tidy, that's for sure,' Alice said. 'Keeps the whole place looking pretty, Jacob do. Trims the hedges, clears out the ditches, looks after the churchyard, does a few gardens – there's nothing Jacob can't turn his hand to. And always got a smile and a cheery word, too. Not like that surly old crosspatch that lives next door to him.'

'Oh well, him and Jed have been at loggerheads for years,' Ted said. 'Not just him, neither – Jed's at loggerheads with everyone in the village.'

'Never mind him,' Val said. 'The point is, is Jennifer going to tell Jacob she thinks he might be her father? How do you think he's going to feel about it?'

They all sighed and looked at each other again.

'I dunno how he's going to feel,' Ted said at last. 'I dunno how I'd feel meself. Not that it's ever going to happen,' he added quickly. 'There ain't been nothing like that here. But in Jacob's shoes – well, I don't know, and that's the truth. And when you comes down to it, it isn't for us to decide, is it?' He nodded towards Jennifer. ''Tis none of our business after all, maid. 'Tis your decision.'

'I know.' She gazed down at the photograph. 'I just can't decide what's right.' She looked up at them again, her eyes shadowed. 'And there's another thing. He probably thinks my mother died then, just as you did. If her parents put that story about in the village, he'd have heard it, too. He must have been broken-hearted!'

Alice stared at her, shocked. 'So he was, the poor dear soul. It took him a long time to get over it – that's why he never married for such a long time. Oh, what a wicked thing for them to do! Not so much poor Liza, because Abraham treated her so bad she'd have been frightened to tell anyone the truth – though it must have been a sore trouble to her, having to pretend her own child was dead – but that Abraham, he was a wicked man, there's no two ways about it, and I hope he's paying for it now, wherever he is.' Her tone left no doubt as to where *she* thought Abraham was now. She turned to Ted. 'This makes it all the worse, don't it? I mean, think how poor Jacob's going to feel when he knows his Susan was alive all that time, not twenty miles away, and had his babby and all. It's going to bring it all back to him.'

They sat in silence for a time, thinking over the problem, and then Alice turned to Jennifer again.

'Why not ask the vicar? You've already talked to him, after all, and I'm sure he'd be willing to help. He knows Jacob well, and he'll never say anything to anyone else.'

'I think that's the best idea,' Ted agreed, and the others nodded. 'Mr Harvey's a funny little chap sometimes, always worrying about being late and that, but he'm a good man and got a wise head on his shoulders when it comes to serious matters. He's the best one to talk to about this.'

Jennifer nodded. 'Yes, I'll do that. He's been very nice to me, and it was him suggested I should come here. I ought to go and tell him what you've told me.' She gathered the scraps of paper together and put them back into their envelope, looking wistfully at the photograph as she did so. 'I wish I could see him, though – my father, I mean. Even if I didn't say anything . . . It would be nice just to see what he looks like – just to *look* at him and think "he's my father".'

'Well, you could,' Val said. 'He's round the village all the time. You've only got to walk round the lanes and you'll bump into him somewhere. You could even stop and talk to him.'

'I don't know,' Jennifer said. 'It would be a bit like spying. I don't think I ought to do that – not until I've talked to Mr Harvey again, anyway.' She put the envelope back into her handbag and smiled round at them. Her eyes were bright with tears. 'Thank you, all of you. You've been a real help. I'll get in touch with Mr Harvey again. But now I ought to be thinking about going back to Plymouth. The last bus goes soon.'

'That's right, maid.' Alice stood up and fetched Jennifer's coat from the hook by the door. 'Now, you come and see us again, whatever you decide to do, won't you? And let us know how you get on – that's if you want to,' she added hastily. 'Like Ted says, it's none of our business, really. But you'm Susan's maid, when all's said and done, and us'd like to know how you go on.'

'I will,' Jennifer said, smiling at them a little waveringly. 'I'll come and see you again.' She looked around the big, warm kitchen with the family sitting at the table, the brown teapot in the middle and a big jug of fresh milk beside it. 'I feel as if I've found a family already,' she said. 'I feel as if Burracombe's my home.'

There was very seldom a day when Val and Luke didn't manage to meet at some point. After Jennifer Tucker had left the farm, Val put on her coat and said she was just going to walk up to the charcoal-burner's cottage to see him for an hour or so. 'Don't wait up,' she said to her mother. 'Luke'll see me home.'

'Well, don't you be too late, mind.' Alice said. 'You've got an early start in the morning and it's been a funny sort of evening. Given us a lot to think about.'

'I won't be late,' Val said, and walked out into the cool night air. Joanna and Tom had gone to their own room, and she sensed that her parents and grandmother weren't sorry to be left on their own to discuss Jennifer's story. There were more old memories there than they had divulged, she thought, and a lot for them to talk about and come to terms with.

Who would have thought that old Jacob Prout might have a daughter! And born out of wedlock, too. Val thought of the sturdy, upright man who worked so hard around the village and was held in such high regard and tried to imagine him as a young man, leaving his home village and going to sea and to war. She thought of the girl he'd left behind. She too had known the aching loneliness of being parted from the one she loved, and the terrible grief of losing him. And there was something else that she and Susan Hannaford had in common . . .

'I felt as if I could share in what she was going through,' she said to Luke as they sat on his old settee in front of the smouldering log fire. 'I felt as if I were Susan herself – having to leave home in disgrace, turned away by her family. It could so easily have been me.'

'Your family would never have treated you like that,' he said, tightening his arm about her shoulder.

'I don't know. Girls did get turned out into the snow with their little white bundles. I knew a girl it happened to and her family have never spoken to her again.'

Luke drew her closer. 'Val, all this must have brought back that time when you—'

'Yes, it did,' she said quietly. 'I honestly don't know what I'd have done if things hadn't turned out the way they did. Not that I was *glad* to lose the baby – he was our baby, and I've grieved for him ever since. I think I always will.'

'There'll be other babies,' he said, and she nodded.

'I know. But never that one. Never that little boy. Oh, *Luke* . . .' She turned and buried her face against the soft wool of his pullover. He wrapped both arms around her and held her close, rocking her gently, his heart aching as he thought of that time, years ago, when he and Val had first fallen in love. It had been an impossible, forbidden love then, but its power had been too great for them, and the hurt it had caused had kept them apart for a long time. Now, at last, they were together, and he felt a sudden urgent desire to make sure that nothing should ever again come between them. He thought of the promise he had made to Ted Tozer on Christmas afternoon, and suddenly it didn't seem so important any more. It was what Val wanted that was imperative to him now.

'Darling,' he said, when her tears had eased, 'don't let's wait any longer to get married. Let's do it as soon as possible, and if we haven't got anywhere in Burracombe to live, we'll go to Plymouth and find somewhere there. I'm tired of having you go back to the farm every night. I'm tired of being engaged. I want to be married!'

She raised her head and looked at him. Her cheeks were wet and her eyes brimming, but her mouth broke into a trembling smile. She tried to speak but a hiccuping sob shook her, and she gasped and felt for a hanky. At last, she said, 'Luke, do you mean it? Do you really want to get married soon?'

'Well, of course I do!' he exclaimed, laughing. 'I'd get married tomorrow if it was possible. But since it isn't, let's see just how soon we can do it. An Easter wedding, perhaps – how about that?'

'Oh, Luke, yes!' she cried, hugging him to her. 'But we won't go to Plymouth – not yet. We'll stay here, in this cottage. I know it's too small and it's cold and draughty, but summer's coming and we needn't be indoors all that much. We'll have months to find somewhere to live before winter comes. And we'll have all that time to enjoy being married.'

'I'm going to enjoy being married for a very long time,' he said, taking her face in his hands and looking deep into her eyes. 'I'm going to enjoy it for the rest of my life.'

Chapter Seventeen

Aggie Madge said she would be delighted to have Stella's sister staying in her cottage.

'I remember her as a little maid,' she said when Felix asked her. 'Proper little ray of sunshine, she were. Everyone loved little Maddy, and Dottie looked after her like a mother.'

'And you don't think there'll be any problem with her staying here – since I'm here as well?' Felix asked, wondering how to put the question delicately.

Aggie stared at him. 'Why should there be a problem? You don't use the spare room for anything.'

'I didn't mean that. I meant . . . well, with me being a single man and—'

'But you'm the *curate*!' Aggie exclaimed. '"Tisn't like you'm an *ordinary* young man, now is it!'

Felix thought that in some respects he was very ordinary indeed, but this wasn't the moment to explain that to Aggie. He hoped the rest of the village would take the same view as her. He was looking forward to having Stella's sister staying in the cottage. For one thing, she was a very pretty girl, and for another, it meant that he would see more of Stella herself.

Felix had begun to feel very fond of Stella, and having the little sports car had helped a lot. Taking her to the cinema had become the highlight of his week, and they'd discovered similar tastes in films, music and even books. Both loved the stories written by Daphne du Maurier, though Felix's favourite was *Jamaica Inn*, whereas Stella liked *Rebecca* best.

It had become an accepted fact that they would spend at least some of their spare time together, and now that the evenings were getting lighter, Felix had plans for runs out across the moor in the little car, and walks in some of the spots that were less accessible by bus or on foot.

He'd been thinking of kissing her for a while before he actually plucked up the courage to do so – and then it wasn't pre-meditated at all, just a spontaneous gesture because she was so pretty and he felt so sorry for the sadness in her life, and because they'd been talking about Burracombe and whether either of them might ever move away; because he'd known, suddenly, that he didn't want to leave the village, and he didn't want Stella to leave either.

Stella's lips had been soft and tasted faintly sweet, as if touched with honey. They'd trembled a little under his, and he'd realised that this was her first real kiss. He'd ended it gently and held her for a moment before turning to begin the walk home.

I must go very carefully with Stella, he'd thought. She's sweet and innocent, and she's been hurt enough already – I mustn't do anything to hurt her more. I must be very, very sure . . .

'Now then,' Aggie was saying. 'I'll have to think how to make young Maddy comfortable. She'm used to something better than an old cob cottage these days, what with living in London and Paris and all them places. My stars, I expect her'll be used to having her own bathroom and everything!' She gazed at Felix in dismay. 'She'll have forgotten what it's like down here, with the bath having to be brought in from the back yard every Friday night and everyone using the same water!'

'I hadn't thought of that.' Felix himself had found this to be quite an embarrassing procedure when he'd first arrived in Burracombe. Some of the larger houses, like the vicarage and the doctor's house and the Warrens', had their own bath-rooms, but most of the cottages were still reliant on tin baths hung, like Aggie's, on a nail outside and hauled in once or twice a week to be filled with kettles of hot water. It wasn't all that long ago, so he'd been told, that some of the cottages hadn't even had their own water supply and had had to fetch supplies from a standpipe or the old well at the far end of the village. Felix and Aggie didn't exactly take turns with the bath, sharing the water as many families did, but since this meant that there wasn't enough hot water for two baths in the same evening, it was still quite a procedure bringing it in two nights a week. With Maddy here, it would mean another night – perhaps more.

'She probably wants a bath every day,' Aggie went on, anxiously. 'A lot of they posh people do, you know. Sometimes twice!'

Felix rubbed his hand over his fair hair, tousling it into a mass of curls. 'You're right, Aggie. I hadn't even considered it. We'd better ask Stella what she thinks. I suppose she could have a jug of hot water in her room every day – you've got that old washstand set, haven't you?'

Aggie thought for a minute. The set Felix meant had been her grandmother's and stood on the washstand in the spare bedroom, almost as if it were ready for use, but Aggie couldn't remember the last time it had been put to its proper purpose. There was a large china washbasin and a big, heavy jug, both patterned with full-blown roses, and there was a soap-dish and a saucer for a flannel or sponge.

'You could have a proper all-over wash in that,' she agreed. 'And it'd be no trouble for me to take up the hot water every morning, so long as she don't mind not having a real bath. It's just as clean, anyway, to my mind. Cleaner, really – you're not laying there in all your dirt, are you?'

'I'll ask Stella,' he said. 'After all, Maddy must know what it's like in these old cottages. She lived at Dottie's for long enough.'

Aggie shook her head, still looking doubtful, and he tried to reassure her.

'She'll be perfectly comfortable here, Aggie. The bedroom's very pretty, and if the bed's as comfortable as mine, she'll never want to get out of it. And your cooking is marvellous.'

'Her won't be having much of that, though,' Aggie said. 'Her'll be having her dinners over at Dottie's with her sister.'

'Well, she'll be having breakfast here, and you know what they say – you should breakfast like a king, lunch like a lord and dine like a pauper. Your breakfasts are fit for any king, Aggie.'

'They might be too heavy for her. Maddy's more like a little princess.'

'Aggie, for goodness' sake! Stop worrying. She'll be perfectly comfortable here. Anyway, we haven't asked her yet – she might want to stay at the Barton after all. That's where she's been before, isn't it?'

'Yes, because Miss Forsyth was a friend of Hilary's mother. But she'm coming on her own this time, to see her sister. I'm sure her'd rather be in the village.'

'I'm sure she would, too,' Felix said firmly. 'And I'm sure this is the best place for her – just across the road, as near to Stella as she could possibly be. Between us, we'll make her as comfortable as any princess could wish. Honestly, Aggie, she'll be as happy as can be staying here.'

'And I'll be happy to have her,' Aggie said, cheering up at last. 'You can tell Miss Simmons that. It'll be a real pleasure to have little Maddy staying here.'

Getting married at Easter seemed less easy than Val and Luke expected.

'But that's only just over two weeks away!' Alice exclaimed, outraged. She was decorating a simnel cake and stopped in the middle of rolling out marzipan balls to stare at her daughter. 'You've not even had the banns called yet. You've got to have at least three weeks, and that's nowhere near long enough to get a wedding arranged proper.' She gave Val a close look. 'There isn't no *reason* for this sudden hurry, I hope, is there?'

'No, of course there isn't,' Val said indignantly. 'It's just that Luke and I are tired of waiting—'

'You only got engaged at Christmas. In my day, engagements lasted a good two years. More, sometimes, while people saved up and the bride got her bottom drawer filled up. I haven't noticed you doing anything about yours, Valerie.'

Alice so rarely used her daughter's full name that Val knew she was seriously disturbed. Lamely, she said, 'Well, we've all been busy knitting for Joanna's new baby . . .'

'Then maybe you shouldn't have been,' Alice said smartly. 'If you were so keen to get married all in a hurry, you should have been thinking about that! There's plenty of time till Joanna has her babby.'

'Mum,' Val said, feeling as if she were a child again, asking for more sweets, 'Luke and I are over twenty-one. I'm almost *thirty*, for goodness' sake! We just don't want to wait any longer.'

Alice looked at her daughter and her face softened. 'Yes, I can understand that. I'm sorry, Val. You've waited a long time for happiness to come to you. But I'd really like you to have a proper wedding – all in white, with bridesmaids and all, and a proper reception with your dad making a speech. I've been looking forward to it for so many years, and if you wants to get married all in a rush, there just won't be time. Don't you want that yourself? Don't every girl want a lovely wedding? A day to remember and look back on?'

Val sighed. She looked at the mantelpiece where a framed photograph of Ted and Alice on their wedding day stood in a brass frame. Her mother never allowed anyone but herself to polish that frame, and Val had seen her fingers lingering over it as she did so. The happy couple looked, in fact, anything but happy, both standing so stiff and formal, Alice in a cream-coloured lace dress, and Ted in the suit he had worn again only a day or so ago for Jem Squires's funeral. But Val knew that they must have been happy inside – warm and excited, filled with joy and anticipation of the life ahead.

That's how I want to feel, she thought.

'You'll enjoy it all so much more if you've done it right,' Alice went on, more coaxingly now. She began to place the marzipan balls around the edge of the cake. 'I know there's a lot of preparation, a lot of sewing and planning, and maybe a few little arguments along the way. Weddings are always like that. But it all turns out right in the end, and it's like everything else in life – you gets out of it what you puts in. That's what makes things worthwhile.' She was silent for a moment, and then she said, 'There's your dad to think of, too. You know he's got his own opinion about Luke – not that he don't like him, mind, it's his job your dad can't seem to understand. Painting pictures for a living – it just don't seem to be proper work, to him.'

'Luke works very hard,' Val said indignantly. 'He's done a lot of training at art college, and he's had exhibitions of his work – think of those pictures he showed in London last year. And he could get a good job as a teacher if he wanted to.'

'Well, your dad might think a bit more of him if he did,' Alice said. She saw the look on Val's face and added hastily, 'Not that he don't like him – I've already said that. And he's agreed he won't say no more about it. You're of age and you love each other, and it's your business. But if you goes on with this idea of getting married all in a hurry – well, he's bound to be upset. And that's not a good way to start off, now is it?'

'I suppose not,' Val said unwillingly. 'Though it's not my fault if he takes that attitude . . .'

'It's your fault if you don't take it into account, though. You can do what you like in this world, Val, but you has to take the consequences. And hurting other people without good reason – if there ever *is* a good reason for hurting someone that loves you and only wants what's best for you – always has consequences. You just think about that before you makes any decisions. In any case,' Alice added, reverting to her first argument, 'you can't get married at Easter because you haven't had the banns called, and that's all there is to it.'

Val thought of saying that they could get a special licence, but decided against it. There was no point in prolonging the argument and she had a feeling that her mother had already won, anyway. She folded her lips tightly and stared at the kitchen table, and after a moment or two, Alice came round and put her arm across Val's shoulders.

'Don't look so miserable, maid. Nobody wants to stop you and Luke from being happy together. We just wants it done proper. Can't you think again – put it off till the summer, perhaps? A June wedding's always nice.'

'I don't know,' Val said miserably. 'I'll think about it. I'll talk to Luke.'

'You do that,' Alice said, satisfied. 'He's a good chap – he'll understand, I'm sure. After all, what's two or three months? Give us all time to get things ready, that will. We wants to give you a day to remember all your lives, don't we.' She straightened up, looking at her cake with satisfaction. 'Now, I'll just put this away in the larder and then I'll make a pot of tea. Your gran will be coming down from her rest soon, and the men'll be in from the fields. I made some flapjacks this morning; they're in that tin if you wouldn't mind getting them out.' She bustled about the kitchen, filling the kettle and setting the big teapot by the hob to warm up, and Val got up, too, and did as she was told. The flapjacks, made of oats and butter and golden syrup, were a rich toffee-brown and smelled delicious, but somehow she had no appetite and when she had put them on the table she turned towards the door.

'I won't stop for a cup of tea, if you don't mind, Mum. I don't feel much like talking, anyway. I think I'll go for a walk.'

'All right, maid.' Alice was busy with the kettle and didn't look round, but once the door had closed behind her daughter, she moved to the window and stood for a moment, watching Val trudge dispiritedly across the yard and out to the track.

It's a shame she's got to wait, she thought, but it's the best thing, really. People never quite forget or forgive a wedding that's not arranged right, and I don't want these two starting off on the wrong foot.

It was something in the story Jennifer Tucker had told them that had set Val off like this, she thought, with a small, puzzled frown. I saw her face then, while she was listening. There was something in that story that upset her, but I don't know what it was.

Still, there were bound to be things in your children's lives that you didn't know – things you never would know. And once Val was safely married to Luke, and everyone happy about it, perhaps whatever it was could be put in the past and not upset her any more.

The kettle began to sing, and Alice heard the voices of the men coming across the yard at the same moment as sounds from above announced that Minnie was on her way down from her afternoon rest. She turned back to her duties, wondering if mothers ever stopped worrying about their children.

'I suppose it was a bit optimistic,' Luke said as they climbed the hill to the Standing Stones half an hour later. Val had found him putting the finishing touches to a painting of a patch of snowdrops they had found along the riverbank a few weeks ago, glowing like pearls in a pool of sunlight. 'I'd thought about the banns, too. I was going to come and see you and suggest we went and had a talk with Uncle Basil about it.'

'We could always get a special licence,' Val argued, unwilling to let go of her dream. 'You can get married in three days, then, can't you?'

'I don't really know. But we don't want to do that, do we?' They reached the grassy plateau where the big, granite Standing Stones formed their ancient circle, and stopped. Luke took her in his arms. 'Val, there really isn't that much hurry. I know we're tired of waiting, all we want to do is get married and live happily ever after – but not in a way that will upset a lot of other people, especially when they're the people we love. Your mother will be terribly disappointed if you don't have the wedding she wants for you, and so will your father. And they're not the only ones—'

'But it isn't their wedding!' Val broke in, angry tears forming in her eyes. 'It's ours! And we should be able to have what we want. We're not just doing it to please other people.'

'No, of course not, and nobody expects us to,' Luke said, not entirely certain that this was true. 'But I thought it was what we wanted – a traditional wedding, with a church service and you in a long white dress, and the bells ringing and everything. And there's no nicer place than Burracombe to have it.' He drew her across to one of the stones, and they sat down on the short, springy turf, leaning their backs against the sun-warmed granite. 'Tell me the truth, Val. Is that what you want? Or have you just been going along with it because you thought I wanted it?'

Val frowned and stared down at her hands. She picked at the turf, tearing out small lumps and piling them up beside her. Then she said, 'Do you know, I've never even thought about it until now. I just took it for granted, I suppose. It's what you *do*, isn't it? I mean, I'd want to be married in the church, of course I would, with all our friends and family

179

around. I don't want something that looks like a hole and corner affair. But it doesn't have to be like that, does it? It can be simple and quiet without being second-rate.'

'Of course it can. It can be whatever you want.' He took her hand and stroked it, rubbing his thumb over her engagement ring. 'But if we're going to have our friends and family there, it's not going to be small, is it? It's going to be over half the village. And there's my family, too. We'll probably fill the church.'

'Oh dear,' she said dismally. 'It's impossible, isn't it? We can't arrange anything like that in a couple of weeks.'

'Not even in a couple of months,' he said. 'I think your mother's right, you know. We're going to have to wait till the summer at least.'

Val nodded, her lips pressed together in resignation. Then she turned her head to look at him and said, 'There's something else I've realised.'

'What's that, sweetheart?'

'This white dress,' she said hesitantly. 'I don't think – it seems wrong to me, to wear that. It's like telling a lie.'

'Oh, *Val*—'

'Well, it is, isn't it! It's a symbol of purity – it's supposed to show that the bride's a virgin. And I'm not.' She turned her head away again and he saw the glitter of a tear on her cheek. 'It's worse than that. I've been a mother.'

'Val—'

'I know he didn't live,' she said tonelessly. 'He wasn't even big enough to be born. But he existed just the same, and I can't go up the aisle in our own church wearing a white dress and pretending it never happened. I just can't!'

Chapter Eighteen

Maddy arrived on the Wednesday before Easter, and Stella met her from the train at Tavistock. She had brought an array of suitcases and Stella looked at them in some dismay as the guard helped pile them on the platform.

'I'm not sure we can get all these in Felix's car. He's waiting outside.'

'Isn't there a taxi?' Maddy asked, looking around the quiet station.

'Well, there are taxis down in the square. I could ask Felix to go down and get one. But I can easily go back by bus, if you can get yourself and all your cases into his car.' She looked doubtfully at the luggage. 'You're staying with him, anyway.'

'Staying with Felix?' Maddy said in surprise. 'Isn't he that rather nice-looking young curate I met at Christmas?'

'Yes, that's right. He lodges just over the lane from me, at Aggie Madge's – you remember her, don't you? She's got a spare room you can have, and you'll have breakfast there but your other meals with me and Dottie. I hope that's all right?' Stella asked anxiously. 'You wouldn't rather be at the Barton, would you?'

'No thanks. We used to stay there when Fenella came down, but that was because she and Mrs Napier were friends. I was always rather scared of Mr Napier and I don't know Hilary or Stephen all that well. I thought I'd be staying at Dottie's, with you.'

'That would have been best, but there just isn't room. Dottie would have moved out of her room, but I didn't think you'd want her to do that. And you'll only be just across the road.' Stella turned as Felix came on to the platform, looking enquiringly at them. 'Oh, there you are. We were just trying to decide what to do. Maddy's got quite a lot of luggage.'

'So you have.' He regarded the pile of suitcases. 'Well, why don't I just cram all that stuff into Mirabelle and take it home, and then come back for you? You can have a cup of tea in Goode's or Perraton's or go for a walk in the Meadows. Show Maddy round a few of her old haunts.'

'That would be nice,' Maddy said. 'Not that I knew Tavistock all that well in those days. We only came here occasionally. But wouldn't that be an awful bore for you?' She gave Felix a bewitching smile and he blinked.

'No, of course it wouldn't. It'd be a pleasure.' Looking slightly dazed, he bent to heft some of the cases into his arms and carried them out of the station. Stella picked up the remaining case, Maddy swung her handbag on to her shoulder, and the two girls followed to find him stacking the cases into the sports car.

'There,' he said, squeezing the last one into the dicky seat. 'Just room. However did you manage on the way down, Maddy?'

'Oh, there are always porters about,' she said vaguely, glancing around the deserted station yard. 'Well, usually. And people are terribly kind and helpful, I always find.'

'I'm sure you do,' Felix said, with a glance at her delicately featured face, framed in soft, pale curls, and the curving lips. 'I should think people fall over themselves to help you.'

Maddy laughed. 'Well, I wouldn't say that. It's Fenella they really want to help. But there was a kind man on the train who put the cases in the rack for me and helped me get them down again. Anyway, never mind that now. Are you really sure you don't mind, Felix?'

'I don't mind at all. I wouldn't have been able to get both of you in the car, anyway – Stella was talking about going back on the bus, but I didn't think you'd want her to do that.'

'I don't mind going on the bus with Stella,' Maddy said at once, but he shook his head.

'Definitely not. You can use the bus other days if you want to, but not today. I'm your chauffeur.' He swung himself into the driving seat. 'I'll meet you in the square in about an hour.'

The little car roared out of the station yard and left silence behind. A moment or so later a pickup lorry came grinding up the hill, and two burly men jumped out with shovels and began to fill it with coal from the huge pile at the end of the yard. Stella took Maddy's arm.

'Come on. We'll go over the bridge and down the steps into the town. It's easier than walking all the way round.'

'I remember this,' Maddy said as they emerged in the main street. To their left and right were rows of shops, with several entrances to the Pannier Market across the road and the tall granite tower of the church dominating the end of the street. There were two or three cafés, and since Maddy declared herself to be dying of thirst, they made for one of these and settled themselves at a table with a pot of tea and a plate of scones.

'We'd better not eat or drink too much,' Stella said, pouring tea. 'Dottie's putting on an enormous spread in your honour. She's looking forward so much to seeing you.'

'I'm looking forward to seeing her again, too,' Maddy said, spreading a scone with jam and clotted cream. 'She was a mother to me. Not like our *real* mother, of course, but you know how warm and kind Dottie is. She really took me to her heart and looked after me.'

'I know.' Stella could hear that her voice sounded wistful. 'You were very lucky, Muriel.' She caught herself up quickly. 'Sorry, I mean Maddy, of course. I've been trying but I still forget sometimes, especially when I think of when we were little.'

'It's all right. I've almost forgotten being Muriel now, because nobody else knows me by that name. I don't mind you using it, though. It makes it rather special.'

The two sisters smiled at each other, then drank their tea, and Maddy began to talk about her recent stay in Paris, where Fenella Forsyth had her own apartment. Stella wanted to ask more questions about her childhood in Burracombe, and in the children's home she had lived in before the actress had adopted her, but she realised that Maddy needed more time, and perhaps this crowded café wasn't the place. There'll be time enough in the next two weeks, she thought, more time than we had at Christmas, when there were so many people about and so much to do. We'll be able to go for long walks together and talk till all hours, just the two of us.

There would be Felix, too, some of the time, she thought with a thrill of warmth touching her heart. Felix, Maddy and me. That's all I want.

Easter Day was fine and sunny, with just a hint of a warm spring breeze to freshen the air. After the sobriety of Good Friday, with all the shops shut and the village feeling more like a Sunday, it was good to wake to a cheerful breakfast of eggs boiled in onion skins or food colouring and walk along lanes sprinkled with primroses and violets to find the church bright with sunlight and spring flowers, and hear the music of the bells welcoming them in with extra joy in their tone.

As usual on Easter Day, the nave was filled with people, all in their best clothes, and there was a feeling of happiness and renewed growth in the air. It was, Stella thought as she sat in her pew gazing up at the jewelled colours of the east window, the beginning of a process that would come to fruition with the Harvest Festival – the start of the most productive part of the year, when seeds were planted, when birds laid their eggs, when lambs were born and trees began to blossom.

And it was the start of a new stage in her own life, too. There was Maddy, who had arrived a few days ago and was sitting beside her now, and there was Felix, coming in with the vicar at the head of the little procession of choirboys and men as the congregation rose to sing the Easter hymn: 'Jesus lives! No longer now, Can thy terrors, death appal us . . .'

Nothing, Stella thought, can 'appal' me now. I've got everything I want. And she watched the sunlight gleam on Felix's corn-gold head, and then turned her own head slightly to see the same rays catch the almost silvery blonde of her sister's soft curls, and wondered how it had come about that her life should have changed, in such a short time, from the loneliness of her years at the children's home to the fulfilment and happiness she had found in Burracombe.

It's this village, she thought. It's such a happy place. It's like a miracle, living here, as if nothing can ever go wrong. It's a magic place.

Near them sat the Tozers, with Ted stiff and smart in his best suit, Alice wearing a pale green costume she had made herself, Minnie in her best feathered hat, Jackie looking bored, and Val and Luke together looking a little wistful. In the front pew were Hilary Napier and her father and, behind them, the Cherrimans, who were so seldom seen in the village that some members of the congregation weren't sure who they were. Constance Bellamy, whose accustomed pew they had taken, had been forced to move back and when she stood up for the hymns her stocky back was stiff with indignation.

As the service progressed, the ringers got up from their seats and made their way self-consciously to the chancel steps, where they formed a semi-circle round Minnie, who was holding up the cards with the bell notations carefully written up by Joanna. The silvery notes made a dainty contrast to the deeper tones of the church bells themselves as they went into the old changes, and then to the more familiar tunes of 'All in the April Evening' and 'All Things Bright and Beautiful', finishing with the stirring chords of 'Jerusalem'. As they ended their recital and returned to their seats, there was a small sigh of approval from the congregation, and if it had been the custom to clap in church, there would have been a burst of applause. Instead, people turned and smiled at each other.

'That was really nice,' Maddy said afterwards as they made their way back to Dottie's for dinner. Felix had been invited as well, and afterwards he was taking the two girls out for the afternoon in Mirabelle. 'They couldn't ring the big bells when I was here, of course, because it was during the war, but Mr Tozer did get the handbells out at Christmas for carols. It was a lovely idea to have them in church today.'

'I wonder if he'd come to the school and teach the children to ring them,' Stella said thoughtfully. 'We could have them as part of our concerts. I'll mention it to Miss Kemp as soon as school starts.'

Dottie had roasted a leg of lamb, boned and stuffed with pork sausagemeat and dried apricots. To go with it, they had new potatoes, carrots and spring cabbage, and for pudding she had made a lemon sponge soufflé, which had magically separated itself into two layers, the top one of feather-light sponge and the bottom of creamy lemon sauce. Afterwards, she made a big pot of tea and they lay in their armchairs or on the sofa, declaring themselves too full to move.

'I shall never need to eat again,' Maddy said. 'I've missed your cooking, Dottie.'

'Go on with you,' Dottie said, looking pleased. 'After all that lovely cooking you get in Paris?'

'It's not the same as yours. Mind you, they do have scrumptious *pâtisseries*. But it's only just starting to come back after the war. They've had rationing, too, you know.' She sighed and stretched her arms above her head. 'Actually, their

186

peasant cooking – the sort they do in the country – is more like yours. *Proper* food – vegetables and things like pigeons and goose and that sort of thing. And they don't waste a single thing – it all gets eaten, one way or another.'

'And when did you ever eat peasant food?' Dottie asked, picking up her knitting. She had begun making things for the Summer Fair and was working on a pale-blue baby's cardigan. 'You and Miss Fenella spend all your time in the city, don't you?'

'No, we go to the country quite a lot. We stay in a château in the Dordogne. As a matter of fact, that's where we're going to live.' A small frown touched her face. 'At least, it's where Fenella's going to live. She's getting married.'

Dottie dropped her knitting. 'Getting married? Miss Fenella? After all these years? I can't believe it.'

Maddy nodded her head. 'Yes, she is. He's a French aristocrat, or he would have been if they hadn't had the Revolution. He owns the château itself, and acres and acres of land, and I don't know how many villages. He's terribly rich.'

'I should think he must be.' Dottie picked up her knitting again. 'Well, fancy Miss Fenella getting married again. I never thought she would.'

'Has she been married before, then?' Stella enquired. 'I never knew that.'

Dottie pursed her lips and nodded. 'When she were a little slip of thing, just twenty-one years old. Had her head turned by an actor in the London theatre – didn't have nobody to advise her, you see, and went and got married without knowing a thing. He was twice her age and a drinker. Drank hisself to death in two years and left poor Miss Fenella alone, a widow at twenty-three. Not that it wasn't a good thing, when you look at it all ways up,' Dottie added, joining on a fresh ball of wool. 'She were well rid of him. But 'twas a hard time for her, all the same.'

'Oh, poor Miss Forsyth,' Stella exclaimed. 'But why didn't she have anyone to advise her, Dottie? Was she an orphan, like Maddy and me?'

'Not exactly, but as good as. Told me the whole story, her did, one day. I'd been working for her as her dresser for a few months then and we got on as well as if we were sisters. It were her dad, you see. Wouldn't countenance the idea of her being an actress, and when her wouldn't give up the idea, he just turned her out of the house. Told her never to go back. 'Twas no wonder her turned to an older man for comfort.' Dottie shook her head. 'Changed his tune after she became a success, but Miss Fenella wasn't having any. She kept in touch with her mother up to the day the old lady died, but she never saw her father again. And after that dratted husband of hers died, she swore she'd never marry again, neither.'

'And so she thought she'd never have any children,' Maddy said. 'That's why she adopted me.'

They sat in silence for a few minutes, thinking over the story and trying to imagine the tragedy and pain that lay behind the words. Then Dottie said, 'And now she'm getting wed again! Well, she ought to be old enough not to make a mistake this time round.'

'Oh, I don't think it's a mistake this time,' Maddy said. 'She really loves him and he thinks the world of her.' But there was a faint note of desolation in her voice and Stella glanced at her.

'What will you do?' she asked quietly. 'Are you going to live in France with them?'

'I don't know,' Maddy said. 'I don't know what I'm going to do.'

After a while, the three of them crammed themselves into the sports car and set off across the moor. Despite Dottie's protests, they had done the washing-up first and left the kitchen clean and shining. They had to be back for Felix to take part in evensong, but apart from that the afternoon was theirs and they felt as free as birds as the little car climbed valiantly up the steep hills and dropped into the hidden valleys of the moor.

'This is Dartmeet,' Felix announced, stopping by a narrow bridge over the flashing river. 'It's where the east and west tributaries of the River Dart come together. There's the old packhorse bridge, see? And there's a nice tearoom, too – we could come back here for tea if you like.'

'I'd like to walk along the river,' Stella said, and they parked the car and set off along the narrow footpath.

'Do you really not know what you want to do, Maddy?' Stella asked after a few minutes. 'Don't you want to stay with Miss Forsyth?'

Maddy, walking just behind, between Stella and Felix, shrugged. She was wearing a flowered dress and a light-blue cardigan, and her fair hair bounced on her shoulders as she moved. 'I don't know what I want to do. It's been lovely until now, travelling about with Fenella – it was exciting and fun when she was still on the stage, and now that she's left it, we've had a good time just visiting all her friends and seeing Europe. She knew it so well before the war, you see, and she's enjoyed showing me France and Italy and Switzerland. And I've enjoyed seeing it all. But now – well, she's not going to need me for company any more, is she? And I feel I ought to be living my own life – earning a living, like you. Only, I'm not trained for anything, and I don't know what I'd be good at. I might not be good at anything.'

Once again, Stella heard the faint note of melancholy in her sister's voice and felt an urge to reassure her. 'Of course you must be good at things. Look at all you've done – the places you've seen. Much more than I have. There must be heaps of jobs you could do.'

'Like what?' Maddy asked. 'I don't think I could teach, and I'd be hopeless as a nurse. I could work in a shop, I suppose.'

'You'd make a jolly good secretary,' Felix said, turning his head. 'You must have lots of experience in arranging things for Miss Forsyth.'

'Yes, I suppose so.' Maddy still sounded doubtful. 'I looked after her diary and did all the travel and that kind of thing. I did learn typing and shorthand at the finishing school I went to, but I've never worked in an office, and I don't know really what else secretaries do.'

'Well, it depends whose secretary they are,' Felix said. 'The thing is, would you like that sort of work?'

'I don't know. I might.' Her voice was so dispirited that they both stopped at once and Maddy walked into Felix and almost knocked him into the river. Stella grabbed them both and the three of them clutched each other, laughing. 'Oh, don't let's bother about all that now,' Maddy exclaimed, resting her head against Felix's shoulder as he steadied her. 'This is a holiday – let's just enjoy ourselves. How far do you want to walk, Stella? I was hoping we could go to Widecombe.'

They turned and walked back to the car, the brief discussion over. As they soared up the steep hill out of the valley, Maddy's spirits seemed to recover, and Stella, taking her turn in the dicky seat, smiled at the sight of the two blond heads so close together. She had no qualms about her sister's ability to find work, if she needed it. But would she actually need it? Fenella Forsyth had looked after her so well until now, adopting her as a daughter and never allowing her to want for anything, that it was difficult to believe that Maddy would ever really need to work for her living. It seemed almost wrong that she should have to – she was so pretty, so enchanting, so different from the plain little Muriel she had once been, that it seemed unnatural to imagine her teaching a class of unruly schoolchildren or serving in a shop. Even sitting at a typewriter . . .

Even if she does have to work, Stella thought, it won't be

for long. Someone will marry her and look after her for the rest of her life. I just hope he's someone who treats her as she ought to be treated.

Chapter Nineteen

'It's this morning Miss Tucker's coming to see me again,' Basil said to his wife at breakfast a few days after Easter. 'I think she's found out quite a lot from the Tozers. Alice wouldn't tell me anything of course, she said she'd leave it to the young woman herself, but it's obvious they know something.'

'Well, if anyone would know, the Tozers would,' Grace said, opening a new pot of homemade marmalade. 'That's if the parents actually did come from Burracombe.'

'I think they must have, or she wouldn't be coming to see me.' Basil folded his newspaper. 'I just hope it won't lead to trouble for anyone. It isn't always a good idea to dig up the past.'

'It's only natural for her to want to know the truth about her parents, though. It's not exactly the distant past, is it?'

'No – it might be better if it were.' Basil dipped a spoon into the marmalade and frowned. 'I believe in the truth as much as any man of my calling, my dear, but I still can't help feeling that some truths are best left untold. But it isn't for me to say what's best in this case. It's Miss Tucker's life we're talking about, and it must be her decision. I'm sure God will guide her.'

'I'm sure He will,' Grace said, smiling. 'And I can't help admitting that I'm very curious to know more myself. Are you ever going to take any marmalade out of that pot, Basil, or are you just going to stir it for a while?'

'Oh – I'm sorry, dear.' He hastily removed the spoon and dropped a dollop of marmalade on the side of his plate. 'Yes, I'm curious, too. But we really ought to set our curiosity aside, Grace. Miss Tucker may have decided to look no further into the matter. She may decide never to say who she believes her father is, and if that's her decision, I shan't question it. Curiosity is a human emotion, my dear – not a godly one.'

His wife smiled again. It might be human, but it was a very healthy emotion, and as long as you kept other people's secrets and never betrayed their confidences, there was no harm in it. It was what kept you interested in your fellow human beings, and that was the most important thing of all.

Grace could understand her husband's reservations, though. A secret like this might be better never told.

'Jacob Prout?' Basil stared at his visitor, too astonished even to close his mouth. *'Jacob Prout* is your father?'

'I believe he is, yes.' Jennifer sat in his study, a cup of coffee on the small table beside her. Basil was opposite her, in his armchair beside the fireplace. The fire was unlit, the room warmed by April sunshine, and through the open window they could hear a robin singing. Basil glanced round, then got up hastily and closed the window.

'Jacob comes and helps in the garden sometimes,' he explained. 'He might easily pass at any minute and hear what we're saying . . . My dear Miss Tucker, are you sure about this? I can hardly believe it. *Jacob Prout . . . ?'* He shook his head and sat down again.

'That's what Mr and Mrs Tozer think,' Jennifer said. 'They knew my mother, you see, and old Mrs Tozer knew my grandmother. They were close friends.' She recounted the story of her grandmother's marriage to the bullying Abraham Hannaford. 'They used to see my mother and Jacob together. She came into the village for dances, when she could get away, and she and Jacob . . .' She raised her eyes to Basil's. 'We don't know for certain, of course. But it really does seem as if he must have been my father. He wrote to her all the time he was away, and then he came back for a while in 1916, when he was wounded. Susan was expecting me when she left the village – when her father turned her out. It *must* have been him.'

'It certainly seems likely,' Basil said slowly. 'And of course I didn't know Jacob then – I didn't come to the village until a good many years after that. But still . . .' He shook his head again. 'Who would have thought it? Who would have dreamed of such a thing?'

'It isn't all that unusual,' Jennifer said defensively. 'People do have babies without being married. I'm sure they *would* have been married, if it hadn't been for the war.'

'Yes, I'm sure they would,' Basil hastened to reassure her. 'I'm not speaking against Jacob, my dear, or your poor mother. It must have all been very difficult for them, especially if she was having such an unhappy time at home.'

'He was a bully,' Jennifer said flatly. 'My grandfather, I mean. He might have been a chapelgoer and read the Bible every night, but he was a bully just the same. He used to beat my grandmother, so old Mrs Tozer says, and probably my mother as well.' She glanced down at her arms and pushed up the sleeve of her cardigan to stare at the faint blue lines beneath the pale skin. 'And this is his blood in my veins. Do you know how that makes me feel?' She leaned forward. 'I need to know who else there was in my life,' she said. 'I need to know who my father was, and to know he was someone good.'

'Jacob is certainly that,' Basil said seriously. 'A very good man – the salt of the earth. But do you really think it matters so much whose blood you have, my dear? It's how you were brought up that's really important, and anyone can see that your mother—'

'Oh, she was a wonderful mother. And my stepfather, too – he was always kind to me, he never treated me any differently from my sisters. But –' she looked at her arm again '– I still need to know about my real father. I'm sorry, Mr Harvey, but I really do need to know.' She pulled down her sleeve and sat back, looking at him almost with a touch of defiance, as if she were presenting him with a challenge.

There was a brief silence. Basil returned her gaze and then picked up his coffee cup. He drank, then put it down again and said, 'Yes. I can see that you do, and of course it must be your own decision. But may I ask what you intend to do next? It's not just curiosity on my part –' he remembered his conversation with Grace and almost blushed '– but Jacob is not only one of my parishioners, he's also a churchwarden and looks after the churchyard. He works closely with me. And while acknowledging that this is really a matter between the two of you, if there's anything concerning his spiritual welfare . . .' He stopped and sighed. 'I haven't the right even to ask you this. It's entirely your business and his. If Jacob wants to confide in me himself, then of course he may. But if not . . .'

Jennifer fiddled with her own cup. 'But I've made it your business, too,' she said at last. 'I came and asked you to help me. And the Tozers as well – I've already involved you all. Are you asking me not to tell him, when you all know already?'

'We don't know,' he corrected her gently. 'Not for certain, anyway . . .' He sighed. 'I think what you are saying is that it isn't fair for so many of us to know – or suspect – while he remains in ignorance. Is that right?'

'Yes, it is,' Jennifer said slowly. 'You were all so surprised, you see. You'd never thought that there might be anything like this in his past. So it's changed the way you think of him. It doesn't seem fair that he shouldn't know that.'

'I hope it won't make any difference to the way I treat him—' Basil began, but she shook her head.

'I don't see how you can help it. You know something he doesn't. Things aren't the same between you any more – they can't be.' She paused, then added, 'I know, because things aren't the same between me and my half-sisters. I'm not saying they've changed in any bad, or hurtful, way, but they're different. It'll be like that with you and Jacob. You and the Tozers know something that he doesn't, and it's something important.'

Basil sat for a few moments staring into the fireplace, filled now with fir-cones for the summer. He gazed at them thoughtfully and at last turned his head and looked back at the woman sitting opposite him.

'You're right,' he said. 'You're quite right. But it still doesn't mean he should be told. Perhaps we should just accept that we know this – or think we know it – and try to adjust. You see, I think it might hurt him very much to know that your mother – his sweetheart – was in such trouble and that he didn't even know about it. And remember that he did, eventually, marry and his marriage seems to have been happy. And your mother, too, seems to have made a good life for herself and for you. After all, she could have contacted him herself, couldn't she? Have you ever wondered why she didn't – before she married?'

'I thought it was probably because he was still away. Or because she knew that everyone had been told she was dead. Her father must have made it impossible for her to come back.'

'Yes, it could have been difficult.' Basil sighed. 'How can we know, so long after the event? But mightn't it still be better just to let things lie? Might you not be able to put this knowledge you have into its own compartment and go on to make your own life? So far, nobody has been hurt by this knowledge, and—'

'Except for me,' she said quietly, and he inclined his head.

'Yes, I'm sorry. Except for you. And I'm afraid it is you

who have to make the decision – whether to go on carrying your secret or whether to approach Jacob. And if you do that, we just don't know what will happen next.'

'He might be pleased,' she said. 'He might be happy to have a daughter. He's never had any other children.' Once again, the challenge leaped into her eyes. 'I'm not a young woman, Mr Harvey, but I'm still young enough to have my own children. He could have grandchildren as well. Wouldn't that make him happy?'

'Yes,' Basil said. 'I'm sure it would.'

They sat silent for a while, then she put her cup back on the table and made to rise. Basil stood up quickly and held out his hand, and she took it in hers.

'Thank you, Mr Harvey,' she said simply. 'Thank you very much. You've given me quite a lot to think about. And I promise I won't do anything in a hurry.' She looked him in the eye. 'I'll promise you something else as well. Whatever I decide to do, I'll let you know first. And if I do tell my father – Jacob – I'll tell him that you know. I don't want anyone else having secrets they can't share.'

Basil nodded, but he still looked doubtful. 'He might prefer to think that I didn't know.'

'But you do,' she said. 'And once we start telling the truth, we're not going to stop. It will all have to come out into the open – every bit of it.'

Basil saw her to the door. As she went out and walked down the path, he caught sight of Jacob himself approaching along the lane. His heart in his mouth, he waited for them to meet, wondering if Jennifer would realise who the man was and whether she would be able to resist speaking to him.

They met at the gateway. Jennifer paused and Jacob stood back a little to let her pass. She said something to him and he touched his cap and dipped his head slightly. Then she walked on past and he came up the path to the door where Basil was still standing.

'Nice-looking little body,' Jacob commented as he came within earshot. 'Haven't seen her around the village before. Visitor, was she?'

'Yes,' Basil said, finding his voice. 'A sort of visitor. She just came to ask me something.' Already, he was realising the truth of Jennifer's words, that the knowledge he had been given was forming a barrier between them. He summoned up all his determination to overcome it, but Jacob's next words almost destroyed his resolve.

'Put me in mind of someone,' the gravedigger said, pushing back his cap to scratch his head. 'Can't quite put me finger on it, though. Maybe she's got family living hereabouts.'

'Yes,' Basil said faintly, 'maybe she has.'

Stella and Maddy met Jennifer Tucker, too, as they were strolling towards the bus stop. They had decided to spend the day in Plymouth, looking at the new buildings and going up to the Hoe.

'There was almost nothing left, you know,' Maddy told Stella. 'The Blitz was over before I came here, of course, and we never went to Plymouth – there wasn't much to go for by then – but Dottie told me about it. She said the flames were so bright when it was burning that you could read a newspaper by their light, all the way out here in Burracombe.'

'I've seen pictures of it,' Stella said. 'Dottie kept a lot of newspapers, and someone put them all into a book. It's like Portsmouth was, when we were little.' They were both silent for a moment, remembering the times their own home had been bombed and that final catastrophic raid when their mother and baby brother had been killed. 'Thank goodness it's all over. I hope we never have a war like that again.'

They came to the bus shelter and looked with friendly interest at the woman already waiting. She smiled back a little shyly and said, 'Going to do some shopping?'

'We're just going for a look round, really,' Stella said. 'My sister used to live here when she was little, but I've only been in the village for just over a year. I haven't been to Plymouth very often.'

'I want to see Dingle's,' Maddy said. 'Dottie told me what a lovely shop it was before the war, and I want to see what it's like now the new one's been opened.'

'That's where I work!' Jennifer exclaimed. 'It *is* a lovely shop – it's really big and open, and there are all sorts of things on sale. I work on the ladies' fashions floor. I'm a senior sales assistant, but I hope to be a buyer.' She looked at Maddy's slender figure and blonde hair. 'Are you a model?'

'Good gracious, no!' Maddy laughed. 'Whatever makes you ask that?'

'With your looks, you could be,' Jennifer said, and Maddy blushed and laughed again. Before she could say any more, they heard the sound of the little country bus trundling along the lane and prepared to climb aboard. The two sisters sat behind Jennifer so that they could continue their conversation.

'Do you mind me asking something?' Jennifer said after a few minutes. She looked at Maddy. 'Your sister said you lived here when you were little. Were you evacuated here?'

'Yes, I was with a children's home – Stella and I lost our parents in the war and we were separated. I was lucky – I was adopted, but my new mother had to be away and couldn't look after me herself, so she left me with Dottie Friend, a village woman that she knew. And Stella lodges with Dottie now, and we found each other again last year!'

'You mean you lost touch completely?'

'That's right,' Stella said. 'I started to try to find Maddy when I came here. It was the first chance I had, you see. But it was pure coincidence that I actually came to the place where she'd been living. Like a miracle,' she added, squeezing her sister's arm. 'You don't know how wonderful it is to find someone you've been looking for all your life.'

'No, I don't,' Jennifer said slowly, gazing at them. 'But I can imagine it . . .' She turned suddenly and stared out of the window.

A little startled by her abruptness, the two sisters glanced at each other and Maddy raised her eyebrows. Stella shrugged and was about to make a remark about the scenery when the older woman twisted round to speak to them again.

'So you're living in the village again now – both of you?'

'No, only me,' Stella said. 'I'm teaching at the village school. Maddy lives in France most of the time.'

'In France?'

'It's where my adopted mother lives,' Maddy explained. 'But I'm not sure I'm going to stay there much longer. Now that I've found Stella again, it would be nice to come back – especially as she lives in Burracombe. It's the place I always think of as home, you see.'

'Yes,' Jennifer said. 'It seems the sort of place where you could really feel at home.'

'Do you know it well?' Stella enquired, thinking that it was their turn to ask a few questions. 'Have you got family in the village?'

To her surprise, the stranger's face coloured and she looked for a moment as if she didn't know how to answer. Then she said, 'My mother used to bring me here when I was a little girl. I don't remember it well, but I've never really forgotten it. I think she had relatives.' Once again she stopped, as if she had said too much, and turned away. Then she looked back and said, 'You know how it's been since the war – people lost touch with each other. Everyone was so busy trying to get back to normal and make new lives for themselves.'

Stella nodded. 'I didn't think I'd ever find my sister again. And we still don't know if we've got any other relatives. I don't suppose we ever will.'

For the rest of the journey they chatted about other things. Maddy was eager to know about the rebuilding of Plymouth after the devastating damage of the war, and Jennifer described the new stores that were being built and the long, straight roads that had taken the place of the narrow streets that had been there before.

'The King himself came to open Royal Parade,' she said. 'I was there – I saw him almost as close as I am to you now. It's a shame he died so young. As a matter of fact, I was in Burracombe the day he died – I was in the church when the vicar came in to tell Mrs Tozer.'

'You know the Tozers, then?' Stella asked, and Jennifer bit her lip, as if once again she'd given herself away.

'Only a bit, just to say hello to. I saw Princess Elizabeth, too, once. She makes a lovely Queen, doesn't she? I'd love to go to London and see the Coronation procession. A lot of people are saying it's going to be on television, but hardly anyone's got it, so I don't see what use that will be.'

'I expect a lot of people will get sets especially to see it,' Maddy said. 'I would.'

By the time they arrived in Plymouth, they felt they were old friends. They got off the bus in Royal Parade, with Jennifer pointing out the big Dingle's store to them and making them promise to come and see her in ladies' fashions next time they came. As they parted, she stood for a few minutes watching them stroll away, arm in arm and chattering like a pair of budgerigars.

She heard Stella's voice in her head: '*You don't know how wonderful it is to find someone you've been looking for all your life . . .*'

Jennifer hadn't been looking for her father all her life. She hadn't even known about him until recently. But that didn't mean he hadn't known about her. It didn't mean he hadn't been carrying his own secret through all these years.

Perhaps *he* had been looking for *her* – or at least missing her – all his life.

Chapter Twenty

The next morning, Stella woke up with a cold. It was the sort of cold that leaps upon you suddenly, rather than creeping up over a few days, so that when she opened her eyes they were already streaming, her throat felt as if it were on fire, and her head was thumping as if half the infant class were banging their tambourines beside her pillow.

'My stars, you look a bit under the weather,' Dottie said, coming in with a cup of tea. Stella had told her time and time again that she didn't have to do this, but Dottie took no notice and this morning Stella was grateful for it. 'You've got that nasty cold that's been going round the village. Mrs Warren had it last week. She couldn't come to the Parish Council meeting and we got through everything in half the usual time.'

'I feel terrible,' Stella said miserably. 'Felix was going to take me and Maddy to Becky Falls today, but I really don't think I can go. Anyway, I don't want to pass it on to them.'

'Do you want me to slip over the road and tell them?' Dottie enquired. 'I'll pop across first and then bring you a bit of breakfast, shall I? I dare say you'll be better by the weekend – you could go then.'

'No, Felix is going to be busy all weekend. He's taking a wedding at Little Burracombe on Saturday and he's going to Exeter to see the Bishop on Monday. Tell them to go without me. It's such a lovely day, and it would be a shame not to make the most of it. It'll probably be raining again by the weekend.'

Dottie nodded and went out, leaving Stella to sip her tea and snuggle back beneath the bedclothes. After a while, she reappeared with a breakfast tray.

'I've been over to see them. Maddy wanted to come and see how you were, but I wouldn't let her. No sense in you catching it, too, maid, I told her, and she knows if she catches a cold it goes straight to her chest.'

'So are they going to go out?' Stella asked, sitting up and wondering how much she would be able to eat of the breakfast Dottie had brought her. 'That looks lovely, Dottie, but I really don't think I've got much appetite.'

'You can manage some Weetabix and a boiled egg,' Dottie said firmly, settling the tray across Stella's lap. 'And there's some nice honey from Iris Tozer's bees, which she keeps up in the corner of the churchyard, to go on that toast. Good for colds, honey is. Feed a cold and starve a fever, that's what I was always told. You've got to keep up your strength when you'm poorly. Now, my blossom, you take your time and eat it all up. You aren't going anywhere else today, not if I've got anything to do with it.'

Stella didn't want to go anywhere else. She ate as much as she could and then put the tray down on the floor and lay down again, feeling exhausted. Outside, she could hear the usual sounds of village life – the clip-clop of horses' hooves as the baker's cart or the milkman went along the road, the cheerful voices calling to each other as the men went to work in the fields and the women came to do their shopping. She heard the church bells chime the hour and the bleating protests of a flock of sheep being driven from one field to another. And she heard laughter coming from almost beneath her window and realised it was her sister and Felix, setting out for their day across the moor. A moment or two later, she heard the sound of the car starting up and roaring out of the village. For a moment or two after that, it seemed as if everything fell silent. It was as if Felix and Maddy had taken all the life of Burracombe with them.

Feeling miserable and bereft, Stella pulled the bedclothes up over her head. I'm being stupid, she told herself crossly. I'm sorry for myself because I've got a cold and I'm missing a day out with my two favourite people. I should be pleased they're enjoying themselves. I *am* pleased.

Tears filled her eyes and she sat up and found a handkerchief to blow her nose. Then she lay down and tried to go back to sleep and not think about Maddy and Felix, together in the little sports car, enjoying their day out together.

'It's such a shame poor Stella's got a cold,' Maddy said, snuggling down beside Felix in the front seat. 'Just when we've got time to spend together and really get to know each other – it doesn't seem fair.'

'You and I'll have to get to know each other instead,' Felix said. 'I'm disappointed, too, but at least Stella and I see each other quite a lot. You'll be going away again soon – back to France, I suppose.'

'I suppose so.' But her voice was unenthusiastic and Felix glanced sideways at her.

'Don't you want to go back?'

'I don't know. It's all different, now that Fenella's getting married. I like Raoul, of course, and I'm really happy for them both, and they both say I'm welcome to stay with them – there's room enough in the château, after all! – but I just don't know what I'd do with myself. Up till now, since I left school, I've been Fenella's main companion. I've looked after her and made sure everything happened properly for her – where she was supposed to go, what she was supposed to do. I've made all our travelling arrangements and that sort of thing. But she'll be living a different sort of life now, and

Raoul has his own people to take care of all those arrangements. There won't be anything for me to do.'

'You could just enjoy yourself,' Felix suggested, slowing to avoid a Dartmoor pony that had decided to amble across the road in front of them. 'I should imagine they'll be having an interesting sort of life.'

Maddy made a face. 'Interesting for people like them, I suppose. Lots of socialising and parties and so on for Fenella. And Raoul has his estates to look after.' She turned her face up to his, regarding his profile as he concentrated on his driving. 'But there's nothing for me to do. I want to feel useful, and I don't think I shall any more.'

'Where will you live, if you don't stay in France?' he asked. 'Would you come back to Burracombe?'

'How could I? I'd need to earn a living somehow. Oh, I'm sure Fenella would want to give me an allowance, and she might find me somewhere to live – a flat or something in London. And I suppose if I said I'd rather stay in Burracombe, she'd help me do that. But I'd still want something to *do*. I can't just spend the rest of my life being a butterfly. Anyway, I'm tired of being kept and looked after. I want to be independent.'

'You'll probably get married,' he said. 'A lovely girl like you isn't going to stay single for long.'

'That's what Fenella and Raoul say. Stella said something like it, too, the other day. But suppose I don't, Felix? Suppose I just never meet anyone I want to marry? Anyway, not all girls get married. Some have careers. Stella and I met a woman on the bus yesterday, she's a senior sales assistant in Dingle's, and she's hoping to become a fashion buyer. She really seems to like it. Maybe I could do something like that. I don't want to get married just so that I don't have to work for my living, Felix.'

They drove in silence for a while, passing the grim buildings of Dartmoor Prison at Princetown and a working party of convicts labouring close to the road. Maddy shuddered and pulled her jacket closer around her.

'Cold?' Felix asked. 'I could put the hood up.'

'No, I love to feel the air. It was just seeing those poor men and thinking of that horrible prison. Imagine spending years and years of your life in a place like that.'

'They probably deserve it,' Felix pointed out. 'They're criminals – maybe even murderers.'

'I know, but it's still horrible to think of. Whatever awful things they've done, they're still human beings. They can still feel desperately miserable.'

'A lot of people would think that was the least of their punishment.' He glanced down at her. 'You're very soft-hearted, aren't you?'

'I suppose so. It's probably because I've been so lucky in my own life. Except for the first few years, I mean – being bombed out and losing my parents and baby brother, and then Stella, none of that was lucky. But afterwards, when Fenella found me and adopted me – well, ever since then I've been very lucky indeed. I've had an easy life – much easier than Stella has.' She thought for a moment or two, then added in a slightly surprised tone, 'And yet, she's the one with a career. She's the one who's got a purpose in her life.'

From Princetown, they drove through a maze of steep, narrow lanes to Widecombe and stopped for coffee at a teashop opposite the church. Its tall tower soared into the air, looming over the little green and the huddle of cottages. Felix and Maddy walked about for a while, and he told her about the famous fair held here every September.

'You wouldn't know the place then. There are gipsies telling fortunes, wags telling jokes, town criers ringing their handbells, children dancing round the maypole, sheep and cattle and ponies for sale – but you must know all about it,' he added. 'Surely you came here when you lived in Burracombe?'

'No, they couldn't hold it during the war. Maybe I could come this year, though.' She looked up at him with shining eyes. 'We could come together! And Stella, too, of course.'

'Yes,' he said. 'Of course.' And they turned and went back to the car, to continue their journey to the famous waterfalls a few miles away at Manaton.

'It was a lovely day,' Maddy told Stella later, peeping in through the bedroom door. Dottie had told her that Stella seemed a bit better now, and so long as she didn't go right into the room, she shouldn't catch the cold, which seemed to be one of those that came suddenly and went just as fast. 'Manaton is so pretty, and the falls were beautiful. And we went to Haytor as well and climbed right up on the rocks – the view from there is wonderful. You can see as far as Exmoor and even to the sea! And there are lambs everywhere now, and Felix says the ponies will be having their foals soon.' She smiled at the thought. 'It's so nice to be back in the country. London and Paris and Rome are all very exciting, but there's nowhere quite like Burracombe!'

'I'm glad you had a good time,' Stella said, trying not to sound wistful.

'Oh, I did! Felix is such good company, isn't he? And he knows just how to look after a girl. He made sure I wasn't cold in the car, and he found a lovely spot to have our picnic by a little stream, and then we had tea at Badger's Holt, like we did when you were with us, and I had junket as well as those special scones they make.' She glanced a little enquiringly at her sister. 'You're very lucky, you know.'

'Lucky? Why?'

'Well, having a nice young man like Felix.' There was still a slight questioning note in her voice, and Stella felt the hot colour sweep into her cheeks.

'Felix isn't my "young man"! We're just friends, that's all.'

'Oh. I thought – oh, never mind. Sorry.' But Maddy didn't

sound sorry; in fact, she sounded rather pleased and Stella felt suddenly depressed. She felt for her handkerchief and blew her nose.

'You'd better go downstairs. I really don't want you to catch this, especially as you'll be going back to France at the end of the week. And I'm feeling a bit tired again.'

'You look a bit feverish to me,' Maddy said anxiously. 'All pink and flushed. I'll ask Dottie to come up and have another look at you in case you've got 'flu or something.'

She disappeared and Stella heard her voice downstairs. A few moments later, Dottie came up and peered at her in concern.

'Are you feeling worse, my flower? I wonder if I should ask Dr Latimer to look in.'

'No, don't do that. I'm all right – it's just a cold. I'll be better in the morning, when I've had a good sleep.'

'Well, we'll see.' Dottie didn't sound convinced. 'If you'm no better then, I'll pop into the surgery.' She plumped up Stella's pillows and smoothed her coverlet. 'Seems like Maddy had a lovely day out with Felix. Shame you couldn't go with them.'

'Yes. I'm glad she enjoyed it, though.' Stella lay down again, still feeling depressed. It's just because I'm not well, she told herself. I really am glad Maddy had a nice day. It's silly to feel left out, when I know they'd have liked to have me with them.

But that was the wrong way round, wasn't it? It shouldn't be *her* going with Maddy and Felix. It should be Maddy coming out with Felix and Stella.

Somehow the balance between the three of them had changed, and Stella wasn't at all sure that she liked it.

Chapter Twenty-One

Miss Kemp had not forgotten the plan she and Joyce Warren had discussed for a dramatic production to be put on by the schoolchildren at the Summer Fair, and she and Stella had agreed that a scene from *A Midsummer Night's Dream* could be quite a good idea. As soon as the summer term began, she decided it was time to start planning.

'We'd better have all the children together in my room,' she said to Stella. 'I'll explain the story to them first. I'm sure they're going to enjoy it.'

Stella, who had never understood Shakespeare when she was a child and wasn't sure of all of it now, nodded a little doubtfully. Still, the play was all about country people and woods, which were familiar to the children, and a lot of the smaller girls firmly believed in fairies, so that was a good start. After those who went home for their dinners had returned, and those who stayed had helped clear the tables, she shepherded her infant class into the larger room and they all settled down to hear the story of *A Midsummer Night's Dream*.

'I knows Shakespeare,' Henry Bennetts announced confidently. 'My dad took me to see it at the pictures. There's this Prince, see, that comes home from school and finds his dad's dead. His dad was King, see, so the Prince thinks he'll be King, like Princess Elizabeth was Queen when our King died, only he's not because his mum's been and got married again and so there's another King. And then the old King comes back to life as a ghost, and—'

'You can't do that,' Micky Coker interrupted. 'You can only be a ghost if you'm dead. If you comes back to life, you must be alive again, so—'

'Well, he'm a ghost, then,' Henry said, determined not to be deflected. 'And he tells 'Amlet that he didn't die natural, he was murdered through having poison poured in his ear—'

'In his *ear*? Why didn't they make him drink it?'

'He was asleep, so they couldn't.'

'They could have waited till he woke up. They could have put the poison in his cup of tea. My mum says she'm going to put poison in my dad's tea if—'

'Micky!' Stella broke in, dismayed. 'I'm sure she doesn't say that.'

'Well, 'tis only a joke,' he admitted. 'But they could have done that, couldn't they, miss?'

'Well, they didn't,' Henry said, beginning to sound irritated. 'They poured it in his ear, and Shakespeare said so, so it must be right. Anyway, then 'Amlet – that's the Prince, 'Amlet – decides to kill the new King, see, and there's this soppy girl who keeps following him about saying she loves him, so he pushes her in the river and drowns her—'

'I'm sure he doesn't do that,' Stella exclaimed. 'Ophelia drowns *herself*—' She caught the huge, horrified eyes of one of the smaller girls and stopped. 'Perhaps we'd better forget *Hamlet* now and think about—'

'But it be a good story, miss,' Henry said, outraged. 'There's skulls in it and people fighting with swords, and in the end everyone dies. I wanted to go and see it again, but my dad said, no, we was going to the football instead.'

'Please, miss,' said Katy, the smallest Culliford girl. 'I don't want to die. Can't us do *Goldilocks and the Three Bears* instead? They done it at Horrabridge last Christmas and it were ever so good. They didn't have proper bears, mind,' she added. 'Just people dressed up with heads on.'

'I wouldn't mind being a bear,' Micky volunteered, but

before an argument could break out between the girls as to who should be Goldilocks, Miss Kemp came in and rang the bell for silence and the children subsided.

'Now, children, you all know what this is about,' the headmistress began. 'We're going to do a short piece from one of the plays written by William Shakespeare, who was a very famous playwright—'

'That's a man that writes plays,' Henry explained in a loud whisper to Katy Culliford, who was sitting next to him. 'I've seen it at the pictures, it's all about—'

'—and this play is called *A Midsummer Night's Dream*,' Miss Kemp went on, fixing Henry with a reproving eye. 'The part we're going to do is set in a big forest—'

'Like Cuckoo Wood?' Jane Pettifer asked, and Miss Kemp nodded.

'Like Cuckoo Wood, only much bigger. In the forest there is a band of fairies, with a king called Oberon and a queen called Titania.' At the mention of a king and queen, Henry, who had been looking mystified up to this point, nodded with satisfaction. 'There's also a little group of craftsmen – a carpenter, a weaver, a tinker, a tailor—'

'Like in *Tinker, Tailor, Soldier, Sailor*,' Jane supplied helpfully, and Miss Kemp nodded again but held up her hand to indicate that she would rather there were no more interruptions.

'—a joiner and a bellows-mender. They're rehearsing a play to perform at a very important wedding. There's also a rather mischievous servant called Puck, who has been sent into the forest by Oberon to find a magic flower. The juice of this magic flower could be squeezed over someone's eyes when they're asleep so that when they wake up they will fall in love with the first person they see.' Miss Kemp paused for dramatic effect, which was ruined by Henry's indignant tones.

'No, miss, that's not right. It's poison that you pour in

their ears so that when they wake up they'm dead! I saw it at the pictures.'

The headmistress stared at him for a moment, baffled, but decided to continue. 'Please be quiet, Henry. I don't know what you saw at the cinema, but it couldn't have been this play. Nobody wakes up dead.' She continued. 'In fact, when Titania, the Queen of the Fairies, does wake up, the first person she sees is the weaver and she falls in love with him. But Puck has been up to mischief again and has given him the head of an ass – that's a donkey, Katy – and as he doesn't realise that he now looks like a donkey and doesn't know anything about the love potion, he thinks the Fairy Queen really has fallen in love with him, and there's a great muddle. But in the end everything is sorted out and the right people get married to each other and Puck comes on to tell the audience he's sorry for all the trouble he's caused and asks them to imagine it was all just a dream.'

She stopped and the children gazed at her in silence. Then Henry, obviously still smarting with indignation, said, 'That's not what I saw at the pictures! There was a ghost in it and a skull and lots of fighting. With proper swords. And a prince called 'Amlet. And everyone got killed. And it *were* Shakespeare, because it said so in the title. I reckon this play you've been telling us about is by a different Shakespeare. And 'tisn't anywhere near as good, neither. This is just soppy.'

'That's right,' Micky agreed. 'I wouldn't mind being in something with swords and skellingtons and things. But I'm not being a fairy. Fairies is girls' stuff.'

'*I'd* like to be a fairy,' Shirley Culliford said. 'I could be the Fairy Queen, couldn't I, miss? I'll still have a bit of time left over from being Festival Queen last year, won't I?'

'No, you won't,' one of the other girls argued. 'There'll be a new Queen by then, won't there, miss?'

'Can't us do *Goldilocks and the Three Bears*?' Katy Culliford asked plaintively. 'Micky Coker says he'll be a bear.'

It looked as if another argument was about to break out; several, in fact, as the girls continued to debate the question of who should be Fairy Queen and the boys began at least two heated discussions about sword fights, skeletons and bears' heads. Miss Kemp rang the bell again and called for silence, and eventually order was restored.

'I think the film Henry saw must have been *Hamlet*,' she said firmly. 'It was certainly by William Shakespeare, and many people think it was his best play, but the play we're doing, which was also by William Shakespeare, is called *A Midsummer Night's Dream*. And if Micky really wants to wear an animal's head, he can play Bottom.'

There was a horrified gasp from the children, who then instantly dissolved into giggles. Micky turned scarlet and Miss Kemp closed her eyes for a moment.

'There is nothing funny about the name Bottom,' she said, raising her voice above the smothered laughter. 'It's the name of the weaver whose head is turned into a donkey's and who falls in love with the Fairy Queen. All the craftsmen have funny names, just like they do in – in –' inspiration struck her '– in pantomimes. In fact, this story is very much like a pantomime. And one of the other craftsmen plays a lion, so nobody need think they're going to look silly or soppy—'

'Well, if it's just a pantomime, why can't us do a proper one, then?' Micky demanded, still crimson in the face. 'I'd rather be a bear than a stupid donkey with a rude name.'

'Us could do *Cinderella*,' Jane Pettifer suggested. 'There's some nice frocks in that, too.'

'Or *Dick Whittington*,' someone else called out. 'I could bring our cat, only I don't think he'd like wearing them boots.'

'I saw *Babes in the Wood*, once, there was robbers in it, and—'

'Why can't us do the one with skellingtons and ghosts?'

came Henry's disappointed voice. 'It were ever so good, and I got a wooden sword with proper silver paint on its blade—'

'Because it's not a pantomime!' Miss Kemp snapped, and then, recalling that they weren't planning to do a pantomime, anyway, added hastily, 'We're doing *A Midsummer Night's Dream* and that's all there is to it.' She inserted a note of encouragement into her voice. 'You'll enjoy it once we start. The boys can play the craftsmen and the girls can be the fairies, so there's something for everyone. Except for Oberon, of course, he'll have to be played by a boy. But I'm sure one of you would make a very good King.'

There was a long silence. The children stared up at their teachers and then looked at each other. They had all heard that tone in Miss Kemp's voice before and knew that there was no point in further argument. They heaved deep sighs and folded their lips in resignation.

Micky had the last word.

'Well, if us got to do it, I suppose us got to do it. But you'll have to change the name of that donkey, miss. I'm not going to be called Bottom, not for nobody.' He looked up at her with pleading eyes. 'Couldn't I be a bear instead, like in *Goldilocks*?'

Maddy had gone back to France after her visit to Burracombe, promising to come again soon. Felix had driven her and Stella to Tavistock to catch the train, and afterwards he took Stella for a cup of tea at Goode's, on the corner opposite Creber's grocery shop.

'I'm going to miss her dreadfully,' Stella said, wiping her eyes. 'Oh, I'm sorry about this, Felix – I didn't mean to be a cry-baby. But we were apart for such a long time, and I didn't know if I'd ever see her again. It makes it harder to part from her now.'

'I know. But I'm sure you're going to see lots of her in the future. I know she's got to go back to France now, for Miss

Forsyth's wedding and everything, but it seems pretty likely that she'll come to live in England once that's over. Maybe even in Burracombe!' he added with a smile.

'That would be lovely, but I don't really see how she could do that, unless—' Stella stopped suddenly and spooned sugar into her tea, stirring busily. Felix cocked an eyebrow at her.

'Unless what?'

'Well, unless she found somewhere to live, for a start. She couldn't lodge with Aggie for ever. And what would she do with her time? I know she talks about getting a job, but she doesn't seem to know what kind of job she wants to do. And she's not used to the quiet country life any more – she's spent the last few years in big cities with really sophisticated people. She'd be bored to death in a few weeks.'

'Do you really think so?' Felix asked. 'Maybe it's the sophisticated people, as you call them, who really bore her. Anyway, there might be an alternative to her getting a job. She could get married.'

'Who could she find to marry in Burracombe?' Stella demanded, and then looked up and caught his eye. Immediately, she felt the hot colour rise into her cheeks. She looked down again at once, furious with herself and trying to ignore the twinge of pain in her heart. I might have known this would happen, she thought miserably. All the breakfasts they had together, the evenings when Maddy went back to Aggie's, that day out they had at Becky Falls. Maddy's so lovely, how could I expect Felix *not* to fall in love with her? And Felix is so kind and funny and good-looking . . . I wish I'd gone over to Aggie's and let Maddy have my room at Dottie's cottage.

'Well, it doesn't have to be someone in Burracombe itself,' Felix said after a moment. 'Once she was here, she'd meet all sorts of people. In Tavistock, for instance, or one of the other villages. You'd like to have her living nearby, wouldn't you?'

'Of course I would. And I'd be very happy for her to marry someone nice. It's all I want, really – for her to be happy.'

Stella paused, then said, 'You know, when we were little, I always used to look after her. She was my little sister, and I always felt I had to be grown-up and take care of her – especially after our mother died and we were evacuated. And then, when we were separated and I didn't know where she was or who was looking after her – or even if *anyone* was taking proper care of her – I used to cry myself to sleep, worrying about her. It was horrible, not knowing where she was. Sometimes I even thought she must be dead.' Her voice broke a little. 'And then, last year, when I found her again, it was like a miracle. All I want now is for her to be happy, and safe, and for me to know about it.'

Felix said nothing for a moment. Then he put both his hands across the table and folded them around hers. She looked up at him, startled, and he said quietly, 'But you need to be happy, too, Stella. You can't live all your life through your sister.'

'I'm not. I've got my teaching, and Burracombe. I've made my home there. I love it. I don't need anything else to make me happy.'

'Don't you?' he asked seriously. 'Don't you remember telling me one day that you'd like to fall in love? Don't you think you'd like to get married one day?'

Stella met his eyes, then looked away quickly. 'No,' she said. 'No, I don't. I'll be perfectly happy to be like Miss Kemp and teach in the village school all my life. I honestly can't think of anything nicer – and if Maddy's happy, too, I shall have everything I want. Everything!'

Chapter Twenty-Two

'So have you got any further with your wedding plans?' Hilary enquired, handing Val a cup of tea. They were sitting on the terrace at the back of the house, looking out towards the sweeping moors. The hillsides were a blaze of golden gorse, and the garden was full of birds. Gilbert Napier's two black Labradors were lying as if exhausted on the flagstones, their paws twitching as they dreamed, and the old tabby cat was curled up at the edge of one of the flowerbeds.

Val took the cup and set it on the low wicker table. 'We have and we haven't. We're definitely getting married this summer, but we haven't actually set a date yet. And we still haven't got any forrader with finding somewhere to live.' She sighed. 'Luke's still talking about getting a job. It's such a shame – he's got a wonderful talent, but he says he just can't sell enough to keep a wife and family. And even if I keep on working for a while after we're married, I'd still have to give up once the family starts. And we do want a family.'

'Of course you do. And I'm sorry I haven't been able to help over the estate house. I really don't know why Arnold Cherriman is so set on staying there. He's still talking about building somewhere new in Plymouth, but I don't know if he actually means it. I know his wife loves the garden, but I got the impression she'd rather go back to her old one.'

'Never mind. Something will turn up,' Val said, not sounding as if she really believed it. 'In the end, I suppose we'll have to live wherever Luke gets a job. And that'll probably be in Plymouth.'

'Well, it's not so far away,' Hilary said encouragingly. 'He could go on the bus if you did find somewhere local. Even if you had to go to Plymouth to start with . . .'

'I know. It's not as if he's talking about going to London.' Val sat staring pensively at the plate of biscuits Hilary had placed on the table. 'We're lucky, really, I know that. It's just that – well, I thought once we'd decided to get married, everything would fall into place. But it hasn't.'

Hilary laughed ruefully. 'It hardly ever does. Are you going to have one of those biscuits, Val, or are you trying to hypnotise them? They're very good – Mrs Ellis made them yesterday.'

'Oh yes – thanks.' Val took one and nibbled it absent-mindedly. There was a small frown between her brows, and Hilary looked at her thoughtfully.

'Is there anything else the matter? Your dad's not still worried about Luke, is he?'

'Mm?' Val looked up. 'No, not really. He'd be happier if Luke got what he calls a "proper job", so at least someone will be pleased when he's a wage-slave. No, it's not that.'

'So what is it?' Hilary asked gently. 'Unless you'd rather not tell me, of course.'

Val chewed her top lip and sighed. 'I might as well. Some of it, anyway. Hil, d'you think I'm too old to wear white?'

Hilary blinked, taken by surprise by the sudden question. 'Too old? No, I don't think so. Why, do *you* think you're too old?'

'I don't really know. I'm almost thirty, after all. It's quite old to be getting married at all, and the thought of a long white dress – well, it seems a bit inappropriate, somehow. I just wondered what other people might think.'

'Does that matter?'

'It would be nice to say no, it doesn't matter at all,' Val said wryly. 'But you know what it's like in a village, Hil. Things do matter an awful lot to some people. I don't care about the spiteful old gossips who have nothing to do with me or Luke, but I do care about the people who are important to me. Like Mum and Dad and the rest of the family, and friends like you.'

'Well, it's not going to upset me to see you in a long white dress, and it wouldn't whatever age you were,' Hilary said roundly. 'I can't see why it should. As far as I can see, it's how *you* feel about it that matters. Would you rather wear a colour?'

'No, that would make me look like a bridesmaid – people would be looking for the bride! But I wondered about a costume. A nice smart jacket and skirt, in a light colour, that I could wear for best afterwards. A pale blue, perhaps. What do you think?'

'I suppose that would be all right,' Hilary said slowly. 'But don't you think some people might feel they'd been done out of seeing a bride in all her virginal glory? It's the white dress that makes a wedding special, isn't it?'

Val put down her cup abruptly, rattling it in its saucer. 'Is it? Is that what you really think? The dress is the most important thing?'

'No, of course not. I didn't mean that at all. I just meant that a lot of people think the white dress is something special. It *means* something. It isn't the most important part of it, though – that's the bride and groom. You and Luke . . .' Hilary looked at her friend again, and then said, 'Val, what's the matter? Why are you so upset?'

'I'm not upset. It's all right, Hil, I know what you mean. I'm just being silly – all this uncertainty's getting on my nerves a bit. Sorry.' Val's voice was tense. 'Is there any more tea in that pot?'

'Yes. Pass me your cup.' Hilary gave her friend another

curious glance. 'Are you sure there's not something else the matter? If there's anything I can do—'

'No, there's not. There's nothing anyone can do.' Val caught Hilary's look and added hastily, 'There's nothing that *needs* doing. Honestly. I'm just a bit fed up, that's all, and I don't have any right to be. I'm getting married to the man I love, and that's all that matters. Let's talk about something else. How's your father these days?'

Hilary pulled a comical face. 'Just the same as he always is – wanting to do too much. He thinks that because he feels all right, he can go back to doing everything he did before. All he wants is to get back to managing the estate. I keep telling him that was what caused his heart attack in the first place and he'll be risking another, but he can't see it. I just wish he'd let me get on with it. I wish he'd *trust* me.'

'I don't think it's that he doesn't trust you,' Val said thoughtfully, glad to have the conversation moved from her own concerns. 'He just can't let go. It must be difficult for him, you know. One minute he was in charge, with the reins firmly in his own hands, and the next it was as though they'd been snatched away from him. And now that he feels he could drive again, he can't get them back. It must be horribly frustrating.'

'Yes, I expect it is, but that's something he's got to get used to, isn't it? Charles has told him he mustn't go back to working as hard as he did before. And part of it was the fact that he used to worry so much about what was going to happen to all this.' She waved her hand at the landscape stretching before them. 'All that fuss over Stephen not wanting to take over. He doesn't need to worry about that any more. He knows I can do it instead.'

'He might think you won't want to do it for ever, though,' Val said. 'Suppose you got married?'

Hilary shrugged. 'I might marry someone who'd be happy to stay here with me. Still, I can see what you mean. But the latest bee he's got in his bonnet is if I *don't* get married. If neither I nor Stephen can produce an heir who'll want to take it over—'

'Oh, for goodness' sake!' Val exclaimed. 'He's worrying about what's going to happen for the next fifty years or more! Honestly, Hil, we could all drive ourselves into the grave if we did that.'

'I know. But you try telling Dad that.'

They were silent for a few moments. Eventually, Val said thoughtfully, 'D'you think if you let him take over some of the work – enough to occupy him for a few hours a day – it would help? Being frustrated isn't going to make him any better – it could do just as much damage as working too hard. You don't really have to do it all yourself, do you?'

'It's what he used to do,' Hilary said obstinately.

'And it's what made him ill.'

'Oh, come on, Val – *I'm* not going to have a heart attack!'

'No, I don't suppose you are. But then, he didn't think he was going to, either. And we're trying to think of a way to help him, aren't we?' Val stood up and brushed down her skirt. 'I'd better be going. I promised to help cook supper tonight and Luke's coming round so I've got to make a good job of it – don't want him backing out now! Thanks for the tea, Hil, and tell Mrs Ellis her biscuits are scrummy and I want the recipe.'

Hilary laughed and got up to walk round to the front of the house with her friend. 'I don't expect she'll give it to you. She keeps her best recipes a secret. I'm sorry about the house, Val. But I'll keep my eyes and ears open. Something will turn up in the end.'

'Hope so.' Val gave her a quick hug and then walked off down the drive. Hilary stood watching her for a few minutes, her face thoughtful. Despite her friend's protestations, she was sure that there was something else worrying Val, something she wasn't prepared to talk about. But then, Val had always played some of her cards close to her chest. Deep though their friendship had grown since those days when they'd been in Egypt together, Hilary had always been aware that there were areas of Val's life that she simply didn't discuss. Not that this present worry could be anything to do with that, she thought, going back to collect the tea tray and take it indoors. Egypt was years ago, during the war. That water had flowed under the bridge long ago.

Her mind turned to their discussion about her father. It was true that Gilbert seemed to be fully recovered from the frightening heart attack he'd had last year, but Hilary was acutely aware of the danger of another one. It was this fear that kept her from letting him take on more of the burdens of the estate work. At least, that was what she told herself.

She wondered if Val was right, and that frustration at not being able to do more might be even more harmful. Could it be true that she just didn't want to let the responsibility go, now that she'd been given it? Was she being selfish?

It was an uncomfortable thought.

As she walked away from the Barton, her hands thrust deep into her jacket pockets, Val's mind returned to the question of the white dress. And it wasn't only that which concerned her. Even more important was the whole matter of whether she should be married in church at all.

The Tozers would not have called themselves a particularly religious family, but they were regular churchgoers and believed in the ethics that they had been taught. The children were baptised as a matter of course and attended confirmation classes when they reached the age of fourteen. Once confirmed, they went to Holy Communion once a month, at least until they were adult. It was true that Tom didn't go so often, and Joanna, who had been brought up differently, only went at Christmas and Easter and a few other occasions, but the whole family was in church for either matins or evensong, with Ted and Tom present half an hour earlier to ring the bells.

St Andrew's wasn't a 'high church', but there were certain rules that were understood. One was that the bride wore white to show that she was a virgin. If you didn't, you were more or less lying. And if you'd been married before and divorced – though that was so rare that nobody could remember it happening in Burracombe – you couldn't get married again in church, at least until your former spouse had died.

So what, Val wondered, was the position of someone like her? How could she put on a white dress and walk up the aisle, as if she were a young girl, innocent and untouched? She would be lying to everyone there. She would be lying to God – except that He already knew . . .

I don't know what to do, she thought miserably. And there's no one I can talk to. Luke's got enough to worry about, what with having to find a job when he ought to be using his talents as an artist, and Mum would be dreadfully upset. And nobody else knows about what happened in Egypt – not even Hilary. There are only the girls who were on the ship with me when I lost little Johnny, and they're scattered all over the country now.

She paused for a moment, leaning on a gate and gazing at a flock of sheep. The lambs had begun their usual teatime games, racing from one end of the field to the other and leaping on and off rocks. One was standing on its mother's back, bleating triumphantly, a sight that usually made Val chuckle, but there was no laughter in her heart this afternoon. Instead, hot tears prickled her eyes and for a moment she almost wished that Luke had never come back.

Shocked by the thought and angry with herself for thinking it, she brushed her hand across her eyes and looked up. The church tower was directly in her view, serene and grey against the tender blue of the sky, and she knew at once who she must talk to.

I'll tell him everything, she decided, pushing herself away from the gate. If he says I mustn't get married in church, then I won't. And if I have to tell everyone the truth, I'll do that, too. I may lose a lot of friends, but I won't lose those who truly love me, and even if my family are upset, I'm sure they won't desert me. But I can't start my new life with Luke with a lie. I just can't.

'It's not just that I need to know my father,' Jennifer said to Basil as she sat once again in his study. They had been talking for some time and had drunk two cups of tea each. 'He may need to know me. Well, not *need*, exactly, since as far as we know he doesn't even know I exist. But if he did know, wouldn't he want to meet me? Wouldn't he want us to have at least some time together, especially as we've missed so much? And we can't be really sure that he doesn't know I exist. He may have known my mother was expecting a baby. In fact, I think he must have done – surely she would have written and told him.'

'It's certainly a possibility,' Basil said slowly. 'What I can't understand is why nobody else seems to know if she did. Minnie Tozer knew Susan was pregnant, and Alice was told later. Were they the only ones? There must have been gossip. Why didn't all that come to Jacob's ears when he came back from the war? Or was it all such a turbulent time that some things just disappeared from people's minds?' He rubbed a hand over his fuzz of silver hair. 'People may have felt sorry for the girl, of course. By all accounts, Abraham was a very strict father—'

'He was a bully,' Jennifer said tersely. 'I should think everyone knew that.'

'Yes. You're probably right.' Basil sighed. 'Not that that helps us to decide what to do now.' He shook his head at himself. 'I'm sorry. As I said last time we met, it's your decision, not mine. I can only tell you what seems right to me, but I could be quite wrong and you have to make up your own mind.'

'But you're not really sure yourself what's the right thing to do, are you?' she asked.

'No, I'm not. And it doesn't really help that I know Jacob so well. Or thought I did . . .' He heaved another deep sigh. 'I suppose when all's said and done, it's truth that matters. People should know their true place in the world. If Jacob is a father – your father – he has a right to know it. And I think you're right – he would be pleased to know.'

Jennifer blushed, and he thought again what a pretty woman she was. Not in the first flush of youth, yet attractive, with a warmth in her face when she wasn't looking anxious. Perhaps knowing her true father would take that anxiety away, and that shadow of loneliness he could detect at times in the grey eyes. It was strange, he reflected, how important a blood relationship was. Jennifer had had a stepfather who loved her, and half-sisters she had grown up with on equal terms. Yet she still hankered after her real roots. And having searched so hard, and come so close, who was he to advise her against taking that final step?

'I'll go and see him,' she said decisively, and stood up. 'I'll go now – this afternoon.' She smiled a little ruefully. 'I feel that if I go back to Plymouth now, I'll lose my nerve!'

'Very well, my dear,' he said, getting to his feet as well. 'I wish you luck. And happiness, too. Jacob's a fine man. I don't know what Burracombe would do without him.' He held out his hand. 'Thank you for taking me into your confidence. I hope all goes well. And if you feel you need to come and see me again – or want to let me know how you get on – the vicarage door is always open to you. You're welcome at any time.'

'Thank you,' she said, taking his hand. He looked at her face and saw that the anxiety had fallen completely away. She looked young and happy and excited. 'You've been a real help. I'll come and see you again, and tell you all about it.'

He saw her to the door, warmed by her happiness, yet still feeling a twinge of anxiety for both her and Jacob. She seemed so sure that she was doing the right thing, that Jacob would take her instantly to his heart and that the lost years could be somehow regained. But Basil's experience told him that this wasn't always so easy. Sometimes things did just fall into place, but sometimes the jigsaw was just too difficult.

As he stood at the door, watching her walk out through the gate into the lane, his wife came to stand beside him.

'Has she made up her mind?' Grace asked, and he nodded.

'She's going to see Jacob now. I hope it won't be too much of a shock for the poor man. You know, even if he did realise that Susan was expecting his baby, he probably thinks they both died, just as the Tozers did. Seeing her now, without any warning, could be like meeting a ghost.'

'You think she should have written, or asked you to talk to him first?'

Basil turned away from the door, shaking his head. 'I really don't know, Grace. Without being able to see into the future, how can we know if any of our actions are for the best or not? We can only do what seems to be right at the time. That's what Jennifer Tucker is doing now, and I only hope she really is right. After all, it may be a shock to Jacob, but it must, surely, be a pleasant one. And there's no other wife or children involved. I don't see what trouble can come of it, do you?'

He went back to his study to finish the work he had been doing when Jennifer had arrived. But before he could gather his thoughts, Grace was at the door again and he found Jennifer's problem driven out of his head by another one, even closer to home.

'Val Tozer's here to see you,' Grace said. 'She says she needs to talk to you urgently.'

He stood up at once, beaming a welcome, but his smile faded when he saw her face. 'Why, Val, whatever's the matter? I thought you were coming to tell me the date for your wedding.'

'I'm not sure there's going to be a wedding,' Val said, and burst into tears.

Chapter Twenty-Three

Basil came swiftly across the room and put his hands on her shoulders, guiding her to the armchair so recently vacated by Jennifer Tucker. He pressed her into it and then took the chair opposite, wishing the fire laid instead of being piled with fir-cones so that he could put a match to it. The afternoon had been warm, but distressed people always seemed to feel the cold.

'Would you like some tea?' he asked. 'Grace would willingly—'

Val shook her head at once. 'No, no, I've just had some at Hilary's. I came straight here. I've decided I must talk to you.' She looked suddenly doubtful. 'You're not too busy, are you?'

'My dear, I'm never too busy to talk to any of my parishioners. Especially when it's you, and you seem to be in such distress. Tell me what's happened. Have you and Luke quarrelled?'

'No. No, it's nothing like that. It's just that—' She began to cry again. 'I don't know how to tell you!'

'Val, please. Surely it can't be that bad.' A number of possibilities flashed through his mind, but he discarded them all. 'I've heard most things in my time as a vicar,' he said gently. 'People think clergymen are easily shocked, but really we're not. We wouldn't last very long in the job if we were.'

Val mopped her face and looked up at him, her eyes still brimming. 'I suppose you've come across lots of girls who have been silly enough to get into trouble before they were married, then.'

'Getting into trouble' was the phrase most used to mean pregnancy. Basil looked at her in some surprise.

'Is that what's happened to you? Well, it's not the end of the world. You're planning to marry soon, anyway – we can arrange it more quickly, if that's what you want.' He frowned, remembering Val's words when she had first come into the room. 'Luke *is* the father, I take it?'

'No!' she cried, and then added hastily, 'Nobody's the father! I mean, there isn't a baby – not now.' She sobbed into her handkerchief while Basil waited, disturbed and anxious. Luke was his godson and, although the boy had had his wild moments, working as a war artist and then contracting tuberculosis seemed to have subdued him, though there could still be a wicked gleam in his eye at times. Basil was extremely fond of him, and of Val, whom he had known ever since she was a young girl.

'Try to tell me all about it,' he said quietly. 'Take your time – there's no hurry. And I think I will ask Grace for some tea, but I'll fetch it myself. I won't be long.'

He got up and slipped quietly from the room, leaving Val by herself. In the kitchen, his wife looked at him enquiringly, but he shook his head and filled the kettle. Grace immediately began to set cups and saucers on a tray and put a few biscuits on a plate.

'Don't bring it in,' he said. 'Just knock on the door and I'll come and take it. Val's in rather a state, I'm afraid.'

By the time he returned to the study, Val had managed to stop crying and was more composed. She gave him a small, rueful smile as he came in and said, 'I'm sorry, Mr Harvey. I didn't mean that to happen.'

'It's quite all right, my dear. It often happens when someone's been bottling up a problem. You have to get the tears out first. Now, Grace is going to bring us some tea in a moment – you don't have to drink it, but you do need to replace those tears! Can you tell me what it is that's upsetting you so much? It's to do with the wedding, isn't it?'

'Yes.' She looked down at the sodden handkerchief she was twisting between her fingers. 'It's nothing that's happened now – I mean, recently. It – it goes back rather a long way.' She raised her eyes again. 'It goes all the way back to the war, when I was in Egypt.'

'Ah.' Basil nodded slightly. 'Egypt. And Luke was there, too, wasn't he?'

'Yes.' She stopped as Grace knocked softly on the door. Basil got up and collected the tray, bringing it over to the table and pouring milk and tea into the two cups. He returned to his own chair and waited again.

'We got to know each other,' Val said tonelessly. 'I was engaged then, to Eddie, but it had been so long since I'd seen him. And there were dances and things. You had to go to them, there wasn't much else to do, and we needed . . . I was a nurse, you see. We really did need to have time to forget – time just to enjoy. Oh, it sounds so selfish!'

'It's not selfish at all,' Basil said. 'You needed the recreation. You couldn't have done your job without it. And I know just how difficult that job must have been at times.'

'Yes. We saw some terrible injuries. It was very hard – they were so young. So when we went to the dances, we sort of let ourselves go a bit. And when I met Luke, we fell in love.' She looked at the vicar as if expecting condemnation, but he merely nodded. After a moment, she went on. 'I never meant to be unfaithful to Eddie. I loved him. But he was so far away, and – well, I *was* unfaithful. Luke never tried to force me or anything,' she added quickly. 'It was my fault as much as his. And I think we really must have loved each other, because we do now, don't we? It wasn't just – you know.'

'I know.' He waited again and then said, 'And what happened then?'

'We had to part – I told him we must. I came back to England. But on the way, I found—' Her voice broke again. 'I found I was expecting a baby.'

There was another silence. Val's eyes were dry now as she stared at the fir-cones piled in the grate. Basil said nothing. He knew she would finish telling her story now, and he was beginning to have an idea as to why she had come to him.

'I lost it,' she said at last. 'I had a miscarriage. It was a perfectly natural one. The baby was very tiny, but I knew it was a boy. I called him John.' She turned back to the vicar. 'We buried him at sea.'

'Did you tell anyone?' Basil asked after a moment. He had told Val he couldn't be shocked, but he had felt his heart quiver as she spoke the words so baldly. It was her pain he was feeling, he thought, the pain that had haunted her all these years. A pain that she had, he guessed, borne all alone.

'No. The girls with me knew – three or four close friends. That's all. I hadn't started to show much, you see, so no one else guessed. And it was so early in the pregnancy that he wouldn't have been counted as a person – not officially. I counted him, though,' she added in a lower tone.

'Of course.' He let the silence continue for a moment and then asked, 'Did Luke know?'

'No. Not then. We'd parted, you see. I'd told him it was over – I was going back to Eddie. I was going to marry him. That was before I knew about the baby, of course. But then Eddie was killed. And I never saw or heard from Luke again until he came to Burracombe. I didn't know his address, and I wouldn't have tried to get in touch with him, anyway. I felt so guilty – even when we did meet again, I could hardly bear to look at him. It was a long time before I could bring myself to admit that I still loved him.'

'And does he know now? About the baby?'

'Oh yes. I told him everything in the end.'

Her throat was dry and she sipped her tea. Basil, too,

picked up his cup, although he felt as if he'd been drinking tea all afternoon. At last he asked, 'So what are you worried about now? I can see that this story is still haunting you – which is only natural, and I'm afraid it will probably do so to some extent all your life – but why do you say that you and Luke may not marry after all? Is it causing him problems? Should I be talking to him as well?'

'No! No, he doesn't even know I'm worried about it. And we *are* going to get married – there's no question of that. It's just that –' she looked at him with piteous eyes '– I don't know if we should get married in church.'

'Ah,' he said, understanding breaking through at last. 'I *see*.'

'Do you?' she asked. 'It's not just the dress – although that was the first thing I thought about. Wearing white, I mean, when I'm not a – a virgin. It's everything else as well. It feels like telling lies. Nobody else knows anything about it. I feel as if I should tell them. But if I did – well, I just don't know what would happen. They'd be so hurt. Mum and Dad and Grandma especially. Everyone else might be just disgusted,' she added forlornly.

'And do you think that would be better than leaving them in ignorance?' he enquired gently. 'Leaving aside those who might be, as you say, disgusted – and I'm sure your real friends and family won't be – let's think about those who might be hurt or disappointed. Your parents, and the rest of your family, for instance. Is it really necessary to hurt them in this way? What happened, happened years ago, in another time and another place. War does strange things to people, and it isn't fair to yourself to judge your actions as though it were peacetime. And you and Luke must have been truly in love. You're marrying now.'

'But I was unfaithful to Eddie.'

'Yes, you were. But isn't that between Eddie and yourself? You weren't married to him—'

'I was engaged.'

'Engagements can be broken,' he said. 'The reasons are nobody else's business but the couple's involved. You'd made no vows in church, and we don't know for certain that you would actually have married him, had he lived. I'm not excusing you,' he added, when Val began to protest again, 'but I want you to think carefully about why you are punishing yourself like this. Is it really about Eddie, or is it about the baby?' He paused, while Val stared at him, her face first crimson, then deathly pale. 'Do you feel it was your fault the baby miscarried?'

'I didn't do anything to cause it!' she burst out. 'I really didn't!'

'But you must have wished it hadn't been conceived. Don't be ashamed of that, Val. Any girl would feel the same in your position. Do you, perhaps, feel that you brought it about just by wishing it would happen?'

Val stared at him. Her eyes were like black pools in her white face. He wondered uneasily if he had gone too far, and when the tears burst forth again, he reached out and caught her by the arms, his hands gentle but firm. She sank forward, crying, and he held her, rocking her a little. I'm not good at this, he thought anxiously. I've said all the wrong things. I've made matters worse.

'Val,' he said, when the storm seemed to be passing, 'these wounds can sometimes take a very long time to heal. Perhaps you buried the pain and are only now having to suffer it properly. You need to grieve for your baby. You have a *right* to that grief.'

'I don't have a right to anything,' she said dully. 'It's all working out so well for me, and I don't deserve it.'

'That isn't true. You do deserve it. Yes, you made a mistake and you did wrong, but you did no more than thousands – millions – of other women have done down the ages. And I think you've atoned for it. What I *don't* think you're entitled to do is pass on your pain to other people. That's what you'll be doing if you tell your parents what happened. You won't get rid of your own pain but you'll give it to others. You'll increase it, and what is the point of doing that? What good is it going to do?'

'But marrying in church—'

'It's not a lie,' he said firmly. 'You made no vows. Remember the marriage service requires you to "forsake all others". It doesn't say that there mustn't have *been* any others. We *are* supposed to be a forgiving church,' he added. 'And you don't have to be married in white. Why not choose a cream dress, for instance? It's not pure white, if that's what's worrying you, but it's near enough for people not to wonder.'

'Do you really think that would be all right?' she asked doubtfully.

'I'd be perfectly happy with it myself. It would suit your colouring, too.'

Val smiled a little at the idea of Basil Harvey as a fashion adviser, and he beamed at her. 'There's that's better. Quite honestly, my dear, I don't mind what colour you wear, so long as you feel comfortable with it. I think a rich, creamy colour would be admirable. Or, if you still feel uncomfortable, a very pale silvery grey. I once married a bride wearing that colour and it looked most attractive.'

'And you don't think I ought to tell my parents about Luke and me and the baby?'

'I can't see any purpose in it at all. What's the point of hurting people with knowledge they don't need? They love you as you are, Val, and whatever has happened to you in the past is part of what has made you what you are. I dare say there are quite a few other things you've never mentioned to them!' He smiled at her and she laughed a little chokily. 'And

234

you have no intention of doing so, either – yet none of them would cause the pain that this could. You don't feel you're lying by not telling them everything you've ever done, do you?'

'No,' she admitted.

'Then why should you feel it about this? You know, we often feel that telling such truths might ease our consciences, but why should we be eased at the expense of others' peace of mind? I've always thought that was rather a selfish way to go about things.' He leaned forward a little. 'What happened was between you and Luke and Eddie – nobody else. What God will have to say about it is a different matter, and I can't speak for Him. I can only try my best to do His work on earth.'

Val sat quietly for a few moments, then she looked up at him. To his relief, he saw that some of the strain had gone from her face and there was a new clarity in her eyes. She nodded slowly and began to get up.

'Thank you very much, Mr Harvey. You've given me a lot to think about, but I can see things a bit more clearly now. I'd better go. I've taken up too much of your time.'

'You haven't at all,' he said, taking one of her hands in both of his. 'It's what my time is for. I hope I've been able to help. The main thing to remember is that once words have been spoken they can't be taken back. Always wait until you're quite sure, and remember that they're often better left unspoken.'

'Yes. Thank you.' She turned to go and he released her hand.

'Come and see me again if you want to talk any more.'

'I will.' The colour had returned to her face, and she smiled at him. 'Perhaps the next time I come, it really will be to set the date of the wedding!'

He saw her to the door and then went back to the kitchen. Grace was peeling vegetables for their evening meal. He went to stand beside her and leaned his head on her shoulder.

'I feel utterly exhausted,' he said. 'I just hope I've said the right things to both those young women.'

'You need a cup of tea!' Grace said, and went to put the kettle on again.

Chapter Twenty-Four

Jacob was working in his front garden when Jennifer arrived. He gave her a friendly look as she stopped by the gate, and straightened up for a moment. Scruff, stretched out on the path, gave a wuff and ran over to sniff her hand.

'I've seen you before,' he remarked. 'Come to live hereabouts, have you?'

Jennifer shook her head. Her heart was beating quickly and she felt a sudden twinge of apprehension. Suppose he didn't want his old memories revived? Suppose he didn't welcome the news that he had a daughter? But she knew that if she left it and went home now, she would only have to come back and try again. She took a deep breath. 'I've been looking for relatives. I think my mother came from this village.'

'Did her, now?' He looked at her consideringly. 'Who would she have been, then? I been living here all my life – maybe I knowed her.'

Before Jennifer could say any more, the door of the next cottage opened and Jed Fisher came out, carrying a long-handled spade. The look he gave Jennifer was as unfriendly as Jacob's had been pleasant.

'More incomers?' he said unwelcomingly. 'Village is full of 'em these days – there's that young woman teacher, hardly old enough to be out of school herself, that idle good-for-nothing what calls hisself an artist and those stuck-up city folk that Squire's let have Woodman's Cottage. Now here's another of 'em, looking to buy up a place where decent village folk ought to be living.' He glowered at Jennifer again. 'Well, mine ain't for sale, I can tell you that for nothing. I'm not going out of here till I goes feet first.'

'And that might be sooner than you reckon, Jed Fisher,' Jacob retorted, his face reddening. 'I can hear you coughing your lungs up every morning through the walls. You want to stop smoking all they fags, you do. They'm doing you no good.'

'S'pose you thinks I ought to smoke a pipe like you do,' Jed said, taking a packet of Woodbines from his pocket and sticking one between his lips. He struck a match and held it up defiantly. 'Fags don't do nobody no harm. I only coughs *before* I has one, not after.' He lit up, drew in a deep breath and coughed.

Jacob gave him a look of contempt. 'Anyway, that ain't no way to treat visitors.' He turned back to Jennifer. 'You don't want to take no notice of this old misery, miss. Most of us in Burracombe got better manners.'

'It's all right,' Jennifer said, rather taken aback by the animosity between the two men. It seemed to sully the idyllic picture she had had of the village, but she supposed that every community had their less appealing characters and their squabbles and feuds. She looked uncomfortably at Jacob, wondering how to broach the subject now that Jed was present. He might well have known her mother, too, she realised, but she certainly didn't feel like discussing the matter with him.

'The vicar told me that you look after the churchyard,' she said. 'I've been looking at some of the graves there. I suppose you'd know everyone who was buried there over the past twenty or thirty years.'

'I can go back further than that,' he said with pride. 'My old dad was the gravedigger, too. Between us, us buried almost everyone in the parish over the past hunnerd years.

Except for Chapel folk, of course,' he added, glancing at Jed. 'They has their own burial ground.'

'An' I looks after that,' Jed said belligerently, as if someone were about to argue with him. 'An' that's what I oughter be doing now, not standing here chewing the fat with all and sundry.' He gave them a look as if to imply that they were keeping him from his work. 'I'll be on me way, if you don't mind.'

'Us don't mind at all,' Jacob retorted. 'Us never asked you to stop in the first place.'

It looked for a minute as if Jed would start a fresh round of abuse, but after a moment's hesitation, he shrugged, spat into the hedge and shouldered the spade he had leaned against the wall. With one last unfavourable glance at Jennifer, he marched away along the lane.

'Good riddance,' Jacob muttered, and then gave Jennifer a wry look of apology. 'I'm sorry about that, maid. He brings out the worst in me, Jed Fisher does, and always has done, ever since we was young fellers, though we got on well enough as tackers. Born within a day or so of each other, we were, and lived in these two same cottages, side by side, since we was babbies, and somehow we got to put up with each other till we dies. But that's no worry of yours.' He looked at her thoughtfully. 'Did you say you got family round here?'

'It seems so.' She hesitated. 'As a matter of fact, it was Mr Harvey who suggested I come and talk to you.' She held out her hand. 'My name's Jennifer – Jennifer Tucker. You are Mr Prout, aren't you? Jacob Prout?'

'I am,' he said slowly, taking her hand. 'I dare say he sent you to me because I been in the village so long – except for a few years when I was away in the Great War. So what is it you wants to know, maid? You said you reckoned your mother come from round here. What was her name?'

Jennifer glanced along the lane. There was nobody about, but she didn't want to be interrupted again. Diffidently, she said, 'I wonder if we could go indoors? It might take a little while . . . '

Jacob looked surprised, then opened the gate and stood aside for her to pass. Her heart hammering again, Jennifer walked past him, then paused at the front door. Jacob pushed it open for her, then bent to take off his boots and followed her in his socks.

'Straight in, maid, and sit you down in the armchair. Push the cat off if her's on it – that's the way.' He came in after her, his feet now encased in brown slippers, and took a chair at the table, leaning his arm on it as he surveyed her. 'Now, what's this all about? I can see there's a bit more to it than just looking for an old gravestone.'

'Yes, there is.' Jennifer stopped again. All the way out here on the bus, she had been rehearsing various ways of introducing the subject, and had decided that it would be best to approach it cautiously, in a roundabout way, so as not to give him too much of a shock. But as she looked at the lined, weatherbeaten face and the direct blue eyes, her carefully prepared speeches fled from her mind and all she could think of was that this was the man her mother had loved, and that she ought to have been living with him her whole life. With tears suddenly choking her throat, she blurted, 'I think you're my father!'

There was a long silence. Jennifer looked down at her lap and then felt in her bag for a handkerchief. She pressed it to her face, blotting the tears from her eyes, and blew her nose. When she raised her eyes again, Jacob was staring at her, his face rigid with shock.

'I'm sorry,' she said. 'I didn't mean to come out with it like that. I meant to be a bit more tactful.'

'Your *father*?' he said at last. 'Why, maid, whatever makes you think that?'

'Because my mother was Susan Hannaford. And Mrs Tozer remembers that you and she were friends. The old Mrs

Tozer was very friendly with my grandmother, and Alice Tozer was about the same age as my mother, Susan. I'm sorry,' she said, thinking suddenly that he might object to his private business being discussed with others. 'I had to try to find out somehow, and I went to the vicar and he suggested I should ask the Tozers. You see, I couldn't find out anything about my mother at first. He had no records, because her family were Chapel, and—'

'But Susan died,' he said, as if he hadn't heard any of this. 'Her died years ago – while I was away in the war. When I come home, 'twas all over. And the babby died, too, so I were told.'

'No,' Jennifer said. 'We didn't die, either of us. My grandfather turned her out and she went to Plymouth. He told her she was never to come back to Burracombe again. And he spread the story that she'd died. He made my grandmother say so, too.'

She looked anxiously at Jacob. His face was white, his eyes almost black. He shook his head slowly and brushed back his hair with a trembling hand, and stared at her again.

'I thought she were dead. All these years – I thought she were dead . . .'

Jennifer got up. 'Can I make some tea? I've given you a shock – I'm sorry. Perhaps I should have written, or asked the vicar to tell you. But I wanted so much to find my father – and when I found out that it was you . . .' She went out to the kitchen and filled the kettle, shaking almost as much as Jacob as she looked around the small, tidy kitchen for the tea and teapot. Both were easily found, and she took two cups and saucers from the dresser, opened the larder door and took the milk from the cold slab on the deep windowsill, and made the tea. By the time she carried it in, Jacob had moved to the other armchair and was sitting with his head bent, staring at the rag rug. Scruff was at his feet, staring up with anxious eyes, and Flossie, the tortoiseshell cat, had climbed on to his lap. He was stroking her absently, as if he barely knew she was there.

'I remember now,' he said as Jennifer put the cup beside him. 'You come round the day the King died. You were asking about graves and such then. You been here a time or two since, I reckon.'

'Yes, I have. I wasn't sure to begin with that it was Burracombe, you see. I looked at other villages as well – I thought for a while it might be Meavy, since there's a green and an oak tree there, too. Or maybe Walkhampton . . . But I always felt it must be Burracombe, because it seemed familiar. My mother brought me here once, when I was very small, and I felt I could remember it.'

'Susan come to Burracombe?' he asked. 'Why did her do that?'

'I don't know. Perhaps it was when her own mother died. I don't remember much about it,' Jennifer said apologetically.

'I never knew,' he said, quietly and regretfully. 'I never knew she'd been here. If I'd just been working in the lane that day, I'd have seed her. I'd have seed you both.' He stared at the mantelpiece. 'I'd have thought she were a ghost.' He turned back to Jennifer, his eyes filled with pain. 'Why didn't her never come to see me? Why didn't her never even write?'

'I don't know,' Jennifer said helplessly. 'She – she did get married, after I was born. Perhaps that's why.'

'Got *married*?' His brows came together and he shook his head again. 'Well, I dare say 'twas the best thing for her. And for you, too, I hope. Treated you well, did he? Looked after you both proper?'

'Oh yes,' Jennifer said. 'He was a good husband and father. They – they had two more daughters. My half-sisters.'

'Two more liddle uns,' he said, almost to himself. 'My Susan. And all these years I've thought . . .' His voice faded away.

'Drink some tea,' Jennifer said gently. 'It's been a shock for you.'

Obediently, Jacob picked up his cup and drank. Jennifer had put in two spoonfuls of sugar, not knowing whether he took it but believing it was good for shock. He put the cup down again without comment and met her eyes.

'Tell me about Susan. Tell me what sort of a life she's had.' A sudden hope leaped into his face. 'Will she come out and see me, d'you reckon? What about her man? Is he still living?'

'No, he died in the war.' Jennifer hesitated, realising that she'd handled this badly and now had to deal him another blow. 'She – she married again, but it was a bad choice and he left and went to London – we've never heard from him again. And I'm afraid my mother died, too, a few months ago. That's why I came to look for you – I didn't know anything about all this until I found my birth certificate.' She stopped and added, 'I'm very sorry. I ought to have told you differently.'

His head drooped again, and his shoulders sagged. Jennifer looked at him with pity. He'd come out to work peacefully in his garden for an hour or two, and now his life had been changed for ever. She didn't know whether he welcomed the news that he had a daughter or not. He was too caught up in his memories of Susan, in the sudden revival of a life he had thought long gone and, more painful still, the resurgence of his loss.

She remembered that he had asked her a question and began, haltingly, to answer him, telling him about her mother, her stepfather and half-sisters and the life they had lived in Plymouth. 'I think she was happy enough,' she said uncertainly. 'I mean, she and my father – my *step*father – got along, they were very fond of each other, and we were a happy family. We didn't have much money, but who does these days? And the war was hard, too – we used to go out to Clearbrook on the bus every night and find somewhere to sleep while Plymouth was being bombed. Hundreds of people did the same. Local people took in as many as they could, or farmers would let you sleep in their barns if there was room, but lots of people just camped on the moor, or even huddled up against the walls and banks.'

'Ah,' he said, and nodded. 'They came out here as well. Maybe your mother's folk would have taken you in, but they were dead by then. Old Abraham's got a lot to answer for,' he burst out. 'Him and his Bible-thumping ways!'

'Once the bombing was over, it wasn't too bad,' she said. 'Our part of Plymouth wasn't flattened like so much of it was. I lived with my mother after I came home. Both my sisters are married, with families.'

'And didn't you never marry, then?' he asked, looking at her as if seeing her for the first time. 'You know, I can see a likeness there now. Not to Susan – I can't see nothing of her in you. But there's a look of her mother, poor soul. Downtrodden, she were, and my Susan was going a fair way to being the same. That's why I wanted to get her away from there and marry her, give her a proper life.' He sighed and looked away again. 'We were proper sweethearts, me and your mother. And I reckon if all had gone the way it should, we'd have stayed sweethearts all our lives.'

'I know,' Jennifer said quietly. 'That's why I wanted so much to come and find you. Because you're my proper father, and if you and my mother can't be together, then at least we can have something of what we all ought to have had all these years.' She slipped out of her chair and knelt on the rug before him, taking his hands in hers and looking up into his face. 'I know you haven't any other children. There's no other family at all, is there? So I hope you'll be pleased that you've got a daughter after all. I hope you'll be pleased to have me as part of your life.'

There was a long silence. Jacob looked into her eyes. She waited, her heart thumping again, for his reply, and was just about to assure him that he didn't have to answer at once, that he could have time to take in all this sudden news, when he drew in a deep breath and spoke at last.

'I'm glad she had a good life,' he said slowly, in a gruff, aching voice. 'I'm glad my Susan found a good man to take care of her and give her more children. I'm glad you took the trouble to look for your real father, and come and told me about it all.' He stopped, and she waited, understanding that he was having difficulty in finding his words. 'But I'm afraid you'm wrong, maid. Susan and me never went that far, you see.' He took another deep breath. 'I'm sorry, maid. The plain truth is, I'm *not* your father.' His eyes were filled with tears. 'I only wish I were . . .'

Chapter Twenty-Five

Ted Tozer was walking his fields when he saw Luke coming towards him. He waved cheerfully, pleased to see the younger man. Since their talk at Christmas, they'd developed a respectful understanding of each other, and Ted was pleased now that Luke was to be part of the family. He'd even been talking of getting a job, and it seemed as if there might be something for him in Tavistock.

'Nice afternoon,' he called. 'I suppose you'm looking for a pretty picture to paint.'

'Partly,' Luke said, drawing closer. 'It's not just that, though. I want to talk to you, Mr Tozer.'

They stopped, facing each other about two feet apart. Something in the young artist's bearing struck Ted as being different; he couldn't put his finger on it, but it made him wary. He waited a moment, watching the long, mobile face, and then said, 'All right, then. Out with it. I can see you've got summat to say.'

Luke drew in a deep breath. 'Yes, I have. It's about what we talked about at Christmas – about Val and me.' He looked Ted straight in the eye. 'I'm going to have to take back that promise I made, Mr Tozer. We don't want to wait any longer to get married. We could do it at Easter, but we want to set a proper date. We thought we'd make it the end of July.'

'July!' Ted stared at him, holding back his immediate response. It was his way to consider first and get his thoughts into order before making any answer. 'That's pretty soon, isn't it?'

'Yes, it is, but we've both had enough of waiting.' Luke took another breath. 'I don't know if you realise how unhappy Val's been—'

'I know she've been a bit under the weather.' His glance sharpened and he asked the inevitable question. 'There's no *reason*, I hope—'

'No! At least, not the one you mean.' Luke took half a step nearer. 'Look, Mr Tozer, I know what I promised you and I meant it. But I didn't really have the right to make that promise – not on Val's behalf. We want to be equal partners in our marriage. I can't make decisions that she doesn't agree with – and she doesn't agree with that one.'

'So you'm putting the blame on her—'

'*No!* It's not a question of blame. It's simply a question of wanting to be together, husband and wife. Somehow, in the next few weeks, I'll find a job that will support us both. But we're not waiting until then to fix our wedding.' He paused, then added, 'I'd wait for ever to marry your daughter, Mr Tozer, if that was the way it had to be. But I don't like seeing her unhappy. I don't like seeing her in tears when all we need to do is walk up the aisle and say "I do".'

'And is that how she's been?' Ted asked slowly. 'In tears?'

'Yes, it is. And I'm not prepared to see it again.' Luke gave him one of his straight looks. 'I'm going to be responsible for Val now, Mr Tozer, not you. If you don't want to take any part in this wedding, then we'll both be sorry, but we're going ahead all the same. And I'm not asking you to pay—'

'Now, you can stop that sort of talk straight away,' Ted broke in. 'Not pay for my own daughter's wedding? What do you take me for, a skinflint? Of course I'll pay for it! It's me privilege and me right. Why, if I didn't give our Val a decent wedding, my Alice would never speak to me again.'

'And you won't object if we set the date for the end of

July?' Luke asked. 'We really don't want to wait any longer than that, Mr Tozer.'

Ted said nothing for a moment. Then he lifted his shoulders and said, 'If that's what you both wants, then I reckon us got to go along with it. To tell you the truth, boy, I *have* noticed the maid looking peaky just lately, and I'm as sorry about it as you. Maybe I was wrong to ask you to make that promise.' He put out his hand and Luke, hardly daring to believe what was happening, took it in his. 'And there's one thing about it – us'll be able to do away with all this "Mr Tozer" nonsense. You can call me Father, like young Joanna does, or Ted if you've a mind. I'll be glad to look on you as a son, and that's the honest truth.'

Luke looked into the weatherbeaten face and saw a smile lurking amongst the seams and wrinkles. He grinned and shook the farmer's hand. 'Thanks, Mr Tozer. Ted. Thanks very much. And I'll make you another promise here and now – one I really do mean to keep. I'll take every possible care of your daughter. I'll do all I can to make her happy.'

'Can't say fairer than that,' Ted said gruffly. 'Now, I got my crops to see to, and you got your picture to paint, so us'd better get on with it. Us can leave the women to organise this wedding, I reckon. That's what *they'm* good at!'

'*What sayest thou, bully Bottom?*' Henry Bennetts demanded in loud, angry tones, and Micky Coker turned to Stella in indignation.

'I'm not a bully, am I, miss? Anyway, that's not the bit we'm supposed to be doing.'

'No, it's not.' The performance had been shortened so much that by now it was a mere snippet. 'We decided to start later in the scene, Henry, don't you remember? And "bully" didn't mean the same then as it does now – it was more like "fine fellow". A term of encouragement.'

The children stared at her doubtfully. She took Henry's

248

book from him and turned over the pages. 'There, that's where we're starting now. Flute, Quince, Starveling and Bottom are in the wood, where they've been rehearsing the play they want to perform at the grand dinner, when Puck comes across them. He stays to watch and when Bottom leaves the scene, he goes after him. The others carry on and when Puck and Bottom come back, Bottom has an ass's head. The others are frightened and run away. We'll start from where Bottom leaves the stage – from *"But hark"*. Say that, Micky, and then just move aside as if you've left the stage – remember, they're in a wood so you'd probably go behind a tree.' The children giggled and she gave them a stern look. 'Micky?'

Micky, who was beginning to fancy himself as an actor, cupped one hand over his ear and said, *'But hark, a voice! Stay thou but here awhile, And by and by I will to thee appear.'*

'Now it's your turn, Flute,' Stella said. *'Must I speak now?'*

'No, miss,' said Brian Madge, who was playing Flute. 'It's me that says that.'

'Yes, I know, Brian. Go ahead and say it.' She smiled encouragingly.

'Must I speak now?' Brian enquired.

There was a long silence.

'Quince?' Stella prompted Henry. 'You have to answer him – see? *Ay, marry, must you . . .'*

'I don't understand that bit, miss. Nobody's said nothing about getting married before.'

'Nobody's said *anything*,' Stella said automatically. 'That's because it doesn't mean "marry" like we mean it today. It means – ' she racked her brains for an explanation '– it means "yes, you have to".' At least, I think that's what it means, she thought. 'You see, what Quince is saying is that Bottom has heard a noise and gone to see what was making it, and will be back in a minute.'

Henry looked at his script and nodded. He planted his feet

wide apart and declaimed, in a hectoring voice: '*Ay, marry, must you; for you must understand he goes but to see a noise that he heard, and is to come again.*'

'Now, Brian, you have to say what Flute is supposed to say in the play. *Most radiant Pyramus, most lily-white of hue . . .*' It's like wading through treacle, she thought as, after another long hesitation, Brian read the speech in a wooden monotone quite unlike his normal lively tones. Henry followed with another tirade, ending with '*Your cue is past; it is "never tire".*'

'I don't see why he got to shout at me like that,' Brian said.

'Well, he could tone it down a bit, perhaps,' Stella agreed. 'But what he's saying is that Flute has said it all wrong. He's said Ninny's tomb instead of Ninus's tomb and he's also saying that Pyramus ought to have entered by now.'

'We haven't got no one for Pyramus,' Henry objected.

'Yes, we have. Bottom is playing Pyramus and he ought to have come in when Flute says 'never tire'. Flute, say your words next. You're repeating the words you said before, you see, so that Pyramus – Bottom – will come in on cue.'

Brian gave her a doubtful look and repeated, in the same monotone as before, '*O – As true as truest horse, that yet would never tire.*'

'Puck and Bottom come in now,' Stella said. 'And remember, everyone, that Bottom has the ass's head on now and you must all look very frightened. You think it's a monster, or maybe a ghost.'

Micky and Shirley Culliford, who was playing Puck, marched in from the side of the space that had been cleared for a stage, and the others struck poses of extreme fear and horror. Well, at least they can do that, Stella thought. She waited for Micky to speak.

'*If I were fair, Thisby, I were only thine,*' he remarked, quite clearly without the least idea of what it meant.

'*O monster! O strange!*' Brian Madge said expressionlessly. '*We are haunted. Pray, master—*'

'No, that's not how it ought to be said!' Henry Bennetts exclaimed, almost beside himself with frustration. 'It's just like what I seen at the pictures. When 'Amlet saw the ghost he was proper frightened, and he were a *prince*, with a sword and everything. Old Brian looks more scared than that if he sees a spider!'

'I don't!' Brian retorted, showing signs of life at last. 'I'm not scared of spiders, Henry Bennetts, and if you says that again I'll knock your block off—'

'*Brian!*' Stella exclaimed. 'How dare you talk like that in my class! Now, say sorry, both of you, and let's get back to what we're supposed to be doing.' She waited while the two boys glowered and shifted their feet and finally muttered a grudging apology. 'Now, you all looked very frightened when Micky came in, but you do have to sound frightened as well. And the word's "monstrous", Brian, not "monster". Try it again. Remember, you are looking at something very strange indeed – a man with a donkey's head. You'd be frightened if you came across that in Cuckoo Wood, wouldn't you?'

'Yes, but I wouldn't hang about saying a lot of stupid Shakespeare,' Brian said, still smarting from Henry's accusation. 'I'd go and get my dad.'

'Well, they did things differently in those days,' Stella said, wondering why Miss Kemp had ever thought this was a good idea. 'Come on now, try it again, and then you all scream and run out. And then we'll stop rehearsing for today and try again tomorrow.'

The promise of release seemed to energise the children's performance and even Brian's voice took on a faint quiver of expression. As soon as he finished his speech – '*Fly, masters! Help!*' – the others joined in with piercing shrieks and everyone made for the door.

'Very good,' Stella called before they managed to get it open. 'All right, you can all go home now. Take your words with you and all try to learn them. We'll need to go on to the next part tomorrow. What's the matter, Shirley?'

'I never got a chance to say my words,' the little girl said tearfully. 'I been practising all day, and you never give me a chance. It was all them boys.'

'I'm sorry.' From the corner of her eye, Stella caught a glimpse of a figure outside the door and knew it was Felix. 'Say them to me now. Start with "*I'll follow you . . .*".'

Shirley, whose family was one of the poorest in the village and had never shown any ability until being made Festival Queen last year, stood very straight. She was dressed, as usual, in a frock that had seen better days, with stains that hadn't washed out and tears that had been clumsily mended, but since her appointment she'd always made an effort to come to school with a clean face, and her fair hair shone. She fixed her large grey eyes on Stella's face and recited Puck's speech.

I'll follow you, I'll lead you about a round,
Through bog, through bush, through brake, through brier:
Sometimes a horse I'll be, sometimes a hound,
A hog, a headless bear, sometimes a fire:
And neigh, and bark, and grunt, and roar, and burn,
Like horse, hound, hog, bear, fire, at every turn.

There was a short silence. Stella was aware of Felix, coming to stand just inside the door. Shirley looked at her anxiously and said, 'Was that all right, miss?'

'It was very good,' Stella said, clearing her throat. 'You spoke it beautifully, Shirley. Do you understand what Puck is saying?'

'Oh yes, miss. He's saying that he'll pretend to be all sorts of different animals and lead them into the bogs. Like we has on the moor. Pixie-led, we calls it. I reckon that Shakespeare must have been to Dartmoor, don't you, or how would he know about all that?'

'Well, Shakespeare might have been to Devon – who knows?' Stella said, struck by this idea. 'But I think the idea of pixies leading people astray happens all over England. Anyway, the main thing is that you understand it and you've learned it beautifully. Well done. Now you'd better go home.' She watched as the little girl scurried away and then smiled at Felix. 'I suppose you've been lurking there for ages.'

He nodded, grinning. 'I heard most of the rehearsal. I was aching with laughter at those boys. How on earth are you going to lick them into shape?'

'I'll call in reinforcements,' she threatened. 'If you've got time to eavesdrop, you've got time to help. Mind you, it all seems worthwhile when a child like Shirley turns out to be such a natural. Who would have thought it this time last year, when she and the rest of the Cullifords were always at the back of the class and nobody thought they'd ever amount to anything? It just shows, you shouldn't judge children by their parents. I wonder what other talents lie hidden in that family?'

'Well, if anyone can bring them out, you can,' Felix said, smiling. 'Now, are you coming for a walk? Dottie caught me as I walked past the cottage and said I've got to come to tea at five, so we've got over an hour. Time to go all the way up to the Standing Stones.'

'All right. Just let me clear up a bit here first.' Together, they replaced the chairs and tables that had been moved to make acting space, and Stella gathered up a few scraps of paper and pencil stubs that had been left lying about. Mrs Purdy could be heard outside, rattling her bucket and mops, and would be displeased if the room was left untidy. She was at the door as Stella closed the lid of her desk.

'Oh, hello, Curate. I didn't know as you were in here. I see someone been sick in the lobby again.'

'It was Betty Culliford,' Stella said. 'I cleared it up as best I could, but the smell never quite goes away. I'm always afraid it's going to affect the others as well.'

'It would if they thought they could get away with it,' the cleaner said. ''Tis all right, Miss Simmons, I'll put down some Dettol. You get out in the fresh air now. Lovely afternoon, it is. I been doing a bit in the garden, them weeds shoot up like rockets the minute you turns your back at this time of year.'

Stella and Felix said goodbye to her and left the school, turning right to walk beside the brook until crossing a cattle grid on to the open moor. From there, it was a steady climb to the stone circle that stood on the hill above the village. They reached the top, panting a little, and leaned against the tall granite slabs.

'It's a lovely view from here,' Stella remarked. 'It's not all that high, yet you can see for miles. Look at the sea glinting in Plymouth Sound. And the chimney on top of Kit Hill, right down in Cornwall. You can even see the china clay dumps near St Austell.'

'Let's sit down for a few minutes,' Felix suggested. 'I've brought a couple of apples. They're the last ones, I'm afraid, until the new ones come along.'

'They look like it, too,' Stella, said, inspecting the wrinkled red skins. 'I'm amazed they've kept so long.'

'So were Aggie and I. She found half a dozen at the back of her shed yesterday – they'd been pushed behind some seed trays and forgotten. But they're all right – just!'

They sat together on the short, springy turf, munching. Then Felix said, 'Have you heard from Maddy lately?'

'I had a letter yesterday. She's awfully busy at the moment – the wedding's next week, you know, and she's been helping with the arrangements. I don't know what she'll do after that; she'll feel rather lost without so much to do.'

'I should think she'd be glad of a holiday. I suppose Miss Forsyth and her new husband will be going away somewhere.'

'Yes, they're going to America for a few weeks. I think there'll be quite a lot for Maddy to do after that – sorting out the château, that kind of thing – but I don't know what her plans are then. I'd like her to come here again, of course, but she hasn't said anything about that.'

'Well, I'm sure Aggie would always be pleased to put her up. And I'd be delighted – I really enjoyed having Maddy around during the Easter holidays.'

'Yes,' Stella said quietly. 'I know.'

Felix glanced at her, but she was looking down at some strands of grass she was plaiting between her fingers. He hesitated, and then said, 'There's something I want to tell you, Stella.'

'Mm?'

He waited, but she didn't look up. He bit his lip, frowned a little, and then reached out, gently removing the grass from her hand. As she looked up at him, a trace of panic flickering in her eyes, the sound of voices on the slope below them made him drop his hand and look away with a small sigh of frustration.

'Well, look who's here!' cried a cheerful voice, and Val Tozer and Luke Ferris came into view over the crest of the hill. 'No, don't move – we'll plonk ourselves down beside you.' Val dropped to the grass beside Stella and leaned back against the stone. 'Phew, that climb doesn't get any easier, does it! Hope we're not interrupting anything,' she added, rather belatedly.

'Of course you're not,' Felix said. 'Stella and I had just come up the other way, from the school. It's too nice an afternoon to be indoors. How are you two getting on? Haven't seen you for a while.'

Val made a face. 'No, I seem to have been working all hours

and Luke's trying to get as much painting done as he can. We're spring-cleaning the cottage, too.'

Stella looked at her. There had been a time when Val had been rather cool towards her, but now that she was engaged to Luke she was friendliness itself. 'Any special reason?' she asked.

'Well, it is spring,' Luke began, but Val laughed and interrupted him.

'Oh, let's tell them! You can be the first to know,' she said, smiling all over her face at Stella and Felix. 'We've set the date for our wedding! It's to be the last Saturday in July. We've just been to see Mr Harvey to make sure he can do it that day, and he says yes! It gives us nearly three months to get ready, which Mum seems to think is the least possible time, and if we can't find anywhere else to live by then, we're going to stay in the cottage.'

'July! Oh, that's lovely,' Stella cried, giving Val a hug. Luke leaned across and she kissed his cheek. 'I'm so pleased. I hope you can find somewhere else to live, though. The cottage is a bit small for two, especially when winter comes.'

'Oh, we're bound to find something by then,' Val said gaily. 'And if we don't, we'll just have to move somewhere else.' She seemed to Stella to have shed ten years. The last few times they'd met, Val had seemed anxious and weighed down, but all that had gone. That's what the prospect of getting married to someone you love does for you, Stella thought.

'Move? Where to?'

'Wherever we can find work and a place to live,' Luke said firmly. 'I've been looking for a job. There's a teaching post advertised in Tavistock that I'm going to apply for – it would give me time to paint in the holidays. If I don't get that, I've been offered work at a picture-framer's in Plymouth. I know what you think,' he said as Val began to speak, 'but we've been through all this before, and it'll be better all round if I can support my wife and family. Living in a shack in the woods and being fed by half the village is all very well for a single man, but it won't do once we're married. We have to face up to it.'

'I'm going to go on working for a while,' Val said to Stella. 'He's doing so well with his painting – look at that exhibition he had last year. I'm sure it won't take long before someone recognises his talent.'

'Well, you have to decide that for yourselves,' Felix said. He was still trying not to show his irritation at being interrupted. 'And I think we'll have to leave you to it for now – Dottie's expecting us for tea at five and we mustn't keep her waiting.'

'Goodness me, no,' Luke agreed. 'If I know Dottie, she'll be taking something delicious out of the oven as you walk through the door. You go on down. Val and I will stay here and enjoy the sunshine.' He lay back on the grass and Stella saw his hand move to stroke Val's waist. 'I'm sure we'll be able to amuse ourselves.'

Stella and Felix set off down the hill in silence. After a few minutes, Stella said, 'They seem very happy, don't they? And it'll be exciting to have a wedding in the village. A summer wedding, too. It's really romantic.'

Felix nodded. He seemed lost in thought, as if he were considering something in his mind. Stella stole a glance at him and saw the expression on his face, and her heart sank. He said he was going to tell me something, she thought. Something about him and Maddy. And she knew, quite suddenly, that she didn't want to hear it – not now. Not on this bright, sunny afternoon, with the sound of Val and Luke's happy voices still ringing in her ears.

'Let's hurry,' she said, quickening her pace. 'Luke's right – Dottie will have been baking something special. And there are one or two things I need to do before tea.'

She walked ahead of him down the narrow path through the old wood, but as they passed the charcoal-burner's cottage where Luke and Val were going to make their home, she slowed down and cast it a wistful glance. Felix saw her expression and the thoughtful look in his eyes deepened. He followed Stella the rest of the way back to the cottage in silence, and although he gave every appearance of enjoying the sandwiches and sponge cake Dottie had prepared, he seemed abstracted, as if his mind were miles away. By half past six he was gone, and the two women were left alone.

'Is anything the matter with the curate?' Dottie asked as they washed up together. 'He didn't seem at all like his usual self.'

'I don't know,' Stella said, although she had a strong suspicion that she did. 'He was quite cheerful earlier on this afternoon.'

'Oh well,' Dottie said after a moment or two. 'I dare say he has his own worries, like the rest of us. Let's hope it's nothing too serious.'

'Yes,' Stella said rather sadly. 'Let's hope so.'

Chapter Twenty-Six

'Don't you ever just sit and admire your garden?' the vicar asked Constance Bellamy. He had been passing her gate when he noticed her wheelbarrow parked in the middle of the front path, and paused to say hello.

Constance, who had discarded her baggy tweed skirt in favour of a drooping cotton one, and her woolly jumper for a man's shirt, straightened up from a flowerbed, a small weeding-fork in her hand.

'Afternoon, Basil. Of course I do. I come out here every day with a cup of tea and settle myself down on that bench over there. But it's only two minutes before I notice something that needs doing – a weed that's popped up overnight, or a shrub that's getting a bit straggly – and I think I'll just see to that before it gets worse, and the next time I think about my tea, it's gone three o'clock and the children are coming out of school. And then I think I might as well carry on for another half an hour before I make myself another one.'

'And I suppose you forget about that one as well,' he said. 'Grace is just the same. I tell her the weeds are God's contribution to the garden, but she doesn't seem to think much of His abilities. Says it's no wonder He had to get Adam in to help Him! But I must say, your garden is looking a picture, Constance. You ought to open it to the public.'

The old woman looked around her at the banks of azaleas, now in full bloom, and the borders, bright with lupins like a colourful army on the march, and spotted with scarlet poppies and red-hot pokers. Geraniums were beginning to flower, too, and on the path lay several trays of bedding plants, which Basil guessed she had been hardening off in her greenhouse and were now ready to be planted out. Once in the ground, cared for by their green-fingered grower, they would leap into action and add to the colour that blazed all around them.

'Do you know, I've been thinking about that,' Constance said. 'Not just my garden, but some of the others in the village. Charge people sixpence or so to go round them and put the money to the Organ Fund.'

'It's an idea,' Basil said. 'I haven't done much about that yet, but we're going to have to think about it. We'll need all sorts of fund-raising efforts, I'm afraid – the renovations are bound to cost a lot.'

'Well, it's something to think about for next year. We could put on some teas in the village hall as well. Mind you, we'd have to be careful whose gardens we chose – some of the best ones are Methodists! They might not be too keen to support the church organ.'

'I'm sure they must need funds as well,' Basil said thoughtfully. 'The village hall itself, too – that needs quite a bit of refurbishment. I don't see why we can't all pull together and split the profits. I'll suggest it at the next meeting, and I'll have a chat with Mr Doidge, the Methodist minister, as well.'

'You might have a chat about Jed Fisher, while you're at it,' Constance observed, bending to pull out a dandelion that seemed to have sprung up even as they spoke. 'That man's getting worse, you know. More bad-tempered and abusive than ever, but it's my opinion he's ill. Sometimes when I hear him coughing, I think he's going to turn himself completely inside out.'

'I know. You can't help feeling sorry for him, unpleasant though he is. I don't know that Arthur Doidge will be able to do much about it, though. Jed looks after their graveyard, after a fashion, but I don't think he ventures in through the door very often. And nobody can force him to see the doctor.'

'We've still got to do our best to look after the old curmudgeon, though,' Constance said. 'Good job Jacob Prout's not like that. It's funny how two men who grew up together and have lived next door to each other all their lives can be so different, isn't it? D'you know, I heard them arguing the other day, at it hammer and tongs they were, and all over nothing at all. They seem to enjoy picking fights with each other.'

'I don't know that Jacob does,' Basil said. 'I'm a bit worried about him, to tell you the truth. He's seemed rather down this past week.' He hesitated, wondering whether to confide in Constance about Jennifer Tucker's belief that Jacob was her father, and then decided that he mustn't. Constance would certainly not pass it on, but neither should he. He looked around the garden again and reverted to their original subject. 'I'll certainly think about your idea of opening several of the village gardens to the public. I'm sure it would attract a lot of visitors – people love seeing what lies behind the hedges! I've often thought a postman's job must be pleasant from that point of view – they have free entry to every garden in the area and can watch their progress right through the year!'

Constance laughed. 'And never have to pull a single weed. I'll consider that, if I decide I need a job. Well, nice to see you, Basil. Tell Grace I've got some bedding plants for her, sowed far too many seeds, as usual. I'll walk round to the vicarage later on with a few.'

Basil went on his way, cheered by the little chat and the colourful garden. The idea of opening other gardens to give people the same pleasure was a good one, he thought. The Latimers' garden was lovely, and so was Joyce Warren's. He wondered if Gilbert Napier could be persuaded to allow visitors to walk in the Barton grounds. And there were probably others he didn't know about. He made a mental note to discuss it with Grace and then bring it up at the next meeting of the Parochial Church Council.

Somewhat reluctantly, he turned his mind to his anxiety about Jacob Prout. The village handyman was definitely upset about something, and Basil was sure it must be to do with Jennifer Tucker. Had Jacob found her news unwelcome? He must have been upset to realise that his sweetheart had been living just a few miles away all those years, married to another man – did he feel betrayed? Whatever the reason, it must have been a shock to discover the truth, and Basil desperately wanted to help him.

I can't broach the subject, though, he thought, strolling along the lane deep in contemplation. I'll have to wait for Jacob himself to bring it up – if he ever does. It was one of the frustrations of Basil's job that people often came to him with their problems but seldom came to tell him when they had been resolved!

'Hello, Uncle Basil. Where are you off to? You look as if you've got the cares of the world on your shoulders.'

Basil looked up, startled, and saw Luke Ferris leaning on the drystone wall and laughing at him. He smiled back, shrugging away his sober thoughts like a dog shaking water from its coat.

'Hello there, Luke. No, just contemplating life in general. I've been into Constance Bellamy's garden. It's a real picture. What a wonderful woman she is, always busy. She does tapestry as well, you know, when she can't get into the garden.'

'I know, I've seen some of her work.' Luke eased himself away from the wall and fell into step beside his godfather. 'I can't tell you how pleased I am that Val and I have got the wedding fixed. I'm taking her up to London at the weekend to meet the family. She's met Ma and Pa, of course, but some of the others are gathering, too, apparently, to give us a belated engagement party. Hope it doesn't put her off marrying me when she sees what a zoo the family is.'

'I don't suppose it will. Val's a tough young woman.' As he said the words, Basil remembered her distress when she'd come to see him a few weeks ago, and wondered if they were really true. 'And she's too fond of you, for some inexplicable reason, to let a mere family change her mind. I think you're going to be very happy together, Luke.'

'So do I. It's like a miracle, finding her again.' Luke hesitated. 'I know she told you about Egypt.'

'Yes. A difficult time for you both, but especially for her. I'm glad it's turned out well in the end.'

'I sometimes feel a bit guilty that her fiancé died and sort of made way for me,' Luke confessed. 'I'm sure she would have married him, you know.'

'We can't know that. She might have felt very differently when she met him again – especially after all that had happened.' They were both silent for a few moments, and then Basil went on more briskly, 'Anyway, it's all in the past now. It's the future you have to think of – and the present as well, of course. Enjoy the one and plan for the other, that's the way I believe we should live.'

Luke laughed and clapped him on the shoulder. 'You can always be relied on for good advice, Uncle Basil! I'll walk back through the village with you – I'm on my way to do a painting of the pool down by the Clam. There was a kingfisher there the other day, and a dipper on the rocks.'

They walked together as far as the green. The great oak tree was in full leaf now, shading the grass with its ancient canopy, and there were a couple of girls in riding gear by the horse trough letting their ponies have a drink. Luke waved his hand and sauntered off in the direction of the river, and Basil went through the lychgate into the churchyard.

Jacob Prout was there, clipping the yew trees. Basil

hesitated, and then as Jacob looked round and saw him, walked over to say hello.

'Is everything all right, Jacob?' he enquired when they had discussed the yew trees, the state of the gravestones and the great-tit's nest Jacob had found in a hole in the stone wall. 'You're keeping well, I hope, are you?'

'Me? 'Course I am. You knows me, Vicar, one cold a year and that's my lot. It's living in the fresh air that does it, and looking after meself proper.'

'That's good. Only I've been a bit worried about you lately. You don't seem quite your usual self.' Having given Jacob the opportunity to say what was worrying him if he wanted to, Basil changed the subject. 'I've just been looking at Miss Bellamy's garden. She does a wonderful job there, doesn't she?'

'She does that, right enough. Mind you, her old mother were just the same, out in the garden in all weathers, she were, and what her didn't know about plants wasn't worth knowing.' There was a short silence, and Basil began to turn away, murmuring something about the church. As he did so, Jacob took a sudden deep breath as if he were diving into a swimming-pool, and said, 'Before you goes, Vicar – if you got a minute, I'd be glad of a word, private like.'

'Of course, Jacob,' Basil said. 'Shall we sit on the bench by the door, in the sunshine? I don't think anyone's likely to overhear us there. Or would you rather go across to the vicarage?'

'No, out in the air's good enough for me.' He wiped the blades of his shears on a piece of rag he drew from his pocket, and they walked over to the bench. There was a good view of the path from the lychgate there and nobody could come upon them unawares. They sat down together and Basil gave the old man an enquiring glance.

'You'm right when you say I haven't been meself lately,' Jacob began after a few moments during which he seemed to be gathering his thoughts. 'I've had summat to think about, that's what it is. Had to turn it over in me mind and sort of find me way through it, if you understands my meaning. I couldn't talk about it till I'd done that.'

'I understand,' Basil said gently. 'Take your time, Jacob.'

''Tis about that Miss Tucker,' he said abruptly. 'I know her talked to you about me.'

'Yes, she did. She came to me for help and then advice. It wasn't easy to know what to say to her, to be honest.'

'No, I don't suppose 'twere. She went to Alice Tozer, too, and old Minnie. By the time she got round to me, her'd got the whole story worked out in her mind.'

'Yes, I think she had.' Basil wondered if Jacob were offended that so many others seemed to know the story before he had done. Yet it was only through talking to them that Jennifer had discovered it. He waited while Jacob seemed to consider his next words.

'Only trouble was,' the old gravedigger said at last, 'that her got it wrong.' He slid his eyes round to Basil's. 'You dunno what I be talking about, do you, Vicar? You dunno what I mean.'

'Well, no, I don't, Jacob. In fact, I'm thoroughly confused. Are you saying that she wasn't Susan Hannaford's daughter after all? But surely—'

'Oh no,' Jacob said. 'Her's Susan's maid, all right. That part's true enough. But she ain't mine.' His voice was low, and the next words even lower as he stared at the earth beneath their feet and repeated in a gruff, almost heartbroken voice, 'She ain't my daughter, Vicar. I only wish she was.'

There was a long silence. Basil looked at the dejected figure beside him, then turned his eyes away. The old man's sorrow was so apparent that it seemed an intrusion to witness it. Nor could he understand what he had just been told. He remembered that at the start of Jennifer Tucker's enquiries, he had warned her that the story might not be as simple as she thought. But she had seemed so sure – the Tozers themselves had seemed so sure – that it must be Jacob. He rubbed his forehead and then the back of his neck, trying to find the right words to speak next.

'Do you want to tell me about it, Jacob?' he asked at last, in a quiet voice.

Jacob nodded slowly. 'Reckon I better had, Vicar. Reckon I got to tell someone or I'll burst, what with it going round and round in me head all the time. And you're the one that knows most about it – you and the Tozers, anyway.' He thought for a moment. 'Reckon I might go and talk to them as well. Alice was a good friend to my Susan and old Mrs Tozer used to go and see her poor mother, too, whenever her had a chance.'

'It is true that you and Susan were sweethearts, then?' Basil asked, feeling his way.

'Oh, that's true enough. Knew each other right through school, us did, and I always had a fancy for her. I used to look after her in the playground, you know, just keep an eye out and make sure none of the others picked on her – you know what devils some little tackers can be. She were such a quiet, pretty little maid, and as she got older she just got prettier, to my mind. Once us all left school, I didn't see so much of her. Her family were chapel so we didn't even get the chance of running into each other in the churchyard of a Sunday. But then we started going to the village hops and dances in old man Tozer's barn and she used to slip down to them whenever she could get away. And we used to meet up on the moor and go for walks. And if it hadn't been for that bloody war – excuse my language, Vicar – I reckon we'd have got wed, never mind what old Abraham thought about it.'

'And you're quite sure that Jennifer isn't your daughter?' Basil asked. 'There's no possible chance. Alice Tozer did seem to think that you might have been home at the right time—'

'Oh, I was home all right! Home with a broken leg!' Jacob

266

gave a short, bitter laugh. 'They sent me back for Mother to look after, and the minute I could walk again I was back to the trenches. I only saw my Susan twice in that time – once when her come to the house to see me, when her father were away at market, and once the day before I went away again, when I met her in Tavistock with her mother. We weren't on our own for more than five minutes either time. And anyway,' he added with bitter regret, 'we never did nothing in that way. I had more respect for her. And I tell you what, Vicar,' he burst out, 'I wish now I hadn't, and if that's wicked of me to say so and goes against God's law, well, I can't help it. It's the way I feel!'

Basil felt his heart go out to the old man, robbed of his sweetheart and not even able to take comfort in the child that should have been his. At the same time, he thought of Val Tozer, who had also borne her lover's child, tiny and unformed though it had been, and suffered her own regrets. He said, 'But if you weren't the father, Jacob, then who was? I suppose we'll never know.'

'Oh, I knows that all right,' Jacob said in a tone of deep disgust. 'I knew she were in the family way, you see, Vicar. It were just after I went back – that's why Alice Tozer and her mother thought it were me. But it weren't. It were that other bastard – excuse my language again, Vicar, but there's times when no other words will do. Always had his eye on her, he did, even though she wouldn't even give him time of day. And I reckon when he saw me out of the way again and saw my Susan all upset, he saw his chance and took advantage of her. Oh, he could charm the birds off the trees in those days, though you'd never think it now, and I dare say he made up to her and offered her a shoulder to cry on, and my poor maid didn't see no harm in taking a bit of comfort. And no more *should* she!' he burst out again, as if Basil had denied it. 'Chapel folk, his family were, same as the Hannafords. She *should* have been able to trust him, now shouldn't she!'

'Certainly she should,' Basil murmured. An idea was beginning to take shape in his mind, an idea that was almost too horrifying to contemplate, and as he asked the next question he almost hoped that Jacob would refuse to answer. But it had to be asked, and it had to be answered. 'So who was it, Jacob? And – before you name names – can you. be absolutely sure, without any possible doubt, that you're right?'

'I'm right. There's no doubt about it, none at all. My Susan wrote and told me all about it. Blamed herself, she did, poor little maid, though no one else would have blamed her, except for that bully of a father of hers. And there weren't nothing I could do about it. Not a blind bloody thing.' He didn't apologise for his language this time. For a moment or two, he stared at the earth path, his jaw clenched and his face set in hard, bitter lines, and then he turned and looked Basil full in the face.

'It were Jed Fisher. That's who it was. Jed Fisher is Jennifer's father.'

'Jed Fisher?' There was a long silence. At last, Basil found his voice. Even though he had begun to suspect it, hearing the words spoken still came as a shock. He stared at Jacob's face, recognising the despair and misery in the other man's eyes, and felt again a powerful compassion. 'But . . . are you absolutely sure?' It was a weak response, he knew. Jacob had already made it clear that he was sure. Yet he could think of nothing else to say, and was once again painfully aware of his own inadequacy.

'I know it for a fact,' Jacob said, returning his gaze to the path. 'I told you, my Susan wrote and told me what he done. All smarm and charm, he were, making out he were my best friend and I'd asked him to keep an eye on her, and then taking advantage of her – filthy bugger!' His voice trembled at the thought of what had happened all those years ago, and Basil marvelled that he had managed to keep it to himself all that time. No wonder he and Jed have always been such enemies, he thought. How could they have gone on living next door to each other with something like this between them?

'Anyway, 'twasn't long before her knowed her was in the family way. I tell you, Vicar, I near enough deserted then to come home to her, but 'twouldn't have done no good. Another bloke in our unit did that one day – turned tail in the middle of all the fighting – and our officer pulled out his gun and shot him. Shot him dead, and us others weren't even allowed to go and get his body. Wouldn't have done my Susan no good for that to happen to me, and anyway, we were in the middle of France somewhere, I don't even know how I'd have got home. And by the time I did –' he seemed to dredge a huge sigh up from somewhere deep within his body '– it was all over. Or at least, that's the story her father put round the village. Said her'd gone off to Plymouth to go into service there, and then caught that 'flu and died of it. And when I went up to the farm one day and asked her mother, she said the same thing. I told her I knew about the babby, of course, and she told me that'd died as well. Wouldn't even say whether 'twas a girl or a boy. And that was the end of it.' Another deep, quivering sigh. 'Or so I thought, until Jennifer Tucker come to my door a week or so back. And now – well, I dunno what to think. It seems like everything's been turned upside down and I don't know how to put it back in its place.' He turned a face full of distress to the vicar and said, 'The worst of it is, I keep thinking she must have waited for me to go and fetch her. She must have thought I didn't want no more to do with her. That's why she went and got married to someone else.'

He fell silent at last, the words that had been spilling from him coming to a sad, despondent end. Basil sat silent beside him, surprised after a moment or two to find his hand on

Jacob's knee. He patted it awkwardly and removed it, and said, 'Have you ever had this out with Jed?'

'Well, what do you think, Vicar? Of course I have. Knocked on his door the minute I got back and found out what had happened – or what I *thought* had happened. His mother come out and saw me and said Jed was away from home, working on some farm up Chagford way. I got it out of her where he was and went off straight away and found him. I told him Susan had told me everything and then I knocked him down. Then I stood him up and knocked him down again.' Basil saw that he was rubbing his knuckles, as if the memory of the force of his blows was still there. 'I reckon I'd have killed him, too, if farmer hadn't come and separated us. He sent us both on our way – threatened us with the law if us didn't go quiet – and us both come home then. There weren't no more I could do about it, so us just went back to ordinary life.' He saw the astonishment on Basil's face. 'Well, what else could us do? Times were hard. There hadn't been the bombing in that war that us had last time – not down this way, anyway – but there'd been thousands of young men lost, *millions* of 'em, and there was work to do. There weren't time for argufying over things that couldn't ever be put right. I never spoke to him more'n I had to and he never spoke to me neither. It was only later, when his mum and dad had died, that he started to go downhill, and that was when he started to shoot his mouth off at me. And I give as good as I got, I don't mind admitting that, and don't see why not, neither. I had more to complain of than he ever had, Vicar, and you can't say nothing any different.'

'No, perhaps not.' Basil sighed and rubbed his face again, still wondering how to deal with the situation. A thirty-five-year-old tragedy had come suddenly to life in this village that, with all its small feuds and fusses, had seemed on the whole to be stable and well balanced. Briefly, he wondered how many worms lay hidden under other stones, and then returned his mind to Jacob's troubles. All this might have happened thirty-five years ago, but the consequences were making themselves felt now, and he was here to help and guide this bewildered man, and the woman who might have been his daughter – but wasn't.

'I can see that this has brought back a lot of painful memories,' he began. 'And some bitter regrets as well. Can you tell me what you would have done if you *had* found Susan – and her baby? How would you have felt about that?'

'Why, I'd have married her, of course.' Jacob sounded astonished that the question could even be asked. 'There's no two ways about it. She were my girl.'

'But what about the baby?' He waited a moment. '*Jed's* baby?'

Jacob, who had seemed to be about to say something more, checked himself. He put his fingers to his forehead and pushed them up through his grey hair. 'I'd like to say I'd have taken her on as well,' he said at last, in a heavy tone. 'But I don't honestly know. She were Susan's babby, and that ought to have been good enough for me – but if every time I looked at her face I had to think of Jed Fisher, I dunno as I could have put up with it.' He scowled at the gravestones all about them, stones that dated from two or three centuries ago and marked graves that might have been dug by his own ancestors. 'I'd like to say I'd have taken her,' he repeated. 'I'm pretty sure I would have done. It was Susan that mattered, when all's said and done, and the babby was as much hers as his. I reckon I could have come to think as much of her as I did of me own, though I dunno how we'd have got on if us had gone on living next door to Jed Fisher.'

'And now?' Basil asked. 'How do you feel about her now?'

This time, Jacob turned again and looked him straight in the eye. 'I'll be honest with you, Vicar. I'll be honest, because there ain't no sense in being nothing else. When that young woman come to my door and told me she thought I was her father, I wanted to believe her. I knew it couldn't be true, but I wanted it to be. She's a nice young woman, and don't seem to have a scrap of likeness to *him*, and in a funny sort of way I felt as if I already knew her. She don't look much like Susan, neither, but there's a lot of her poor old gran in her, and I suppose I warmed to her because of that.' He fell silent for a moment. 'It was one of the hardest things I ever did in the whole of my life, to tell her that she wasn't mine. And even then, I couldn't bring meself to tell her the whole truth.' His eyes reddened and brimmed with tears, the tears he should have shed thirty-five years ago. 'I couldn't bring meself to tell her she was Jed Fisher's maid. It would have been like handing my Susan over to him all over again, like I felt I did when I went back to the trenches and left her on her own. I just couldn't do it.'

He dragged a large red handkerchief out of his pocket and buried his face in it. Basil waited, his heart filled with pity, and after a few moments he asked his final question.

'And now? What do you think you must do now, Jacob?'

The old man seemed to shrink into his heavy work clothes. He looked ten years older. He heaved a sigh so deep that it seemed to come all the way up from his boots, and said in a dispirited, hopeless sort of voice, 'Well, I got to tell her, haven't I? I got to tell her the truth.' He shook his head and then looked at Basil again. 'Why is it that a devil like Jed Fisher can do that sort of thing, Vicar? Where's the fairness in it? He had my Susan, and now he's going to have my daughter as well – or her that ought to have been my daughter. Because she *felt* like mine, even when I knew she couldn't be.' He shook his head again. 'I don't understand it, Vicar, and that's the truth.'

'I don't understand it myself, Jacob,' Basil said honestly. 'It's a tangle. But I don't think you should despair. There's still a strong link between you and Jennifer. You were the one that Susan loved. She isn't going to forget that. And I think she may need you in the months ahead. It may not be easy for her, when she knows the truth.'

'Easy!' Jacob said with a short bark of laughter. 'It ain't going to be easy for *any* of us.'

Chapter Twenty-Seven

'I think it's a lovely choice,' Dottie said, gazing with satisfaction at the yards of lace swathed over her kitchen table. She draped some of it over Val's bare arm, admiring the effect. ''Tis as fine as gossamer. You'm lucky to find such beautiful stuff for your wedding-dress.'

'I know.' Val stroked the delicate fabric. 'And I never would have if it hadn't been for Stella thinking to ask Maddy if she knew of anywhere to get it. Imagine me, having a wedding-dress made of French lace!'

'Not that we can't make good stuff in England, too,' Dottie said at once. 'Right here in Devon – think of Honiton lace. They use that for royal weddings, you know. Why, one of my own great-great-aunts helped make the lace for Queen Victoria's wedding-veil. But this is handsome, there's no denying that.'

'And you think the colour's all right?' Val enquired a little anxiously.

Dottie nodded vigorously. 'I do. It's such a pale bluey-grey it looks almost silver. It suits you, and it's a bit different. After all, you'm not a young girl and white can be a cruel colour to wear. Now, what sort of pattern have you got? You ought to have it fitted to your waist, princess-style, and maybe with a little bolero jacket. Or draped sleeves, like bats' wings.' She held the material up against Val's body, her head on one side as she considered.

The back door opened and Stella came in, already talking.

'Honestly, Dottie, I can't think what possessed Miss Kemp to agree to do *A Midsummer Night's Dream*. It's more like a midsummer night's nightmare! Oh, hello, Val. Is that the material for the wedding-dress? Oh, how *lovely*!'

'D'you like it?' Val asked a little shyly. She watched as Stella touched the lace with gentle fingertips. 'It's beautiful, isn't it? Maddy's been so kind, taking the trouble to find it and have it sent over.'

'I think she enjoyed it. She's coming over herself soon.' Stella was still looking at the cobwebby fabric. 'It's so unusual, too. You'll look gorgeous, Val.' The two young women smiled at each other. 'I can see life is going to be all lace for the next few weeks, while Dottie's working on this!'

'You won't tell anyone else, will you?' Val said, suddenly anxious. 'Luke mustn't hear about it. It's got to be a complete surprise for him.'

'I won't say a word. And we'll have to make sure he doesn't come calling unexpectedly.' Stella looked at the lace again. 'What's going underneath?'

Val held up a roll of satin, exactly the same shade of silver-blue as the lace.

'Oh yes, that'll look lovely. How many bridesmaids are you having? Is Dottie making their dresses, too?'

'Three. Our Jackie and two little ones – my cousin's little girls, June and Patsy. They're only a year apart and look like twins, with curly fair hair and the most enormous blue eyes. They're wearing sky-blue. I've got a bit here . . . ' Val fished around and found a scrap of taffeta, which she held against the satin and lace. It made the pale colour look even filmier, and Stella nodded.

'It's going to be lovely. All of it. I'll have to get something new. Oh!' She put her hand to her mouth. 'Listen to me! I don't even know if I'm invited!'

'Well, you'll have to be now!' Val laughed, and then as Stella began to protest, 'It's all right – I was going to ask you, really I was. In fact, I think we're going to have to ask almost all the village. With one or two exceptions, perhaps,' she added almost under her breath.

'That Jed Fisher for a start,' said Dottie, never one to mince her words. 'You wouldn't want him like a skeleton at the feast.'

'Well, no. And he really is beginning to look more like a skeleton every day,' Val said. 'I saw him this morning. His skin looks really yellow. I don't think he's at all well.'

''Tis all they fags he smokes,' Dottie said. 'Always got one stuck in his mouth. I reckon if he smokes one a day, he smokes fifty or sixty – must be one of Jessie Friend's best customers. Stands to reason it can't do your chest no good. Jacob says he can hear him through the walls of a morning, coughing so bad he wonders he don't bring his lungs up.'

'I can't help feeling sorry for him,' Stella said thoughtfully. 'I know he can be very unpleasant, but he has a miserable life. Nobody seems to like him.'

'And that's nobody's fault but his own,' Dottie said. 'Now, Val, let's have a look at they patterns and decide what you want, a little bolero jacket or those long draped sleeves. I can do either, it's no trouble, and 'tis your day so you must have whatever you want.'

Val produced a sheet of paper with various styles drawn on it and they bent their heads over it, holding up swathes of fabric and letting it fall this way and that as they tried to decide which looked best. Stella left them to it and went up to her bedroom. She had her own problems with the costumes for the play, and had been busy for the past fortnight gradually building up an ass's head with papier mâché.

As she added another layer of scraps of newspaper and flour-and-water paste to her model, she gazed out of the window and thought about her sister. Now that Fenella Forsyth's wedding was over, Maddy would soon be coming back to England, and Stella wondered what her plans were.

The last time she had been here, she'd seemed unsettled and uncertain about her future. She didn't want to stay in France with Fenella and her new husband, but she was anxious that she had no qualifications for a job. Not that there was any real need for her to work – Fenella had promised her a good allowance – but although Maddy had grown up as a privileged young woman, her childhood had been that of an ordinary little girl in an ordinary family: first in a pleasant house in one of Portsmouth's quiet streets, then in the small, neglected two-up, two-down terraced house that they'd been allocated after their own home had been bombed. Stella still grimaced when she thought of the state of that house when they'd first moved in, with no electricity and gas lamps only downstairs, and the smell of cats everywhere. But their mother had scrubbed and cleaned and made a home of it, and they'd been happy enough until the night when that, too, had been bombed and the two girls left motherless.

After that, they'd lived in a country village not unlike Burracombe, billeted at the vicarage with Tim and Keith Budd from a few houses away, and life had been more settled – until their father had been lost at sea, and they were separated from each other and swept up into a world of orphanages.

Even after Maddy had been found and adopted by Miss Forsyth, she had been brought to live with Dottie in this very cottage – once again, the life of an ordinary child, where grown-ups had to work for their living. It wasn't until she left school that she began to travel and live in smart hotels. It was no wonder that now that phase of her life was over, she was unsure what direction to take.

'I feel a bit like a ship at sea, with no rudder,' she'd told Stella and Felix one evening before she'd gone back to France. 'Once Fenella's wedding is over, I'll have nothing to do but go around in circles. Up till now, I've always felt useful – now, I won't be any use to anyone.'

'Of course you will!' Stella exclaimed, distressed, but Maddy had shaken her head.

'I want to earn my living, like you do. But what can I do? Nothing – except maybe work in a shop.'

Maddy's words came back to Stella's mind now, as she sat at Dottie's washstand working away at her ass's head. She thought of the lovely materials downstairs, found and chosen by Maddy and sent over from France, and at the same time she remembered the woman she and her sister had met on the Plymouth bus not long ago. Jennifer Tucker, that was her name. She was a senior sales assistant in Dingle's – perhaps she would know of something Maddy could do. Maddy knows about fashion, Stella thought, and didn't Miss Tucker say that Maddy had the looks to be a fashion model?

She made up her mind to go to Plymouth on Saturday and ask her. Surely a big, smart shop like Dingle's would be pleased to have someone like Maddy working for them!

'Saturday?' Felix said thoughtfully, when Stella suggested a trip to the city. 'I'm sorry, I can't – I've promised to go to Dorset to see my uncle. Perhaps we could go another week.'

'I suppose we could,' Stella said a little reluctantly. 'Maybe I'll just go on my own. It's not your favourite idea of a day out, I know.'

Felix grinned. They had been to Plymouth together before, and enjoyed walking up the Hoe and down to the Barbican where all the fishing boats brought in their catch, early in the mornings, but he was like any other man when they went to the shops, although his natural good manners prevented him from showing just how bored he was. 'I must admit, I'd rather spend my time off out in the country,' he said. 'But I don't mind going with you, if you really want me.'

Stella shook her head. 'I'll go by myself.' She hadn't yet mentioned her reason for going, and decided not to. There was no point in talking about it, if the idea came to nothing. 'I need to look for something to wear to Val's wedding, anyway. It would be very dull for you.'

'Won't Dottie make you a new dress?'

'Dottie's going to be too busy making Val's wedding-dress and the bridesmaids' frocks. I could make my own, but I don't think the sewing-machine's ever going to be free. Anyway, I thought I'd splash out a bit. There are some lovely new summer things coming in now.'

She set off on the morning bus, having decided to make a day of it. Jennifer Tucker might only work on Saturday mornings – or maybe not at all – but someone at Dingle's ought to be able to give her a message, and Stella could think of no other way to contact the other woman. She got off at the bus station and walked up to Royal Parade, thinking how smart and wide it was. She had never known Plymouth before the war, but Dottie and others had told her how narrow and cramped the streets were before the Blitz had destroyed them, and how the city planners had taken the opportunity to rebuild in modern style. The rebuilding was still going on, but Dingle's, and the other big department store, Spooner's, were both open, along with a number of other shops along the new streets, and Stella thought that Plymouth people must be very proud of their city, rising like a phoenix from the ashes.

Occupied with these thoughts, she went in through the big glass doors and stood for a moment getting her bearings. The ladies' fashions were on the first floor, and there was an escalator leading up, so she stepped a little gingerly on to that and found herself in the middle of a vast array of women's clothes displayed on racks and models.

For a while, she wandered amongst them, vaguely looking for something that would be suitable for the wedding and wishing that Maddy could be there to advise her. At the thought of Maddy, she remembered her other reason for coming, and looked around for Jennifer Tucker. Eventually, she approached a sales assistant and asked her.

'Miss Tucker?' The woman was middle-aged, with a rather supercilious expression and dressed smartly in a black skirt and white blouse, making Stella feel like a country bumpkin in her cotton frock and cardigan. 'Does she know you're coming? Perhaps I can help you with whatever it is you want.'

'No, but she said to call in at any time.' Stella was determined not to be bullied. 'It's a personal matter.'

The assistant looked even more disapproving. 'Staff are not supposed to attend to personal matters during shop hours.'

'I'm sure they're not,' Stella said with a smile. 'And I know Miss Tucker is a senior assistant here, so I expect she's busy. But I won't take up much of her time. If you could just tell me where I might find her . . . ?'

The assistant looked for a moment as if she might refuse, but at last she said grudgingly, 'She'll be having her coffee-break at the moment, so I suppose it's all right to disturb her. I'll send one of the juniors.' She lifted her hand to summon a frightened-looking girl of about fourteen who was folding jumpers in a corner. 'Go into the staff canteen, Miss Jenkins, and tell Miss Tucker there's a lady here to see her. On a personal matter,' she added with a frown.

The girl scurried off, and the assistant moved away as if she had more important things to attend to, although Stella noticed with some amusement that they didn't seem to include folding the jumpers. Instead, she began to shift some dresses on a rack, keeping an eye on Stella at the same time.

I hope Miss Tucker remembers me, she thought with sudden anxiety. It was a few weeks ago that they'd met, and the invitation could well have been one of those things you say out of politeness and then forget. And it was Maddy she really noticed. By the time the junior returned, followed by a puzzled-looking woman in a crisp blue suit, Stella was beginning to wish she hadn't come.

To her relief, Jennifer's face cleared as she caught sight of Stella, lurking amongst the dresses, and she came quickly forward, smiling. 'You're one of the girls I met at Burra-combe. The two sisters who found each other after years apart. How nice to see you again. Is your sister with you?'

'No, it's only me. I – I wanted to talk to you – to ask you something. I'm sorry to disturb you at work. I didn't know how else to find you.' Stella looked at the assistant who was hovering nearby and Jennifer's lips twitched.

'It's all right. It doesn't matter at all. Look, I have my lunch-hour at twelve – why don't you come back then and we'll go somewhere together? I'll meet you at the main door.' She gave the assistant a cool glance. 'Thank you, Miss Smith. It was kind of you to send Miss Jenkins to find me. It's a private matter so we won't take up any more time now, and since there are just a few minutes left of my coffee-break, I may as well not bother to go back to the canteen.' She guided Stella through the maze of clothes and said, 'I'm senior to her really, but she's never been able to accept it – she's been with the company for years and is rather officious. That poor little junior is terrified of her!'

'So was I,' Stella said. 'She made me feel as if I ought to have worn my best clothes just to come through the doors.'

'Luckily, not all the assistants are like that. Most of them are very friendly and helpful. Now, you just browse around and I'll see you at twelve.' They parted at the top of the escalator and Stella descended, making up her mind to go to British Homes Stores or Marks & Spencers for her shopping. Dingle's was lovely, and she would still look around the store, but the prices were beyond her budget.

Jennifer came out promptly at twelve and suggested a café down the road. They walked there together and found a table by the window. When they had both ordered shepherd's pie and rhubarb crumble, they looked at each other a little shyly.

'I hope you don't mind me coming to see you,' Stella began. 'Only I wanted to ask your advice.' She explained about Maddy. 'It would be lovely if she could find something she's really interested in, and could live near Burracombe. Or better still, in the village itself. What do you think?'

'There might be something,' Jennifer said thoughtfully. 'She's a very pretty girl. And there's some talk of our starting up a sort of fashion show in the restaurant – girls wearing our clothes, showing them off while people eat their lunch or afternoon tea. Your sister would be ideal for that. It's only part-time, of course, and the girls we'll be employing will probably be from a model agency. Would she be interested in that, do you think?'

'She might be. But I think she'd rather have a job in the store – something like yours, perhaps. She knows quite a lot about fashion. I know she'd have to start as a junior – maybe as a sales assistant – what do you think?'

'I'll find out if there are any openings,' Jennifer said. Their shepherd's pies arrived and they began to eat. Then she said, 'And how is everyone in Burracombe?'

Stella looked at her with some surprise. 'I didn't realise you knew many people in the village. Or did you say you had relatives there? I'm sorry, I don't remember exactly what you said.'

'I don't think I did say much.' Jennifer hesitated a little. 'I've met the Tozers and the vicar. And Mr Prout,' she added after another slight pause. 'Do you know him? Jacob Prout.'

'Oh, everyone knows Jacob! He's a dear old man. I don't know what the village would do without him. Do you know him well?'

Jennifer didn't answer for a moment. She seemed to be concentrating on her shepherd's pie, and when she spoke again she seemed to have forgotten Stella's question. Instead, she said, 'You told me about how you and your sister were separated during the war. It must have been lovely for you to find each other again.'

We've said this before, Stella thought, but she smiled and answered, 'Yes, it was. We hadn't got any other family, you see, and I didn't know what had happened to her. It was like a miracle, finding that she'd actually lived in Burracombe.'

'Families are important, aren't they?' Jennifer said thoughtfully. 'You don't really feel complete without them.'

'No. And we'd lost both our parents in the war, so there were only the two of us.'

'But at least you knew about each other. And you knew your parents, too. You knew who they were.'

'Well – yes,' Stella said uncertainly, wondering what Jennifer meant. 'But then, most people do, don't they?'

'Probably, but not all.' Jennifer looked at her as if trying to decide whether to go on. At last, she said, 'I never knew my father. Not my real one. I had a stepfather, and he was very good to me, but he wasn't my *real* father.'

'Oh,' Stella said blankly, not knowing what to say. She stared at her plate, feeling uncomfortable, but Jennifer went on without seeming to notice.

'I didn't even know until quite recently – but once I found out, I just felt I needed to know the truth. That's why I came to Burracombe.'

Stella looked up in surprise. 'You mean that's where he came from? But how did you know that?'

'I didn't know, for sure.' Briefly, Jennifer explained how she had looked at several villages before coming to Burracombe and half remembering a visit she had made there with her mother. As the waitress came and took away their empty plates and replaced them with bowls of crumble and custard, she told Stella more of the story. 'And then I felt sure I knew who he was. But when I talked to him, he told me I was wrong.' Her eyes filled with tears.

Stella felt a rush of sympathy. 'Oh, how sad. So won't you ever know?'

'Oh yes,' Jennifer said, poking at her crumble with her spoon. 'I'm going to know. I've got to, you see. I've got so far, I can't stop now. I'm going to go out to Burracombe again and see him – the man I thought was my father – and ask him to tell me the truth. He knows, I'm sure of it. And he loved my mother, I know that. I'll *beg* him to tell me.'

Chapter Twenty-Eight

The ass's head was finished at last and Stella took it to school. In the midst of all her other work, Dottie had found time to knit a cover for it in grey wool, and make two long ears, which Alf Coker had fixed on wire loops so that they stood up. Two large black buttons were sewn on for its eyes, and the whole thing fitted together over Micky's head in two halves before the grey cover was pulled over the top.

'I can't see nothing!' came Micky's muffled voice from deep within.

'Oh dear,' Stella said. 'I never thought of that. Can you breathe all right?' She had made holes for nostrils, roughly where she thought Micky's nose might be. 'That's more important – we can always push you into position.'

'It smells all woolly,' he complained, and the others giggled.

'You don't have to wear it for long,' Miss Kemp said. 'I think Miss Simmons has made a very good job of it. You look very lifelike.'

Micky started to drag the head off and Stella hastened to help him. 'You have to take off the knitted cover first, or you'll get stuck. That's why I made it in two halves – you'd never get it on otherwise.' She smiled at his red face. 'Goodness, you do look hot.'

'I'm going to boil,' he said irritably. 'Why can't one of the others be Bottom? I never wanted to be him in the first place.'

'It's too late to change now. And we needed a really good

actor for that part. Bottom is the most famous person in the play – in that part, anyway. Now, how are the rest of the costumes getting on?'

The other children produced their costumes and Stella and Miss Kemp inspected them. It had been decided that the play would be performed twice – first at the school at the end of term and then at the Summer Fair. Stella had heard that morning that Maddy would be here by then, and she had agreed to present the prizes. She was going to stay at Aggie Madge's cottage until she had decided what to do next.

Stella didn't know whether to be pleased or sorry about this news. Ever since the Easter holidays, she thought she had detected a slight cooling in Felix's attitude towards her. He and Stella still spent time together, going for walks or to the cinema, but he had never kissed her again and remained no more than friendly, whereas he was always talking about Maddy and looking forward to her return. Sadly, remembering how she had begun to grow fond of Luke Ferris last year and then been disappointed, Stella told herself that it was too much to hope for that Felix should prefer her to her pretty sister, and she too began to withdraw a little. She hadn't gone to church the day after her trip to Plymouth, and when Felix looked in at the classroom door after school on Monday, she'd told him she was too busy for a walk. It was now four days since they'd spent any time together and although she missed him badly, she told herself that it was best that way. Maddy would be here soon, and Felix must feel free to court her, if that was what he wanted.

As she walked home from school, Stella thought again about Jennifer Tucker's story. Jennifer hadn't told her who she'd thought her father was, but Stella hadn't missed her enquiry about Jacob Prout. She wondered if it could be him. There had been mention of the Tozers, too – a rather mysterious mention, now Stella came to think about it. Could Jennifer have thought Ted was her father? He was about the right age. Maybe he'd hinted that it was Jacob; or perhaps it was the other way about. Whichever it was, it was a muddled situation and one that would surely cause problems if Jennifer insisted on being told the truth.

That's why she was so interested in Maddy and me, Stella thought. It's all about families being separated and trying to find each other. It's about wanting to know who your real family are. But Jennifer Tucker did have a family – she'd had a mother, and a man she'd believed was her father, and sisters as well. Why isn't that enough? Does it really matter that another man was her real father? Does she really have to find him, even if it means trouble and heartache for other people?

Which was more important – the person who gave you your life or the one who looked after you and brought you up? In which case, who was more important to Maddy – their own mother, Kathy Simmons, who had been killed by a bomb, or Fenella Forsyth, who had adopted her, or Dottie, who had taken care of her through the rest of her childhood?

Stella shook her head. It was too difficult to decide. And before she could worry about it any more, Felix's voice jerked her out of her troubled thoughts. She looked up and saw him crossing the village green towards her.

'I thought you weren't going to speak to me,' he said as he came closer.

'I didn't see you. I was miles away.'

She looked at him a little uncertainly, trying to assess whether his smile was as warm as ever and thinking that he looked slightly uncomfortable. There was a small hesitation, then he said, 'Are you on your way home to tea?'

'Yes, we've just been rehearsing the *Dream* again. I think it'll be all right in the end. Shirley Culliford has a real talent – she's a surprising little girl. Only needed to be given a chance. It makes me wonder what other gifts the children have that we don't find.'

'If they've got them, they'll find some way of expressing

287

them,' Felix said. 'Do you mind if I walk home with you? There's something I need to see Dottie about.'

'Of course not,' Stella said, surprised. A few weeks ago, he wouldn't have asked; he'd have just fallen into step beside her. It just shows how far apart we've drifted, she thought sadly.

They walked along together, talking politely, and Stella felt even sadder. We're almost like strangers, she thought. However did it happen?

Once in the cottage, they were both warmed by Dottie's normal friendly welcome and the atmosphere eased. They sat in the battered armchairs, drinking tea and enjoying crisp, oaty flapjacks, and admiring the progress of the wedding-dress, and things seemed to be just the same as ever. But when Felix got up to go, their constraint returned, and there was no arrangement made for a walk or a visit to the cinema. He stood for a moment in the doorway, his head bent a little beneath the low ceiling, and they looked at each other doubtfully. Then he stepped into the sunshine and walked away down the short path to the front gate.

Stella came back in and closed the door.

'Is he all right?' Dottie enquired, her head bent over her sewing. 'He don't seem quite himself these days.'

'I expect he's just busy,' Stella said vaguely. 'There's a lot happening at this time of year, isn't there? Weddings and garden teas and all that sort of thing . . . And he's helping a lot over at Little Burracombe. The vicar there's not at all well.'

'No, he isn't, poor old man. Never properly got over that bronchitis he had backalong.' Dottie threaded a needle and bit off the end of the cotton. 'Well, so long as everything's all right between the two of you.'

'Of course it is. Why shouldn't it be? We're just friends, that's all.' Stella's voice was sharper than she intended, and as Dottie glanced up at her she flushed and bit her lip. 'Sorry, I didn't mean to snap. It's this play we're doing, it's getting me down a bit. I'll go upstairs – I've got a few things to see to for tomorrow.'

'That's right, my pretty, you do that,' Dottie said peaceably. 'I'll just finish this hem and then I'll start thinking about supper. I went into Tavistock this morning and got a nice piece of smoked haddock. And there's strawberries from the garden for afters – the first ones.'

'That sounds lovely. Give me a call if there's anything I can do.' Stella went up the narrow stairs to her room and shut the door. She stood for a minute or two looking out of the window, and then sighed and turned away to unpack her school bag.

If Stella had stood a minute longer at her window, she would have seen the local bus that connected with the main route through Yelverton pull up beside the green and Jennifer Tucker climb out.

Val Tozer was walking by at that moment, and the two young women smiled and greeted each other. They stopped and Jennifer said, 'I'm glad I've met you. I was thinking of coming up to the farm. You don't have time for a few words, do you?'

'Of course,' Val said. 'Come up and have some tea.'

Jennifer hesitated. 'Well – maybe in a minute. But I'd quite like to talk to you on our own. It's all a bit difficult, you see. I know your parents and your granny know my story, but . . . well, let's find somewhere quiet and I'll tell you what's happened.'

Curiously, Val led her along the lane and through the gate that led to the path up through the woods to the charcoal-burner's cottage. 'It's where Luke and I are going to live after we're married,' she explained. 'We'll need to find somewhere else as soon as possible, because it's not really suitable for two, especially in winter, but we don't want to wait any longer. We can talk privately there – Luke's gone to Tavistock for an interview at the school.'

'Is he a teacher?' Jennifer asked in surprise. 'I thought he was an artist.'

'He is, but he says he can't earn enough from his paintings. I don't want him to get a job – I think he ought to use all his time for painting – but you know what men are, they feel they've got to support their wives. And I'll make sure he does plenty of painting in his spare time!' She opened the door of the ramshackle little cottage. 'Come in. I'll make a cup of tea.'

Jennifer sat down in one of the wooden carver chairs, looking around. There were only two rooms – the main living-room where they were sitting, which served as a kitchen as well, and what she guessed must be the bedroom through an inner door. The only furniture was two chairs, a small, elderly settee and a kitchen table. Luke's easel stood in one corner and there were paintings everywhere, stacked together on the floor and leaning against the walls.

'I can see why you want somewhere else to live,' she said. 'There's hardly room to swing a paintbrush.'

Val chuckled. 'I know. It's going to be a bit like camping. But we've known each other a long time.' She turned from the tiny cooking-range and glanced at her visitor, grinning a little awkwardly. 'Longer than most people realise, to tell you the truth. Anyway, we just don't want to wait any longer. I'm almost thirty, you know, and if we want to start a family we've got to get on with it.' A shadow crossed her face, but she turned away without saying any more and poured boiling water into the fat brown teapot.

Jennifer accepted a cup of tea, and Val sat down in the other chair. They looked at each other and then Val said, 'Did you go to see Jacob?'

Jennifer nodded. 'That's what I wanted to talk to you about. You see, it's all turned out differently from what I expected. Your mother and grandmother – they were wrong about him.' She stared out of the open window. It looked out through the trees, with their bark green with moss, and up the hill towards the Standing Stones. A few birds fluttered amongst the branches; the two women could hear the piping voices of tits, the trill of a robin and the harsh screech of a jay. Jacob and Susan would have walked up that path, past this cottage, and done their courting within the ring of granite stones on the brow of the hill, just as countless lovers must have done through the ages, and probably still did. Tears pricked her eyes as she felt a sudden deep longing to know that she had been conceived there, in love and happiness, but the longing was swiftly followed by the sorrow of knowing it was not true; and the lonely desolation of perhaps never knowing the truth.

'I don't understand,' Val said after a few moments. 'How do you mean, they were wrong about Jacob? Wasn't he Susan's sweetheart after all?'

'Oh yes. They were sweethearts – he told me that. He really loved her, Val, you can see it in his eyes even after all this time. It broke his heart, what happened. But he's not my father.' She turned her head and met Val's startled gaze. 'He says he couldn't possibly be my father. They never went that far, you see.'

'But – but Mum says he was home at the right time. He'd been wounded, hadn't he?'

'Yes, she's right about that. But then he went away again. And it must have been soon after that that it happened.' Her voice was low. 'Someone else came along and – well, I suppose she was lonely and upset, and whoever it was didn't have the same scruples as Jacob. Oh, Val!' she burst out. 'I *liked* Jacob! I wanted him to be my father! I still do – I felt as if I *knew* him, even though we'd never met before. But instead . . . he's no relation to me.' She fell silent for a moment, then added tonelessly, 'I feel that if we could have found each other again, it would have made up, somehow, for all he'd lost. All they'd both lost. And now – well, I'm back to the beginning again. Worse than that, I've upset that nice old man. I wish I'd never started it.'

She buried her face in her hands, while Val watched helplessly. After a moment, she moved across and knelt beside the other woman, putting her arm across Jennifer's shoulders, patting her gently. At last she said, 'And didn't he ever find out who the man was?'

Jennifer dropped her hands and lifted her eyes towards Val's face. Her cheeks were wet with tears, and Val felt for a hanky to give her, but she shook her head and took her own from her pocket. 'He wouldn't say. And I couldn't ask him – not then. It was all such a shock, for us both. But I think he knows who it was, Val.'

'Do you think he'd tell you? Do you still want to know?'

Jennifer didn't answer at first. She stared out of the doorway, as if still thinking about it, and then she nodded slowly.

'Yes, I do. Whoever it was – and however it happened – it's still part of my mother's history, and mine. I won't feel easy until I know.' Her lips twisted wryly. 'I may not feel easy then either, but at least I'll have found out all there is to find out. I'll have done what I set out to do. The thing is, *will* he tell me? I just don't know, Val. I can't upset him any more than I already have. I can't *make* him tell me. But I feel I've got to ask him, just once more.' She drew in a deep, shuddering breath. 'That's why I was coming up to the farm. You see, I don't know how it might affect him. I thought I'd ask you and your family before I go to see him again.'

'I see.' Val moved away and returned to her chair. 'I don't honestly know what to say,' she confessed. 'I've known Jacob all my life, and he's always seemed a very steady sort of man – not the sort to get upset easily. Unless it's with Jed Fisher, who lives next door,' she added with a grin. 'They're always at loggerheads! But apart from that, he takes life as it comes.

292

I've never seen him in this sort of situation, of course,' she added.

'What about when his wife died? Do you remember that?'

'Not really. It was during the war – I was away from home. Mum wrote and told me about it, of course, but by the time I came back, it had been over for ages and Jacob seemed to have settled down to being on his own again. I'm not really being much help, am I?'

'I can't expect anyone to help me, really,' Jennifer said despondently. 'I wonder sometimes if I'm being selfish. What good is it going to do to anyone for me to dig up all these old stories? They can still hurt people, you see, and I don't think I'd ever realised that before – not completely. What's the point, except to satisfy my own curiosity?'

Val thought of her own story, and her talks with Basil Harvey on whether the truth should be told, even years later. He had guided her towards the decision that if it were only to result in pain for other people, it might be better kept secret. Was it the same in Jennifer's case?

'The thing is,' she said, 'you've done it now. You've brought it to light for Jacob, and now he knows that Susan didn't die all those years ago. There might not be anyone else he can talk to about it – only you. All his memories might be welling up – he may really need someone to talk them over with. And you're the only one who can tell him about your mother – Susan – during the last thirty-five years. I think you should go to see him, Jennifer. Not just to ask him your questions, but to let him ask you his.'

Jennifer stared at her. Her face was pale and there were fresh tears in her eyes. She shook her head slowly.

'I must be the most selfish person on earth,' she said. 'I never even thought of that. I knew I didn't want to upset him, but it never occurred to me that he would want to know about my mother. It never occurred to me that he might need me to talk to.'

'So will you go to see him?' Val asked quietly, and she nodded.

'I'll go now. I won't ask him who my father was – not yet, anyway. I'll just let him talk, if he wants to. I'll try to get to know him before I go any further.' She began to get to her feet. 'I'm not going to cause poor Jacob any more pain. But I still hope he'll tell me. I'll always want to know who the man was, Val. I can't help wanting to know that.'

Chapter Twenty-Nine

Jacob was lying back in his armchair, his feet up on his mother's old sewing-stool and Flossie on his lap, when he heard the knock on the door. For a minute or two, he didn't move, then, slowly and reluctantly, he lifted the cat down to the floor and heaved himself up. Whe he opened the door and found Jennifer standing there, he hardly knew whether to be glad or sorry.

'Jacob,' she said quietly, 'can I come in?'

The old man rubbed his eyes and forehead with the back of one hand. For a moment, he seemed about to refuse, then he stood back a little and made a small gesture. 'Come you in. I was just having a bit of a rest.'

'I don't want to disturb you—' she began, but he shook his head.

'You've come all the way out from Plymouth special, I dare say. Sit down –' he shifted two or three newspapers from the other armchair '– and I'll make a cup of tea.'

Jennifer did as she was told and looked around the room. It was less tidy than on her last visit, with papers on the table, dust on the dresser shelves and dirty dishes beside the sink – more than Jacob would have used for one, or even two, meals. Scruff, the dog, came over to sniff at her, wagging his stumpy tail, and she bent to fondle his ears, feeling anxious. She'd caught only a glimpse of Jacob before he'd turned away, but he didn't look as if he'd shaved that morning. Her impression of him before had been of a man who took care of himself and his surroundings. Now, he and his home looked slightly unkempt.

Jacob shuffled over in his socks and put a cup down beside her. He went back to his own chair and sat looking at her, and Jennifer fidgeted uncomfortably.

'Well?' he said at last. 'You've come to ask me summat, I suppose.'

'No,' she said quickly. 'I haven't. It was my reason in the first place, I've got to be honest about it – but I've had second thoughts.' She faced him. 'Perhaps I should never have come here at all, but when I found that my father was a different man from the one I'd always thought – a man I didn't even know existed – I felt I had to know who he was. I tried to forget it, but I couldn't. It was on my mind all the time – day and night. In the end, I had to do something about it. I looked in a lot of different places, and eventually I came to Burracombe. And I found you.'

'And I told you—'

She lifted one hand and he fell silent, still watching her. 'You told me you weren't my father. It was a shock, Jacob. I felt, when we met, that there was some strong link between us. I *wanted* you to be my father. I really believed you were. But—' Her voice broke and she shook her head, unable to go on. Jacob filled the silence.

'So you've come to ask me who he was.'

Again, she shook her head. 'No. I don't think it's right to make you go over it all. I've caused enough upset for you. I've come because I thought you might want to talk to me about my mother. I thought you might want to know what her life was like, after she left Burracombe. And – and if you can bear it, I'd like you to tell me about her when she was young. Because there's no one else who can do that – not in the way you can.' She met his eyes. 'I won't ask you about – about *him*. And if you don't ever feel you can tell me, then that's an end to it.'

There was a long silence. Scruff settled down at Jacob's feet and Flossie climbed back on to his lap. He stroked her absently, his fingers moving slowly down the soft, tortoise-shell back. His eyes were veiled as he looked down at the cat, and Jennifer waited with a thumping heart. If he told her to go now – if he said he didn't want to go over those old memories and open up those old wounds – then that really was an end to her search. She would never know who her father was. Nor – and, to her surprise, this suddenly seemed more important – would she ever really get to know this man whom her mother had loved.

''Tis good of you, maid, to come and talk to me like this,' he said at last. 'I won't say 'twasn't a shock to see you, and hear that my Susan had been alive all these years. It's taken a bit of getting used to, and I don't seem to have had the heart for much else these past couple of weeks. But you'm right. It *has* brought back old memories – and there hasn't been no one I could share them with. Maybe it'll be a good thing to chew 'em over with you. Otherwise, seems to me they'll just keep turning round and round in me own head, with nowhere else to go.'

Jennifer let out her breath and relaxed a little into her chair. Jacob had stopped speaking, but she sensed that he still had more to say. She waited, quietly, wishing that she too had a cat to stroke. After a few minutes, the old man spoke again.

'But you'm wrong to think I can't tell you who your own father was. Seems to me, if we'm to be able to talk about these things honestly together, we both got to know the truth from the start. It'll never be satisfactory if there's a secret between us. Not a secret like that, anyway. It'll stand in the way all the rest of our lives.' He raised his eyes and looked at her, and she knew that she was about to hear the truth of what had happened all those years ago.

'It isn't summat I finds easy to talk about,' he said in a dry, rusty voice, 'so you got to bear with me if I don't put it well.

And I dare say there be more to the tale than even I knows. Things that only *he* knows – and I wouldn't trust him to tell them, neither, not honest and truthful. He don't know the meaning of the words.' He caught himself up, hearing the bitterness in his own voice, and his mouth twisted. 'But there – 'tis of your father I'm speaking now, and I got to remember that. But we been at odds for years now – ever since it happened – and old habits die hard.'

Jennifer stared at him. Little as she knew of Burracombe and its inhabitants, she had heard enough to suspect what Jacob was about to tell her. She felt a dread settle over her heart, and almost cried out to him to stop, she didn't want to hear the name, didn't want to know the truth. But she had come too far now and couldn't turn away because it was harsher than she had thought.

Jacob leaned forward a little, and she leaned automatically towards him in turn. In a quiet voice, and turning his eyes towards the wall of the adjoining cottage as he spoke, he said, 'The man who took advantage of my Susan and fathered her babby – fathered *you* – lives next door. We grew up together, living side by side, and we'll live side by side until one or t'other of us dies. You saw him, last time you came here. His name's Jed Fisher.'

Jed Fisher. She thought of the scrap of paper, the last few words of the letter Jacob himself had written to her mother. The initial J that was his and hers – and, by heartbreaking coincidence, her father's as well.

The man who had stared at her with such hostility, who had ranted at Jacob in the front garden, who was dirty and unkempt and repellent, and apparently disliked by the whole village – that man was her father, whom she had thought of, dreamed of and sought to complete her own life story.

A sick, dizzy feeling swept over her and she put her hand to her forehead. She felt Jacob's big, strong hand on her arm, steadying her and then on the back of her head, pushing it down between her knees. After a moment or two, the dizziness faded and she sat up, trembling a little. He held the cup of tea to her mouth.

'Have a sip of this, maid. It's been a shock for you, and no wonder. Maybe a drop of brandy – I got some in the cupboard, for medicinal purposes.'

'I'm all right now.' She sipped the tea and then gave him a shaky smile. 'Sorry about that.'

'Bless your heart, maid, there's no need to be sorry. Seems we gives each other shocks.' He gave her a wry smile and she gave him a faint one back. 'That's the trouble with telling the truth. It ain't always what folks wants to hear.'

'No,' Jennifer said. 'We always think it's going to be something better.' She looked at him again. 'I really did want you to be my father, Jacob.'

'Ah,' he said, nodding slowly, 'and I wanted it, too. But 'twasn't to be, maid, and us got to accept that. And I'll tell you something else, too.' Jennifer looked at him enquiringly, and he went on with a heavy note to his voice, 'Right's right, and if we'm going to do this thing proper, to my way of thinking we got to go the whole way. 'Tidden easy for me to say this, considering how I've felt about it all these years, but that old so-and-so next door – begging your pardon – has got his rights, too, whatever he done. He may not deserve to be, but he'm your father and seems to me he got a right to know it. Now, you don't have to agree with me, and to tell you the truth, I'll not be sorry if you don't, but you got to think about it, at least. Do you tell him, or don't you? That's the next thing to look at.'

Once again, there was a silence. Jennifer thought of the choices that lay before her. She could take her quest no further; ignore Jed's existence, pretend that he had no part in her life and build up a relationship with Jacob himself, telling herself that his love for her mother was enough. Yet how was that any different from the relationship that she and her mother had had with her stepfather, Arthur Tucker, whom she had believed for years to be her father? If she had been satisfied with that, she would never have started on this search.

'How do you think he'll take it?' she asked at last. 'He might deny it – pretend nothing ever happened. He might say you're lying.'

'Well, us'll be no worse off, in a sense, if he do,' Jacob said. 'And whatever else happens, maid, you and me'll be friends. If that's what you wants.'

'Yes, it is,' she said at once, and simultaneously they reached across the hearthrug and shook hands.

'Well, then,' he said with a smile that showed he felt more at ease now, 'what do you want to do next?'

'I want us to talk,' she said. 'I'll think some more about what you said about Jed. I know you're right, but I'm not quite ready to talk to him yet. All this –' she waved a hand '– all this has come so suddenly. But I want you to tell me about my mother, when she was young. And I'd like to talk about her to you, too, if you'd like that.' She returned his smile. 'We've got thirty-five years to catch up on! We'd better start straight away.'

They talked for hours. Jacob made more tea, and then he noticed the time and realised that his visitor must be hungry. There was an enamel dish in the larder with some bacon and four thick sausages – 'Cokers' – in it, and he fried these along with some mashed potato left over from his dinner and some tomatoes from his garden. He cleared the papers from the table, apologising again for the 'mess' and laid it with a red checked cloth and old, bone-handled knives and forks. 'These were my granny's,' he said. 'Look after 'em right and never put the handles in water and they'll last for ever.'

They sat down to their meal, still talking. While Jennifer kept an eye on the sausages, he had shaved at the kitchen sink, using a cut-throat razor, and then he slipped upstairs and came down in a fresh, clean shirt. 'I'm ashamed you found me like you did. Been letting things go, I have.' He glanced around the room, noting the dust on the dresser. 'I'll give this place a good go tomorrow, get it back up to scratch.'

Jennifer didn't ask why he'd been letting things go. She felt a pang of guilt, realising that her sudden arrival in his life had brought back painful memories, and understanding that he had been tormented by his own conscience during the past fortnight, knowing that he must tell her the truth. If it had been anyone but Jed, his enemy . . . But when she mentioned this, Jacob shook his head.

'Jed and me were pals up to then. Always together, when us was little tackers. Well, us would be, wouldn't us, living next door to each other and our parents friendly as they were. But he were always a bit wilder than me, Jed was, and as us got older things started to change. Didn't go to chapel any more, and I didn't like his way with the maids. Didn't seem to have proper respect for 'em, somehow. And then, when the war broke out and he wouldn't join up – managed to get exemption on account of *flat feet* or some such excuse – I'll be honest with you, Jennifer, I was proper riled about that. His feet had never stopped him doing nothing before that!' He took a bite of sausage and chewed fiercely. 'And I used to think even then that he had an eye for my Susan. Not that I thought she'd ever fancy *him*, but I didn't like the way he looked at her.'

'And then you came home and found she'd gone. That must have been dreadful.'

'Ah, it were a bad time.' He told her the story he had told Basil, about his visit to Chagford and the fight with Jed. 'And since then, I've done me best to pretend he's not there, but it's not been easy and for the past few years we been snapping and snarling at each other like bad-tempered dogs. I ain't proud of it, but there you are, 'tis the truth. I reckon it got worse when my Sarah died,' he added thoughtfully. 'Seemed to bring it all back, being on me own again. I don't say I wasn't proper fond of my Sarah, I was, but I couldn't help wondering sometimes if me and Susan would still have been together, if things had been different. And I'm not very proud of that, neither,' he added.

They finished their meal and Jennifer helped him wash up. It was getting late now and she looked at the grandmother clock that stood in his front room and said, 'I'd better be going. I'll have to walk out to the main road to catch the Plymouth bus.'

'I'll walk with you, maid.' He hesitated. 'You won't be calling on him next door now?'

'Not tonight. I'll have to come out again. I can't do it until next Wednesday, though – that's my afternoon off, when the shop's closed. I'd come on Sunday but I don't know how he'll react . . . I wouldn't want to cause trouble in the village then.'

Jacob nodded with understanding. 'There's no knowing what line he'll take, and us hears his voice shouting the odds enough during the week. He generally do keep it down a bit of a Sunday, ever since the minister had a word with him after he went over to Arthur Culliford and started effing and blinding, if you'll excuse the term, about their eldest boy kicking his football over Jed's fence.' He gave Jennifer a sharp look. 'I don't say as he'll do that to you, maid, but I reckon it'll be a good idea if I'm about when you comes.'

'You don't think that would make him worse?' Jennifer asked doubtfully, wondering whether she really wanted to go through with this encounter.

Jacob folded his lips together and nodded. 'I dare say it might, at that. All the same, I wants to be on hand. Tell you what, maid, I'll be here indoors and keeping an eye and an ear out, and if I thinks you need a bit of help, I'll come out. Otherwise, I'll keep to meself. How's that?'

'That sounds ideal,' she said gratefully. 'I have to admit,

I'm not looking forward to this. But I do think I've got to do it. I've got to talk to him – no matter what he did, he's my father and I'll never be able to rest if I haven't looked him in the eye at least once.'

Jacob nodded again and took his jacket down from the hook behind the door. 'I'll walk up to the main road with you now and see you on the bus. And –' he hesitated for a moment '– I'd just like to say, whatever happens with him, you'm always welcome here. And I hope you'll come out and see me, regular, if you feels like it. You'm my Susan's babby, and you'm special to me.'

Jennifer felt the tears prick her eyes. Impulsively, she leaned forward and kissed him on the cheek. 'You're special, too, Jacob,' she said tremulously. 'I'll come out to see you whenever I can – whatever happens with Jed.'

They walked through the lanes in the gathering dusk, to reach the main road where the Plymouth bus was already in sight. Jacob stuck out his hand and the big vehicle pulled in and stopped. Jennifer began to climb aboard, then paused and turned back to give him a hug.

'I meant what I said,' she told him. 'I'm glad I found you.'

Jacob stood at the side of the road, watching as the bus disappeared into the twilight, then turned to walk back through the lanes that he and Susan had known so well, towards Burracombe. And Jennifer Tucker, the woman who ought to have been his daughter, stared unseeingly out of the window as the bus took her back to the city where she had grown up.

Her feelings were in turmoil. She wanted desperately to be able to think of Jacob as her father, yet she knew that the truth was very different and stemmed from a tragedy that had begun before she was born. It was up to her now whether she took it any further, and revived more memories – and a truth that would be painful for both her and Jacob himself.

I don't have to do it, she told herself. I could stop now. I
don't have to go any further.

But she knew that she would.

Chapter Thirty

'There's a letter for you from France,' Dottie said as Stella came through the door the next afternoon. 'It's Maddy's writing on the envelope.'

'Oh, perhaps it's to say when she's coming home.' Stella seized the envelope and tore it open eagerly. She scanned the sheet of paper inside. 'She's coming to England at the weekend! She'll be staying in London first for a few days, then coming here. We must see if Aggie can put her up again.' She laid down the letter. 'It's such a shame she can't come here.'

'Well, I could go over and stop with Aggie for a day or two—' Dottie began, but Stella shook her head.

'Of course you can't! We can't push you out of your own home. Anyway, we don't know how long she means to stay. It could be for good!' She read the letter again. 'She doesn't say anything about that. Just that she's coming as soon as Fenella and her husband get back from their honeymoon. Oh, Dottie, won't it be lovely to see her again! I wonder what she plans to do. I know she'd like to have a job of some sort, but I don't suppose there's any hurry. We could spend the whole of the summer holiday together!'

'It'll be a treat to have her about the place again,' Dottie said, her round face beaming with pleasure. 'I hope she don't find anything too soon. She'd have to go away again, for certain – I can't think what there'd be for her to do in Burracombe. None of the shops needs anyone, as far as I know, and there's only the pub, or one of the big houses, and I don't think they'd suit her neither, not after the life she's led.'

'Well, let's hope we needn't think about that just yet,' Stella agreed. 'I'll go over and see Aggie straight away, and see if she can give her a room. I hope she hasn't got any other visitors coming!'

She dropped her school bag on a chair and hurried out of the cottage and across the village to Aggie Madge's house. Felix will be pleased, too, she thought, with a little less pleasure, and wished again that Maddy could be staying at Dottie's. But there really wasn't room, and Aggie Madge was the only one that Stella knew of who let her spare room. All the same, Stella found herself hoping that she had already booked in some holidaymakers. In that case, Maddy could go and stay at the Barton, where Hilary Napier had told her she was always welcome.

Felix came to the door, smiling, and before she could speak he said, 'I know why you're here. Maddy's coming! It's good news, isn't it? You must be delighted.'

Stella stared at him, feeling a little deflated. 'I am. But how did you know? Has she written to ask Aggie for the room?'

'Not really, although she does ask that. She wrote to me.' He stood back to let Stella enter, and waved a sheet of paper at her. 'I had a letter this morning. I was going to come and meet you from school, but I had to go over to Little Burracombe and see Mr Berry. He's ill again and I'm taking Sunday services for him.'

'Oh dear. I'm sorry.' Stella was diverted, but only for a moment. 'Maddy wrote to you? But why? She must know I'd tell you.'

'Well, she does write to me now and then, just a friendly letter, you know. And as I say, she did ask about the room as well.'

'Yes, I see.' Stella was silent for a moment. 'And can Aggie take her? She hasn't got anyone else coming? I know she has a couple who come quite regularly each summer.'

'They're not coming this year – they wrote a few weeks ago to let her know. So she can take Maddy for as long as she wants to stay. A long time, I hope,' he added, beaming. 'You must be hoping that, too.'

'Yes, I am.' But there was none of her previous enthusiasm in Stella's voice. 'Well, it seems as if that's all settled, then. I needn't have rushed over.'

'Of course you need! You know I'm always pleased to see you.' He looked at her uncertainly. 'There's nothing the matter, is there?'

'No. What could be the matter? I expect I'm just a bit tired, that's all. It's a busy term, what with Sports Day and the play, and the classes all thinking about moving up after the holidays. The top class will be leaving, you know, and going on to Tavistock, and then we get the babies coming in. There's a lot to think about.'

'I know there is.' He took her arm and guided her towards a chair. 'Sit down and rest for a minute. I'll get Aggie to bring us some tea. And then maybe we could go for a walk before supper.'

Stella shook her head. 'No, thanks. I've got to go back. I promised to go up to the Tozers' farm to see Val – Dottie wants her to come down for a fitting. And I've got to do something to Micky Coker's head – his ass's head, I mean – it got a bit knocked about during the rehearsal yesterday.' She was already turning back towards the door. 'So I don't need to write and tell Maddy it's all right about the room, then, do I? I expect you'll be doing that yourself.'

'I certainly will,' Felix replied cheerfully. 'And I can't wait to see her. We've got a lot to talk about.'

'Yes,' Stella said, opening the front door and stepping out on to the path. 'I expect you have.'

The June sunshine seemed a little less bright as she walked

back to Dottie's cottage. And her pleasure at the prospect of seeing her sister again had also dimmed.

Maddy arrived at Tavistock station on the one o'clock train from London, and Felix took Stella in the car to meet her. Once again, she was surrounded by a huge pile of luggage and together they hauled and squeezed it into the seats and luggage space, until there was barely room for Felix. He inserted himself into the driver's seat and grinned at them as he set off back to Burracombe, promising to return in an hour or so.

'Honestly, I could just as easily have got a taxi,' Maddy said as they walked down the steps to the town. 'It's silly for Felix to do all this ferrying back and forth.'

'He likes to think he's doing something for you.' Stella led the way to their favourite tearoom. 'He's really pleased that you're staying at Aggie's again.'

'So am I. After Dottie, she's the person I'd rather stay with than anyone in the whole world. I've promised to go and see Hilary, of course, but I don't really know her all that well. She and Stephen were away so much when Fenella and I used to stay at the Barton. Stephen's coming home on leave sometime this summer, did you know that?'

'I think I heard something about it,' Stella said vaguely. She had met Stephen Napier a few times before he joined the RAF to do his National Service but hadn't seen him now for some months. 'What are you having? Just a pot of tea?'

'Goodness, no! I'm having a full cream tea – scones and strawberry jam and lots of cream. You can't get this sort of thing at all in France, you know.' Maddy leaned her elbows on the table, rested her chin in her hands, and gazed round with satisfaction. 'It's *so* good to be back. The last few months have been just frantic, getting ready for the wedding and then sorting everything out afterwards. You know, I think I could set up in business organising big society weddings. I don't suppose there's much call for that, though.'

'There might be. Not just weddings, but big events. Someone has to do it, and I don't suppose the people who hold them are always that experienced. You'd be really good at it, Maddy.'

Maddy shook her head and laughed. 'Well, I'll bear it in mind. But I might be doing something else.' Her eyes sparkled and when Stella looked at her questioningly, she pressed her lips together and shook her head again. 'No, it's a secret at the moment – just in case it doesn't happen.'

'You're not thinking of being a fashion model, are you? Jennifer Tucker said you'd be good at that, too. Or doing the sort of job she's doing, at Dingle's. In fact, she told me she'd look out for any openings for you.'

'That's nice of her, but I don't think I'll need to do that. And it's no use looking at me like that, Stella, I'm not going to say another word. It's not just my secret, you see. Now, tell me about everyone in Burracombe. How's Val Tozer getting on with her wedding preparations? I don't suppose she needs any help with the organisation, does she?' She laughed at Stella's expression. 'I'm only joking!'

'It all seems to be pretty well sorted out.' Their tea arrived and Stella began to pour milk into the cups, hiding her disappointment. What was so secret that Maddy couldn't share it with her? And who was the other person whose secret it was? She thought of Felix and his delight at knowing Maddy was coming home, his insistence on coming to meet her, the warmth of his kiss when they'd met, and her heart seemed to weigh more heavily within her.

For the rest of the hour, Maddy chatted eagerly about Fenella's wedding, about her journey from Paris and the time she had spent in London, staying with friends. She had been to the theatre to see Moira Lister in *The Love of Four Colonels* and to Covent Garden to see *Coppelia* and *Giselle*. 'It was simply wonderful,' she said. 'I'd love to take you to see the ballet. Tell you what, we'll go to London during your summer holidays. The Festival Ballet's doing *Giselle* and *Nutcracker* at the Festival Hall in August. We could stay with my friend Alison, she's got a spare room, and I could show you round some of the sights.'

'I saw the Festival Hall last year, when we took the children on the outing to the exhibition,' Stella said. 'We didn't go in, but it looked lovely.'

Maddy nodded. 'It is. And London's looking so much better now that they're doing so much rebuilding. You'd hardly know there'd been all that bombing. Have you got any other plans for a holiday?'

Stella shook her head. 'I was just going to stay in Burracombe. There's always plenty to do there – I haven't explored half the places around. And Felix—' She stopped suddenly, then went on rather lamely, 'Felix was talking about going on walks and picnics when he has time, but I don't know if . . . ' Her voice trailed away.

Maddy looked at her thoughtfully. 'Don't you think he meant it? You do spend quite a bit of time together, don't you?'

'Well, up till now we have, but – well, there's nothing serious in it,' she said quickly. 'We're just friends, that's all.'

'I see.' Maddy split the last scone and spread the two halves with strawberry jam and clotted cream. 'Here, share this with me. So that's settled. We're going to London for a few days in August.' They heard the sound of a car drawing up outside the café and looked out through the window. 'And we'd better finish this quickly, because if I'm not much mistaken, that's Mirabelle and Felix now!'

Felix bounded over the low door of the sports car and met them on the pavement, his face alight with pleasure. 'There you are! I thought I was going to have to come in and hoik you out. Where are you going to sit? Stella, d'you want the front seat?'

'No – let Maddy sit there. I'll squeeze into the back.' She clambered into the dicky seat and the other two arranged themselves in front of her. As they drove along the main street of the market town and through the big square, with the impressive stone-built town hall on one side and the imposing church on the other, she looked at their two heads, so close together – Felix's hair a darker blond than Maddy's shimmering gold – and felt a mixture of happiness at having her sister back and sadness at the loss of something that had perhaps never really been hers. I imagined it all, she thought. The happy times we've had together, the day he kissed me, the look I thought was in his eyes sometimes – they were all in my imagination. It's Maddy he loves, and because I love them both, I just have to step back. And be happy for them.

She didn't even have to wonder what Maddy's secret was – or who the other person was who shared it with her.

Val was on her way up to the Barton when she saw Felix's sports car round the corner into the village, filled with laughing faces. She waved and the car came to a halt beside her. Maddy leaned out.

'Hello, Val. I'm back again, like the bad penny. I hear your wedding's all arranged now.'

'Yes, and you're invited,' Val said, smiling. 'I hope you'll be here then.'

'I wouldn't miss it for the world. How's everyone at the farm? And at the Barton? I must go and see Colonel Napier and Hilary sometime – Fenella's sent some presents for them.'

'I'll tell them you're on your way. Stephen's coming to the wedding, too,' Val added. 'He's getting a fortnight's leave at just the right time.'

Felix put the car into gear and they roared away again. Val

continued up the drive to the Barton and found Hilary in the stable yard, just dismounting from Beau, her bay gelding. She rode him as often as possible, frequently using him to visit tenants or parts of the estate that were more easily reached on horseback than by road.

'There's a good chap,' she said, patting his white nose. 'Can you hang on, Val, while I give him a rub-down and pop him into the field?'

'Of course. We can talk while you do that. I just saw Maddy Forsyth coming home. She was in Felix's car – he and Stella had been to collect her from Tavistock.'

'Oh, that's good. Stella will be pleased to have her sister back again. She always strikes me as being a bit lonely.'

'She hasn't been lately,' Val observed, fetching a brush from the stable. 'She and Felix have been seeing quite a lot of each other.'

'Mm.' Hilary had been the one to see quite a lot of the curate the previous year. 'He's a nice man, but I'm not sure he's serious. I think he just likes to have a girl to take about in that flashy car of his.'

Val raised her eyebrows a little. 'That sounds a bit sharp, Hil.'

'I didn't mean it to.' Hilary had finished rubbing Beau down and began to lead him through the yard. 'It's just that he got a bit keen on me last year, but he didn't seem all that upset when I turned him down. Some people are like that, you know – they think they're serious, but they're not really. I hope Stella realises that.'

'I'm sure he wouldn't do anything to hurt her,' Val said. 'Mind you, he did look rather pleased to have Maddy beside him in the car. Maybe you'd better get Stella and Stephen together while he's here, just in case her heart gets broken.'

'Oh, I think Stephen's even worse!' Hilary said with a grin. 'He seems to have a different girlfriend every week, from what he says in his letters. Anyway, it's not for us to interfere.

Have you had any news about a house or anything since I last saw you?'

Val shook her head and held the gate open while Hilary walked Beau through and unclipped the lead rein. 'No, we're staying in the charcoal-burner's cottage for the summer, but we really will need to find somewhere else then. I'm having to leave almost all my stuff at the farm as it is. Luke's waiting to hear if he's got the job in Tavistock, so if he does we'll start looking there, too.'

'Well, that wouldn't be too bad.' They watched as Beau tore up mouthfuls of grass and then collapsed in the muddiest patch he could find and began to roll, kicking his legs in the air. 'Honestly, I wonder why I bother . . . It would be a shame not to have you in the village, but Tavi would be better for you than Plymouth.'

'Oh yes. We might be able to rent one of the Bedford cottages. They're quite nice, especially the ones by the river. Luke could paint lots of river scenes from the garden! And I could carry on working at the hospital for a while. I don't see any point in giving up until I have to.'

'Nor do I. You'll need all your savings when the family starts coming. How's Dottie getting on with the dress?'

'She's nearly finished mine and it's lovely, Hil. I had a fitting yesterday and couldn't believe how beautiful it looked. And the bridesmaids are going to look sweet. Well, Patsy and June are – I'm not so sure about our Jackie!'

Hilary turned away from the gate. 'Don't be silly. Jackie's a pretty girl. And she's bright, too. She really ought to be doing something more with her life. Is she still writing to Roy Pettifer?'

'Oh yes, but I don't think she looks on him as her boyfriend any more. She's been out a few times with a boy from Yelverton. I don't think it's serious – she seems to have learned her lesson there.'

The two women looked at each other with understanding,

knowing the fright Jackie had had last year over her romance with Roy. She'd had a lucky escape, Val thought; she wasn't likely to make that mistake again.

'And how are things with you, Hilary?' she asked. 'Has your father come to terms with you managing the estate yet?'

Hilary shrugged. 'As much as he ever will, I suppose. We've come to an arrangement now – he looks after certain things and I do the rest. He can drive the car again, so he can go round and visit the tenant farmers. And listen to this – he's thinking of writing a book about the family! It started when he did that village archive last year – he got interested then and started looking out old documents, and he's decided we need a family history. It won't be published or anything, of course, but he's thinking of getting a few copies printed and bound, just for family members.'

'That's a wonderful idea,' Val said. 'It'll keep him busy and interested without putting too much pressure on him, and it'll be something he can be really proud of. How far back can you go? Did your ancestors come over with William the Conqueror or anything like that?'

'Well, they might have done, but the name Napier isn't Norman. It's what's called an "occupational" name – like Butcher or Baker.' Hilary laughed at Val's expression. 'Not nearly so upper-crust! But even the Normans must have had butchers and bakers, so who knows? Anyway, "napiers" would have looked after the table linen in a great household. The linen itself was called "napery" you see.'

'And little bits would be called "napkins"!' Val exclaimed. 'Isn't that interesting!'

'Well, I don't know if everyone will think so,' Hilary admitted. 'But I hope Dad will put it in, because I think that's the sort of thing people like to read, more than long lists and family trees and things. Anyway, as you say, it will keep him busy and be a nice thing to pass on to future generations. If there are any,' she added, pulling off her riding-boots at the door. 'Can't see much likelihood of that at present.'

'You'll meet someone one day,' Val said. 'You're bound to.'

'Maybe I won't want to. I quite like the independent life, you know. I certainly don't need a man to keep me, anyway.' Hilary led the way indoors. 'I think it'll be up to Stephen – he's got the name. Even if I did have children, they wouldn't be Napiers.' She went over to the kitchen sink and filled the kettle. 'Why the sudden interest in matchmaking? In the past half an hour you've discussed the marriage prospects of half the village – me, Stella Simmons and Maddy, anyway! It must be because you're getting married yourself. You just want to drag everyone else in with you.'

Val sat down at the table and laughed. 'I'm not dragging anyone! But maybe you're right. It's because I'm happy. I want all my friends to be happy, too.' She leaned her elbow on the table, cupped her chin in her hand and gave her friend a dreamy smile. 'I never thought it would happen to me, you know. But it did – so I don't see why it shouldn't happen to you as well.'

Hilary took a biscuit tin out of the cupboard and placed it on the table.

'You're getting maudlin. Have one of Mrs Ellis's flapjacks and talk about something sensible, for goodness' sake!'

'There is nothing,' Val said with dignity, 'more sensible than getting married and being happy. Nothing in all the world.'

Chapter Thirty-One

For Jennifer Tucker, there was nothing more important now than resolving the question about her father.

Until she had faced Jed Fisher, she felt she would never be quite sure. Although Jacob seemed to have no doubts that it was Jed who had fathered Susan's baby, she still felt that he might not know the whole truth. She knew she couldn't voice these fears to Jacob himself, who would have been even more hurt by any further slur on Susan's name, and she knew in her heart that Jed was the most likely culprit. If he were her father, she had to talk to him, even if he refused to listen.

It was the middle of June when she came out to Burracombe again. The fine weather had given away to cloud, and as the bus trundled out on to Dartmoor she saw the shadow of rain falling over Princetown. It seemed several degrees cooler when she got off at the village green, and she shivered and pulled her raincoat closer around her as she set off towards Jed's cottage.

She had written to tell Jacob that she would be coming this afternoon and he had agreed to stay indoors and be ready to come out if she needed him but otherwise keep out of the way. As she passed his window, she caught a glimpse of him inside but made no acknowledgement. Jed might be watching, too, and the situation was delicate enough without giving him cause for another tirade.

She paused for a moment before pushing the rickety gate open. The patch of front garden was an even wilder tangle of weeds now, and brambles caught at her legs as she walked up the path. She knocked on the peeling front door and waited, her heart thumping so hard that she thought he would hear it above the sound of the knocker. For a moment, she hoped he wasn't in.

A scuffling noise from inside dashed her hope. She heard a muttering, and then the sound of a bolt being drawn. The door creaked open and the old man's face peered at her with rheumy, suspicious eyes.

'What be you after?'

'I'd like to talk to you for a minute or two, if you've got time,' Jennifer said, her voice shaking a little. 'Could I come in?'

'You selling summat?' The door began to close again in her face. Jennifer put her hand against it and spoke quickly.

'No, I'm not selling anything. I just want to talk to you. It's a personal matter,' she added desperately as the door pushed against her hand. 'Please, Mr Fisher. It's about . . . it's about Susan Hannaford.'

The door stopped moving. There was a long pause. At last, the gruff voice said, 'Susan Hannaford? Her that lived up at Whinberry Cross?'

'Yes,' Jennifer said. 'She was my mother.'

The door opened a little wider. She could see his face now, grimy and unshaven. He gave her a distrustful stare.

'Susan Hannaford died years ago, and her babby with her.'

'No, she didn't. I've got her papers here.' Jennifer took an envelope from her bag. 'Her birth certificate and her death certificate. And her marriage lines,' she added.

'Marriage lines? You mean her got wed?' He seemed to be having difficulty in taking it in, and Jennifer gave the door another gentle push. 'But her died of the 'flu years ago—'

'Please let me come in,' she repeated gently. 'I don't want to talk about it on the doorstep. Please, Mr Fisher.'

For another long minute, he stood irresolute; then, to her

317

relief, he pulled the door wider open and turned back into the cottage. 'Come you in then, if you must,' he said brusquely, and she followed him into the disordered room, trying not to wrinkle her nose at the smell of dirt, neglect and cigarette smoke.

Jed dropped into an old, sagging armchair with cushions that looked as if they hadn't been washed for years, and waved a grudging hand towards the one on the other side of the fireplace, which was cluttered with old Woodbine packets and other rubbish. He picked up a cigarette that was smouldering in an old saucer beside him.

'You can sit down if you wants to.'

Jennifer looked dubiously at the chair and perched on the edge. For a minute or two, they regarded each other with caution, and then he said in a hostile tone, 'I seen you before. You been in next door a time or two, cooking up some fiddle or other with that old schemer Jacob Prout. What's it all about, eh? What you trying to get out of me? I ain't saying nothing.' He began to haul himself out of the chair, already waving one arm threateningly. 'You better get out. Go on with you! Out of my house!'

'Please, Mr Fisher!' Jennifer forced herself to stay where she was. 'You must listen to me. It'll only take a minute. I promise you, there's nothing going on, and I'll leave straight away if you want me to, if only you'll listen to what I have to say. Please.' She saw him hesitate, and then, terrified that he might once again order her out, or even that he might strike her, she added desperately, 'I think you may be my father!'

Jed Fisher froze. She saw his face turn pale under the grime, and his upraised arm dropped slowly to his side. His body trembled and she half rose, afraid that he might fall. Then he sank slowly back into his chair, staring at her. He took a long puff of his cigarette and then stubbed it out in the saucer.

'You think *what*?' he whispered at last, hoarsely.

Jennifer relaxed slightly against the cushions, then remembered the state of them and sat up again. Slowly, quietly, she repeated her words: 'I think you may be my father. Susan Hannaford was my mother. She left Burracombe almost thirty-six years ago, when she was pregnant.' Jennifer paused. 'She was pregnant with me.'

Jed's eyes never left her face. He shook his head slowly. 'You ain't nothing like Susan.'

'I'm like her mother. My grandmother, Liza Lilliman. Minnie Tozer says that's who I look like, and—'

'Minnie Tozer?' he broke in. 'You been discussing my private business with they Tozers?'

'I didn't know it *was* your business,' she pointed out. 'When I talked to the Tozers, I didn't know who I was looking for. I didn't even know for certain if my father came from Burracombe. And they had no idea it might be you.'

'No,' he muttered, lighting another Woodbine, 'no more they would. There wasn't nobody that knew.'

Jennifer stared at him. 'So it's true?'

'I never said that,' he countered quickly. 'I wants a bit more information from you before I starts giving any out. If Minnie Tozer didn't know nothing about me, how come you fetched up at my door?' As he stared at her, she saw comprehension dawn. 'It's that old bastard next door!' he burst out. 'That's who sent you here! Sticking his nose into my private business!' He began to get to his feet again. 'I'll tell him! I'll give him what for! I'll—'

'Mr Fisher, *please*!' Even now that she was almost certain he was her father, Jennifer couldn't bring herself to address him in any other way. 'Please, let's just talk about this. I haven't come to cause trouble—'

'If you didn't want to cause trouble, you shouldn't have come at all. What else did you think it would do but cause trouble? Didn't it never cross your mind that there'd be trouble?'

319

The old man was off again, but Jennifer had had enough. Rising to her feet, she stared down at him and, every word hard with anger, said, 'All right, Mr Fisher, I won't ask you again. I'll go. I wanted to talk to you, that's all. I wanted to find my father. Well, a lot of people told me I might regret it, and now I know they were right.' She half turned towards the door, tears of disappointment welling up in her eyes, and then turned back. 'But you might just remember this. It isn't me who's caused any trouble about this. The trouble started thirty-six years ago – and it was *you* who caused it. You, and nobody else!'

She held his gaze. Like a dog being scolded, he tried to look away, but had to look back. At last he said in a gruff, quiet voice, 'You'd better sit down again, maid. I thought all that was over years ago, but since you'm here, us might as well have it out. I suppose the Tozers sent you to Jacob Prout, thinking it was he, did they?' He uttered a short laugh, entirely without mirth. 'Well, I bet that put a bit of tarnish on that shiny halo of his. No wonder he ain't been out much lately – too ashamed to stick his nose out of his own front door!'

'Jacob has nothing to be ashamed of,' Jennifer said angrily. 'And if he hadn't thought, like everyone else, that my mother and I had died, he would have gone to find her and married her – even though I wasn't his child.'

'Well, *that* weren't my doing, any road,' Jed snapped. ''Twasn't me put that story out. That were *her* father, old Abraham Hannaford. Told everyone she were dead, he did, but wouldn't say a word about where she was or where she were buried. I'd have gone to see her grave if I'd knowed that.' His voice dropped and there was a sadder note in it as he added, 'I'd have took flowers.'

Jennifer gave him a curious glance. 'Were you really fond of her, then?'

'Fond of her?' He snorted. ''Course I were fond of her!

320

Always had an eye for Susan, I did, only she never took no notice of me, 'twas always Jacob Prout for her. Even when he first went away to war . . . I used to ask her out then. Just for a bit of a walk, or maybe some dancing in old man Tozer's barn. But no, her had to stay true to *him*.' He jerked his thumb at the wall. 'My only hope was that he might get hisself killed. Well, and why not?' he demanded as Jennifer drew in her breath. 'All's fair in love and war, ain't that right, and us *was* at war. He'd have been a hero, got his name on the village cross and all, and I'd have had Susan. Seemed fair enough to me. Anyway, it never happened, so it don't matter.' His head drooped and he seemed to sag in his chair. For a moment, Jennifer seemed to glimpse his life through his own eyes; wasted and endured, all because he had lost the girl he loved; because the one chance he might have had with her had been misused and resulted in heartbreak.

Yet Jacob had lost her, too, and Jacob hadn't wasted his life. He had overcome his sorrow, gone on to make a happy marriage. He was loved and respected throughout the village. Why had one man achieved so much and the other so little?

'I really didn't come here to upset you,' she said at last. 'If you want me to go, I will.'

He sighed and shook his head. His lank hair looked unwashed and straggly, as if he cut it himself with a knife and fork. His skin had a yellowish tinge and seemed to have tightened over his skull, as if he were shrinking. She felt a sudden regret for his poorly spent life, and wished it could have been different.

'No, you'd better stop now,' he said. 'Us can't wind back the clock. You can tell me a bit about Susan, now you'm here. When did her die, if 'twasn't back in 1917?'

'It was just a few months ago,' she said. 'Not long before Christmas. She had a happy life, I think. We were a happy family, at least until Dad – my stepfather – died in the war.'

'That were the chap she wed?'

'Yes. I was about two then. I always thought he was my father until I found the papers after she had died. Then I realised that there'd been someone else, and I wanted to find him. I wanted to meet my real father.'

'And this other bloke,' he said, the words coming out slowly and painfully, 'did he treat her right?'

'Yes, he did. They loved each other very much.'

Jed was silent for a while. Jennifer looked around the room, noting the piles of yellowing newspapers on the windowsill, the cobwebs in the corners of the dirty windows and hanging between the beams of the ceiling. Through the door she could see the scullery, little more than a cubbyhole with a deep sink, chipped and smeared with grease, a few used dishes stacked carelessly beside it. Her pity grew, mixed with disgust, but although part of her wished she had never started on this quest, another part knew that she could not abandon him now. Finding her father, she thought, seemed to bring with it responsibilites she hadn't imagined.

'And she never gave you no hint that he weren't your proper dad?'

'No. I think she brought me here once, when I was little. The first time I came, I felt as if I recognised the green and the oak tree. But that's all. And she had other children, too. I've got two sisters – half-sisters, really.'

He nodded. 'Her always wanted little 'uns, Susan did.'

Jennifer waited a moment or two, then asked, 'Can you tell me what happened, Jed? After Jacob had gone away that time? Did it start then, or were you and Susan already—'

'No!' he said with sudden vehemence. 'No, 'tweren't nothing like that. Us were friendly, like, but never no more. You got to remember, maid, I got exemption from the Army, and that didn't go down too well with folk round here. It were different in the Great War. Men were supposed to volunteer, and if they didn't, folk thought they was cowards. You got spat on in the street, and women walked about with bags full

322

of white feathers to hand out to any young chap who wasn't in uniform. If you went to see the music hall down in Plymouth, the women singers and dancers would shout out for volunteers and chaps'd feel forced to go up on the stage and sign their names. I never tried to get out of it. I went along same as all the rest and had me medical when it first started, but the Army doctor said I had a weak chest. I didn't know if it was true or not, it'd never given me no trouble, but that's what he said. But folk didn't like it. Someone put it about that it was flat feet got me off, and I just let 'em think that, if that's what they wanted. Seemed to me, if they couldn't be bothered to listen to the truth, I wasn't bothered to tell 'em. Susan Hannaford was the only one who'd give me time of day then. Reckon she knew what it was like to be treated like an outcast.'

Jennifer listened in dismay. Nobody had given her this picture of Jed, a young man told he wasn't fit to serve his country and then treated like a coward. She tried to imagine him, returning to his village to be spat upon and handed white feathers. No wonder he had turned in on himself.

He spoke again, smoking and staring into the cluttered fireplace as if gazing down the years. 'But it weren't till after Jacob come home with his broken leg and then went back again that it got really bad. There was him, going back to fight even after he'd been wounded, and me safe at home with nothing wrong with me. Didn't matter about me chest when it come to doing a good day's work, but I couldn't put me nose out of the door without someone passing some remark, and folks even started to turns their backs on my poor old mother. I had enough of it then. Got a job over Chagford way and left the place.' He paused. 'I was on me way when I run into Susan, and her stopped to tell me how sorry she was about it all. And somehow or other, it all just seemed a bit too much for me. I'd always fancied her, but it were Jacob Prout she'd got her heart set on. *Jacob Prout!*' He spat suddenly into the fireplace and Jennifer started back, shocked. 'Couldn't do no wrong, could he! Blinking golden boy, he was – went off to war, come home a hero and then bloody went back for more. The whole village turned out to see him off, but did anyone give *me* time of day? Not them. They just turned their backs. And he'd got Susan, too. It was all too much for me,' he repeated heavily, and then, in a voice so low that Jennifer had to bend close to hear it, 'God knows I never meant to do it. I was brought up God-fearing chapel. I never meant to hurt her.'

There was a long silence. Jennifer felt the tears hot in her eyes. She thought of Jed, walking away from his home bitterly resentful, spurned by all those who had known him all his life, doomed to unfavourable comparison with his boyhood friend. She thought of him meeting the girl he loved but could never have, and she tried to imagine the sudden welling up of all his anger, his bitterness and frustration, into an uncontrollable passion. That girl was my mother, she thought. And that was the day when I was conceived.

'Well,' Jed said at last, 'now you knows. I dunno what you wants to do about it.'

'No,' she said quietly, 'neither do I.'

Chapter Thirty-Two

They talked on through the afternoon. At one point, Jed got up and made tea, but although Jennifer accepted the cup that he washed cursorily in the sink, running his fingers round the inside in an attempt to remove the stains, she let it go cold. Now that Jed had begun to talk, it seemed that he didn't know how to stop, and all the bitterness and regrets of thirty-five years poured forth in a torrent of disappointment and misery. It was as if he had held it back all this time, and now the dam had burst.

'I knew straight away I'd done wrong,' he said. 'It was in her face – in her eyes. She looked at me as if I was dirty – as if I'd made *her* dirty. I reckon that was how she felt, an' all. And nothing I could say made any difference. I told her I was sorry. I tried to tell her what it was like for me, but her couldn't understand. I don't blame her for that, mind,' he added quickly. 'How *could* her understand? Her just an innocent maid, and me – me the village outcast.' He paused, remembering the scene on the lonely moor, with the gorse in flower close by and the Standing Stones looming on the skyline. 'I said I'd see her home, but her wouldn't have it. Ran off, her did, ran off sobbing her poor innocent heart out, and left me there to think about what I'd done. I'd sinned,' he said, meeting Jennifer's eyes. 'I knew that. I'd sinned in the eyes of my Creator, and I never went in the Chapel again if I could help it. I didn't have the right.'

'But you look after the Chapel graveyard, don't you?'

'I does whatever I can,' he said, 'but it'll never be enough to make up for what I done to Susan.'

There was a short silence. Then Jennifer asked, 'Did you see Susan again after that?'

'Once,' he said. 'Her come up to me when I were working out in the fields, and told me her was going away. I'd got her into trouble, and her father had turned her out. Didn't want no more to do with her. I said I'd stand by her – offered to wed her. It was what I wanted, after all. But no, her wouldn't have that, and I knew she wanted to wait for *him*, if he ever come back.' Jed jerked his head towards the adjoining wall and gave a snort of mirthless laughter. 'I dunno what he'd have made of it, mind, taking on my by-blow. Begging your pardon,' he added, remembering that Jennifer herself was the by-blow. 'But I dare say he'd have done it, if only to spite me. Anyway, that was the way of it, off her went to Plymouth and the next thing us knew was that her'd died of the 'flu, and the babby with her. Not that Abraham admitted there *was* a babby,' he added bitterly, 'until I went and asked him straight out, and then he told me both of 'em had gone. Blasted liar!'

Jennifer could find nothing to say. The tragedy of the unkempt and unlikeable old man before her seemed greater, at that moment, than the sadness she had felt for Jacob himself. How different might life have been for him, if he had been allowed to stand by her mother? And how different for Jennifer herself? She glanced around the dilapidated cottage, realising suddenly that this might have been her home. Either of these cottages might have been her home – and either of these men, for all she would have known, might have been her father!

Jed had fallen silent, but suddenly he was overtaken by a fit of coughing and Jennifer gazed at him in alarm. This was the coughing Jacob could hear through the walls, and she wondered if he was there now, listening and thinking of her in here with his enemy. She half rose from the chair, anxious to do something to ease the racked body, but Jed waved her away and she sank back.

'That's a terrible cough,' she said, when he subsided at last and lay back in his chair, his chest heaving. 'Have you seen the doctor about it?'

Jed snorted with contempt. 'Nothing he can do! Had it for years. It's what they said at the medical – a weak chest. They were right, see. Nothing nobody can do about that.'

'Has he said so?' Jennifer persisted. She wanted to suggest that he smoked less – he had lit one Woodbine from another ever since she had come into the house – but she knew that he wouldn't take kindly to her interference. His daughter she might be, but you needed years of companionship before you could start to criticise your father's way of life. 'Have you seen him lately?'

'I never goes near him,' he growled. 'I told you, the Army said I had a weak chest and so I have. There ain't nothing doctors can do about it. It'll carry me off in the end, and I don't reckon that's all that far off now.' He started to cough again. 'Every time it gets a hold of me, I thinks maybe this time's the last,' he wheezed eventually.

'Jed, you mustn't say that! I'm sure the doctor could help. Would you like me to—'

'You keep out of it!' he rasped, and she shrank back again. 'I knows you're my girl, but that don't give you the right to come telling me what to do.' As if his own words had brought the truth home to him, he stared at her and said in a lower voice, 'My girl. That's what you are – my own flesh and blood.' His eyes, which had watered freely during his coughing bouts, grew moist again. 'I never thought to see the day.'

Jennifer swallowed her distaste. She thought of the neat cottage next door, the man who took such pride in his work and himself, and with whom she had felt such rapport. If only he could have been her father . . .

Instead, she had found this scruffy, uncombed and bitter man; yet, repellent as he was, she couldn't find it in her heart to reject him. Whatever he was now, he was her father, and had become so through real passion. Despite the dreadful ordeal he had put her mother through, Jennifer still felt an unexpected compassion for him; he had given way to a rush of feeling, made up of the rejection by the people he had grown up with, the resentment of being called a coward and compared with the shining Jacob, and the hopeless love he had felt for Susan Hannaford. It was almost impossible for Jennifer to imagine what it must have been like; she could only accept him as he was. She had set out on this quest and must take the consequences.

'I shall have to go soon,' she said quietly. 'I have to walk out to the main road to catch the bus back to Plymouth.' She realised that she had told him almost nothing about herself, and felt in her bag for a scrap of paper and a pencil. 'I'll leave you my address. If you want to get in touch—'

'Ain't you coming again, then?' He looked up at her with sudden anxiety. 'I suppose now you know who I am and what I'm like, you won't want to know me no more.'

'Of course I do!' The assurance came swiftly, without need for thought. 'You're my father, Jed,' she said, and reached out for his hand. It felt as thin, as bony and as dry as a chicken's foot. 'I know it hasn't been easy, having me come to the door without any warning. You'll have a lot to think about. But if you want me to come again—'

'You'm my maid,' he said. ''Tis only right.'

There was a short silence. Jennifer released his hand and stood up. Jed made no effort to rise, no offer to walk to the road with her; he sat with his head bowed, his cigarette packet beside him. Then he looked up again and she saw in his eyes the pleading that belied the brusqueness of his words.

'I'll come again next week,' she said softly, and turned to let herself out of the cottage.

At the gate, she hesitated, wishing she could go to Jacob. But she knew that Jed would be peering, narrow-eyed, through his own grimy window, and with a small shrug of regret she passed along the twilit lane, and set out on the walk to the main road.

As she walked by the window, she saw a flicker of movement within Jacob's cottage and knew he had been watching out for her.

Dottie Friend happened to glance out of the window, too, as Jennifer Tucker passed by. She paused for a moment and said, 'There's that young woman who's been coming out here to Burracombe lately. Didn't you say you'd met her in Dingle's?'

'That's right.' Stella craned her neck to see out past Dottie's plump figure. 'Yes, that's her. She's nice. I wonder—' She bit back the words. Jennifer hadn't asked her to remain quiet about her quest to find her father, but Stella still felt it would be wrong to discuss it, even with Dottie. Particularly as Stella had no idea as to who the man might have been. She remembered wondering if it could have been Val Tozer's father, or Jacob Prout. No, it was better to say nothing. 'I wonder where she's been at this time of the evening,' she finished lamely.

'Well, 'tis none of our business,' Dottie said comfortably, returning to her sewing. She began to fold up the blue material that Val had chosen for the bridesmaids' dresses. 'I'll have to get Patsy and June to pop in soon to try these on. Then there's only Jackie's to make and they'll be finished. I might get some material for a frock for myself then. A nice flowery print, I thought, and then it'll do for a Sunday dress for the rest of the summer.'

Stella sat down by the window. It had been a warm day and Dottie had kept it open, but once the evening started to close in and the lamps were lit, she had shut it to stop insects flying in. The room was still full of the orange-blossom scent of the philadelphus, which had thrown itself like a green-and-white coverlet over the garden fence, and the sweetness of honeysuckle from the mass of soft golden flowers that climbed up the walls of the cottage. The front garden was filled with roses, their perfume vying with the others so that it was as if the room held a huge, unseen bouquet of summer flowers. Even with the window closed, Stella could still hear the evening song of the blackbird in an apple tree across the lane, and of its rival the thrush perched on a gate-post as it waited for snails to come out of their cracks in the stone walls.

'And where have Maddy and Felix been off to today, then?' Dottie enquired, packing away the last of the shimmering blue satin.

Stella turned and looked at her in surprise. 'Maddy and Felix? Well, Maddy was talking about going to Exeter on the train, but I don't know about Felix. Wasn't he going to visit his uncle in Dorset?' Not so long ago, she thought regretfully, she would have known exactly where Felix was going on his day off, but they seemed less likely to confide in each other these days.

'Exeter?' Dottie repeated. 'No, maid, I think you've got that wrong. They went off together in that little car of his, not long after you went to school. I saw them when I was on my way to the pub, to clean through. I suppose he could have been giving her a lift to Tavistock, but they didn't go in that direction. Didn't her say nothing?'

'No, she didn't,' Stella said thoughtfully. 'I expect she just changed her mind – you know, they were probably talking over breakfast and she decided to have a day out with him instead. Or maybe he offered her a lift as far as Exeter. They're probably both home by now, anyway.'

Again, Dottie shook her head. 'The car wasn't there when I popped over to Miss Bellamy to borrow some blue Sylko. And there was no lights on in the front of Aggie's cottage.

Not that I noticed particularly,' she added quickly, in case Stella thought she was being inquisitive. 'You just see these things, don't you?'

'Yes.' Stella glanced towards the window, now a square of deepening twilight. Where had Felix and Maddy been until this time, if they'd set out at nine o'clock that morning? And why had neither of them mentioned their outing to her? 'I expect Maddy'll tell us all about it tomorrow,' she said. 'She's coming to the school to see the dress rehearsal. The play's next week, you know, on Sports Day. I hope you'll come and see it.'

'Wild horses wouldn't stop me,' Dottie declared, getting up and putting her sewing away in the cupboard. 'Now, it's a bit warm for cocoa tonight – shall us just have a glass of homemade lemonade and some of they strawberries I picked this afternoon for our bedtime snack? And then I'd better boil up what's left of the milk, or it'll turn sour overnight for certain. We can have the top of it on our cornflakes in the morning.'

Stella smiled but shook her head. 'I won't have any more now, thanks, Dottie. I'll just have a glass of cold water and go to bed. I'm rather tired.'

She filled her glass at the sink and went up the stairs. It was true that she did feel unaccountably tired, yet when she climbed into bed between the cool white sheets she could not drop off to sleep. Instead, she lay staring through the open window at the stars. Try as she might, she could not get that question out of her head: where had Maddy and Felix been all day, and what were they doing?

Chapter Thirty-Three

Basil Harvey was wondering about his curate, too. The young man was a good clergyman, but he did seem rather susceptible to female charms. I hope he's not going to get himself into a tangle over those two nice young women, the vicar thought as he went over to the church to lock up a day or two later. It would be a good thing if he could marry one of them and settle down – but which one? Perhaps that was his problem, trying to decide between them.

As he came out of the church, he noticed Jacob Prout leaning on one of the flat tombstones in the far corner, smoking his pipe. The aroma floated down through the dusk like perfumed woodsmoke, and Basil hesitated, wondering whether to approach the old man. As he paused, Jacob turned and waved his hand, and Basil climbed the sloping churchyard towards him. Scruff ran to meet him, sniffing at his trouser turn-ups.

'Evenin', Vicar.'

'Evening, Jacob. How are you these days? We don't seem to have had much time to talk lately.'

'No, to tell you the truth, I ain't been all that sociable.' The gravedigger cupped his hands round his pipe and drew on it until a tiny red spark glowed in the depths of the bowl. 'Had a lot to chew over in me mind.'

Basil murmured something and waited, knowing that if Jacob wanted to tell him what was on his mind, he would take his own time in doing so.

'It's about that young woman that came out here,' Jacob said at last. 'That Jennifer Tucker. Her come and talked to you first.'

'Yes, I remember. And then she came to you. A sad story, I thought.'

'I suppose that's one word for it. Sad for anyone to find out they'm related to that old scoundrel next door to me. Told you about that, didn't I, Vicar?'

'You did, Jacob.' He waited again, and eventually Jacob gave another snort and decided to continue.

'I had to tell her. 'Twasn't no way out of it, see. I had to break it to her that I wasn't her father, nor no kin at all when you comes down to it, and I had to tell her who was. It come as a shock, I could see that. Her'd made up her mind, see. Her didn't know what to think after that. Proper upset, her was.'

'Yes, I see.'

'Anyway,' Jacob said after another long pause, 'her come out again day before yesterday. Never come to see me, though. Didn't even knock on the door. Went in to see *him*.'

'I suppose she felt she had to,' Basil ventured.

'Oh, I knows that, Vicar. I knowed she were coming. Told her I'd be handy, just in case her wanted me, and so I was. Stopped in all afternoon, never even went out in the garden, for all it were a warm day. Stopped in and done a few jobs round the place, and just kept me ears open.'

'And did she call you? Did she stay long?'

'Stopped till it were nearly dark,' Jacob said, shaking his head in wonder. 'I saw her leave, just as the sun were going down. I thought her might come in then – might ask me to walk to the main road with her, seeing as *he* obviously wasn't going to, but her never did. Just walked past the window as if us had never said so much as a good morning to each other.'

Basil could hear the hurt in his voice and felt sorry for him. 'Perhaps she felt she couldn't come to you straight after talking to her— to Jed. And I expect she had a lot to think about.'

'I dare say her did,' Jacob said. 'Her'd only seen Jed Fisher the once, but that were enough to show her what he were like. And I don't like to think what it's like inside that dump of a cottage of his now. I'm just surprised her managed to stop there as long as her did.'

Basil was quiet for a moment, and when Jacob seemed to have nothing more to add, he said, 'I expect she'll come out and see you again, Jacob. She didn't strike me as the type of person who would drop someone she felt was a friend.'

'Maybe not. That's if her *do* look on me like a friend, after what I had to tell her.'

'That was hardly your fault. You told her the truth. It was what she was looking for.'

'That's as maybe. Her didn't know how the truth was going to turn out, did she! Her might have rather I never said nothing. After all, I could have done, couldn't I? – there's nobody but me and Jed knows the truth. I could have just let it lie.'

'I don't think you could, Jacob. I'm sure she realised that you knew. And I don't think you would have felt easy, keeping it back from her.'

'I don't feel easy now,' the old man said morosely. 'So I don't know as that would have made all that much difference.'

'Well, we can't take it back now,' Basil said. 'I think you must just wait patiently, Jacob, and hope she comes again. I'm sure she will. I don't think she'll leave matters now. She'll come and see Jed again, I expect, and this time she'll probably call on you as well.' He thought for a moment. 'I wonder if you ought to talk to Jed yourself.'

'Me, talk to that cantankerous old blackguard? And what would I have to say to him, Vicar? Wish him a happy birthday? I'm sorry to say it to you, being as I've always had respect for you, but that's daft.'

'So it may be,' Basil said mildly, 'but it may come to that in the end. If you both have Jennifer's interests at heart . . .'

Jacob sighed heavily and pushed himself away from the tombstone. His pipe had gone out and he stuffed it into his pocket and turned towards the lychgate. The sky was almost dark now, the first tiny pinpoint of a star showing in its depths, and Basil could no longer see his expression. After a moment, he spoke in a gruff voice.

'I can't speak for him, Vicar. Nobody can. But I can say this: I'll always have her best interests at heart. Her might not be my daughter, not by blood, but if wishing could make her so, her would be. And her's my Susan's maid, and that's the next best thing as far as I'm concerned, no matter who fathered her. By all the rights there are, her ought to have been mine.'

He walked slowly down the path, Scruff at his heels, and Basil fell into step beside him. He could feel the old man's turmoil like an aura around him; his bewilderment, his sorrow, his struggle to understand. And he felt his heart go out to them all – to the two men who had competed all those years ago for the love of a young girl, to the girl herself and now to the young woman who was trying to pull together the ends of this heart-rending triangle.

I don't think there can ever be a happy ending to this story, he thought, bidding Jacob goodnight and turning his footsteps towards the vicarage. It was doomed from the very moment one young man went off to war and the other stayed at home.

Jacob could, in fact, have contacted Jennifer without waiting for her to come to Burracombe again. She had given him her address in Plymouth and he knew that she worked at Dingle's. When he went home, he took the piece of paper she'd given him from his mother's old writing-bureau, where he kept all his bills and important papers, and turned it over between his fingers. A letter wouldn't do any harm, surely. Just a few lines, hoping she was as well as it left him now and might see her way clear to calling in next time she was out this way . . . The sentences formed in his mind as if he were writing them down. Then he sighed and put the paper away again. He would have to be patient for a little longer. Give the poor maid time to get over the shock of finding that Jed Fisher was her father. That's if she ever could!

Scruff ran over to his water-bowl and drank noisily, while Flossie raised her head from her cushion and opened a sleepy eye. Jacob bent to rub her head and then went out to the scullery to make himself a cup of cocoa. The cottage was as neat and tidy as ever, and he felt ashamed of his lapse into neglect. The maid must have thought he was as bad as old Jed, he reflected, filling the kettle. He wouldn't let that happen again. Next time she came, she'd find the place spick and span, neat as a pin. He wouldn't let himself be lumped in with Jed Fisher and his slovenly ways. Not in front of Susan's girl.

When the cocoa was ready, he took it into the living-room and settled himself in his armchair to drink it. The two animals curled themselves close to him, and he felt warmed and comforted by their presence. At least I made a decent life for myself, he thought. I had a good wife, I've made myself useful, and I've been no nuisance to nobody. That's more than him next door can say.

It was very quiet in the cottage. Darkness had fallen and only one lamp cast a pool of glowing light on the table beside him. His library book lay open, ready for him to read a few pages before he went to bed, as he always did, but he was too deep in thought to pick it up just yet. He drank his cocoa, finding comfort in the hot drink, and leaned back against the cushion of his chair.

The coughing startled him from a light doze. He jerked awake, almost spilling the last few drops of cocoa, and put the cup down hastily on the table. It was Jed next door, sounding worse than ever. Jacob listened uneasily as the racking noise went on. It seemed to fade once or twice and he relaxed a little but then, as if Jed had paused only to draw painful breath for a fresh onslaught, it started again. My stars, Jacob thought, if he goes on like that he'll blow the roof off. And then, with an unexpected pang of pity, it sounds as if that hurts, and hurts bad. I wonder if I ought to do summat?

As he sat there, trying to decide what to do, the coughing stopped and there was silence. That was even worse, he thought. Suppose the old pest had had a stroke or a seizure or something and was laying there on that dirty floor of his, breathing his last? Jacob got to his feet and stood staring indecisively at the party wall. I'll have to go in, he decided at last. It's a flaming bloody nuisance, but I'll have to go and see if he's all right . . .

He was halfway to his front door when he heard a movement and then another bout of coughing. Thankfully, it didn't sound as bad this time, and after it had stopped, he heard heavy footsteps on the stairs that went up beside his own. The old misery was going to bed. Well, that was all right, then. Best place for him. If he died in the night, at least he'd die decent in his own bed, and be no further bother to anyone.

Feeling slightly ashamed of this thought but blaming Jed for being the sort of person you'd have such thoughts about, Jacob made his own preparations for bed. He took out his teeth and gave them a good scrub before putting them in a glass of clean water, where they grinned at him from his bedside table, and then he changed into his pyjamas and got into the iron-frame bed he had shared with his wife, Sarah. Then he turned out the light and settled himself for sleep.

A final cough from next door brought back the irritation he always felt at the reminder that Jed was so close, and his last thought as he drifted off was that if Jed's cough didn't get better soon, someone was going to have to do something about him.

Chapter Thirty-Four

'We ought to be thinking about this wedding,' Alice Tozer said when all the Sunday-dinner dishes had been washed up and put away. 'There's a lot to decide. So far, it seems to me the frocks are the only things anyone's given a thought to.'

'Oh, come on, Mum,' Val protested. 'You know I've booked the village hall for the reception, and Dottie and Mrs Dawe are going to help with the food—'

'Mrs Dawe!' Tom interrupted. 'What are we having, a school dinner?'

'Don't be dafter than you can help,' his sister admonished him. 'Mrs Dawe's a good cook. And Dottie's going to ice the cake, which I made weeks ago, if you remember . . .'

'Oh, was that your wedding cake? I thought you were just getting ahead with next year's Chrismas puddings.'

'If you go on like that, you won't be invited. There are three tiers—'

'I expect we'll all be in tears.' Tom ducked as Val aimed a cuff at his head. 'All right, all right, I'm sorry. Anyway, you won't need me here, will you? I don't see that I can be any help.'

'You never are, so that's no change. But you can't go away. You're going to be the chief usher.'

'What, like at the pictures?' He caught her eye and subsided, grinning. Joanna came to Val's rescue and put her hand over her husband's mouth.

'Take no notice, Val. He's overexcited because he's never been an usher before.'

'What do ushers have to do, anyway?' Jackie enquired, and answered before her brother could speak, 'I know, they say "ush" when people talk in church! Well, our Tom won't be much good at that. He never shuts up.'

Alice rapped on the table. 'Isn't there anyone here who can talk a bit of sense? Look, I've got some paper and a pencil here and I want to get a few things written down. First of all, has everyone sorted out what they'm going to wear?'

'Well, I have,' Val said. 'And so's Jackie. I don't know about the rest of you.'

'I suppose I'll have to wear my best suit,' Ted said in a tone of deep gloom. 'And a tie.'

'You'll all have to wear your best clothes. Tom, you're all right, you can wear the suit you had for your own wedding. What about you, Joanna?'

'I thought I'd borrow that marquee we used for the teas at the pageant last year,' Joanna said, looking down at her swelling figure. 'I'll be enormous by then. I don't want to be in any photographs, Val, all right?'

'You could stand at the back of the group photos and look over people's heads,' Tom said helpfully. 'Nobody will see how big you are then.'

'Well, I certainly can't stand in front!' She caught her mother-in-law's eye. 'It's all right, Mum, I am taking it seriously, honest. I'll wear that nice maternity dress I had with Robin. The one with flowers on that Tom said made me look like a municipal park.'

'You looked very nice in it,' Alice said, frowning at her son. 'What about Robin?'

'He can wear those dark-blue shorts and the little blazer I got in Plymouth. And a blue tie – I got one at the same time. He looks so grown-up, and it almost exactly matches Jackie's dress.'

'And I've got that lovely costume I bought at Sweet's,' Alice said. 'It's fuchsia-pink, so it won't clash with any of the bridesmaids. I hope Luke's mother doesn't wear the same colour.'

'When are they coming?' Ted enquired.

'The day before the wedding. I wish we could meet them beforehand and get to know them a bit, but his father can't get away before that.'

'He's very busy,' Val said. 'But you'll like them, Mum. They're really nice people.' She had been to visit Luke's family two or three times now and felt at ease in their company. 'And they're staying over the weekend. They want you to go and have lunch with them at the Bedford Hotel on Sunday.'

'Well, that seems to be all right, then.' Alice put on her glasses and peered at her list. 'Now, you've got the bellringers all sorted out, have you, Ted?'

'They're queueing up to ring. And we'm going to have the handbells, too, while the bride and groom are signing the register. Vicar suggested that and I think it's a good idea.'

Minnie nodded. 'I'm arranging some music specially.'

'Not the "Wedding March", I hope,' Tom said facetiously, and Alice sighed.

'That'll be for the organ to play. What about the flowers?'

'I'm having a bouquet of deep-red roses,' Val said. 'And the bridesmaids are having pink posies.' She and Alice had been to Tavistock the day before and looked at several different styles. 'And guess what? Miss Bellamy stopped me in the village street the other day and said I can have whatever I want from her garden for the church! Wasn't that kind of her?'

'She's a good soul,' Alice said. 'And that garden of hers is a picture. Us'll have to make time to go and see what there is a few days beforehand, Val, and then get them all picked and arranged on the Friday.' She frowned again. 'That's going to take a bit of time.'

'I could do that,' Joanna offered. 'And I'm sure Miss Bellamy will help. We can do the arrangements together.'

'That'll be a help. Now, Ted, is your Norman going to get that friend of his over Walkhampton way to do the photos? And how's our Val going to get to the church? You'll need to scrub out the pony-trap well if her's going to use that.'

'Can't she walk?' he asked. ''Tis only a footstep to the church from here.'

'Of course her can't walk! And what if it's pouring with rain? She'll look like something the cat's dragged home.' Alice threw down her pencil indignantly and everyone laughed. 'For goodness' sake! Am I the only one who's taking this wedding seriously?'

'No, of course you're not,' Val said, still giggling. 'But you don't need to worry about the trap. Hilary says I can borrow their gig, the little black one that Mrs Napier used to go to church in. And the bridesmaids can have the bigger pony-trap. She's going to have them all polished up and decorated with flowers and ribbons.'

'Well, isn't that kind of her!' Alice exclaimed. 'That'll look lovely, Val. Well –' she looked at her list again '– I reckon that's just about it, don't you? I'll talk to Dottie and Annie Dawe about the food. It'll be ham salad, and some nice puddings for afters. Ted, you'll need to sort out the drinks – sherry for when people arrive, and then cider or lemonade with the meal. And, Tom, you can make yourself useful and see to the chairs and tables. Us'll need plenty of white sheets for tablecloths, and plenty of china and glasses too – I'll have to see who can lend us some. There's only a few old cups and saucers in the hall cupboard, for teas.'

'It's time they got crockery and stuff down there perma-nent,' Minnie observed. 'People are going to want to use it more for weddings and parties.'

'Perhaps some of the money they raise at the Summer Fair could be used to buy some,' Val suggested.

'Well, perhaps it could, but that's for the committee to decide and it won't help us with the wedding.' Alice drew a line on her sheet of paper. 'Now, does everyone know what they've got to do?'

The family nodded and scraped back their chairs, eager to bring the meeting to a close. Tom pulled on his boots and Joanna went to fetch Robin from his afternoon nap, ready to take him for his Sunday-afternoon walk. Ted disappeared into the front parlour, where he would pretend to read the *Sunday Express* and fall asleep within minutes. Jackie slipped out to meet some of her friends, and Val wandered away to find Luke, who had talked of going somewhere along the riverbank to find a new subject for a painting.

'It's going to be a lovely wedding,' Minnie said to Alice as she stumped to the back door to sit in the garden. ''Tis going to be a pleasure to see our Val settled at last.'

'Yes, it is.' Alice followed her mother-in-law with some cushions to lay on the wooden bench where she would sit and enjoy the sunshine for an hour or so. 'I don't mind telling you, a year ago I was wondering if she would ever be really happy again. But now, you only got to look at her face to see that she's found the right man. I just hope they don't move too far away, that's all. 'Tis a problem knowing where they're to find somewhere to live.'

'You don't want to worry about that,' Minnie said, leaning back and closing her eyes. 'Something'll turn up. Something always turns up, in the end.'

Alice looked down at her. Minnie was well into her eighties now and had lived through two world wars, as well as the Boer War. She had seen enormous changes in the world, some good and some bad. She had seen tragedy in her own life and the lives of others. Yet she could still, on this quiet Sunday

343

afternoon, sit in the sunshine in her own garden and say that 'something would turn up'.

Us ought all to learn from her, Alice thought as she went indoors to fetch a bit of sewing to do. Worrying never solves anything. If you can't do nothing about it, just let it be. Something will turn up, in the end.

Luke had walked quite a long way before Val found him at the old stepping-stones, almost a mile from the village. He was sitting on a moss-covered rock, his easel propped up in front of him, looking thoughtfully at a large gorse bush that was overhanging the tumbling water. The rocks in the stream glittered in the sunlight, and as Val came round the bend she saw the brilliant-blue flash of a kingfisher.

'You've frightened him away,' Luke said, putting out an arm to draw her against his side. 'Never mind, he'll be back if we keep quiet. He's got a nest over there – see the hole in the bank?'

'It could be a she, then,' Val said, settling herself on the rock beside him.

'Could be. But they both look after the nest and the young. Look – there he is again. Or she,' he added with a grin.

They both watched as the bright bird flew like an arrow up the stream and came to rest on a low branch. It was carrying two small fish in its beak, head to tail, and turned its head, peeping from side to side to make sure it wasn't observed, before diving into the hole Luke had pointed out. A moment or two later, it emerged, minus the fish, and shot off again.

'Oh, how lovely!' Val exclaimed softly. 'It's got babies. Or maybe the other parent's inside, sitting on eggs. Did you know it was here, Luke?'

'I had an idea there was a nest the other day. I've walked along this stretch of the bank quite a bit lately and I noticed a lot of coming and going. I hope they'll get used to seeing me here – I want to paint that gorse bush over the river. The sun catches the gold of the flowers and the ripples in the water so well.'

'It'll be a lovely picture,' she agreed. 'Oh, Luke, I wish you didn't have to get an ordinary job. Your paintings are so good, you shouldn't be wasting your time doing anything else.'

'It's no bad thing to be teaching other people to paint, though. I owe my own teachers a lot – I think it'll be rather satisfying to pass some of it on.'

'Mm. I suppose so.'

'And I'll still have time to paint. Evenings and weekends, and holidays.'

'I know. But it's not just that.' She slid down to the cushiony moss and leaned her back against the rock. 'Look at what you've been doing this week – coming out here at all times of the day to see just when the sun catches the gorse and the water in just the right way. You won't be able to do that if you have to be in school in Tavistock all week.'

'I'll be able to bring home a proper wage, though,' he said, and bent to kiss the top of her head. 'That's important, too.'

'A wage-slave! That's what you'll be. I want you to be *free*, Luke, as an artist should be.'

Luke was silent for a moment. 'It's not going to be a real problem to you, is it? Me being a "wage-slave", I mean? You won't think less of me?'

'Of course I won't!' She spoke more loudly than she had intended, and the kingfisher, which had just come to perch on its branch again, flew off in alarm. 'Oh, I'm sorry – I didn't mean to shout, and now I've frightened him away. Don't take any notice of me, Luke. I'll love you whatever you do, you know that. In fact, I'm very proud that you're prepared to give up your way of life because of me. I just wish you didn't need to do it.'

'Ten years ago,' he said, 'men were having to go to war, and their wives were wishing they didn't need to do it. Going to Tavistock to teach children to draw and paint doesn't seem all that terrible to me.'

'No, it isn't, when you put it like that,' Val said soberly. 'Look, he's coming back. I'll be quiet and watch, while you start your painting.'

They were still there an hour later, Val half asleep in the sunshine while Luke stared first at the scene before him and then at the painting that was taking shape on his canvas, when Felix and Maddy came along the path. They stopped when they saw Luke and Val, and sat down on the rocks to watch the kingfisher and talk for a few minutes. When they went along their way, Val and Luke looked at each other.

'And what do you suppose is going on there?' Val enquired. 'I thought Stella was rather keen on the curate.'

'So did I.' Luke frowned uneasily. His friendship with Stella the year before had left him with a protective feeling towards the young schoolteacher. 'I hope she's not going to get hurt.'

'Felix isn't the type to play fast and loose,' Val said thoughtfully. 'And I'm sure Maddy wouldn't do anything to hurt her sister. But people don't always fall in love to order, do they? And none of us can help what we feel.'

Their eyes met as they thought of their own story, begun so many years ago when passions had run high and falling in love had certainly not been 'to order'. And then Luke shrugged and said, 'There's nothing we can do about it, anyway. They'll have to sort out their own lives – we've got our own to worry about.' He started to put away his paints. 'Come on. Let's pack up now and walk home the long way round. Your mother's not expecting us for tea just yet, is she?'

'Not today. She's just putting out sandwiches and cakes and things for everyone to come and have whenever they're ready.' Val stood up and stretched her arms above her head. 'It's such a lovely day, it seems a crime to go home at all. Let's stay out all night!'

Luke, kneeling on the ground to fasten the straps of the rucksack he used to carry his painting gear, looked at her and felt his heart quicken. He stood up and took her in his arms.

'Not long now, my darling,' he murmured into her hair, 'and we'll be able to stay out all night, every night. We can sleep under the stars for the rest of the summer, if that's what you want. I don't mind what we do – or where I work – so long as we can be together.'

Felix and Maddy strolled slowly on along the riverbank. They had had Sunday lunch at Dottie's, but when Felix had suggested a walk, Stella had shaken her head and said she had some work to do for school the next day. They'd come out alone, saying they'd be back by five as Felix was taking evensong in Little Burracombe.

'It's a shame Stella wouldn't come,' Felix remarked. 'It's too nice an afternoon to be stuck indoors. She's working too hard, you know.'

'It's the play,' Maddy said. 'It's getting close now and she's so anxious that it should go well. I know it's only a short scene, but Shakespeare isn't easy for young children. I've told her they ought to try something simpler next time – a pantomime or something.'

'Miss Kemp will never agree to that. They always do a nativity play for the Christmas term. Poor Stella! If this one's a success, she'll get roped in for that, too. Mind you,' he added thoughtfully, 'I wouldn't mind trying a pantomime with some of the older villagers. I was in an amateur-dramatics group myself once, and it was great fun. Mrs Warren started one a while ago, but they haven't actually done anything yet.'

'That's a good idea. We could do plays as well.' Maddy turned to him eagerly, and then shook her head. 'Except that we might not both be here! Oh bother.'

'Well, who knows where we'll be?' They looked at each other and laughed. 'Shall we tell her soon?' he asked.

'I think we'd better!' Maddy giggled. 'She's beginning to suspect something. I hope she'll be pleased about it.'

'Of course she will,' Felix said. He put his arm round Maddy's shoulders and gave her an affectionate squeeze. 'All Stella wants is for you to be happy. You know that.'

'I know. All the same . . . she might not be happy about me not being in Burracombe. Still, I never said I'd stay here for good. And she knows I've been restless since Fenella got married.'

'It's all going to work out beautifully,' he said with confidence. 'I'm just glad I was here when you came home again. It's been a lovely few weeks, Maddy.'

'For me, too,' she said, and they stopped. Maddy turned to him and stood on tiptoe to give him a kiss. 'Thank you, Felix.'

'What for?' he asked in surprise, and she laughed again.

'For – oh, for everything. For just being here, on this lovely afternoon. For helping me to be happy . . .'

Chapter Thirty-Five

'I been thinking about writing to you,' Jacob said. 'I weren't sure you'd be coming out to Burracombe again. Not after you'd been in next door.'

'Of course I've come again,' Jennifer said. 'He's my father. And I wanted to see you again, too.'

Jacob gave her a sharp look. 'That true, is it? Well, I been wanting to see you as well. I sort of hoped – well, even though things haven't turned out the way either of us might have liked them to, I hoped us might keep in touch.'

'I hope so, too,' she said quietly. They were sitting in Jacob's front room, drinking tea. 'That's why I've come in to see you first. I didn't want you to be upset that I hadn't called in the last time I was here. It wasn't because I didn't want to. It just – well, it didn't seem right, somehow. And I had a lot to think about.'

'I'm sure you did, after being in that dump,' he said grimly. 'Mind you, I ain't been in there meself for years, not since the old lady died, but I can guess what 'tis like. You only got to look at the front window. I don't suppose he's done any cleaning since his poor old mum passed over.'

'I don't think he has,' Jennifer admitted. 'I don't think he's had the heart for it.'

'Heart! That old misery ain't got no heart!' Jacob bit back the words and shook his head. 'Begging your pardon, maid, seeing as he'm your flesh and blood, more's the pity, but it's true. Never cared a tuppenny damn for nobody except hisself, that's Jed Fisher all over.'

'I don't think that's quite true,' Jennifer said gently. 'You were good friends when you were younger, weren't you?'

'When us was tackers and didn't know no better.'

'And when you were older – when you were young men.'

'We got along all right,' he allowed grudgingly. 'Most of the time, anyway.'

'There must have been something for you to like, then.'

'What *is* all this?' he demanded. 'Got you on his side, has he? Even when you seen what he's like and how he lives? Even after what he done to your own mother?'

'Well, I wouldn't be here if he hadn't done it,' Jennifer said, and then added quickly, 'Not that that makes it right. But I'm not sure that you really understand—'

'There isn't nothing to understand! He took advantage of her – there's no other word for it. Well, there is, but 'tis not one I'd want to say with a lady present. And he done it when he knowed her were upset because I'd gone away again, and already been wounded once. *In action*,' Jacob added fiercely. 'Which was more'n he was ever likely to be, with his flat feet or whatever he got the medical men to say was wrong with him. Flat feet!'

'It wasn't flat feet. It was a weak chest, and—'

'I don't care what it was!' Jacob was on his feet now, his mouth working with rage. 'He stopped at home when better men went off to fight for their country, and he took advantage of my Susan when her was upset and got her into trouble so that old bully of a father of hers chucked her out, and all these years I thought her was dead, and the babby along with her. And that was all Jed Fisher's doing, and he can cough his weak chest inside out for all I cares, and next time I hears him I'll just stop in here and listen, and be glad of it! I *will*!'

Jennifer stared at him, shocked, and after a moment or two he sat down, breathing heavily and looking shamefaced. 'Well,

I don't suppose I will, not when it comes to it,' he muttered after a while. 'I was in two minds whether to go over to him the other night, to tell you the truth. I thought he was going then. I couldn't just listen to him die, in all Christian charity I couldn't.'

'No,' Jennifer said, still shaken by his outburst, 'I don't think you could.'

'What I don't understand,' Jacob said after another pause, 'is why you'm sticking up for him. You say he'm your father, and I know that's true, but that don't mean you got to have any loyalty towards him – not the way it come about. Do it?'

'Well, it depends how it came about, doesn't it?' Jennifer said, feeling her way. 'I know what you believe happened, but—'

'He haven't managed to persuade you she done it willingly!' Jacob burst out. 'Not my Susan! Because I'll never believe that, not if you sits there for a hundred years!'

'No, I don't think it was like that. But I do believe he truly loved her. He told me he'd always been fond of her, but it was you she wanted—'

'That's true enough. Even he couldn't deny that.'

'He doesn't. That's what I'm saying. He always knew it was you—'

'And he was jealous.'

'Well, probably he was. But that wasn't—'

'So why did he do it, then?' Jacob burst out again. 'Why did he have to do that to an innocent maid like my Susan? I had more respect for her than that – why couldn't he?'

Jennifer didn't reply at once. Then she said, 'If I tell you what he said, will you listen to me? Really listen? And try to imagine what it must have been like for him, how you would have felt yourself, in his place?'

'I wouldn't never have *been* in—' Jacob began, then caught the look in her eye and sank back into his chair. 'Oh, all right,

351

then. Go on. I'll listen – but don't expect me to be sorry for him, because I won't. He don't deserve it.'

Jennifer took a deep breath and began to tell Jed's story. She told it as briefly as possible, knowing that Jacob would resent any attempt to guide his thoughts and emotions towards sympathy for Jed. When she came to the end, she said simply, 'I think he's lived with a bad conscience ever since. I think that's why he's gone the way he has, and wasted his life.'

Jacob was silent for a long time. At last, he said, 'I dare say you'm right about that. A bad conscience'll turn anyone sour. But look at it this way, he had plenty to feel bad about.'

'Yes,' she said. 'He did.'

When she left Jacob at last and went next door, Jennifer was struck even more by the contrast between them – the one so neat and tidy, the other so neglected. It seemed to epitomise two very different attitudes to life itself, and she wondered whether Jed would have ended up like this if he had not been rejected for the Army, or if he had not had that encounter with her mother. He might have been killed and had his name engraved on the village war memorial as a hero, she thought. And either way, I would never have been born.

Jed opened the door and peered at her in his usual suspicious manner. His skin looked even more sallow, she thought, and the dull colour had even seeped into his eyes. He seemed to have lost weight even in the short time since she had seen him last.

'Hello, Jed,' she said quietly. 'Can I come in?'

'I s'pose you'd better,' he said, turning back into the dim recess of his room, where even the afternoon sunlight had difficulty in bringing light through the dirty windows. 'I didn't think you'd bother coming again.'

'I said I would.' She sat down gingerly on the edge of the armchair and began to unpack the shopping-bag she had brought with her. 'I thought you might like a few bits and pieces. Some biscuits, a nice Victoria sponge, a packet of tea, half a dozen oranges, a few bananas and a piece of cheese. I hope you like the tasty sort.'

He stared at her. 'All that's for me?'

'I didn't know what you liked,' Jennifer said apologetically. 'Just tell me if there's anything you'd rather have. Oh, and I've got something for your cough.' She pulled a bottle of dark liquid from the depths of the bag. 'How is it now?'

The old man shrugged. 'Same as always. Chemists' jollop ain't going to make no difference to that. I've had it too long.' As if to prove his point, he began to cough and Jennifer watched in alarm as he heaved and retched, the blood suffusing his face and eyes. When she went to help him, he waved her away angrily, and when the attack was over, he lay back in his chair, panting.

'I really think you should see the doctor,' she said at last, when he was able to take notice again. 'That's more than just a cough.'

'And what would he do, eh? Put his stethyscope on me chest and tell me to take more care of meself. He can't do nothing for what I got.' His thin, claw-like hand was spread across his chest and Jennifer's anxiety grew.

'Why? What do you think it is?' The dreaded word 'tuberculosis' passed through her mind. In the conditions in which Jed lived, any germs could multiply. 'Jed, I'm sure he could do something. You ought to be in hospital—'

'I ain't going to no hospital!' His voice rose, but she realised that even when he shouted, he lacked the strength she had heard when he'd abused Jacob, the first time she had ever seen him. 'Wire me up to a lot of machines, that's what they'd do, and I'd die just the same. Go into hospital and you never come out again, not when you're like me.'

He might very well be right there, Jennifer thought, but she didn't say so. Instead, she said gently, 'Would you like me

353

to make you a cup of tea? You could have a piece of sponge cake with it – I made it myself.'

He stared at her, and she realised that he had probably not had a cup of tea made for him for years. Her eyes suddenly wet, she got up and took the groceries out to the cluttered scullery. I ought to have brought some cleaning things as well, she thought, filling the rusty kettle, but he might have been offended. It can't be good for him to live like this, though. He's killing himself.

'Have you got any milk?' she called, not liking to open cupboard doors without his permission. He might live in dreadful conditions, but he still had a right to his privacy.

'In the larder. By the back door.'

The larder was surprisingly large and had its own window, with a deep sill. As might be expected, it was cluttered and untidy, but there was an array of tinned foods on the shelves and a jug of milk on the windowsill. Jennifer found a bag of sugar and opened her own packet of tea. The teapot was full of swollen leaves, and as she took it outside to empty it, she wondered if he simply put in more each time he made a fresh pot, without bothering to tip out the last lot. Either that or he liked it extremely strong.

While she was waiting for the kettle to boil, she surreptitiously wiped the kitchen sink, but it was too greasy to benefit much. It wants some really hot water and carbolic, she thought. In fact, that's what the whole place needs, including the man who lives here!

At last the tea was ready and she carried it in. She had found a dinner plate for the sponge cake, and two smaller plates, and after she had cleared a space on the table, she cut a couple of slices of cake and gave one to Jed. He looked at it as if he'd never seen cake before.

'You made this for me, special?'

'Yes. I hope the crumbs don't make you cough,' she added anxiously. 'What sort of cake do you like best?'

'My mother used to make a good fruit cake,' he said, lifting the slice of sponge and turning it this way and that, as if he wasn't entirely convinced that it was real. 'Mind, I dunno if me teeth would stand up to it now. She used to put a lot of nuts in it.'

'I could make you one without nuts,' Jennifer offered, and he gave her one of his narrow looks.

'Why? Why should you do that? Hoping I've got a fortune to leave you?'

'Of course not! I don't want anything. I just want to do something for you. You're my father.'

'More's the pity,' he grunted. 'I dare say that's what you thought, anyway, when you found it 'twas me and not that Holy Joe next door.'

In all honesty, Jennifer couldn't deny this, so she said, 'It's best to know the truth. I think so, anyway.' She paused and went on tentatively, 'Are you sorry I found you, Jed? Would you rather I hadn't come at all?'

He took a noisy slurp of tea. 'Never thought about it. You come, and that's all there is to it. No use being sorry.'

'I hoped you might be pleased,' she said a little wistfully, but he shrugged. Perhaps, she thought, he had forgotten to feel any emotion other than bitterness, and she remembered her comment to Jacob about a 'wasted life'. Whatever the rights and wrongs, it was a sad thing to see.

She stayed with him for over an hour, telling him about her life with her mother and her sisters and asking him about Burracombe. He seemed to listen to her stories, but talk of his own home village only brought out more bitterness and she veered away from it. He had another coughing fit just before she left, and once again she tried to persuade him to see the doctor.

'I told you, he won't do me no good. Only give me more medicine, and I won't take it, I tell you that now. It tastes horrible.'

'I'm sure he could help you more than that,' she began, but he shook his head.

'He'd send me to hospital. I told you, I'm not going to no hospital. I'd rather die!'

At least you'd die clean and in comfort, she thought wryly, but all she said was, 'He might not do that. He could send in the district nurse to look after you.'

'And I know what her'd do, as well. Clean me up, that's what. I don't want no district nurse round here, telling me I got to have a bath and clean the place. I'm all right as I am.'

Jennifer saw that it was no use arguing, and left it, but as she walked back through the village she made up her mind that she wouldn't let it go. She couldn't pretend that she felt any love, or even affection, for Jed, but she did feel a tie that couldn't be ignored. He was her father, and couldn't be left to cough himself into his grave with nobody to care for him.

Jacob wasn't in his cottage as she walked by, but she heard the church bells ringing and remembered that he was a ringer. He was probably in there now, pulling on his rope; a part of the village community and its activities that Jed had never been.

Compassion grew within her heart for the life that had been so wasted – and yet had given her her own life. It was very hard to understand, but knowing what she must do was simple enough.

Her quest had been to find her father, but there was another side to this. For Jed Fisher, his 'wasted life' had brought him a daughter.

Chapter Thirty-Six

'Why don't we go over to Little Burracombe with Felix for evensong?' Maddy suggested as they sat round Dottie's table having their tea. It was salad, with the first crisp lettuce, radishes and spring onions from Dottie's vegetable patch and hard-boiled eggs from Constance Bellamy's hens, which were laying at the moment as if they'd been charged with sustaining the entire population of the village. 'Mr Harvey won't mind, and it'll make a nice walk.'

'That's a good idea,' Felix said eagerly, and as Stella began to shake her head he added firmly, 'You're to come as well! You've been stuck indoors all afternoon.'

'Yes, you can't possibly have any more work to do,' Maddy agreed, and Dottie joined in with her own opinion.

'You need some fresh air. You'm looking proper washed-out.'

'Well, thank you!' Stella said with a laugh. 'All right, I'll come. It's a nice idea.' But she still sounded less than enthusiastic, and the others looked at each other with some concern.

'You're not feeling ill or anything, are you?' Maddy asked. 'Dottie's right, you do look a bit pale.'

'I'm fine, honestly. It's just that this is such a busy term, what with the play and Sports Day and everything. And I have to do reports on all the children in my class who will be moving up into Miss Kemp's next term, as well as the ordinary end-of-term reports. And then there's—'

'You definitely need some time off,' Felix interrupted. 'So that's settled – we're walking over to Little Burracombe as soon as we finish tea . . .

'It'll be a good thing when this term's over,' he added later as they set out for the footpath down to the Clam. 'You need a break. I'm glad Maddy's taking you to London for a few days.'

'Yes, I'll enjoy that,' Stella said tepidly.

The other two glanced at each other. Stella caught the tail of their glance and felt her misery deepen. What had they talked about that afternoon? she wondered. They'd come back with bright eyes, wind-blown hair and the air of a secret. Whatever it was – and she thought she could guess – she wished they would come out with it soon. The sooner she knew the truth, the better, even though she felt certain she wasn't going to like it.

They must never know how I feel about it, she told herself. I've got to keep it to myself for the rest of my life. They mustn't ever know how unhappy they're making me . . .

Little Burracombe, sitting close to the river on the other side of the valley, was not much more than a handful of cottages clustered round its ancient church. Like Burracombe itself, it had once been a mining village and there had been almost as many pubs as houses, but now there was only the Rose and Crown, almost next door. The vicarage was on the other side and Felix knocked on the door to let Mrs Berry know he had arrived.

'Oh, hello, Felix,' she said, and smiled at the two sisters. 'How nice of you to come. John's rather poorly today, I'm afraid – I won't ask you to come in after the service, if you don't mind.' She looked anxious, despite her smile, and Felix laid a hand on her arm.

'Don't worry about that, Mrs Berry. I wouldn't want to disturb him. Just let him know that I'm here, and if there's anything he needs to know about, I'll slip in and tell you afterwards. Otherwise, we'll just go straight home.' As the three of them went back down the garden path, he said, 'I'm afraid the poor old man's fading away. He looked like a ghost the last time I saw him – almost transparent against his pillows. He doesn't seem to be suffering much, though, which is something to be grateful for.'

'Poor Mrs Berry,' Stella said. 'I wonder what will happen to her if he dies? Will she have to leave the vicarage?'

'Probably, but I don't think that'll be a problem. They've got a niece in Ashburton – she'll probably go and live there. She talks about it quite practically, but it's obviously going to be very sad for her to lose him.'

They went into the church. Felix walked round to the vestry while Stella and Maddy found seats near the back. Quite a few people had already gathered for the evening service and there were nods and smiles from those that knew them. The church door was left open and they could hear birdsong rising above the soft notes of the organ. When Felix emerged from the vestry, clad in his white robes, a shaft of evening sunlight beamed through the west window and turned his hair to the rich gold of ripe corn.

Stella knelt to say her prayers, and thought about the happy times she and Felix had enjoyed together – the walks and the picnics, the drives in Mirabelle. It seemed that they were about to end – in truth, they already had ended. There would still be walks, picnics and drives, but it would be no longer she and Felix alone. It would be Felix and Maddy, with Stella invited to join them only some of the time. Felix would still be a part of her life – but as a brother; not, as she had begun to hope, as a lover and a husband.

I've got to stop thinking about myself, she told herself, and think about them. I love them both and I always will. I want them to be happy.

Perhaps here, in the small, quiet church with the organ

sounding softly in her ears and the song of the birds drifting in on the scented air, she would find the strength she needed.

'Let's sit here by the river for a while,' Felix suggested. 'It's too nice an evening to go back yet.' He led the way along the riverbank to where a large slab of rock made a seat large enough for the three of them, and sat down in the middle. The two girls sat on either side of him and they watched the water break into showers of glittering spray over the rocks.

'We used to come swimming down at the Clam,' Maddy observed. 'There's a deep pool quite near the bridge, but it can be dangerous. I remember a little boy being drowned once in a whirlpool, after we'd had a lot of rain.'

'Oh, how sad. Were you there?'

'No, and Dottie never let me go swimming there again. Everyone was very upset.'

'So they would be.' Stella stared at the water, which had looked so beautiful a moment ago but now appeared threatening and treacherous, and Felix gave her a quick glance and squeezed her arm.

'It's no use letting yourself grieve over everyone who's ever died, Stella. The Reverend Berry, small boys – it's always sad, but it's natural as well. You know that.'

She nodded, but could find nothing to say. Despite her prayers and despite the beauty of the evening and the company of the two people she loved best, she felt shadowed by sadness. I'm just a selfish person, she thought bitterly, thinking of myself all the time. It's no wonder Felix loves Maddy instead of me.

'Shall we tell her now?' Maddy said suddenly, and Stella turned her head. Her sister's face was alive with excitement, and Stella felt a sudden sinking of her heart. The moment she had half dreaded, half longed for, if only so that she could know the truth, had arrived.

'I think now would be a very good time,' Felix said softly. 'She knows there's something in the wind, anyway.'

'Weren't you ever told that it's rude to say "she"?' Stella asked, rather more tartly than she'd intended, and Maddy laughed.

'Mummy would have said that. She'd have said, "*She's* the cat's mother"! Wouldn't she, Stel?'

Stella felt a sudden pricking of tears. The occasions on which she and Maddy reminisced about their childhood and their parents had brought them closer together, but they hadn't yet reached the stage of bringing them into the conversation casually. She stared at the rock beneath her hand and didn't answer, and after a moment Felix went on.

'You tell her, then, Maddy. It's your news, really.'

'Only because of you.' But Maddy leaned over and touched Stella's hand. 'It's good news, Stella. At least, I hope you'll think so.'

'I'm sure I will.' Stella looked up and smiled at her sister. 'Come on, then. Tell me what it is – as if I couldn't guess.'

'You can't. Not in a month of Sundays.' Maddy took a deep breath and then said, 'I've got a job!'

The news was so unexpected that Stella didn't take it in at once. She stared at the bright face, then looked at Felix as if asking him to interpret. Both he and Maddy burst out laughing at her expression and she felt a momentary irritation.

'You're teasing me,' she said. 'What do you mean, a job? What sort of job?'

'I don't know why you're so surprised,' Maddy said, pretending to be hurt. 'You're not the only person who can earn her own living, you know. Anyway, you knew I was looking for something.'

'I know, but I thought—' Stella stopped herself before she could say what she'd thought. Whatever this job was, it didn't mean her suspicions were wrong. 'Well, what is it, anyway?'

'I'm going to be a secretary,' Maddy said importantly. 'I'm going to be secretary to the Archdeacon of West Lyme!'

Stella stared at her. 'The Archdeacon of West Lyme? But—'

'My uncle,' Felix said. 'You knew he was an archdeacon, didn't you? I'm sure I've mentioned it.'

'Practically everyone in your family is an archdeacon or a bishop or vicar of somewhere,' she told him. 'Is this the one in Dorset?'

'Well, since West Lyme is in Dorset . . .'

'All right! You can stop laughing, both of you. It's just come as a surprise, that's all.' She looked at their faces. 'You both look very pleased with yourselves. I suppose this is why you've been making all these secret trips to Dorset . . .'

'Only two,' Maddy protested.

'Well, it seems like more. And you went to Exeter one day.'

'We did meet him there as well,' Felix admitted. 'He was coming to the cathedral for a special service and it seemed like a good opportunity for me to introduce him to Maddy. I knew he needed someone, and I thought she'd be ideal, with all her experience with Miss Forsyth. And he thought so, too.'

'Being companion to an actress is a bit different from being an archdeacon's secretary,' Stella said.

'Oh, I don't know,' he said thoughtfully. 'The Church and the theatre have quite a lot in common . . . But it's mostly all the social arrangements – travel and meetings and so on – that he needs Maddy for. There's not much difference there.'

Stella was still struggling to come to terms with the news. 'But where will you be living? West Lyme's quite a long way away.'

'Not all that far. You can get there in a couple of hours by train. We'll be able to visit each other. You can even come to stay.'

'To stay? Have you found lodgings?'

Maddy shook her head. 'I'll be in the Archdeacon's house.

It's quite big – I'll have my own little flat, with a spare room for visitors. You can come as often as you like.'

Stella looked at Maddy's bright face and reached across Felix to take her hand. 'I'm really pleased,' she said warmly. 'It sounds ideal and I'm sure you'll be good at the job. And as long as you're not too far away . . .'

'I'd never go too far away from Burracombe,' Maddy said softly. 'There's too much here to make me want to go very far.'

As Stella lay in bed that night, looking at the night sky through her open window and breathing in the scented air, she tried, as she always did last thing at night, to organise her thoughts about the day that had just passed.

It doesn't mean they're not in love, she thought. Just because Maddy's going to be living in West Lyme . . . It's only a couple of hours on the train – or by sports car . . . And she's going to be working for Felix's uncle – living in his house . . . They can still see each other often . . . It doesn't mean I was wrong . . .

Unable to lie still, she got out of bed and sat by the window, gazing out into the night. The moon was rising over the horizon, shedding a cool pale light over the rolling moor and throwing the Standing Stones into dark silhouette. Beneath her, the white flowers of the philadelphus bush gleamed like snow and the scent mingled with that of the honeysuckle on the wall and a cluster of tobacco plants just below. The hollyhocks had begun their annual climb towards the roof of the cottage, and as she leaned out of the window she heard the hoot of an owl and saw the pale glow of its wings, like a giant moth, drift across the garden.

This time last year, she thought, I was happy here, living in Dottie's cottage and getting towards the end of my first year at the school. All I wanted to make my life complete was to find my sister again. It was my one dream, and it came true.

And if Maddy and Felix are really in love, they'll stay in my life. I'll have a brother as well as a sister.

She climbed back into bed, once again reproaching herself for her selfishness.

What right did she have to feel sad now?

Chapter Thirty-Seven

'I got the doctor off me own bat,' Jacob said. 'I couldn't stand it no longer, hearing him coughing and hawking in here. It sounded too bad. I couldn't have lived with meself if he'd died in here all by hisself, and nobody to give him a bit of comfort, the old misery.'

'You did the right thing,' Jennifer said. She was standing with Jacob in Jed's living-room, while Charles Latimer was in the room overhead. Jacob had telephoned her at Dingle's and she'd left work straight away and caught the next bus, arriving within an hour.

'How long has the doctor been here?'

'Come five minutes before you did. He were out on his rounds when I went up to the house, or he'd have been here sooner. I rung you as soon as I'd been there and then come straight back.' Jacob shook his head. 'He's in a poor way, mind. Didn't make no fuss when I told him he oughter be in bed. Well, it shows how bad he is that he even let me through the door.'

'Oh dear.' Jennifer looked at the chair she usually sat in, wanting to sit down now but thinking of her business suit. 'I wonder what the doctor will say. Jed hates the thought of going to hospital.'

'Well, none of us wants to finish up there,' Jacob said, as if it were prison. 'I don't see what else he can do, though, if the old misery's really bad. There's no one to look after him, and I don't reckon he'm fit to look after hisself. To tell you the

365

truth, maid, I had a shock when I saw him. I ain't laid eyes on him for the past fortnight and he seems to have shrivelled up in that time. He looks just like a peanut.'

'A peanut?' Jennifer echoed, startled, and Jacob nodded.

'One in its shell, I mean, all pale and wrinkled up.' They both turned as the doctor came down the stairs and looked enquiringly at Jennifer.

'I'm Jennifer Tucker,' she said, holding out her hand. 'Jed's daughter.'

'His *daughter*? I didn't realise . . . ' Charles Latimer looked from one to the other and decided not to ask any questions just now. 'Well, Mrs Tucker, I'm sure you realise that your father's quite ill. He's been going downhill for some time, I'm afraid, and he's not been looking after himself at all well.'

'I know. I've been trying to get him to come and see you but he wouldn't.' She hesitated. 'Will he have to go to hospital?'

Charles Latimer sighed deeply. 'It would be the best place for him – he'd get proper care there, certainly. But I'm not sure there's anything anyone can actually do to help him, other than that. The illness has progressed too far. And when I mentioned it, he got very upset.'

'He says if he goes into hospital he'll never come out,' Jennifer said, and the doctor looked at her thoughtfully.

'I'm afraid he's probably right, although not for the reasons he believes. Mrs Tucker, may I speak freely?'

'Yes, of course,' she said. 'But I'm not Mrs – I'm Miss.' She flicked a look at the ceiling, wondering how much Jed could hear. Jacob saw her glance and interpreted it correctly.

'Why don't we all go next door to my place?' he suggested. 'Nobody won't overhear us there, and we can all sit down decent.' He indicated Jed's chairs and the doctor smiled.

'That's a good idea. Do you want to let Jed know?'

Jennifer shook her head. 'I'll come back as soon as we finish.' They followed Jacob out of the door, through the

366

tangled garden and back into his own neat abode. Jacob pushed Flossie off his chair and gestured towards the others.

'She don't sit on those – you won't get hairs all over your clean clothes. So what do you have to say, Doctor?'

'I'd rather know the truth,' Jennifer said quietly.

'Well, as I said, it's not good news. I haven't seen Jed professionally for a long time, not since he cut his arm rather badly with a sickle, but of course I've seen him about the village and I've been aware for some time that he's not a well man. All the same, I'm shocked by his condition now. He seems to have gone down so suddenly.'

''Tis the way he lives,' Jacob said. 'Never cleaning the place up or washing hisself properly like a Christian soul should, and feeding out of tins all the time. I don't reckon he's ever cooked hisself a proper meal, ever since his mother died, poor old lady. Stands to reason a body'll go downhill, living like that.'

'I'm afraid you're right. But there's more to it than that. I think Jed has a serious illness.'

'Is it TB?' Jennifer asked. 'All that coughing . . . '

The doctor looked at her. 'No, I don't think it's TB. I think he has cancer. Lung cancer.'

The room seemed very still. 'Cancer' wasn't a word you spoke out loud. It was something to be talked of in hushed whispers, something that nobody could do anything about. Jennifer had known a woman once, one of her mother's friends, who had had breast cancer – a 'growth' as people more usually termed it – and stubbornly refused to go to her doctor until it was too late. She could have been saved, Susan had said, because the doctors could cut off a breast. But could they take away an old man's lung? And what if it had attacked both lungs?

'Isn't there anything . . . ?' she began, but the doctor shook his head.

'I really don't think there is. As I say, he could go to

367

hospital where they'd make him as comfortable as possible, but they couldn't really do any more than could be done for him at home, if he had someone to look after him. And the upheaval of taking him there, especially if he were to be taken against his will – well, that in itself could kill him.'

'How long do you think he has?' Jennifer asked in a low voice. She was surprised by how upset she felt. Unlikeable though Jed was, he was her father, and the tie she'd been aware of seemed even stronger than she'd thought.

Charles sighed again. 'It's impossible to tell exactly. But in his poor condition – undernourished and weak – and by the signs of jaundice in his skin and eyes, I'd say it's no more than a matter of weeks. And not many, either. Two weeks – a month at most.' He turned to Jacob. 'If it hadn't been for you calling me this morning, it might only have been days.'

'I oughter have called you before,' Jacob said heavily. 'I've heard him in there night after night coughing and moaning, and I've never done a thing about it. I oughter have done something, even though we've been at loggerheads for the past thirty-five years or more.'

'You mustn't blame yourself,' the doctor said. 'We've all known Jed wasn't well, but nobody could force him to seek help.'

'And I tried to make him come to you only last week,' Jennifer said. 'He wouldn't hear of it.'

They sat in silence for a few moments, each lost in thought. Then Jacob said, 'So what shall us do now? Be you going to take him to hospital, Doctor?'

'You can't,' Jennifer said. 'You heard what the doctor said, Jacob. It would kill him.'

'Seems like he's going to die anyway,' Jacob began, but she shook her head and turned back to the doctor.

'Dr Latimer, is there anything else we can do? What about a district nurse?'

'Nurse Petherell could come in each day, certainly,' he

agreed. 'But Jed really needs someone here all the time. This last attack has left him very weak. The disease is accelerating, you see. I doubt if he could manage to do anything for himself now.'

'Then I'll come myself,' Jennifer said decisively. 'I'll get leave from the shop. I've got my summer-holiday leave allowance coming up, and I can ask for extra. I'll come and live here and look after him for as long as he needs me.'

Jacob stared at her. 'What, and live in that dump? You can't mean it, maid.'

'Of course I can. What else can I do? He's my father.' She saw the flicker of pain in Jacob's eyes. 'I'm sorry, Jacob,' she said softly. 'But it's the truth. I have to do it.'

Charles Latimer looked from one to the other. There was something here he didn't understand, a story he knew nothing about. But it wasn't his business just now, and he was relieved to think that Jed Fisher, the most unpopular man in the village, had someone to care for him at this last, desperate time of his life. All the same, he felt he had to warn Jennifer of what lay ahead.

'It won't be easy. Jed's small and frail now, but he'll still be surprisingly strong. He may be in a lot of pain and he'll probably become delirious. Nurse Petherell will help with bathing and lifting him, but he'll need a lot of nursing the rest of the time. You need to be very sure you can manage it.'

'I know. I nursed my mother through her last illness not long ago.' Jennifer met his eyes. 'So long as I can have help, I think I can manage. And if I really can't – well, then I suppose he'll have to go to hospital. But I'll do my best to see that he spends his last days at home.'

'And I'll be around to give you a hand,' Jacob said gruffly, and she turned to look at him in surprise. 'It's all right, maid. I know we been at each other's throats all these years, and you and me both knows why, but I wouldn't be able to call meself a Christian if I couldn't put that on one side while he'm

369

dying. You can come in to me any time you needs me. Just knock on the wall, that's all you need do.' Their eyes met and he put out his hand towards her. 'It seems a funny business, but it's like it's the last thing I can do for my Susan, to help her maid when her needs me. Even if it do mean helping that old misery as well!'

Jennifer went straight back to Plymouth, first to Dingle's to arrange her leave, and then home to pack a case. Before leaving Burracombe, she had gone back to Jed, venturing up the stairs to his bedroom, to tell him what she meant to do.

'You'm coming to look after me?' he wheezed painfully. Like Jacob and the doctor, she was shocked by the change in him, even in the few days since she had last seen him. I ought to have realised how ill he was, she thought remorsefully. I ought to have insisted he saw the doctor then.

Not that it would have made any difference. Dr Latimer had explained that the course of the illness was already irrevocably under way, and had been for some time. Nothing could have been done for him other than what was being done now. And at least the old man had the pride, such as it was, of knowing he had kept his independence until the last possible moment.

Now, however, it seemed as if he'd given in. Lying on an old iron bedstead between thin grey sheets, he looked half the size he'd looked before, the yellow, wizened skin of his face shrunk back against his skull. His eyes were sunk back into dark hollows, and his almost colourless hair lay in thin, greasy strands across his head.

Gazing down at him, Jennifer could well believe that he had only days to live.

'Yes, of course I'll look after you,' she said gently. 'I have to go back to Plymouth to collect some things and let them know at the shop, but I'll be back by teatime. I won't leave you on your own now.'

'I dunno where you be going to sleep,' he grunted. 'There's only my old bed in t'other room but there be a lot of other stuff there, too, stuff I didn't want to throw out.'

Jennifer could believe that, too. She would have been surprised to find that Jed had thrown out anything at all during his entire life. Old newspapers, tins, bottles, jars, a broken radio set that looked as if it had been homemade sometime before the war, and tattered clothes lay everywhere. The smell of neglect permeated the whole cottage.

'I think some of it will have to be thrown out now,' she said. 'Or at least shifted about a bit. Will you mind very much if I clear out the other bedroom so that I can sleep there?'

He shrugged a thin shoulder. 'Do what you like, maid. I'm fed up with the lot of it.'

'I'll need to tidy up downstairs, too,' she warned him, hoping that he would not take instant offence. 'And clean round a bit as well. I don't suppose you've felt much like it, just lately.' She didn't want him to feel that his home was being taken over, but she knew that she couldn't possibly stay in the cottage as it was.

This time, he didn't even bother to shrug; he simply closed his eyes and turned his head away. He's exhausted, poor soul, she thought. He's past caring what anyone does now.

By the time she returned from Plymouth, Jed was awake again and Alice Tozer was in the cottage scrubbing the sink. She turned as Jennifer came through the door.

'There you are, maid. I've give him his tea and I thought I'd just try and get a bit of the grease off this sink. I don't reckon it's been cleaned in years. Filthy, the whole place is.' She caught sight of Jennifer's suitcase. 'You'm not planning to stop here, surely?'

'Of course I am,' Jennifer said. 'I can't leave him alone in that state. He needs someone here all the time.'

'Well, I know that,' Alice said, 'but the thought of you

sleeping here . . . Have you seen that room upstairs? It's not fit for a pig to sleep in.'

'I'll clean it up. I've brought some of my own sheets for the bed.'

'You'd have done better to bring a mattress as well,' Alice said grimly. 'Nothing but a nest for mice, that one be – that's if you can find it at all under all the mess and rubbish he's piled on top of it. Listen to me, maid, you come and stop up at the farm tonight and me and Val will give you a hand doing a bit of spring-cleaning.' She wrinkled her nose. 'It wants proper fumigating, but we can bring along some carbolic and disinfectant and a couple of scrubbing-brushes. And we can shift the rubbish outside – Ted'll bring the tractor along and take it down the dump.'

'I don't think we ought to do too much without Jed's agreement,' Jennifer said. 'It's his home, after all. I don't want him too upset, while he's so ill.'

'Well, maybe you'm right about that,' Alice allowed. 'But you still can't sleep in that bedroom until it's had a proper turn-out, and this kitchen's unhealthy the way it is now. I'd be frightened to eat anything made here. Now, we'll never get that room sorted out by tonight, so why don't you come and stop with us, like I said, and we'll sort it out in the morning? Jed won't hurt for one more night. Doctor popped in again while he was having his tea and said he'll most likely sleep now he's got some decent food inside him.'

Jennifer hesitated, but as they were talking Jacob had come in and stood listening. He said, 'You could stop in with me, maid, if you likes. I don't get many visitors, but there's a spare bed, and 'tis clean. And you'll be close enough to hear the old blighter if he starts coughing in the night or calls out. You could be round here in a couple of minutes.'

'That sounds a good idea,' Jennifer said gratefully. 'Thanks, Jacob, I'll do that. And thank you for your offer, too,' she said to Alice. 'If you really don't mind giving a hand with the cleaning—'

'Bless you, my bird, of course I don't. And Val's a registered nurse, you know, so she can give you a hand when Bet Petherell can't be here. We'll all rally round, never you fear.' She came closer and laid her hand on Jennifer's arm. 'I know old Jed haven't been the best-liked man round here, but he'm one of us just the same, and there's nobody would see him suffer on his own, not like this. And I hope you don't mind, but Jacob here told me what 'twas all about – you know, about your poor mother and him. Seeing as we already knew some of the story, as it were.'

'That's all right,' Jennifer said, feeling the tears in her eyes. 'I'm glad he told you. In fact, I don't mind if everyone knows now – do you, Jacob? I'd rather the truth was known.'

Jacob hesitated, and she wondered if she'd upset him. He might not want the old story brought to light again, a subject for gossip in the cottages and pub.

'It's your story, too,' she added gently. 'Alice won't spread it around if you don't want it.'

'No,' he said after a moment. 'I think you'm right, maid. 'Tis best for it to be out in the open. I don't suppose many folk will care that much, anyway. They'm too interested in their own concerns. Nine-day wonder, it'll be.'

Alice nodded. 'They'm bound to be a bit curious about Jennifer and why she's suddenly turned up in Burracombe.' She finished scrubbing the sink and dried her hands on a scrap of towel she had obviously brought with her. 'If there's nothing else you needs me for now, maid, I'll be getting off home. There's the family supper to get . . . Now, you'm welcome to call up at the farm any time you wants to, and Val and me'll be along in the morning with our scrubbing-brushes. Do you want to come up a bit later on for a bite to eat? I've put a few eggs and some butter and a jug of fresh milk in the larder, along with a loaf of bread. Ted's mother made it.'

Jennifer shook her head. 'That's really kind of you, but I think I'll stay here. I've got enough for supper tonight and breakfast, and I'll do some shopping in the morning.' She sighed, looking out of the window at the untidy garden. 'It seems such a shame that anyone can let themselves go like this. I know he's not an easy man, but I would like to make these last few weeks a bit more comfortable for him, if he'll let me.' She smiled ruefully. 'I hope he'll let me wash his face, at least!'

'Bet Petherell will see to that,' Alice said. 'She won't stand no nonsense. And it won't be just his face, neither. I have to say, I don't envy you that!' She unwrapped her apron and stuffed it into the shopping-bag she had brought with her. 'Well, I'll be on my way. Now, you know where we are, and us'll be expecting you to drop in, so don't wait to be invited, will you? And Val and me'll see you in the morning. Goodbye, Jacob. You look after her, now.'

'I'll do that,' he said as the farmer's wife bustled out. 'As if her was me own daughter.' And then, with a surprisingly shy glance towards Jennifer, he added in a mumble, 'I know you'm not, maid, and I know you've got *his* blood in your veins, but seems to me you'm as *close* as a daughter.'

'Yes,' Jennifer said. 'It seems like that to me, too.'

Chapter Thirty-Eight

It took only a day or two for the news of Jed's illness and Jennifer's arrival to spread round the village, and she was astonished by the number of visitors who began to knock on the door. Most were genuinely concerned, admitting that Jed had been deeply unpopular, but still ready to help Jennifer in her difficult task. Most were also, she realised, as curious as they were concerned – the sudden appearance of a daughter in Jed's life, and the reawakening of an old story involving one of the most well-liked people in the village, was enough to provide food for gossip for well over the nine days Jacob had predicted.

Even Joyce Warren and her husband came along one day, arriving while the doctor was there. The three of them stayed in Jed's bedroom for some time, while Jennifer and Alice gave the kitchen a thorough spring-clean. By the time they came down, it was as near gleaming as a kitchen, undecorated for at least twenty years and equipped with what looked like museum pieces, could be. Joyce Warren looked around in disbelief.

'It's hard to imagine that anyone could have managed in a place like this! You're saints, both of you, to take on such a job.'

'It's got to be done,' Alice said, wiping her hands on a roller towel Jacob had hung on the back door. ''Twasn't healthy the way it was. I'm surprised Jed didn't poison himself years ago.

How is he this afternoon, anyway? Must be in a chatty mood. Visitors don't usually stop with him that long.'

'He's certainly not very well,' Joyce said. 'It's very sad to see someone in that condition. So you're staying here to look after him?' she added to Jennifer. 'I must say, I do admire you for that. And you didn't even know him until quite recently?'

'That's right.' Although she had said she wanted the story known, Jennifer found it embarrassing to talk about it, especially to this woman who was so different from the villagers she had met so far. 'I couldn't leave him on his own.'

'Well, he's very lucky to have you,' Joyce said, and turned as her husband and the doctor appeared. 'I'm just saying how lucky Jed is to have his daughter to look after him.'

'He is indeed.' The doctor ducked his head to come through the door. 'I've been meaning to ask you, Miss Tucker, have you sent word to the Methodist minister? I'm sure he'd want to see Jed.'

Jennifer nodded. The minister, who looked after two chapels, lived some distance from the village. 'He came yesterday. He's very concerned. He says Jed didn't go to chapel much, but he always looked after the graveyard.'

'In a manner of speaking,' Alice said grimly.

'He's coming again tomorrow,' Jennifer went on. 'Jed seemed a bit easier in his mind after he'd talked to him for a while.'

Henry Warren, a quiet, grey-haired man in spectacles and a business suit, nodded. 'He seems well enough in that respect. Just very tired and obviously not at all well.' He turned to his wife. 'I'm afraid I have to be going back to Tavistock now, I've got a number of matters to attend to in the office . . .'

'Yes, dear, we'll be on our way. I'm sure these two good ladies want to get on with their work. There's certainly a lot to be done here.' She glanced around with an expression of distaste, and then smiled kindly at Jennifer. 'I really do admire you, coming here like this and making such sacrifices.'

376

Jennifer returned her smile but said nothing. Henry Warren nodded and said goodbye, and the doctor stayed for a moment.

'Mr Warren was right about Jed's state of mind. He's well enough at the moment – understands all that's going on, even if he doesn't like it. But I'm afraid that will start to change soon. He's going to suffer quite a lot of pain, and the drugs I give him will make him very drowsy.'

'I know,' Jennifer said. 'It's all right, Doctor. I know just what to expect and I'll do my best for him.'

'You'll get help from Nurse Petherell, of course.'

'And me and Val,' Alice said. 'She'll not be short of helpers, Dr Latimer.'

He nodded. 'I'm sure of that. Burracombe wouldn't be the village it is if people didn't rally round in times of need. Well, I'll look in again tomorrow, Miss Tucker, but call me if you're at all worried.' He let himself out.

'Well!' Alice said, turning back to her cleaning. 'I wonder what that was all about.'

'All what? I know the doctor's a bit anxious about how I'm to manage, but—'

'No, not that. I mean that Mrs Warren and her husband coming to see Jed. She never had a good word to say for him, and you hardly ever see Mr Warren around the village, he'm always so busy.' She came closer and lowered her voice. 'If you want my opinion—'

Her voice was drowned by a sudden fierce knocking from upstairs. Jed was banging on the floor beside his bed with the knobbly walking-stick Jennifer had found in a cupboard.

'Well, the old termagant hasn't started to feel drowsy yet, that's for certain,' Alice observed. 'I'll tell you something else, too – he hasn't taken long to get used to being waited on, either. That old busybody Mrs Warren was right about one thing – you'm a saint, and he's lucky to have you.'

*

'It's not Jed they're helping,' Val said later, when she came in to help Jennifer get her father ready for the night. 'It's you. Not that they wouldn't help him, I'm not saying that, but I don't think he'd get quite so many visitors if he hadn't had a long-lost daughter turn up to look after him.'

'You mean it's just curiosity?'

'Well, a large part of it is. It's only natural – all the older ones knew Jed and Jacob when they were younger, but nobody ever knew what really happened to Susan. There was talk about a baby, but no one knew if it was true, and they'd have all thought it was Jacob's. It's bound to have caused a lot of interest, to know what really happened. And you coming just when Jed's in such a poor way—'

'They don't think I'm after his money, I hope!' Jennifer exclaimed, and Val hooted with laughter.

'What money? Has he got a sockful under his mattress? Well, I suppose there are always one or two who've got nasty minds, but you don't need to take any notice of them. Anyway, if there was any money – which I'm sure there isn't – I'd say you were earning it now. It's not the most pleasant of jobs, looking after someone like Jed.'

'I suppose you're used to it,' Jennifer remarked. 'Are you going to go on working at the hospital after you're married? It's not long now, is it?'

'Three weeks! We had the banns called for the first time last week. I'll go on for a while – there's not much point in stopping, really. There's not much housework to do at the charcoal-burner's cottage! We might as well have the money while I can earn it. Dad doesn't approve, of course, he says a man ought to be able to keep his wife, but I tell him if I stop nursing he'll be asking me to help out with things on the farm, so I'll still be working but not getting paid! That shuts him up.'

Jennifer laughed and they went upstairs to give the invalid his final wash, a drink and the medicine that Dr Latimer had prescribed. As he had foretold, Jed was now beginning to suffer more pain, and the sedatives were starting to have effect, but he was still aware enough to know what was happening and to protest at the indignity.

'I ain't been seen in me underwear since I were a babby. It isn't decent.'

'Don't be silly, Jed,' Val said firmly. 'I'm a nurse and Jennifer's your daughter. There's nothing indecent about it. And these are pyjamas, not underwear.'

'I had that nurse round here this afternoon, bathing me as if I were a babe in arms,' he continued indignantly, although his voice was weakening. 'I'd have showed her the door if I'd had the strength to do it. Taking advantage of a poor old man!'

'I don't think anyone's likely to take advantage of you,' Val told him. 'Now, let me prop you up while Jennifer gives you this drink. It'll help you sleep.'

'What is it? Milk?' He made a face of disgust. 'Can't a bloke have a pint of beer in his own home no more? That old skinflint up at the pub would send one down in a tankard if you paid him. Here, and that's another thing –' he reared up in bed so that Jennifer almost spilled the cup she was trying to hold against his lips '– he've got my old pewter tankard up there, the one I always has me beer out of when I goes in there. If I can't go in there no more, I want it back. You go up straight away and fetch it.'

'Not tonight,' Jennifer said. 'They'll be closing soon. I'll fetch it tomorrow and you can have all your drinks out of it.'

'Not milk,' he said, sinking back and allowing her to feed him at last. 'I wouldn't give it the insult.'

After that, he seemed to recede into a muddled, half-dreaming world of his own, rambling and incoherent. Eventually, he drifted into sleep and the two women went downstairs, feeling exhausted. The living-room was reasonably clean and tidy now, though the distempered walls and bare floor gave it a bleak and inhospitable air, and Jennifer made cocoa for them both. They sat down in the armchairs, their old covers thrown away and replaced by clean blankets Jennifer had brought out from Plymouth, and gave each other a little sigh of relief.

'I hope he sleeps well tonight,' Jennifer said. 'He's had dreadful nights just lately. I really do feel sorry for him. I think if Jacob hadn't called the doctor and got in touch with me, he could have died here, all by himself with no one to care.'

'It's a horrible thought,' Val agreed soberly. 'Yet I expect a lot of people would say it's no more than he deserves. He really has been an unpleasant man, all his life from what I can make out.'

'I don't know – even Jacob says they were friends when they were young. I think what happened to him in the war, and what happened with my mother, just turned him in on himself. He hated himself for what he'd done, and he hated everyone else for treating him as a coward. And he must have felt as if he was responsible for my mother's death, too. It was cruel of my grandfather to tell those lies.'

Val looked at her thoughtfully. 'It seems strange to hear you talking about them as your father and grandfather, especially when you've had other relatives. Doesn't it feel peculiar to you?'

'Yes, it does. I think about it a lot. I'll always think of my stepfather as my real father, in a way. And his parents were my granny and grandad. Nothing will ever change that. But with Jed, it's a different feeling. I can't think of him in the same way, but I can't pretend he doesn't exist. I feel a sort of tie. I can't just walk away and leave him to die alone. And then there's Jacob. He *ought* to have been my father, yet if he had been, I wouldn't have been me!' She shook her head. 'It's all so complicated, it makes my head ache so I've decided to stop worrying about it and just do whatever feels right. And that means looking after Jed.'

'And what about afterwards?' Val asked. 'Will you stop coming out to Burracombe then?'

Jennifer looked up and met her eyes. The room was almost dark, and they could only just see each other across the small space. She reached out and lit the old table lamp beside her.

'No,' she said. 'I'll never stop coming to Burracombe. I'll always want to see Jacob.'

Chapter Thirty-Nine

Jed died in the early hours of the morning, four days later. His decline, once begun, was rapid and after his remark about the pewter tankard, he did not speak coherently again. Jennifer was by his side almost all the time, sleeping only when too exhausted to stay awake and only when someone else could be with her father. She had been in her own bed for less than an hour when Jacob, who was sitting beside his old enemy, woke her up.

'You'd better come, maid. I think this is it.'

She was up almost before he had finished speaking, pushing her feet into slippers and pulling her dressing-gown around her. Together, they went into the next room, where the frail, shrivelled body was shifting restlessly, the bony, yellow fingers picking at the sheets. A voice that sounded quite unlike Jed's was mumbling on and on, as if commentating on an endless procession of events, and sometimes he sobbed. Every now and then a harsh rattle sounded in his throat, and Jacob gave Jennifer a significant glance.

'That's the death rattle, that is,' he muttered. 'Won't be long now, maid. You don't have to stay if you don't want to.'

'Of course I will.' She took the chair by the bed, and Jacob moved round to the one they had placed at the other side. She picked up one of the restless hands and held it, stroking the thin fingers gently. 'Jed. Can you hear me? It's Jennifer.'

'Jennifer,' he muttered. 'Don't know no Jennifers.'

'Yes, you do.' She took a breath. 'I'm your daughter, Jennifer. Susan's girl. You know me.'

'Susan? My Susan?'

She heard a sharp intake of breath from the man on the other side of the bed, and gave Jacob a swift glance. 'Susan Hannaford,' she said steadily. 'My mother.'

'Susan,' he whispered. 'Sweet little maid, her was . . . I were sorry after . . . I told her I were sorry . . . I'd have gone after her, but 'twas no use . . . Where's my tankard? I told that woman I wanted my tankard.'

'It's here. Would you like a drink?'

'I got to go to work.' He began to struggle, his feeble body suddenly strong, so that it took both of them to hold him in the bed. 'Job over Chagford way. I got to go, Mother.'

'It's all right, Jed. You don't have to go.'

'Hens to feed . . . Lambing-time . . . I got a grave to dig.' He began to struggle again. 'Bury my Susan.'

'Jed, it's all right.' Jennifer leaned close and spoke in his ear. 'There's nothing you have to do. You can rest now. Rest easy. Rest . . . ' She spoke in soothing whispers, hoping that the tone of her voice at least would penetrate his confused mind. 'Just lie quiet and rest, Jed. Just let yourself rest . . .'

Whether he understood her or not, she couldn't tell, but his breathing, shallow and ragged as it was, grew very slightly easier and his struggles eased. He lay flat in the bed. He was so shrunken now that the bedclothes barely rose above him. He kept turning his head restlessly from side to side, his free hand still picking endlessly at the sheet. As the hours dragged on, every breath seemed to pain him more and the rattle sounded more and more often in his throat, frequently ending with a cough that threatened to tear his body to pieces. Once or twice, Jacob got up and went quietly downstairs, returning with a cup of cocoa for them both, and once Jennifer asked if they ought to call the doctor again. He shook his head.

383

'Nothing he can do for him now, poor old sod. 'Tis just a matter of time.'

'It seems to be taking so long. He's so frail, I can't understand how he can go on breathing.'

'The body don't want to let go. Us'll do all us can to stay alive, that's what it is. I seen it before, when my old father went, and again when it were my Sarah. Not many of us has it easy.'

She nodded and stroked Jed's forehead. It was cold and clammy, as if he were half dead already, and she wondered if he had slipped away while they were talking. But the breath was still coming, so shallow that it was a wonder it got as far as the destroyed lungs, and as she looked down on the skeletal face, the hollow eyes opened suddenly and looked straight at her.

He knows who I am, she thought. He's lucid again.

'Jennifer.' A shaking hand reached up to her face. 'You'm my Susan's maid.'

'She weren't never your Susan!' Jacob burst out, unable to restrain himself, and the yellow face turned to him.

'Be that you, Jacob Prout?'

'It be,' Jacob growled. 'I been here these past three days, on and off, only you never knowed it.'

'Wanted to be in at the death, eh?'

Jennifer gasped in shock, but Jacob shrugged his shoulders. 'Maybe. I was there at the start, might as well be here at the end.'

The dying man was silent for a moment. But he still seemed lucid as he whispered in his painfully grating voice, 'I were proper fond of her. I never meant to hurt her.'

Jennifer glanced at Jacob, and since he seemed unlikely to answer, she said, 'I know. We both know. It's all right, Jed.'

'And if it isn't,' Jacob said, 'you'll have someone bigger than us to answer to, before the night's out.'

Jed closed his eyes and Jennifer wondered if they should

have called the minister. He'd been in that afternoon and spent an hour or more with Jed; if he'd been a Roman Catholic, she thought, he would probably have given him the Last Rites. Perhaps the minister's visit would have had the same effect, leaving Jed at peace. To make sure, as best she could, she said quietly, 'My mother forgave you, Jed. She never bore any grudge against you.'

'Susan?' he whispered, his senses failing fast again.

'That's right. Susan. And so do I.' She touched his papery cheek. 'Go to sleep now, Jed. Go and rest.'

The hollow eyes looked into hers. Slowly, the bony head turned, and he cast a last look at his childhood friend and enemy. Then Jed Fisher gave one last, tremulous sigh and one last faint rattle, and his eyes closed as if in sleep. The room was suddenly silent. 'He've gone,' Jacob said after a moment, and Jennifer nodded. Her eyes were filled with tears.

'I know.'

They sat quietly for a few minutes and then, taking a deep breath, she folded the dead man's hands on his chest and drew the sheet over his face. Jacob rose to his feet, still looking down at the bed.

'He were a miserable old sod,' he said. 'But us had good times when us were tackers. I reckon that's what I ought to remember.'

'I think so, too,' Jennifer said. 'He didn't start out bad. It was what happened to him.' Her voice broke suddenly. 'Oh, *Jacob*!'

'There, there,' he said, moving round the bed to put his arms round her shoulders. 'Don't take on, maid. 'Tis the natural way of the world, and you did your best for him.'

'It seems such a waste,' she wept. 'Oh, Jacob, I never thought, when I started looking for him, that it would end like this.'

'I don't suppose you did,' he said thoughtfully. 'The thing

is, are you sorry you done it? Are you sorry you started to look in the first place?'

Jennifer took her hands away from her face and looked up at him, the man she had thought was her father, the man who she still felt *ought* to have been her father, and she shook her head.

'No. I'm not sorry. Because I've made things right for him now. I've found you – and we've both found out the truth. I'll always be glad I came to Burracombe.'

Chapter Forty

The Church of St Andrew was packed when Val Tozer finally walked up the aisle to marry Luke Ferris. They had been welcomed by the silvery pealing of the six bells, captained today by Jacob Prout, since Ted Tozer was occupied with giving his daughter away, but all the ringers were in their best suits and filed into seats at the back as soon as they had finished ringing. Everyone was invited to the reception in the village hall.

Stella was there with Maddy, sitting halfway back behind the Tozer family and keeping a place for Dottie, who was in the porch putting the finishing touches to the dresses. She scurried up the aisle just before the signal was given to the organist to strike up with 'Here Comes the Bride', and slipped into her pew. Then the bells stopped, the music started, and Luke – who had been fidgeting anxiously in the front pew for the past ten minutes with his brother, Simon – stood up and turned to greet his bride.

As the congregation caught their first glimpse of Val, tall and slender in her drift of pale blue-grey, a sigh of pleasure ran round the church. Her rich brown hair was caught in a veil of lace, cascading down beneath it in a tumble of gleaming curls. She looked proud and happy, her face glowing as if she were walking into a dream, and as she came to stand beside Luke and they looked into each other's eyes, it was as if the promises to be made between them were encompassed in that moment and the rest of the service no more than a formality.

Basil Harvey was taking the service, with Felix standing close by. Stella gazed at him, standing tall behind the short, rotund vicar, his corn-gold hair lit by the sunlight that flooded through the windows, and thought wistfully of the hopes and dreams she herself had had. Since that evening when the three of them had sat by the river and Stella had heard for the first time about Maddy's new job with Felix's uncle, she had had very little time alone with him. School had taken up so much of her time, and Felix had spent more and more time at Little Burracombe, where John Berry was failing fast. Maddy herself had been in West Lyme for the past fortnight, learning about her new duties from the Archdeacon's present secretary, who was leaving to get married, and had come home for the wedding before taking Stella to London for the promised holiday, after which she would be moving to her own apartment. It was all changing, Stella thought; all except her own life, which looked like going on just the same. And that's good, she told herself fiercely. It's what I wanted. I've got *everything* I wanted . . .

Jennifer Tucker was sitting on Stella's other side. She and Val had become close friends as they tended Jed together, and she was staying with Jacob, who had told her that the spare bedroom was now hers whenever she wanted it. 'You can't stop in that dump next door,' he'd told her bluntly. 'Wants stripping out and starting all over again, that do.'

The wedding was the second big event in the village in the past week or so. Jed Fisher's funeral, held in the Chapel, had also been well attended – better than anyone who had known him could have expected. Jennifer suspected that many of them might have come out of curiosity, having heard the story of herself and Jed, and those who had already met her were present to lend her their support. But there were others, especially the older villagers, who seemed to have come for a different reason. Perhaps they remembered Jed from his younger, happier days; perhaps they felt a vague guilt at the way he had been treated; perhaps it was just because he had been a part of their lives and of the village for so long that they felt compelled to wish him goodbye.

Jacob himself had dug the grave. He had never dug a grave in the chapel graveyard before, since Jed himself had done that, but although the minister could have asked a gravedigger from another village to do the job, Jacob had gone to him the day after the death and asked for it.

'Us lived next door to each other all our lives, and us were pals when us were youngsters,' he said. 'I'd like to see to the old misery's last resting-place.'

'Like to make sure he's properly buried, that's what he really means,' some of the other villagers commented on hearing this, but the minister agreed to Jacob's request and he was a pall-bearer as well.

Jennifer, as chief mourner, had felt a deep sorrow at the passing of this sad old man, whose life had been poisoned by bitterness and regret. She gazed at the coffin, standing before them as they sang their last hymn, and thought how prejudice and false assumptions had started the poisoning. Who was really responsible – bullying old Abraham, her own grand-father, who had driven his daughter away and then lied so cruelly about her death? Those who had scorned Jed for being rejected by one over-zealous Army doctor? Or Jed himself, for allowing the bitterness to rot his soul? Well, there was no way of knowing now, and all anyone could do was learn from his wasted life – if anyone ever did learn from someone else's mistakes. All our mistakes are our own, she thought, unique to ourselves – can we ever learn from someone else's?

Today was a happier day, however, she reminded herself as she watched Val turn to hand her bouquet of cascading deep-red roses to her sister, Jackie. Ted, having handed her over to the vicar, stepped back to stand in the front pew beside Alice, resplendent in her fuchsia-pink suit and hat. She was glad to feel a part of the Tozer family and their celebration, glad to feel a part of the village. It was strange to think that what had happened to Jed – what had seemed a wasted life – had brought all this about for her. There really was no understanding it, and all you could do was get on with life as it happened to be.

Hilary Napier was sitting just in front of them, with her father and brother, Stephen, who had managed to 'wangle' his leave to coincide with Val's wedding. Tall and handsome in his RAF uniform, he had given Maddy an interested glance as he passed her to enter his pew. They knew each other, of course, since Maddy had often stayed with the Napiers when she had been with Fenella Forsyth, but it was some time since they'd met and clearly Stephen was impressed by the changes he saw in her.

Hilary noticed the smile that passed between them and murmured, 'She's very pretty, but I don't think you've got a chance – she's been seen about with the curate rather a lot just lately!'

'Are they engaged?' he whispered, and she shook her head. 'Not as far as I know.'

He sat back with a wicked grin. 'All's fair in love and war, then! And I think my uniform's better than his!'

Hilary stifled a giggle. She was feeling especially happy today. Her father had made a start on the family book and become almost completely absorbed in it, leaving her free to administer the estate as she wanted to. He spent his mornings in his study, his head buried in old documents and photographs, and in the afternoons he either accompanied her on a visit to one of the tenants – taking the opportunity to acquire more old tales – or took the dogs out on the moor. Charles Latimer had told him that steady exercise was good for him, and he would walk for hours as the dogs dashed around looking for rabbits.

There was another reason for Hilary to feel cheerful today. Arnold Cherriman and his wife had come to dinner a few evenings before, to play bridge, and Arnold had announced that he had at last decided to move back to Plymouth. 'We're converting the old house into flats and building a new house in the garden,' he'd said. 'The whole place is too big for us now. There's over an acre of garden, you know – plenty for Evelyn to play about with, and to give us privacy. There's a big demand for decent homes in the city now, so I'm going to retire. Play a bit of golf, enjoy the fruits of my labours all these years.'

Hilary's heart had leaped. 'How long do you think it will take?' she asked, thinking of Val and Luke. What news she would be able to give them at their wedding!

'Oh, a year or more. Builders are all pretty busy, and we've got to get an architect to draw up plans and all that. So we'll be wanting to stay on in the estate house for a while yet. But you'll need to be thinking about new tenants, and I may be able to help there—'

'Oh no,' Hilary said hastily before her father could show interest. 'I think we'll be able to find tenants, thank you, Mr Cherriman.'

A year or more, she thought. Would Val and Luke be able to manage for that long in the charcoal-burner's cottage? It was so small and not at all suitable for winter. They'd hoped only to have to live there for the summer . . . But even if they had to move into Tavistock, where Luke was to take up his teaching post in the autumn, it need only be until the Cherrimans moved. They would know that they'd soon be able to move back to Burracombe.

The bride and groom were making their vows now, and everyone concentrated on hearing their voices. Sometimes a bride spoke so quietly that you could barely hear her, and even the grooms almost lost their voices at this moment. But Val's voice was clear and strong, and Luke's deep and firm. They obviously meant their vows to be heard by all present, a confirmation of their love and determination, and the silence after they spoke their last words was broken only by a small sob from Alice and another from Luke's mother. Tears were on many other cheeks, too, but no other sounds were heard and Basil's voice rang out as he lifted the clasped hands and made the exhortation. 'Those whom God hath joined together, let no man put asunder!'

While the register was signed, the handbell-ringers filed out to the chancel steps and rang Minnie's special adaptations of 'Ode to Joy' and 'O Perfect Love'. Then the ringers hastened back to the ringing-chamber at the back of the church, the organ pealed out the notes of the 'Wedding March', and Val and Luke, husband and wife now, emerged beaming from the tiny vestry and led the procession of families down the aisle, smiling and nodding at all their guests as they came. There were more tears on many faces as they gazed at Val's radiant face and the pride with which Luke bore her on his arm, but by the time everyone was out in the sunshine, milling about the churchyard and trying to get in – or out of – the photographs, the tears had dried and there was nothing but laughter.

'It's a wonderful wedding,' Stella said as she stood with Jennifer and Hilary, sipping a glass of sherry in the village hall. 'The first I've been to in Burracombe. Are they all like this?'

Hilary laughed. 'Some of them! Others are smaller and people have the reception at home, just for their family. But the Tozers are such a big family, and so well known that they couldn't really have it anywhere smaller.'

'Well, I'm really pleased to have been invited – after all, I've only been in the village five minutes. They didn't have to ask me.'

'Or me,' Jennifer said. 'I don't even live here.'

'You'd have been almost the only ones left out. Well, along with the Cullifords and a few others, perhaps! How are you, by the way? You must be looking forward to the holidays –

the summer term's a busy one, I know. I enjoyed the play, by the way.'

'It went quite well in the end,' Stella agreed. 'It was a shame that Sports Day was the only wet day in the whole month, but we managed to have it last week, and it did give us a bit more time for rehearsals. The children worked very hard to get it right, although my heart was in my mouth when the ass's head tipped over sideways.'

'Has Felix said anything to you about starting up a dramatic society?' Hilary asked. 'He was talking about it the other day when we met over at Little Burracombe – Father and I had gone to see poor Mr Berry. He seems quite keen and I'd rather like to have a go. I loved acting when I was at school.'

'I know he's been thinking about it,' Stella said, 'but I haven't seen much of him lately.' She looked round as Val and Luke came up to them, hand in hand and wreathed in smiles. 'You two look very pleased with yourselves.'

'And so we should,' Val declared. 'It's the best day of our lives.'

'So far,' Luke added. 'Unless you mean it's going to be all downhill from now on!'

'I don't mean that at all!' She slapped his arm. 'I can see I'm going to have trouble with you.'

'I've got some news for you,' Hilary said, and they both looked at her expectantly. Stella and Jennifer started to move away, but she gestured to them to stay. 'It's not private – at least, I don't think it is – but it's very good news.' Her voice bubbled with excitement. 'The Cherrimans are going back to Plymouth! That means you'll be able to have the estate house after all. Not straight away,' she added as Val turned to Luke with an exclamation of delight. 'They're building a new house in Plymouth so it'll be at least a year. But even if you move into Tavistock in the autumn, you'll know it needn't be for long. You'll be back in the village by the end of next year.'

'Oh, that's wonderful,' Val cried. 'We'll stay in the cottage as long as we can in the autumn and look for something in town – it won't seem nearly as bad moving to town if we know we're coming back so soon.'

'But you don't have to do that,' Jennifer said suddenly, and they all turned to stare at her. 'You don't have to move into Tavistock. You can have my cottage.'

'*Your* cottage?' Val said blankly. 'But which – do you mean *Jed's* cottage?'

'Yes. He left it to me. Mr Warren came one day and made out his will – you remember, Val, your mother was there and we wondered why the doctor had brought them along. I didn't even know he was a solicitor. I didn't know anything about it until after the funeral. But it was quite true – everything was left to me. I suppose he had no one else to leave it to,' she added a little sadly.

'But won't you want to live there yourself?' Val asked.

Jennifer shook her head. 'Not yet. I'm sure I will eventually, but I don't want to rush into anything. Jacob says I can come and stay with him any time I like, and I need to be in Plymouth for my job. And I do have my sisters and their families there, as well – I've rather neglected them lately.'

'And we really could rent the cottage from you?' Val asked, dazed.

'Yes, of course. But it needs an awful lot doing to it. You wouldn't be able to move straight in.'

'That doesn't matter. We could do it ourselves, during the summer holidays. Then it will be ready for us by winter – the charcoal-burner's cottage is so tiny, and with no running water or proper cooking facilities it would be dreadfully uncomfortable then for two people. Oh, Jennifer, that's lovely! It's made a perfect day even perfecter!'

They all laughed, and the ushers began to move them towards the tables that had been laid for the wedding meal. Dottie and Mrs Dawe, with a small army of helpers, had been busy all the previous day and again this morning, and it looked, as Alice herself had said when she came that morning to take a look, as good as a dining-room in any fine hotel.

Val and Luke and their families seated themselves at the top table. Jennifer was with Jacob, and Hilary with her father. Stella and Maddy found themselves seated with Felix between them, and Stephen on Maddy's other side.

'It's a great day, isn't it?' Felix said cheerfully, passing a bowl of steaming new potatoes to go with the ham salad. 'Nice to see two people so happy.'

'It is.' Stella smiled at him, determined not to let her own personal disappointment show. 'I wonder who'll be the next in the village to get married.'

'Who knows? Life is full of surprises.' He helped himself to half a dozen potatoes. 'And now that the term's almost over, maybe you'll have a few yourself.'

'What do you mean?' She looked at him in sudden dread. Please don't let them announce it now, she thought. Not today, not here amongst all these people. 'Has Maddy planned something special for our holiday in London?'

'I've no idea! Well, that's not quite true. There is something special planned, but it's not Maddy who's been planning it. It's me.'

He grinned at her, but Stella could only gaze back in dismay. Hastily, she said, 'Don't tell me now, Felix. Save it for later.'

'But I want to tell you now. I've been keeping it to myself for too long – you've been so wrapped up in school things for the past few weeks I've hardly had a chance to talk to you on your own. And once this meal's over we'll have to listen to speeches and drink toasts, and then there'll be dancing and I might not get another chance. I've got to say it now, while you're trapped here and can't get away from me.'

'Felix—'

'Be quiet,' he said. 'Eat your nice salad and listen to me.

And there's to be no arguing, understand?' As she gazed at him, mute, he went on with a touch of drama in his voice, 'When Maddy takes you to London, you're not going on your own. I'm coming with you!'

Stella stared at him. 'You? But—'

'Even curates are allowed to have holidays, you know,' he said. 'Maddy and I have been talking it over, and she wants me to come, too. You see, Fenella Forsyth, or whatever her French name is, is coming to London just then, and wants Maddy to spend a few days with her. And Maddy doesn't want to leave you on your own, so it seems the perfect solution.'

'But—' Stella began again, and he put his finger to her lips. She felt her cheeks colour and turned her head away quickly. 'Felix, don't.'

'I want to,' he said quietly. 'I want to touch you. I've wanted it for so long, but these past few weeks you seem to have drifted away from me. Tell me it's all right, Stella. Tell me everything's the same between us as it was that day I kissed you on the bridge.'

Slowly, unbelievingly, she turned back and met his eyes. With doubt in her voice, she said, 'But you and Maddy . . .'

'Maddy and I what? What do you mean?'

'I thought you and Maddy . . . I thought you . . . I didn't think you wanted me any more. I thought perhaps you never had.'

Felix stared at her. 'You thought that? But I thought you were still in love with Luke!' He glanced towards the top table. 'That day we met them up by the Standing Stones – the way you looked at the cottage when we walked down the hill . . .'

'I was thinking how lucky they were to have found each other,' she said. 'That's all. I got over Luke long ago.'

'And have you got over me?' he asked.

396

Stella shook her head, knowing that this was a moment for truth. 'I don't think I'll ever get over you, Felix.'

'Nor will I get over you,' he said softly, and felt for her hand beneath the table. 'Oh, how I wish I could kiss you now! But that's something I really will have to save for later.'

'I'll look forward to it,' she whispered, curling her fingers in his, and they both smiled. Then she said, 'Although I'm sorry, in a way, that it isn't you and Maddy after all. You'd have made a very nice brother-in-law!'

Felix chuckled. 'Well,' he said with a nudge, 'you may find yourself with one who's equally nice.' And as she looked past him at her sister, who was openly flirting with Stephen Napier, Stella laughed with amusement, relief and an overwhelming rush of love.

A sudden sharp rap from a gavel on the top table brought them all to attention. Luke's brother, Simon, was on his feet, and the speeches were about to begin.

'Here's to Val and Luke,' Felix murmured, touching his glass to Stella's as Ted Tozer rose to his feet, red-faced and clutching a sheet of paper. 'Here's to love and marriage. And here's to us.'

'To us,' Stella echoed softly.

available from

THE ORION PUBLISHING GROUP

☐ **Goodbye Sweetheart** £6.99
LILIAN HARRY
978-1-8579-7812-4

☐ **The Girls They Left Behind** £6.99
LILIAN HARRY
978-0-7528-0333-3

☐ **Keep Smiling Through** £6.99
LILIAN HARRY
978-0-7528-3442-9

☐ **Moonlight & Lovesongs** £6.99
LILIAN HARRY
978-0-7528-1564-0

☐ **Love & Laughter** £6.99
LILIAN HARRY
978-0-7528-2605-9

☐ **Wives & Sweethearts** £6.99
LILIAN HARRY
978-0-7528-3396-5

☐ **Corner House Girls** £6.99
LILIAN HARRY
978-0-7528-4296-7

☐ **Kiss the Girls Goodbye** £6.99
LILIAN HARRY
978-0-7528-4448-0

☐ **PS I Love You** £6.99
LILIAN HARRY
978-0-7528-4820-4

☐ **A Girl Called Thursday** £6.99
LILIAN HARRY
978-0-7528-4950-8

☐ **Tuppence to Spend** £6.99
LILIAN HARRY
978-0-7528-4264-6

☐ **A Promise to Keep** £6.99
LILIAN HARRY
978-0-7528-5889-0

☐ **Under the Apple Tree** £6.99
LILIAN HARRY
978-0-7528-5929-3

☐ **Dance Little Lady** £6.99
LILIAN HARRY
978-0-7528-6420-4

☐ **A Farthing Will Do** £6.99
LILIAN HARRY
978-0-7528-6492-1

☐ **Three Little Ships** £6.99
LILIAN HARRY
978-0-7528-7707-5

☐ **The Bells of Burracombe** £6.99
LILIAN HARRY
978-0-7528-7804-1

☐ **A Stranger in Burracombe** £6.99
LILIAN HARRY
978-0-7528-8277-2

All Orion/Phoenix titles are available at your local bookshop or from the following address:

Mail Order Department
Littlehampton Book Services
FREEPOST BR535
Worthing, West Sussex, BN13 3BR
telephone 01903 828503, *facsimile* 01903 828802
e-mail MailOrders@lbsltd.co.uk
(Please ensure that you include full postal address details)

Payment can be made either by credit/debit card (Visa, Mastercard, Access and Switch accepted) or by sending a £ Sterling cheque or postal order made payable to *Littlehampton Book Services*.
DO NOT SEND CASH OR CURRENCY

Please add the following to cover postage and packing

UK and BFPO:
£1.50 for the first book, and 50p for each additional book to a maximum of £3.50

Overseas and Eire:
£2.50 for the first book plus £1.00 for the second book and 50p for each additional book ordered

---

BLOCK CAPITALS PLEASE

name of cardholder .... *delivery address*
.... *(if different from cardholder)*
address of cardholder ....
....
....
....
postcode .... *postcode* ....

☐ I enclose my remittance for £ ....

☐ please debit my Mastercard/Visa/Access/Switch (delete as appropriate)

card number ☐☐☐☐ ☐☐☐☐ ☐☐☐☐ ☐☐☐☐

expiry date ☐☐☐☐   Switch issue no. ☐☐

signature ....

prices and availability are subject to change without notice